Shadow of the Rock

Thomas Mogford

W F HOWES LTD

This large print edition published in 2012 by
W F Howes Ltd
Unit 4, Rearsby Business Park, Gaddesby Lane,
Rearsby, Leicester LE7 4YH

1 3 5 7 9 10 8 6 4 2

First published in the United Kingdom in 2012
by Bloomsbury Publishing Plc

A CIP catalogue record for this book is available
from the British Library

ISBN 978 1 47120 609 2

Typeset by Palimpsest Book Production Limited,
Falkirk, Stirlingshire

Printed and bound by CPI Group (UK) Ltd,
Croydon, CR0 4YY

For Ali Rea

There is shadow under this red rock,
(Come in under the shadow of this red rock),
And I will show you something different from
either
Your shadow at morning striding behind you
Or your shadow at evening rising to meet you;
I will show you fear in a handful of dust.

T. S. Eliot, *The Waste Land*

The girl gasps as his fingernails rake the soft skin of her inner thigh. She reaches for the whisky bottle and takes a long slow drink, clear brown liquid spilling down her lips and chin. She passes the bottle to the man beside her; he screws it back into the corpuscular imprint it has formed in the sand.

Across the Strait of Gibraltar, just a few miles distant, the lights of Europe flicker, losing their strength to the dawn. The girl manoeuvres herself onto all fours, facing out to sea as the man kneels behind to hoist her thin dress to the small of her back. The first glow of the sun starts to redden the Straits; this, and the electricity spreading up the girl's spine, convince her, ever superstitious, that her decisions must be right, that today's actions will be vindicated.

Warm water laps at the girl's splayed hands. The tide is coming in; she pushes herself back and forth onto the man's strong extended fingers, grinding her knees down into the sand, watching the European shoreline lights vanish as the sun unsticks bloodily from the mire.

The man reaches forward, easing down the straps of her dress, stroking a shoulder blade. Her head lolls, hanks of dark hair hanging over multi-pierced ears. Out to sea, the morning breeze gusts on the water, drowning out the break of the waves.

The girl sucks in a sudden breath. She feels a sharp, chilly sting on the side of her neck, as though more whisky has dripped down, or some insect or jellyfish has been brought in by the tide. She tries to exhale but the breath will not come. Lifting a hand to her neck, she senses the warmth between her thighs matched by a thick, sticky gush, as a high-pitched whine distinguishes itself above the waves, like a mosquito, the girl thinks dreamily, or a punctured lilo held to the ear.

Her elbow collapses, face slapping down hard onto wet sand. Rich red pools in the film of water, turning to pink before it drains away. The girl sees his shadow darken the sky above, then feels something spatter her cheek. The spittle clings to her eye socket, quivering with the last spasms of her body. Somewhere behind, a call to prayer rings out, marking the start of another Tangiers morning.

PART I

GIBRALTAR

CHAPTER 1

Spike Sanguinetti stared across the water at the shimmering lights of Africa. A breeze was whipping in off the Straits; he held his cheek to it, testing for the dry heat of a Saharan southerly. Instead came the same moisture-laden levanter. There would be no sun in Gibraltar tomorrow.

He turned back towards Main Street. Cobblestone lanes that a few hours earlier had been jostling with tourists were now deserted – safely back aboard their cruise ships, or cloistered over the Spanish border in the cheaper *pensiones* of La Línea de la Concepción. The grilles of the duty-free shops were down, wooden pub tables tipped on their sides, gleaming in the lamplight from closing-time scrub-downs but failing to dry in the humidity. Spike pulled his tie free, folding it into his suit pocket. Then he turned off Main Street and entered the steep-rising maze of the Old Town.

The ancient, crumbling houses clung precariously to the skirts of the Rock. Spike climbed past them, lulled by the routine, into backstreets and alleyways too tight to permit traffic. The

Church of the Sacred Heart gave a solitary toll, while high on the Upper Rock, mist was muting the floodlights, lending a yellow sodium glow to the residential buildings below.

Spike stopped as he entered Chicardo's Passage, suddenly alert. Twenty metres ahead, silhouetted in the spectral light, stood a figure. Thickset, with a man's broad shoulders, standing directly in front of his house. Spike watched, heart quickening, as the figure took a silent step forward, then tested the door handle.

'Hey!' Spike called out.

Flinching at Spike's voice, the man turned and launched into a heavy-footed sprint. Spike waited until the figure had reached the end of Chicardo's Passage, then doubled back the way he had come in, pacing himself for the climb ahead.

Tank Ramp, Bedlam Court, Devil's Tower Road: Gibraltar street names were the hallmarks of its bloodstained past. After crossing a narrow passageway, Spike ran up a high-walled set of steps. A fig tree had seeded itself in the ruins of an old victualling yard; he caught a hint of mustiness in the scented leaves and raised a hand to the branches, sending a large grey ape bounding away into the darkness.

Tongues of fog licked at Spike's face as he burst onto Castle Road, the last demarcation before the Rock became too sheer to colonise. Cars and scooters were parked tightly on the cramped pavements; he zigzagged between them, stopping at the point where Fraser's Ramp met the road. Head resting against damp concrete, he waited, allowing his breath to steady. The levanter swept through the Rock scrub above. More low cloud drifted past floodlights. It was then that he heard the noise.

A soft scrape of shoes on flagstones, followed by a coarse, asthmatic panting. Spike edged closer, stopping as the squat dark figure appeared on the road, chest heaving, hands on thighs. As soon as the man straightened up, Spike stepped out of the shadows and grabbed his arm.

A dusty old Fiat was parked ahead on the pavement; Spike slammed the man against it, pinning his thick neck down onto the sloping rear window. In the half-light, he made out pouchy cheeks and round, gold-rimmed spectacles. 'Solomon?' he said.

CHAPTER 2

Solomon Hassan leaned against the passenger door of the Fiat, arms by his sides, staring down at the pavement. He wore a pinstripe suit, the right trouser leg torn and the white shirt stained. His black hair was wet with grease or sweat, a tuft at the back sticking up.

'Why did you run?'

'It was dark,' Solomon replied, speaking English in the same lilting accent as Spike. 'I wasn't sure I had the right house.'

A light flashed on opposite, and Solomon raised his head. His small, circular glasses were unhooked from one ear; he reached up to straighten them, hands shaking. 'I need your help, Spike.'

The sash window across the road began rattling up, so Spike turned and walked quickly down Fraser's Ramp, Solomon following behind. They came into Chicardo's Passage by the opposite way. After unlocking the front door, Spike ushered Solomon into the hallway, then through the bead curtain into the kitchen. 'Keep the noise down.'

General Ironside gave a low growl as Solomon

passed. Spike raised an admonitory finger at the dog basket, then clicked through the bead curtain himself.

Solomon was standing by the pine kitchen table, head bowed, hands clasped behind back. Beneath the hanging bayonet bulb, Spike could see him more clearly. He was still as short as in their schooldays, but his chest was stockier, pectoral muscles bulging as though from assiduous gym time. The stains on his shirt were of a rusty-brown colour, the tear in his pinstripe trousers just below the knee, giving him the air of a smartly dressed postman savaged on his round. Solomon held himself there, letting Spike's eyes range over him, absent-mindedly picking at his left thumb with the sharp nail of a forefinger. The wooden wall clock ticked; Spike spread his jacket over the back of a chair and sat down heavily.

'Got anything to drink?' Solomon whispered.

'Nothing grown-up.'

'*Agua de beber?*' Solomon added, switching to *yanito*, the patois of Spanish, Genoese, English and Hebrew used by native Gibraltarians.

'*Por bashe.*'

Solomon plodded across the buckling cork-tile floor. A tumbler had been upturned by the sink, alongside a pharmacy-shelf windowsill of pills; he filled it and drank, stubbly cheeks puffing. After blinking over at Spike, as though momentarily puzzled as to who he was, he drew out a chair and sat. 'It's all a misunderstanding,' he said, mopping his brow with his suit sleeve. 'I'm in trouble, Spike.'

'Financial problems?'

Behind Solomon's glasses the whites of his eyes were striated with red, like two semi-precious stones. 'Murder.'

Spike shifted forward in his seat, reassessing the dark stains on Solomon's shirt.

'It's just tomato juice, Spike,' Solomon said. '*Los tomates*.' He bunched up his shirt tail, revealing a braille of dried seeds. 'Eight hours in the back of a lorry . . .' His eyes focused on a knot on the pinewood table, as though he were viewing images within. 'There was this girl.'

Spike raised a dark eyebrow.

'It was three days ago,' he said. 'Feels like more.' He straightened up a little, chest puffing. 'I'm based in Tangiers now: I imagine you've heard. She was new in town. We went to a bar on the beach, took our drinks down to the shore, sat for a while, watched the sunset. Then she leans in and kisses me.' Solomon scratched again at his thumb; Spike saw a drop of blood ooze from the pink, porous scar tissue around the nail. 'So I pull away. I'm only meant to be showing her round, plus she's crazy this girl, tattoos, piercings, the lot. She grins at me: "You know," she says, "I only kissed you because you're such" . . . *Empollón* was the word she used.'

'A nerd,' Spike translated, almost suppressing a smile. 'Spanish?'

'My boss's Spanish stepdaughter. You can see why I didn't want to start anything with her.' Solomon sat back, eyes concealed by two suns of light reflecting from his glasses. 'I get to my feet. It's not completely dark, plus she's no kid. So I left her there, Spike. On the beach.'

'Anyone see you go?'

'Even if they did, you'd never find them. No one in Tangiers talks to the police.'

'But someone saw you come home.'

Solomon shook his head.

'CCTV?'

'Unlikely. It's more in rural, isolated areas. So I go up to my flat. Watch a football game . . .'

'Since when do you like football?'

'There's not a lot to do in Tangiers. Next morning I go into work. When I get home there's a police car outside my apartment block.'

'How did they find you?'

'I used my card in the bar.' Solomon worked a finger beneath his spectacles, itching at his left eyeball. 'A policeman gets out: "Are you Solomon Hassan?" et cetera. He can see I'm uneasy so he goes back to his car. On the passenger seat there's an envelope of black-and-white photos. The top one . . .' Solomon withdrew his finger and ran it beneath his nostrils, laying a gleaming snail trail on the hairy knuckle. 'She was lying on her back, head against the sand. Her eyes were all milky . . . like an old fish. And her neck – the mark was so small, Spike, like a tiny dash in biro. There was no blood. I asked if she was sleeping and the policeman said the tide had come in and washed the blood away.'

'You went with him?'

'Of course. To the station on the Avenue d'Espagne. Full of Moroccans in djellabas, rocking on their hunkers. He took me into a back room. Stacks of papers everywhere. I told him what I told you. The tape wasn't working so I told him again. Then he let me go.'

'What language?'

'English . . . French at the start.'

'You speak French now?'

'Like I said, Spike, there's not much to do in Tangiers. So I lie awake that night. The Tangiers police . . . they're like animals. If they can place you anywhere near a crime, that's it, they make the arrest, get the stats up. Plus for me . . .'

'What?'

Grinning sourly, Solomon rubbed his finger up and down the bridge of his nose. 'Jews are hardly flavour of the month in Morocco. The next morning I look out onto the street. A police jeep. Same guy as before but talking to two meatheads with sub-machine guns. The doorbell starts to ring; I grab my passport and run down the service stairs. I assume there'll be police on that side of the building, but there aren't, so I catch a *petit taxi* to the harbour.'

'Not stopped by immigration?'

'There's a Gibraltarian who works the port. Slip him enough euros and he'll get you over.'

'You mean you crossed illegally?'

'In the back of a lorry. Six hours before the catamaran even left. The waves . . . felt like my belly was being sucked dry. We got to Gib and the lorry rolled off. Let me out at Casemates. Imagine how it felt to see the Rock again.'

'There was too much cloud,' Spike said.

'Sorry?'

'There was too much levanter cloud to see the Rock.' Spike stroked his jaw thoughtfully. 'Why not go to your mother's?'

'You crazy? She'd have a heart attack. No, I think, my old pal, Spike Sanguinetti, he's a lawyer. I remembered where you lived. Or thought I did.'

'I'm a tax specialist, Solomon.'

'You're a friend,' Solomon said, holding out his shaky palms in supplication.

'You shouldn't have run.'

Solomon snapped closed one hand. 'And *you* don't know Tangiers.'

Spike looked over to the wall, at his father's blurry watercolours. All showed the Rock: from below, from the side, from above with HMS *Victory* towing in Nelson's body, pickled in a barrel of cheap Spanish brandy. He got to his feet. 'I'm going upstairs. When I come back down, you may be gone. You may even have crossed the border to Spain. I doubt the Moroccan authorities will have had time yet to alert immigration. Or,' Spike added, turning from the curtain, 'you may still be here. If you are, this is what happens. You'll surrender your passport and I'll make a call to Jessica Navarro. She'll drive you to prison where you'll be remanded overnight. After that, a criminal barrister will come and find you.'

Spike pushed through the beads to find General Ironside asleep in his basket. He creaked upstairs; from outside his father's door he heard erratic, laboured breathing.

The tap in Spike's sink snarled like an ape. He splashed his face and tasted salt. The house's plumbing was so antiquated that seawater still seeped into the mains.

Downstairs, Solomon was standing by the side-board, examining a silver photo frame. 'My mother always said your father was the most handsome man on the Rock.' He held the picture out; Spike looked down at the tall, laughing man in his elegant waistcoat and sombre tails. Even with the fading of time, Rufus Sanguinetti's piercing blue eyes stared back fearlessly: northern Italian blood, as he still liked to insist. Beside him, Spike's mother – a foot shorter even in heels – gazed up quizzically, as though unsure of what was to come, but guessing it would at least be amusing. Her left hand held a small bouquet of ivory roses, contrasting with the dark, delicate features of her face.

'You look a lot like him,' Solomon said.

Spike replaced the photo on the sideboard. When

he looked back, Solomon had the crumpled purple rectangle of a British Gibraltar passport in one hand.

'All right,' Spike said, taking it. 'Let's get this done.'

CHAPTER 3

By 7 a.m., Spike was at his desk. The ceiling fan whirred soporifically above as he picked up a remote, switched off the fan, then picked up another and turned on his iPod speakers, feeling the humidity rise as the first arpeggios of Caprice No. 5 filtered through. Spike could do ten minutes of music with no fan, ten minutes of fan with no music, but combining the two created a discord that made work impossible.

The tax statute had downloaded; Spike checked an appendix, fountain pen in hand. Ahead, a pair of high French windows gave onto a paved patio. A date palm had centuries ago cracked through its flagstones to provide shade, not that that were needed today – the levanter breeze had drawn in a blanket of thick, humid cloud, shrouding the entire peninsula of Gibraltar, while out in the Straits, the sunshine blazed.

Spike heard the distant scrape of chair legs on parquet. The offices of Galliano & Sanguinetti had once been a grace-and-favour residence for various Royal Navy sea lords. Spike liked how their conversion reflected Gibraltar's shift from military stronghold to financial centre. Liked that more than the work.

A rap came from the door. 'Keep it on, keep it on,' Peter Galliano said as Spike stretched for a remote control. 'Anything to distract from this *pipando* closeness.' He sank down into the leather armchair opposite Spike's desk. 'Your fellow Genoese?'

Spike nodded.

'Didn't he sell his soul to the Devil?'

'Paganini had Marfan syndrome,' Spike said. 'A rare disorder of the connective tissue.'

'Sounds like the Devil's music to me,' Galliano replied, still arranging his bulky frame in the armchair. 'Anyway, speaking of crafty Devils . . .'

'The Uzbeks?'

'Back in town and meaning business.' Galliano shunted forward in his seat. He was wearing his three-piece houndstooth suit today, a sign of an important lunch. There was even a spotted kerchief in the breast pocket, which he took out to dab at his fleshy brow. '*Jodido* levanter,' he murmured.

Spike switched the music for the ceiling fan, the rush of air making the documents on his desk tremble.

'Why you won't let me buy you an air-conditioning unit,' Galliano said, 'I shall never . . .'

Spike let him finish, waiting for the double blink that signified his mind was focused. 'The key,' Spike began, 'is to impress on them that Gibraltar's ten per cent headline rate is for keeps. Other tax havens may give better short-term deals, but their fiscal future is uncertain. Gib will still be here, same as before. Minor expenditure for major security.'

'Safe as the Rock of Gibraltar?'

'You got it.'

'And the sovereignty issue?'

'There's a new Foreign Office report out. Print it off.'

Galliano waved a pudgy palm. 'Too much detail looks like weakness to your Uzbekistani.'

'Where are you planning to take them?'

'I thought the Eliott.'

'There's always that new vodka bar in Ocean Village.'

'*Ochen horosho.*' Galliano prised himself up using both armrests. With one hand he smoothed down the goatee beard he'd grown in an attempt to reclaim a long-lost jawline. In the three years since he and Spike had started up on their own – escaping the open-plan uniformity of Ruggles & Mistry, their previous employer – Galliano had had to make numerous adjustments to his wardrobe. Lunching for victory, he called it. 'Still on that e-gaming SPV?' he asked, seeing the statute open on Spike's laptop.

'Yes, but for a different company.'

He gave Spike a sideways bear hug, wafting cologne. 'Goods and services, young Sanguinetti,' he said, wheezing at the effort. 'A few more years of this and think of all the goods and services. Your own palazzo in Genoa. Yo-Yo Ma playing

Paganini at your dinner parties . . .' He was still muttering as he picked up his briefcase and huffed into the entrance hall. Spike heard him curse as he met the butterfly-house humidity outside, then pause to light a Silk Cut Ultra as the doors clicked closed behind him.

Spike switched the music back on. On his desk sat a more recent photograph of his mother. He stared at her, embarrassed to be startled yet again by her beauty. He tried to catch her eye, but she was gazing out to sea, dark glossy hair tied back in a ponytail, snapped unawares on a family holiday a lifetime ago.

The intercom buzzed. 'I know,' Spike said, 'goods and services . . .'

Instead of Galliano's jocular tones came a brusque female voice. 'Mr Sanguinetti?'

'*Sí.*'

'It's Margo Hassan. Solomon's mother.'

Spike's finger hovered over the button. He depressed it and switched off the music for good.

CHAPTER 4

Spike indicated the leather armchair Galliano had just vacated.

'I'd rather not,' Margo Hassan replied curtly, 'you'll probably bill me.' She stood with her legs apart on the frayed Moroccan rug that covered the office parquet. Above her faded black jeans, a scooped green top revealed a seamed and sun-weathered neck.

Spike leaned against the panelled wall, arms crossed. He remembered Mrs Hassan from his schooldays, waiting for Solomon by the gates. She'd always been a favourite with the older boys – the dyed brown hair was shorter but her sharp eyes and red lipstick remained the same. Spike had seen her around from time to time, in the way the thirty-odd thousand residents of Gibraltar did as they went about their business: a nod here, a smile there; too much courtesy and you'd never make it past your front door.

'I've seen him,' Margo Hassan said.

'I told him to keep it quiet.'

'The warder told a friend and that friend told me.' Her lower lip began to quiver, sending a wave of irritation through Spike. '*Patitu*,' she murmured. 'I'm a bit . . . May I?'

'Of course.'

They both sat down, Margo Hassan neat and bird-like in the armchair. Spike pointed behind him to a shelf of leather-bound spines. 'Tax books, Mrs Hassan. I haven't taken a criminal case in years.'

'He wants you.'

'Drew Stanford-Trench read law at Durham.'

'Solomon says lawyers only practise in Gib if they can't make it elsewhere.'

'I'm here.'

'That's different.'

'How?'

Margo glanced at the portrait on Spike's desk, giving him another stab of irritation.

'He says Stanford-Trench drinks.'

'This is Gibraltar, Mrs Hassan.'

'That he doesn't know about extradition treaties.'

'Nor do I.' Spike stared at her across the desk. He had only the vaguest memories of Mr Hassan, a short, bearded man in a skullcap who used to carry Solomon through the streets on his shoulders. He'd left Gibraltar when Solomon was still young. Just cleared out one morning – the talk was he'd wound up in Tel Aviv with a new family.

'Please,' Mrs Hassan said. 'I know you two weren't the greatest of friends at school. But this is Solomon we're talking about. Solly. He can be pushy, ambitious. But *this*?' Her voice caught as she traced four red nails across a fold of her neck. ‘He doesn’t even know *how* to lie. As a boy, I’d say, Do the right thing when you go to a friend’s house – even if you don’t like the food, say you do. But he never could.’

Spike remembered that attitude crucifying Solomon in the playground. ‘Mrs Hassan,’ he said, ‘there are more lawyers per capita in Gibraltar than in any other town on earth. If your son doesn’t like Drew Stanford-Trench, I can find him someone else.’

‘I want you.’ She stalled, casting about. ‘You . . . won that scholarship.’

The clouds parted behind the French windows, sending a contre-jour sunbeam onto Margo Hassan’s face. Spike took in the notches around her mouth, the translucency of her skin as it hung at a slight remove from her skull. The sky reclaimed the sun and her face darkened. ‘He won’t last five minutes,’ she said.

‘I’m sorry?’

‘As a Sephardi. In a Tangiers jail. Not five minutes.’ She rose from her armchair, still staring over at Spike. ‘It’s always come so easily to you, hasn’t it?’

‘What has?’

‘I mean . . . just *look* at you.’

‘I’ll walk you out,’ Spike said, but she was already in the hallway, pushing through the doors onto the street.

CHAPTER 5

The Union Jack flapped impatiently from the portico of the Convent, the pretty pink building that was home to the governor of Gibraltar. Opposite, the beer garden of the Angry Friar pub was bustling with punters: tax-free shoppers, baffled Japanese, small-time Costa crims leafing through the day's *Sun*. The pub was named after the Brotherhood of Franciscans evicted from their monastery – *convento* in Spanish – to make way for the British gubernatorial household, after Spain had lost Gibraltar in 1704. A group of shirtless youths was marching towards it, tattooed forearms swinging in formation. Their leader – best man, probably – glanced up at the sky, frowning at Gibraltar's curious subtropical microclimate before joining in with his friends' football chant.

Spike shouldered past them, the sharp iron railings of the law courts to his right, a gravel pathway running between beds of orange orchids towards a knot of chain-smoking locals awaiting their turn in the dock. The crowds grew denser; interspersed with the British high-street brands were independent Gibraltarian shops: VAT-free drink and fags, gold, perfume, electrical equipment. One name, Booze & Co., caught the tone nicely. Inside, Spike saw the shopkeeper heaping litres of Gordon's and cartons of Winstons into the greedy arms of expats. They'd be back over the Spanish border by evening, driving their booty down to Sotogrande for a weekend pool party. A leather-faced Brit looked Spike up and down. He stared back and she winked a lazy, turquoise-lidded eye.

Behind the Horseshoe pub, pigeons pecked busily at a heap of carroty vomit. A herring gull waddled over to chase them from their savoury syllabub. As Spike climbed higher, the tourist droves began to thin and the urban beautification so beloved of the Gibraltar government – brass plaques, hanging baskets, ceremonial cannons – ceded to flaking stucco and unionist graffiti. *With Britain till death do us part* was daubed on one block of houses; *We shall fight to the last but never surrender*, a legacy of the constant threat that British sovereignty of Gibraltar be shared with Spain.

Above lay Chicardo's and home; Spike turned left, skirting over Main Street, heading for the easternmost edge of the Old Town. Casemates Square sprawled below, the hub of Gibraltar, formerly a soldiers' barracks and site of public executions, now full of karaoke bars and fish'n'chip stalls. Beyond spread the frontier traffic of Winston Churchill Avenue, queues of overheating cars tooting in frustration as the Spanish border officials deliberately slowed them down: the unnecessary search of the spare-tyre axle, the drawn-out phone call to check a valid EU passport. Gib was like a wart to the Spanish. Pull the noose tight enough and eventually it would drop off.

On the corner of Hospital Hill, Spike saw a group of kids, probable truants from the Sacred Heart Middle School. 'Check it,' the youngest one said, pointing up at the cemetery. '*Macaco*.'

Spike looked up to where a female ape perched on a headstone. Clinging to its underside was a fluffy brown ball with eyes, its fur darker than the light-grey pelt of its mother. Appropriate insulation for the snows of the Atlas Mountains in Morocco, where the apes were said to have originated, less suitable here. The mother gave a hiss, flashing yellow sabre-tooth fangs. Patrolling the unweeded graveyard below was a stocky male, moving on all fours with a swagger that would have impressed the stag parties down on Main Street. Its naked pink face and absence of tail gave it a disconcertingly human quality. It made a lunge for the female, which bounded off the headstone onto a wall – baby still hanging – before thumping down onto the roof of a transit van.

'*Muncho* cool,' the youngest kid said. Time for a cull, Spike thought to himself as he walked away – when the ape colonies grew too large and started encroaching to the Old Town, the government would send in the sharpshooters with silencers.

Ahead rose the Moorish Castle, dominated by

the Tower of Homage, built by the Moors when they'd captured Gibraltar in ad 711. They'd held it until the reconquest, seven centuries later, and their leader's name had stuck, *Jebel Tariq* – Mountain of Tariq – had stuck, morphing over time to Gibraltar. Beneath the stone battlements ran dark, sweaty stains where the Moors had poured boiling pitch onto besieging Spaniards. Spike stared up at them, marvelling as ever at their longevity, as he came into Upper Castle Gully. Then he saw Jessica Navarro standing by her Royal Gibraltar Police van.

CHAPTER 6

Jessica took off her chequered hat, pinioning it beneath her short-sleeved white shirt as Spike stooped to kiss her cheek. He still had a hand on her shoulder as she drew away; she hesitated, then moved back in for the second peck.

'How's your schedule fixed?' Spike said.

'Pickpocket. Due in the Mags at half two.'

'Looked pretty busy down there.'

'Thought you'd given all that up, Tax Man.'

They both turned, looking up at the Rock, at the gulls circling and squawking as they dipped in and out of a grey discus of cloud. 'Humid one today,' Spike said.

'*Muy mahugin.*'

Spike looked back. The smooth olive skin of Jessica's forehead betrayed no hint of sweat. Her chestnut hair was gathered in a silky knot, the better to fit beneath her police hat. 'So what do you think?' she asked, managing to hold Spike's eye. 'Guilty?'

'Solomon's a chartered accountant, Jess. He's capable of many things but I don't think murder's one of them.'

'People can change.'

'I'm glad you think so.'

She looked away. 'Maybe you're right. He's got that feel about him. Wrong place, wrong time.'

'How do you mean?'

She shrugged, breasts shifting beneath her black stab vest. 'He was hysterical when we brought him in. Freaking out in case he had to share his cell. But when we stuck him in solitary, he just sat there on the bunk and bowed his head. Like he was used to life doing him over. Expected it.'

'What's the commissioner's take?'

'He's waiting to hear from you. Seems we all are.' She stared up again. 'You know,' she said, 'when I saw your number come up, I assumed you actually wanted to talk.'

'I've been busy.'

He watched her beautiful eyes narrow with anger. 'Don't work too hard,' she said. 'All that paper-pushing is ageing you.' She half reached up to touch his face, then let her hand fall as a clank came from above. The portcullis door of Her Majesty's Prison opened to reveal a junior warder accompanied by a sullen, handcuffed youth in a tracksuit.

Spike walked Jessica up the slope. She signed a clipboard, escorting the pickpocket back down to her van as Spike and the warder continued on to the entrance, the fifteen-yard passage that represented the thickness of the castle's thousand-year-old walls. There'd been attempts to move the prison wholesale to a shiny new facility on the other side of town. It still hadn't happened.

Before going inside, Spike turned to see Jessica sharing a joke with her ward. Then she slammed the double doors behind him.

CHAPTER 7

Alan Gaggero stood up from the front desk. Behind him rose a bank of elderly CCTV monitors. Spread before him was the *Gibraltar Chronicle* crossword.

'Stuck?'

Gaggero grinned. His grey comb-over and kindly eyes were unchanged. 'What's it been now, Spike?' he said. 'Two years?'

'Three.'

'Three years,' Gaggero repeated as he ran Spike's briefcase through the scanner.

'Thought they were shutting this place down,' Spike said.

'Overspill.'

They headed in single file down the side stairs. 'How's your old man doing?' Gaggero asked.

'*Está haleto*. But he can still finish the crossword in ten minutes flat.'

'I'll have to up my game then.'

Gaggero jangled his key fob and unbolted the steel door. 'Back in a mo,' he said, leaving the door ajar.

Spike listened as Gaggero's rubber soles squeaked away down the corridor. The off-white walls of the interview room were windowless and the strip lights hummed. The air smelled of disinfectant and was as dank as might be expected in the deepest reaches of a medieval castle. A table was nailed to the lino, carved like a school desk with initials and incomplete slogans of protest. In the corner, a black CCTV camera peered from its bracket like an alien eye.

Once Gaggero's footsteps had faded, Spike walked over to the far wall. Leaning back against it, he took a tissue from his pocket and worked the two leaves of the material apart. He tore off a fingertip-sized piece, which he moistened with his tongue. After checking the door, he reached up and stuck the tissue to the CCTV lens. Then he returned to the table.

Tipping one of the chairs onto its side, he brought a brogue crashing down on the pivotal leg. With a few more kicks, the wood splintered. He propped the chair back up in front of the table, then went round to the other side and sat down.

His briefcase held a single-deck tape recorder, which he took out and positioned on the table. Moments later, the door opened fully and Solomon Hassan appeared, Alan Gaggero behind. 'You remember the form,' Gaggero said, gesturing at the wall buzzer beneath the camera.

Spike nodded.

'*Vale*,' Gaggero said. 'Enjoy.' He withdrew, sliding the bolt into place.

Solomon was back in his supplicatory position, head bowed, hands behind back. He wore prison denims now – belt-free trousers, coarse button shirt – and tatty flip-flops with, for some reason, a minute Brazilian flag on the straps. His skin was paler and his plump cheeks stubblier, like wintry copses seen from the air.

'Have a seat,' Spike said.

The chair leg gave way at once. Solomon let out a yelp, making a lunge for the table but toppling sideways onto the lino.

Spike moved round to his side. 'You all right there, Solly?'

Solomon lay on the floor in the foetal position, snapped chair beside him.

'Here, let me help. Have mine.' Spike hauled him up and brought his own chair round. Solomon sat down carefully, shaking his head.

'I'll perch,' Spike said, sitting on the table. 'So are they treating you OK?'

'I have a slop bucket in my cell.'

'Ouch.'

'And the guy next door keeps praying. I can't sleep.'

'It is called the Moorish Castle, Solomon. You didn't care for Drew Stanford-Trench, they tell me?'

'He was vague on extradition treaties.'

'Well, I'm briefed on those. Want to hear?'

'Yes.'

'There's good and bad news. The good is that you won't have to see Drew Stanford-Trench again.'

Solomon gave a nod.

'Nor me for that matter.'

Solomon wrinkled his nose as though confronted by a sudden stench.

'Because the bad news is that there's a new Order-in-Council, extending the Extradition Act 1870. Only passed at the start of the year, part of a broader deal made by the Gibraltar government. Trying to seem squeaky-clean to the EU – any fraudsters skip across the Straits, we get them back. But it cuts both ways. So if the Kingdom of Morocco requests the company of Mr Solomon Hassan, they need only say the word.'

'But I haven't done anything.'

'They just need a prima facie case.'

'They don't even have a proper justice system.'

'Oh, I hear Moroccan public defenders can be pretty good. Some of them even speak English.'

Solomon laid both hands on the table. His thumbs were criss-crossed with dark-flecked scabs. 'Why are you –'

'They've still got the death penalty in Morocco, you know that, Solly? Not used much, but in your case, a defenceless girl, a foreigner –'

'I'm innocent, Spike.'

'You ran.'

'I told you, as a Jew –'

'Where are the witnesses who saw you leave? Where's your alibi?' Spike dismounted and came round to Solomon's side. 'Let me tell you what I think,' he said. 'Stop me if I veer off track.' He crouched down to Solomon's level. 'You're on the beach, right? The sun is setting; it's romantic, almost.'

Solomon stared into the middle distance, picking at his thumbs. Spike leaned in closer. 'This girl's new in town, and she likes you, you can tell. You've had a few drinks, you're sitting on the sand, and then suddenly you realise. This is it. This is why you left Gibraltar. This is what you've been pumping iron for all those nights alone in your flat. So you lean across and kiss her. And it was that way round, wasn't it, Solly? But she just laughs. She doesn't say "Sorry" or "Can't we just be friends?" She just laughs in your face. And it all starts to come back. Solly the Wally. Simple Solly. Shoved around the playground by the younger boys. You thought you'd left all that behind, the big shot who went to Africa to make his fortune, but now you see that's how it's always going to be, and something inside you snaps. You smash your bottle of beer, or maybe you use something on the beach. You jab forward and suddenly she's not laughing any more. Stop me if I'm wrong, Solly.'

Solomon blinked behind his spectacles; Spike

reached to the floor and picked up the broken chair leg. 'Take it,' he said, wrapping Solomon's thick fingers around the shaft. 'How does it feel? That weight in your hand. Is that how the knife felt?' Solomon's right fist gripped the chair leg, veins rising on the back like worm casts. 'She was laughing at you, Solly, and she's Spanish, and God knows, we Gibbos have all had enough of that. So you lunge at her, and now you're staring at a corpse, and something takes over, an instinct, and you're rolling her into the water, but she's heavy, you can't get her far, but the tide will come in, won't it, so you're running from the beach, slowing as you reach the coast road, then it's home safe to a football match, just to say you've done something, and in the morning even you can't believe it, *did* you do it? Except the police turn up. They're all corrupt in Tangiers, who wouldn't run? And here we are.'

Solomon was trying to speak.

'Sorry?'

He shook his head, blinking.

'When did your father leave?' Spike said, moving in closer. There were flakes of dandruff in Solomon's hair, dazzling against the greasy blackness. 'Twenty years ago, was it? Left you and old Mother Hassan behind. She came to see me, Solly.'

Solomon's head turned a fraction. The red lines in the whites of his eyes were back.

'That's right,' Spike went on. 'Came to my office this morning, low-cut top, legs akimbo.'

Solomon's fist clenched more tightly around the chair leg.

'After your dad left, *ima* kept you close, didn't she? No one good enough for her boy. But you got away. Made it over the Straits, promised to send her money, got to Tangiers where no one was watching. Somewhere you could make a move on a girl. Somewhere you could punish a girl.'

Solomon's teeth gritted. The chair leg rose, angling towards Spike.

'Away from old *ima* nothing counts as much, so when a girl laughs at you, the one girl you thought might actually like you, you can shut her up and it won't matter at all.' At the periphery of his vision, Spike checked the dimensions of the room. 'Murders happen all the time in Tangiers, who's going to notice some Spanish *chochi* who drank too much and –'

There was a clatter as Solomon's grip slackened and the chair leg dropped to the ground. His head slumped down, two oily lines exuding from behind his spectacles. 'No,' he said. '*No.*'

Spike moved behind him, laying a hand on his shoulder, feeling the surprising tautness of the muscles. 'It's OK,' he said. 'I just had to check.'

As soon as Solomon's sobs subsided, Spike sat down on the table and hit 'record' on the tape recorder. 'Twenty-first of August, fifteen twenty hours,' he said into the speaker. 'Room 2, Moorish Castle Prison. First client interview.'

Solomon glanced up.

'Mr Hassan, why, in your opinion, is it unsafe for a Jew to be held in prison in Tangiers?'

'Is this –'

Spike nodded.

'But you –'

'Answer the question, please, Mr Hassan.'

Solomon took off his glasses, dabbing at the teardrops with his denim shirt. 'There was a home-made bomb. Six months ago. At a synagogue in Casablanca.' He sniffed moistly. 'The King rounded up all the Islamists. There've been reprisals in the prisons.'

'Presumably Jewish inmates are held in separate wings.'

'The attacks happen in the yard. In the canteen.'

'Is this documented?'

Solomon slid his glasses back on. The lenses were still mottled. 'The media still gets censored. But people know.'

'And you're a Sephardic Jew?'

Solomon nodded.

'Speak up, Mr Hassan. The machine doesn't register gestures.'

'Yes-I-am-a-Jew.'

Spike clicked off the tape as Solomon's lips peeled back. 'What the hell was *that*?'

'My peace of mind.'

'Your what?'

'If I'm going to represent you.'

There was fresh blood on Solomon's thumbs.

He continued to pick at them, oblivious. Spike reached over to stop him and he snatched both his hands away, hiding them beneath the tabletop. 'So I won't have to go back to Tangiers?'

'We can try and stall them on the Jewish angle,' Spike said as he walked over to the wall buzzer, 'but no promises.'

After counting to ten, Spike peeled the flake of tissue from the camera lens. Thirty seconds later, the metal bolt began to slide.

'Find out the time of death,' Solomon said hurriedly as the door creaked open.

Spike looked round.

'The precise hour. Someone from that bar must have –'

'Twelve and a half minutes,' Gaggero said as he came in. 'You'll tell your old man that, won't –' Gaggero broke off, seeing the carcass of the chair on the ground.

'One too many halal burgers for Mr Hassan, I'm afraid,' Spike said, giving the chair back a prod with his shoe. 'It just went.'

Gaggero frowned, then tapped Solomon on the back. As Solomon rose, Spike thought he saw the ghost of a smile on his mouth. Maybe it was a grimace. 'The girl's name,' he said. 'It was Esperanza.'

Spike nodded, then put away the tape recorder and returned to the office.

Galliano was still out to lunch. Spike sat

motionless at his desk until the harsh staccato notes of Caprice No. 9 reached their climax. Then he picked up the phone and placed a call to the court of assizes in Tangiers.

CHAPTER 8

Spike watched the paintbrush swish back and forth: the cyan sea, the outline of a boat. A moment later, the Rock of Gibraltar began to loom from the centre of the canvas as Rufus's long thin fingers worked the brush, each tapering down to a dainty nail.

'It comes to eight pills a day,' Spike said, looking back down at his list. 'Four lots of two.'

Rufus began smudging the area beneath the Rock with his thumb, creating the impression of a dark, foreboding shadow cast over the Straits.

'Dad?'

Rufus winched up his head, frowning like a hermit disturbed.

'I've written down all the times.'

'Pills, pills, pills,' Rufus said. 'Pure buggery quackery.'

'The fridge is fully stocked, Dad. Any problems, just give me a call. Day or night.'

Rufus peered from behind his bifocals, blue eyes freakishly magnified. Silver hair curled onto his shoulders like the tendrils of the spider plants that grew upstairs in his study. 'It's you we should be worrying about, son.'

'Why's that?'

'Tangiers. Easy place to get entangled.'

'I'm just gathering evidence for an extradition hearing. Three nights, max.'

'City of Perfidy, Jean Genet called it.'

'I'll bet he did.'

Rufus laid down his paintbrush. 'I used to go there every month in the seventies. When the generalissimo had closed the border with Spain. Ferry to Tangiers, transfer, wait, ferry to Algeciras. Ten-hour round trip to go the best part of a mile. A man needs to watch his step. Could run into trouble like the Hassan boy.'

'I really wouldn't worry about it.'

'There's always baksheesh, of course. Financial inducement. Foul and filthy lucre.' Rufus combed his fingers through his hair. 'Maybe I'll pay a visit to Mrs Hassan. Damned handsome woman.'

'You just take it easy, Dad.' Spike stood to help him tidy away the watercolours. He slipped an arm beneath Rufus's shoulder but he shrugged it away. 'I'm fine, son. *Entro en pala.*'

Beneath the table, General Ironside's tail tapped out a steady tattoo before he appeared with a scratch of unclipped claws on cork. Spike fell in behind both man and Jack Russell as they creaked upstairs.

'Get some sun in Morocco,' Rufus said, turning once they reached the landing. 'You look worn out.'

'I'll bring you up a cup of tea, Dad.'

CHAPTER 9

Spike stood in front of the mirror, pushing his dark hair back from his forehead and forcing a smile. Jessica was right. Crow's feet crinkled the corners of his eyes. He let the smile fall. The resemblance to Rufus was there in his height and blue irises, but his full mouth and dark Latin skin were his mother's. He rotated his shoulder blades, searching for traces of pain. Fifty-fifty, the Spanish doctor had said, that Marfan syndrome passed from father to son.

Setting the music to low, Spike stretched out on his bed, watching the curtains swirl as the violin strings hit an uncomfortable pinnacle. He'd always been more of a Mozart man, much to Rufus's disapproval, but now that he'd reached Caprice No. 10, he had to admit there was something haunting in those shrill, tremulous notes.

Through the open window, the terracotta roofs of the Old Town concertinaed down to cranes and high-rise apartments. Luxury tax-exile accommodation built on land reclaimed from the sea. On the far side of the Straits, the lights of Africa pulsed, as though flashing out signals that Spike was supposed to decipher.

He tucked his hands behind his head, thinking back to the doctor's lame attempts at reassurance. The list of famous people who'd managed to thrive with Marfan's had not been long. Initially the name of Niccolò Paganini had not stood out; indeed, it was only when Spike had learned that Paganini had originated in Genoa that he'd taken an interest, ordering a collection of the caprices online, twenty-four solo pieces designed, so far as Spike could tell, to showcase the composer's unnatural capabilities. According to the CD sleeve, he could play up to twelve notes a second, handspan stretching over three octaves.

No. 11 was a caprice too far; Spike reached over to kill the music. A cacophony of karaoke drifted up from Casemates on the levanter. Folding his hands across his chest, Spike pushed the image of Solomon's bespectacled face to the back of his mind, then willed himself to sleep.

PART II

TANGIERS

CHAPTER 10

Spike Sanguinetti stood on the wooden deck of the catamaran, watching the Bay of Tangiers emerge from the heat haze. He'd been here once before, perhaps a decade ago, accompanying an English girlfriend on a quest to buy some authentic Moroccan saffron. They'd arrived in the morning and left by the afternoon. Spike hadn't stuck around long enough to find out if the mother had liked her present.

Much of the city resembled a wasps' nest – box-shaped, paper-white houses clustered on a hillside. The steepest and brightest part was the Medina, a walled zone that still followed the contours of the ancient Roman settlement, stone towers and minarets jutting towards a blurry skyline. Stretching around the bay were the more modern tenement buildings and broader boulevards of the Ville Nouvelle. Curving in front of both was a dark yellow scimitar of sand.

The breeze fell as the catamaran slowed. The crossing had been calm, belying the dangers Spike knew lurked beneath. British sailors nicknamed this stretch of water 'The Gut', due to its hidden, churning currents. The rivers flowing into the Mediterranean replaced only a third of the water lost through evaporation – as a result, extra water was needed from the Atlantic, so speeding up the movement on the surface of the Straits. The denser, more saline waters of the Med, meanwhile, sank down to the seabed and spilled out into the Atlantic, causing the currents at the top and bottom of the Straits to flow in opposite directions. It was what one couldn't see that needed to be feared.

An announcement crackled through in English on the tannoy. By the time it had been repeated in Spanish, French and Arabic, its information was outdated. They were already at their destination.

Grizzled Moroccans in Western dress began filing onto the deck, yawning as they shielded their eyes from the glare – manual workers who'd spent most of the crossing asleep on the bench seats inside. Gibraltar had opened her borders to them in the 1970s, when Franco had shut the frontier with Spain, and labour had been needed in the commercial dockyard. The younger ones were still employed, and this Friday afternoon catamaran brought them home to their families, bundles of Gibraltar pounds sewn into their trousers, plastic tartan holdalls zipped at their feet.

After passing an industrial mole – cranes, bunkering equipment – the catamaran eased into a buoy-marked lane. From the lower deck, ropes weighted by miniature cannonballs were flung onto a jetty by unseen hands, collected by dark-skinned men in white djellabas, who lashed them to iron ringbolts, creating a creak as the hull battled its restraints.

The air smelled of diesel and woodsmoke. Spike leaned his forearms on the railings and looked down into the murky water. Just below the surface, a large grey mullet was swimming in a circle. It kept stopping and flipping onto its side, white belly glinting in the sun. After sinking down a foot or so, it would right itself and swim back up to continue its circle. Its spine was kinked, Spike saw, injured by a boat propeller or malformed through pollution.

The jaws of the catamaran began to gape as the vans and lorries rolled out. Painted on the side of one, Spike saw a cartoon tomato in sunglasses. As he waited for the passenger gangplank to lower, he took a notebook from his leather overnight bag. Below, the kinked fish still described its circle.

CHAPTER 11

On the far side of customs, families were gathered, women in headscarves trying to sneak a look past each other's shoulders, toddlers pincering their legs like stag beetles. Spike slid over his passport. The immigration officer had a mongrel look, oily dark hair hanging over a pallid, sunken-eyed face. A Gibraltarian kind of look, Spike thought. '*Nulli expugnabilis hosti*,' he said as he stamped Spike's passport.

No enemy shall expel us – the Rock's official motto. 'I'm surprised you left then, *compa*,' Spike replied in a thick Gibraltarian accent.

The officer gave a smile, rubbing his thumb on his first two fingers in the universal gesture of money. Spike pushed on through to arrivals.

The moment Spike entered the hall, a crowd of hawkers surrounded him like a celebrity lawyer leaving a courthouse. The swiftest on their feet wore knock-off Levi's and trainers, those behind more traditional white tunics and sandals. 'Hey, Jimmy,' called one. 'Hotel? Lovely price.'

'*Amigo!*' cried another, scrumming over his rival. 'Guide for the Kasbah?'

'DVD film, *mein Herr*?'

A tangle of arms extended. '*Uzbek*,' Spike said firmly.

The hawkers stared up in puzzlement as a teenager with a downy moustache tugged at the sleeve of Spike's suit. '*Du kif, monsieur?*' he whispered.

'*Uzbekistan*,' Spike repeated, and the hawkers switched their attention to an American backpacker who'd just come in through the gate.

By the main exit, Spike saw a European holding up a placard. He wore a seersucker jacket and mirrored Oakley shades. As Spike approached, he pushed his sunglasses up onto his high freckly forehead. His eyes were watery blue with sandy lashes, the thinning blond hair side-parted.

'That'll be me,' Spike said, indicating his misspelt name. Above it was a logo, 'DUNETECH', the 'N' stylised to look like a desert sand dune.

The man held out a signet-ringed hand. 'Toby Riddell.'

'Spike Sanguinetti.'

'Crossing OK?'

'Incident-free.'

Riddell smiled slightly as he walked down the steps. Out in the sunshine, a queue of lorries was waiting to exit the port complex, harbour guards in Aviators checking documentation. Gulls circled above, cackling as though some stale old joke had set them off.

They headed towards a silver Mercedes saloon.

A hunched, toothless man emerged from the shadows, fingering a necklace of tasselled fez hats. 'Special price –' he began, but Riddell interrupted him with a palm to the forehead, handing him off like a rugby player. The man clattered back against the barbed-wire fence that ran along the pavement.

'They're like dogs,' Riddell said without breaking stride. His shiny black shoes ticked on the flagstones like a metronome.

With a satisfying bleep, Riddell unlocked the Mercedes. As soon as Spike got in, they accelerated away beneath an archway dedicated to private cars. The guard waved them through at once, and they came out onto the coast road, the Medina rising above, various official-looking port buildings to the left. The roadway was divided by a central reservation of dried yellow grass, on which clusters of men in prayer robes sat eyeing the traffic as though plucking up courage to leap before it.

Riddell drove with a single, freckled finger on the wheel. 'So how is old Solly-man?' he said.

'Bearing up.'

'At least he's back among his own –' Riddell broke off to hoot at the moped in front, on which two men in tunics were perched, one clamped to the other. A container lorry was blocking the right-hand lane; Riddell drew up so close to the moped that his bumper was almost touching its back wheel. The driver glanced right before wobbling sideways, wing mirror inches from the lorry's rusty steel slats. Spike saw wide, terrified eyes as they passed.

'Give this mob half an inch,' Riddell said, 'and they'll half-inch a mile.' He adjusted the wheel with a fingertip to avoid a *petit taxi*. 'So how's business in Gib? Economy booming?'

'Ticking over.'

'I suppose there are enough Solomons and Abrahams to keep it that way. Angry Friar still open?'

'Was yesterday.'

'Quite a boozer.'

Spike didn't need to ask how Riddell knew the Rock. Gibraltarians had sensitive antennae when it came to spotting the British military. The sun reflecting in Riddell's over-polished black shoes had spoken eloquently.

Spike looked out at the beach below the coast road. Hand-painted signs protruded from the sand. Before Spike could read them, Riddell had veered right and they started to climb a cross street up the hillside. An entire block of buildings had collapsed here, leaving a landslip of rubble and weeds. Some entrepreneurial opportunist had taken advantage of the unexpected exposure to the coast road by scrawling '*Garage mécanique: 933317*' on the wall of the house behind.

They turned onto a broader, French-style boulevard. Rather than plane trees, date palms lined the pavements. The windows were barred with wrought-iron balconies, while interspersed with the apartment blocks were *pâtisseries*, *épiceries*, *pharmacies*. On the roof of one, a billboard proclaimed 'DUNETECH'. Beneath its logo was a phrase: *Powering a Greener Future*. The next hoarding advertised a failed bid for Tangiers to host the international Expo. Spike checked the date: four years ago.

Riddell drove the Mercedes into a large commercial square. A fountain trickled in its centre, a bare-chested old man washing his prayer robes in its stone dish. 'This is us,' Riddell said, breaking sharply. 'You get out and I'll park the steer.' His accent was a carefully neutral English, as though a posher edge had been planed off.

As Riddell sped away, Spike realised why he'd been dropped in this position. Distance was needed to take in the scale of the Dunetech building. It dominated the entire south-facing end of the square, rising at least ten storeys higher than the shabby concrete office blocks on either side. Blue-tinted mirror glass burnished all four walls, gleaming in the mid-afternoon sun as though God had just finished buffing it with His own chamois leather.

Spike watched his reflection elongate as he approached. The revolving doors were mirrored, the Dunetech logo etched above them in a tastefully discreet font. It didn't need to be any larger; the point had been made.

CHAPTER 12

Spike sat on a cream-coloured sofa at the edge of a cavernous atrium. The Dunetech headquarters had a hollow centre, offices rising up around the sides, fewer than might have been expected from outside. Three potted palm trees stretched towards a skylight roof, newly arrived, judging by their greenness. The floor was of black polished limestone, the desk manned by a deeply tanned girl sporting excessive lipgloss. Behind her, an electronic turnstile protected a bank of glass-fronted lifts.

The receptionist shot Spike a smile. He'd been sitting for ten minutes and not a phone had rung nor a person come or gone. From the far wall issued a hi-tech whirr: one of the lifts had started to descend. A moment later the glass doors opened to a tall man in an immaculately cut pinstripe suit.

Spike rose.

'So sorry,' the man called out, rotating the turnstile with a clip of his hip. 'Nothing worse than being kept waiting after a long journey. I'm Nadeer Ziyad. How do you do?'

Spike shook a dark, slender hand.

‘So very pleased to meet you,’ the man said. He looked mid-thirties, Spike’s age. His face was long and angular, his nose hooked like a hawk’s and his eyes sparkling with the green and yellow glints that were the hereditary mark of the Berbers, the original inhabitants of North Africa. ‘Let’s go upstairs,’ he said. ‘You all right with your case?’

Spike swung his leather bag onto his shoulder and followed Nadeer towards the desk. As Nadeer passed, he whispered something in Arabic to the receptionist, who lowered her head before opening a drawer and taking out a remote. A rich air-con whoosh came from on high as they moved through the turnstile.

Nadeer adjusted his carefully crafted Windsor knot as he stepped into the lift. ‘These country girls,’ he said with a smile. ‘They rate forty degrees as mild.’

The speakers were piping out an instrumental version of ‘Candle in the Wind’. As the lift began to climb, Spike saw the receptionist stand from her desk. Her black pencil skirt rucked up her thighs as she crossed the marble to a cabinet beyond the palms. ‘So Tobes picked you up OK?’ Nadeer said.

‘Seemed most efficient.’

The lift stopped and Nadeer extended an arm for Spike to exit. A row of doors ran along one side of a white-carpeted corridor, with a waist-high Perspex screen giving onto the atrium below. Cream-cushioned chairs with plastic covers still on seats had been placed between each doorway. 'Developers are the same the world over,' Nadeer said as he strolled away. 'Take the estimate, double it and add a year. Don't you find?'

At the end of the corridor, Nadeer held open the door to an enormous corner office. Two of the walls consisted of floor-to-ceiling glass, the others solid and decorated with Rothkoesque sunscapes: burning reds, yellows, tangerines. In front of the tinted glass stood a heavy mahogany desk, to one side of which, propped against the skirting board, leaned a framed photograph of the King of Morocco.

'On a clear day we can see your homeland from here,' Nadeer said, striding over to the glass. 'Like God reaching out for Adam's fingertip, as my father likes to say. The continent of the past giving its blessing to the continent of the future.' All Spike could see through the haze was a parasailor being towed around the bay, motionless in his harness like a hanged man. 'Does the mirror glass power the building?' he asked.

'It will do,' Nadeer said, pressing his palms together. He smiled, eyes glittering like a tiger. 'Have a seat, Mr Sanguinetti. Please.'

Spike sat down on a stool opposite the desk, as Nadeer settled into a high-backed swivel chair. Spike caught a monogrammed flash of 'NaZ' on the lower left side of Nadeer's shirt. He checked the cuffs of Nadeer's blazer: the last button was undone, a subtle signal that the suit was bespoke.

Nadeer clicked down an Apple laptop, planting his elbows on the desk and resting his narrow chin on interlaced knuckles. 'So,' he said, 'how is he?'

'Still in a state of shock.'

He closed his eyes, breathing deeply. 'It's unbelievable. If there's anything we can do. Anything.' He opened them again, watching.

'We're going to fight extradition on human rights grounds,' Spike said. 'Article 5, Security of Person. We'll argue it's unsafe for a Jew to be held in custody in Tangiers.'

'Would that my country were a signatory to the Convention.'

'Gibraltar is. And so long as Solomon remains on Gibraltarian soil it applies.'

Nadeer tapped a nail against a pearly front tooth. 'You'd need proof of a genuine threat, of course.'

'That's why I'm here.'

He canted his head. 'Morocco is not Gibraltar, Mr Sanguinetti. It is perhaps a little less about what you can prove than who you know.'

Spike glanced over to the picture of the King of Morocco; Nadeer followed his gaze. 'Cup of tea?'

'Not for me, thanks.'

'No, no. I insist.' He lifted the phone without pressing a button and murmured in Arabic. 'All this sunshine,' he said, cupping the receiver, 'and I still miss England.' He smiled and hung up. 'The grey skies. The theatre. Annabel's. Do you get to London much?'

'Enough.'

'And Gibraltar's always been home?'

'University and law school in London. Since then, yes.'

'Doesn't it get . . . claustrophobic? Same size as Hyde Park, I seem to recall.'

'Minus the Rock.'

'Ah yes, the Rock, the great symbol of –'

A tap at the door mercy-killed the small talk as the receptionist teetered in with a silver tray. Nadeer remained seated as she lowered it onto his desk; he reached forward, raising the teapot lid, then dropping it with an icy clatter. Within the faint, rasping Arabic Spike recognised the words 'Earl Grey'. The girl began to slide the tray backwards.

'Mint tea's fine.'

'Sorry?'

'I've come all this way so it's a shame not to drink it.'

Nadeer nodded and the girl crept away. Smiling flatly, he arced a caramel spout of liquid through the strainer into Spike's cup. 'Human rights grounds,' he repeated as he poured a cup for himself. 'I suppose I could have a word with our local governor. Though he might not welcome accusations of anti-Semitism.'

'Nor global media coverage of a murdered Spanish girl on the beach.'

Nadeer puffed on his tea.

'Has there been much coverage of the death?' Spike said.

'Not thus far.'

'Of course,' Spike went on, blowing on his tea as well, 'one good thing about the size of Gibraltar is there's only one proper newspaper. The editor's a close friend.' He took a sip: sickly sweet, sugared in advance in the pot.

'Too sweet for you?'

'I like it that way.'

'Have you got a business card, Mr Sanguinetti?'

Spike put down his cup and reached for his wallet.

'"Somerset J. Sanguinetti",' Nadeer read aloud. '"Barrister at Law". Your people Italian?'

'Genoese, originally.'

'Escaping Napoleon?'

'In 1798.'

Nadeer turned the card over where the same information was written in Spanish. 'You know,' he said, tucking it beneath his phone, 'we're like blood brothers, Moroccans and Gibraltarians. Colonised. Oppressed. How many wars have you had against the Spanish?'

'Ten sieges and counting.'

'Ten sieges . . . I used to talk to Solomon about it. Ours are more recent – 1860 and 1926. Then there's the Spanish Civil War. Franco press-ganged 100,000 Moroccans to fight for him. Wiped out half my family.'

'But you work for a Spaniard, don't you? Esperanza's father.'

'Stepfather. We work together. But we can forgive him that. He's a phenomenal engineer. A visionary.'

'Is he in town?'

'Still in Madrid. Mourning.'

Spike sipped at his dark brown tea. 'Did you know Esperanza well?'

'She came by the office once or twice. Something of a wild child, I believe. Hardly Solomon's type.'

'Did you see her the day she died?'

Nadeer narrowed his green eyes. 'Toby and I were at a board meeting in Rabat with my father. Why?'

'Trying to piece together her final movements. Is Solomon's office in here?'

'Yes.'

'May I take a look around?'

Nadeer put down his cup. 'The police have already been through it with their usual grace but . . . I don't see why not. I can trust you not to remove anything?'

'I'm a lawyer, Mr Ziyad. Trust is our watchword.'

The frown translated into a smile.

'I couldn't use your . . .?' Spike stood, motioning to his teacup.

'Of course. Through there.'

Spike crossed the white shagpile carpet to a doorway. The cubicle had a porcelain sink at one end and a wooden-seated lavatory at the other. The walls were papered with red-and-green stripes; propped on the gleaming cistern was another picture still to be hung, a house photograph from Eton College, dating from twenty years ago. The names of the tail-coated boys were given in italics at the bottom. Spike scanned for 'Nadeer Ziyad' and found him at the back, small and shy with a neat centre-parted haircut. As he replaced the photograph, his eye was caught by the face of a boy in the bottom row, seated beside the housemaster. He had thick blond hair and a cool gaze levelled at the camera. His arms were folded across a polka-dot waistcoat, its garish design in contrast to the dull, uniform black worn by all the other pupils. Spike looked down at the list of names: 'The Hon. Tobias Riddell, Capt. of House'. He flushed the cistern and left.

CHAPTER 13

The next-door office was marked with a shiny brass plaque: 'Toby Riddell, Head of Corporate Security'. Spike tried the handle: locked. The adjacent door had two empty boreholes in the wood. Spike opened it and stepped inside.

A flat-pack desk faced a bare wall, the only window covered by a venetian blind with dusty blades, which Spike tugged up to a view of the neighbouring building's featureless concrete. There was an empty space on the desk where a laptop might once have sat, a number of tiny yellow Post-it notes dotted around it: 'NB future oil crunch for presentation'; 'Mamma's birthday – card *and* flowers'. Solomon's precise, careful handwriting looked unchanged since their schooldays. Already it had the quality of a relic.

Spike tried the desk drawer. Alongside a tray of golden paper clips was a plastic cylinder, 'CALIFORNIA MUSCLES' emblazoned on the front above an image of a bronzed he-man giving it the flex. Spike undid the taped-down foil, sniffed the powder, then put it back in the drawer.

Behind the desk stood a metal filing cabinet, a 'Gibraltar Rocks!' coffee mug on its top, encrusted with the same vanilla-scented powder. Five green suspension folders hung inside. Spike ran a fingertip over the tabs: 'DUNETECH Phase 1', 'DUNETECH Phase 2', 'Q1 Budget Review', 'Zagora Zween', 'Legal'. He drew out the last and opened it. Most of the correspondence was with Ruggles & Mistry, Spike's former employers. A cursory scan of the documentation revealed that Dunetech were looking to expand operations, keen to use Gibraltar's competitive tax rates to minimise their liability. So far so sensible, but if Solomon were already instructing Ruggles, why not ask them to represent him now? They had the best criminal practice on the Rock. Professional embarrassment, presumably.

Footsteps outside; Spike quickly replaced the file, knocking a Post-it to the floor. As he crouched to pick it up, he noticed something behind the back of the desk. He strained forward to a stiff card invitation: 'Dunetech Investor Roadshow'. Voices now; Spike folded the invitation into his inside pocket and walked out.

Nadeer's door was wedged open on the carpet. Ahead, Spike saw the crumpled back of Toby Riddell's seersucker jacket. Nadeer had his elbows on the desk, talking in an undertone. He broke off when he saw Spike. 'Find any lead piping? A candlestick?'

Riddell turned. The mirror shades were off,

exposing a pink V on the bridge of his nose. In his right hand he cupped an olive-green squash ball, which he compressed back and forth like a miniature heart.

'I'll have Tobes run you back to your hotel,' Nadeer said. 'Where did you say you were staying?'

'I didn't. Hotel Continental.'

Nadeer waved a hand like the choppy sea. 'Traditional, I suppose. How long are you with us?'

'Three nights. Maybe less.'

'Well, I've got your card. In the meantime, enjoy our fine city. It's still Ramadan, so everyone's a bit grouchy, but it'll liven up after sundown.' Nadeer stood, running his fingers through his wavy black hair before limply shaking Spike's hand.

Spike turned at the door. 'Either of you know the Sundowner Club?'

Riddell pumped at his squash ball.

'What's that?' Nadeer said.

'Some kind of beach bar, I think. Esperanza went there the night of her death.'

'Oh, that place,' Nadeer said as he sat back down. 'Those cathouses change their name by the week. Go there by all means, but if you're thinking of late-night entertainment, I'd advise you to tread carefully. Tobes?'

Riddell escorted Spike down the corridor. 'Give 'em half an inch,' he muttered.

'I'll walk from here,' Spike said as the lift arrived. 'Get my bearings.'

CHAPTER 14

The tight, whitewashed streets of the Medina were a hotchpotch of religious dress. Men wore beige hooded cloaks, or candy-striped djellabas, or immaculate white robes with perforated *kufi* caps; the few women wore black veils with eye slits, or embroidered kaftans, or jeans with bandannas over mouths and chunky black Ray-Bans perched on noses. Sub-Saharan Africans strode among them, broad-nosed Nigerians in tribal dress, gangly Masai with tartan blankets draped over shoulders. It was as though the continent of Africa had been tipped upside down and shaken like a pepper pot.

Schoolboys in tunics poured from a side door of the Grand Mosque. Seeing a shadow beneath a scooter trailer, one of them jabbed in a sandal. A kitten darted away as the boy high-fived his friend.

Rugs had been laid out on the road, heaped with pyramids of prickly pears, baskets of star anise, packets of crispy sunflower seeds. The rugs were for sale as well, judging by a merchant thumbing the weave at Spike. A barefoot man in rag trousers staggered by with a tray of samosas on his head, brown chair hooked over a browner arm.

Spike continued up the concentric circles towards the Kasbah, the fortified complex at the top of the hill that had once been the Sultan's palace. When he saw the white, crenulated walls, he knew he'd gone too far. He tried a different route down, passing an American woman of a certain age arm in arm with a handsome Moroccan youth. The irresistible pheromones of the green card.

Just around the corner was an alley lined with beggars. Spike dropped all his coins into the lap of a cowl-draped amputee. As he rounded the next corner, he found a woman with glaucous eyes, rocking on her hunkers.

Hawkers appeared, the first tapping at a bongo. Offers were made in a babel of languages but Spike strode away, dragging the more persistent in his slipstream. He was closer to the sea now, the air fresh and saline, blending with the fragrant smoke of joss sticks that were wedged in the shutter hinges of leather shops. The owners sat on stools outside, fiddling with prayer beads, watching the sky, waiting.

A cross-eyed man crawled by on his knees, scouring for cigarette ends. Spike watched him stop and pick up a twig, then jam it upright in a drain as though it were the centrepiece of some elegant flower arrangement. Two boys in fake Barcelona football shirts crunched it down as they passed by hand in hand, chatting.

At last Spike saw the sign, painted on a stucco archway. *Hotel Continental.* Rufus had made the recommendation. 'An institution, son,' he'd promised, 'good enough for Winston Churchill.' Spike entered the courtyard, where a uniformed security guard sat in a fogged-up hut watching football. He glanced over at Spike, then returned to his black-and-white TV.

Two men stood together at the reception desk. On the counter in front of them sat a triangular cardboard sign: *Together Against Terrorism*. The floor was of chequerboard marble, with a grand piano with the lid down and a smoked-glass art deco chandelier hanging from the wooden latticework ceiling. The curved staircase looked like it hadn't been dusted since Churchill's last visit.

The receptionist was jotting down directions on a free map. The guests said '*Shukran*' in a Spanish accent, then walked away. One had a shaven head with sideburns like drips of dried blood, the other peroxide hair and sugary aftershave. Both made a moue at Spike as they left.

'Single, please,' Spike said. Though old and grey, the receptionist had a chubby, beatific face. He wore the standard white djellaba and sandals but with silver stubble rather than full beard.

'Is the restaurant open?' Spike asked once he'd checked in.

The receptionist handed over the key. 'Hunger is housed in the body, satisfaction in the soul.'

Spike waited for further enlightenment, but the

receptionist returned to his seat to pick up a book.

The third-floor landing was decorated with framed maps of Tangiers through the ages: as a Roman provincial capital, a Portuguese colony, an English naval base, and more recently as a hedonistic international freeport, independent of the French and Spanish protectorates that ruled the rest of the country until 1956. Tangier, Tanjah, Tanger, Tangiers – even the present-day name seemed hard to pin down. As Spike passed a doorway, he heard a film blaring within. The adjoining room was his; groaning slightly, he slid his key into the lock.

Wooden-framed bed, cracked dressing-table mirror, en-suite bathroom with inevitable dripping tap. Spike took off his suit, feeling the office lift away as he stripped down to his boxers to unpack his overnight bag: fresh white T-shirts, loose cargo trousers, crisp linen shirt. He'd forgotten his sunglasses, he realised as he stowed the empty bag inside the cupboard. The shutters were closed; he pushed them open to a rooftop vista of water tanks, aerials and washing lines. Doves cooed. The sky was pink, the sun finally gone.

Sitting at the foot of the bed, he picked up the TV remote and found it mummified with yellowing Sellotape. He took out his phone instead as the film soundtrack throbbed through the walls.

'Been to prison yet?' said Peter Galliano.

'Tomorrow.'

'Is that your squeaky fiddler playing?'

'It's the next-door room.'

'Good hotel?'

'Charming. Listen, Peter . . .'

Spike told Galliano about his meeting with Nadeer Ziyad. 'He was talking about getting me an audience with the governor of Tangiers. I promised him a media blackout as long as the trial takes place in Gib.'

'What does he care?'

'There's been nothing so far in the Moroccan papers. Dunetech won't want any bad publicity, particularly as an eco company.'

'So what's he like, this Nadeer Ziyad?'

'Not short on confidence.'

'To those who have, Spike, shall be given. And you really feel we can keep the media at bay?'

'All that matters is they think we can.'

'I've already had the Moroccan authorities on to me. They want a DNA swab.'

'Do it. Keep 'em sweet on the small stuff.'

'Still no bail though. Flight risk.'

'Ask Alan Gaggero to schedule me a phone call with Solomon. If Alan's off duty, try Jessica Navarro. Just don't say it's for me. Anything from the Uzbeks?'

'They liked the vodka bar.'

'*Grevi*. I'll call you later then.'

'Careful, Spike. I know that tone.'

'*Non me voy de weeken.*'

The soundtrack next door had taken on a pornographic slant: moaning, panting. Spike hoisted the shower head to the top of its mast, washed, changed, then descended into the Tangerine dusk.

CHAPTER 15

The sand felt warm between Spike's toes. Seeing a discarded syringe ahead, he dropped his espadrilles back to the ground and kicked them on. The breadth of the beach had been a surprise, more than half a kilometre wide, continuing all along the inlet of the bay, port to the left, hills to the right, bright wasps'-nest city rising behind.

Waves lapped at Spike's feet, propelled by their cross-mix of currents. A shelf of sand rose at the tidemark: if someone had wanted to sit by the sea they could lean on the sandbank and be out of sight of anyone walking behind. Washed up against it was a mêlée of debris: punctured lilo, toothbrush, a plastic doll with a melted face.

Spike took a bite of sandwich. The flat, semolina-dusted bread was spread with a sour and rather delicious goat's cheese. He looked out at the late sun, spray-painting the crests of the wavelets blood orange. It was a still evening, the beach a biscuity colour in the fading light. In its hard-packed centre, street kids were playing football – the ball spilled to Spike and he side-footed it firmly back.

Beyond, the lights of Spain gave a watered-down glow. There was something tantalising about that view, Spike thought, close by yet out of reach.

He walked past the footballers towards the road. The row of beach bars was set beneath it, most of them little more than concrete bunkers. Some had gone for a Miami deckchair look, others fenced-off dance floors. Spike took in the plagiarised names: 'Snob', 'Pasha', 'Ritzys'. Most looked defunct – boarded-up windows, trussed parasols, tubs of dead hydrangeas with fag butts jammed into soil.

Spike was about to climb back up to the road when he stopped. Thirty metres ahead, a whitewashed customs depot marked the end of the beach. Just in front, sunk into the sand at an angle, was a wooden sign. Half a setting sun surmounted by a curving word, 'Sundowner'.

The terrace was enclosed by screens of palm fronds and gated by a plywood panel. Spike gave it a shove. It swung open and he crouched through past crates of empty beer bottles and a teetering stack of plastic chairs.

The back door was of salt-corroded steel; Spike put his shoulder to it. Ahead, a corridor led to a screen of velvet. A muffled throb came from behind; Spike felt his way along the cool concrete, then separated the curtains.

Through rotating disco lights, Spike made out the long pale back of a woman. She wore a thong and black, knee-length PVC boots. Her hands cupped her breasts, crimson bra straps dangling as she perched on a small round stage, hip against a pole. Facing her in the middle of a cushioned, seraglio-style set of bench seats sat a suited man. It was too gloomy to see features beyond a pair of large black-rimmed glasses.

Opposite the stripper was another, unoccupied stage, while along the back wall ran a bar with five or six stools. A Moroccan in a leather waistcoat manned it, standing by the sink, topping up a vodka bottle from the tap. The air smelled of perspiration and essential oils.

Spike sat down, and the barman straightened up, replacing the bottle on the mirror-backed shelf behind. '*Vous connaissez cette boîte, monsieur?*' he snapped.

'Vodka. No ice. And no water.'

The barman was bald on top but had contrived to scrape together a ponytail from the lank crop on the sides. He reached behind for a different bottle as Spike swivelled his stool. The stripper was facing him now, hands still teasingly over breasts. She had Eastern European hair and a body so thin the ribs stuck out like the timbers of a shipwreck. She bent down, twitching the T-strap of her thong in her client's bespectacled face. A smack rang out; Spike saw the stripper flinch, then reaffix her come-hither smile.

Spike listened as a techno version of an old Police number started playing, 'Tea in the Sahara'. A thumb-smeared tumbler slid his way. He took out his wallet and let the barman drink in the notes. 'Keep the change.'

A hundred-dirham note disappeared into the leather waistcoat with card-sharp dexterity. 'You like a dance?' the barman said. 'Some . . . private room?'

Spike sniffed his vodka.

'Karim, he dancing later.' The barman flicked his flaccid double chin at the empty stage. 'Two hundred dirham.'

Another slap from the podium, as the barman reached below the counter. Lifting out a crate of limes, he started cutting them into quarters with unnerving speed and skill. Spike looked beyond him to a pinboard of photographs: men hugging women, men hugging men, women hugging women. The blade of the kitchen knife ticked back and forth. The sliced limes rolled into a chrome bucket and the crate returned beneath the bar.

'You know Esperanza?' Spike said.

The barman smoothed back his ponytail.

'Esperanza,' Spike repeated loudly, eyes on the stripper, who tensed up her thighs, thumbs hooked beneath her G-string. The barman lowered his chin into a neck brace of fat. 'So many girls.'

'This one's dead. Found on the beach last week.'

'You from the Sûreté?'

'No.'

'Is like I say before – I never working that night.'

Another slap: Spike glared at the businessman, who was standing to get a better purchase. The stripper was naked now apart from her boots, crouching with one arm linked around the pole. Her face was still turned to Spike.

Spike laid three hundred dirham on the bar top. When it had disappeared, he stepped off his stool and moved to the end of the bar.

'She come in often time,' the barman said as he sidled over. Spike caught something sour on his breath that reminded him of the junkies he'd defended while working at the criminal bar in Gibraltar.

'Western slut,' he went on. 'She go with man, woman. Drugs and drink. Oh yeah.' He sucked in air through his widely spaced teeth. A gold molar glinted.

'What about the night she died? Did you see who she was with then?' Spike reached again for his wallet, laying down another hundred dirham.

'Oh, the little Jew,' the barman replied as he took the money. 'He follow her to the beach. Then? Who knows.'

Spike made a feint at the barman's waistcoat; he skipped back with the certainty of a creature which knows the dimensions of its cage. His hand moved upwards to adjust a spotted dicky bow.

'You can do better than that,' Spike said.

'I never see the Jew.'

'So someone told you. Who?'

'No one.'

'Did they argue?'

'He quiet man. Good money.'

'Did she argue with someone else?'

Spike caught an infinitesimal flicker of the eyelid. He laid down another two hundred dirham. The stripper was on her front now, boots apart as the businessman crouched forensically behind. The barman made a grab for the money but Spike got there first, slamming his palm down. 'Who?'

'One girl,' the barman said, backing away.

'Her?'

'Different. Maybe two week ago. This one, she throw a drink at Esperanza. They shout so I pull them apart, like two dogs fucking. Few days later Esperanza dead. Throat open like a baby lamb at the Eid. Yessir.'

'Which girl threw the drink?'

'She gone now. Owes me money.'

'Her name?'

Spike crammed the note into the barman's hand, folding his clammy fingers around the paper. With a smile and surprising grace, the barman pirouetted to swipe a photograph from the pinboard. Two shiny-faced jocks had their arms around a dark-skinned girl. Spike could see only part of her face: high cheekbones, serious expression, black hair tied back with a single strand over one eye. 'Her name?'

'Zahra.'

'Zahra who?'

'Bedouin bitch. No family name.'

'Dancer?'

'Waitress.'

Another slap; the stripper was trying to stand

but the businessman had a fist on the small of her back. The barman gazed on, polishing an earhole with a twisting index finger.

'Second thoughts,' Spike said. 'I will have that dance.'

The barman's pink gecko tongue flapped up and down. 'Five minute.'

'Now.'

'Mo' money.'

Spike gave a nod and the barman reached below to stab a button beneath the bar top. The businessman glanced up as the music stopped. The stripper drew in her bony knees.

'What's your name?' Spike said.

'Marouane.'

'Did you tell the police, Marouane?'

The barman shook his ponytail.

'When Zahra comes back,' Spike said, taking out his business card, 'you give me a call. Understand?' He picked up the photograph and walked towards the stripper.

CHAPTER 16

The girl was climbing onto a tiny plywood podium. There was barely room for the pole.

'Sit with me,' Spike said.

'Cost extra.' Her accent was French with a rough-grained Arabic underlay.

'Just to talk.'

The girl stepped down, stilettos scraping the porcelain. Spike glanced around. The 'private' room appeared to be no more than a converted lavatory: red drapery on the walls, two plastic chairs by the stage, floor-to-ceiling tiles exuding an ammoniac tang of a thousand drinkers' pit stops.

The girl took one of the chairs, spun it and pleated her long, smooth legs around. Close up, Spike could see the dark roots of her platinum hair. 'What's your name?'

'Tatiana.'

'Real name?'

'Tatiana,' the girl replied with a smile.

'Don't hear that one so much in Morocco.'

The girl arched an over-plucked eyebrow. Spike

held out a note which she rolled and slid into her boot. 'From Algeria. Annaba City. Ten year ago.'

'How much do you make a night, Tatiana?'

'You like to take me home?' She stroked her chin. There was a short, deep scar at its base which no amount of foundation could mask. 'Five hundred dirham, maybe I –'

'I'll give you five hundred just to talk.'

Tatiana started to stand, but Spike caught her wrist. 'It's OK,' he said. 'I'm a friend of Esperanza's.'

She glared down, then draped herself uncertainly back over her chair. 'You from Spain?'

'Nearby. You knew her?'

'I dance for her.'

'She liked women?'

'She liked . . . everyone.'

'Did you see who she was with that night?'

'I no working.'

'It seems the club was running itself.'

She smiled again. 'You friend for Marouane?'

'No.'

'Marouane here . . . all times.' She reached over and ran a long, fake fingernail up and down Spike's inner forearm.

'Marouane sells drugs?'

'If you like, I can –'

'He sold drugs to Esperanza?'

She folded her arms over the chair back, hiding her chin on top.

'Do you know who killed Esperanza?'

The coquettish expression slipped. In repose, her

face looked very young. 'Esperanza go to the beach,' she said. 'There, *avec les sans-papiers –*'

'*Sans-papiers?*'

'They coming into Tanger. *Pour passer le détroit.* All of Africa, waiting. No place for sleep. Sleep in park, cemetery, beach. Dangerous *abid* man. Eating cats and dogs.'

'And Zahra is a *sans-papier*?'

'You know Zahra also?'

'She argued with Esperanza, right?'

'One time.'

Spike held out another note which Tatiana tucked into a different boot. 'Esperanza come into the club,' she said. 'She see Zahra, and when Esperanza see . . .' Suddenly she climbed to her feet, enjoying the pantomime now. Through her lace bra Spike made out large, dark areolae. 'Zahra shout at Esperanza. Then . . .' She stabbed forward with an arm.

'She cut her?'

'Champagne wine. In her face. Then Esperanza stand and leave.'

'Why did Zahra throw the drink?'

'Maybe Esperanza touch her wrong. Or . . .'

'What?'

Another hundred dirham gone.

'Two days later,' Tatiana said, 'I see Esperanza's jeep. Zahra inside.'

'Are you sure?'

'I *see*.'

'Where does Zahra live?'

'In Chinatown. Like all the girls.'
'Where's Chinatown?'
'In the hills.'
'Address?'
Tatiana smiled. 'No address for Chinatown, *estúpido*.'
'Does she have a mobile number?'
Tatiana hovered above Spike. 'You strong tall man,' she said. 'But gentle eyes.' She reached out a hand. 'You put contact lens for the colour, no?'
Spike caught a hint of sugar almonds on her skin. He'd known a girl once who smelled like that. She hoisted a leg over Spike's lap. 'Sometimes I like to know a man,' she said, lowering herself down, 'before I give him secret . . . informations.'
Spike raised his hands to her sides, feeling the jutting prominence of her ribs as he eased her down onto his own chair. She edged her thighs apart; the gusset of her thong was dark-stained. Spike reached again for his wallet. 'Here's two hundred more. Now go home. And be careful who you dance for.'
The girl snapped closed her thighs. 'I prefer a man who *fuck*,' she said, fluffing out her crisp white hair. 'Maybe you only talk because you cannot fuck. Spanish *zamel*.'
Spike held open the door back into the club. A new song blared: 'Rock the Casbah' by The Clash. The girl pushed past, the top of each buttock embossed with a cherry-red welt.
Marouane was standing behind the bar, hunting

for scurf in hishair. On the previously empty podium, an Arab boy in cut-off shorts and Cleopatra eyeliner was humping a pole. Beneath, Spike recognised the two Spaniards from the reception of the Hotel Continental.

The bespectacled businessman drank alone, scouring the room, legs folded daintily among the cushions. Spike walked over, leaned in close and whispered a few words in his ear. Then he left.

CHAPTER 17

Spike crossed the waiting hall of the Sûreté Nationale on Avenue d'Espagne. The fissured marble floor was covered by men reclining in traditional dress. The air smelled like a classroom in midsummer.

At the desk, a duty sergeant was reading the *Journal de Tanger*. Spike asked for Inspector Eldrassi; without looking up, the duty sergeant waved a benedictory hand across the silent, waiting congregation. Spike saw they formed a sort of queue. He asked when Eldrassi would be available. '*Demain*,' the sergeant replied, flipping to the sports section.

Outside, dusk clung on, as though afraid to surrender to night. The restaurant terraces were bustling with men eating sweetmeats. Spike realised Tatiana was the only woman he'd exchanged words with since arriving.

There was a bank opposite; Spike went to the cashpoint. A heavily armed security guard stood by as he made the withdrawal. On the other side of the avenue, three young black men looked on. *Sans-papiers* probably, awaiting their chance to steal across the Straits. Spike had read countless articles on the risks involved – bloated, cracked bodies washing up each month on Spanish beaches, victims of unscrupulous boat runners, victims of the Gut.

A *petit taxi* swerved to a halt, responding to Spike's European height and clothes. The driver had a package of greaseproof paper on the passenger side; he drew it onto his lap as Spike got in and shunted back the seat. 'Chinatown.'

'*Comment?*'

Spike pointed up the hill to where the city rose. The driver shrugged. '*On va à Chinatown, donc.*'

CHAPTER 18

Spike forced down the stiff window to let the curried air circulate. Once they'd passed through the Ville Nouvelle, with its ornate, Parisian-style apartment blocks, they crested the hill and rolled down the other side. Vandalised, half-finished buildings – breeze blocks and rusting girders – protruded from a cacti-studded wasteland. The road began to dispense with pavements, then markings, then traffic altogether until a jeep drew up behind. Once it had grasped that the taxi couldn't speed up, it overtook on a blind corner.

The driver braked suddenly as a tall man with a long white beard emerged from the wayside, guiding some goats over the road. Kids crossed behind, bleating. Somewhere a dog barked.

They drove on, turning left down a potholed track. The food parcel bounced on the driver's lap. He stopped the car. '*C'est Chinatown.*'

Spike stared down the slope to a line of low-slung brick buildings clustered at the bottom of the track. The light was poor but they appeared to have sprung up in a dip between two hills, like fungus on a moist enclosed part of the body.

'It's a shanty town?'

'*Bidonville.*'

'Can you get any closer?'

The taxi driver crunched on his samosa. He was a small, bug-eyed man with pictures of small, bug-eyed children gummed to his glove compartment. Spike took out his wallet and removed a hundred-dirham note.

The driver shook his head. 'Bad place for taxi.'

Spike looked again down the slope. A few lights were visible. It clearly had electricity. 'Why's it called Chinatown?'

'No laws for building.'

'Seems quiet.'

'People working. In the city.'

'Bedouins?'

The driver coughed a flake of samosa onto his beaming children. '*Tu parles des bédouins?*'

'Do Bedouins live in Chinatown?'

'Desert peoples . . . *C'est bien possible.*'

Spike put away the note and held up a two hundred. The driver restarted the engine and they continued another fifty metres up the road before turning left. This time they drove further down the rough, unsurfaced track. Reeds sprouted by a stream; a patch of dusty scrubland revealed two burnt-out cars, kissing bumper-to-bumper like some untitled art installation. More brick buildings ahead; the driver switched off the engine.

'Twenty minutes,' Spike said, signalling the number with his fingers. As Spike opened the door, he felt a tap on the shoulder. '*Attention, uh?*'

Outside, the air smelled sulphurous. Spike removed some low-denomination notes from his wallet and stuffed them in the top pouch of his cargo trousers. The driver watched on in silence, chewing his samosa.

CHAPTER 19

The ground consisted of layer upon layer of trodden rubbish: flattened cans, shredded sackcloth, powdered glass. A stream snaked between the brick shacks. Its stench – eggs and rotten meat – suggested open sewer. The tall, nuclear-green reeds grew on one side only, giving Spike a glimpse of a brownish sludge oozing through the centre.

Covering his mouth and nose, he followed the stream between the buildings. The walls, he saw, had plywood embedded in the brickwork. Sticking from the top of one was an incongruously modern satellite dish.

Spike gagged as he neared the water. Beneath the surface lay an eyeless mongrel puppy, its chest swollen, guts flapping in the current like pink pondweed. He put a hand to his neck as he passed, folding a soft mosquito beneath.

The stream continued on through the settlement, forming a muddy half-moon-shaped bank. A few plastic tables had been pushed together, at which a group of men sat smoking clay pipes and playing cards. All wore thick black moustaches, their faces darker than the other Moroccans Spike had seen, Indian almost. Paired with white djellabas were coiled, light-blue turbans.

Candles guttered on tables, an electric light fizzing behind, dive-bombed by suicidal, shiny-backed beetles. A woman in a headscarf sat cross-legged on the mud, shelling pods with a knife as a child played nearby with a food wrapper. The cables feeding the naked bulb looped away over corrugated roofs – illegally siphoned electricity, Spike supposed. '*Zahra, por favor?*' he called, holding out the photograph of the girl.

The child stared up, open-mouthed, as her mother continued shelling. One of the card-players crooked a fingertip to the left. Spike gave a nod, hearing urgent, whispered rasps as he walked away.

Of the twenty minutes Spike had asked the driver to wait, five had elapsed. A thicker, more faecal smell began to coat the back of his throat as he turned into a gap between the huts. Through an open door he saw the flicker of a TV, a rag-draped figure prostrate before it on a camp bed.

Despite the condition of the buildings, Chinatown appeared to follow a grid system of sorts: parallel roads intersected by narrow alleyways. Spike continued left. Scrawled on a door was a painting of some rapt children with the words *École Primaire Mohammad VI*. The dark, plastic-sheeted windows were too murky to see through. Spike glanced up to the sky: the last of the sunlight had gone.

On the opposite side of the road, a bulb gleamed

from an open-fronted shack. A youth appeared by Spike as he crossed over, cycling tight against him, aligning his wheels in the tyre tracks scored in the dried mud. He was staring so fixedly at Spike that his front axle caught in the furrow and he almost fell.

The facade of the shack was made of sliced-up plastic pallets. A man was sitting inside, eating with his fingers as a TV blared out Al-Jazeera news. A balding parrot clattered above him in a cage.

'*Hola?*'

The man suspended his fingers by his lips as Spike drew closer. '*Zahra la beduina?*' he said. '*Dónde?*'

'*À gauche*,' the man said. '*Gauche, gauche*.' He crammed his fingers to his mouth. The parrot chewed at the bars of its cage.

The moon was visible, just a nail clip of white in the hazy, blue-black sky. Ahead in the street, Spike saw the boy on the bicycle joined by four other youths. They were all watching him too.

He turned into the next alley. Some sort of shop, a rack of exhausted-looking vegetables outside and an old, aproned woman hunched on a stool, serving a girl. As Spike drew closer, the girl glanced round. Then she picked up her plastic bag and walked quickly away.

CHAPTER 20

Spike kept ten metres behind the girl. Her black kaftan flowed outwards, a sequinned headscarf concealing her face as she glanced around, increasing her speed. They were one behind the other now, following the raised, mud-packed ridge between the tyre tracks.

'I'm a friend of Esperanza's,' Spike called out.

The girl crossed the road beside a half-built breeze-block wall.

'I've spoken to Tatiana.'

She dropped a handle of the plastic bag. Tomatoes and aubergines bounced to the ground. She cursed, crouching as Spike loomed above. Behind, a vehicle began to glide silently along the road. Spike turned to look: a jeep. He took a step closer to the girl. 'I've been to the Sundowner Club.'

She continued gathering groceries.

'You're Zahra, aren't you?'

'Why don't you fuck off back to Ángel?'

'I'm sorry?'

'Or I'll scream,' she added in surprisingly clear English.

A tin can had rolled into the tyre tracks; as Spike

bent down for it, he glimpsed the girl's tight denim jeans stretch beneath her kaftan. The sequins on her headscarf began to glitter in a beam of light; the jeep had performed a U-turn and was peeling back towards them. It traversed the road until it was facing the girl, stopping twenty metres shy, engine on, headlights blazing through a bull-bar bumper.

Spike picked up the tin can, then heard the engine rev. 'Zahra!'

The girl snapped up her head as the jeep roared towards her. Sprinting over the road, Spike launched himself into the air. He smelled her sharp, citrus perfume as he pressed himself against her clothing, bruising his shoulder as they thudded down together onto the hard ground. She elbowed him in one kidney, then scrambled to her feet.

The lights of the jeep glowed red. Hubcaps scraped against ridges of crisp mud. Zahra crouched again, gathering her shopping.

'What are you *doing*?'

The reverse lights of the jeep had been replaced by sharp yellow beams. Spike gave Zahra a shove; she took a step forward, dropping her bag before starting to run. Spike followed her into a narrow side street. Headlights tickled its mouth, disappearing before returning more strongly. 'Down here,' Spike said.

The walls on either side of the alley were made of cemented, blue-grey breeze blocks. Glassless windows above revealed dark figures silently watching. Rats scuttled in front, shifting one behind the other like a relay team. A pothole of stinking softness slurped at Spike's foot as Zahra streaked ahead with long strides – she seemed focused, unsurprised.

Spike heard the engine rev behind them. 'Stop,' he called, catching her up. She spun round, fist emerging as though to strike him.

'We can't outrun it.'

The headlights gleamed into Zahra's almond eyes; she glanced back, then dashed towards the side wall.

The breeze blocks were piled seven feet high. Zahra leapt up and got her hands on the top, holding herself in position before slipping back.

Spike dropped to his knees like a sprinter. 'Stand on my back.'

'What?'

'Go on!'

Spike felt pressure on his spine as Zahra's feet pressed downwards. He forced his neck up, her weight finally lifting as she got a hold on the wall above.

The headlights were almost on him. In a single fluid motion, Spike got to his feet and threw himself at the wall. His fingers gripped the top edge and he held himself there, lungs burning, espadrilles paddling against rough breeze blocks.

He hauled his legs into the air as the jeep sped beneath him. Further along, it stopped. There was a sharp double click of doors opening.

Spike felt a touch on a sinew-twisted shoulder. He pulled himself higher, scraping his stomach muscles until he came to rest face down in a flat, asphalted space. Feet pounded the mud below. A flashlight raked up and down the wall.

Spike's shoulder joints sang in a hot and not unpleasant way. The girl grabbed his hand; he'd cut himself, he saw as he stood. They edged for a while along the platform until Spike felt his neck jerk back, the top of his head slamming into a low-hanging pole. He put a hand to his hair, testing for blood, then felt Zahra touch his arm, steadying him. They crouched together in the darkness, the only sound now the pitch and fall of their chests. From below came the slam of car doors. An engine restarted.

Spike sat down, leaning dizzily against the surrounding wall. He felt her breath warm his face. 'Thank you,' he heard her say. Then he closed his eyes.

CHAPTER 21

The back of Spike's head was leaning against a rough surface, sandpaper or pebble-dash. The air smelled of hot cat piss. He groped in his pocket for his phone, then manoeuvred it over his eyes. He'd only been out for five minutes. And she was gone.

He hauled himself up. His head throbbed; he explored with his fingers, finding a large bump above the hairline. The skin of his forehead felt taut, uneven with mosquito bites. Balance regained, he edged along the platform, waiting for his eyes to adjust. A makeshift frame of bamboo scaffolding seemed to be holding the structure up, a dusty back road three metres below.

After testing the bamboo, Spike started to climb down. His shoulders ached. There were more bites on his ankles, slick blood on the back of his wrist. He licked it and tasted ferrous grit.

Once on the ground, he saw stars spangling the night sky like the sequins on Zahra's headscarf. At the end of the street, a bonfire crackled, three or four silhouettes gathered round, turning some kind of meat on a spit. Woodsmoke and burnt flesh carried in the air. Beyond, Spike made out the jagged shape of a bicycle.

Fresh tyre tracks scored the mud; Spike kept to the shadows until he caught the first whiff of the stream. The outdoor café appeared, card-players gone, bearded proprietor slowly clearing tables.

Jogging now, Spike followed the bank, dry-retching as the miasma strengthened. Two bristly yellow dogs burst from the rushes and ran at his ankles, thrilled at the speed. Once past the brick buildings, Spike felt his heart lift as he saw the triangular roof panel of the *petit taxi*.

The driver was slumped at the wheel; Spike tapped on the window and his head shot up. Blinking bulbously, he reached over and tugged up the passenger lock.

'Hotel Continental,' Spike said, and the driver twisted on the headlights.

As they reversed, Spike saw a figure appear between the buildings. They rumbled away, pursued by the barking pack of dogs. The figure was gone.

CHAPTER 22

The cafés on the Avenue d'Espagne were busy, black-tied waiters shuttling between groups of locals and tourists. Seeing a table of tanned, laughing Europeans, Spike felt a powerful urge to go and join them.

'Slow here,' he said as the police station came into view. A youth with a fishing rod over one shoulder was arguing with a man in chef's whites, their dispute overseen by a harassed-looking sergeant. Spike caught sight of a crowded hallway behind. 'Forget it,' he said. 'Carry on.'

They stopped at the walls of the Medina, the streets above too narrow for cars. The driver hit a button on the meter: '*Bonne continuation*,' he grinned once he'd registered the size of the tip.

A few late-night hawkers ambled over but their hearts weren't in it. As Spike passed the Grand Mosque, he saw a strip-lit room where lines of men chanted, kneeling and bowing in unison. Looked like good exercise.

Outside the hotel, the guard was watching football in his cabin, devouring couscous from a paper plate. Spike strode past him to reception.

The lighting from the chandelier created a soothing atmosphere as the receptionist perched contemplatively at his desk. 'A good night, *monsieur*?' he said.

'Eventful.'

'The variety of the rainbow creates its appeal.'

'If you say so,' Spike replied as he went upstairs.

Nearing his room, he heard screeching tyres and machine-gun spray. He stopped, rapping at the door. He thumped harder until it was opened by a tall, well-built black man with shoulder-length dreadlocks. '*Ouai?*' The air behind him stank sweetly of hashish.

'Can you turn that down?' Spike shouted. '*Menos ruido?*'

The man shook his head, dreadlocks held in place by multicoloured beads.

'I'm in the next-door room,' Spike said, feeling fatigue drape him like an oppressive cowl. He tucked his hands pillow-like behind an ear.

The man's face brightened. '*Ah. Mes excuses.*' As he turned away, Spike made out a glowing bank of TV monitors. The noise quietened and he reappeared, smiling. 'Jean-Baptiste,' he said, proffering a pink-palmed hand. The skin was rough yet soft, like the bottom of a dog's paw.

'Spike.'

Jean-Baptiste's eyes fell to Spike's cut. '*Tu veux du . . .*'

Spike shook his head, then went next door, collapsing on his bed as the fan wheeled above.

He shut his eyes, trying to think of the name Zahra had used when he'd approached her. What had it been? Sleep tugged at his brain like a crafty hand on the corner of a blanket.

CHAPTER 23

After bandaging the cut on his wrist, Spike stared at himself in the bathroom mirror. The pink domes of mosquito bites spotted his forehead. He threw cold water over his face, remembering a story he'd read about Paganini. In the winter of 1786, when Paganini had been four years old, his parents had thought he'd died of measles. They'd laid him to rest in a chilly pauper's grave until the undertaker had seen a wisp of condensed breath emerge from his shroud. The boy had been removed from the coffin and nursed back to health, and the next year his father, a mediocre mandolin player, had pressed a violin into his bony hands. The ghoulish rumours had started when the boy had begun composing sonatas aged seven. They'd stepped up a level when he'd played his first solo concert at nine. Look closely, the people of Genoa whispered, and you will see the Devil guiding his elbow.

The receptionist was still at the desk.

'Don't you ever sleep?'

The receptionist looked up from his book. 'How short is the night for those who sleep well.'

'What are you reading there?'

He held up a front cover marked by curly Arabic script.

'Quotations?'

'A man must take his wisdom even from the side of the road.'

'I'll remember that,' Spike said as he handed over his room key.

The dining terrace of the Continental overlooked an apron of shipping containers. A female dog was lying in their shade as a male sniffed her rear. The female kept her tail down, head firmly on forepaws.

The Arabs were fasting, the Europeans breakfasting. Spike sensed the Spanish couple observing him from behind. The man with the sideburns now had a split lip. Spike wondered what adventure they ascribed to the wound on his wrist.

He drank his coffee – warm and milky, better than the reconstituted orange juice that had preceded it – and stared out at the Straits, where a succession of freight and cruise liners was coming and going from the quayside. On the furthest coastline, his father Rufus would be eating his breakfast egg, slippered, dressing gown gaping as he fed the occasional buttered soldier to General Ironside. Routine: the doomed attempt to defeat the march of time. The past wasn't truly past if it could be repeated.

Spike stood and headed for the coast road.

CHAPTER 24

The duty sergeant was reading the next day's *Journal de Tanger*, but the rest of the waiting room had emptied out. Spike walked past him to a side door, where a man at a desk was scowling at a large computer monitor, as though not quite sure what it was, still less how it had come to be there. He wore a brown corduroy suit rather than the sky-blue shirt and peaked cap of the sergeant outside. Beside one hand lay an overflowing ashtray.

'Inspector Eldrassi?'

The man raised his eyes, face long and grey, like a lolly sucked dry of flavour. Contrasting with the sallow skin was a suspiciously dark moustache.

'Jessica Navarro gave me your name. *Hablas inglés?*'

His expression animated, as though he'd been flicking through a mental file of e-fits and come across a match. 'The beauty from Gibraltar,' he said, laying his cigarette in the crematorium of its predecessors. 'They send me there for trafficking conferences. I speak the best English.'

'Spike Sanguinetti.'

The man stood up properly. 'Inspector Hakim Eldrassi. You are also a policeman from Gibraltar? Here on holiday?'

'Lawyer. Here on business.'

Hakim withdrew his hand and rubbed it on his brown corduroy trousers. He motioned with his chin to a chair opposite the desk. 'Five minutes.'

Spike sat down. 'I represent Solomon Hassan.'

Hakim shook a cigarette from his pack even though the previous one was still smouldering. 'He is on his way back to Tangiers, I hope?'

'We're seeking to prevent extradition.'

Hakim's eyes closed in weary disbelief. 'There is an arrest warrant, Mr Sanguinetti. He has a case to answer.'

'We consider Tangiers Prison to be unsafe for a Sephardic Jew. Even if my client were only in custody overnight, that would still represent a breach of his human rights.'

A smoke ring hung in the air, stretching to a Munch-like skull before disappearing. 'Why are you here?' Hakim said.

'Seeking evidence of anti-Semitism within your penal system.'

'But here,' Hakim went on, 'in front of me. Now.'

'Have you been to the Sundowner Club?'

'In this room,' Hakim said, 'we do not care for it when people answer a question with a question.' He threw some ash into the tray with a practised flick. On his desk Spike saw the same triangular card he'd seen in the hotel: *Together Against Terrorism*.

'It's a clip joint,' Spike continued, 'on the beach. The murder victim, Esperanza Castillo, was there the night of her death.'

'With your client, no?'

'Did you know Esperanza was involved in a fight at the Sundowner a few days before she died? With a waitress.'

Hakim sucked hard on his cigarette, as though it were somehow to blame. 'We are considering no other suspects until your client comes back to answer the charges against him.'

'You're not following other leads?'

'Guilty men run, Mr Sanguinetti. Your police friend, Miss Jessica, will tell you that. In fact, she is the only reason I am still talking to you.'

'And I'm the only person doing your job.'

Hakim frowned.

'Last night I went to see this waitress. A jeep tried to run us over.'

'Where?'

'Chinatown.'

Smoke flowed simultaneously from Hakim's mouth and nose. The laugh changed to a cough, which racked his wiry chest until he covered his mouth with a fist, spitting then swallowing. 'Chinatown,' he gasped. 'Normally they just beat you to death with a baseball bat then try to sell your organs. Did you see the number plate?'

'Too dark. But it was a black jeep with tinted windows. Bull-bar bumper.'

'You should not go to Chinatown, Mr Sanguinetti. Especially at night.'

'Like I say, I'm being forced to do your job for you.'

Hakim's face settled into a glare. At the end of his office sat a plywood cabinet, a plastic-framed photo of the King on the wall above, so standardised that Spike realised the one in the Dunetech office must have been a personal gift. Hakim rose, walking over and rattling open a drawer. Ash crumbled down as he drew out a Manila folder.

Back at his desk, he shoved a bulldog-clipped sheaf of forensic photographs into Spike's hand. The top one was a black-and-white head shot. Esperanza's dark shoulder-length hair was washed back from her forehead. Her face was paler than the sand around her and her upper lip shadowed by a faint moustache, like a self-portrait by that Mexican artist. She wore a bolt through one eyebrow and a metal stud beneath her lip. Her cheeks were plump and her eyes open, milky-white, as Solomon had said, with a vacant upward stare that chimed somehow with her strange, otherworldly beauty. Spike brought the photo closer: the cut was just a nick to the left-hand side of her neck, no bigger than a comma. The only indication of depth was the blackness and bruising around.

He turned to the next photo, in colour this time, taken from further back. A juvenile crab was entwined with her armpit hair. Bangles racked up her right forearm.

'So,' he heard Hakim say as he fired up another cigarette, 'the victim and your client are having a drink on the beach. Your client removes the victim's underwear – still missing, if she had any – and they engage in sexual activity. Digital penetration, say forensics; finger-fucking, you might call it.'

Spike reached for the last photo, a full body shot. Esperanza's floral dress sheathed her thighs, revealing a dark raised triangle beneath the cotton. The straps were a rusty brown.

'Your client is carrying a knife,' Hakim went on. 'He leans into the girl, who trusts him, and slits her external jugular with a flick of the wrist. Then he drags her body into the sea – which destroys any traces of DNA – and escapes to Gibraltar.'

Spike turned over the last photo: stamped in red on the back was 'Sûreté Régionale de Tanger'.

'And you,' Hakim said as Spike reaffixed the bulldog clip and slid the pictures back, 'wish to free this murderer on a technicality.'

'We just want him tried in Gibraltar.'

'Because it is more likely he will escape conviction.'

'What if he's not your man?' Spike said. 'Have you even entertained that possibility?'

'He has no alibi.'

'Nor motive.'

'A man, a woman – what more motive do you need?'

'Have you checked for CCTV footage?'

'There were no working cameras on his route home.'

'And no witnesses to prove he was even on the beach at the time of death.'

'The time of death is not yet confirmed.'

'How long?'

'A second post-mortem is being done in Madrid.'

'Why?'

'At the request of her stepfather. A powerful man, I am told.' Hakim began tidying up the photographs.

'Inspector Eldrassi,' Spike said, 'I've known Solomon for thirty years. He's not capable of murder.'

'Sometimes the less you know, the more you see.'

'Is that the motto of the Sûreté Régionale?'

Hakim grinned hazelnut teeth. 'You introduce me to someone you know. You are affected by your experiences of them. I *see* the person.'

'Maybe you see a quick prosecution to keep the governor of Tangiers happy.'

'I see you, Mr Sanguinetti,' Hakim said, face shrouded in smoke like a cheap mystic. 'You are familiar with death, for example.'

'Oh?'

'When you looked through those pictures your face was still. No shock, even when you saw the crab. You have known death. A parent perhaps. A sister.'

Spike felt his jaw tighten. 'Maybe I see you, Inspector Eldrassi.'

'Oh?'

'You've lost your religious faith. But it's not that which keeps you awake at night. It's fear. Fear because you can't shake off the thought you'll still go to hell.'

'Why do you say that?'

'Because you look exhausted. And you're smoking in the daytime during Ramadan.'

Hakim smiled and nodded slowly. 'Your five minutes are up, Mr Sanguinetti,' he said as he crossed the room.

'Go back to the Sundowner Club,' Spike called over. 'Have a chat to the barman, Marouane. He's a small-time drug dealer.'

Hakim shut the folder away with a definitive thunk. Moving to the doorway, he stuck an arm into the entrance hall.

'That cut,' Spike said, rising to his feet. 'It looked precise. Stanley knife? Scalpel?'

'The pathologist believes it was done with an Eid knife; just the tip pressed into the vein.'

Spike shrugged.

'You know of Ramadan but not the Eid? Maybe you have no religion either. It is a festival twice a year. Once to mark the end of Ramadan, another a few months later. Sometimes we kill a lamb to celebrate. A symbol of Ibrahim sacrificing his child, Ismail. A small, sharp knife cuts the throat. They sell maybe five thousand a year in Morocco.'

'Solomon Hassan is Jewish.'

'Jews slaughter lambs, do they not, for Passover?'

Hakim ushered Spike through. 'I'm a busy man, Mr Sanguinetti. Until your client comes back, the case is on hold.'

'Can I have access to Solomon's flat?'

'No.'

'Will you get me into Tangiers Prison?'

'You do not stop, do you?' He lifted a hand to Spike's shoulder. 'You are intrepid; I respect that. But if your case against extradition depends on information about our prison, I suggest your client will be back here sooner than you think. Two places a foreigner does not go. One is Tangiers Prison. The other is where you went last night.' Hakim patted himself down for more cigarettes. 'Catch the next boat home, Mr Sanguinetti. And send your client back the other way.'

Two beefy policemen were coming through the main door, sub-machine guns at their sides. They nodded respectfully at Hakim as they passed.

Spike stepped out onto the street, where the late-morning sun was already blistering. A black jeep was parked on the pavement, 'Sûreté Nationale' painted on the side, windows tinted. Spike stood back and snapped a picture on his mobile phone.

CHAPTER 25

Shaded beneath a date palm near the police station, Spike dialled Nadeer Ziyad's number. Opposite, on the central reservation, a young black man was asleep in the sunshine. Spike wondered at the thickness of his woollen roll-neck, before realising he must have climbed the Atlas Mountains to get here, trudging through the Sahara. Even summer nights in the desert were said to be bitterly cold. Where had he started his journey? Mali? Cameroon?

No answer from Nadeer; no voicemail facility either. Spike put away his phone and drew out the invitation he'd taken from Solomon's office. 'Dunetech Investor Roadshow, Saturday 24th'. The 24th was today. A business conference was surely improbable on a Saturday, Spike thought, until he recalled that the Muslim day of rest was Friday. Hence yesterday's skeleton staff at Dunetech, perhaps.

There was a map on the back, which he followed into town, thinking as he walked of Zahra, of the close fit of her jeans beneath her kaftan, of her excellent, foul-mouthed English, husky-voiced as though recovering from a bout of karaoke the night before. He checked the photo he'd taken of the police jeep, trying to remember if there'd been any side markings on the vehicle which had rammed them in Chinatown. It had been too dark to be certain.

The El Minzah Hotel was just past the souk, its sparkling glass doors manned by three porters in fezzes. Seeing the stars arching resplendently above the name, Spike wondered, not for the first time, why he'd heeded his father's advice on accommodation.

'*Je peux vous aider, monsieur?*'

'Here for the Roadshow.'

'Start ten minute ago.'

'My driver got lost.'

One of the porters led Spike through the lobby. The front desk was adorned by a vase of white Casablanca lilies and a crystal decanter of brandy. Past a bank of old-fashioned payphones, a side door was guarded by another porter. The A-board outside welcomed investors to 'The Dunetech Roadshow'; Spike flashed his invitation and was shown into murmuring, air-conditioned darkness.

At one end of the room was a stage, above which a film was projected onto a state-of-the-art screen. Rows of folding chairs were set out in front, an aisle in between. Spike spotted an empty seat near the back by the DVD trolley.

Faces turned, European mainly. Symphonic music and a recorded voiceover were emanating from the stage. Spike heard '. . . over two thousand megawatts of energy . . .' spoken by an actor whose tones he vaguely recognised. Most of the audience wore lightweight summer suits. Spike was in espadrilles, cargo trousers and a T-shirt.

'The sands of time are running out,' the actor's voice said, 'so the time is right . . . for Dunetech.'

The rear wall was lined by soft velvet curtains; Spike backed along them before stepping forward into the aisle. A young Moroccan glanced over from the DVD projector, then resumed pressing buttons.

A prospectus gleamed on the chair, which Spike scooped onto his lap as he sat. The film had switched to sweeping silent images, aerial shots of rows of solar-power units, squatting like triffids in the desert. Their numbers began increasing exponentially, demonstrating how much larger the power field could grow. The last shot panned across an army of mirrored machines, massed to the furthest horizon before the screen switched to black and the Dunetech logo faded in.

Enthusiastic applause swept the room. A woman sitting close to Spike – Japanese or Korean – leaned into a male colleague, whispering in his ear before clapping like an apparatchik.

The projectionist began fiddling with a control panel. The lights came on. The applause ramped up further as Nadeer Ziyad stepped onto the platform. He soaked it up, then raised his arms. '*Shukran*,' he said, stepping higher onto the lectern.

'*Namaste. Arigato. Sheh-sheh.* Thank you.' He slid on a pair of rimless specs.

'Ladies and gentlemen, the nature of solar power is such that –' Abruptly he glanced up and removed the glasses. 'My country,' he said, smiling as he leaned a forearm on his notes, 'my beautiful, crazy country.' He looked around the room. 'How much of our energy do we import from abroad? Twenty per cent? Thirty?' He shook his head. 'Ninety-six. *Ninety-six* per cent! No oil to speak of, nor natural gas. In order to make our energy affordable, it must be heavily subsidised by the government. Unfortunately, this eats up resources which could otherwise be dedicated to helping wipe out Morocco's most dreadful affliction.'

Spike saw the audience transfixed as Nadeer penetrated them one by one, giving each a taste of those glittering tawny eyes. 'Investing in Dunetech,' he continued, sliding his spectacles back on, 'is not just about buying into the most democratic and politically stable of all North African countries. It is not just about the provision of renewable, environmentally friendly energy as the world's oil and gas supplies run dry. It is about an immediate and urgent need. A need that will only grow more acute as global climate change exacerbates. One last chance to eradicate the scourge of modern Morocco. Poverty.'

Nadeer turned his head as a series of images of rag-doll children and lean-to huts appeared on the screen. Spike thought he recognised the effluent stream of Chinatown.

'What has traditionally constrained our ability to tap into the immense power of solar energy,' Nadeer resumed sadly, 'is what we in the industry call the three Cs. Cabling, cost and collection. If I may, I will explain to you how Dunetech plans to revolutionise these one by one. First . . . cabling.' The images switched to a diagram as Nadeer began talking about how Dunetech had secured permission to lay cables from the Sahara, over the Atlas Mountains and into the major cities of Tangiers and Rabat. Spike's neighbour began taking conscientious notes.

'. . . using technology designed exclusively by Professor Ángel Castillo . . .' Spike tuned back in. *Fuck off back to Ángel*, Zahra had said. So Ángel was Esperanza's stepfather. How had Zahra known his name?

Spike opened the prospectus. The first pages were dedicated to exploring the science behind a 'heliopod', one of the futuristic triffids he'd seen in the promo. Hourglass-shaped, each unit stood two metres tall, with a smooth metal base leading up to two concave solar panels. The panels seemed capable of movement, opening and closing like a clam shell as the sun passed overhead.

Spike flicked onwards, stopping at the 'Who we are' section. The first photograph showed Nadeer, narrow chin pinched pensively between thumb and forefinger. His bio revealed him as the son of Yusuf Ziyad, a personal adviser to the King of Morocco – educated at Eton College, Cambridge

University, Harvard Business School . . . Spike flipped over to the head shot of Ángel Castillo. The eyebrows were bushy, the salt-and-pepper goatee a luxuriant oval. Bags hung like dried apricots beneath his eyes, creases ran between his nostrils and mouth, and the dismissive smile suggested he had better things to do than pose for a publicity shot. The blue cravat under the collar gave a slightly nautical look. 'Educated at the Complutense in Madrid,' the prospectus said, 'and now tenured at the Universidad de Sevilla, Professor Castillo has worked all his life in Africa and lived in Morocco for the last decade, using his expertise to assist the country's poor. Known affectionately in renewable energy circles as the Sun King, his patents in solar technology have . . .'

Spike returned his eyes to the stage, where Nadeer was onto the final C, Collection, explaining how a single concrete storage tower could regulate energy distribution both at night and in the rare event of cloudy weather. The screen faded back to the Dunetech insignia as Nadeer tucked his glasses into the breast pocket of his suit. 'I thank you all for your patience. Now, any questions?'

'Will Professor Castillo be speaking later?' came a Texan drawl.

'Ángel is slightly unwell. Upset stomach. Incidental pleasure of living in Tangiers.'

A ripple of uneasy laughter.

'When will he be back?'

'This afternoon, inshallah.'

Another hand at the front, a Scandinavian lady

enquiring after the timeline of 'Phase Two Expansion'. A moment later, the curtains behind Spike opened to reveal trestle tables of champagne and canapés. Nadeer stepped down to another volley of applause. Spike picked up the prospectus and followed him out.

CHAPTER 26

Spike declined a smoked salmon blini. Beyond the buffet, a bank of sliding glass doors gave onto the hotel swimming pool. Spike watched a pale, expensive redhead sway across the suntrap terrace, fanning a hand down the back of her bikini before diving neatly into the water. In the main room, the Roadshow guests seemed more interested in networking than refreshments. Spike looked over as the young projectionist struggled to fit the DVD unit back into a cardboard box. 'Need any help?'

The projectionist shrank back as though he'd done something wrong. The rims of his ears broke the sheen of his hair like two dolphins breaching.

'*Ayuda?*'

Understanding now, the projectionist passed Spike one half of the unit, which they lowered into a Japanese-marked box. '*Shukran*,' he said, eyes drifting hungrily to the buffet.

Nadeer was in the centre of the room, trailed by the immaculate Scandinavian, who kept staring into his eyes as though he were imparting religious homilies. Three Asian men lurked behind, prospectuses under arms. Outside, the redhead drew herself sleekly out of the pool.

As Spike closed in, Nadeer appraised him with an impassive glance, before turning the whole of his head. 'We've already secured second-round investment from – Mr Sanguinetti, what a surprise.'

'I was thinking of upgrading hotel. Saw the Dunetech poster outside.'

'Of course. Miss Solness? This is Mr Sanguinetti.'

The Scandinavian held a Mont Blanc in one hand and a reporter's pad in the other. She bestowed a tight, glossy smile on Spike before turning back to Nadeer, who opened his mouth to continue.

'How did you get on with the governor?' Spike interrupted.

'I'm sorry?'

'Have you fixed up a meeting yet?'

'There's a function tomorrow at my villa. I'll have Toby furnish you with the details.' He turned back to the girl, who swept a manicured hand through her ash-blonde bob.

'Is Ángel Castillo in town?'

One of the Asians stepped forward. 'Castillo,' he repeated, nodding approval as his colleagues did the same. The Scandinavian's gaze dipped from Spike's dark stubble to his red espadrilles.

'As I mentioned earlier, he's not been well,' Nadeer replied. 'Though hopefully,' he added with a smile to the Asians, 'he'll be sufficiently recovered to attend this afternoon's session.'

‘I wanted to ask him about Esperanza’s final movements.’

The Scandinavian frowned at this new name, and Nadeer gave a subtle nod to the middle distance; almost instantaneously, Spike felt a hand on his shoulder. He turned to see Toby Riddell behind him. Riddell’s open-necked shirt revealed a sandy patch of chest hair. His Adam’s apple was prominent, one or two reddish whiskers missed on the gristle.

‘Toby will be delighted to answer any questions you may have,’ Nadeer said, turning back to the Asians.

After tossing a nod at the Scandinavian, Spike followed Riddell to the door. In his right hand he was still pumping that squash ball, back and forth.

CHAPTER 27

No one accosted Spike in the cooler lanes of the souk. The covered stalls offered meat, fish, herbs and vegetables, their clientele local, no call for the tourist buck. Craggy Berber ladies in straw hats sold mountain cheeses, while high on butchers' shelves, rows of skinned lambs' heads seemed to follow Spike, eyeballs bulging as though still coming to terms with their unexpected deaths.

Stepping out onto street level, Spike jumped as an engine roared by. Just a rusty three-wheeler, belching fumes. He walked on into the Medina.

A hawker was flogging pirated DVDs; Spike showed him the map that Riddell had sketched out on El Minzah notepaper. Once the hawker had adjusted to the role reversal, he pointed up the hill towards a small enclosed square. The Arabic street sign had a French translation beneath: *Petit Socco.*

The stones of the Petit Socco undulated with the ancient, lumpy quality that suggested continuous use throughout the many guises of Tangiers.

The proximity of its two main cafés, Tingis and Central, put Spike in mind of other famous rivalries: Florian and Quadri, Flore and Les Deux Magots, Rick's and the Blue Parrot. An elderly man passed by, dragging a wooden cart as he croaked out his wares, three plump silvery fish reclining behind him on crushed ice. Above, on the wooden balcony of a *pensión*, a woman in a diaphanous veil crooked a long, pink finger Spike's way.

A waiter from the Café Central directed Spike to a lane climbing towards the Kasbah. He passed beneath an arch, turning into a narrow alleyway to find a wall tile painted with the words, 'Numéro Seize'.

An Arabic voice crackled from a speaker in the wall; Spike said 'Ángel Castillo' and the voice fell silent. He took a step back: the facade was blue-and-white-tiled, delineating its boundary from less salubrious neighbours. The front door was of thick, carved oak, the louvred shutters closed, as were all the shutters on this side of the alley. Those opposite were open – it seemed that in the Kasbah, where the streets were too narrow for both sides to open their shutters at the same time, the residents divided their use to one half of the day each.

Spike buzzed again. This time he added the word 'Dunetech' and the catch snapped. He pushed into a gloomy hallway. A shuffling came from above; after climbing a few steps he made out a small, shadowy figure.

'*Duna, duna*,' came a voice.

He climbed further to find an old woman in a black shawl standing in the doorway. She waved him into a long reception room with an intricately-carved arabesque ceiling. A garish acrylic of the Kasbah dominated one wall; on another hung a bank of carved African fertility masks, black-stained and with deep, empty holes for the eyes. The marble floor shone like a mirror; Spike saw a stepladder ahead, its bottom rung draped with a cloth.

'*Min fadhlek*,' the woman said, jabbing forward with her broomstick. Spike slid his rope soles over the gleaming floor. To the left was a tiled room of cushioned marble benches with a plasma TV; to the right, a corridor cross-hatched with light. A spiral staircase rose at the end; the woman pointed towards it.

The staircase led to a cramped doorway. As Spike hunched to step outside, the sunlight stung his eyes. Shielding his face, he crossed a roof terrace surrounded by trellises. A hot tub bubbled in the centre like a cauldron. Beyond stretched a wooden bar backed by shelves of dusty glasses. A table stood to one side with four heavy-looking teak chairs. Slumped in one was a man.

'*Hola?*' Spike called out. The hot tub was redolent of chlorine and something worse; as Spike passed he saw a dead chick churning in its filthy froth. In front of the bar was a binful of empties, fizzing with wasps. The man half sat up: a glass was raised to the mouth, then replaced on the table.

Spike recognised Ángel Castillo from the Dunetech prospectus. He wore beige chinos and a navy, horizontally striped polo shirt. His greying hair and goatee were damp with grease or perspiration. Cracked lips moved as though in silent prayer; a whisky bottle stood at his naked, sunburnt feet.

'*Profesor Castillo?*'

The man squinted up. '*Heebralta?*' he said. His voice was croaky, as though it hadn't been used in a while.

'*Sí.*'

'Here to replace the Jew?' he asked, switching to a serviceable English.

'In a sense.'

'Have a drink, then. *Cagana*, I believe you call it in your Gibberish.'

Spike helped himself to a tumbler at the bar. Ángel picked up the bottle, sloshing brown liquid into Spike's glass before topping up his own. His hand shook; Spike waited for him to raise his glass and drink. 'The answer is no,' he said once he'd managed to put the tumbler down.

Something flashed in the sky above, a swallow, dipping down to the hot tub, chattering as it skipped up over the wooden trellis then down across the rooftops of the Kasbah.

'No to what?'

'I will not come. You can tell him that yourself.'

Spike breathed in the fumes of his glass. 'I'm not from Dunetech,' he said, eventually. 'I'm a lawyer from Gibraltar. I represent Solomon Hassan.'

The swallow swept back over. The bubbles stopped and Spike saw that the chick was still paddling in the water with a wing. Ángel's eyes were closed; Spike stood and went to the water's edge. The mother swallow boomeranged past as Spike cupped his hands into the hot froth and scooped out the chick. Black claws scratched feebly at the decking. Spike returned to the chair.

'There is a nest in the eaves,' Ángel said, eyes still shut. 'It was learning to fly but it fell.'

Spike paused. 'I'm sorry about your stepdaughter, Professor Castillo. You have my sympathy.'

Ángel refilled his glass.

'But I do need to ask you some questions.'

He drank deeply, spilling whisky on the thigh of his chinos.

'Do you believe Solomon Hassan killed your stepdaughter?'

He shrugged.

'Do you know who might have?'

He shrugged again, wincing this time; beneath the sweat-soaked collar, his neck was tender from the sun.

'Do you *care* who killed her?'

'Caring does not bring her back.'

'But you do want justice?'

Ángel reached back for the bottle but found it empty. Returning to the bar, Spike found a plywood case in a cupboard, its side plastered with yellow customs stickers. He drew out a fresh bottle of J&B, glancing through the trellis as he walked back – another landslip below, beggar-built shacks in the rubble. One seemed to be constructed from a framework of shopping trolleys.

'*Gracias*,' Ángel muttered, 'you understand drunks.' He refreshed his glass with a steadier hand. 'You know,' he said, 'my work has taken me all over Africa, but never have I seen poverty like Morocco. Supermodels partying in Marrakesh while children rot on the streets. New luxury hotels in Rabat, while the population flocks in from the countryside with nowhere to live. Rising birth rate, falling employment, corrupt politicians, and not a thing done to change it.' He smiled, teeth indecently white among the raw stubble. 'Until now.'

The bubbles came back on in the hot tub.

'Do you know how many lives Dunetech will save?' Ángel said. 'In five years, it can free up more than one hundred million euros for the King to use against poverty. Think how many deaths that can prevent. Millions.'

'I'm afraid my humanitarian work is on a smaller scale,' Spike said. 'My client is facing a potential death penalty, or an extradition order that amounts to the same thing. Did you see Esperanza the day she died?'

'She was staying here; I saw her every day.'

'And that day?'

'We had lunch together at the Café Central. She went for a beauty treatment – hot wax, I believe.' His tone was of bitter irony.

'Then?'

'She saw a fortune-teller about her luck.'

'Who was he?'

'Some street rat. The police picked him up. Esperanza was superstitious, like her mother. They both had to believe in something.'

'And then?'

'She met the Jew. He was showing her round town.'

'She hadn't been here before?'

'Hadn't wanted to.'

'What changed?'

'She got older.'

'Did she like Solomon Hassan?'

'Did anyone?'

'Did you?'

Ángel drank again. 'He was back office; I rarely saw him. When I did, he was always keen . . . to ingratiate himself.'

'Did your stepdaughter have enemies?'

'She was a *child*.'

Spike paused. 'Have you heard of a girl called Zahra?'

'No.'

'A Bedouin?'

'*Qué dices?*'

'*Beduina?*'

Ángel suddenly drew himself up, grabbing the whisky bottle and slamming its base onto the end of the table. Shards of glass skittered across the decking. He held out the dripping, jagged stump, hooded eyes peeling back. 'You use that word,' he said, 'in *my* house?'

Spike edged towards the bar, Ángel jabbing at him with the sawtooth end.

'Get out.'

'Easy, pal.'

'Out!' Ángel's bare soles had found an unexpected nimbleness on the decking. The swallow chick, semi-recovered, flopped back into the hot tub. 'OUT!'

The doorway part-opened to reveal the maid, beckoning as though afraid to emerge fully. Spike looked back at Ángel's now unshaking hand, then ducked beneath the lintel. '*Samt*,' the maid said soothingly, '*la taklak*.'

On his way out, Spike paused at a room off the hallway. The walls and ceiling were tiled like a Turkish hammam; in one corner stood a wooden console table covered in picture frames. All showed Esperanza, alone or with friends. She looked thinner, younger. Innocent.

Outside, the maid was mopping up Spike's footprints. She murmured to herself as she worked; Spike thought he recognised a word. '*Beduina?*' he repeated.

Head down, with a low guttural sound, the maid sliced a broad thumbnail across her throat. She was still mopping as Spike crossed the sparkling marble floor back down to the street.

CHAPTER 28

Spike sat beneath the awning of the Café Central, eating an *omelette au fromage*, the cheese just a rubbery orange bookmark between two fluffy folds of egg. He mopped up the sunflower oil with his bread before pouring himself another cup of super-sweet mint tea. The perforated silver pot had a pleasing ability to yield up another cup just when it looked like supplies had run dry.

A bearded Moroccan with a shaven moustache was watching him from across the square. Spike stared back and the man crept furtively away, up the hill towards the Kasbah. Strapped to his back was a small red rucksack.

At the table to Spike's right sat a couple of gap-year girls, German or Austrian. They kept glancing at him before returning to their guidebooks, giggling as he met their gaze. He had a missed call, he saw – number withheld. He took a punt and rang.

'Hello, Tax Man.'

'Hi, Jess. Did you call?'

'Nope. I'm on foot patrol in Irish Town. So how's Tangiers?'

'They don't seem to like me much.'

'That makes a –' Jessica checked herself. 'Where are you staying?'

'Hotel Continental.'

'*Una tanita?*'

'Seen better days.'

'And you hooked up OK with Eldrassi?'

'Yeah. You sure he's straight?'

'As they go.'

'How's Solomon?'

'Still complaining.'

'I need to talk to him.'

'I've scheduled you a call for 4 p.m. tomorrow.'

'*Tenkiu*, Jess. And let's have that drink when I get back.'

'You OK, Spike?'

'Why?'

'You sound . . . different.'

Spike paused. 'What do you know about Bedouins?'

'Bedouins? Come from the desert. Move about a lot. Big on honour codes, like most nomadic people. Not many left in Morocco, I think. Why?'

'What sort of honour codes?'

'Blood feuds, that sort of thing. Why? Have you fallen for one?'

'A whole tribe. So I call the Castle tomorrow at four?

'*Está penene*, Spike.'

The sun was passing above the square, dragging its shadow line over the cobbles like a tarpaulin drawn by invisible ball boys. Spike's phone rang again. 'Yes?' he said irritably. Damp breathing poured down the line. 'Hello?'

'Is Marouane.'

'Who?'

'From the Sundowner. You come now. Alone.'

The breathing was replaced by dead air.

CHAPTER 29

Swimmers and sun worshippers disported themselves in the distance. At this end of the beach, clusters of men loitered in full-length robes, cupping illicit Ramadan cigarettes, chatting surreptitiously as they glanced out to sea. A father and son flew a home-made kite, a mongrel gleefully chasing its shadow. Spike skirted around them to follow the perimeter fence of the Sundowner Club.

The gate hatch was open; Spike ducked beneath and slipped through the metal door. The velvet curtain was hooked onto a nail in the concrete; ahead, Spike saw the back of Marouane, bucket at his feet as he slopped down the bar top. He wore pink Hawaiian shorts, Jesus sandals and a hard-rock T-shirt. His hair was loose, lank black locks spilling over narrow shoulders.

Spike gave a sharp enough whistle to be heard above the brutal music. Marouane turned, tossing his cloth into the bucket. 'You happy with your Marouane,' he shouted. 'Yessir.'

'Turn the music off.'

After glancing left and right, as though appealing

to an imagi nary referee, Marouane moved to the bar top and turned the music down.

'Off. *Apagada.*'

Finally, silence. 'Vodka?' Marouane said, but Spike ignored the offer, drawing up a chair beside the bench seats. As Marouane came over, he paused by the podium to lick a fingertip. A trail of crusty powder ran along the black-painted plywood; Marouane reconstituted it with his saliva, dabbing the ball of a finger onto his tongue. He grinned. 'You like Tatiana, no?'

'You asked to see me.'

Marouane sat down on the sticky bench seat. 'Marouane must eat, you know?'

'Is Zahra back?'

'Fuck that Bedouin bitch. I see her, I cut her. No . . . Better.' He stood and went to a doorway adjacent to the 'private room'. Spike heard two short, crisp sniffs from inside before he re-appeared, handbag over shoulder, sauntering towards the bench seats, hips jigging, one wrist cocked as he placed the handbag on the podium. Sitting back down, he pinched both nostrils, eyeballs bulging.

The handbag was made of expensive brown leather with a zip down the middle. 'One *thousand* dirham,' Marouane declared, holding out a hand, then shaking his head in frustration, hair exuding a stale pomade. Picking up the bag, he set it on the bulge in his Hawaiian shorts, unzipping it and drawing out a wallet with a familiarity that suggested lengthy acquaintanceship. He slung the wallet at Spike's chest; it fell into his lap.

Spike picked it up. Spanish driver's licence in the gauze flap: Esperanza Castillo, smiling, neat collar of a white frilly blouse around her neck. 'Did you show this to the police?' Spike said.

Marouane flashed a gold molar. 'Police don't pay.'

Spike opened the opposite flap – Spanish ID, picture more recent, plumper, scowling – as Marouane removed a tampon from the handbag. Using his right hand, he formed a tunnel into which he jabbed the tampon back and forth. 'Uh, uh, uh. Big bitch,' he chuckled.

Spike stuck out an arm. 'The bag.'

As Marouane passed it over by the strap, Spike caught his hand, wrapping his fingers around the knuckles. Marouane frowned; Spike gave a brisk and vicious twist. His free hand grabbed at the source of the pain.

'Drop it.'

'I'm trying to.'

Spike twisted further until Marouane began to screech, clawing at Spike's forearm. Finally he managed to release the strap, huddling back into the bench seat, hand to his stomach, rocking. 'You break my fuckin' *arm* . . .'

Spike reached down for the handbag, then stood.

'Hey!' Marouane called out. 'One thousand dirham.'

He flicked a twenty note on the ground. 'For

the coat check.' He was almost out of the door when he heard Marouane call after him: 'You a dead man. You cunt.'

Spike turned. Marouane's left hand held up his business card. The wrist drooped: he transferred it to his right. 'I find you, cunt. Maybe Tangier. Maybe your home. But I find you.'

'I look forward to it,' Spike replied as he headed back out to the sunshine.

Walking along the pavement above the bar, Spike saw blood spreading beneath his bandage. A young woman was closing in; he recognised Tatiana, casually dressed in stonewash jeans and a paisley headscarf. She stopped, eyes on the ground. 'Zahra,' she said, 'she gone.' Her left eye was puffy, flaking with foundation, the scar on her chin unmasked and prominent.

'Gone where?'

She stared across the Straits. 'Sometimes when a person leave, first they make visit to the Café des Étoiles.'

'Here in Tangiers?'

'Ville Nouvelle.'

Spike nodded. There was fear in Tatiana's good eye as it flitted from the cut on his hand to the handbag on his shoulder. 'Listen,' Spike said, 'Marouane's in a bad mood. *Mal humor.* Take the day off.' He gave her a two-hundred note, then continued along the pavement.

CHAPTER 30

Stretching out on the unmade bed, ankles dangling, Spike listened to the rapid-fire finale of Caprice No. 13 in B flat major. No wonder they called it 'The Devil's Laughter'. He stared at the handbag, then reached for the central zip. It felt like opening a body bag. Sitting up properly, he emptied out the contents onto the bedclothes.

Condoms, aspirins, golden tube of lipstick. Well-used pack of tarot cards, screwed-up receipts . . . Spike checked for credit cards or cash. Not so much as a coin.

As he refilled the handbag, his hand brushed something solid. He stood and carried the bag to the light of the window. Drawing the two sides apart, he found a concealed zip at the base. He slid in his fingers and worked out a slim mobile phone.

He tried the on button: the screen flashed white then went dead. He pressed it again and nothing happened.

Turning the device over, he found a hole for the

charger. He unplugged his own phone and tried it. Too small. He checked the make: Arabic.

The soundtrack of an action film boomed from next door. Picking up Esperanza's phone, he stepped out onto the landing.

CHAPTER 31

Jean-Baptiste rolled his eyes, the whites reminding Spike of the skinned lambs' heads in the souk. 'Relax,' Spike said. 'It's not about the noise. I want to take you up on your offer.' He held out his wrist.

Jean-Baptiste glanced down at the bloodied bandage and made a series of clicking noises with his tongue. He stepped inside, leaving the door half open.

Spike followed him in. The shutters were closed, the air sweet and stale, the only light issuing from a line of four TV monitors, side by side at the edge of the room. The same film seemed to be showing on each; Spike recognised a starlet of the moment, doing 'scared' in the hallway of an ultra-modern house.

'Wait here,' Jean-Baptiste said. His accent was French, deep and languid. On the screens, the girl had responded to the danger by slipping off her hot pants and creeping through the house in her underwear. Spike looked about: four DVD players lay interconnected on the floor. A glinting pillar of blank discs stretched halfway to the ceiling. Turning to the bedside table, Spike saw a photograph taped to the wall, a hefty matron beaming beneath a floral headdress.

'You like movies?' Jean-Baptiste said as he upended an iodine bottle onto a cotton-wool ball and swabbed it over Spike's cut. Spike felt a sting then saw yellowness stain the skin. The film soundtrack changed to urgent strings as the killer snuck up. 'She should run away,' Spike said.

'They never do. *Voi . . . là.*'

Spike drew back his wrist then took out Esperanza's mobile. 'You wouldn't have a charger for this, would you?'

Jean-Baptiste examined the handset. '*C'est d'ici, uh?*'

'Belongs to a friend.'

With a knowing grin, Jean-Baptiste crouched down to the bedside table, plunging his hand into a vipers' nest of cables. He seemed able to navigate expertly in the half-light. Spike watched him try various pins until at last he saw the blue-white glow of a phone screen. Jean-Baptiste looked up. '*Tu veux du kif?*'

Spike suddenly felt very tired. 'Why not?'

Jean-Baptiste's teeth flashed like bone as he reached for a drawer and took out a toffee-sized lump of hashish. Sitting back on the bed, he burnt a large crumb onto a DVD case, mixing it with sprigs of tobacco which he stuffed into the mouth of a clay pipe. The cop launched into a showdown with the killer as the girl lay unconscious, breasts straining against her bra.

Spike caught the familiar sweet herbal smell as Jean-Baptiste puffed on the pipe then handed it over. He sucked on the end, hot ash catching at the back of his throat. The iodine on his cut began to throb.

'*Oro negro*,' Jean-Baptiste said. 'Black gold from the Rif Mountain. *Le kif est dans le Rif, uh?*'

'Mercy,' Spike replied, finally letting the smoke out.

'*Tu parles français?*'

'*Pas un word.*'

Jean-Baptiste took a few more puffs. A new sound from the TV, like two men in the distance sawing a tree in half. Spike felt the mattress vibrate then realised Jean-Baptiste was laughing. 'What?' Spike said.

'*Pas un word . . .*'

Spike found he was laughing too. He took another puff, feeling tears prick the corners of his eyes. Jean-Baptiste sat back, sighing.

'So how did you get into all this?'

'Into what?'

Spike forgot what he was going to say. They smoked some more until he remembered. 'The technology. *Technologie*,' he added in a Clouseau accent.

Jean-Baptiste cleared his throat, suddenly serious. 'In the Côte d'Ivoire. Abidjan. I work for the radio.

Producteur de radio. One day I make a programme the police do not like. My mother' – his eyes flicked to the bedside table – 'she give me money for Europe. All her money.' He puffed out slowly as though trying to cool the memory. 'I cross to the north. Burkina, Mali. Into desert. Three thousand kilometre. Bus, lorry, *camionette*. One month in the desert. When I reach here, I think, it is time for Europe. But for Europe you need money and now my money is gone. So I earn' – he gestured at the screens, as the hero cop and the starlet embraced – 'and I wait.'

'DVD sales holding up?'

'Not just DVD,' Jean-Baptiste said defensively. 'I make slide show for tour companies. Business conference for hotels–'

'The El Minzah?'

'Sure. El Minzah, Mövenpick, Intercontinental.'

Spike received another numbing hit of smoke. 'Did you meet many Bedouins in the desert?'

'*Les bédouins?*' Jean-Baptiste nodded vigorously. '*Très costauds*. Tough man, tough woman. Berber, Tuareg, black man – all are the same to *les bédouins*. First, *les bédouins*, then all else. Not like in Tanger. Know what they call me here?'

'What?'

'*Abid*.'

'Abid?'

'Slave.'

Spike passed back the pipe. 'I get that sometimes.'

'*Tu parles de la merde*, white boy,' Jean-Baptiste muttered.

'In Gibraltar,' Spike went on. 'The Spanish. They call us Chingongos.'

Jean-Baptiste paused. '*Chingongo*,' he said, trying to replicate Spike's accent. 'What is that?'

'A remote tribe of people who are interbred.'

Jean-Baptiste looked puzzled.

'*Incestuoso*,' Spike explained. 'Have sex with their family.' He contorted an eye and let his tongue loll. '*Chin-gon-go*.'

Spike saw Jean-Baptiste's face scrutinise him in the glow of the credits. He looked preoccupied, then his eyes creased and he spluttered out a long, hacking laugh. '*Abid*,' he sighed, '*et Chingongo*.' He pointed at Spike; this set him off again until he wiped his eyes and crouched down to the nearest DVD player. Spike felt his inner thighs squeak as he adjusted his position on the bed. For a moment he envied the flowing cotton lightness of Jean-Baptiste's djellaba. 'Do you know the Café des Étoiles?' he said.

Still on all fours, Jean-Baptiste worked himself round. 'Is like my *salon*. You want to go there, *Chingongo*?'

'*Mais oui, mon ami*.'

Jean-Baptiste gave another serious look. Then he burst out laughing again as he pressed a DVD into its plastic case.

CHAPTER 32

The sun was setting, the cafés and takeaway stalls abuzz. Spike and Jean-Baptiste wove through the labyrinth of lanes, towering over the locals. Every third step Jean-Baptiste seemed to stop to greet a vendor or glad-hand a shopkeeper. As he chatted to two weary-looking men with Afros, Spike asked him to wait and went down to the coast road.

The police station was starting to fill up. Spike handed over Esperanza's handbag wrapped in a hotel laundry bag, a letter taped to the front. 'For Inspector Eldrassi,' he said to the duty sergeant. 'Tell him it's to do with the Solomon Hassan case. Solomon Hassan, you got that?'

'Hassan. *Wakha*.'

Jean-Baptiste was waiting outside the police station. He carried his bulky canvas duffel bag with ease. 'You go in there for your friend?' he said.

'*Oui*.'

He nodded, satisfied, and they continued up the coast road. The wind was picking up, billowing out the burka of a lady coming the other way like some funereal ghost. A set of three-footers broke on the beach, the Gut doing its hidden work, roiling and churning beneath the surface.

CHAPTER 33

The Café des Étoiles occupied the tongue-shaped end of a shabby block of the Ville Nouvelle. Two boulevards crossed at its facade; a black bin bag had been kicked into one, clipped by cars, spilling its guts. A cedar tree grew outside the main door, gnarled after a lifetime of being kicked by passers-by and urinated on by dogs, one of which cocked its leg as Spike and Jean-Baptiste passed, observing them with pink discomfited eyes.

The brown-stained interior was a fug of malodorous smoke. 'I visit to maître d',' Jean-Baptiste called over the din. 'Ski-Coca for later?'

'Ski?'

'Whi-ski.'

Spike watched him edge through the crowd, somehow avoiding the cul-de-sacs as he moved to a doorway in the back wall. In front, the low tables were crammed together, the spaces between filled by punters talking over the heads of those seated. At one end stood a platform where a trio of rictus-grin musicians were struggling to make themselves heard. The two men on double bass and drums were North African, the keyboard player white. A fellow European, Spike assumed, until he passed and saw he was a freckled, albino black.

Spike sensed eyes on the back of his head. Someone hissed up, 'Change money, friend?' but he continued on by to an empty bar stool, where a white-haired barman was crushing mint with a pestle. Spike shouted out his order; a minute inclination of the head suggested the barman had heard.

He sat down. The two men on adjacent stools turned. One wore an ill-fitting suit, the other a hooded beige burnous. Spike took out his wallet; they glanced at one another then resumed their chat. He caught a glimpse of what looked like a European passport beneath the bar.

'*Vingt dirhams, monsieur.*'

Spike paid up as a giant West African entered the postage-stamp-sized space by his stool. Gathering his drinks with a sweep of the arm, Spike withdrew to sit beside a poster advertising last decade's visit of the Cirque du Maghreb.

After pressing his forehead against the tepid Coke bottle, Spike took a swig, then removed Esperanza's mobile phone from his pocket. His fingertips looked large and clumsy on the keys. No more hashish – ever. The screen lit up – 'Maroc Télécom' – showing two bars of battery but a full signal. He checked the call list: nothing. The inbox contained four texts, each from Maroc Télécom offering hearty welcome in English, French,

Spanish and Arabic. Three weeks old: evidently a local mobile had been a recent acquisition for Esperanza.

Another gulp of Coke, then Spike moved to 'Sent items'. A single message this time, sent to a contact saved as 'Abd al-Manajah'. Written out in Spanish: '*Vengo mañana como fijado*'. *I will come tomorrow as agreed.* Sent on the 16th, the day before Esperanza died.

Spike checked 'Contacts'. One name again: 'Abd al-Manajah'. He looked over at the bar: the two men on stools had been replaced by newcomers. Pressing the phone to one ear and cupping the other with his hand, Spike hit call back. Five rings, ten . . . He thought about Ángel Castillo's account of Esperanza's last movements. Tarot cards from a fortune-teller. A trip to the beautician. Fifteen rings, twenty . . . In the dark, uneven mirror on the wall, he saw Jean-Baptiste's head bobbing towards him over the customers.

Spike hung up and reached beneath the bar stool. '*Merci mec*,' Jean-Baptiste said as he accepted his drink. After downing it in one, he did a jig on the spot, dreadlocks clacking. 'Now I buy for you,' he said, turning to the bar. 'Happy hour for *Chingongo et Abid*.' His duffel bag wilted emptily on his shoulder.

As soon as Jean-Baptiste left his sightline, Spike saw something glitter at a table ahead. He crouched down, trying to catch a view through the tangle of limbs. A girl in a sparkly headscarf was passing something to a man with a bushy beard and shaven upper lip. The girl received a package in return, which she tucked into the pocket of her kaftan. As she drew back her hand, she met Spike's eye, then looked hurriedly away, reaching over to touch the arm of her companion before turning for the exit. 'Got to go,' Spike said to Jean-Baptiste.

'*Comment?*'

'See you back at the hotel.'

Spike launched into the crowd as Zahra gracefully circumnavigated the table. He collided with a youth with gaps shaved into his eyebrows, who shoved him back, spitting out insults in French.

A channel opened up; Spike plunged into it. Zahra was almost at the door. 'Wait!' Spike called out.

A hush swept through the bar, broken only by the tuneless rendition of 'Summertime'.

'I'm a friend,' Spike said. 'I've seen Ángel.'

The bar hum began to reassert itself as Zahra exited. Through the misty window, Spike saw her hesitate on the pavement outside, then beckon with a hand.

CHAPTER 34

Spike had forgotten how tall she was. ‘Come,’ she said in her husky voice, ‘not too close.’ He kept a few metres behind her, breaking into an occasional jog. Most of her face was hidden by her headscarf, the only clear features her flashing eyes and a loose strand of black hair, swaying in the breeze.

They entered the café-clogged Place de France. On the roof of a medium-rise building, backlit so as to be visible at night, Spike saw a Dunetech billboard. *Powering a Greener Future* . . . Beside it was a panel advertising ‘33 Export’ beer. Alcohol was banned within the Medina and Kasbah; outside, most things seemed to go.

Zahra exited the square along an avenue of palm trees, stopping as the pavement widened out to provide a viewing platform over the Straits. Four black ceremonial cannons were pointed out to sea, primed as though to repel intruders. Moored in the bay was a green-lit cruise ship, dull Europop throbbing from its deck.

Zahra sat down on the retaining wall, folding her kaftan beneath. Some Moroccan teenagers gathered further along glanced over. When Spike appeared, they resumed their kif smoking, inured to courting couples. Spike's legs hung beside hers above a shadowy bed of bougainvilleas.

'You know this place?' Zahra said.

'No.'

'It is the Terrasse des Paresseux. The Terrace of the Idle.' She stared out to sea. 'Who are you?'

'A lawyer.'

'You don't look like a lawyer. Where are you from?'

Spike pointed over the Straits to the lights of Gibraltar; Zahra inclined her eyes to see. 'The magical island for the idle English.'

'English speakers. And it's not an island. It's attached to mainland Spain.'

She turned her head properly. Her dark, almond-shaped eyes held Spike's own, causing him a momentary, unfamiliar slide in his stomach. 'Why are you following me?' she said.

'I want to talk to you about Esperanza.'

'Why should I listen?'

'I represent a man called Solomon Hassan. He's the chief suspect in Esperanza's murder.'

'So this is about money for you. Tax-free, I assume.'

'Do you know him?'

She shook her head.

'You argued with Esperanza. Why?'

She turned back to sea.

'Why did you throw a drink in Esperanza's face?'

She pulled up the sleeves of her kaftan, giving Spike a glimpse of smooth, coffee-coloured skin beneath. 'Esperanza used to come into the club,' she said. 'She was friendly at first. Then I processed her card and saw she was a Castillo.' A muezzin began to wail from a distant minaret; Zahra waited for him to finish. 'My father was head of the Bedouin council in my village. Eight years ago, some men from Ángel Castillo's company came to see him. They wanted to buy some land. A Bedouin burial site. Two weeks later my father disappeared.'

'Where?'

'Nobody knows. The elders say he took a bribe. That he's in Rabat, spending the money on women.' Her voice hardened: 'He liked women.'

'And the land?'

'Sold. Most of the Bedouins now have jobs on the site.'

'Did you tell Esperanza about this?'

'At first she just laughed. Then we fought.'

'But you saw her again?'

'She came back to the club. She was upset. We went for a drive and she told me she'd confronted her father. The next day she was dead.'

'Stepfather,' Spike murmured. 'So who killed her?'

Zahra shrugged. 'When I found out what happened I kept away. Then you turned up in Chinatown and we had our fun with the jeep.'

'Do you know who was driving?'

'I thought you might.'

'Why?'

'Because,' she said, turning again, 'it looked like it was trying to hit you.'

Spike paused. 'A police vehicle?'

'Maybe.' Her gaze returned to the European shoreline.

'Where were you the night Esperanza was killed?'

'Fuck you.'

'Could Marouane have killed her?'

'He tried to touch me once. He didn't do it again. He's a parasite, not a killer.'

'What were you buying just now in the café?'

She started to stand, so Spike reached into a pocket for his wallet, stopping only when he saw her look of contempt. Shaking her head, she walked away.

'Wait,' Spike said. 'I've got Esperanza's phone.'

'A lawyer *and* a thief,' Zahra called back. 'How unusual.'

Spike stood and dug into another pocket. 'There's a text on it,' he said. 'From an Abd al-Manajah.' He approached her; she was just a half-head smaller. 'I think Esperanza had arranged to see him the day she died.'

Zahra looked down at the phone. 'It's a Bedouin name. Used for the city. Abd is for Abdallah. Al-Manajah is the name of the tribe.' She passed the phone back.

'Do you know him?'

Before she walked away, Spike thrust a business

card in her hand. 'Call me if you remember anything,' he said. 'Especially about Abdallah al-Manajah.'

Zahra turned the card upside down. 'No baksheesh?'

'Do it for Esperanza.'

'Why should I care about her?'

'Because she's dead.'

Zahra strode away into the darkness. Spike checked to see if she'd dumped the card. When he looked back up, she was gone.

CHAPTER 35

An empty police jeep was parked on the pavement above the Sundowner Club. Street kids milled around it, kicking the tyres before running away. Spike crossed over and started climbing up to the Medina, where men were streaming out of cafés, plastic carrier bags in hands, chatting as though leaving a sports event.

Stopping at a food stall, Spike bought an avocado milkshake and some dusty unleavened bread. As he paid, he saw a bearded man watching him from beneath a street light.

Spike continued up the hill, chewing on his bread. When he looked back, the man was still following. He turned into an alleyway, then up a wider lane towards the Petit Socco. The man was still behind, his step quick and athletic. Around the next corner, Spike ducked into the first open shop he could see.

The shelves were lined with pots and jars like in an ancient apothecary. The owner creaked up from a stool, as though surprised by the custom. In the back room, Spike saw a shawled woman clipping her toenails as a tajine crock simmered before her.

‘*Bon prix pour épices, monsieur?*’ the owner said. ‘*Guter Preis?*’

There was a barrel in the middle of the shop; Spike crouched behind it as his pursuer appeared at the window. His beard was bushy, his upper lip entirely smooth. He carried a red rucksack on his back, which he swung off to remove a slim mobile phone. Still by the window, he made a call, talking animatedly, glancing about before finally moving out of sight.

The owner reappeared with a glass jar. Spike watched him tweezer out a series of fragrant, russet stamens, holding them one by one to the light. Spike bought the bag of saffron for old times’ sake, then chose a different route back to the hotel.

CHAPTER 36

'An offence by one villain may injure a million.'

'Room 303.'

'You had a visitor.'

'Quotation or fact?'

'A police inspector.'

Spike picked up his key. 'What did he want?'

'To come back tomorrow.'

Spike started walking up the stairs, then stopped. 'Do you have a telephone directory?'

'*Comment?*'

'A big book. With phone numbers.'

The receptionist turned to a shelf behind the computer point. 'A book is a garden you carry in your pocket,' he said as he heaved the directory onto the counter.

'You'd need pretty big pockets for this one. *Merci* and . . . *bonne nuit*.'

'*À vous aussi*.'

Silence from Jean-Baptiste's door, the frosted panel above it dark. Spike unlocked his own room. The bed was as he'd left it: no turndown service at the Continental. He pulled off his T-shirt, opening the shutters to breathe in the warm spiced air. A pale crescent moon hung above the Straits.

After clearing a space on the dressing table, he selected Caprice No. 16 in G minor, composed by Paganini in Lucca in 1805 while he was working as court musician for Napoleon's sister, Elisa Bonaparte. Paganini had conducted an affair with Elisa while also giving private violin lessons to her husband, Felice. The Devil looks after his own . . . The cadenzas seemed to clamp Spike's temples like a vice. He forced himself to keep listening, shutting his eyes and seeing Arabic script and musical notes flit interchangeably beneath his lids. The caprice ended; he snapped back to life and picked up the phone directory.

Half the names were in Arabic, half in French. The same names in both languages? No 'al-Manajahs' anyway. He searched for 'Abdallah' as a surname and found two entire pages.

Reaching for his notebook, he began making a list. *Ángel Castillo. Nadeer Ziyad. Toby Riddell. Marouane. Abdallah al-Manajah. Zahra* . . . He tore out the sheet, crumpling it into a ball and basketball-pitching it into the bin. He was here with a simple task: delay an extradition demand. And what was he doing? Drawing up a list of suspects like some backwater Poirot. His penultimate night in Tangiers and he'd achieved nothing save for a possible meeting with the local governor. The prison . . . He needed to go to the prison, seek out some hard evidence.

Grabbing the phone book again, he flicked through for the most common Jewish surnames: Benunes, Israel, Larache, Levy . . . His mobile phone was ringing; he hit 'pause' on the iPod. Number withheld. 'Hello?'

'It's Galliano.'

'*Qué pasa?*'

'I'm afraid there's been some news.'

Spike shot up from his chair. 'Dad?'

'What? No, no. Nothing like that.'

Spike felt his lungs deflate as he sat back down.

'They've done the second post-mortem in Madrid.'

'And?'

'Traces of DNA.'

'I thought they'd been degraded by the salt.'

'Not on the body.'

'The knife?'

'No.'

'Underwear?'

'It seems that no good deed goes unpunished, Spike,' Galliano said. 'The girl was two weeks pregnant. And there's a ninety-nine per cent genetic match with Solomon Hassan.'

CHAPTER 37

After a night of disturbing dreams, Spike awoke to find the city back in Ramadan mode. The Mendoubia public park was strewn with *sans-papiers* face down on the grass, as though there'd been a street festival the night before and they hadn't quite made it home. Tethered goats grazed around outstretched limbs.

Once through the commercial zone, the *petit taxi* drove past various small-scale industrial concerns – brickworks, sawmill, bus depot. Spike assumed they'd reached the prison when he saw a gate topped with razor wire; instead, the hand-painted Coca-Cola billboard above the walls revealed it as a bottling plant.

The road grew narrower, flanked by scrubland and the occasional caved-in building. Past the next hill, Spike saw Chinatown nestling in its sweaty hollow. The taxi began to slow, stopping at another set of gates. A Moroccan flag dangled from a pole, blood red with a green star in the middle. A metal car barrier was presided over by CCTV cameras.

Spike paid the driver and got out. Two women in

burkas were chatting on the pavement, each with a child tugging at a black-cloaked arm. Spike buzzed the door panel. '*Visita*,' he said as a Coca-Cola lorry lumbered behind.

As he reached to buzz again, a jeep with tinted windows turned off the road. The barrier bounced up and the gates began to open. Spike waited, then followed the jeep inside.

The gates clanked closed. The air throbbed with stillness. Somewhere a cicada buzzed.

Passing the entrance the jeep had taken, Spike saw a courtyard of parked cars. He stopped at a wooden hut, occupied by a heavy man sharing a spicy dish with the flies.

'*Visita*.'

The man stashed his carton guiltily out of sight. His face was so fat that the flesh pushed his eyes shut, reducing his vision to a slit of skin.

'*Visite*,' Spike tried, guessing at the French. 'Levy,' he added, handing over a sheet of paper on which the receptionist had written out the surname in Arabic. The guard slimmed his eyes still further, then picked up a Bakelite phone and waited for the connection.

Just past the hut, a two-tiered gate gave onto one of the yards of the prison. The ground was dusty and sun-drenched; in the only shady corner sat a group of men hugging their knees.

Spike moved towards the bars. One of the men shielded his eyes then stood. He took a step forward as another prisoner yanked him back by the tunic. He broke free, loping across the yard. His beard was russet, his forehead pink and flaky. He hurled himself at the bars, one sandal still on, the other left behind in the dirt, shouting in a language Spike did not recognise.

'*Hellas*,' he yelled, just inches from Spike's face. '*Hellas, Hellas . . .*'

One of the other prisoners was striding over, dark tufty beard down to his chest.

'Greece,' the sunburnt man shrieked, '*ambassada, ambassada . . .*'

With a creaking of hinges, the guard emerged from his hut. Drawing his truncheon, he strolled towards the gate, shouting as he swung at the bars. The man gave a bird-like cry as the truncheon crushed his knuckles, and fell to the ground. The prisoner behind him laughed as the guard raised his truncheon again.

'Hey!' Spike called out, stepping between the guard and the gate. '*Visite*.'

Tucking the truncheon under his arm, the guard took Spike's piece of paper out of his pocket and tore it neatly in two. Spike swore at him in English, then turned to the sound of a clank from the opposite end of the walkway. Another jeep was driving in.

The gates were starting to close. Spike set off rapidly towards them, hearing the guard shouting behind him as he slipped between the gap.

The ladies in burkas were still on the pavement.

Spike walked past them, waving down a *petit taxi* on the other side of the road. 'Medina,' he said, and the cab performed a U-turn and headed back to town.

CHAPTER 38

'Right then, you *charavaca*,' Spike swore down the phone, 'one more lie, one more half-truth, and I throw you to the wolves. Do you understand?'

'Yes.'

'How long do we have?'

Solomon gulped at the other end of the line. 'Twenty minutes.'

'Then get ready to talk. Did you kill her?'

'God, Spike. *No*.'

'But you were sleeping with her.'

'Yes.'

'How many times?'

'Twice . . . once.'

'Which is it?'

'I don't know. The first time didn't . . . work.'

'Didn't work?'

'Couldn't.'

'Where?'

'We went to the Museum of Ethnography. Then to a hotel bar, the El Minzah. She had a few drinks, then went crazy. Pulled me into the toilet but I was too . . . taken aback. So I asked her to dinner at my flat. I'd ordered up some pills online. Things went . . . better. I told her I wanted to see her again. When I asked her if she was sleeping with other people, she just laughed.'

'Which other people?'

'Men she picked up. Women.'

'Their names?'

'I don't know, Spike, I just know there were others. A few days later, we arranged to meet at the club. We watched a woman and a man dance. I didn't like it so we went outside. The rest is as I told you.'

'So who killed her?'

'I don't know. Someone on the beach. Or from the club.'

'The barman?'

'I really don't know.'

'Why did you lie before?'

'I thought you might not take my case.'

'Why?'

'If you knew I was sleeping with her you'd think I had motive.'

'You do have motive, *cortapisha*. Did you know she was pregnant?'

Solomon paused. 'If I'd known . . .'

'You wouldn't have killed her?'

'No! I wouldn't have left her on the beach.'

'Why didn't you use a condom?'

'We did. It broke.'

'Did you use a condom the night she died?'

'It never went that far, Spike. We argued then I left.'

'Argued?'

'About her not wanting to be faithful.'

From next door came a leonine MGM roar. '*Bezims*,' Spike cursed.

'What's that?'

'Who's Zahra?'

'Who?'

'Waitress from the Sundowner Club?'

'Never heard of her.'

'Did Esperanza talk about people trying to hurt her?'

'No.'

'Friends of hers in trouble?'

'She didn't have any friends.'

'Did you hear anything about a Bedouin going missing?'

'Sorry?'

'To do with Dunetech?'

'A Bedouin? No . . . I mean, Bedouins are important to Dunetech, we employ them on-site. They're good workers, rank and file.'

'What about Abdallah al-Manajah?'

Solomon went quiet.

'Abdallah al-Manajah!'

'Please,' Solomon said, 'I'm trying to think. Yes . . . he came into the office a few times. I remember him, fat guy in his sixties. Dirty clothes.'

'Bedouin?'

'I think so . . . He was dark like a Bedouin. He used to work in Zagora Zween in the early days. Before my time. Phase 1 site manager, something like that.'

'What's his connection to Dunetech now?'

'Probably consulting on the expansion programme.'

'You didn't ask?'

'Why should I? People came and went the whole time.'

'Did Esperanza know Abdallah?'

'I doubt it.'

'Could she have done?'

'It's possible. She came to the Dunetech offices. That was how I met her. She could have seen him there, I suppose.'

'Did she talk about meeting him the day she died?'

'I told you, Spike, she never mentioned his name.'

'What else did she do that day?'

'Went to see some crystal-gazer. She was into all that crap.'

'But no mention of Abdallah al-Manajah?'

'No, Spike. Why do you keep asking?'

'What about the stepfather? Castillo. What's his story?'

'They didn't get on. She said he made her flesh creep. That's why she hadn't seen him in years.'

'Why change now?'

'How the hell should I know? Maybe she liked the sound of Dunetech. Wanted to give him a second chance.'

A Hollywood symphony filled the silence. 'What about Toby Riddell?' Spike said.

'What about him?'
'Trustworthy?'
'Decent enough, if a little slow. I think he went to school with Nadeer in England. Couldn't get into university so he tried Sandhurst. Saw some action in Northern Ireland. Then Gib. After that he was decommissioned and got in touch with Nadeer.'
Spike heard Solomon's hoarse, asthmatic breathing.
'Spike?'
'Yes?'
'They're going to send me back to Tangiers, aren't they?'
'Almost certainly, pal.'

CHAPTER 39

The *petit taxi* puttered along the brow of the hill. Spike stared out at another flawlessly clipped lawn. A sprinkler clicked and whirred as a green-uniformed gardener tilled the soil. 'What do you call this area?' Spike said.

The driver grinned. His two front teeth were missing and he worked a furry tongue through the gap. 'Is La Montagne. Or Beverly Hills. See here?' He pulled up beside a red all-weather driveway leading to a pair of spiked gates. Two armed soldiers guarded the posts. 'Here is the summer palace for our King.'

'Is he in?'

The taxi returned to the main road as one of the guards stepped forward. 'It is Ramadan – the King is in his castle in Rabat. And here –' they passed a higher set of gates; above, Spike saw the top half of what looked like a replica of the White House – 'here is for Sheikh Ben-Adis, Prince for Saudi Arabia. And here –' the driver pointed to another neo-Palladian Christmas cake – 'is for Mister Forbes.' *Fourbez*, he pronounced it.

'American magazines. *Multi* million.' He sawed his tongue back and forth. 'And here –'

'OK,' Spike said. 'I get it.'

They continued along the ridge, a medley of gardeners and security men sending over heavy, sweaty glances. Below, the Medina and Kasbah were clustered neatly on the hillside. To the right, the Straits glowed tangerine in the setting sun.

At the next corner the taxi pulled up. Two life-size stone lions guarded a pair of iron gates. '*Voilà*,' the driver said. 'La Villa des Lions.'

An open-doored sentry box stood to the right, from which a mustachioed security guard emerged. The driver rolled down his window as the guard peered past him to Spike. 'Name?'

'Sanguinetti.'

'Uh?'

'San-guin-etti.'

Back in his cabin, the guard spoke into a phone; a moment later the gates began to open.

'You like Mister Fourbez,' the driver said, tonguing his teeth.

The driveway was lined on each side by sickly, thin-trunked palms. Between them, Spike caught a glimpse of a concrete helipad on the grass. Thirty metres on, the driveway opened into a turning circle, an umbrella pine spreading in its centre. Parked around the outside like dates in a box were twenty or so executive cars, chauffeurs at the wheels, capped and bored.

A rectangular yellow building blocked the far

side of the circle, a smartly dressed flunkey already striding from its central archway.

The taxi driver started to reverse into a space beside a Bentley, leaving Spike room to get out, but squeezing his own door so close to its bodywork that the uniformed chauffeur glared up from a paperback.

The footman wore full livery. For a grim moment Spike thought the function might be fancy dress. He turned to the driver. 'Wait here. OK?'

The footman opened Spike's door as the taxi driver killed the engine.

'Welcome, Mr Sanguinetti, please.'

They crunched over gravel towards the gatehouse, Spike smoothing the creases from his blue linen shirt. After passing through the arch, they emerged into a terrace to the sound of soft music and chatter.

The pool was long and broad, mosaic-tiled and with shallow marble steps at the end. On one edge Spike saw a heliopod solar-power unit, both panels splayed open, crouching like a hothoused carnivorous plant patiently waiting for prey.

The guests were gathered in the last of the sun on the opposite edge of the pool. Moroccan girls in black, sunray-pleated skirts sashayed between them holding trays. A jungle of palms and sunflowers lined the terrace, fed by a serpentine watering system. In front of the main house, a tablecloth-draped bar was staffed by three men, to the right of which a band of traditionally dressed

Berbers were knocking on drums and tootling on flutes.

'Most welcome, sir,' the footman concluded, sweeping an arm over the guests. Spike continued onto the bar, recognising faces from the Roadshow. 'Coca-Cola,' he said. 'Cold as you can.' The barman decapitated a bottle with a flair that suggested Spike's order left him seriously under-used.

Spike stood with his back to the bar. The pool lights flashed on, sending turquoise sea snakes shimmering through the water. A waitress with hoop earrings offered him a canapé; as he passed up the chance for a second, he made out Nadeer Ziyad among the guests. Eschewing his Savile Row threads, Nadeer sported a full-length burnous, yellow and white striped with a baggy, hanging hood. On his head was a tassel-free fez; on his feet, soft babouche slippers. He raised an arm and started walking over, arching an eyebrow in a manner that suggested he was no fan of this frippery either. 'Hello, mate,' he said. Rather than a handshake, he went for the full body-clasp. 'Thank God you're here. Some sanity at last.'

He joined Spike by the bar. Guests kept shooting looks their way. On the other side of the pool, Toby Riddell was telling a story to a group of Middle Eastern investors, pointing towards the heliopod. He wore a brass-buttoned blazer and high-waisted chinos. His black shoes gleamed.

'There comes a point in a man's life when he

must say, No, there shall be no more vol-au-vents.' Nadeer smiled. 'So how's tricks?'

'There's been a development.'

Nadeer pinched his hawk's nose. 'Yes, I heard about the post-mortem. Not good. Not good at all.'

'Is the governor here?'

Nadeer's irises glittered like champagne diamonds. 'The governor is what my father likes to call a dear, dear friend. He doesn't blow out a Ziyad.'

With a firm but gentle grip, Nadeer took hold of Spike's hand. Though Spike had seen men walking this way in the Medina, he still let go after a few paces, and they continued onwards to an urn of sunflowers, where a suited Moroccan was chatting to a blonde girl. Spike recognised Miss Solness, the Scandinavian from the Roadshow, slick in a trouser suit, kitten heels and silver top. Her companion glanced over as they approached. His shaven scalp had a covering of stubble midway up, as though a tide of skin were rising. He whispered something to Miss Solness; she looked on nonchalantly, sipping from a foliage-stuffed tumbler.

When the Moroccan was close enough, Nadeer put an arm around him. 'Spike Sanguinetti,' he said, 'I'd like you to meet His Excellency, the Governor of Tangiers.'

The governor looked barely older than Spike. His smile reconfigured to gruff mistrust. 'Let's go inside,' he grunted, accent tinged with American.

Nadeer turned to walk back across the terrace, Spike and the governor following behind like a couple of international bodyguards. The governor gave Spike a glance, then increased his pace to catch Nadeer up. The band played faster – as they passed through the sliding doors to the main house, the lute player was strumming like a North African Paganini.

The hallway was paved in stone, bisected by a staircase with a curving silver banister. A chandelier hung above a table fanned with copies of *Country Life* and *The Field*. A vase of orchids gave off the fleshy scent of carrion.

On the stairs hung a full-length portrait of Nadeer, leaning on a rifle, foot pressed triumphantly down on the tongue-lolling head of a leopard, the backdrop mountainous and romantic. Neither Nadeer nor the governor looked at the painting, passing instead through a padded doorway.

Spike followed them into an oak-panelled study. Another portrait of Nadeer graced the empty fireplace, his wavy hair slicked back, pastel jumper lightly laid over the shoulders of an open-necked shirt as he perched on a boardroom table.

The governor slumped into a knobbly leather armchair, Nadeer sitting down next to him, Spike opposite.

'You see,' the governor began, as if picking up on an earlier conversation, 'the situation is very delicate.' His voice was deep and slow, as though distorted for a ransom demand. Nadeer kept his eyes on Spike, smiling expectantly like the giver of a present gauging the recipient's reaction.

'It's a mess that just keeps on getting messier,' the governor said. 'And now I hear about some pregnancy?' Flecks of spittle flew from his mouth as he rasped the 'r'. 'And another arrest?' He turned to Nadeer for confirmation. 'A barman?'

'He works in the nightclub where the girl was last seen,' Spike said. 'He had her handbag. I told the police.'

'Ugly,' the governor replied. 'Ugly, ugly, ugly.'

'Have they pressed charges?'

The governor waved a hand as though swatting away a mosquito. 'The issue is as follows. Your client's former employer is about to sign a deal of great importance to the future of this region. It cannot be jeopardised by the death of some Spanish whore.' He stared at Spike, his eyes a nervous brown, ill-suited to the strong, gravelly voice. 'Nadeer tells me you're well connected in Gibraltar?'

'It's a small place.'

'The deal signs sundown Thursday, the last day of Ramadan. The court of assizes will waive extradition on one condition. That you delay the trial until at least three months after the Dunetech deal is concluded. I make that –' the governor glanced down at a chunky sports watch – 'November the 29th. So roll out the red tape. Sit on your hands. Slow-walk the situation. You people do that better than anyone.'

'And any trial will take place in Gibraltar?'

'Agreed.' The governor thrust out a hand. It quaked a little, like a drinker's. Spike reached out and shook it, then followed him and Nadeer out of the study, wondering why he didn't feel quite as elated as he might.

CHAPTER 40

The governor strode beneath the gatehouse arch, the liveried footman slipping in behind him. 'He's a cold fish,' Nadeer said. 'But effective. Tourism on the up.'

'How old?'

'Thirty-eight.'

'Your voters like 'em young.'

'Regional governors are still personally appointed by the King.'

'I thought you said Morocco was a democracy.'

'Even with our Arab Spring, there are many ways to define the word.'

The party had hit a pitch that suggested the barmen now had the chance to express themselves. Guests kept trying to catch Nadeer's eye. He reached again for Spike's hand. This time Spike reduced the contact to an elbow-touch.

'He's certainly right about the mess though,' Nadeer said once they were at the bar. 'Best to get it cleaned up. Sorted.'

Spike heard a discreet phut, then saw the barman expertly tip a flute.

'At least it's good news for Solomon,' Nadeer said, turning.

'He faces three months in Gibraltar without bail.'

'Well, hopefully the evidence stacks up against this other suspect. The barman or what have you.' He passed Spike a glass of champagne. 'Of course we'd have Solomon back here like a shot. Exciting times ahead at Dunetech. Need minds like his on board.'

'He was hardly Brain of Britain at school.'

'But you can't teach business acumen, Spike. It's like courage. Or survival instinct. Either you've got it or you don't.' He held up his fizzing flute. 'To Solomon and the future.'

Spike smelled the sour tang of bursting bubbles. 'Fuck it.'

'What's that?'

'It's how we say cheers in Gibraltar.'

Nadeer grinned. 'Fuck it,' he repeated, and they chinked glasses.

Eyes closed, Spike took a deep, sparkling gulp. Then another. When he opened his eyes, Nadeer was watching, drink untouched, smile on his delicate lips.

'Impressive set-up you've got,' Spike said, wiping his mouth.

Nadeer scanned around. 'I suppose so. The firm's based in Tangiers, so there's a certain pressure to appear . . . settled.'

'And your father still lives in Rabat?'

'Yes.'

On the opposite side of the pool, Toby Riddell was pointing a group of Asian investors towards the heliopod. One of the panels moved, making them jump in fright, then laugh nervously at their mistake.

'Ever heard of a man called Abdallah al-Manajah?' Spike said.

Nadeer's champagne flute stopped en route to his mouth. 'Don't think so.'

'One of your employees?'

He lowered his glass. 'That doesn't narrow it down.'

'Solomon seems to think he might work for Dunetech. A Bedouin?'

'The Bedouins are our main source of human capital,' Nadeer replied as though that settled it. 'Our site is close to a Bedouin village so we provide jobs for what's a largely disenfranchised section of society. They're far less numerous than the Berbers, Tuareg or Reguibat, and as such are treated as second-class citizens.' He nodded towards an overweight American-looking man. 'Duty calls,' he sighed. 'Got to press the flesh. And by the look of it, there's a fair old bit of it over there.' He gazed past Spike to the heliopod. 'Christ. What a sunset. Enjoy the party.' Snatching Spike's hand again, he gave it a squeeze.

Spike turned back to the bar. 'Another, please,' he said, putting down his flute, 'this time with some booze in it.' He pointed to a brandy bottle behind.

Drink fortified, he walked over to the far side of the pool. The band were playing the same tune on repeat, some facile flute jig. Ahead loomed the heliopod. At any point it looked as though it might swivel on its stand and blast Spike like some intergalactic droid.

'You like?'

Spike turned into the pale, laughing eyes of Miss Solness.

'Not much.'

'See that mirrored panel? It reflects the sun onto the darker-coloured cells, so they get the natural *and* reflected rays. Doubles the output.'

'The Sun King rules OK.'

Miss Solness smiled. '*And* the panels clean themselves of sand as they move. My name's Regina.' The 'G' of her Christian name was hard, her English as faultless as most Scandinavians'.

'Spike.'

Spike saw that the tip of her nose was peeling. She followed his gaze. 'What can I say? I'm Norwegian. Land of the snow-white tan. You?'

'From Gibraltar.'

'Investor?'

'Not today.'

'You seem pretty close to the money though.' She glanced over to the other side of the pool, where Nadeer was working the crowd. 'You know,' she said, passing her tongue across her pink, chapped lips, 'what the best thing is about Dunetech?'

'What is the best thing about Dunetech?'

She tucked a hank of shiny hair behind her ear. 'Once they get the power into Tangiers, they can start laying cables over the Straits.'

'Underwater?'

'HVDC – high voltage direct current.' She prodded the ground with a diamanté-encrusted sandal: a thin black wire stretched from the base of the heliopod to the side wall of the house. 'Barely any energy-loss. And once you're over the Straits, you can plug into the European grid and sell to the whole of the West. No more worries about Russia dominating the market.'

'Is that part of the official business plan?'

Regina leaned in close to let Spike light her thin cigarette with a tea light. Her scent was sharp and musky, like a man's cologne. 'It's what's exciting investors, I can tell you that much. Why else headquarter the company in Tangiers? It's smaller than Casablanca and Rabat. But closer to Europe. Isn't that what's always made Tangiers special?'

Spike put down the candle and reached over to the shining shaft of the heliopod. He whipped back his hand: felt like he'd just been stabbed with a pin.

'Ouch,' Regina said.

'Not such a friendly source of energy after all,' Spike said, shaking his fingers.

Regina took a step forward. She had a pair of oversize designer sunglasses hooked to her top, their weight tugging down the silk to reveal a smooth arc of breast. 'I'm stuck here with my trade mag till they sign,' she said. 'Want to grab a drink in town?'

'Maybe some other time.'

She tapped at her clutch bag. 'Not tempted by the local specialities?'

Spike shook his head, and Regina shrugged, sliding on her sunglasses and setting off in the direction of the house, a swarm of eyes following her haunch as she swayed across the flagstones. When she was gone, Spike looked down at his hand. A small, greenish burn scored the index nail.

CHAPTER 41

High-wattage uplights blazed from the terrace. A cicada in an olive bough duetted with an unseen sprinkler. Spike zoned in on it, amazed as usual that something so small could create such a racket.

Alongside the panel that controlled the pool lights was a doorway. Still facing the terrace, Spike leaned against it, feeling behind for a handle. It twisted and he held it down, kicking backwards with his heel. Another quick glance at the guests, and he stepped inside.

The air had the close, mushroomy smell of an old cellar. Spike felt for the switch and watched the strip lights wink and flicker, eventually revealing a damp concrete stairwell. Downstairs was another switch. A dingy, gaping underground space emerged.

Ranged along one side of the garage was a collection of gardening equipment: rakes, hosepipes, shiny four-pronged forks. Beneath the mouldy ceiling ran a bank of video monitors, each displaying black-and-white images of the terrace, the driveway, the gatehouse, the turning circle, two cars already pulling out . . . Spike located his *petit taxi*, still parked beside the Bentley. A row of numbers updated at the base of the screen. Beneath lay a metal chair flanked by an ashtray and a Moroccan newspaper.

On the other side of the garage, four vehicles were parked, noses pointed towards a ramp which appeared to lead up to the turning circle. A yellow Ferrari, a Hummer with glittering wheel spokes, the silver Mercedes which had picked Spike up. And a jeep with tinted windows and bull-bar bumper.

The jeep was painted electric blue. Putting his champagne flute down on the concrete, Spike delved into his pocket for a ten-dirham coin, then crouched to the mudguard and scraped at the bodywork. Nothing happened so he twisted the coin in a circle. Powdery flakes came away; he brushed them off and saw jet-black paint beneath.

A metallic clank sounded from upstairs. Spike crouched behind the jeep. Footsteps on the concrete, slow then quick; flattening himself, he peered beneath the chassis and caught a flash of diamanté.

Spike rose to his feet. Regina's long legs were tensed in their gleaming heels. Her tuxedo jacket was draped over her forearm like a sommelier's towel. She threw it onto the metal chair and it fell to the floor. Her bra was a similar pale pink to her skin.

'Bit hot up there, is it?' Spike called out, glancing

suspiciously over her shoulder. As he stooped to pick up her jacket, he checked her eyes. The pupils were dilated, rolling back and forth in her head as though drawn by a magnet.

Regina smiled lazily as she put down her handbag. A new image was flickering on the monitors above her head: a black-and-white Toby Riddell, striding across the empty side of the terrace. As Riddell reached the heliopod he paused, hand testing for something tucked in the waistband of his chinos. Spike turned to the opposite wall, where a small black CCTV camera was fixed. On one of the monitors, Riddell's arm was extending for the gatehouse door.

Spike looked back to Regina. Her bra was unfastened, exposing two neat, coral nipples. She beckoned at Spike, pupils still rolling, and he stepped forward to kiss her. Her saliva had a sharp chemical taste. 'Fuck me,' she hissed in his ear, Scandinavian accent thickening. 'Fuck me on the Ferrari.'

Spike felt her tongue probe forcefully against his. From upstairs came a creak; he slid his hand across her stomach and cupped a breast.

'Squeeze it,' she breathed. 'Harder.'

Taking the stiffening nipple in his fingertips, Spike steered her round until she was facing the stairwell. She'd unclipped her trousers: no underwear, the smooth, pinker skin between her thighs hairless save for a slim strip of blonde. She reached down to his flies: 'Hel-*lo* . . .' she began, before suddenly tensing up and drawing her elbows across her chest.

Spike turned to see Riddell on the bottom stair, hand still tucked beneath his jacket. He drew Regina close, face twisted in disgusted shock. 'Some privacy, maybe?' he shouted.

Riddell continued to stand.

'Piss *off*!' Regina snarled, pressing her half-naked body to Spike's.

Riddell took a hesitant backward step, catching the leather sole of his shoe and stumbling, hand still beneath jacket. He held his watery eyes on Regina, before turning and climbing back up to the door.

'Pervert,' giggled Regina, leaning in and gnawing at Spike's lower lip. He drew away and pointed at the camera. 'Not sure we want to end up online.'

'Oh, I don't know. Behind the Hummer?'

'Probably best not.'

Regina started to blink, as though slowly becoming aware of where she was. She shook her glassy eyes in an attempt to focus, then reached down for her trousers. Spike passed over her bag and jacket, zipping himself up and taking her hand to lead her, dressed, up the car ramp at the other end of the garage. There was a red lever box on the wall; Spike yanked it down and the gates began to open.

They emerged at the edge of the turning circle. Most of the cars were gone but the *petit taxi* was still waiting. Regina laid her head on Spike's shoulder, twining a white lock of hair around one finger. 'Feel a bit sick,' she said in her sing-song accent.

Spike stuck a thumb up at the taxi driver. 'Still time for a loosener?' he asked Regina.

She brightened, lifting her head, and they walked back through the tunnel to the pool terrace. There were fifteen or so guests left, all gathered by the bar. The band had packed up; of Nadeer and Riddell there was no sign. Seeing Nadeer's overweight American friend, Spike led Regina over. 'Do you two . . .?'

'Oh sure,' the Texan drawled. 'Reggie's gonna do a piece on me.'

'Maybe you could give her a lift into town.'

'If she'll wait till this numbskull masters the mint julep.'

Spike turned to Regina. Her jawbone poked in and out as she chewed her teeth.

'Got to go,' Spike said.

'What?'

'Boat to catch.'

'But –'

He squeezed her hand – 'Sorry' – then set off back to the turning circle.

CHAPTER 42

The usual traffic hierarchy had been reversed, cars waiting for pedestrians, the road a pavement, choked with people, the majority fighting their way towards a single narrow gateway in a whitewashed wall.

'What's going on?' Spike said.

'Le Jour Sacré,' the taxi driver replied. 'When the Gates of Heaven are open to all.'

'Is there another way through?'

White minivans were parked on the pavements, either having disgorged their passengers or abandoned their journeys altogether. Blankets patchworked the road, women in headscarves selling branches of foliage, slowing progress further as the customers haggled and paid. From behind the walls came the distant sound of chanting.

'Marshan Cemetery,' the taxi driver said. 'Oldest for all Tangiers.'

'I'll walk then,' Spike said. The taxi driver counted his notes, tonguing the gap between his teeth more quickly.

Once through the gate, the cemetery sloped ahead, an uneven rectangle the size of two football pitches, ended by clifftops and the sea beyond. The gravestones were intersected by pathways, the widest running down the centre, lined by beggars, wailing as they held out warty, palsied palms in supplication.

The crowd swept Spike on. The chanting and incense grew heady, intermingled with saline gusts from the sea. Spike turned onto a smaller path: the graves were like concrete bathtubs sunk into the ground, headstones where the taps might have been. Some sprouted with grass, mulched by sprays of decaying flowers.

Spike watched a man and woman approach, escorted by a beggar with a hoe who set to work scraping away the weeds. The woman carried a water bottle; she sluiced it over the headstone, cleaning off the dirt, worrying at the engraving with her fingernails. Her husband beckoned to a holy man, who came over and planted joss sticks in the soil, reciting from the Koran as the woman pressed her face into her husband's chest.

Spike walked to the cliff face, sitting down on a bare patch of dirt. White horses reared in the Straits: the Gut, twisting away with its secret currents. Sickle-shaped swifts screamed above, preparing to migrate south. The murmur of the crowd started blending with the chanting, as though the mourners were singing their own requiem.

Spike took out his phone and texted Galliano: 'Extradition dropped. Taking night boat home.' Then he stood and went to a side exit.

CHAPTER 43

'O*uai?*'

'It's Spike.'

The door opened. Jean-Baptiste's chest was bare above a pair of baggy Aladdin trousers, his brown nipples like tired eyes above the round prurient mouth of his navel. Spike followed him in, bag over shoulder. The air reeked sweetly.

'Where you go last night?' Jean-Baptiste said as he picked up a remote control and sat down on the bed.

'Business.'

'Your friend?'

Spike nodded as the sound of the TV monitors muted. On-screen, an actor with a widow's peak was pinned against a wall, knife point stretching to a nostril.

'I'm going home,' Spike said.

Jean-Baptiste picked up a rubber band and fastened his dreadlocks into a ponytail.

'Can I buy you a drink at the port?'

'Have to finish this movie, uh?'

Spike laid a hotel envelope on the mattress.

'No money . . .'

'Good,' Spike said, 'because there isn't any. I've got a friend in Gibraltar called Sebastian Alvarez. He runs cigarettesover the border to Spain. If you can make it into Gib, he'll get you across in his fishing boat. Phone number's in the envelope.'

Jean-Baptiste prodded the envelope with a finger.

'There's a Gibraltarian on the dock who can arrange passage. He takes euros.'

'My Chingongo,' Jean-Baptiste said, smiling. 'Maybe I do come for –'

'Be seeing you, Jean-Baptiste.'

Downstairs, Spike settled up. 'Money is like a rose,' the receptionist said as he handed Spike his receipt. 'Smell it and pass it onto the next person.'

'Did the policeman come back?'

'Not yet.'

Spike reached over the counter. 'It's been a pleasure.'

'Life without friends is like couscous without salt.'

'What *is* that you're reading?'

'Mysteries are the –'

'OK, OK.'

Down by the quayside, Spike purchased a half-bottle of whisky and waited at a café, plugged into his iPod. The lights of the catamaran began to approach, passengers already out on deck. He looked down at his ticket. Gibraltar, *Jebel Tariq* . . . The screen of his mobile illuminated and he swatted out his earphones. 'Yes?'

'It's me.' The voice was husky and low.

'Zahra?'

'I found his address.'

'Whose?'

'Abdallah al-Manajah's.'

'In Tangiers?'

'Terrasse des Paresseux. Half an hour.'

Out in the Straits, the catamaran slotted into the port like the last missing piece of a jigsaw.

CHAPTER 44

Zahra was waiting in the shadows on the Terrasse des Paresseux. Her headscarf was tied beneath her chin to reveal a large mobile mouth with dark, cushion lips. She wore a white dress over her kaftan, fastened with a sash. Her smile vanished as quickly as it had arrived. 'You smell like cheap perfume.'

'Whisky.'

'Yesterday kif, today whisky?' She strode away along the line of cannons into the Place de France. The cafés were closing, a seller of individual cigarettes padlocking his wooden cart for the night.

Spike adjusted his overnight bag on his shoulder and caught her up. 'I didn't think you would call.'

'Esperanza wanted to see Abdallah al-Manajah,' Zahra said. 'Maybe he will know something about my father.'

The sky was a dark, denim blue, the moon still too thin to shed light. They crossed over the rue de Belgique. The smaller residential streets had potholes in the macadam and beaten-up cars on the pavements, the apartment blocks seeming to date from an earlier, more optimistic period, acanthus scrolls crumbling above doorways like in old-world Paris.

'How did you find the address?' Spike said.

'I asked a friend.'

'The man with the red rucksack?'

'Who?'

'From the Café des Étoiles?'

Zahra stopped. 'You are spying on me now, Somerset?'

'It's Spike.'

'Why "Spike"?'

'Because it's better than Somerset.'

'Is Somerset a family name?'

'My mother was a fan of the English short story.'

A white, Velcro-strapped trainer emerged from Zahra's dark robes as she picked her way across the rubble. 'It's 13C, rue des Rosiers.'

The bell pushes were unmarked. Zahra pressed the third one down. Nothing happened so she tried the same on the next column.

A light flashed on; someone was coming out. Spike and Zahra drew back like caryatids on either side of the entrance as it opened to an old woman in black. As soon as the woman stepped into the road, Spike moved forward and caught the door. She turned and stared; Spike stared back and she shuffled away into the darkness.

'After you,' Spike said as Zahra came forward, ducking elegantly beneath his arm like an Elizabethan dancer. Inside, envelopes marked with dirty footprints littered the doormat. The ground-floor flat was 13A; they climbed the drab stairwell to 13C.

The doorbell was silent so Zahra knocked instead. 'Why don't you try his phone?' she said, turning to Spike.

'He never answers.'

Zahra stared at him until he took out Esperanza's mobile. From inside they heard a long, distant ringtone. She cast him a querulous glance then rapped again. As she turned to leave, he dropped to his knees and slotted an arm through the letter box.

'What are you *doing*?' she hissed.

'Just watch the stairs.'

He contorted his arm upwards. Blood poured into his head as he strained his fingertips towards cold metal. With one last surge he got hold of the latch and yanked it down. The door shifted, tugging at his shoulder blade. He released the latch and removed his hand.

'You're very flexible.'

'I think it runs in the family.'

The door fell an inch open, releasing a dank putrid aroma. Spike put his shoulder to the frame. Something was blocking it. 'Hello?' he called through the gap. 'Can you try in Arabic?' he said to Zahra.

'You think that makes a difference?'

'Could do.'

'*Salaam?*' she said. '*Billatí?*' She withdrew, wrinkling her nose in disgust. Spike barged the door again. It moved a foot this time, allowing him to edge crabwise inside, arm extended for the switch. She followed him in, momentarily throwing them into darkness as she blocked the gleam from outside. Sweeping his hand up and down, he found metal again and the lights crackled on.

The flat was open-plan with a high-beamed ceiling and a mezzanine level accessed by a fixed wooden ladder. A halo of bulbs shone above a motionless fan; there seemed to be a problem with the circuit as they kept flickering on and off.

'*Ya Allah*,' Zahra said.

At first Spike assumed the flat had been ransacked. It looked as though the contents of a skip had been emptied out. The door had been blocked by an armchair, one of three crammed next to each other, springs jabbing one to the other. A racing-green picnic table was heaped with string-bound Arabic newspapers, a tangle of anglepoise lamps beneath.

Zahra shoved the door closed. On top of a stack of microwaves sat a gramophone, vinyl records in a crate alongside. She drew one out, nose still wrinkling: the sleeve showed a Moroccan in a handlebar moustache and seventies string vest. She reached into the gramophone cylinder, emerging with a tangle of round spectacles, most missing a lens. 'Doesn't he throw anything away?'

Spike glanced to his left. Along the far edge of the flat ran a kitchenette, its floor space covered in empty jars and cans, a knife block on the work surface over-jammed with blades. The aroma of rotting food seemed to issue from there. The lights went out again; Spike heard a clatter as Zahra grabbed his shoulder. 'What was that?'

The lights blinked on to reveal a tabby cat slinking through the detritus. It turned to Spike and Zahra, stripy tail swishing, before hopping onto the arm of a sofa.

Spike squeezed between the furniture towards the only clear space, a nook beneath the mezzanine where a free-standing plasma TV rose like an altar before a canvas director's chair.

'Look,' Zahra said. He turned and saw her spinning a blue plastic globe. The cat reappeared, perching on a heap of stepladders. It rubbed the side of its head against the metal, clear liquid drizzling from its mouth. Then it sprang down to the floor beneath the mezzanine. 'Maybe no one lives here,' Zahra said, 'and people just use it to dump –'

The bulbs fizzled out. In the silence, Spike heard pulsing purrs. When the light returned he saw the pink rose petal of the cat's tongue rasping up and down the bare floorboards. It slunk away, licking its lips.

Spike looked up at the mezzanine ceiling. A small, dark circle stained the wood. A bead of moisture stretched to a point, then dripped down into Spike's face. He clawed a hand to his eye.

'What?' Zahra called.

Redness smeared his palm. The lights crackled out again. 'Stay there.'

'What?'

Spike felt for the TV, then knocked into it, sending the tabby scurrying for cover.

'*What?*' Zahra said again.

When the lights came back on, Spike found himself in front of the steps that led up to the mezzanine. He glanced back at Zahra, then put a finger to his lips.

CHAPTER 45

Light drifted dingily up onto floorboards of stripped pine. Spike made out a single bed in front, a window with the curtains closed, a set of wooden railings protecting from the drop to the main room.

'What's going on?' Zahra called from below.

'Stay where you are.' To his right, Spike saw the silhouette of a floor lamp; feeling forward with a foot, he pressed down. Brightness flooded the mezzanine. As his eyes grew accustomed, he saw that the metal-framed bed was strewn with magazines. Slowly his gaze turned to the floor.

The man lay naked on his back in the space between the bed and the railings. The skin of his soles was cracked. A stubby yellow penis rested on the heaped, distended mound of his belly.

'Don't come up here, Zahra,' Spike called down. He crept forward until he could see past the paunch to the face lying on the wood. The eyes were closed and the lank grey hair oiled back. Stubble pierced wan, sagging cheeks. The neck was visible – skin lacquered bright red – with the hands out in front, clasped together on a hairy pigeon chest as though in prayer. A knife protruded from the right fist, its small curved blade encrusted with blood.

Spike heard a creak. 'I told you not to –'

Zahra put a hand to her mouth. Something twitched on the man's body: a shiny brown cockroach bobbing and weaving over his mountainous belly, clipping the head of his penis before beetling off through the dark red oval that had seeped across the floorboards on either side of his neck.

Zahra spoke between her fingers. 'I recognise him from my village,' she whispered. 'From Zagora Zween.'

At the sound of her voice, the man's lashes flickered. Zahra took a step forward and his eyes flew open, lids stretching wildly.

'Ambulance,' Spike said. 'What number?'

'Fifteen.'

'Are you sure?'

'Fifteen, fifteen!'

Abdallah's eyes bulged as though he were drowning. Pink froth bubbled from the gash in his neck, followed by a high-pitched whistle, like gas escaping. Spike connected to the operator, as Zahra crouched down to Abdallah, who was blinking up at her now, desperate, trapped.

'Don't touch him,' Spike said, cupping the handset.

The whistling deepened to a rasp. Zahra tilted her head towards Abdallah's mouth. His eyeballs looked poised to spray from their sockets.

As Spike hung up, the tip of Abdallah's grey tongue emerged to dab at the canal of Zahra's ear. She recoiled in panic, losing her balance, palms slipping in the ooze that blotted the floor.

Spike helped her up. Her eye was caught by a smear on the front of her white dress. She started rubbing at the blood; Spike grabbed her wrist, loosening his grip when he saw the pallor beneath her natural tan.

'It's OK,' he said. 'Take deep breaths.'

When Zahra's colour began to return, Spike released her. 'What did he say?'

'He was asking for his mother.'

He caught her arm again as she backed away. 'You can't leave a crime scene.'

She wrested herself free. 'You can in Tangiers.'

Lowering a trainer onto the ladder, she turned. 'Last night,' she said. 'At the café. I was buying a train ticket home. Tanger Ville Station, 11.30 p.m.'

Spike looked back to Abdallah. His eyes were closing, froth popping on the bristles of his stubble as his breaths grew more shallow. Below, Zahra was creeping through the flotsam. Spike moved to the railings and the lights went out. When they flickered back on, she'd reached the door. The stain on her dress bloomed like a rose. 'Tanger Ville Station,' she repeated. 'Eleven thirty.'

CHAPTER 46

'So what you are telling me,' Inspector Hakim Eldrassi said as he drew deeply on his cigarette, 'is that you entered this apartment illegally.' He and Spike sat on the arms of opposing sofas. Upstairs, the floorboards creaked with activity. In front of them, a bearded man in shirtsleeves was perching on a stepladder, tightening light bulbs.

'Esperanza had an appointment to see Abdallah al-Manajah on the day she died,' Spike said. 'It was imperative I talk to him in the interests of my client. When I got here, the door was unlocked. I entered and found Mr al-Manajah upstairs.'

The lights grew steady and the bearded man descended. He picked up a camera from the kitchenette and began snapping photos of the mezzanine ceiling, calling out a question to Hakim, who answered in Arabic, casting about half-heartedly for an ashtray before finally tapping his ash on the floor.

'First,' Hakim resumed, 'you lead me to a barman who you claim was in possession of Esperanza's handbag. Now you bring me here, where a man who supposedly met Esperanza just before she died is killed with a knife on the Jour Sacré, the very day when guilty souls may enter Heaven.' Hakim's sallow eyes managed a twinkle. 'So I ask myself: How far will a lawyer go for his client? Will he seek to incriminate others? Cast seeds of doubt?' He turned, surveying the flat with what looked like sadness. 'Of course, you cannot leave the country now. Not until the coroner has his verdict.'

'I have commitments in Gibraltar.'

'I presume you know the law, Mr Sanguinetti.'

'How long?'

'We bury the dead fast in Tangiers. Two days for the coroner. Another for your statement.'

Spike took out the penultimate business card from his wallet. 'You dropped by my hotel yesterday. Who told you where I was?'

'The Sûreté is capable of a certain degree of efficiency.' Hakim stubbed out his cigarette on the spinning globe. 'So he was alive when you found him?'

'He opened his eyes. We thought it best not to move him.'

'We?'

'Sorry?'

'You said you were alone.'

'The royal "we", Inspector Eldrassi. An English idiom. We did this. We did that.'

Hakim's moustache twitched. 'Not an idiom with which I am familiar.'

'You should spend more time in Gibraltar.'

A creak came from behind as a pair of uniformed legs appeared on the stairs, followed by one end of a black ziplock bag on a stretcher.

'I have circulated your details to the port authorities,' Hakim said, eyeing Spike's suitcase, 'in case you felt the same . . . call for home as your client.'

A policeman passed Hakim a sealed exhibit bag. Inside it was a phone, Esperanza's mobile number displayed on the screen as a recently missed call. Hakim nodded and the policeman began to clear a passageway through the junk for the cortège.

'What makes a man live like this?' Hakim said, shaking his head. 'Burying himself alive.'

Spike picked up his bag. 'May I go?'

'Your prints,' Hakim said, sliding what looked like a cigarette case from his inside pocket. On one side was a spongy black pad, thick white card opposite. Spike pressed five fingers onto one then the other.

'I shall be in touch, Mr Sanguinetti,' Hakim said as he snapped the case closed. 'Until then, I advise you to be careful. The barman from that nightclub had an alibi. We had to release him. He is not your friend.'

On the pavement outside, Spike saw the old lady in black being interviewed by a policeman. She turned to look at him as he walked towards the rue de Belgique. A phrase his father had used echoed in his head: *City of Perfidy . . . City of*

Perfidy. He rubbed the ink from his fingertips and hailed a *petit taxi*.

'*Vous allez où, monsieur?*'

Spike checked the time. Through the taxi windscreen, the lights of Europe looked that little bit further away.

'*Monsieur?*'

PART III

ZAGORA ZWEEN

CHAPTER 47

Spike woke on his side, vibrations jolting through his body. He had slept on his left arm, which felt numb through lack of blood. He tried to roll over but a wooden board blocked his way. Opening his eyes, he made out a shape beneath the blanket on the opposite bunk: Zahra, her hair thick and loose. He felt a small pang as he saw the dark strands dampened to her forehead as on a sleeping child.

The window of the couchette was covered by a blind marked 'Office National des Chemins de Fer'. Sunlight lanced through it into Spike's eyes. He rolled out his legs and saw he was still wearing last night's clothes. After feeling beneath the bunk for the reassuring bulk of his bag, he forced the carriage doors apart and stepped out into the corridor.

Rather than coast or scrubland, he saw lush green fields. The train was moving along a ridge, with orchards of pears or apples extending down the slope. He pressed his face to the glass, seeing shaggy sheep driven by a herdsman in a wide-brimmed hat. The herdsman stopped and raised a hand; Spike waved absently back, before realising the man had only been screening his eyes against the glare from the train. Verdant hills rose beyond, mountains in the distance, purple-peaked. In the railway siding, the green fingers of what looked like wild cannabis plants spread from the shingle.

Spike's phone claimed 6.40 a.m. Gibraltar was two hours ahead.

'Dad?'

'Mm?'

'It's Spike.'

'Oh.' He heard a deep sigh. 'Oh.'

'Are you having breakfast?'

'Still in bed.'

'How come?'

'It's . . .' He sighed again. 'Got that thing again. With my chest.'

'Palpitations?'

'Somewhat.'

'That's what the beta blockers are for, Dad. Have you been taking them?'

'They give me diarrhoea.'

'It's better than the palpitations. They're on the list, two a day.'

Rufus's voice sounded distant and small. 'You're coming home soon, aren't you, son?'

'Got to stay in Tangiers for a few more days.'

'Not got ensnared, have you?'

'Just a couple of things to sort out.'

'Don't tell me you're off the wagon?'

'Go to the doctor, Dad. If you go late morning, there's no queue.'

Rufus swallowed at the other end of the line. 'Might just lie here a bit longer. I had a call from Mrs Hassan yesterday. Says you deserve a medal. Got her boy out of trouble.'

'He stands trial in Gibraltar not Morocco. That's it.'

'No better place to be. The levanter's finally shifted. We've a nice dry southerly. I can hear the gulls outside.'

'You'll get up soon, won't you, Dad?'

There was a sudden shriek as the train switched tracks. Spike put a hand out smartly to the carriage wall.

'Where are you, son? Sounds like a tramp steamer.'

'Better go, Dad. Bye.'

The sun changed angle, exposing Spike's reflection like a ghost in the window. He called a different number.

'All hail the conquering hero,' Galliano said. 'What time did you get in?'

'I didn't.'

'Delayed?'

'There's been a complication.'

Spike told Galliano how he had discovered Abdallah's body. 'I can't leave the country now until they've established cause of death.'

'*Ten cuidado*, Spike.'

'I'm just going to lie low for a few days.' Spike

heard a door open at the end of the corridor. A man appeared; he wore a prayer cap and a full beard with a clean-shaven upper lip. He withdrew abruptly, giving Spike a glimpse of red rucksack as the door slammed behind him.

'Spike?'

'I need you to do something for me, Peter.'

'You name it.'

'Dunetech, Solomon's company. I think it's time to shine a bit of light on proceedings.'

Spike heard a pen and paper readied.

'It's a clean technology business, right? Backing from sovereign investors. Renewable energy funds. Philanthropists with an eye on the buck. They're using Ruggles & Mistry to sort out their tax liabilities in Gibraltar.'

'So?'

'This is a sensitive time. Chequebooks readied. New offices built. I think Esperanza may have stumbled onto something at a crucial moment.'

'Such as?'

'Just see what you can dig up on the founders, Nadeer Ziyad and Ángel Castillo. And an ex-British Army officer called Tobias Riddell.' Spike heard Galliano chuck away one pen to pick up another. 'Maybe you could talk to Belinda Napier at Ruggles. Ask her for the skinny on Dunetech.'

'Think I'm still *persona non grata* with Napier.'

'Take her to a vodka bar. And can you drop in on my dad? Check he's OK?'

'Will do. So when are you back?'
'Looking like Friday.'
'Sorry?'
Spike checked his phone screen: half a bar of reception. 'What kind of thing,' he heard Galliano say as he put the handset back to his ear, 'might –'
The line went dead. Outside, the landscape had lost its verdure: pebbly ground, rocky outcrops. Hearing footsteps, Spike turned to find Zahra in the corridor. She wore baggy drawstring trousers and a long-sleeved black T-shirt. Her headscarf was off and her hair free; she was older than Spike had thought, early thirties probably. As she rubbed her eyes, he saw faint frown lines on her forehead.
'What time is it?' she yawned.
'Coming up to seven.'
She turned and gazed out of the window. 'Hopefully we'll make the next bus.'
'How long's the journey?'
'Couple of hours, if it doesn't break down first. *Tired*,' she added in an elongated voice. When she yawned again, Spike caught her eyes dart his way. The pupils were cold and alert.

CHAPTER 48

The bus had been driving for two hours and there was still no sign of the desert. The road followed a gorge with a river below and steep, crumbly walls of orange rock above. They were travelling downhill, but only just; the watercourse was deep and sluggish, content to creep along the base of this narrow fissure, spreading its goodness to the limited flat space on either side, where belts of almond groves grew interspersed with the occasional cuboid mud hut.

Spike stared out of the bus window, sunshine slanting through onto his forearms. He wondered not for the first time if a person could get burnt through glass. Zahra sat beside him, hair still loose, waving intermittently at a small, silent boy who kept peeking from between the foam-spilling seat backs.

The brakes mewled plaintively as the bus slowed into a corner. Outside, Spike saw three grey apes sitting on an outcrop of rock, two adults and an infant. 'Barbary macaques,' he said, looking back round. 'Same as in Gibraltar.'

'You have monkeys in Gibraltar?' Zahra said, craning her neck to see.

'We call them apes, because they don't have much of a tail. Only place in Europe where they're wild.'

'How did they get there?'

'In reality, pets for the British garrison. But according to legend, they crossed over from the Atlas Mountains in a secret tunnel beneath the Straits.'

'Maybe this is the start of that tunnel. The old caravan route from the desert.'

Spike stared up at the vertical walls of orange rock.

'You know,' Zahra said, 'I think that's the first time I've seen you smile.'

He ran a hand through his short dark hair and looked ahead.

Zahra waved again at the child, who was encouraged back round by its mother and presented with something sticky to eat from a rolled-up handkerchief. Spike cleared his throat. 'So you slept OK?'

'Yes.' She breathed out. 'Thanks for coming, Spike.'

'I can't leave the country anyway.'

'I suppose not.'

Another rickety single-decker came tearing round the corner. Spike saw the bright polka dots of headscarves leaning on the windows. 'There's a bus every day,' Zahra said. 'You can be back in Tangiers by tomorrow night.'

'Is there phone reception in your village?'

'Not sure. These days.' She reached into a woven handbag for a bottle of water and offered it to Spike.

'You first.' As she drank, he watched her larynx glide up and down her tanned, glistening throat. When the bottle came to him, he was careful not to finish it. The water had a hot saline taste, filled from the tap at Meknes station. Zahra's bag shifted forward as a wooden toy rolled from under the seat in front.

'I've never seen a dead body before,' she said, putting a foot down on her bag.

Spike turned. 'Are you sure he was only asking for his mother?'

'*Sakarat al mowt.*'

'Sorry?'

'Death noise.'

'Death rattle?'

The mother stood to retrieve her child's toy.

'Yes,' Zahra said. 'Death rattle.'

CHAPTER 49

The river broadened out and the gorge on either side of the road reduced to friable, horizontal shelves of rock. Spike saw a man in a turquoise turban leaning against a dead tree, smoking a roll-up as the bus sped by. The driver changed up a gear, heedless of potholes and boulders.

Spike felt a tap on the shoulder. Zahra was mouthing at him; he plucked out his headphones.

'What are you listening to?' she said.

He showed her the iPod screen with its image of an emaciated man in black, hair tied back in a ponytail, violin at his chin. 'Niccolò Paganini,' she read aloud, putting the stresses in the right places. He reached over to tuck a plug into her neat little ear. She screwed up her face at once. 'Is a string broken?' she shouted.

He lowered the volume. 'Paganini was the greatest violin virtuoso of his era.'

'I'll take your word for it,' Zahra replied.

He unlinked them, then plugged himself back in. Outside, the road emerged into a wasteland of stones and shrunken shrubs. The river was just a trickle now, a green ribbon vanishing into the hazy brown horizon. From the corner of his eye, he saw Zahra slip a mobile phone out of her bag. He turned down the music; she spoke in a strange kind of Arabic, quick and low. She flashed him a look, then put the phone away.

A range of hills rose in the distance, the parched, cracked earth before them like a dried-out seabed. Shimmering at their base was a Legionnaire-type settlement: fortified terracotta walls, minarets poking above. 'Is that your village?' Spike asked, switching off his music altogether.

'It's where I went to school. Erg Makeem.'

'Is it near your village?'

'An hour's walk. Then a bus.'

'Every day?'

'Twice.'

Spike steered a finger along the soused sponge of an eyebrow. The sun seemed low in the sky.

'My cousins are going to pick us up,' Zahra said.

'Is that who you were phoning?'

'I was just updating them.'

'So they do have signal.'

'Landline.'

'What did you tell them about me?'

She pursed her lips. 'They know I want to move to Europe. That's why I learned English. When I said I was bringing you, they just . . . assumed.'

'Assumed what?'

'That you would be helping me.'

Spike reached automatically for his pocket,

checking for the sweaty rectangle of his passport against his thigh.

'I had to tell them something,' Zahra protested. 'They're very traditional.'

A billboard flashed by the roadside. 'DUNETECH,' it read. '*Powering a Greener Future.*'

CHAPTER 50

The bus pulled over at a crossroads as Spike, Zahra and three men in turquoise turbans got out. The driver's assistant clambered up a ladder to the roof and unfastened the guy ropes holding down their bags. Somehow carrying all of them at once, he bundled back down and dumped them on the stony ground.

Spike's leather bag felt hot to the touch. The sun was directly above yet still seemed low in the sky, as though it had decided to set where it was. A single-storey building with a reinforced door stood back from the road, a camel lying in its shade, chewing on a bridle of chains with long, hairy lips. A small man emerged, overwhelmed by his white robes; Spike caught a glimpse of shelves of canned food behind him. 'Is that your cousin?' he said.

He had to squint to see that Zahra was smiling. 'He's here for the tourists.'

'What tourists?'

'Camel safaris into the desert.'

Zahra spoke to the man in the same rapid language she'd used on the phone. He reached into his robes and took out a coiled black ammonite. When she added something else, he carried the fossil reluctantly back inside.

The bus rumbled away, revealing a dusty lay-by where a white pickup was parked by a minivan. Zahra and the three other passengers set off towards it.

Spike could feel the heat of the sun on his hair. 'Have you got a spare headscarf?' he called out to Zahra, but the wind gusted and she didn't hear.

The strap of Spike's bag kept slipping on his collarbone. He raised his eyes to the sky: the sun seemed even lower, a huge orange saucer docking overhead, pushing downwards.

As the minivan drove away, Spike saw a face pressed to the window. Black beard, shaven moustache . . . He seemed to be staring down at Spike with what looked like a patient smile.

The pickup was still parked in the lay-by, white and new-looking. Its doors opened simultaneously and two men got out. Both wore turquoise turbans and button-down beige djellabas. The driver stuck out both arms, letting Zahra walk into the hug. Drawing back, he rubbed his nose three times against hers. His companion did the same, then all three turned to stare at Spike.

The face of the driver was elongated, a thick black moustache curving above a deep, prominent jaw that seemed out of kilter, as though the top half had not been designed to go with the lower. Stopping a few metres shy of Spike, he gave a stage bow, one arm tucked into his stomach, the other sweeping the dusty earth below. Sweat dripped into Spike's eyes as he nodded in response.

The younger man stepped towards him, almost handsome butburdened with a similar jaw. Spike stuck out a hand, but he only wanted the bag.

Zahra came over, touching the sodden back of Spike's T-shirt. The driver glanced round as he walked towards the truck.

'That's Othman,' Zahra said quietly. 'Salem's his kid brother. We'll do the introductions later.'

Both doors slammed as Zahra climbed up over the tailgate and sat down. Once Spike had joined her, they pulled out of the lay-by and onto the road in the direction of the hills they'd seen from the bus. Wedged in by Zahra, Spike stared out at the dust cloud burgeoning behind. The metal had started to burn through the material of his T-shirt; the breeze gave relief, but he knew he was still in full glare, so looked about for a cloth or oilskin. Nothing but a spare tyre with a petrol can inside. He drew his T-shirt over his forehead. The metal seared his back so he held himself away from it, stomach muscles straining.

Zahra turned and smiled. 'Now you are a Bedouin,' she shouted above the engine.

The dust cloud made it hard to see behind, but left and right there stretched nothing but a flat, shimmering void. Spike tucked his forearms beneath the tail of his flapping T-shirt. Zahra had an elbow on the side of the pickup, oblivious to the heat, staring out in silence.

The bumps became less frequent as the dust cloud reduced. Spike peered over the edge: the road looked like a First World dual carriageway, four lanes of dark, puffy tarmac. No other vehicles passed. On the wayside, Spike saw a Dunetech billboard, this time in Arabic.

Zahra moved to her hands and knees, edging around until she stood with her head up above the driver's cabin. Spike did the same. '*Estoy en babia*,' he exclaimed.

Rearing above them was a vast, apricot-coloured cathedral, smooth-sided and with a peaked, snaking crest along the top. At least a hundred feet high – like the southern tip of the Rock. A similar-sized dune stood adjacent, with a rippled, broader base; smaller dunes continued either side, blending into one another, interlocking like giant orange knuckles.

Zahra's headscarf streamed behind her in the wind as she turned to check Spike's reaction. 'He smiles again,' she shouted.

The road continued on between the dunes. Walls of orange sand blotted out the sun, spatula-smooth. The wind fell and then there was no sound beyond the turning of the engine.

'This is the holy place,' Zahra said quietly. 'The burial land my father would not sell.'

The narrow, shady strip was half filled by road. Outcrops of rock rose on either side, holding in the sand dunes, presumably the reason for the formation of this passageway in the first place.

Spike saw what looked like carvings on their flanks. 'Was the road here before?' he asked.

'Just a track.'

The sun came blazing back as they emerged on the other side. Spike had been expecting a vista of soft rippling sand but instead there stretched the same brown, pebble-strewn crust. As the road curved left, he saw that the rocky outcrop continued all around the base of the sand dune, a few mud huts huddled against it. Beyond, Spike made out the first row of heliopods, glinting in the sun like a silent, waiting army.

CHAPTER 51

Still on their feet in the back of the pickup, Spike and Zahra stared out at the village. The first buildings they saw were new-looking single-storey Portakabins. To the rear of each, an identical white picket fence delineated a patch of desert garden – had one picked up the Portakabin, the fence would have come with it. Most seemed unoccupied, the only signs of life stripy woven sheets hammered into the back walls to create makeshift tents.

A pack of beautiful mongrel dogs chased the pickup as it passed a concrete warehouse. Tipper trucks and caterpillar diggers were parked outside. Some kind of open-plan marketplace lay beyond – food stalls, goats, queue of people waiting at a well.

'It's all so different,' Zahra said.

'When were you here last?'

'Six years ago.'

'Imagine how it'll look in another six.'

The plastic-looking minaret of a new-build mosque poked upwards as the track began to rise. Spike stared up the slope. The mud houses were embedded into the rock, their colour the same as the dunes behind. The pickup slowed to a woman in a blue headscarf standing cross-armed outside the entrance to a house. Smoke rose from a hole in the roof behind her. Hens pecked at her feet.

'That's Salwa,' Zahra said as Othman and Salem got out, 'Othman's wife.' Zahra moved her face towards Spike's. 'Don't mention the Sundowner Club. They think I work shelling prawns in a factory in Tangiers.'

'Understood.'

'And don't say you're a lawyer either.'

Spike jumped down. One of the dogs came over, tail rigid as it sniffed Spike's trouser leg. When Salem made to kick it, it bolted off and stood at a distance.

Salwa was joined at the doorway by a drowsy little boy with tangled hair. She stood on her tiptoes to perform the same nose-rubbing ritual with Zahra. Spike heard his name mentioned in a rush of low, coarse sounds. Salwa blinked over, eyes limpid and black, skin as wrinkled as a lost balloon. The child gazed up at him.

Othman and Salem strode past through the open doorway. The entrance was just an antechamber to a deeper, shadier cavern, carved into the rock, its floor covered by a threadbare rug in the centre, various faded cushions around it. Dark, stripy drapes hung on the walls and passageways disappeared into the rock behind. One section was divided off by a curtain fixed to the roof, a waft of smoke and oily food issuing from behind.

Salem barked something, and another woman appeared from behind the screen, brushing down her robes. She wore the same nun-blue headscarf as Salwa, but it framed a younger, sweeter face. When she lowered a hand from her mouth, she revealed a neat cleft palate, the upper lip arching into a pink marquee, tab of dry white tooth below.

Zahra introduced her as Fatiya, wife of Salem. 'Fatiya was at school with me,' Zahra said, voice echoing off the walls. 'She still speaks a bit of Spanish. *Español?*'

Fatiya grinned, then covered her mouth. '*Poquito.*'

The toddler made a dash for Spike, but Salwa stuck out an arm and caught him by the hair. He didn't cry, just sat down on the dirt floor, rubbing his matted head.

'And that's little Rami.'

Salem carried their bags into one of the tunnels. Spike had to hunch down as the temperature cooled. The tunnel curved right into a chamber lit by a brass oil lamp. Salem turned up the flame to reveal a cave of soft cushions and colourful kilim blankets. In one corner sat a broad ceramic bowl with a dented pewter jug of water. Salem said something to Zahra, then backed away like a courtier. She threw Spike an apologetic glance.

'Don't worry about it,' he said, unzipping his leather bag.

Zahra began picking up cushions and dividing

them into piles. There was a fetid chill to the air, tomb-like. She ran a finger down the rocky wall, testing for moisture. 'This was where my father slept,' she said.

Spike found what he was looking for in the side pocket of his bag.

CHAPTER 52

They sat in a circle on the mud floor of the main chamber. Light shone in through the open doorway, motes of dust spinning like planets in its beam. Spike looked down at his earthenware pot and dipped in some flatbread. The goat stew was spicy but he still regretted adding so much yogurt: it fizzed with a sour, unpasteurised rawness. Due to Ramadan, he was the only one eating – he'd tried to refuse but Zahra had insisted. Bedouin hospitality. The others watched him as he chewed, analysing the size and constitution of each mouthful.

Conversation comprised Othman talking to Zahra, who would then translate to Spike. A tune played over in Spike's head as he sipped his sage tea. 'Tea in the Sahara . . .'

'Othman wants to know what you do.'

'Tell him I'm a teacher. *Profesor.* I teach history and English in Gibraltar.'

Fatiya peered from behind the curtain to check Spike's bowl. As she seemed to be head chef, Spike had made the gift of the bag of saffron to her. Since then, she hadn't stopped staring. Salwa hissed at her unseen, and she retreated back behind the curtain.

'They want to know if you earn well as a teacher.'

'Fabulously well. Can you ask them if they both work for Dunetech?'

At the sound of the name, Othman and Salem swivelled their heads like owls.

'Dunetech?' Spike repeated, looking at each in turn.

Othman shielded his mouth and whispered something to his younger brother. They'd both removed their turbans, their cropped black hair displaying the same dainty ears as Zahra.

'They want to know where you heard about Dunetech,' she said.

'Tell them I saw it on the billboard. Is it possible to visit the site?' Spike focused on Othman as he spoke.

Zahra translated again; Spike thought he caught the word 'al-Manajah' in the reply.

'Othman says we can drive down there this afternoon.'

Spike nodded his thanks, and Othman and Salem rose to their feet, the sound immediately drawing Salwa from behind the curtain. Fatiya followed with another earthenware pot; Spike shook his head regretfully. '*No más, gracias.*'

Fatiya moved behind him, hitching up her robes as she sat. Spike glanced over at Zahra, who smiled.

'*Muy calor-o,*' Fatiya said in her faltering Spanish.

He heard a cork stopper removed, then felt a cool sensation on his forehead as Fatiya leaned forward to rub in some unguent. Despite himself, he shut his eyes in relief. When she reached the back of his neck, her fingertips began describing circles, working the fatty paste into his tanned skin as she murmured, '*Duna, duna . . .*'

In the corner of the room, Spike made out a small dark shape. The little boy, Rami, watching on in silence.

CHAPTER 53

Salem had stayed at home so Spike and Zahra were sitting up front with Othman. As they raced along the tarmac road, Spike made out the first line of heliopods glinting in the distance, a tall white tower looming over them like a sentinel.

To the left of the road, a patch of green stood out from the hazy emptiness. Spike thought he saw tents erected amid the palm and acacia trees. Zahra was jammed against him, right thigh pressed forcibly to his; she pointed through the open passenger window and said something to which Othman grunted a reply.

'What was that?' Spike said.

'Othman says the older generation doesn't want to settle in the village. They're still camping at the oasis.'

'Does the river resurface there?' Spike said.

'Yes, but it's salty.'

'How come?'

'This part of the Sahara used to be an inland sea. There's still salt in the sand and rocks. It seeps into waterholes.'

'How do you get drinking water?'

'You have to dig down deep.'

Spike saw a plume of smoke rising from the oasis. 'Did you say "al-Manajah" just then?' he asked.

Othman peered round and grinned, eyes away from the road. 'Al-Manajah,' he repeated.

'The al-Manajah are the main tribe,' Zahra said. 'In winter they roam with their livestock, then come back here in summer.'

Othman was still grinning across at Spike; fortunately the road was straight.

'Just thirty thousand Bedouin left in this part of Morocco,' Zahra said. 'Tuareg in the desert, Berbers in the mountains. We're a bit like you, clinging to your piece of rock.'

'Clinging to your sand dune.'

Another off-road vehicle was coming the other way. Spike caught a glimpse of a bearded driver with something red beside him on the passenger seat. 'Did you see that?' he said as he clambered back round.

'What?'

'That was the man from the train. And the bus.'

'Sorry?'

'You were with him in the Café des Étoiles.'

Zahra gave Spike a concerned look, as though the heat were getting to him. He shut his eyes and rubbed his forehead, still sticky with Fatiya's unguent.

Othman slowed the pickup. The lines of heliopods

extended on either side of the road, twenty or so in a row, each unit five metres apart. The concrete tower above them was fifteen metres high, black cables snaking up its edges, a hollow diamond shape at the base and an upper ledge lined with similar small black cameras to those in Nadeer Ziyad's garage. In front of the tower spread an open-ended hangar. Othman parked beside it. The bonnet ticked. Othman got out and Spike followed.

As soon as Othman reached the nearest heliopod, he stuck out a sandal and slapped it down on the circular concrete base. '*Sssswww*,' he said, waving a hand. He picked up a handful of dust, which scattered at once in the breeze.

Zahra followed Spike and Othman into the hangar. A heap of orange sand was piled at one end beside an industrial cement mixer and a fleet of wheelbarrows.

'This is where they make –'

'The concrete for the bases?'

'I see you've picked up Bedouin dialect.'

'Ask him how many more units they're going to put in.'

Zahra translated, then listened to the answer. 'He doesn't know the exact number. But they start the day after Ramadan.'

'How many workers?'

She asked again. 'Hundreds. Half from the village and half on their way back from the desert. The Bedouins can work in the heat.'

Othman was beckoning to Spike to admire the

cement mixer, but he went back outside. A clicking came from overhead: he looked up and saw a heliopod's mirrored panel rotating. Dust trickled down. There were more clicks as the rest of the row followed.

Spike squinted into the distance. The sand dunes blocked off the route to the foothills of the mountain range they'd crossed on the bus. 'Is there a back road that leads to the site?' he asked Zahra when she came out.

'Don't think so.'

'Could you ask?'

Zahra called back to Othman, who was marching out of the hangar, gait stiff. 'No,' she replied, 'nothing but desert between here and Algeria.'

'Can you move the sand dunes? Dynamite them?'

'They're protected by law. Anyway, the wind would blow them back.'

'Rendering your burial ground rather a valuable point of entry,' Spike said.

Othman began climbing into the pickup, clench-jawed. From behind came more clicking as the next row of heliopods followed the movement of the sun.

CHAPTER 54

The intervening hours had not improved the goat stew. The front door was closed – the wind was getting up – and the room eye-wateringly smoky, illuminated by oil lamps which gave off waxy, aromatic fumes.

Othman had taken to staring at Spike as he spoke, using Zahra as an unacknowledged interpreter. Spike kept hearing the word '*Visa*', the 'V' pronounced as a 'W'. 'Just tell him I'll sort everything out,' Spike said, getting to his feet.

Salem sat up at once on his cushions. Both he and Othman followed Spike with their eyes, moustaches gleaming with oil from their hastily eaten meal. Salwa and Fatiya were on stools by the stove, bowls on their laps like air hostesses in the galley. They started in surprise, then bowed their heads.

'*Disculpe*,' Spike said.

'*De nada*,' Fatiya murmured in Spanish, hand over her pink cleft.

'It's the other way,' Zahra called from the opposite side of the curtain. Spike re-emerged and walked into the tunnel at the far end of the chamber, unlatching the back door and entering the desert night. An outhouse stood in an open yard; he navigated through the darkness, stumbling in a foxhole. Those heliopods were not doing their job yet – at least not in Zagora Zween.

The lavatory was just a drop into the earth; Spike smelled faeces disturbed as his urine spattered. He threw down a scuttle of sawdust, then set off back for the house. The wind had started to gust, warm as a hairdryer. A nice Saharan southerly . . . Spike wondered how long it would take to reach Gibraltar and his father.

A hatchway off the corridor was ajar, light filtering from within. Spike eased it open and saw a handmade wooden crib inside, presumably containing little Rami. Propped on two nails above the crib rested a heavy-looking rifle. Spike listened for a child's breathing, then returned to the main chamber.

The crockery had been cleared and a shisha pipe lit. Spike settled back onto his cushions as Othman bubbled smoke through cloudy water. The odour was of apples and cloves; Salem inhaled, then passed the tube to Spike. It didn't taste like cannabis; didn't taste like tobacco either. Coals glowed; Spike offered some to Zahra, sensing the gaze of Othman and Salem as she accepted, sucking in and coughing.

Salwa appeared with coffee. She pursed her lips in disapproval as she gave a glass to Zahra. When the pipe came back, Spike drew in more smoke. This time when he passed it to Zahra, he wasn't sure who was watching.

The coffee was granular: pungent and strong. Salem lit some incense in a chalice lined with mother-of-pearl. Outside, the wind swept through the desert. Spike caught Zahra's eye and they both smiled.

Othman was speaking; Zahra kept her gaze on Spike. 'He wants to know what your father does.'

'Retired.'

'From?'

'Guess.'

'Teacher?'

'Correct.'

Othman spoke again.

'He wants to know –' Zahra began.

'What?'

'If your mother is respectful.'

Spike forced a smile. 'Was respectful . . . Not especially, which was one of her most endearing qualities.'

Othman started to stand, grunting at the curtain as Salwa appeared, headscarf off, black hair halfway down her back. Fatiya followed, hair also loose, a strand gripped in her cleft mouth.

Othman grabbed Spike's hand. '*Yalla ruh*,' he said, shoving it into Zahra's.

Fatiya giggled as Spike and Zahra entered the tunnel in the rock.

CHAPTER 55

Zahra sat down on a cushion at the edge of the chamber. Spike turned up the oil lamp, catching his fisheye reflection in its tarnished amber: cheeks dark-stubbled, forehead still shiny with unguent. He sat down heavily beside her, their shoulders touching momentarily as the waxy smell of burning carbon crept through the room. One of the women had tidied away Spike's bag: his clothes were folded carefully by the wall.

'Embarrassing,' Zahra sighed.

'Don't worry about it.'

They stared ahead, chests sinking and rising in time.

'I'm sorry about your mother,' Zahra said.

Spike altered his position on the cushions.

'What happened?'

'Why do you want to know?' There was a pause. 'She killed herself.'

He sensed Zahra's gaze but refused to meet it. He knew how earnest her look would be. They always were. Lying back, he stared up at the dirty, red-draped ceiling. 'She was a musician,' he said, 'Maltese, originally. Twenty years younger than my father. They worked together at the same school in Gibraltar. After I was born, she changed to giving violin lessons at home. Bit by bit, she stopped practising altogether. She used to like a gin and tonic in the evenings; after a while she'd be drunk by lunch. One afternoon, she cancelled a lesson and took the car out. Drove off the edge of a cliff.' Spike made a sharp whistling between his teeth, indicating the sound of the wind rushing over the bonnet. 'My father always said it was an accident. Banned alcohol from the house. Bought a dog and that was the end of it.' He glanced over at Zahra, who'd drawn up her knees beneath her kaftan. 'Everybody has their tale of woe, Zahra. How about you? Where's your *mamma*?'

'Dead.'

'How?'

'Giving birth to me.'

He softened his tone. 'So it was just you and your father here?'

'It was different then. Everyone knew everyone. In the mornings we used to climb the sand dune behind the house. You can bathe in sand before it gets too hot.'

'And now your cousins have taken over the house?'

An echo came, a groan of sexual activity – Spike thought back to his room at the Continental. Zahra waited for the noise to fade. 'When my father went away, yes.'

'What do they think happened to him?'

'They don't want to know. They're both illiterate anyway.' She undid her headscarf and her inky hair came free. 'Tell me,' she said. 'How does a Gibraltar lawyer end up in Chinatown? That was a strange thing to do.'

'Blame my father.'

'The teacher?'

'Last year he was diagnosed with a rare illness. He needs special medication so I have to go to the Spanish pharmacy each month in La Línea de la Concepción.'

'La Línea de la Concepción,' Zahra repeated.

'It's a town just over the Spanish border. It's dirt poor so they hate Gibraltarians. They wake up every morning and see the Rock with all its expensive new buildings. They see a car with Gibraltar plates, they scratch it. They find a Gibraltarian alone, they shout abuse.'

'I thought Gibraltarians were basically Spanish.'

'We've been cut off from Spain for so long that there's not much Spanish blood. Italian and Portuguese, Maltese and Jewish. A bit of British, with all the soldiers who've been there.'

'Is that where you get your blue eyes?'

Spike gave her a quizzical look. 'So one evening I was taking a short cut home. A gang of Spaniards followed me. I saw one flash a switchblade and thought, Run. But they knew the streets better than me. So I walked right up to them. Offered them a cigarette. And nothing happened. People always expect you to run. So I do the opposite.'

'Luck can run out,' Zahra said. 'And we had to run, didn't we?' The grunts became more urgent. 'What do you think happened to Abdallah?' she asked after a moment.

'We'll find out when the post-mortem comes in.'

'You put a lot of faith in the Tangiers police.'

Spike turned to look at her. 'I think I found that jeep,' he said.

She propped herself up on one elbow. The oil lamp projected long, wavy shadows onto the stone walls, intermingling with Spike's own.

'It belongs to a man called Nadeer Ziyad,' he said. 'Heard of him?'

Zahra shook her head.

'Co-founder of Dunetech.'

'You think he was driving?'

'Not personally.'

'Then what . . .?'

Spike propped himself up too. 'I've got a couple of theories.'

Their eyes met.

'The first is the obvious one. Esperanza dislikes her stepfather. You bump into her at the Sundowner Club and make her even more suspicious. She goes and talks to an ex-employee, Abdallah al-Manajah, trying to dig the dirt. Abdallah is crazy – you saw his flat. He's so thrown by this pretty girl coming to see him, he kills her then himself a few days later.'

'And the other?'

'The other is more . . . complicated.'

Their eyes locked.

'That burial site between the sand dunes,' Spike said. 'It's in a strategic position. Dunetech would have needed it to build their road. Otherwise they couldn't get in construction supplies. I don't know your father but . . . let's just say they did pay him off. That's an illegal bribe. Maybe Esperanza found out about it. Contacted Abdallah to learn more. That's why they ended up dead.'

'You think Dunetech would kill them for that?'

'They're about to sign a massive deal. They can't afford for anything to surface about the company. Especially as they're pitching themselves as such a socially responsible business.'

Zahra moistened her lower lip as she thought. 'But why go after us?'

'After you, I'm afraid. They knew you'd met Esperanza. They were worried Esperanza might have told you about the bribe.'

'How did they know I'd met Esperanza?'

'Maybe they were following her. Or they spoke to Marouane, found out about your argument. Anyway, yesterday afternoon I mention Abdallah's name to Nadeer. Three hours later, Abdallah is dead. There's a pattern emerging.'

'How about your client?'

'Solomon? He just happened to be the last person seen with Esperanza.'

'You don't think he's involved?'

'No.'

'How can you be sure?'

'I know him.'
'You're very confident about people.'
'We were at school together. Twelve years.'
'So he's your friend.'
Spike's mind drifted back. 'He used to get a hard time in the playground. I helped him once – got punched a few times, punched a few people back. After that he wouldn't leave me alone.'
A louder moan rang out, as though the two brothers were competing.
'How long will you stay here?' Spike said.
'A week or so. See if I can get any answers about Ibrahim.'
'Ibrahim?'
'My father.'
'And then?'
'Back to Tangiers to apply for another visa.'
'You've tried before?'
'Five times.'
'No luck?'
'You think they want some Bedouin girl in Europe?'
'But your English –'
'Means nothing.'
'Well, I probably ought to get back tomorrow.'
'Don't worry,' Zahra said tersely. 'I've spoken to Othman. He'll drive you to the bus stop in the morning.'
Spike reached for the oil lamp. 'Mind if I turn this down?'
'Off is better.'

Spike extinguished the flame. In the darkness he heard a swish as Zahra removed her kaftan. He caught a waft of citrus perfume, then rolled over to face the wall.

CHAPTER 56

Spike woke after dreaming of a thunderstorm. His bladder felt taut, his lungs shrunken and dry, reminding him of why he'd given up smoking. After a minute of trying to go back to sleep, he pushed himself up, cursing under his breath.

A faint glow was coming from the tunnel; Spike used it to locate his trousers, espadrilles and a fresh white T-shirt, glancing, as he dressed, at the heap of blankets on the far side of the room. He was impressed by how silently Zahra slept, until he realised she was gone.

He walked through to the main chamber. The open doorway spread a runner of lemony light over the mud-packed ground. The stove was still smouldering as a man lay on the central cushions, arms splayed, cotton nightdress revealing hairy ankles. Spike heard a loud, moist snore: Salem, flat on his back, unmarked bottle by an outstretched hand.

Spike strode carefully past him to the corridor, catching a whiff of yeasty hooch. The back door was double-bolted; Spike turned round, poking his head through the hatch to check the peaceful shape of Rami, still sleeping in his cot.

Outside, the light was pale and washed-out, the sun concealed, the stillness of the air oppressive. Desert mornings were not as chilly as he had been led to believe. Moving to one side, he saw a plastic tub soaking last night's crockery. He unzipped his flies in a corner by a thorn bush. A cockerel crowed. Dew clung to prickly foliage. The rich orange sand dune formed a sharp contrast to the brilliant blue sky.

From the corner of his eye, he saw a tall, shawled figure emerge onto the dirt track. He zipped up. The sun rose over the top of the dune, and he saw a headscarf sparkle: Zahra. She was walking quickly, glancing occasionally behind.

Spike stepped out onto the track. Two stray dogs were lying opposite one another, touching paws, enjoying this tranquil, human-free moment. Zahra was about forty metres ahead, skirting the village along the line of the dunes. Spike thought about calling out, but didn't.

Approaching the rock face at the base of a dune, he caught the sweet-sour tang of sun-warmed rubbish: the village midden heap, carved into an indentation. A small fox with bat ears watched from amid the rubbish bags and oil drums. Hens pecked on the path. The fox followed Spike with its yellow eyes.

Zahra had passed the prefabricated houses and was climbing the rocky mound that marked the end of the village. Spike saw her glance left and right; he readied himself to raise a hand in greeting, but she disappeared down the other side.

A breeze tickled the nape of Spike's neck as he reached the top of the mound. To his right ran the wide road that led to the heliopods – Zahra was walking parallel to it over arid, featureless scrub. A hundred metres ahead of her lay the green oasis.

A single needle of light fired from the solar-power site. One became two, until an entire pincushion was gleaming back, bright as magnesium. The sun had mounted the dune behind and caught Spike up.

He descended the slope, keeping his espadrilles square-on to avoid slipping. Once on flat ground, he felt solid slabs of bedrock beneath the sand. Three-inch thorns grew between; a pale, translucent scorpion fled Spike's foot, tail curved like a cracked finger as it plunged into a bolt-hole.

Spike walked on, feeling the hot roughness rise through his rope soles as the sun teased a first bead of sweat from his brow. Zahra was fifty metres ahead now. He checked behind: the hillock he'd just climbed obscured the village, and for a moment all he could see was the crumbly orange rock and the smooth sand of the dune. This absence of human habitation caused a brief, seasick feeling before he turned back round, taking comfort in the distant tents pegged out around the oasis.

He increased his pace. The sun troubled him less as the breeze picked up. It gave a sudden blast, like a blow from bellows, prickling his neck with grit. Then the air went still.

Ahead, Zahra was almost at the oasis. She was jogging now, keen to escape the sun. Spike wondered if he should shout out; instead he looked back round to check his location.

Head turned, he stared into the distance. The sand dune behind the village appeared to have changed position. It was as though it had stepped forward from the other dunes in order to move up the line. Spike's eye muscles relaxed and he looked out more clearly. The momentary pleasure at being able to see without squinting ebbed when he realised that the sun had gone in. He glanced up at the sky. A cloud of dust was blotting it out.

He swivelled back round and started running. The shadows grew darker. 'Zahra!' he called, and saw her glance over one shoulder before the dust cloud blurred her to brown.

Visibility faded further until Spike could see no more than a metre ahead. He slowed down. Was he even going in the right direction? He tried to look around but the sand was too painful. The whistling grew shrill, like a train conductor's signal. His damp, prickly T-shirt puffed out in front; the ankles of his cargo trousers billowed as he jumped in the air and felt himself carried a metre. The smell was of hot sawdust.

He could barely see his shoes now. He shouted

and felt sharp salty powder coat his throat and nose. An image flashed into his mind of the concrete bases of those heliopods: he crouched into a ball as the sand squalled on his neck and scalp. What if he were buried here? Shielding his eyes, he caught a glimpse of the dune ahead. That meant the road was in the other direction. If he could find the road, it would lead him back to the village.

He shunted back round until he was facing the opposite way. Still crouching, he placed one espadrille in front of the other and fought to make progress forward. A plastic bag flew by, inflated like a toy parachute. The noise was all around, increasing in strength like a jumbo preparing for take-off.

Heart thumping, Spike wrinkled his nose to breathe. His head felt light, but like a tightrope walker he managed to construct a forward line with his espadrilles, one step at a time. His clothes were clinging to his chest and thighs; the skin on his head felt like it was being rubbed with sandpaper.

In front stretched a perpendicular line. He half straightened up and was nearly blown over; hunching again, he shuffled forward until he felt the soft spring of tarmac beneath his feet.

Grit gouged at the corners of his eyes. Slowly he manoeuvred himself round into the direction he hoped was the village. The prickling on his face was unbearable. He turned back – better to head for the site, find shelter in the concrete hangar. If that was locked, he could use the walls as a break.

The wind was on his back now, propelling him on. After a few steps, he heard a noise. Distant and hollow, like a foghorn in the Straits. He forced his head round and saw the muffled glow of headlights. The vehicle was moving almost as slowly as he was. It drew up beside him. A white pickup.

'Hey!' Spike called, and more dust flew into his mouth.

The passenger door opened a fraction, then slammed closed. Straining against the wind, it started to reopen. Spike edged towards it, hands over ears. He looked up to see Othman hunching on the road, headscarf flailing behind him like a ship's pennant.

Othman's jaw was clenched. His arm began to rotate as though he were bowling a cricket ball. Something hard hit the top of Spike's head. The wailing of the wind grew still.

CHAPTER 57

Spike tried to swallow but his mouth was too dry. He gave a cough and felt a salty bolus of sand scrape down the back of his throat. Breathing through his nose, he opened his eyes. His chin lolled forward; he started to raise it but felt a pain in his head, as though someone were grinding a finger down on the skull.

Blinking crust from his eyes, he stared lazily ahead. He was slumped in a chair at the edge of a room paved in concrete. He heard a voice and saw a man in a blue turban sitting cross-legged in front of him, heating something on a Campingaz stove. Othman. The hangar. The pickup truck . . . Spike snorted and felt a plug of sand pop from one nostril. What an idiot he'd been venturing out like that.

He pressed down with his feet. Nothing happened. He tried to move his arms: still nothing. A first squirt of adrenalin washed through him. 'Othman?' he managed to say, voice coming out as a croak.

He heard a sudden clatter of cooking utensils as Othman shot to his feet. Salem appeared beside him, overbite clamped shut as though he had grave news to impart.

Spike felt his head pulse as he flicked his eyes to the doorway. A woman was standing beside it: Fatiya.

'*Dónde Zahra?*' Spike mumbled.

Fatiya gave a giggle, covering her mouth with one hand. Othman called out and she came and stood in front of Spike.

'*Bisha'a*,' she said with a coy grin.

He tried to stand again but something was restricting his ankles. Looking down, he saw his feet strapped to the front two chair legs. He tried to move his hands: they were bound to the top of the back legs.

He raised his eyes to Fatiya's face. Her small white tooth rose like a tusk. Salem passed her a square of paper. Spike recognised his business card.

'*Abogado?*' Fatiya said with a smile. Lawyer.

Spike snorted again; they must have been through the wallet he'd left in his chamber.

'*Abogado, no profesor*,' Fatiya continued, as Salem passed her a larger piece of card, face as serious as a court official. '"Dunetech",' Fatiya read aloud. She held up the invitation to the Investor Roadshow. '*Abogado para Dunetech*,' she concluded.

Spike half shook his head. '*Abogado, sí*,' he groaned. '*Para Dunetech, no*.'

Fatiya translated this to Salem; he moved

towards Othman, who was cross-legged again in front of the stove. In one hand Othman held a large serrated knife with a blue plastic handle. He turned the flat of the blade in the roaring flame.

Spike looked more urgently at Fatiya. He tried to move his legs but succeeded only in shuffling the chair. He strained outwards with his hands; the rope seemed less tight on his left wrist. He started to rotate the joint.

Othman called something to Fatiya, which she mangled into harsh, accented Spanish. '*Tú es abogado para Dunetech. Sí o no?*'

'*No*,' Spike said.

'*No?*'

'*No, no, no.*'

Salem hove back into view, a small wooden box in his hands. Keeping his distance, he circled Spike like a matador. A moment later Spike felt hands clasp his forehead from behind. The skin stung; he struggled but Salem's grip was too firm. The wooden box dipped before his eyes, open-sided like an insect inspection chamber without the glass.

Spike struggled again as he felt the box pressed into his mouth. Shutting his lips and teeth, he heaved in air through his nose. Salem had managed to hook Spike's forehead in the crook of his elbow, lowering his free hand to his mouth, fingers working open the lips. Spicy-tasting nails slid beneath Spike's teeth; he opened his jaw, then snapped it closed.

'*Neik!*' he heard as the box and the hand disappeared. Spike's breath rasped again as another blow hit the top of his head.

CHAPTER 58

Spike's neck was tilted backwards. His jaw ached. He flopped down his chin, feeling drool spill from cracked lips. Fatiya was standing in front of him, still holding his business card in one hand and the Dunetech invitation in the other. Her expression now was more intrigued than amused.

When Spike tried to close his mouth, he found an object wedged between his teeth. He probed with his tongue and felt the rough grain of wood. A splinter came off and he drew his tongue back in, breathing through his nose.

The raised voice of Othman echoed from ahead. Fatiya glanced round and nodded, smile returning. '*Bisha'a*,' she said. '*Verdadero o falso. Si ambollaz, falso. Si no ambollaz, verdadero.*'

Spike couldn't speak with the box in his mouth. *Ambollaz* . . . what the hell did that mean? Steps now on the concrete floor; Othman above him, brandishing the knife.

Now Spike struggled properly, twisting his wrists back and forth, feeling the rope scrape against the cut he'd got in China-town. Kicking with both legs, he slid the chair backwards as Salem appeared at Othman's side, left hand bandaged in tissue paper, right holding a pair of cooking tongs.

Spike gave a grunt, flailing forward with his legs. For a moment he was free, but then his shoulder slammed down onto the concrete floor as the chair toppled over.

Salem yanked him back up, muttering disapproval. Spike felt queasy as the room twisted then straightened. Othman returned to the Campingaz, blade in the blue flame. Spike continued to swivel his wrists but his strength was failing.

Salem had vanished. Spike felt him make another grab at his forehead, then lose his grip on the slippery skin. He came back round to the front, kneeling as he cradled Spike's jaw from below. Now Spike could only shift his head from side to side like a fish trying to dislodge a hook.

Head cocked in concentration, Salem inched the tongs towards Spike's mouth. He tried to spit out the box, but his jaws were clamped around it. He felt the chilly metal slip through the side of the box to explore the cavity of his mouth. It nuzzled at his tongue then pinched down hard on the tip.

Slowly, Salem began to draw Spike's tongue out through the open sides of the box. Othman reappeared; Spike's eyes flitted between the two of them. The blade of the knife glowed red as Othman leaned in close, Spike trying to withdraw his tongue, but the grip of the tongs was too firm. He spat but nothing came. When he coughed, droplets of saliva crackled and slid on the fiery knife blade.

Spike closed his eyes, breathing in deeply. The image of the red-hot metal glowed beneath his eyelids like the sun. He tried to detach himself, send himself floating over the Rock, looking down at the levanter cloud, at the moat-like Straits, at his father, shuffling alone through the backstreets . . .

The scream seemed to issue from elsewhere, a bestial shriek, a stuck pig or a lamb at the point of slaughter. Spike inhaled desperately as the pain spread through his lips, his throat, the deep-set nerves of his teeth. He smelled sweet burnt flesh, then felt a wad of something soft come away as the blade was withdrawn. He sucked in his tongue, tucking it beneath his dry lower lip.

'*Bisha'a*,' he heard in Fatiya's giggly voice. '*Bisha'a*.'

CHAPTER 59

When Spike next opened his eyes, his tongue was throbbing in concert with his heart. He tried to close his mouth but the box was still there. Othman, Salem and Fatiya surrounded him in a circle. Salem held the tongs, stepping forward to Spike's face. Rather than suffer the sharp indignity of the metal, he lolled his tongue out through the gap in the box. It felt as fat and raw as marinated meat.

Othman and Salem both tilted their heads, staring down like a pair of fastidious dentists. '*Shouf*,' Othman said. '*Shwíya*.' They withdrew to the Campingaz.

'*Ambollaz*,' Fatiya grinned, wagging a finger. '*Falso*.'

Ambollaz . . . *ampollas*: blisters. Silence until Spike felt a tap on the shoulder.

'*Tú*,' Fatiya said. '*Por qué estás aquí?*'

Spike let his eyes close as the fingers worked out the saliva-soaked box from his mouth. His jawbone gaped, giving a sweet moment of respite before the throbbing restarted.

'*Por qué estás aquí?*'

His head dropped. Strings of white saliva hung from his mouth. *Why are you here?*

'*Duna?*'

'Mmm.'

'*Qué?*'

'*No.*' The word came out as a cough. He felt his jaw gripped again, fingers pinching his nose. The attempt to resist was mental only. He opened his mouth to breathe, and the box slotted back into place. The roar of the Campingaz cranked up.

The tongs again; Spike felt the heat of the blade as it hovered over his upper lip. He shut his eyes, trying to remove himself once more, when a shout came from up ahead: '*Ey!*'

The heat reduced; Spike opened his eyes and saw Zahra standing in the doorway.

'*Iryaa!*' she shouted, and everyone stopped moving. Spike had time to wonder why her arrival signalled such authority. Then he saw that she was holding in her arms the rusty hunter's rifle he'd seen hanging above Rami's crib.

'*Iryaa!*' she shouted again, advancing past the threshold.

Slowly, Othman placed the knife down on the floor. Zahra jabbed forward with the rifle and Othman, Salem and Fatiya all moved backwards.

As Zahra edged closer to Spike, Othman stepped away from the group. The rifle wavered in Zahra's hands. Then she shut her eyes and squeezed the trigger.

The kick caused the barrel to wheel up violently. There was a smack like the flick of a towel, then a deep gonging as the bullet collided with one of the wheelbarrows. Spike heard something fizz not far from his face, then a neat rustle as the bullet ricocheted into the heap of orange sand on the other side of the hangar.

Othman, Salem and Fatiya crouched down, hands on heads. Zahra yelled again, and they dropped to their knees.

She continued towards Spike. He widened his eyes in greeting. A warm stream of saliva spilled down one side of his chin.

'*Wakafy!*' she cried. A sharp smell of cordite hung in the air. She transferred the rifle to her left arm; now it pointed directly at the concrete floor. With her right hand, she reached for the box in Spike's mouth. The rough-grained wood tore at the wound on his tongue, making him twist his neck in pain. She glanced over, nostrils flaring, then gently drew the box out.

The relief was even sweeter than before. His head fell forward and more saliva spilled. Just letting his jaw hang was the most exquisite feeling. He came back to attention as Zahra made a grab for the rifle.

Othman was up on his feet. Spike saw Zahra squeezing the trigger again. 'Reload,' he tried to say, but only a tired exhalation emerged.

Othman's jaw was clenched so hard that rivets seemed to extend from its sides. His eyes were black. Two metres ahead of him lay the knife. He stepped towards it.

'Lever,' Spike grunted. 'Got to reload.'

Zahra lowered her gaze, then slid her hand up from the stock to draw back the bolt. A thin metallic chink broke the silence, like a triangle at the end of a symphony. Spike saw the empty shell come to rest by his feet. Othman saw it too and stopped moving.

Zahra bent down, eyes on Othman as she stuck out an arm for the knife. Rifle barrel scraping over concrete, she backed towards Spike, knife in her left hand. When she reached his chair, she shouted again, and Othman returned to his knees. He lowered his head, but Spike could see he was still watching.

The barrel of the rifle lay on the floor to Spike's right. He felt a shaky pressure as Zahra began sawing at the ropes binding his hands.

Now it was Salem creeping forward, head down. 'Zahra,' Spike said, hearing the clatter of the knife as she picked up the rifle and stood.

Spike swivelled his wrists, straining them apart, feeling the rope start to fray. With another twist, it gave. The same relief he'd felt in his jaw flooded through his shoulders as he moved his arms forward. He reached for the knife and cut free his ankles. His knees sagged as he got to his feet, forcing him to grip the chair back for support.

Zahra stood by his side. She yelled again and they drew back towards the open doorway. Othman and

Salem both raised their heads. As soon as Zahra was at the door, she turned and started to run. Spike lumbered after.

The pickup was parked outside; Spike went to the passenger side as Zahra climbed in behind the wheel, gun pointing down between her legs.

She twisted the key; nothing happened. Othman appeared in the doorway, running towards them. This time, the engine caught and the pickup screeched away. Spike saw Othman sprinting after them in the rear-view mirror before he was lost in a cloud of dust.

Spike put a hand on Zahra's thigh. She jerked the wheel in shock, making the pickup veer right. She straightened up; Spike saw his overnight bag in the footwell below. He leaned his head back against the rest and closed his eyes.

What felt like seconds later, he lurched forward as Zahra braked. She opened her door, took out the rifle and threw it side-on into the desert. The wind had dropped. Ahead shimmered millions of acres of emptiness.

When Zahra got back in, she reached over to Spike's face.

'Water,' he said.

CHAPTER 60

The thorns, the sand, the rocks, the dust, the bus, the gorge, the plateau, the train . . .

Spike came to in the half-light, Zahra sitting beside him on the hard mattress of the couchette, rubbing aftersun into his face, neck, ears. She reached down for a bottle of water and tipped some in his mouth. He closed his eyes, letting her rub cream into the lids. Then she lowered her head and kissed him.

She held her lips there, as though afraid to go further, before easing her tongue downwards. Spike's eyes prickled with tears: it felt like he'd just swallowed a sea anenome. He let out a muffled cry, like a scuba diver in distress. Zahra drew back.

'Not on the lips,' Spike managed to say.

She gave an involuntary snort of amusement.

'What?' Spike said. The pain made him laugh as well. Zahra whispered an apology, then kissed his cheek, gently at first, then more passionately, moving her mouth over his, pausing just long enough to see his alarmed expression, before grinning again as she dipped down to his neck.

Once the stinging in his mouth had subsided, he

slid his hands beneath the light cotton of her kaftan, running his fingertips up the smooth skin of her stomach until he found the dome of a breast, feeling her hips buck as he touched a small, stiff nipple.

She stopped, sitting up so abruptly that he thought he'd pushed things too far. Swinging one knee over his waist, she straddled him, drawing her kaftan over her outstretched arms and throwing it against the couchette wall.

Spike stared up. Seeing him try to swallow, she bent down for the water bottle, sluicing it into his mouth then over her firm, dark breasts, dripping it warmly from her body to his. He reached forward, undoing his trousers and letting her sit up as he inched them down to his calves. She kissed his bare chest; he wrapped his arms around her back, fingers tracing the half-pipe of her spine. Her skin was as soft as damask. His nose filled with the scent of sweat and suncream.

She moved her face above his, smile replaced by an intense, almost angry, look. He watched her pupils dilate. 'Are you sure you're well enough?' she said.

'Definitely.'

'Do you have any . . .?'

'In my wallet.'

She reached behind, fingers seeking the small foil square, which she tore in two to work out the shiny pink mollusc inside. With a small, backward shuffle, she hoisted him up. He felt a sharp electric tingle as she pressed the greased cap hard down.

He took her hand and then they were both rolling down the long, ridged condom. Cupping her buttocks, he brushed a thumb over the slick fold between. Breathing more quickly, she reached down and drew aside her knickers.

Spike felt the abrasive cotton edge as she eased herself up and down, head back, one hand on his ribs, the other squeezing her left, then right nipple, almond eyes half closed, long hair coiled over one shoulder. He raised his hands and eased her onto her back. He tried to relax his body, to empty his mind, but now she was grinding back into him, and then there was nothing he could do, the shivers were intensifying, throbbing in time with his tongue, pain mixing with pleasure, everything drawing to a point, like the blood on Abdallah's ceiling, like jagged violins, her moan rising at the same time as his.

The carriage, the seagulls, the hawkers, the *petit taxi*, the sound of her breathing . . . Sleep.

PART IV

TANGIERS

CHAPTER 61

Spike was sure he was home in Gibraltar. He heard the creak of floorboards and assumed his mother was bringing him up a mug of tea. Instead, on opening his eyes, he saw a figure crouching beside the bed. She picked up his trousers, slipping a hand into one pocket and taking out his wallet. After placing it on the dressing table, she reached for another pouch. His passport; now she was creeping towards the door.

'Zahra?' Spike groaned, his voice a full octave lower than normal. He swallowed and felt his throat scrape.

Zahra turned. 'I didn't know you were awake.'

'Mm,' Spike said.

'The receptionist called. He wants a copy of your passport. At least, I think that's what he wants.'

The door closed, leaving just the helicopter whirr of the ceiling fan above. Tentatively, Spike touched his head, feeling a double quail's egg on the crown. Two separate headaches were battling it out in his brain, jockeying for position. He sucked on his tongue: the upper half was swollen with fluid, twice as fat as the lower. The main discomfort, though, was in his throat.

The hotel bedroom at the Continental was either the same as before or of identical layout. The sheets beside him were disturbed. On the dressing table, next to his wallet, lay two mobile phones, his and Esperanza's. He crawled over the bed towards them.

Having retrieved his phone, he lay back. 8 a.m. on Thursday. *Thursday?* He'd lost a day somewhere. He could remember the sandstorm, the knife, Zahra, the rifle. But how he'd got back here he had no idea.

Two voice messages, the first from Inspector Eldrassi, asking him to come by the station, the second from Galliano, asking where the hell he was.

He could see Eldrassi today. That would free him up for the night-boat home, get him back to civilisation, out of this godforsaken country forever. He rolled out of bed and went to the bathroom, stopping as he passed the mirror. His left eye was black, the lid two-thirds closed as a purple sunset blushed through the socket. His forehead and neck were a fuchsia pink; he opened his mouth and saw pale clusters of ulcers crowding his tongue. 'Jesus Christ,' he muttered as he steered a tangerine cord of urine into the lavatory. Water droplets covered the bathtub as though someone had just showered. His stomach rumbled.

Back in the bedroom, he saw Zahra's woven handbag on the floor. Something bulky lay beside it. He stooped down; orange sand shifted from black plastic as he picked the package up. Hearing the door handle turn, he replaced it and rolled back into bed, wincing at the sudden movement.

CHAPTER 62

Zahra passed him two veterinary-sized aspirins, which he swallowed painfully with mineral water. The shutters were closed; she sat down at the dressing table beneath them. 'Are you hungry?'

'Beginning to be very.'

'How's the tongue?'

'It only hurts when I breathe.'

She smiled for a moment, then became serious. 'It's called *Bisha'a*.'

The soft sibilants of the word transported Spike back to the hangar.

'It's an ancient Bedouin tradition. Supposed to be illegal but it's still practised in rural areas.'

'I don't see why they bothered. I'd have told them anything.'

'They call it trial by fire. They use it instead of courtrooms.'

Spike kept crackling the plastic water bottle in one hand; he put it down on the floor.

'If the defendant's tongue blisters, it means he's lying. If it doesn't, he's telling the truth. Apparently it's quite accurate. Your mouth gets dry when you lie, so . . .'

'Sounds about as effective as witch ducking.'

Zahra frowned, not understanding the term. 'Do you want me to take you to the hospital?'

'No way.'

'Well, if it's any consolation, I can never go back to my village now.'

'It's no consolation.'

'At least we're even. You rescued me in Chinatown. I rescued you in Zagora Zween.'

An uncomfortable silence passed. 'Thank you,' Spike said eventually.

Zahra undid her headscarf and shook back her still-damp hair. Something in the motion made Spike's groin stir, as though it knew something his mind didn't. 'What time did we get in?' he asked.

'About 10 a.m. You kept repeating "Hotel Continental" so we came here. You've been asleep. You had a fever.' She smiled, as though waiting for something more. He felt as though he were missing a detail. 'What were you doing,' he asked, 'in the desert?'

She lowered her eyes. 'I went to find something.'

'What?'

'A secret.'

'Abdallah's secret?'

'Yes.'

'More than just a death rattle?'

She stood and went over to the plastic-wrapped package. More sand trickled to the floor.

'So what did he say to you?' Spike asked as she brought it over.

'At first I thought he was asking for his mother.'

'But?'

She sat down on the bed. 'He was telling me to *see* his mother. To ask for what was hidden.'

'So you went to her tent by the waterhole . . . Did you tell her that her son was dead?'

'She was old; I thought it best not to. She hardly had any possessions. Except this.' Zahra held up the package. 'Buried in the sand outside her tent.'

Spike stared at the layers of faded masking tape around the plastic.

'When the storm died out, I walked home,' Zahra said. 'Salwa told me Othman was angry. I saw he'd been through your stuff. The pickup was gone and I guessed where he might have taken you.' She pressed a nail through the plastic and tore it open. Another plastic bag inside; she repeated the process, then drew out what looked like a blue hardback book.

Digging her fingers beneath the lid, she bit her lower lip, giving Spike another strangely erotic flashback. The hinge wouldn't come so she passed it over.

Spike's sunburn pulsed as he prised the case apart. Inside lay a videotape; he turned it over in his hands. Twice the size of a normal VHS, a sticker of bleached spidery Arabic on the front. 'What does it say?' Spike asked.

'*Play me.*'

The celluloid band was warped. 'Easier said than done, I suspect.'

From next door came a 20th Century Fox fanfare. Spike smiled as he climbed out of bed.

CHAPTER 63

Jean-Baptiste's dreadlocks dangled over his face. He flicked them up when he saw Spike. 'Chingongo! I thought you go.'

'Change of plan.'

Jean-Baptiste peered over Spike's shoulder, widening his eyes. '*Bien évidemment, mon frère*. What happened to your face?'

'Beach football. Got out of hand.'

Zahra stepped forward. She still had her hair free. Jean-Baptiste took her hand in greeting, sucking in his small pot belly. '*Enchanté*,' he said, planting a noisy kiss on the back of her hand.

'Jean-Baptiste? Zahra.'

'*Za-rah*,' Jean-Baptiste repeated. 'She speak French?'

'*Mieux en anglais, si possible*,' Zahra replied.

Jean-Baptiste widened his eyes still further. 'She burn you up,' he whispered to Spike as he held open the door.

The room was glowing with its usual bank of monitors. 'Sorry for chaos,' Jean-Baptiste muttered, picking up a pair of Y-fronts, 'sometimes, you know, *pour la créativité* . . .' He turned down the volume, then opened the shutters. 'Now, what is it I can do for Chingongo and his . . .'

Zahra sat down on the bed and drew the tape from her kaftan. Jean-Baptiste frowned as he sat beside her. He examined the tape in his large hands.

'Can you get it to play?' Spike said.

Jean-Baptiste puffed on the celluloid band. 'Not easy like with mobile phone. Model is eight . . . maybe ten year. Where is it from?'

'Home video.'

Jean-Baptiste looked at Zahra. 'You have CCTV in your home?'

'Her father's a judge. Now can you do it?'

Zahra said something in French to which Jean-Baptiste shrugged a response. She added another comment and he laughed.

'What was that?'

'I said it had been in the sand,' Zahra explained.

'And?'

'He told me the damage was from the sun not the sand. I said in the desert you can't tell the difference. He agreed.'

'Is there anything you can do?' Spike said. 'There's money in it.'

Jean-Baptiste clicked his tongue. 'I think impossible. Maybe at the Café des Étoiles . . .'

'What time?'

'I go for usual hour. Five o'clock?'

Zahra reached back for the tape. '*Non*,' Jean-Baptiste said, lifting it away. 'You leave with me. You have the box?'

'It broke,' Spike said. As they made to leave, Jean-Baptiste went to his bedside table and took out the envelope Spike had given him. 'Maybe I talk to your contact soon,' he said. '*La vida española*, uh?'

'Catch you later, Jean-Baptiste.'

CHAPTER 64

'Are you sure we can trust him?'

'Yes.'

'The great expert on Morocco,' Zahra muttered as she went over to the landing wall with its framed maps of Tangiers. 'Tourist bullshit,' she said. 'What was in that envelope?'

'Information.'

'What kind of information?'

'I said I could help him get to Spain.'

'You say a lot of things.' She turned away from the wall. The frankness of her glare took Spike back to the sleeper. His memories were still blurred: it was hard to know what was real. 'Look, I'm sorry,' he said, stepping towards her. 'I think I had sunstroke. On the train . . . that actually happened, didn't it?'

'I'm glad it was so memorable.' She walked past him to the hotel-room door. 'Forget it, Spike.'

The door was locked.

'Do you want to grab some breakfast?' Spike said.

'It's Ramadan.'

'Still?'

'The last day.'

'After sundown?'

'I'll be at my friend's house.'

'Which friend?'

'The one I've been staying with since you came to Chinatown.'

'The man with the red rucksack?'

'Not this again. Can I have the key?'

'Why do you need to see him?'

'For my papers.'

'Why do you need those?'

'You don't remember that either?'

He gave her the key and she went inside. As she gathered her bag, he reached out and took her hand. 'I do remember,' he whispered in her ear.

She tried to pull away but he had a hand on her hip. Leaning forward, he kissed the nape of her neck. She turned and faced him. Her lips were swollen, her breath warm. He smelled her sharp scent as she dropped the bag and slid her hands up beneath his T-shirt.

CHAPTER 65

Zahra had two little dimples on the small of her back, one each side of her spine. Light, wavy lines traversed her skin, fading into dark treacle. On her right shoulder rose a neat oval bruise where the rifle had recoiled. 'What?' she said as she stepped into a pair of pink knickers.

'Just looking.'

Tutting as though he were a deviant, she pulled on jeans and a tank top. After crouching to her trainers, she held the black kaftan over her head and let it unfurl downwards.

'I think it's depressing.'

She moved to the dressing table beneath the window, using the cracked mirror to tie back her hair. 'What's depressing?'

'The whole covering-up thing.'

'My *foulard*?'

'Your what?'

She gestured at her sequinned headscarf, which she was positioning over her ponytail.

'All of it,' Spike said, lying back. 'The suggestion that if men actually see what you look like, they can't be answerable for their actions.'

'Coming from a man with second-degree sunburn, that sounds a bit naive.' Zahra stood and gave a rich, croaky laugh. 'I find it comforting,' she added, knotting the headscarf beneath her chin. 'I would still wear it in Europe.'

A beat passed. 'I will help you,' Spike said. 'I'll help with your visa. Act as a referee.'

'You don't have to do anything for me.'

'I want to.'

'That's not why I slept with you.'

'Of course.'

She sat down on the side of the bed. 'Show me.'

He stuck out his tongue.

'Better.'

'So I'll meet you at five at the café?'

'Or four? For the application . . .'

'OK.'

'Or five?'

'No, four's fine.'

Zahra took his hand, caressing the palm. 'Look at your long fingers. Like a musician.' She leaned in and kissed him, reaching below the covers, breathing rapidly before drawing away. 'Better not. I have enough praying to do as it is.'

She glanced back from the door and smiled. When she was gone, he slid out of bed and searched through his trousers. His passport was still missing. He checked the dressing table, then heard the bedside phone ring. 'Yes?'

'It's Nadeer. I'm down in reception. Mind if I pop up?'

CHAPTER 66

There was a rap at the door. 'Tracked you down at last,' Nadeer said, coming in unasked as Spike stood bare-chested by the bed. 'Christ alive, what happened to your face?'

'Too much sun.'

'I thought you were going home.'

'Got held up.'

Nadeer was back in his suit, a tan leather satchel slung over one shoulder. He looked down at the floor where a 'Rock Hard' condom lay replete and exhausted.

'Have a seat,' Spike said, toeing the condom beneath the bed and sitting up against the headboard.

Nadeer took off his satchel and sat down at the dressing table. 'I was starting to get worried,' he said. 'I called your office and was told you weren't there.'

'I'm touched by your concern.'

'I wanted to check how Solomon was.' As Nadeer reached forward to open the shutters, his reflection caught in the dressing-table mirror. The crack bisected his forehead, warping his face into two distinct parts like a fairground hall of mirrors. 'So what have you been up to, buddy?' he said, sitting back in the shadow.

'Taking some downtime.'

'Here in Tangiers?'

'Yup.'

'That's odd. Because I came by the hotel on Tuesday. They told me you'd checked out.'

Nadeer nudged something along the table with a manicured nail: a hairclip. 'I passed a young lady on the stairs.'

'Oh?'

'A rather pretty young lady. Looked to me like she came from the desert. You know, we have a proverb here in Morocco: "A Bedouin took his revenge after forty years. It was said he was in a hurry." Heard that one?'

'Have you been talking to the receptionist?'

Nadeer stared across. 'Be careful you're not being played, Spike. That's all I'm saying.' He stood. 'Miss Solness was asking after you. You're quite the dark pony. Quite the dark pony.' There was a spot of orange sand on the floor; Nadeer dipped in a finger, checking the colour. Ahead in the corner lay the plastic tape box. 'What's that?' he said, straightening up.

'What's what?'

He walked over and picked up the box, gripping both sides then pressing them together.

'It was here when I checked in.'

From next door came the first notes of a movie

soundtrack. Nadeer turned to the wall, then back to Spike. 'I was talking to Professor Castillo. He told me some thug from Gibraltar had been harassing him just when he was at his most fragile.'

'Riddell gave me his address.'

'I wouldn't pay too much heed to Tobes – he's just a donkey I've comfortably stabled.' There was a pause. 'I asked you to my party, Spike. We cut a deal, I seem to remember. It involved you going home to help delay a trial. Call me old-fashioned, but I don't see much evidence of you fulfilling your side of the bargain.'

'Maybe I prefer the long goodbye.'

'There's a ferry to Gibraltar this afternoon. I'd really hate to see all the good work you've done for Solomon go to waste.' He threw the tape box onto the bed, then picked up his satchel and left.

CHAPTER 67

'The whole world united cannot harm you as much as you yourself can.'

'Have you got my passport?'

The receptionist opened a drawer and handed it over. 'Shall I put you down for another night?'

'Why not?'

'May your God go with you, friend.'

'And also with you.'

Spike stepped out into the late Tangiers morning, face immediately throbbing in the heat. Sunscreen and refreshment, his two main priorities. He passed the guard hut then came out onto the street. A man was waiting with his back to the white-washed wall that ran around the hotel. He was squeezing a squash ball in one hand.

'I hear you're catching the 3 p.m.,' Riddell said.

'You working on commission now?'

'Comm-iss-ion,' Riddell repeated, aping Spike's accent. 'Is it Spike or Spick, by the way? I never could tell.' He detached himself from the wall and followed Spike up a narrow lane at the edge of the Medina. 'Saw your lady friend back at the hotel,' he called out.

'Always the voyeur, Riddell.'

'How much she set you back?'

Spike stopped. 'What did you say?'

'Your Bedouin whore. I hear they fuck like bitches in season. Arseholes even wider than their –'

Spike slammed Riddell back against the wall, one hand on each shoulder. His balding sandy head knocked against the stucco. He looked shocked for a moment, then grinned his stained teeth. With a double sweep of the arms, he pushed Spike's wrists away, using the heel of his hand to jab at the lower part of Spike's stomach. Spike felt his lips open as a pocket of air puffed between them. He tried to breathe in but nothing happened. Riddell kicked his feet away and he fell to his knees. Riddell kicked him again; he slumped to his side.

Men in djellabas bustled by, eyes carefully averted. 'You Gibbos are all the same,' Riddell said as he stood over Spike. 'Piggyback on the garrison for three centuries, then on the banks once the garrison's gone. Inbred camp followers. Leeches.' Spike felt something warm spatter his cheek.

'Now run along and catch your boat, little Gibbo, and go get your kike out of jail.' He walked away, leather soles ticking on the cobbles.

There was spittle on Spike's left cheek. He wiped it off and staggered to his feet, leaning against the wall until he got his breath back.

CHAPTER 68

'A mere two days late,' Inspector Hakim Eldrassi said as he stood up from his desk. 'Ouch. I hope that barman didn't catch up with you.'

'May I?' Spike said as he sat down.

Hakim cleared the clutter from his desk, then pushed a sheet of paper towards Spike. 'The translation on the top is my own.'

Spike scanned through. 'Suicide?'

'I was a little surprised myself,' Hakim said, screwing a cigarette between his lips. 'Especially as handwriting samples suggested Mr al-Manajah was left-handed and the knife was found in his right. But there you have it. He was a Bedouin. They go a bit crazy when they leave the desert. Hence all the . . .' Hakim waved his cigarette over the room; seeing the state of his own furniture, he drew it back to his mouth.

Spike read the rest of the statement. 'And the Arabic corresponds to the English?'

'No doubt you will extricate yourself on a technicality if there are any problems.'

Spike signed, then handed it back. 'Any chance of a copy?'

'In . . . theory.' Hakim turned to lift two styrofoam cups from the antique photocopier. 'I'll telephone the port authorities and have your name removed from the list,' he said. 'You should be pleased. Passage home. Trial in Gibraltar. No extradition for your client.' He dropped the blurred copy onto Spike's lap.

'So what happens now?'

'I celebrate the Eid ul-Fitr with my wife and daughters,' Hakim replied as he sat down. 'Watch the fireworks. Come back on Monday to deal with a tourist mugging.' He turned up the corner of a piece of paper. 'Round up a few of the more persistent *sans-papiers*.' He turned up another. 'It's most odd. All the big crimes seem to have disappeared.'

'Have you heard of a man called Nadeer Ziyad?'

Hakim grinned through his fug of smoke. 'Do you remember the advice I gave you when we first met?'

'Remind me.'

'There's a catamaran to Gibraltar at 3 p.m.' Hakim reached into the bin for a scrap of paper. 'I'll need to liaise with your friend, Sergeant Navarro,' he said. 'The Hassan file will have to be conveyed to Gibraltar. This is my mobile number. Tell her to call me.'

Hakim clipped the scrap of paper to the photocopied statement. Spike read it as he came out onto the street. Beneath the digits were the words 'CATCH THAT BOAT'.

CHAPTER 69

A bandstand and bunting-clad Bedouin tent were being erected on the beach below the police station. Spike walked away up the coast road, pausing as a lorry rumbled by, its rear compartment stacked with crates of wide-eyed lambs. He passed a travel agent on the Place de la Marche Verte, where a poster advertised twice-weekly ferries from Genoa to Tangiers. He wondered how things might have turned out had his forebears made that journey across the Mediterranean instead of to Gibraltar.

As he climbed the winding alleys of the Medina, the hawkers recognised him, steering their approaches elsewhere. '*Uzbek*,' one of them said. '*Ma ka'in mushkil*.'

There was a charge in the air, the streets even busier than usual, shopkeepers swabbing foamy terraces, trailer mopeds making deliveries. Spike took out his phone; Galliano picked up at once. 'Spike! *Cacarruca*. Where have you –'

'Out of reception.'

'Are you home?'

'Almost.'

'All OK?'

Ahead, a man with a lank ponytail was queuing at a butcher's shop. His flaccid double chin quivered as he haggled over price . . . Spike wheeled into a back alley.

'Spike?'

'Did Nadeer Ziyad call the office?'

'Don't think so.'

'Didn't leave a message?'

'Not that I know of. Listen, Spike, I've been looking into Dunetech. I even winkled some info out of Napier. It's not millions we're talking about. It's billions.'

'Dirhams?'

'Euros.'

'How many?'

'A brace, and that's just the first round of investment.'

Threads of silk wound down the alleyway, taut against the tiled walls; Spike followed them until they disappeared through the doorway of a fabric shop.

'How's the fund structured?'

'From what I could tell this is Nadeer's chance to persuade Daddy he can run the show on his own. I went down to Companies House, and you're right, the holding vehicle is registered in Gib. Forty-nine per cent held by third-party outside investors. Thirty per cent by the Ziyad Family Settlement – that's Nadeer and his old man. Ten per cent by Ángel Castillo. Six in a charitable trust called the

Ziyad Foundation. And the remaining five has been siphoned into a separate vehicle called "Interzone Holdings".'

'Who's behind Interzone Holdings?'

'Couldn't penetrate it. Senior management, perhaps.'

'Or the governor of Tangiers. Any mention of Toby Riddell?'

'Checked Google, Lexis. Nothing.'

Spike jumped at a whip-crack: a woman emptying a bucket.

'Spike?'

'Yes.'

'I think you should come home.'

'You're in good company. Did you check on my dad?'

'Alive and well. Bit bolshie.'

'Taking his medication?'

'So he says. Look, Spike, you've done what you set out to do. There's talk of getting Solomon bail.'

'I'll give you a call when my boat gets in.'

CHAPTER 70

From the terrace of the Café Central, Spike watched as a chef took receipt of a lamb and led it bleating by a string through the kitchen back door. The Petit Socco hummed and bustled, shoeshine boys doing a brisk trade, elderly fish seller completing a sale. Spike turned up his iPod.

The last caprice, No. 24 in A minor. Spike listened to the crazed pizzicato, thinking about how Paganini's sun had started to set from this point on. His life as a travelling virtuoso had taken him to Paris, where he'd poured his earnings into setting up the Casino Paganini. The venture had been such a disaster that he'dhad to auction off his musical instruments to pay the debts. With failing health he'd returned south, refusing the last rites of a priest and dying alone aged fifty-seven, spindly arms draped over his last remaining violin, before being buried – toothless and emaciated – in unconsecrated ground.

Spike checked the time, wondering what aphorism the receptionist might have for this career arc. The boat for Gibraltar left in an hour. He didn't even have Zahra's phone number. Another girl cut adrift.

He switched off the music; the bustle of the Petit Socco refilled his ears. After paying up, he set off towards the Kasbah.

CHAPTER 71

The maid jabbed upwards with her broom as Spike climbed the spiral staircase. When he reached the door, he slid the small brass key out of the lock. The sun dazzled his eyes as he stepped out onto the terrace. Closing the door, he locked it and slipped the key into his pocket.

The hot tub burbled, murkier than before, a decomposing lump bobbing in the surface scum. Ángel Castillo was slumped in the same wooden chair.

'*Profesor Castillo?*' Spike called out.

Ángel's polo shirt was streaked with sweat and whisky. His beard had grown thicker and his deeply tanned cheeks drooped beneath the rose-coloured blotches under his eyes. At his feet lay a half-empty bottle of J&B and a round cardboard box of Moroccan sweets and pastries.

Spike touched his shoulder and he gave a groan. He shook him and there was a sudden intake of breath, followed by a hacking clearance of the throat. Then he smacked his lips and lowered his head again.

Spike slapped him hard across the chops; this

time his head shot upright, bloodshot eyes blinking as they took in Spike's backlit presence.

'Aren't you going to offer me a drink?' Spike said.

A smile spread across his cracked lips. For a moment Spike saw he must once have been very handsome. 'It got to you too,' he said.

'What did?'

'This city. It got to you in the end.'

Spike moistened his blistered tongue. 'I suppose it did.'

Ángel began to laugh; Spike picked up his glass and sloshed it full of whisky. The smile died. 'I told you not to come back, *Heebralta*.'

'Today's different. I've got the tape.'

Ángel squinted upwards.

'The tape from Zagora Zween.'

His sunburnt knuckles whitened as he clenched his glass.

'So I'll ask you one last time: who killed your stepdaughter?'

'You,' Ángel sighed, whisky dripping down his stubble. 'Me. Everyone.'

Spike took out his mobile phone. 'Just one call,' he said, holding it up. 'One call and the tape goes to the police in Gibraltar.'

'What *tape*?'

'Abdallah al-Manajah's tape.'

Ángel clumsily put down his glass, wiping his mouth with his sleeve.

'Tell me the truth,' Spike said, 'and you get the

tape. Lie, and I make the call.' He stepped forward. 'You raped her, didn't you? You raped your own stepdaughter, then murdered her.'

Ángel made a sideways chop with one hand, sweeping the tumbler off the table where it skidded unbroken into the hot tub. He made a grab for the whisky bottle but Spike got to him in time, digging a forearm beneath his throat and pressing a knee into his thigh. He spoke quietly: 'When I send that tape to the police everything you've worked for will end. Your Dunetech legacy will die. No more Sun King, just a common criminal.' The hot tub came back on. 'Nod if you understand.'

Ángel's throat made a rattling like Abdallah al-Manajah's.

'Nod . . .'

Ángel nodded and Spike withdrew, hearing him gulp in air then cough it back out. He held up a hand as though asking for time; Spike walked back to the bar, returning with a fresh tumbler which he filled to the brim.

Like a priest giving communion, Spike held the whisky to Ángel's mouth. He gulped it down as easily as apple juice, then shivered his head, spitting twice onto the decking. '*Vale*,' he said. 'We went to meet the Bedouin ourselves.' He coughed. 'At Zagora Zween.'

Spike held up his mobile phone as if to remind Ángel of the threat. Feeling for the recording function on the side, he slid the button forward with a thumb. 'Who's we?'

'Me and Nadeer. And the site manager, Abdallah. We assumed he wanted more money. Drove him down to the land, told him we would only widen the road, a road that was already there. But that stupid peasant *cabrón* wouldn't listen.'

'Then?'

'We took him to the site. I showed him a heliopod, explained how much larger the power field could become if only we had the proper access. But still he refused. We had the cash ready, thousands in US dollars. When I opened the briefcase, he shoved it back in my face. Cut my lip. Banknotes everywhere, blowing in the wind. He slipped, hit his head on the base of one of the units. At first we thought he'd just knocked himself out, but then I saw the blood.' Ángel's hands were steady enough now for him to feed himself.

'Go on,' Spike said.

'We panicked. This was Ibrahim al-Mahmoud, the Bedouin elder. The leader of his people. Abdallah told us he knew where the concrete was still wet. We threw the body into the foundations of the hangar, waited until it sank. Abdallah gathered up most of the cash. We told him he could have it if he kept quiet. Then we drove back to Tangiers.'

'But he didn't keep quiet.'

'There was a video – CCTV from the storage tower. Abdallah said he wanted a monthly stipend or he would take the tape to the villagers. He didn't ask for much. We paid up and that was the end of it.'

'Until now.'

Ángel grinned. 'Abdallah heard about our expansion plans. He got greedy. Came to my office; came here, we argued. Then he saw Esperanza.'

Spike paused. 'So Abdallah killed Esperanza because you wouldn't pay him more money?'

'No,' Ángel said forcefully. 'I think Abdallah told the Bedouins in the village. The relatives of Ibrahim. He told them what we had done, and they killed my stepdaughter to avenge the death of their leader. And to punish me.' Ángel poured himself another glass, eyes starting to glaze. 'So you are right, *Heebralta*. Maybe I did kill her.' He gazed through the trellising. 'They will come for me next. They are down there, waiting. I have always known it. *Los beduinos*.' The hot tub stopped bubbling, exposing a clatter from the doorway. Ángel finished his drink and lowered his head.

Spike was still on his feet, phone held out. 'I've just come back from Zagora Zween. The Bedouins couldn't give a fuck about Ibrahim's disappearance. They only want to keep their jobs. Abdallah didn't avenge himself by telling *them* what you did to Ibrahim. It was Esperanza he told. After that, Esperanza threatened to go to the police, so you cut her throat before she could.'

Ángel's neck began to sag.

'You killed your own stepdaughter, then had Abdallah killed as well.'

'*No*,' Ángel murmured. '*La quería*.' *I loved her.*

The terrace door shook. Spike switched off the

record button and returned to the bar, placing the last two bottles of J&B beside Ángel's chair leg. As he unlocked the door, he found the maid huddled behind it. He passed her the key then went downstairs, Ángel still repeating in the background, '*La quería . . . la quería . . .*'

CHAPTER 72

Spike strode up the rue de Belgique. He'd listened to the recording twice but all that was audible were his own questions and the steady burble of the hot tub. Too much ambient noise. He swore under his breath as he inputted a number.

'I was about to call you,' Hakim said. 'We need you to come back to the station. There's been a problem with your statement.'

'Forget my statement,' Spike said. 'I've got a body for you.'

'I'm sorry?'

'In Zagora Zween. Sunk into the concrete beneath a hangar at the Dunetech site.'

'I don't understand.'

'A Bedouin elder called Ibrahim al-Mahmoud. Killed by either Ángel Castillo or Nadeer Ziyad. They may be responsible for the murder of Esperanza too. Do you understand me?' Grilles were rattling up from shop windows. People kept staring.

'There is a witness,' Hakim resumed, 'who says she saw you and a girl enter Abdallah al-Manajah's flat. You never mentioned any girl. You told me you were alone.'

'I'm giving you the solution to a murder and you're quibbling over witness statements? If you've got all this time on your hands, why not drive down to Zagora Zween with a pickaxe and smash up some concrete?'

'Are you at the Hotel Continental, Mr Sanguinetti?'

Spike stopped. 'How did you know I wasn't on the boat?'

Silence at the other end.

'You asked me to catch the 3 p.m. boat,' Spike went on. 'Who told you I wasn't on it?'

'Where are you, please, Mr Sanguinetti?'

Spike switched off his phone and continued up the rue de Belgique, hearing the distant wail of a police siren as he neared the Café des Étoiles.

CHAPTER 73

The café was empty save for the same white-haired barman washing glasses. Spike checked the time: 3.50 p.m. Zahra was due at four, Jean-Baptiste at five. He ordered a Coke and sat at a stool, looking ahead at the door through which Jean-Baptiste had disappeared the last time they were here. Moving his drink to one of the low round tables, he waited until the barman had his back turned.

After knocking on the door, Spike heard the sound of chains being removed as a young Moroccan with severe acne appeared in the gap. Behind him, Spike sensed the familiar glow of monitors. '*Jean-Baptiste, por favor?*'

The boy shook his head, then closed the door. Spike looked back at the barman, who was staring at him. '*Mon ami,*' Spike called over.

The chain jangled to reveal Jean-Baptiste, tall and stern in his white prayer robes. 'We say 5 p.m., no?'

'Have you seen Zahra?'

'*Qui ça?*'

'The girl. Zahra.'

Jean-Baptiste shook his head.

'Does the tape work?'

'I do not try. Later.'

'Can you try now?'

Someone called from behind him in Arabic. 'I go,' Jean-Baptiste said. 'I find *you*, uh?'

The door closed and Spike returned to the table. Another police siren droned outside. The barman continued to stare.

Spike pressed in his solar plexus, bruised from where Riddell had hit him. It was after four . . . maybe he should just hide out here until the night boat. He drank some more Coke. His phone rang. 'Zahra?'

'It's Nadeer.'

Spike put down his bottle.

'I've heard about the videotape,' Nadeer said. 'You still there?'

'Yes.'

'It's a fake, of course, but an irritant. You have it with you?'

'What if I do?'

'I understand you and your Bedouin sweetheart have been rubbing the police up the wrong way. Something about a false witness statement? We could probably make that disappear.'

'I've got a different idea,' Spike said. 'You get Ángel Castillo to give a full confession to Esperanza's murder and I'll consider not posting the tape to Gibraltar.'

'Now you're being silly.'

'If you say so.'

'Your girlfriend's rather keen for you to bring the tape here. Isn't that right, Tobes?'

Spike heard a muffled scream in the background. 'Bullshit,' he said.

'Well, she's not with you, is she? What colour are her panties, Tobes?'

'Pink,' Spike heard shouted in the background.

'Pink,' Nadeer repeated. 'So bring the tape with you in half an hour. You remember the villa. Send the taxi away then ring the bell on the gatepost.' There was a pause. 'Half an hour, Spike. Don't make her wait.'

The line went dead. Spike felt his heart banging against his ribs like a prisoner in a cell. He stood and walked to the café entrance, glancing left and right up the street. Four thirty. His head felt dizzy; he waited for his breathing to regulate then returned inside, hammering on the back door.

Spike barged in as soon as the teenaged boy opened up. Rather than TV monitors, the glow was from laptops. The room smelled of weeks of stale perspiration.

Jean-Baptiste and a crew-cut Moroccan sat staring at a fold-up screen. Displayed was a black-and-white image of heliopods, filmed from above. Numbers ticked along the base.

Jean-Baptiste turned his slack face. 'That tape,' he said.

'Have you made a copy?'

Jean-Baptiste said something to the Moroccan,

who hit a key on the computer. 'We burning DVD now,' Jean-Baptiste said.

'I need the original.'

He spoke again to his colleague. 'Is it . . . real?'

'Yes. Can I have the original?'

'Not finished.'

'I need it right away.'

'You want help, Chingongo?'

'Just the tape. The tape and a pen and paper . . .' Spike scoured the cluttered room and saw a printed sheet on a table. 'Pen, pen . . .'

The boy gave Spike a chewed biro and he wrote out the home addresses of Peter Galliano and Jessica Navarro on the back of the sheet. On the screen, the black-and-white image was forward winding. Nothing changed but the numbers at the base.

'*Beaucoup* bad shit,' Jean-Baptiste said as he ejected the tape and handed it over.

'Listen,' Spike said, 'I've got to meet someone. If I don't come back, you're to post DVD copies of the tape to Gibraltar. I've got money . . .' He laid out a two-hundred-dirham note.

'What you mean, don't come back?'

Spike moved to the door, then turned. 'The El Minzah Hotel. How good are your contacts?'

Jean-Baptiste stuck up a thumb.

'One more favour, Jean-Baptiste, and I'll buy you a first-class ticket to Madrid.'

CHAPTER 74

Spike held down the buzzer as soon as the taxi pulled away. There was no one in the sentry box, just the same stone lions eyeballing the road. A small black CCTV camera peered down from the gatepost.

'Yes?' came a voice.

'It's Sanguinetti.'

The mechanism began to whirr, and Spike slipped at once between the gap. Cicadas pulsed in the palm trees lining the driveway. Strips of late sun shone between their trunks, heating Spike's skin as he passed through them. In his right hand, in lieu of the tape box, he held a plastic carrier bag.

The dizziness returned as he remembered Zahra's smile as she'd left the hotel room. He'd let her go, failed to protect her . . . He stopped, wiping a sleeve across his forehead. He needed to concentrate. He continued up the curved section of driveway into the turning circle.

No cars, no liveried butler to welcome him. He crunched over gravel to the gatehouse tunnel. Another CCTV camera tracked his paces.

The swimming pool glowed in the last rays of the sun. Squatting like a silver toad at its rim was the heliopod.

Spike walked up the right-hand edge of the pool. The doors to the main house began sliding apart, and Toby Riddell stepped outside, frowning at the sun, a smile on his freckled face. He wore a navy, brass-buttoned blazer and high-waisted chinos. His sandy hair was combed back, as though he were ready to go out for the evening. His black shoes glinted.

'You've got the tape then,' he called out.

Spike held up the plastic bag.

'Great,' Riddell shouted. 'Bring it over, then you can take the girl.'

Spike took a step towards the heliopod, then stopped. 'No,' he said. 'Zahra first. Then the tape.'

Riddell glanced over Spike's shoulder at the doorway which led down to the underground garage. 'Uh-uh, sunshine,' he replied. 'Other way round.'

As Spike started to turn back towards the gatehouse, he saw Riddell's right hand dip beneath his blazer. Spike would have thought that the pistol was fake, but for the long black silencer screwed to its muzzle.

'Hands nice and visible,' Riddell called out.

Spike raised the plastic bag up above his head. Riddell was coming towards him over the terrace.

'Higher. Where I can see them.'

Using his fingertips, Spike felt for the handles

of the plastic bag and knotted them together. Riddell was almost at the heliopod now, skirting towards him along the edge of the pool. Spike could see his yellow teeth as he smiled, piggy eyes squinting at the sun.

Breathing out slowly, Spike transferred the plastic bag to his left hand. It dangled down. He swayed it back and forth. Then he looped it into the air so that it landed with a plop in the middle of the pool.

Riddell's smile disappeared. He steered his gaze to the pool, where the tape was floating, buoyed by the air in the bag. 'That was stupid,' he said, looking back at Spike.

'You'd better get it before it sinks,' Spike replied. 'Or you'll never know if it's genuine.'

Riddell twisted both hands, angling the pistol, as though aiming up beneath Spike's chin.

'And if it's not genuine,' Spike called out, 'then I'm the only person who can tell you where the original is.'

Riddell glanced again at the plastic bag. 'Not one fucking muscle,' he said, as he backed along the edge of the pool.

The water darkened Riddell's chinos as he splashed down the steps. The plastic bag was creeping towards the deep end, drawn by the cleaning current. Riddell was up to his waist, still pointing the pistol at Spike. His blazer tails swirled. The bag was just three metres in front. When he turned his eyes to check its position,

Spike sprinted towards the heliopod and crouched down behind it.

There was no bang from the gun, just a cymbal-like reverberation as the bullet hit the side of the heliopod. A higher-pitched clang followed, as Spike crouched down lower, protected by the metal shaft. In front, he could hear Riddell thrashing about in the water, trying to get an angle for the shot.

Grimacing, Spike placed his hands on the shaft of the heliopod and shoved outwards. The current prickled his palms as though he were gripping the stem of a rose. The heliopod started to rock as the metal clanged again, right by Spike's ear. Directing all his strength into his arms, he heaved again until it tipped on its stand, landing with a heavy splash in the water.

Sharp droplets sprayed up onto Spike's face; he was teetering on the flagstone edge, hands clawing at the air, trying to switch his momentum backwards. Elbows by his ears, he held himself there, looking down and seeing Riddell frozen in the middle of the pool, plastic bag beside him, one hand still on the pistol, the other clutching back and forth, sinews on the side of his neck like ropes as his face angled upwards to the setting sun.

A crackle came from the water: the heliopod was sinking, drawing its forked tail of wires behind it. Now Riddell's entire body was convulsing. As Spike finally fell back onto the terrace, he heard Riddell give out a long falsetto scream. Then there was nothing but the rhythmic saw of cicadas and the slow, steady chug of the filtration system.

CHAPTER 75

Spike glided like an automaton, a torso on mechanical legs. The lights were on in the gatehouse; he descended to the garage, taking the steps three at a time. Then he saw her. Sitting on a metal chair in the middle of the concrete floor, motionless, brown hessian sack over her head. 'Zahra!'

Her shoulders began to twist; he pulled off the sack and saw her eyes wide, hair lank and sweaty, electrical tape over her mouth. She kept glancing beyond him, blinking as though in warning.

'It's OK,' Spike said, 'you're safe now.' He moved behind her; her wrists and ankles were taped behind the chair.

With unsteady fingers, he set about unpeeling the tape. Her hands came free first; he knelt to her ankles and untied them too. She stood shakily and threw her arms around him. The strip of tape on her mouth had been softened by saliva; Spike eased it off and pressed his lips to hers. As they kissed, he stroked the damp hair back from her face.

Above them stretched the bank of CCTV units. One monitor showed the driveway, one the pool terrace. Spike reached up and pressed eject: a large black cassette slid out, the same make as the one he'd just thrown into the pool. He ejected the others and slung them in the hessian sack.

Zahra was still tearing off the last of the dangling strands of tape. 'They grabbed me outside the hotel,' she said, 'they wanted the tape –'

'Are you hurt?'

She shook her head. 'One of them kept touching me. I've seen him before at the Sundowner, he was –' She stopped. 'He had a gun.'

'Not any more.'

'How did . . .?'

'Shh,' Spike said. 'We can talk later.'

He steered her up the vehicle ramp. The lever drew no response so they turned and ran up the garage stairs to the terrace.

'*Ya Allah*,' Zahra said, covering her mouth with a hand.

Riddell was floating face down in the water. His legs dangled and his wrists hung limply by his ears. On the tiled base of the pool, the heliopod lay side-on like a space-age shipwreck. The plastic bag containing the tape had caught on a mirrored petal; it flapped in the current beside the set-square shape of the pistol. Above, in the filtration system, bobbed a dark, oily squash ball.

'Let's get back to the road,' Spike said, and they turned and ran down the tunnel.

CHAPTER 76

They pushed through the shadowy shrubs of the El Minzah gardens. A street band was playing, the music blending with the cheers of a crowd. A police siren shrieked behind; they waited until the blue flashing lights had passed, then carried on through the foliage.

Empty wooden sunloungers surrounded the hotel pool. The underwater lights were on, the sight of the shimmering water giving Spike a queasy feeling in his stomach. He blinked away a flashback of Riddell's floating body.

They continued towards the glass doors. The first two were draped by velvet; through the next two along Spike made out the same trestle tables he had seen at the Roadshow. He turned back to Zahra, who kept tightening and loosening the knot on her headscarf. 'You surviving?' he said. Taking her hand, he led her to the darkest spot by the windows. 'I've got to find Jean-Baptiste. Will you wait here?'

She sat down on a sunlounger; he leaned in and kissed her.

The first glass doors were locked. Spike tried

the next, flattening his palms to the glass. The panes came apart; he glanced back at Zahra, then slipped quietly inside.

The buffet was even more lavish than before, skewers of rare lamb, samovars of mint tea, flaky Moroccan pastries, soft cloying nougat oozing with fondant. The curtains at the far end were closed. Indistinct voices came from behind.

Spike crept forward, seeking the midpoint of the curtains. Parting them with his thumbs, he peered through. Nadeer Ziyad was standing at the lectern. Among the Americans, Chinese, Japanese and Europeans in the audience, Spike saw more Moroccans than before, some in traditional dress, most in suits. The blonde bob of Regina Solness leaned towards the governor's shaven head.

'The festival of Eid ul-Fitr is a time for thanks,' Nadeer was saying, 'a time for universal gratitude. What better day, then, to . . .'

Spike widened the curtains further. The DVD trolley lay ahead in the aisle; beside it, in the same seat that Spike had taken at the Roadshow, Spike saw the lofty, proud head of Jean-Baptiste, dreadlocks tied back in a ponytail.

The screen behind Nadeer was down but it didn't look as though there were plans to use it. Two porters in fezzes flanked the door. They seemed as transfixed by Nadeer as everyone else.

'After this long period of hardship,' Nadeer continued, 'it is only natural to look forward to something bright, to a chance to make good the . . .'

A black cable snaked up the aisle towards the DVD player. Spike crouched down, feeling under the velvet until he had it in his hand. Looking again through the gap, he gave the cord a tug. There was a click of plastic on wood; he yanked again and saw Jean-Baptiste's head turn.

'A truly *global* initiative,' Nadeer was saying, 'which the rest of the world will look upon as . . .'

Jean-Baptiste stepped into the aisle and moved behind the DVD trolley. A constellation of red and green lights twinkled on the unit.

'. . . the *genuine* sense that history – Actually,' Nadeer broke off, 'we didn't book any VT for tonight, so –' The screen behind him lit up. The porters, not understanding Nadeer's English, reached for the switches by the door and turned off the lights.

'*Ama nas aghbiaa*,' Nadeer hissed in Arabic, but all eyes were on the screen now, making Nadeer himself turn.

The footage was silent. In grainy black and white, two men were arguing. Only one of their faces was visible, a tall handsome man in a turban. His indignant expression was one Spike had come to know well. The tall man raised his hands as though making an emphatic point. Suddenly his turban unravelled like a ribbon, arms falling limply by his sides as he sank to the ground out of shot, as quickly as if someone had flicked an 'off' switch. The man he had been arguing with leapt back in panic: Spike caught a glimpse of the thick salt-and-pepper hair of Ángel Castillo. A third man appeared in shot, face to the camera. His dark wavy hair was shorter but the glinting eyes and hawk's nose were unmistakable. Nadeer held a pistol with a silencer in one hand. He pointed it downwards; it kicked back and a cone of light flashed from the muzzle.

There was an intake of breath from the audience. A woman screamed. Nadeer looked round from the screen. 'I don't know what kind of prank this –'

The sequence restarted: Jean-Baptiste had edited it into a loop. A murmur rose as the turbaned man fell again from shot. 'This is outrageous . . .' Nadeer said as he stepped down from the lectern. He shouted in Arabic, then began striding down the aisle towards Jean-Baptiste.

The *danse macabre* was on its third showing; Spike heard a low sobbing from behind. He spun round to see Zahra watching the screen from over his shoulder.

Nadeer was running now towards the DVD unit as Jean-Baptiste backed up the aisle.

'*Oho*,' Spike heard behind. '*Oho, oho* . . .'

Most of the audience were on their feet. Heads turned as Zahra lurched for the gap between the curtains, flailing her arms at Nadeer, who stopped now, staring at her, face transformed for a moment into the small, scared boy Spike had seen captured in a school photograph.

The DVD was still playing as Jean-Baptiste came marching through the curtains and helped Spike drag Zahra, shrieking and clawing, back through the glass doors.

CHAPTER 77

They sat together in the darkness beneath the Medina walls. 'I've just spoken to my friend,' Spike said to Jean-Baptiste. 'He'll get you into Spain by tomorrow night. From then on, you're on your own.'

Spike turned to Zahra. Her arms were clasped around her knees, forehead leaning against them. Her shoulders shook. 'Zahra?'

She looked up, eyes brimming.

'We should get going. The man said we have to be there in half an hour.'

Zahra swallowed then gave a weak nod.

The three of them looked up as a firework exploded above, fired from the festival celebration on the beach, arcs of red glittering streamers embracing the night sky. Spike got to his feet, Jean-Baptiste following.

Zahra was still sitting; Spike reached down and took her hand. She stood, then hugged him, closing her eyes as the unshed tears spilled. 'Feels like my heart has been cut out,' she whispered.

'It's better to know,' Spike said.

Another volley of fireworks; Spike held Zahra's

hand as they set off up the coast road. A few metres on, Spike turned. Jean-Baptiste was still standing beneath the walls of the Medina, chin raised defiantly to the burning sky. 'What can I say?' he called out. 'I must like this city.'

Spike smiled and continued hand in hand with Zahra towards the port.

PART V

GIBRALTAR

CHAPTER 78

Spike threw open the French windows. It was a fine day outside, a few wisps of cloud, not too much wind. A new collection of Paganini's chamber music was playing on the iPod dock. Spike detected the gentle, fast-fading notes of a mandolin beneath the violin and bassoon. Altogether a more charming tone than the caprices. He wondered if he shouldn't take a trip to Italy when the weather cooled, see if he couldn't find the run-down quarter of Genoa that had produced this strange, lugubrious man.

The tax books were up on the shelf; open on Spike's desk were Blackstone's *Criminal Statutes* and a copy of the Immigration, Asylum and Refugee Act, the latter coffee-stained with scrutiny.

After switching off the music, and enjoying a brief but necessary burst of the ceiling fan, Spike put on his suit jacket and stuck his head into the adjacent office. 'Making any sense?'

Galliano looked up. He'd trimmed his goatee into a pointy, Lenin-style prong. A pudgy arm was bent protectively around the documents on his desk. 'I'll let you have a butcher's once I'm done.'

Loose sheets of paper littered the floor; billowing from his picture rail was a large white dress shirt. 'See you at the party later?' Spike said.

'*En plan* nice.'

Spike strolled up Main Street towards the Moorish Castle. Two police vans were parked outside; he buzzed himself in and approached the front desk.

'You can't seem to keep away these days,' Alan Gaggero said, looking up from his crossword.

'Got a secret crush on you, Alan.'

'I'll ask Ida to take you down. I-*da*! Long queues today at the border, they tell me.'

'That's the Spanish for you, Alan. *Slopis* and *chiteros* all.'

The stout form of Ida Milby-Low materialised to escort Spike past the scanner and into the dank, lower reaches of the castle.

CHAPTER 79

Spike stood beneath the CCTV camera and planted a flake of tissue on the lens. He stepped away from the wall just as the door opened. 'Quarter of an hour do you?' asked Ida.

'Better make it half.'

'*Vale vishi*.'

The moment the bolt closed, Spike pulled the detainee towards him. They kissed for a full minute, each holding the other close. Spike heard Arabic words rustle in his ear like palm fronds in the levanter.

'What does that mean?' he asked as he sat down at the table.

'I'll give you a full demonstration once I'm out of here,' Zahra replied.

Spike bent down to remove a stack of papers from his briefcase. 'The good news is we've been able to fast-track your application,' he said. 'The hearing's set for Wednesday. I just need you to initial this.'

Zahra took the pen then signed.

'Aren't you going to read it first?'

'I trust you.'

Spike reached over and turned the page. 'We're going for "Asylum from Persecution". Given the latest events in Tangiers, I can't see there being a problem.'

Zahra initialled the other document, then sat back, slim arms folded across her kaftan. Her face was drawn but her eyes were bright. 'Tell me,' she said.

She knew the first part already. After the unexpected screening at the El Minzah Hotel, all foreign investors had withdrawn from the Dunetech deal. In an investigation led personally by the governor of Tangiers, the hangar at the Dunetech site had been dug up and the concrete-embalmed body of Ibrahim al-Mahmoud discovered. Nadeer Ziyad had been arrested on suspicion of murder and his alibi for the night of the death of Esperanza Castillo re-examined – he had indeed been in Rabat, yet flight records revealed he had returned by helicopter and could therefore have been back in Tangiers by late afternoon. Solomon Hassan had since been released, all charges dropped.

'Now they're reinvestigating Abdallah's death too,' Spike said. 'Basically, whatever the Moroccan authorities can throw at Nadeer, they will. A modern-day Icarus, my father keeps saying. Anything to keep soaring higher.'

'He's a coward and a murderer. And Ángel Castillo?'

Spike reached for his briefcase and took out a Moroccan newspaper. 'Jumped off his roof last week. Landed on a shack made of shopping trolleys.'

'And you think this will help my application?'

'Nadeer still has a lot of influence in Morocco. Two Bedouins dead. Not safe for you to go back.'

Zahra shut her eyes. 'They buried my father yesterday. In the sacred place. I spoke to Othman on the phone.'

The sound of that name caused Spike's tongue to throb. He put the documents back in his briefcase.

'How about the other man?' Zahra said.

'What other man?'

'In the swimming pool.'

'Oh, him,' Spike said. 'Inspector Eldrassi concluded he must have accidentally brushed against the heliopod, received an electric shock, and ended up pushing it and himself into the water. Funny that, as it was almost impossible to tip over.'

Zahra gave Spike an ironic look. 'How about the gun?'

'Oddly enough, that didn't seem to come up.'

A heavy steel clank cut the air.

'Two more days,' Spike said, making a 'V' for victory. 'Just two more.'

CHAPTER 80

Spike, Rufus and General Ironside walked side by side beneath Southport Gate, where the faded coat of arms of Charles V of Spain still showed on the pink stucco. Rufus's short-sleeved shirt revealed scrawny, liver-spotted wrists. A canvas tote bag was hooked over one shoulder, which he had refused to let Spike carry.

Spike encouraged General Ironside's lead away from a lamp post. As they passed the entrance to the Trafalgar Cemetery, Spike glanced in at the neat gravestones, thinking of the disordered chanting of the Marshan. A Coke can had been jammed on one of the spikes of the metal railings, like some dire medieval warning to soft-drink fans.

'And you think Margo Hassan will be there?' Rufus said.

'She wouldn't miss it.'

'Good-oh,' said Rufus, brushing back his mane of silver hair, 'there's one waiting.'

They crossed the forecourt to the ticket hut. Spike took out a ten-pound note but the pretty salesgirl shook her head. 'You with the Hassan party?'

'That's right.'

'All taken care of. *Pish pine.*'

Rufus batted away Spike's hand as he tried to help him into the cable car. By degrees, Rufus rocked himself inside before lowering himself painfully down onto the furthest bench. Spike gathered the General in his arms and climbed in too. The cogs began to crunch as the car soared into the void.

Spike stared out. The unadorned facade of the Great Synagogue appeared to the right, the first to be built on the Iberian peninsula after Spain had expelled the Sephardic Jews in the fifteenth century. A Hindu temple stood alongside, while on the far left rose the mosque and minaret of Europa Point, with the Catholic and Anglican cathedrals emerging slowly into view in front.

'Had a letter from Malta this morning,' Rufus said.

Spike looked round. Rufus's narrow, sockless ankles were exposed where his trousers had ridden up. 'From your uncle and aunt. They want us to come over in May.'

'Why the sudden olive branch?'

'It would have been your mother's sixtieth birthday.' Rufus turned and gazed out as another no-frills jumbo banked round to land on Gib's tiny, aircraft-carrier-sized runway.

'Want to go?' Spike said.

Rufus jutted a non-committal lip.

'We could stop off at Genoa. Make a holiday of it.'

'Maybe, son. Maybe.'

Spike craned his neck as they passed beneath the final pylon. The Upper Rock was closed to tourists at this hour but the cable-car terrace was swarming with people. 'Looks like he's hired out the whole place.'

'Man of means,' Rufus said, reaching down to tickle General Ironside's ribs.

CHAPTER 81

As soon as they were up the steps, Rufus tottered away towards Margo Hassan, who broke off a conversation to kiss him hello. Over by the bar, Peter Galliano was puffing on a Silk Cut Ultra as he relayed a lengthy anecdote to two bearded men wearing yarmulkes.

A Spanish waitress passed with a tray of tumblers; Spike took two. 'Told you we'd have that drink,' he said as he gave one to Jessica Navarro.

'It doesn't count if it's free.'

They stepped out of the bar area onto the rear terrace, a semicircular platform protruding from the flank of the Rock. The sun was setting, pinking up the water that surrounded on three sides, Mediterranean to the east, Atlantic to the west, Straits interlinking. Ahead, the thin sandy isthmus that connected Gibraltar to Spain pointed at La Línea like an accusation. In contrast to the marshy flatlands of the *campo* beyond, the Rock rose as dramatically and mysteriously as a sphinx.

'I hear she's very beautiful,' Jessica said.

'Who's that?'

'Oh, don't be coy with me, Spike Sanguinetti.

Just your type, too. Ripe for the rescuing.' Above her white capri pants, Jessica wore a silver satin top that reminded Spike of Regina Solness. Her chestnut hair was loose from its bun, thick and glossy. 'Know what they're calling you at the station now?'

'Surprise me.'

'The Devil's Advocate.'

'Bit harsh.'

'One week in Tangiers and everyone ends up dead.'

Spike switched his empty glass for a full one from a passing tray.

'Prison looks like it's done him good,' Jessica said, gesturing across the terrace to where Solomon Hassan was working the crowd, clean-shaven in an oxford shirt, pressed chinos and navy docksider shoes. His pouchy cheeks had been levelled off and he seemed taller somehow, shoulders back, barrel chest out. Comb grooves remained in the slicked, dark hair and his little round spectacles had been replaced by designer tortoiseshell frames.

'You scrub up pretty well yourself,' Spike said. 'Your hair looks good down.'

Jessica gave a grimace. 'Please, Spike.'

Feeling a tap on the shoulder, Spike turned to see Margo Hassan, head bowed, palms out. 'What you've done,' she said, voice quaking, 'it's beyond . . . just *beyond* . . .'

Jessica mouthed 'I'll leave you to it' and headed back inside to the bar. Mrs Hassan thrust out both arms, drawing Spike into the same low-cut green top she'd worn in his office. Her perfume was excessive.

'He'll reward you, of course,' she said as she reached up to dab her lipstick from Spike's face. 'He told me so himself.'

'He's already paid my fees and expenses.'

'I mean personally. He'll be a rich man soon.'

'Will he?'

'Well, someone has to resurrect Dunetech. It's a good company. Millions of lives to be saved.'

'I think Solomon may be some way down the pecking order.'

Mrs Hassan looked askance. 'My Solly? I wouldn't be so sure.'

Inside, Rufus was sitting by the picture window, watercolour pad on lap, General Ironside dozing beneath his chair. He beckoned to Margo Hassan, who squeezed Spike's hand before walking over.

On the far side of the terrace, Solomon was listening to the chat of a rival lawyer. He lowered his gaze as Jessica passed him, clamping his eyes onto the tight fit of her trousers, scanning from her bare calves to her neat behind. Seeing Spike watching, he returned to his conversation.

Spike felt his face grow hot as he sipped his drink. From the corner of his eye he saw Solomon coming over. 'My friend and saviour,' Solomon said, arms cruciform, mineral water in hand.

'I hear you're off back to Tangiers,' Spike said.

Solomon lowered his hands. He had two skin-coloured plasters around the thumbnails. 'Be a shame for a few bad apples to spoil the barrel.'

'Thought you'd have had enough of that place.'

'Got a meeting with the governor. See what we can salvage from the wreckage.'

'No catamaran till Friday.'

'I chartered a Sunseeker. Wanted to return in more style than I left.'

'Leaving tonight?'

'At nine. But feel free to stay on. The bar's open late.'

Spike felt the blood start to thump in his ears like a drum.

'You OK, *picha*?' Solomon said. 'You look a little flushed.'

'Must be the punch.'

'Tequila sunrise,' Solomon corrected. 'Seemed . . . appropriate.' He raised a hand to his ear in a 'call me' gesture as a suit left the party.

'What's Interzone Holdings?'

Solomon's bull neck swivelled Spike's way.

'How much is it worth to you? Thirty million? Forty?'

Solomon's new spectacles were of a clearer glass, the large empty pupils behind them reminding Spike of something he couldn't quite place. 'Let's imagine a scenario,' Spike said quietly. 'A young man in a hurry is promised a chunk of a company that's about to become very valuable. A girl is threatening to reveal something that will compromise that value.

The girl is stubborn and won't be persuaded. A man like that might take . . . desperate measures.'

Solomon shrugged. 'That man is Nadeer Ziyad.'

'What if Nadeer were just mopping up your mess?' Spike hissed. 'If Nadeer committed his crime years ago, then was forced to keep yours hidden from investors when you lashed out at Esperanza?'

Solomon stared back blankly until his face selected a smile. He threw a heavy arm over Spike's shoulder, exposing a dark oval of perspiration on his shirt. 'I know your games by now, Mr Sanguinetti,' he grinned. 'They're what make you such a formidable advocate.'

Disco music started in the bar. More tequila sunrises circulated. Spike freed himself from Solomon's grip and took out his mobile phone. 'There's still an hour till your boat goes,' he said. 'Let's get some air.'

Spike pushed through the crowd, sensing Jessica and Galliano's enquiring stares. Solomon remained behind, dead-eyed, an amused smile still playing on his lips.

CHAPTER 82

Spike walked away from the cable-car station up the footpath that ran along the top of the Rock. The ground above was screened off by the barbed-wire fence of an MI6 listening post, one of the last remaining British military installations – a giant golf ball on a tee, rows of satellite dishes, a barred roadway leading down to a secret network of caves and tunnels inside the Rock.

A musty, damp-dog smell came from up ahead. Three grey apes were lounging in the dust, circles of bluebottles orbiting their heads. Fruit and vegetables were provided in the Apes' Den, but they were always greedy for that extra stolen snack. Spike made a lunge at them with his arms; they consented to hop lazily onto a limestone outcrop.

At the point where the music from the party had dulled to a distant throb, Spike stopped on the path. A crumbling stone platform extended outwards, with a low parapet wall protecting from the drop down the Rock, part of the eighteenth-century fortifications built to provide flanking fire on besieging Spanish troops. A thousand feet below looped the coast road; Spike recognised the spot where his mother's Sunbeam Alpine had smashed over the cliffs all those years ago. A herring gull displayed its broad, off-white wingspan in the nothingness. Beyond, the last rays of the sun bloodstained the Straits.

A noise came from behind: Spike spun round to see Solomon Hassan striding up the path. The apes watched on from their crag. The limestone of the Rock glowed a soft red.

'You intrigue me, *compa*,' Solomon called out as he joined Spike on the platform. His smile remained in place but moisture beaded his upper lip.

Spike still had his phone in his hand; he held it out and snapped a photo, hearing the camera give its ersatz click. As he checked the picture, he realised what Solomon's empty pupils reminded him of – the stained, wooden masks hanging on the walls of Ángel Castillo's house. He swivelled the screen to Solomon, now just a foot away. 'Look at yourself.'

Solomon tilted his head. Shoulder muscles rippled his sweaty shirt.

'That fat, feeble face.'

Solomon frowned, then turned to glance out to sea. Spike followed his gaze to where a sleek Sunseeker motor yacht was heading for Marina Bay, cruising effortlessly over the hidden currents.

'At the party just now,' Spike said, still holding out the photo, 'I remembered something Jessica Navarro told me. That you had a smell about you. One of life's fall guys. A born loser.'

Solomon looked back at his own image, then took a step forward, forcing Spike closer to the parapet.

'And suddenly it made sense,' Spike said, edging away from a gap in the wall. 'Nadeer hung you out to dry, didn't he? He asked you to get close to Esperanza, to persuade her not to tell the police about the Bedouin's murder. So you befriended her. Slept with her. But still she wouldn't budge. So back you went to Nadeer, explained the situation until he sweetened the deal, set up Interzone Holdings, a slice of the action if you could shut her up for good. You knew Dunetech had the police in their pocket – all you needed to do was pluck up the courage, buy a knife, then choose a discreet location. But Nadeer double-crossed you.'

Solomon looked above the handset into Spike's face, his irises swallowed up by pupils as dark and deep as tunnels. 'Nadeer behaved exactly as I thought he would,' he said. 'As did you, my friend.'

It was Spike's turn to frown. 'I don't follow.'

'Of course not, Spike. Because you're always one step ahead.'

Spike edged further along the wall. 'You mean you *knew* the police would come after you?'

'I suspected they might.'

'Then why risk killing her? I don't . . .'

Spike watched Solomon turn and glance up at the satellite dishes which crowned the peak of the Rock.

'You always knew about the videotape,' Spike said.

'Who do you think paid that fat fuck his hush money?'

'You were drip-feeding me information . . . just enough to help me to find the tape.'

'I knew you'd get there eventually. You never could resist a damsel in distress.'

'And once the tape was found,' Spike went on, 'you knew it was inevitable that the crime you committed would be pinned on Nadeer.'

'Or Castillo. Let's not forget he was in the video too. Joint enterprise murder, if my legal research is up to scratch.'

'Leaving you in full control of Dunetech.'

Solomon's thick lips formed a smirk.

'How about Toby Riddell? How could you know that –'

'Riddell would just have followed the pay cheque,' Solomon said. 'A mere foot soldier, Spike, same as you. Same as most people.' He removed a BlackBerry from the pocket of his chinos. 'It's hardly a fucking war crime, anyway,' he muttered as he twisted the cog. 'Christ. Get over it.'

With a slide of the thumb, Spike clicked off the record button on his phone and walked back up to the path. A cluster of stone-pine saplings had seeded themselves in the scrub; Spike drew their resinous, Mediterranean perfume deep into his lungs as he found play on the handset and put it to his ear. Solomon's voice returned unencumbered by ambient noise: '*You're always one step ahead . . .*'

Switching off the recording, Spike dialled Jessica Navarro's number. As he waited for her to pick up, he stared out from the Rock. The sun had finally gone and the Straits were cast in shadow. Spike looked away and continued up the path.

MARJORY HARPER is Professor of History at the University of Aberdeen, and Visiting Professor at the Centre for History, University of the Highlands and Islands. Her book *Adventurers and Exiles* won the Saltire Society Award for the Scottish History Book of the Year in 2004, and *Scotland No More?* was shortlisted for the same Saltire Society Award and won the University of Guelph's Frank Watson Prize. Her current teaching responsibilities focus on directing the University of Aberdeen's innovative online Masters Programme in Scottish Heritage, which was launched in September 2017, and she is involved in an ongoing oral history research project, as well as research into health and migration.

By the same author:

Adventurers and Exiles, Profile, 2003
Scotland No More?, Luath Press, 2012

Testimonies of Transition

Voices from the Scottish Diaspora

MARJORY HARPER

Luath Press Limited

EDINBURGH

www.luath.co.uk

To Andrew

First published 2018

ISBN: 978-1-912147-31-1

The paper used in this book is recyclable.
It is made from low chlorine pulps produced in a low energy,
low emissions manner from renewable forests.

Printed in the UK by Bell & Bain Ltd., Glasgow

Typeset in 11 point Sabon by Main Point Books, Edinburgh

Contents

Acknowledgements

THIS BOOK HAS been a labour of love. It has taken me to three continents, reuniting me with old friends and introducing me to a host of new ones. Where personal visits were not possible, the ever-advancing wonders of technology allowed me to engage in many enlightening conversations with people whom I have not yet been able to meet.

Wherever I have gone, I have been received with warmth, hospitality and encouragement. In Australia, I am immensely grateful to Rob and Jane Linn, Kirstie Moar, and Graham Hannaford, for their hospitality, practical support, and wise insights, which allowed me to make best use of my time in Adelaide, Toowoomba and Canberra respectively. An invitation from Flinders University to participate in a seminar in honour of my friend and colleague, Eric Richards, generously provided the initial opportunity to go to Australia, and at that very happy gathering in 2015 I engaged with colleagues from across the world. Thanks to the Board of Trustees of Newstead House, Brisbane, and Kirstie Moar, I was able to deliver a public lecture in Brisbane, which in turn led me to a number of new interviewees. In Canberra, the staff of the Oral History and Folklore Section at the National Library of Australia kindly invited me to give a public lecture on oral testimony and emigration, and devoted a day to discussing my project with me and showing me around the library. I am particularly grateful to Marian Hanley, Kevin Bradley, Shelly Grant and Margy Burn for their interest and support. Thanks are also due to the National Library of Australia for permission to quote from two of their oral history collections in this book.

In 2010, a kind invitation from Angela McCarthy of the University of Otago, and a grant from the Royal Society of Edinburgh, enabled me to visit Dunedin, where in the course of a week I met several new friends, and conducted a number of interviews. As well as the interviewees, I am particularly grateful to Denise Montgomery, Kathy Petrie, and Jill Harland for their continuing friendship and support. Elsewhere in New Zealand, I am indebted to Megan Hutching for granting me access to the documentation associated with her oral history study, *Long Journey for Sevenpence*.

During many visits to Canada, I have benefited from long-standing connections with the Scottish Studies Centre at the University of Guelph, Ontario, and the Scottish Studies Centre at Simon Fraser University, Vancouver. As well as providing me with opportunities to share my research through public lectures, seminars and workshops, my involvement with these Centres has allowed me to identify and meet a number of interviewees. I am also grateful to Maureen and the late Ray Eagle of Vancouver for their hospitality and for putting me in touch with a number of interviewees in and around that city. In Halifax, Nova Scotia, I received invaluable assistance from the staff of the Canadian

Museum of Immigration at Pier 21, where oral historians Steve Schwinghamer and Sinisa Obradovic have provided me with helpful statistical information. Elsewhere in Canada, Georgina Taylor initially alerted me to the riches of the Saskatchewan Archives Board's pioneer questionnaires, and in Ottawa I continue to enjoy frequent discussions about oral history with Marilyn Barber of Carleton University. In the United States, during a visit to New York City in 2013 I enjoyed the hospitality of Camilla Hellman and Alan Bain of the American-Scottish Foundation. In the south-west USA, the wisdom and encouragement of Margaret Connell Szasz and the late Ferenc Szasz, both of the University of New Mexico, have been of incalculable benefit to me for more than two decades.

Back in Scotland, I am indebted to my former Head of School at the University of Aberdeen, John Morrison, for allowing me to pursue my research and writing agenda unhindered. My colleague Andrew Dilley supplied me with helpful references to material in the National Archives of Australia, and Ted Ranson regularly alerts me to relevant snippets from the archives of the American and Canadian press. Archivist Angus Johnson from Shetland Archives has drawn my attention to numerous articles about emigrants in the *Shetland Times*. Jim Hunter, Professor Emeritus of the Centre for History at the University of the Highlands and Islands, is a constant source of support, as is the current Director, David Worthington, and indeed all the staff at the Centre, with which I am privileged to maintain a connection. In Edinburgh, I am grateful to the staff of the Edinburgh Theological Seminary for providing, once at very short notice, a comfortable and quiet venue in which to conduct interviews, and to Ewen Cameron of the University of Edinburgh for similar assistance.

Three individuals – Lauren Brancaz, Kirstie Moar, and Kirk Reid – have rendered huge assistance in compiling meticulous written summaries of a number of interviews, and Kirstie also undertook four interviews on my behalf in Queensland. A grant from the Research Institute of Irish and Scottish Studies at the University of Aberdeen generously funded the preparation of the summaries undertaken by Kirk and Lauren.

My especial thanks go to the interviewees themselves, who have given generously of their time in telling me of their experiences as emigrants, sojourners and returners. In meeting these individuals, and recording their testimony, I have been richly rewarded. Not only have I been able to compile a rich databank of evidence and insights: I have made many lasting friendships, not least with those whom I have met on more than one occasion. As I have been deploying their testimony to illustrate the themes of this book, their accents, idioms, enthusiasms – and occasionally their sorrows – have resonated through almost every page. This book has only come to fruition because of their interest and encouragement, and I thank them profoundly for their involvement in that collaborative effort. I hope they have enjoyed the experience even half as much as I have.

CHAPTER 1

Listening to Emigrants:[1] Evaluating Personal Testimony

Introducing the evidence

'I HAVE NOT regretted, even for two minutes, that I came here.' Murdo MacIver's ringing endorsement of his decision to settle in Vancouver in 1953 contrasts starkly with the painful experiences of his fellow Hebridean, Ena Macdonald, who emigrated to Australia a decade later. 'I was homesick before I even went,' she recalled. 'It was crazy, absolutely crazy. I should never have gone.'[2]

Personal testimony provides a powerful lens through which to view the complex and often contradictory saga of Scottish emigration. Not only does it offer multiple narratives of the motives, expectations and experiences of successive generations of individuals and families: it can also be used to explore broader issues about the cultural and political spirit of the age, as well as the socio-economic context that triggered tidal waves and trickles of emigration. By adding participants' voices to top-down, policy-based studies, personal testimony combines solid academic credentials with popular appeal, by demonstrating – through individuals like Murdo and Ena – the practical impact of principles and procedures on the lives of real people, with whose sentiments we can readily identify.

Since the 1980s we have seen the ever-expanding public celebration of Scotland's global heritage. New York's Tartan Day, organised in 1982 as a one-off event, has been absorbed into Scotland Week, North America's 'annual celebration of all things Scottish'.[3] Australia and New Zealand followed suit in 1989 with International Tartan Day, and in 2006 the Scottish Argentine Society inaugurated a Tartan Day parade in Buenos Aires.[4] The Scottish government climbed on the bandwagon in 2009 with the first 'Year of Homecoming', repeated in 2014, although Shetland had seen the commercial potential of wooing homecoming tourists as early as 1960, when it organised its first 'hamefarin' celebration.[5] As these events demonstrate, Scotland's history cannot be separated from the saga of its diaspora: the millions of emigrants who in various ways implanted aspects of their Scottish identity in the lands where they settled or sojourned. And at the heart of that dispersal lie stories of human adventure, achievement and adversity, experiences which are best expressed in the participants' own words. Some of their stories emerge in the ensuing narrative, which draws, first and foremost, on an extensive collection of interviews to explore aspirations and decision-making processes; recruitment strategies; physical transitions; adjustment and integration in home, school, workplace and community; dealing with adversity; attitudes to Scottish identity; and experiences of 'homecoming'. The oral evidence is taken from an ongoing interviewing project, entitled 'Emigrant Voices', which documents Scottish emigration in the 20th and early 21st centuries through my recorded conversations with over 100 individuals over more than 15 years.

In order to contextualise the interviewees' relatively recent experiences, their opinions and recollections are blended and compared with emigrant testimony taken from other collections, earlier periods, and different genres. AJP Taylor may have dismissed oral history as nothing more than 'old men drooling about their youth',[6] but since he made that notorious pronouncement in 1972, oral testimony has become a well-established analytical tool, skilfully wielded in the hands of pioneers like Paul Thompson, Rob Perks, Alistair Thomson and Alessandro Portelli, and enthusiastically adopted by armies of amateur researchers.[7] As Portelli has pointed out, the innovative elements of oral sources include the collaboration involved in dialogue, where 'the historian's agenda must meet the agenda of the narrator'; illumination of the relationship between events themselves and their significance within the lives of the narrators; and a foregrounding of the role of 'memory, narrative, subjectivity [and] dialogue' in historical analysis.[8]

In 1999 Alistair Thomson reviewed the scholarship with specific reference to migration, which he claimed was 'one of the most important themes of oral history research'.[9] As well as giving access to the complex 'internal worlds' of the participants, interviews with migrants demonstrated the dynamic relationship between memory and identity at different stages in the lives of individuals, families and communities.[10] Since Thomson's article appeared a few more historians have deployed oral testimony in studies of emigration to the Antipodes and North America, using either their own recordings, or existing published collections of interviews.[11] Some of the examples that are used in this book to amplify the study or expand its chronology are taken from well-known archival collections in the United States, Canada and

Australia, but the treasure hunt also extended to more obscure materials lodged in state or provincial repositories, heritage societies and local libraries. These recordings have been consulted *in situ*, purchased, or accessed online. The Ellis Island Oral History Project, initiated in 1973, has recorded the recollections of almost 1,900 of the 12 million individuals (including around 600,000 Scots) who passed through the portals of the United States' main immigrant processing station in New York harbour between 1892 and 1954. The interviews document the origins, motives, journeys, arrival and settlement of the immigrants. Across the border in Nova Scotia, the Canadian Museum of Immigration in Halifax has, since 2000, assembled a growing collection of interviews with immigrants (currently over 900 individuals from over 80 countries), many of whom entered the country through the portals of Pier 21 between 1928 and 1971. It includes 26 interviews with Scots.[12] On the other side of Canada, Simon Fraser University's Centre for Scottish Studies in Vancouver hosts 'Scottish Voices from the West', an ongoing oral history archive, inaugurated in 2003, that includes four of the individuals featured in the 'Emigrant Voices' collection. Australian material has been sourced from the National Library of Australia's Oral History and Folklore Division, specifically from the recent 'Scots in Australia' pilot oral history project.[13] Recourse has also been made to an older collection, the New South Wales Bicentennial Oral History Project, which interviewed 200 people – including Scots – about their recollections of the period 1900–1930.[14] That venture was triggered by the concern of the Ethnic Affairs Commission of New South Wales that 'the experiences of large numbers of migrants who had come to Australia' – albeit mainly those from non-English-speaking backgrounds – were not being recorded and preserved and therefore 'would not be reflected in writing about and understanding modern Australia.'[15]

The preservation of oral testimony in its raw form, and our ability to savour its orality, became possible with the invention of the reel-to-reel tape recorder. The concept of an oral history archive was pioneered by Allan Nevins, an American historian and journalist, who in 1948 established the Oral History Research Office at Columbia University, New York. Nevins, however, did not value the orality of his interviews with elite businessmen and politicians: his objective was to transcribe the recordings into typed manuscripts for the use of researchers, without necessarily preserving the interviews themselves.[16] It was some time before oral history was institutionalised, first in the United States, where the Oral History Association was formed in 1967. Britain, Canada, Australia and New Zealand followed suit by inaugurating similar national organisations in 1973, 1974, 1978 and 1986 respectively,[17] but in 1973 TC Smout was pessimistic about the future of oral history in Scotland. Speaking in Edinburgh at the inaugural conference of the British Oral History

Society, he singled out the neglect of emigrant testimony as a particularly glaring historiographical omission which had wider implications. Seven years earlier Gordon Donaldson's pioneering book, *The Scots Overseas*,[18] had turned the spotlight on the significance of the Scottish diaspora, and Smout's plea was for more attention to be paid to the (literal) voices of ordinary emigrants, in the context of his general concern to promote social history:

> Large Scottish emigrant colonies exist abroad, some of them Gaelic speaking – but attempts to record their oral history are scarcely afloat, and little effort seems to have been made to discover in a systematic way whether or not foreigners are doing the job for us in countries where the diaspora live [sic]. A very good case indeed could be made out for substantial backing for all these ventures, but unless Scotland is prepared to enter the fray and approach with zestful leadership and well thought-out projects, Scottish oral history... will be left behind [and] the whole study of history in Scotland will suffer again.[19]

Scotland did indeed enter the fray, though not immediately, and not specifically in pursuit of emigrants' stories. Edinburgh University's School of Scottish Studies, established in 1951, already had a sound archive, which included material from the diaspora, but its emphasis was on oral *traditions*, rather than oral *history*. It was only in the 1990s that dedicated oral history projects were inaugurated, with the establishment of Strathclyde University's Oral History Centre, followed by 'Lives in the Oil Industry', a joint venture between the British Library's National Life Story Collection and the University of Aberdeen. These Scottish developments were part of a wider international pattern of increased activity, which simultaneously reflected and stimulated the acceptance of oral testimony as a scholarly methodology. The availability of more sophisticated, less intrusive, technologies (cassettes and then digital recorders) also gave rise – sometimes haphazardly – to numerous community ventures, as well as private collections compiled by individual researchers.

As portable equipment and interaction with other disciplines expanded the scope of field work, so the objectives of the interview and the techniques of the interviewer have also changed. In particular, Nevins' elitist approach has been replaced by an emphasis on ordinary life histories whose content is steered by the story-teller, rather than the interviewer. The rigid questionnaires which framed – and constrained – interviews conducted by the first generation of oral historians have given way to semi-structured, more fluid agendas which allow the interviewing project's particular themes to be woven into a broader tapestry of whole life stories. The significance of orality has also been recognised in a way that was not the case in the early days of practitioners like Nevins, when it was common practice, particularly in the US, to destroy the audio tapes once the interviews had been transcribed.[20]

It is perhaps not surprising that questionnaires were frequently deployed by early oral historians, for – in terms of eliciting personal testimony – the questionnaire was the predecessor of the interview. During the Depression, it was used in the United States, when more than 6,000 writers were recruited by the New Deal Federal Writers' Project, to interview over 10,000 ordinary Americans about their everyday lives.[21] The questionnaire had a particularly long pedigree in Scotland. In the 1790s Sir John Sinclair badgered the country's 938 parish ministers to answer 160 questions about past and present life in their parishes, information which he then used to compile his renowned 21-volume *Statistical Account of Scotland.* Sinclair's survey set a pattern of questionnaire-based statistical investigation and reporting that in the following centuries was adopted or adapted by generations of royal commissions and select committees. Rooted in the oral or written evidence or traditions of witnesses, some of these reports turned the spotlight on the causes and consequences of emigration, while their methodology reflects the filtering of personal testimony and memory through a mediator's pen.[22]

Written questionnaires were also used to elicit reflections from emigrants once they had reached their destinations, and two such collections occasionally play a walk-on, comparative role in this book. During the 1950s the Saskatchewan Archives Board commissioned a major survey of pioneers whose memories stretched back to the 1870s. A set of 11 questionnaires sought information on reasons for emigrating, housing, health, diet, religion, education, recreation, farming, folklore, local government, and Christmas from settlers who had come to the prairies between 1878 and 1914. Each questionnaire comprised a minimum of 40 questions, and the survey elicited over 3,500 replies.[23] Four decades later, and on another continent, approximately 280 questionnaires were collected by Megan Hutching as part of her preparatory research for an oral history of post-war assisted immigration to New Zealand, and the collection was donated to the National Library of New Zealand in 2006.[24]

If oral history is still a relatively 'new kid on the block'[25] and responses to questionnaires are limited by the prescriptive format of many such surveys, there is another source of personal testimony that offers both chronological spread and huge breadth of content. Emigrant letters have been around for as long as there has been emigration. They have been preserved by recipients at both ends of the process, have been pored over by scholars, and are injected into this book from time to time in order to strengthen the comparative roots in which the analysis of oral testimony is embedded. Until the coming of the telephone, and in the absence of personal visits, the exchange of letters was the only means of transmitting information between emigrants and their homeland. They retained their dominance until the invention of the internet, for international telephone calls were expensive, and generally made only at times of crisis or celebration. Letters, however, were a common and expected form of regular communication, so any delay or cessation in their delivery was likely to cause disappointment, and sometimes consternation or alarm.[26] James Adam, an emigrant who was sent back to Scotland as a recruitment agent for the New Zealand government in the 1850s, wrote of having met 'an aged mother [who] requested a prayer on behalf of a careless son in New Zealand who had *never* written to his sorrowing mother'.[27] Adam's guidebook advised every emigrant to write home once a month, but some wrote weekly or even more frequently, and these missives were eagerly anticipated. In their study based on the oral testimony of English settlers in Canada since 1945, Marilyn Barber and Murray Watson highlight the importance of frequent air letters, many of which were retained in family archives.[28] Annie MacRitchie, who emigrated from the Isle of Lewis to Detroit in 1953, has preserved several boxes of correspondence that she both received and sent, and still remembers the thrill of receiving news from home:

> Every day I wrote, and every day I got plenty of mail from my parents, my sister – my sisters – my brother, all our relatives, and all my friends. So every day... my treat was looking forward to the mail man.[29]

The foundations for such regular communication had been laid during the previous century, when mass emigration, coupled with an expanding international business traffic, gave rise to modern postal systems that in turn encouraged further epistolary exchanges.[30] It is impossible either to identify the full extent of emigrant correspondence, or to calculate the percentage that survives, but in 1885 the New Zealand Post Office and Telegraph Department estimated that almost 1.1 million letters had left the country for Britain and Ireland that year, equivalent to five letters for every UK-born resident, or about a letter a month for each household.[31] 'Immigrant letters', David Gerber asserts, are 'probably the largest single body of the writing of ordinary people to which historians have access',[32] and they provide a powerful lens through which to scrutinise individuals' attitudes and emotions, as well as their actions and experiences. At the same time they can illuminate broader trends about the spirit of the age, and the circumstances that triggered emigration as a generic movement, rather than simply being the outcome of multitudes of individual decisions.

Private letters were generally conversations between correspondents who knew each other. Even if the exchange was sometimes sporadic, and only one side of the dialogue has been passed down, they can offer a different, more contemporary, and more intimate insight into emigration than the retrospective, semi-public and perhaps more guarded reflections of interviewees who are conversing with strangers. Of course, letters had multiple purposes, and not all were neutral or personal missives. Some correspondents had a self-conscious agenda to vindicate their decision or publicise their experiences. 'You will show this letter to as many of our friends as possible', was John Mackie's instruction when he wrote from South Australia's Clare Valley to his brother in Aberdeenshire in 1851. He suggested that 'perhaps the best way' to spread the good news that he was 'living and liking the Antipodes well' would be to publish his lengthy letter in the regional newspaper, a suggestion which was duly followed.[33] Letters from overseas might also be passed around the emigrants' home communities, sometimes with the deliberate objective of stimulating further emigration. Some went further, and enclosed a remittance or prepaid ticket. Recruitment letters were didactic compositions, similar in style and content to the masses of published guidebooks, which themselves relied heavily on anthologies of emigrant correspondence to spread their evangelistic message. In other cases letters were simply diaristic descriptions of daily life, close cousins of the journals kept by emigrants in transit or (less commonly) after they had reached their destination. A handful of such diaries completes the supporting cast of written sources that help us listen more effectively to the emigrant voices that take centre stage in this study.

Evaluating emigrant testimony

We can only listen effectively if we are aware of bias, which in turn requires some knowledge of context. Whether we are hearing or reading, we have to ask: who is speaking or writing, to whom, when, where, and why? A diary was, in David Gerber's words, essentially 'a dialogue with oneself', even if reconfigured into letter form for transmission to the homeland.[34] Diarists ranged from the utterly self-absorbed to individuals who engaged reflectively with their companions and surroundings. Unlike the retrospective testimony found in memoirs and most interviews, these texts can shed a useful light on the immediate reactions of emigrants to the situations in which they found themselves, most commonly in the early stages of transition.

Emigrant correspondence is a popular and multi-layered source, which has to be handled with particular care. The sheer volume and varied provenance of emigrant letters, as well as their vast range of objectives, constituencies and styles, defy categorisation. Since letters generally tell a story, usually in an accessible way, they are attractive to researchers and readers, who may use them simply to illustrate particular projects while neglecting to probe the generic significance of the medium or the value of theoretical perspectives.

We must also read between the lines in order to detect how the attitudes and emotions expressed in letters, as well as their actual structure, were shaped by the interaction of factors such as the writers' gender, age, education, and family and cultural background.[35] The reasons for self-censorship and silence have to be taken into account, as does the transmission of misleading information, either deliberately or inadvertently, as correspondents underplayed or overstated problems and achievements. As Mary Chamberlain discovered, Barbadian immigrants to the UK after the war did not want to upset families who had loaned them money for the journey by admitting that their image of the welcoming 'mother county' had been shattered by the realities of racial discrimination and menial work.[36]

These influences are subtle and often more difficult to detect than the obvious propaganda in published collections of correspondence that were commissioned, selected and subsidised by charitable emigration societies (with a view to fund-raising for specific groups) or government agencies (in order to trigger a further outflow of targeted categories).[37] Editorial intrusion also affected the selection of letters that appeared in newspapers, the emphasis on encouragement or warning being dictated by the publication's attitude to emigration. Anthologies compiled by genealogists or local historians have their own agendas. Yet even without editorial filtering, and despite their ubiquity, letters can never fully represent the emigrant experience. Correspondence which found its way into the contemporary public domain was generally written by articulate individuals who had a case to make and were aware of the power of the pen.[38] But only a small minority of emigrants belonged to an educated elite. Some were excluded from letter-writing because they were illiterate, others by the cost of postage. Still others had no need or desire to maintain ties with their homeland – for instance, if an entire family or community had emigrated, or if the emigrant deliberately wanted to close the door on an earlier chapter of their life. Some were too busy to write, or did not want to report disappointment or failure. Very few maintained a consistent correspondence across their lifetime, the tendency being to write most frequently in the early years of settlement. The long-term survival of letters was dependent mainly on a deliberate decision by the recipients, and those which dealt with crucial business interests, family landmarks or inheritance issues were most likely to be retained. Moreover, coverage is often asymmetrical, since letters written by emigrants to the homeland seem to have a better survival record than those which were sent in the opposite direction.

Problems of bias and selection are not confined to letter-writers. Illiterate emigrants did not keep diaries, nor did they return questionnaires. The standardised structure of a questionnaire may generate consistent responses which can be quantified and compared, but at the expense of detailed reflection.[39] Open-ended discussion is difficult to achieve in a reactive, perhaps impersonal format which requires answers to be given to questions which are dictated solely by the questioner. Yet not all questionnaires are rigid and impersonal, and the semi-structured interview guide which is used by many oral historians encourages both interviewer and interviewee to give shape to their discussion and jog memories without imposing a straitjacket on the interview.

That is not to say the gathering of oral evidence through interviews is uncontentious: far from it. Although AJP Taylor's dismissal of oral history has been discredited, the methodology is subject to the same challenges of bias and selectivity as written testimony, as well as the charge that interviewers and users fail to apply the rigorous rules of historical scholarship to the analysis of what people *say*, as opposed to what they *write*. Verbal evidence, like correspondence or questionnaires, confronts us with a collection of individuals whose initial identification may reflect the contacts of the project organiser, the circles in which the interviewer moves, the choice of advertising medium, or the power of personal persuasion. Those individuals within the initial group who respond positively to an invitation to be interviewed impose another level of self-selection and bias through their willingness to speak about (and generally validate) their experiences, and possibly by recruiting others of similar background through a snowball mechanism. The interviewing procedure itself is subject to the potentially distorting presence of the interviewer, whose preoccupations and questions can dictate the discussion, promoting or ignoring certain themes. On the other hand, non-intervention can produce an unfocused, tangled, narrative, or a monologue of unrelated and highly subjective anecdotes which cannot be analysed meaningfully. It is an unstable, variable medium, for the changing relationship between interviewer and interviewee means that the same question, asked at different stages in the conversation, may well elicit a different answer, perhaps once the participants have relaxed in each other's company.

The unreliability, instability and selectivity of memory have also been the target of critics who – invoking Taylor's image of 'old men drooling' – highlight the impact of old age and the passage of time on personal and collective recollections, as well as the subtle pressure to conform to a dominant version of a past event or experience.[40] In the context of Highland emigration, for instance, this might mean that a decision which at time of leaving was articulated as a straightforward quest for betterment was subsequently reinterpreted as an enforced exile, to match both the prevailing historiography and a context in which victimhood had become a desirable, and frequently expressed, attribute. Critics also cite the tendency to telescope two or more events into a single memory, or to claim personal recollection of incidents, particularly from childhood, which had only been experienced vicariously, through parents or newspapers. We must therefore evaluate processes of forgetting as well as remembering, whether events have been erased from individuals' minds deliberately or inadvertently, by collective myth-making, painful recollections, or simply the passage of time.[41]

Even those who advocate oral history do not all sing from the same song sheet. Collective interviews, whether they involve only two people, or a much larger group, can stimulate interaction, raise new topics for discussion, challenge interpretations, and correct mistakes. On the other hand, apart from being technically more challenging, the group (or dominant voices within it) can create a pressure to conform to a single narrative, and, in such a public forum, the nuanced, thoughtful and specific responses that are engendered by an atmosphere of privacy may give way to bland generalisations. Other discussions concern the strengths and weaknesses of video rather than audio recording; and the ways in which to use memory aids such as photographs, maps and letters. It is the processing of evidence, however, that has generated most debate. Arguments about the merits of transcriptions and summaries reflect different definitions of oral history and its objectives. Those who simply use oral testimony as an adjunct to documentary sources often favour full transcription, which allows evidence to be scrutinised on paper, without any requirement to listen to the actual voices of the interviewees. Others, however, emphasise the importance of the source *per se,* particularly its aurality, and are more concerned with the archival value of the material than with the uses to which it is put. Transcriptions, it is argued, alter the source fundamentally. As Portelli has pointed out, the filter of language is crucial: 'The transcript turns aural objects into visual ones, which inevitably implies changes and interpretation.'[42] To rely on a written transcription also deprives the researcher of the intonations, irregularities and rhythms that are integral to the spoken word, and which cannot be reproduced in written form. Neither Murdo MacIver's enthusiasm, nor Ena Macdonald's anguish, can be conveyed adequately without listening to their voices. It is only by hearing the voices, too, that we can begin to appreciate disparities in the retention or loss of accent, even among individuals who emigrated at a similar age, in the same era. In practical terms, the pedagogical case for aurality – for the importance of *hearing* the evidence – has also been reinforced in recent years by the way in which the digital revolution has made the spoken word available (and searchable) at the click of a computer mouse.

Many of the challenges raised by critics of oral history can be addressed by applying the same rules of structural rigour, corroboration and internal consistency as when using documentary sources. Additional requirements for an interviewer include meticulous preparation; the patience to listen; the skill to intervene judiciously in order to ensure thematic coherence without imposing their own voice or agenda; the avoidance of overly complex or leading questions; and a recognition of the interviewees' interests, sensitivities and silences. As Gould Colman commented more than half a century ago: 'The interviewer is researcher, audience, and avenue to posterity.'[43] Rapport is the key to a fruitful discussion, but the participants must simultaneously balance the intimacy of a personal dialogue with an awareness that the conversation will also become public property for future researchers. This may raise ethical issues relating to confidentiality or even defamation.

Some particular characteristics of oral testimony that have been denounced as weaknesses can be seen, paradoxically, as strengths. Interviews do not have to be rigidly restrictive or formlessly flexible. Nor does the presence of the interviewer, armed with an outline interview guide and an open mind, necessarily intrude on the process or distort the product unhelpfully. In an ideal scenario, a dynamic conversation develops between interviewer and interviewee, leading to a product which is the shared outcome of their interaction. Unlike written documents, which are static, the content of an interview is shaped by the organic relationship of questions and answers, corrections and clarifications, and perhaps by the location in which the interview takes place. This makes oral testimony a much more nuanced source than simply a verbal record of the past, and also means that an interview, even under identical conditions, 'is never the same twice'.[44]

The subjectivity, inconsistency and diversity of memory can be used to our advantage. Memories are constructed and reconstructed not simply by the lapse of time and the onset of old age, but by the political, cultural and personal context in which recollections are invoked and interpreted. Memories also shape – and are shaped by – perceptions of identity, perhaps especially among emigrants who have had to transplant or reconstruct their identities. Memory is therefore not 'a passive depository of facts, but an active process of creation of meanings'.[45] By conforming to a dominant community memory, family legend or national meta-narrative, interviewees reflect and reinforce that orthodoxy, and revisit their past experiences through the lens of present attitudes and circumstances. Conversely, those who do not recognise or accept the dominant collective narrative may either remain silent or articulate 'oppositional memories', which also remind historians of the dynamism, complexity and interactivity of the phenomenon of remembering.[46] The particular memories invoked, and the way in which policies, processes and procedures are interpreted – including factual inaccuracies and ambiguities – can therefore be important constituents in developing a more nuanced insight into interviewees' understandings of the events in which they had participated.

Interrogating the evidence: the core issues

Such perspectives provide invisible theoretical scaffolding for the conversations which populate this book, and the blending of autobiography and history that lie at its core. The first interview was recorded in 1994, but it was in 2005 that the project got underway with a view to ultimate publication of its findings. Material from the collection was first published in 2012 in a general study of 20th century Scottish emigration, *Scotland No More?*, the final chapter of which dipped a toe into oral evidence to amplify themes that had been scrutinised from documentary sources in earlier chapters.[47] *Testimonies of Transition* has been written in order to give those 38 individuals, and subsequent interviewees, a specific forum for the detailed articulation and analysis of motives, attitudes and experiences that received only passing coverage in the previous study. Although there is inevitably some overlap, interview extracts quoted in *Scotland No More?* have only been reused when such repetition has been deemed necessary for context and understanding.

The databank of oral testimony (which continues to be built up) contains, at time of writing, 91 interviews with 106 individuals, 49 men and 57 women. The conversations were conducted face-to-face or by telephone or Skype in Scotland, Canada, Australia, New Zealand and Hong Kong, intermittently over 23 years, but primarily since 2005. The average length of interview was one hour, though some were as short as 30 minutes, and occasionally a conversation lasted for more than three hours. Of the participants, 88 had left Scotland to live overseas, and a further five were born abroad. Thirty-seven interviewees had either returned to Scotland after living overseas, or (in the case of the five born abroad) had come back during childhood. The oldest participant was aged 100, and the youngest was 26. Of the emigrants, 75 had left Scotland as adults, and 17 as children.[48] The majority of adult emigrants had been married when they left Scotland: 21 of the men and 25 of the women.

Most interviews were one-to-one conversations, but on 13 occasions a husband and wife participated together, on one occasion two sisters-in-law, and on one occasion a mother and daughter. Two nonagenarian mothers and their sons were also interviewed together,[49] and on another occasion three siblings shared their childhood memories of Canada between the wars.[50] Four other participants spoke vicariously about the emigration of family members, and one interviewee had come in the opposite direction, as an immigrant into Scotland. Five participants (three individuals and one couple) were interviewed twice, and one individual – the late Murdo MacIver – was interviewed on three separate occasions. As ambiguities or further questions emerged during the writing of this book, a number of original interviewees were contacted for follow-up information by email, letter or telephone, and a handful of new participants supplied information by phone or email, rather than in a formal interview.[51]

The emphasis is, not surprisingly, on the post-war decades, but two individuals, both now deceased, left Scotland in the 1920s. Only three interviewees requested anonymity, one man being given a pseudonym and the other individuals being referred to simply by their initials. In all but those cases the participants are identified by their real names. Women who changed their names when they married are referred to in the text by whatever surname they used at the time of the events discussed in their testimony. For both pedagogical and practical reasons, the geographical emphasis is on North America and the Antipodes. These were the regions which attracted most Scottish emigrants in earlier centuries, and which have continued to dominate the exodus.[52] Since North America and the Antipodes are also the locations on which most studies of the Scottish diaspora have focused, modern oral reflections can also be compared relatively easily with older written testimony. For the same reasons, it has been possible to tap into networks of scholars, family history societies and Scottish associations in Canada, the United States, Australia and New Zealand, and thereby to identify interviewees. Other parts of the Scottish diaspora are represented however, in a handful of interviews from South America, Africa, and Asia, as well as in conversations with Scots who returned to their homeland after sojourning in these and other locations. Thirteen interviews with Scots in England have so far been confined only to those who went to the identifiably Scottish enclave of Corby, and have not been included in this study.

Interviewees are recruited through various mechanisms. Some have answered advertisements in family history society publications; others have responded to appeals made during evening classes, public lectures or conferences held in different parts of Scotland, Canada, New Zealand and Australia. Sometimes direct contact is made with Scottish organisations overseas or with individuals who have come to notice through exhibitions, newspaper articles, radio or television features. As with the actual decision to emigrate, the recruitment of interviewees also owes much to the snowball effect of word-of-mouth encouragement from participants. Potential interviewees are sent an explanatory letter, along with a permissions form to cover copyright clearance, deposit and subsequent use of the interview and related material. As far as possible, meetings are held in a location chosen by the interviewee, often their own home, but in 15 cases, practical difficulties associated with distance and time have required a phone conversation, and two later interviews were conducted using Skype. Remote conversations are less than ideal, both in terms of the recording's technical quality (particularly in the early days), and because the participants do not generally have an opportunity to develop the rapport that comes from a face-to-face dialogue.

The content of the discussion is framed, but not dictated, by an interview guide, which encourages participants to root their emigration experiences within the context of whole life narratives. The thematic pattern (which is replicated in the book's chapter structure) is a familiar one in migration studies.[53] Basic biographical questions are followed – for those who emigrated as adults – by enquiries about their upbringing, education, accommodation, employment, standard of living, travel history, and social life in Scotland. The circumstances surrounding their emigration are then explored in some detail. Questions include the triggers for leaving Scotland; the key sources of information and persuasion; the choice of destination; the significance of the Commonwealth and/or the role of subsidised emigration in deciding where to go; the nature and extent of prior knowledge about the chosen location; the process of making application and travel arrangements; the length of time between conception of the idea and implementation of the decision; and the attitude of parents, children, friends and workmates. Two interviews with recruitment agents – an elusive category – approach the issues of reaching and effecting a decision from the perspective of the advocate or sponsor, rather than the client.

The next set of questions moves the narrative on to the interviewees' physical relocation, probing the emotions of those leaving and staying, as well as practical details of the journey. The spotlight then shifts to the new country, with questions about first impressions, employment, housing, education, living standards, climate, and social life. The objective here is to elicit information both about practical matters and the conjunction or disparity between the interviewees' expectations and experiences. The discussion subsequently shifts from habits, processes and procedures to explore more cerebral issues relating to adaptation, integration and assimilation, with particular reference to homesickness, interpersonal relationships and cultural attitudes. That in turn opens up the important but elusive field of identities or identifications, those interests and attitudes which might be transferred or transformed in the course of emigration and settlement. Such issues can be explored partly through specific questions about letters and phone calls; or about the emigrants' involvement with Scottish clubs, societies and informal networks – the so-called 'associational culture' that has attracted a lot of scholarly interest in recent years.[54] A different, more open-ended approach enquires about definitions of 'home', probes interviewees' views on their ethnicity, and asks whether they would describe their emigration as transplantation or uprooting. Finally, the spotlight is trained once more on Scotland, in order to explore the motives and experiences of emigrants who have returned to their homeland, either permanently, recurrently, or just once. The expectations and feelings of their overseas-born families are also woven into this section, especially in terms of their perceptions of identity.

The actual discussions, of course, do not follow such a prescribed format, but range back and forth across these – and many other – topics. In the course of the project it became evident that it is not only emigrants' memories that are reshaped by the political and cultural context in which the conversation takes place. In recent years discussions about personal identities and images of Scotland have embraced the emigrants' perceptions of their homeland against the backdrop of an upsurge in nationalist sentiment, especially the referendum of September 2014 and (to a lesser extent) Brexit. Interviewees' attitudes towards Scottish independence have now become a key part of many conversations, injecting a unique element into a study which in all other respects does not support a case for Scottish exceptionalism: in general, the experiences of Scottish emigrants seem to echo those of their counterparts from other parts of Britain whose testimony has been analysed in other recent studies.[55]

Further themes which are not addressed explicitly in discussion, but emerge from subsequent analysis of the interviews, include the appearance of family patterns: what Alistair Thomson has called the 'intergenerational dynamics of migration'.[56] For example, Calum Murray from Shader in the Isle of Lewis was one emigrant who followed very clearly in the footsteps of his father, who before the First World War had travelled between Canada and the Hebrides, working on grain elevators in Ontario and British Columbia. In due course Calum too became a long-distance transatlantic commuter, spending 30 summers from the early 1950s freighting grain on the Great Lakes.[57] What has *not* emerged so far from any of the interviews, however, is the intergenerational tension noted by Janis Wilton among emigrants to Australia.[58] There are also very few examples of spousal disagreement about the decision to emigrate or where to go. Those silences do not necessarily indicate the absence of tensions: as interviewer, I was sometimes unwilling to ask potentially intrusive questions, and most interviewees would probably not volunteer such information unprompted. Two other themes that are not addressed through specific questions, but develop organically from some of the discussions are the significance of gender and emigrants' relations with indigenous people. A deliberate characteristic of the collection is that it tells the stories of ordinary individuals and families, not the high-profile, much scrutinised emigrants such as children who were so controversially despatched overseas by orphanages.

In quoting the interviewees' testimony, their words have been reproduced as they were spoken, though generally with the omission of interjections and filled pauses such as 'you know' and 'er'. There has been minimal grammatical intervention, but where words have been added or deleted in order to enhance fluency and comprehension, the insertions have been enclosed in square brackets, and the deletions indicated by ellipses. Non-spoken communications such as laughter, tears, or significant pauses have also been identified by inserting these words within square brackets. When interviewees have laid particular stress upon a certain word, this has been indicated by the use of italics.

The hundreds of hours of conversations that have taken place can be heard as well as read. Once all the material has been processed, the digital recordings will be deposited in the audio collections of the Special Libraries and Archives at the University of Aberdeen, along with summaries, or – in the case of seven interviews – full transcriptions.[59] Listening is just as important as reading, since the reproduction of narratives on the printed page gives only a partial glimpse into the richness of the source. In analysing and quoting from interviewees' recollections, it is almost impossible to convey the cadences and emotions of the spoken word that resonated through every conversation, and which for me are the most powerful legacy of the project. Yet, even without the auditory dimension, the interviews offer a vibrant mosaic of autobiographical and historical insights, and it is to these conversations – contextualised by other sources – that we now turn in seeking to chart, evaluate and comprehend the persistent phenomenon of Scottish emigration in the 20th and early 21st centuries.

CHAPTER 2

Pulling up the Roots: The Smorgasbord of Decision-making

'ABROAD WAS WHERE it all happened' was the optimistic perception that in 1954 propelled Ian Skinner into a career in shipping management which took him to Singapore, Hong Kong, Japan and ultimately back to Scotland. More negatively, 'disappointment [in the workplace] and the fact that I couldn't get decent housing' persuaded Easton Vance to exchange Motherwell for Vancouver in 1956, the year that Scots supplied 13.1 per cent of Britain's emigrants.[1]

The multi-hued tapestry of influences that triggered and shaped the decision to leave Scotland is firmly woven into the testimony of interviewees. Their recollections echo the sentiments which were articulated by earlier generations of emigrants – explicitly in response to official investigations or publishers' overtures, and implicitly in correspondence with family and friends. This chapter identifies and analyses various categories of catalysts that shaped the initial decision, choice of destination, and particular pattern of migration. As well as giving voice to the concerns and ambitions of different generations of interviewees, it also draws on written testimony from much earlier periods to provide a wider comparative context within which to understand continuities and changes in the complex process of reaching the decision to emigrate. While the basic question that frames the chapter is whether emigration was triggered by austerity, despair and necessity, or prosperity, ambition and choice, examples from the experiences of real individuals inject vital nuances and human dilemmas into that simplistic theoretical dichotomy.

Yet we cannot always take assertions at face value. The caveats that apply to the reliability of personal testimony in general have particular resonance when we evaluate statements about the reasons for emigrating. In retrospective accounts, the temptation to make the motive match the subsequent experience may unwittingly colour memories whose sharpness has faded with the passage of time. Long residence in a country or ethnic community with a dominant narrative of settlement may also shape retrospective explanations of motives, especially if the history of emigration is contentious. Emigrants who wrote letters for distribution around their home communities, or for wider dissemination through the press described and defended their decisions with a carefully crafted self-consciousness. Those whose views were solicited by contemporary policy-makers, later investigators or recruitment agents generally said what was expected of them, responding to leading questions or presenting formulaic comparisons of conditions in homeland and hostland. Testimony that was published in guidebooks or the fund-raising pamphlets of emigration societies was also carefully selected and edited to achieve the maximum impact – and income.

Most interviewees, however, had no obvious axe to grind or advocacy to pursue, and some had very clear recollections of the circumstances that had led them to emigrate. From their wide-ranging and varied testimony it is possible to identify several recurring preoccupations. The clearest thematic shift in attitude from earlier generations is that in most narratives the glass had become more explicitly half full rather than half empty. Emigrants were proactively grasping opportunities overseas, not fleeing from destitution or despair. Although some were frustrated with limited opportunities in Scotland, few felt that staying was the economic equivalent of drinking in the last chance saloon. Many were seeking career advancement, in both trades and professions, but there was – not surprisingly – a marked absence of the farming ambitions that had once dominated emigration rhetoric. As gender roles became less defined, and the employment market expanded, there was also an increasing similarity in the aspirations of male and female emigrants. Perhaps it is a reflection of creeping globalisation and ease of travel that the long-standing perception of emigration as a momentous, life-changing decision was not generally articulated by interviewees. While some fitted it into a wider pattern of career mobility, others regarded it as an extended but temporary holiday or an experiment which could easily be reversed if expectations were not met.

Voices from different constituencies populate the following analysis of overlapping influences. We hear first from those who, having emigrated as children, could only reflect vicariously on decisions made by their parents. Among those who planned and implemented their own decisions the triggers to be highlighted include: the dislocating impact of war and austerity; the pursuit of advancement or adventure in work and leisure; and family traditions of mobility or existing overseas support networks. The vital role of sponsorship and professional canvassing is addressed in Chapter 3, which juxtaposes emigrants' recollections with some rare testimony from the other side of the recruitment desk.

Vicarious decision-making: the recollections of child emigrants

Those who emigrated as children speak only in a minor key in this chapter. They did not play an active part in the decision to leave, and their opinions about their parents' motives are filtered second-hand accounts rather than personal recollections. It is also difficult to offer a wider chronological context for a child's eye view of why their families emigrated. As well as it being unusual for letters to raise issues that would have been discussed prior to departure, the Victorian concept that children should be seen and not heard extended into the realm of emigrant correspondence. We have few letters or diaries written by children, the main exception being the formulaic compositions that appeared in the promotional magazines of child emigration societies.

Children may not have played an active part in the decision to emigrate, but their well-being and prospects often had a considerable influence over that decision. The desire to offer them a better future – cited by several interviewees – echoed the common aspiration of parents in every era. In 1774 William Gordon from Sutherland told a government enquiry that he 'was induced to emigrate for the greater benefit of his children' as a consequence of high rents, cattle losses, and the encouragement of two other sons in North Carolina.[2] In Victorian and Edwardian times the emigrants' goal was frequently to bequeath to the next generation economic security and social status (deemed impossible in Scotland) through the inheritance of a freehold farm, especially in the apparently boundless and empty lands of the Empire. It was an aspiration that propelled numerous settlers to the Canadian prairies at the turn of the century, when federal government propaganda fuelled confidence in the 'last best West'. Mrs AH Padgham (née Gray) was one of the 67 Scottish pioneers who offered testimony to the Saskatchewan Archives Board in the 1950s. She had arrived in the province in a family party in 1906, at the age of 17. Her father, she recalled, had decided to leave Edinburgh partly because 'there would be more opportunities for a large family in this new country', coupled with the encouragement of his eldest son, who had taken up homesteading near Battleford a year earlier.[3]

Similar sentiments were evident in the inter-war period, when land-hungry Hebridean emigrants contrasted their poverty at home with promises of opportunity in Canada. Although interviewee Morag MacLeod did not have 'a clue' why her parents took their seven children to Alberta in 1923, 'because my father dealt with that', she probably reflected the subsequent family narrative in her comment that 'there was nothing there in Benbecula for the family, for the boys'.[4] That negative sentiment was confirmed by her own impression of the island during a visit in the 1990s. On the other side of the border, some of the Scots interviewed by the Ellis Island oral historians suggested – albeit not explicitly – that the betterment of the next generation had played a part in their parents' decision to leave the uncertain economic environment of inter-war Scotland. Nine-year-old Helen Baxter from South Queensferry emigrated to Indiana in the same year that Morag went to Alberta. Her father had gone on ahead, to a job in the steel mill at Gary, where there was 'a regular Scotch colony… a bunch of people who came like my father did, and we did, for a better life'. The following year John Will's father brought the family from Cupar to California, when John was seven.

> The primary reason for emigrating was lousy economic conditions and it didn't look like very much opportunity for his kids, and he brought us all here… to a place where we had opportunity.

When ten-year-old Anne Reilly from Paisley arrived in 1928 with her parents and younger brother, she attributed the decision to her mother, who was fulfilling a youthful dream of coming to 'the land of opportunity', as well as re-joining her five other children and two siblings, who were already in the United States.[5] Among my own more recent interviewees, several who emigrated to New Zealand as children after the war acknowledged that parental concern for their future had been one ingredient among many deciding factors. Cathy Donald was ten when she and her parents left Burntisland for Dunedin in 1953. She recalled:

> My father had two aims. He wanted me to be educated, which for someone who was really quite chauvinist, that was a huge thing for him, but he believed in education that he hadn't got. He didn't see that I would get to university in Scotland. Ten years later it might have been different, I think, but I probably would have ended up as a secretary, or in a bank or something – slightly better than being in a factory. And the other thing was that housing was a difficulty. Because we had this little extra box room and only one child – it was a council flat – they said, 'We're not going to rehouse you, because you've got enough space.' I shudder to think what it would have been like as a teenager.[6]

A year later Morag Callander's parents took their three daughters from Glasgow to Australia, when Morag was four. She believed the decision was made partly on health grounds, 'because I was asthmatic as a baby; *possibly* because of the assisted passage that was available; and also possibly because I think they thought there was a bit more of a future than what was available in Scotland.'[7]

A similar cocktail of reasons led Brian Coutts' parents to emigrate from

Edinburgh to Dunedin with their two sons in 1955. Brian's father had

> seen a bit of the world and I think he thought there was possibly better places to live... I think he thought there were better opportunities for my brother and I. My brother was six years older than me, so he was born in 1941. There were better opportunities overseas, and New Zealand was advertising and seemed to be like a South Sea paradise, and that might be the place to go. And my mother's health. She had suffered from pleurisy and the Edinburgh winters, and I think, now this is only surmise now on my part, but I think that they may have been given the message that her survival might depend on finding a better climate.[8]

Like Brian, Jim Wilson also moved from Edinburgh to Dunedin with his parents and elder brother, arriving in 1959, when Jim was six. He recalled that whenever he asked his parents about their motives for emigrating, 'the reason they gave "was to give the boys... a better chance in life"' than they would have had in post-war Edinburgh, which 'was a drab, dreary place'. He added, however, that no single reason dominated their decision, and referred to the widespread sense 'that anyone with any get up and go got up and went'.[9]

The impact of war and austerity

The complex interweaving – and different hierarchies – of objectives that fed into the decision to emigrate are already evident from the filtered, partial recollections of those who were taken overseas as children. They are no less obvious in the statements of those who made their own decisions. The juxtaposition of economic maladies and opportunities was a dominant and recurring trigger, whatever the era. Back in the 18th century unemployment and looming destitution were the hallmarks of many Scots whose reasons for emigrating were solicited by a two-year enquiry into transatlantic emigration launched in 1773 by a government alarmed at the extent of the outflow. The resulting *Register of Emigrants* published testimony from individuals who were crossing the Atlantic 'for poverty and to get bread', to 'better their fortune', and because of encouragement from family members who had preceded them.[10] Half a century later a flood of petitions in support of State-aided emigration after the Napoleonic Wars spoke of unemployment and destitution among demobilised soldiers, handloom weavers, and evicted Highlanders. By the 1840s the Highlanders' pleas had intensified in the face of famine, and their plight was echoed 40 years later as witness after witness to the Napier Commission testified to a lingering legacy of economic hardship and social alienation. 'We and our fathers have been cruelly burnt like wasps out of Strathnaver', declared Angus MacKay of Farr, who went on to describe the barren coastal strip to which they had been evicted, and the 'tyrannical' estate officials who raised their rents 'at every opportunity'.[11]

Similar concerns and bitterness were highlighted in the oral testimony of 20th century emigrants, although Scotland's ills were perceived as more chronic than acute. Oral evidence collected by the Provincial Archives of British Columbia confirms that such perceptions preceded the First World War. When George Bowman Anderson and John Donaldson left Scotland for Canada in 1905 and 1909 respectively they were both influenced by mass lay-offs, low wages, and poor working conditions, as well as by the encouragement, in each case, of a brother who had preceded them across the Atlantic.[12] Subsequently, the pessimistic assertion of the nationalist journalist, George Malcolm Thomson, that in the 1920s Scots were a 'dying people' inhabiting a 'slum-poisoned' economic and social wasteland[13] seemed to be borne out in the dominant memories of those who, as adults, had fled from post-war austerity to better themselves in countries of apparently greater promise. Further examples of economic threats and opportunities – as well as other catalysts – are given in Angela McCarthy's testimony-based comparative analysis of Irish and Scottish migration between 1921 and 1965.[14]

In the island of Lewis, the legacy of the war was particularly poignant because of the tragic loss of the *Iolaire*, laden with returning servicemen. Only 79 of the 284 on board survived the shipwreck, in the early hours of New Year's Day 1919.[15] One of them was Murdo Macleod from Bayble, who, his niece Donna recalled, emigrated to Vancouver shortly afterwards because he was wracked by survivor guilt. In the small island environment, it was too painful for him to encounter the widows, children and parents of men who had not survived, and respond to questions about the last moments of their loved ones. In building a new life in the Pacific north-west, Murdo attempted to erase the tragedy from his mind, and it was only after his death that his twin daughters learnt, from Donna, of the event that had triggered their father's emigration.[16]

While economic conditions and prospects still dominated the thinking of many interviewees who emigrated in the 1950s, the level of hardship was less after the Second World War, and no one claimed to have been haunted by the spectre of the interwar Depression. Emigrants were now more consciously preoccupied with seeking comfort than escaping crisis, and their interests embraced cuisine and climate, as well as employment, accommodation and social life. The inconvenience and duration of rationing, mentioned by some interviewees, were clearly of a different order to their impoverished predecessors' quest to 'get bread', but frustration with ongoing economic austerity was for several a deterrent to remaining in Scotland. Alison Thornton's father was the parish minister at Newmachar in Aberdeenshire when he decided to emigrate to New Zealand in 1947 with his German-born wife and two young children. His health had suffered under rationing, and he also thought that 'Britain was finished after the war'.[17] Alec Miller, another emigrant to New Zealand, recalled 'pretty good' food on the voyage, and contrasted the experience of shopping in Glasgow and Dunedin, where he arrived with his family in 1953:

> Coming from Britain after the war, I mean, you couldn't go down to the butcher's and say 'I want this, I want that.' It was still rationed. Then we come here... and went to Green Island, this little place, and there was the butcher's shop, full up with meat and veg. You could go in and buy *anything* you wanted. So that was quite an experience, having been stuck with one egg a week.[18]

A few months earlier, Annie Matheson had left Lewis for Detroit. She described the *Queen Elizabeth* as being like a 'floating luxury hotel' whose groaning tables were a huge contrast to the austerity of Hebridean life:

> Everything was rationed when I left. You could only get half a pound of sugar per person per week, half a pound of butter. Things were very scarce... In Britain I had started working at 16. I was working in a clothing store, and my wages were 30 shillings a week, with Sunday and half a day off a week. And then after being there eight years I was making three and a half pounds a week... And in the US it was about ten times that much that you got for your weekly wages, plus your food and your lodgings were supplied.[19]

Canada seemed to offer a similar improvement in living standards. Margaret Gillies Brown, who emigrated to Alberta with her husband and family in 1959, remembered it being portrayed as

> an up and coming country, with a lot of hidden riches. And you would get freedom there. And you could – there was hope – you had heard that you would have a house, and within five years you might have a cabin by the lake and you would have all the things that it seemed almost impossible *ever* to have in Britain, especially at that time when things were so – well they were coming off – they *were* off the rationing but there was still – things weren't too good. And they just saw it as a land of hope.[20]

John Nelson was a Scottish veterinary surgeon practising in Evesham, Worcestershire, when, in 1956, he went to Canada with his wife and two small daughters, initially to a temporary job as a meat inspector in an abattoir in Edmonton, but subsequently – and primarily – to undertake a Master's degree at the veterinary school in Guelph. Although rationing had ended two years earlier, his recollection of a fairly grim existence suggests that living standards were not necessarily any better in England than Scotland, even for those in professional work. The persistence of austerity was compounded by foreign policy humiliation and petrol rationing during the Suez Canal crisis:

> The background to that [the decision to emigrate] is, it was still austerity. It was miserable, actually. You still had to queue up at the butcher and all this nonsense... It was a cumulation [sic] (culmination) of living very close to the edge, and nothing but work, because we didn't get a day off. We were on all the time. And I'd been doing that for years... And the political situation got bad at that time. There was Suez, and that annoyed me.[21]

As most of these interviewees testified, the dislocation induced by war and its protracted aftermath was harnessed to a resolution to seek better opportunities overseas. Military service itself sometimes provided a direct opportunity to implement that desire, for it had traditionally been a trigger for emigration, especially from the Highlands, and had contributed intermittently, but significantly, to overseas settlement since the 18th century. Following the Seven Years' War, lands north of Albany in New York were granted to officers and men of the 77th and 42nd Highland Regiments, while the aftermath of the American Revolution saw several Scottish regiments rewarded for their service with land in British North America. In 1807, Angus MacEacharn, a Scottish priest in Prince Edward Island, wrote to his bishop in Edinburgh about a significant emigration of 'your countrymen the Barra sharks', who 'have begun two or three settlements on the Bras d'Or Lake' in Cape Breton, as a result of glowing accounts brought back to Barra by three soldiers four decades earlier.[22] After the Napoleonic Wars, the British government's policy of rewarding discharged soldiers with land was extended to include civilians, notably in the Perth settlement in Upper Canada, where the Scottish settlers included many unemployed Lanarkshire weavers. The practice was revived, with new clothes, in the soldier settlement scheme of 1919–22, and its extension to civilians under the Empire Settlement Act, which remained on the statute book for half a century. The ex-service free passage scheme was again resurrected – partially and controversially – for a decade after the Second World War, when it assisted almost 50,000 British veterans to Australia.[23]

Against such a backdrop, it is perhaps surprising that military service did not feature more explicitly in the recollections of interviewees who emigrated in the 1950s. The most direct connection was made by Charlie Law, who identified post-demobilisation restlessness as the initial trigger in his father's decision to respond to an offer of work in British Columbia:

> In 1950 my father and mother went to Vancouver, Canada. My father had come out of the army in 1946, 47, couldn't really settle – he worked for the Electric Company in Aberdeen. Him and a few others went to a seminar on Canada in the Music Hall, and a few of them had got together – I met them – they used to come to the house, and they were all talking about going to Canada, a place called Ocean Falls in northern British Columbia, where they had – it was a pulp and paper mill town. It had a population of about 3,000, and they were looking for people to work. Because of the isolation of British Columbia they had huge turnovers the whole time because people would just work there for a little while and go back to the big city, so they were looking for people who would maybe settle there. I think there was quite a few came from Aberdeen.[24]

Sandy Fox (whose testimony was recorded for the National Library of Australia's Oral History Collection) suggested, slightly more tentatively, that his father's war service was a contributory factor in the family's emigration to Australia:

> My dad, Jack, was a bricklayer, and he had always wanted to come to Australia from his demobilisation from the forces in the Second World War, but my mother, who was one of five siblings, and her parents, didn't want to leave her family, from the small town of Dalkeith, which is seven miles to the south-east of Edinburgh, a little market town, and she just didn't want to go. Anyhow, a couple of years later, a cousin of the family, who had been in Australia since before the First World War, decided to visit, and that cousin convinced Dad that he should come to Australia. So he got that cousin's return ticket and used it, and came out here, and bought us a house, and 12 months later the whole family joined him.[25]

Sandy arrived in Australia as a teenager on a ten-pound passage in 1952. Seven years later, six-year-old Christine Matheson emigrated from Invergordon to New Zealand with her parents and three siblings, a move which she also attributed to the lingering legacy of the war. Her father, who had been one of the first cohorts to undergo commando training at Spean Bridge, and had been present at the Normandy Landings, 'was quite restless after the Second World War. I think he was attracted by a new start in a sort of youngish country.'[26] Having trained as a mathematics teacher, he took his family to New Zealand's North Island when in 1959 he secured a teaching position in Gisborne.

National Service in the 1950s helped to trigger a similar restlessness in some young Scotsmen. In 1954 and 1956 Paddy McFarlane and Easton Vance had both recently completed their National Service when they sought better opportunities in New Zealand and Canada respectively. Paddy 'decided to look for greener fields' than he could find in Edinburgh after finishing an engineering apprenticeship which had been interrupted by two years' National Service.[27] Easton's National Service in the RAF had brought him into contact with servicemen from across the Commonwealth, as well as taking him out of Scotland for the first time in his life. As he explained in an interview in 2008, he was awakened to 'the lure of different places... so I got a little bit of a wanderlust'.[28] During a follow-up conversation in 2017, he confirmed the significance of National Service in laying the foundation for his subsequent emigration to Vancouver, where one of his RAF comrades had settled. 'No question about it – that's what did it for me... It opened my eyes and gave me an experience I would not have done [sic], so there was some good about the thing.'[29]

In a similar vein, peacetime service in the merchant navy and army helped to fuel the wanderlust and global perspective of Murdo MacIver from Lewis, AM from Glasgow and Edwin Millar from Dundee, all of whom emigrated to Canada between 1952 and 1980. Glaswegian Jock Baird's experience as a ship's cook led him to enlist for similar employment in the Royal Australian Air Force in 1970, at the age of 41. His disillusionment with a succession of low-paid jobs was compounded by the frustration of living in a one-room, third-storey tenement with his wife and baby, with 'no sign of me getting a house'.[30]

For a few interviewees, climate was a component in the complex assortment of catalysts that led them to emigrate. Sometimes – as with Gail Anderson or Brian Coutts' mother – there were anticipated health benefits, in marked contrast to expectations and probabilities in pioneering days. Often, however, there was simply a perception that monotone dreariness could be exchanged for colour and warmth, with a sub-text of economic and social betterment. Environmental contrasts, particularly with the Empire, had been exploited by generations of propagandists, who injected the glamour of overseas frontiers into the drab, predictable lives of those whose horizons were bounded by the farm, or – increasingly – the factory or office. On the other hand, recruiters' encouragement was countered by detractors who invoked the weather weapon as a deterrent, warning would-be emigrants against exiling themselves to a snow-bound Canadian wilderness or a sun-scorched Australian desert.

When John and Joan Noble emigrated to Canada with their two sons (aged two and four) in 1966, they eagerly anticipated not a snow-bound wilderness, but the benign climate of Vancouver Island. Joan – a native of the Isle of Lewis who had studied in Glasgow and moved to Aberdeen when she married – emphasised that the couple did not conform to the stereotype of unwilling exiles:

> When people talk about emigration, they talk, especially in the Highland areas, there's such a lot of literature about, you know, the literature of exile – sad songs, sad poems, the anguish of exile, and the sorrow and so on. Well, that's how it used to be, 'cos it was not by choice that they came in the past. But we came by choice, and it's been nothing but good things. We came not because we needed to – John was deputy of a school in Aberdeen, and we had a lovely life in Aberdeen, but, I don't know, there was some kind of restlessness in the air in the '60s. A lot of people came to Canada in the middle '60s. And the weather had become absolutely abysmal. We could never get a nice summer, my children were never outside playing the way I wanted them to be. I had to put them into sou' westers and little wellies and all that, you know. And we got a little restless, and we began talking about going somewhere.[31]

Two years later Allan Bruce left Dundee to work as a VSO-funded art history teacher at Khartoum University. In 1969, when he was home on holiday, a military coup in Sudan meant that he was unable to return to his job, but he was determined not to move back to Scotland, where he said 'the pay for teachers and for nurses was the lowest of all professions'. His comments about the environmental deterrents focused on drabness:

> I'd always hated the climate in Dundee. I'd always thought of Dundee as a big, grey place – grey skies, grey buildings, grey river, people wearing grey clothes, grey faces. And having been in more exotic climes and warmer places, it was terribly hard resettling.[32]

Allan's words were echoed almost verbatim by another interviewee, medical doctor AS, who returned to Edinburgh for Christmas in 1970 after a year in Canada. In portraying Scotland as a place where 'everything was grey', she hinted at a connection between the weather and a depressing cultural climate, suggesting that the literal greyness of clothing, complexions and landscape was compounded by the defeatist attitude of a population which 'didn't seem to have the will to do anything... And I thought "I don't want to come back here"'.[33]

The image of leaden skies and attitudes has persisted, for when six Scots expatriates were asked by *The Scotsman* newspaper in April 2016 to comment on the pros and cons of living overseas, Ally Brown – who has lived in Bogota, Colombia, since 2012 – declared that on return visits to Scotland: 'I was struck by how grey everything seemed, and how ill everyone looked.'[34]

Ten years later a similar charge was levelled, more emphatically, by Edwin Millar, the only interviewee to assert that political disillusionment in the wake of the 1979 devolution referendum was the decisive factor in his decision to emigrate. In the early 1970s while living in Dundee and working as a merchant seaman, he had 'got very involved with the Scottish National Party', particularly the two election campaigns of 1974, both of which returned Gordon Wilson to Parliament for the constituency of Dundee East. 'I was in both of them up to my neck,' he recalled. After Wilson was returned with an increased majority at the October election, which also saw the party's representation rise from four to 11 MPs, 'things looked good'. In 1979 however, the failure of the devolution referendum to secure the required majority of forty per cent of the eligible electorate was followed by a General Election which returned only two SNP MPs.[35] Edwin – who by that time was working in an unfulfilling job at Loch Awe power station – was disgusted when the ambiguous result, which he attributed to constitutional sleight of hand, was received with apathy rather than outrage:

> Then there was the referendum. The referendum. For devolution. I worked hard for that. I thought it would be a great stepping stone. The first step. And then the votes came in, and the majority of voters had voted *for* devolution... And there was no protest. There were no demonstrations. There was no riots. Nothing! So I started looking for a place to get out of here.[36]

The quest for adventure and advancement

It is impossible, of course, to disentangle the negative and positive threads that were woven into the decision to emigrate. That has always been the case, and – as demonstrated in the testimony already quoted – is just as evident in the recollections of modern interviewees as in statements made to the customs officials who compiled the *Register of Emigrants* in the 1770s. The key difference, however, is that, as time went on, decisions were driven increasingly by positive incentives, often by specific job offers rather than vague optimism, and applied to a much wider spectrum of emigrants. The starting point was not the existence or prospect of grinding poverty, but a quest for adventure or advancement, over which the emigrants themselves exercised personal choice and agency.

Some testimony exudes a straightforward taste for adventure, not least among single women. Such attitudes were not unknown in the 18th and 19th centuries, but it was the 1920s that saw the noticeable emergence of a more confident generation of young female emigrants. Ellis Island interviewees like Mary Dunn, Marge Glasgow, Maisie Pedersen and Agnes Schilling were only in their teens when they emigrated alone, Marge and Agnes being just 15.[37] 'I just knew that there was something better', Agnes recalled, when she was interviewed in 1992, aged 86.[38] Margaret Kirk, who was 22 when she emigrated in 1923, told the Ellis Island interviewer in 1994 that 'I was just like my mother – adventurous... I would have gone anywhere, I was going to travel.' Since 'everybody wanted to come to America' after the war, and 'America sent out signals that everything was wonderful here', she thought she would jump on the bandwagon, though not with any initial intention to settle there permanently.[39]

Like Margaret, Minnie Anne Fraser from Sutherland had to wait two years for a visa and work permit, and also save up enough money to go to the United States in 1926. She had loosened her roots four years earlier when she left her home in Halladale to work (like her sister before her) as a maid for the bank manager in Dornoch, 62 miles to the south-east. 'I just had a fancy to go', she told her daughter in 1996,[40] though she was also aware that domestic service was better paid and less onerous in a country where labour-saving electrical appliances were already popular. It is evident, moreover, that her decision was also shaped by previous emigration from Halladale, specific encouragement from the friend who accompanied her, and practical assistance from her employer, who had given personal loans to previous emigrants, and provided her with a testimonial:

> Oh yes, yes – from Halladale they had gone many years before and hadn't come back [except] on holiday. But my age group, it was just young folks in Dornoch. The girl in particular who I went out with, she was the one that more or less encouraged me. When she was going, I thought I could go. She was a couple of years older than me. She was Jean Grant, from Embo... I think Mr and Mrs Bell [her employers] were with me from the beginning, 'cos they never discouraged me to go, as long as I got in with somebody who could train me.[41]

Minnie Anne's parents, she recalled, took her decision very calmly, and she was given a send-off and a 'wee presentation' by neighbours, who 'wished me well – possibly they thought I was daft'.[42]

All the Ellis Island interviewees, as well as Minnie Anne, worked in the traditional field of domestic service, but as the female employment market expanded after the war, so did the scope for women to put their specific trades and professions to use. In 1957 Sally Blake left her post as a teacher in Dumfries to take up a position teaching English to senior school students in Digby, Nova Scotia. She had been 'completely turned off' her initial intention to forge a career as a journalist when her first employer, the *Glasgow Evening News*, 'would not give a female any work in anything except the women's page'.[43] Then, after training as a teacher, she discovered she was confined to elementary and junior high school teaching because she did not have an honours degree. Her choice of destination was determined by her older brother having moved to Nova Scotia, but, as she explained, the province was desperate for teachers with ordinary as well as honours degrees:

> Well, actually, the Minister of Education had been in Scotland, recruiting at Jordanhill, and for some reason, I can't tell you why, I did not get in on that, but I found out from my brother, pretty quickly, that they were still desperate for teachers. You see, they'd built all these large high schools, and started closing the one- and two-roomed schools, and they found that they didn't have any teachers with degrees, so those of us who had degrees, we were very precious, so much so that the plane I flew over in from Prestwick was absolutely full of British teachers. Every one of us on the plane. The plane was paid for by the Department of Education in Nova Scotia. They were that desperate. Because before that their high school teachers had all been people with one year of normal school, or two years of normal school, and that was it. There were very few people with degrees.[44]

Dumfries also offered limited horizons to Alison Gibson and her elder sister, Edinburgh University graduates who in the 1960s wanted to spread their wings beyond their birthplace:

> We found the town – my sister and I – very small, growing up. There seemed a lot of the world outside that we'd like to explore. And we also were fairly well known because everyone knew our parents, so life seemed very restricted. We were looking for adventure, both of us, when we left home.[45]

The siblings found work in London, Alison as a computer programmer:

> From there I went to Canada with a friend I met working there [in London], who was very keen to emigrate – to go to Canada, at least for two years. I was sort of interested in going. I enjoyed my time in London, but it wasn't a place that you would want to settle, in the conditions and with the salaries we had. I was intrigued to go and explore with her, but only if I had a job to go to.

> That was in 1967, when it was Canada's centennial year, and so there was a lot of publicity about Canada, especially because of Expo 67. So we and several other people of our age in their mid-20s then were drawn to Canada, and we applied for three jobs that were advertised in the British papers, and ended up in Halifax, Nova Scotia, which is the job we got offered… We went, thinking we'd have, well, the adventure, but also the salaries were double what we were earning in London, which seemed very good… At that time, there were a lot of young people going out, and I think then it was much more for adventure than for necessity.[46]

Looking to the other side of the world, Isobel Gillon was determined not to be fobbed off with unskilled work when she applied to go to New Zealand in 1958. She had qualified as a dressmaker in Gorebridge and then took a diploma in invisible mending at Netherdale Technical College in Galashiels. She opted to emigrate alone after her travelling companion had to withdraw from the adventure:

> Now, at this point they said to me at the mill, 'Oh, Isobel, that's a shame, 'cos you were looking forward to going there.' And all of a sudden I thought, 'I can still go.' 'Oh, you won't go away over there on your own, will you?' I says, 'yeah, I'll go over there for two years and come back. Yes, I can.' I says, 'You watch me.' And from there – on my last interview in Edinburgh, the man said to me, 'Now', he says, 'we've put you down for general factory work.' I said, 'Well, what do you mean, general factory work?' He says, 'Well, we can't guarantee we'll get you into textiles,' he says. 'It could be a shoe factory, it might be a biscuit factory.' I says, 'No, no, no, no.' I says, 'If you can't get me into my trade, cancel my application. I've sat and got my diploma, and that's why it would take me out there.' So they in turn then contacted the New Zealand government, and Ross & Glendining were bringing quite a lot of textile workers, not just menders, out, which then took me to another interview in London, and they said 'Yes, you'll be hearing from us,' and I got a letter in December to say that I was to report to the hotel in London on the 7th or 8th of January.[47]

Ten years later Sheena McBean from Inverness applied to emigrate to Western Australia, along with a college friend. As recently qualified primary teachers they were recruited by the State government, which was making 'quite a big push' to tackle a shortage of primary teachers. For Sheena, however, the job (which she had secured before leaving Scotland) was a means to an end:

> Myself and a friend were particularly keen on going to see the world. Because

> that was basically it. It wasn't so much for economics or anything like that – we just wanted to see the world, and I had family that had travelled beforehand, and I had relations in different parts of the world.

When her friend submitted to maternal pressure and backed out at the last minute, Sheena thought her parents would be reluctant to let her go alone, but the sponsor bent the rules by putting her in touch with another travelling companion, a woman from Edinburgh who was in the same position.

Most interviewees were reflecting on decisions made several decades earlier, but Rachel Minton was only 27 when interviewed in 2010, almost five years after she moved to New Zealand. Her testimony reflects the same quest for adventure as single women in previous generations, albeit within a more explicitly global context. Brought up on a croft at Dundonnell in Wester Ross, Rachel left home at 16, worked in Edinburgh and London, and travelled through the USA and Australia before moving on to Auckland, and then Dunedin:

> After living in various different places in the UK, I decided I would come to New Zealand, mostly because most people come to Australia. Everyone comes to Australia, and I said, 'I'll be a wee bit different.' I hadn't done any travelling before. I'd been to a couple of places in Europe, and I thought, 'It's an easy place to go to, everyone speaks the language, the differences aren't huge, but it'll be a great starting point to see a bit of the world and maybe carry on from there.'[48]

Alison Inglis had also been considering going to New Zealand for a couple of years when she saw an advertisement in the *Journal of the Law Society of Scotland* for a legal practitioner for the Falkland Islands Government. She arrived in the Falklands in 1997, four years after qualifying as a lawyer in Edinburgh. Working in Fife, she missed the scenery of Argyll, where she had been brought up, and went to the South Atlantic knowing 'virtually nothing' about the Islands and nothing at all of their heritage of Scottish settlement. Aged 29, her objective was 'to get out of a rut, travel abroad, and on return settle in Oban or Fort William'. She came from a family where approximately one quarter of each generation had either emigrated permanently or spent long periods working abroad, and her decision came as no surprise to close friends, who attributed it to her 'adventurous personality'. While Alison's father was envious of 'all the wonderful stories' she would be able to tell later in life, her mother was 'appalled' by her choice of destination, and, as Alison recalled 'kept sending me literature on Canada, Australia, New Zealand, and even South Africa, despite my intense dislike of the heat and of South African politics in the 1990s'. Her intention to return to Scotland changed when, six months after arriving, she met an islander. They married two years later.[49]

Twenty-two female interviewees accompanied or followed their husbands or fiancés overseas as they pursued a variety of industrial, professional, farming, academic and commercial opportunities. Like their female counterparts, male interviewees were generally in their 20s or 30s when they left Scotland, and the decision to emigrate was related to particular life stages such as leaving school and embarking on a career; getting married; pondering the future for a young family; or seeking a promotion that was beyond their reach in Scotland.

The three young men who upheld the long-standing Scottish tradition of employment with the Hudson's Bay Company were all bachelors from north-east Scotland who responded to press advertisements. First to go was Angus Pelham Burn from Craigellachie. After leaving agricultural college in 1951, 20-year-old Angus was wondering what to do next when he saw two advertisements in the local paper, one for lumbering in Queensland, and the other to 'join the romantic fur trade' in Canada. He applied to both, but only the Hudson's Bay Company responded.[50] Four years later Les Ford (aged 18) from Aberdeen was attracted by the wages of around $135 a month quoted in a similar press advertisement, which 'seemed like a lot of money' compared with the pay of 28 shillings a week he was then earning with British Rail.[51] And in 1966 John Wallace, also from Aberdeen, was a few months short of his 18th birthday when his sense of adventure was piqued by an advertisement in the *Evening Express*. His mother contextualised John's decision by explaining that when he was at school 'he'd done a big project on Manitoba, and even then he used to say "I think I'll go to Canada"'.[52]

Opportunities for skilled tradesmen attracted a number of interviewees, including two couples who emigrated twice to Canada. In one case the comings and goings were shaped by a mixture of parental encouragement and economic fluctuations in the international paper industry. We have already met Charlie Law, whose parents left Aberdeen for British Columbia in 1950. They were followed three years later by Charlie himself, because his parents thought it would be a good place for him to find work after he had finished his engineering apprenticeship in an Aberdeen shipyard. He got a job in the maintenance department of the pulp and paper mill at Ocean Falls in northern British Columbia, where he was joined in 1954 by his fiancée, Molly Lennie. Twelve years later, having received newspaper cuttings from Molly's mother about Wiggins Teape's new pulp and paper mill that was under construction near Fort William, Charlie 'decided we'd give it a try', and he and Molly returned to Scotland with their four children.[53] Charlie applied successfully for a job and a council house, and they stayed in Corpach for

15 years, before returning to Canada in 1981 when the Corpach mill was in difficulties. Once again Charlie found work in a British Columbia paper town, Kitimat, where his son had been working since 1976.

Hamish and Isla Robertson from Morayshire also followed employment opportunities back and forth across the Atlantic, with regular career moves that both reflected and reinforced their tendency to get 'itchy feet'. They first went to Canada as newly-weds, 'looking for a new life'. On leaving school in Tomintoul, Hamish had moved to Glasgow to serve his apprenticeship as a shipwright. He emigrated to Montreal in March 1966, ten days after getting married, to take up a job with Vickers on the building of an ice-breaker. Isla, a teacher, followed him four months later at the end of the school term. In 1969 they moved west to Toronto, where Hamish worked for McDonnell Douglas on the development of the DC-10 jet airliner, before returning to Scotland in 1970 to a job with Lithgow's shipbuilders in Port Glasgow. They lived in Paisley, which Isla 'really hated', and when Hamish was offered a job in Collingwood, Ontario, in 1974, they decided to return to Canada. Unexpected delays with immigration procedure meant that in the end he took up an alternative employment offer in Vancouver, where they settled permanently.[54]

There were also good openings for career progression in the professions. Two young surgeons were influenced by a mixture of job opportunities and previous positive experiences in Canada and New Zealand respectively. Roddy Campbell was looking for a consultancy when he decided to emigrate to British Columbia in 1969. He found himself in a remote village on the shores of Upper Arrow Lake in the west Kootenay mountains:

> In 1966 I got married, and I thought my career wasn't going to be very good in Britain at the time, it was very hard to become a consultant surgeon. Eventually I would probably get a place, but it might be in the Black Country or somewhere like that, and I didn't fancy that, so I saw this advert in the *British Medical Journal*, telling me that a place was available in Canada at Nakusp. I had never heard of Nakusp, but I had been to Canada before, working on a farm in Ontario, and I really liked the country very much. So, with my wife and new-born child, we headed for Nakusp.[55]

William Gillespie was also a surgeon – in orthopaedics – who was so impressed by New Zealand when he did a year's exchange in 1973 that he decided to return later:

> I remember being hugely impressed by the impression that this was a country where almost everyone had jobs and the gap between the haves and the have

> nots seemed incredibly small compared with what I'd seen in Britain. And I thought it was an attractive society, and they'd made an extraordinary effort to reach an understanding with the Maori people... it was a more even relationship than Australia.

Another orthopaedic surgeon, David Knight, was 55 when in 2011 he gave up his employment as a consultant in Aberdeen and moved to China. After a period of language learning, he secured a position teaching foreign medical students (in English) at Kunming Medical University. His interest in Asia had developed over the years since 1973, when as a schoolboy in Elgin, he had been part of the winning team on the BBC quiz programme, *Top of the Form*. The prize was a two-week trip to Hong Kong, during which the Elgin Academy team not only triumphed in a match against an Australian school, but also had ample opportunity to tour Hong Kong. David recalled looking across the border to the closed land of mainland China, never thinking that 18 years later he would be able to spend six months working in Beijing as part of his orthopaedic training. Having become increasingly aware through his reading of the foundational role of Scottish doctors (not least from Aberdeen) in medical education in both Hong Kong and China, it seemed appropriate to him to follow a similar path when the opportunity arose.[56]

Several decades earlier, the Reverend Henry Thornton had been frustrated not only with post-war austerity, but with the intellectual limitations of his life as a country clergyman, and since he 'really wanted to be in university teaching', in 1947 applied for a lectureship in Philosophical Psychology at the University of Otago.[57] By the post-war era, increasing secularisation meant that clergymen made up only a handful of emigrants. This was a marked change from the 18th and 19th centuries, when ministers and priests were heavily involved in the business of overseas settlement, either spearheading a movement, or answering the call to serve an existing diasporic congregation. Their letters and reports – often preserved in institutional archives – not only testify to their own experiences, but reflect the prevailing culture of donor and host societies. Deep-rooted denominational rivalries surfaced in repeated allegations about the poaching of isolated, unchurched emigrants. Gaelic-speaking crofters on the Canadian prairies were 'in the midst of Protestants and they cannot safely be left a long time', wrote the Catholic archbishop of St Boniface to a Scottish bishop in 1884, while from the opposite end of the theological spectrum some Presbyterians cultivated an acerbic anti-Catholic rhetoric.[58]

By the mid-20th century most denominations had abandoned such negative preoccupations in favour of a less combative concern for pastoral care among the wider community, as well as their own countrymen. Only one Scottish clergyman – Baptist minister Arthur Russell – appears in any previously published oral collections,[59] and for many interviewees, religion was either an irrelevance or an optional extra, rather than a pivotal point of the emigrant experience. There were notable exceptions. A handful of interviewees emigrated under the auspices of churches or missionary societies to follow a particular vocation. From 1976 to 1996, Billy and Elizabeth Graham worked in South Africa as missionaries with the Free Church of Scotland, while in the same era John MacPherson taught, also under the auspices of the Free Church, at Colegio San Andrés (St Andrew's School) in Lima, Peru.[60]

Founded in 1917 as the Anglo-Peruvian School, Colegio San Andrés has included among its alumni some of Peru's most notable businessmen, academics, politicians and clergymen, and has had a significant impact on Peruvian life. Another missionary, former geography teacher Moira Campbell from Aberdeen, spent almost 30 years in a very different culture, that of Taiwan, where from 1967 to 1996 she was involved with youth work among minority people, mainly students, through a number of churches and para-church organisations.[61] Taiwan was also the first destination of doctors Cameron and Ishbel Tallach and their children. In 1974 they went to Taipei to work in the Christian Clinic alongside Dr Donald Dale, whose Scottish parents had been medical missionaries in southern China, where Donald was born. When the Tallachs moved to Hong Kong in 1979, they continued to work with Dale in Vietnamese refugee camps, until the refugees were gradually repatriated to other countries. Cameron and Ishbel then took over the running of the Peace Medical Clinic in Hong Kong, returning finally to Scotland in 2003.[62]

Peer pressure, family and community traditions, and networks

When Samuel Johnson and James Boswell visited the Highlands in 1773, they were struck by the 'epidemick desire of wandering' that had convulsed the region. In Skye, Boswell wrote, 'we performed, with much activity, a dance which... seems intended to shew how emigration catches, till a whole neighbourhood is set afloat'.[63] The influence of peer pressure, precedent and professional propaganda in luring emigrants across the Atlantic was a recurring refrain in the testimony of other 18th century commentators, in a cause-and-effect pattern that became more and more significant with each passing year. Not surprisingly, these traits were confirmed and reinforced by the departure of two million Scots overseas in the 1800s, and the continuing coalescence of economic opportunities with family and community networks throughout the diaspora is evident in much of the

20th century testimony already cited.

Successive centuries of emigration undoubtedly contributed to an attitude that leaving Scotland – either permanently or temporarily – was a natural part of the life cycle. Against a backdrop of constant demographic upheaval, the decision to emigrate was not necessarily remarkable, suggesting that it might be appropriate to ask why Scots stayed at home, as well as why they left. Traditions of emigration, albeit with lingering connotations of clearance and exile, were particularly strong in the Hebrides, where press coverage of the mass exodus of islanders in April 1923 injected a slightly more optimistic tone into the familiar narrative of lamentation.[64] Within a single week 595 men, women and children had embarked on two Canadian Pacific liners, the *Marloch* and the *Metagama,* which called at Lochboisdale and Stornoway respectively, in scenes reminiscent of late 18th century departures. Several Hebridean interviewees mentioned the iconic *Metagama,* which has become embedded – not always accurately – in the folk memory of Lewis, as 'everyone says that they went on the *Metagama*'.[65] Further south in the Long Island and five years later, John Macdonald's emigration from North Uist to Canada was triggered, his son Charlie speculated, by family precedent and a venturesome spirit. 'A lot of people from here, like the previous generation, two of his uncles and his aunt had gone to Canada, so it was quite the sort of done thing to go to Canada by that time. Oh, he just went for an adventure, I suppose.'[66]

John Macdonald was also accompanied to Canada by a cousin from North Uist and an acquaintance from Lewis. In earlier generations, emigration, particularly from the Highlands, had often been a collective activity, as whole shiploads embarked together to form recognisable ethnic enclaves in places like the Eastern Townships of Quebec, the prairie settlements of Killarney and Saltcoats, or – from the Lowlands – the Free Church colony of Otago in New Zealand. By the 1920s the denuding of entire communities by highly visible bulk departures was very unusual, and the remarkable Hebridean haemorrhage of April 1923 was a final throw-back to a much earlier age. Decisions might still be made collectively, however, for example by groups of Glasgow shipyard workers who worked in teams, lived in the same streets in company-owned tenements, and emigrated together when their yard's empty order book threw them on to the dole queue.[67] A supportive network of fellow-travellers, or the mutual encouragement of one or two friends, could be decisive, not least among female emigrants. Several testified that they planned and implemented their emigration in tandem with others. It was while working for the banker in Dornoch that Minnie Anne Fraser heard about emigrants whom he had sponsored to go from that locality to the United States. She herself was persuaded to go to there in 1926 by a slightly older friend, and they travelled with a few other girls from East Sutherland.[68]

Four years later Agnes Lawrie followed in the footsteps of her friend and workmate, whose own decision had been triggered by the incredulity of American cousins that she was working for a pittance in London.[69]

Although the culture of individualism that characterised the second half of the 20th century was reflected in the increasing 'privatisation' of emigration, some interviewees who were not leaving as part of a nuclear family still made joint decisions to leave or sought the company of others. When Isobel Gillon's friend pulled out of going to New Zealand in 1958, Isobel carried on alone, but when Sheena McBean was faced with a similar situation ten years later, she was able to find another fellow teacher to accompany her to Western Australia. Maggie McEwan was halfway through a mathematics degree in 1961 when a friend talked her into applying to accompany her to Canada. The friend, who was a shorthand typist, was accepted, but Maggie was told to wait until she had graduated. Subsequent encouragement from her friend played a part in rekindling her interest:

> Why did I personally want to move to Canada? Well my girlfriend, as I say, had been successful 18 months before I reapplied. She came back to Southport for a Christmas vacation and she spent three weeks feeding me top level propaganda about how much I would enjoy Toronto, how much I would fit in even better than she did, and that it would be an experience.[70]

Maggie emigrated in autumn 1962. Five years later, Alison Gibson's interest in Canada was kindled by the friend with whom she emigrated to Nova Scotia, while Shona Morrison from Beauly went to Australia with her cousin in 1972.[71] Some interviewees fell subconsciously into lifestyles or careers followed by their forbears or neighbours. Transatlantic sojourning had characterised fur trade employees in earlier generations, while the merchant navy was a traditional outlet for Scotsmen, not least Highlanders. It was an occupation which continued to offer global travel throughout the 20th century. In 1954, after some years in the merchant service, Calum Murray from Shader in Lewis embarked on a 30-year career as a seasonal emigrant, commuting between summer work in Ontario and all but one winter with his family back in Lewis. He was following in the footsteps of his father, Donald, who in 1907 had gone to Ontario to work on grain elevators in Thunder Bay, and had returned to Canada following war service. In 1927, by which time Donald was working on elevators in Prince Rupert, British Columbia, he was joined by his wife and children, but after he died in an accident in 1933, his widow brought her six children, including 15-year-old Calum, back to Lewis. Twenty years later, when Calum 'just had that sort of feeling' to return to Canada, his uncle helped him find a job, which involved transporting grain from Thunder Bay as far east as Montreal.[72]

Meanwhile Calum Murray's younger sister Cathie had also inherited the urge to travel. In 1947, with 'nothing much going' in Lewis, she had gone to work for the NAAFI in Germany. While there, she decided to apply to return to Canada, but when her letter to Canada House went unanswered, she took the advice of a workmate from New Zealand to switch her attention to the other side of the world. After the New Zealand authorities answered 'right off', completion of the application form was straightforward, and Cathie arrived in Wellington on a ten-pound passage, 'the best ten pounds I ever spent', she recalled.[73]

Five years later, Annie Matheson joined 'several hundred' people from Lewis who had settled in Detroit. Her decision to emigrate was triggered both by post-war austerity and by a long-held ambition to see the country of which she had heard so much while growing up in the village of Coll:

> In my childhood we were one of the youngest families in the village. Most of the families around me were older, and they had people who emigrated in the '20s and before then – early '30s. And the way of life in the country then – when you were three years old you would walk to your neighbour's house and walk in any time, you didn't knock at the door. I practically lived in the neighbours' houses, and most of them had family in the US, and I used to hear them talk about the family, and I was just interested in what was going on in the US, because it was another part of the world. Then I used to see packages coming from them, and things that I had never seen before, and things that I coveted. And I said to myself, I was very young, 'I'm never going to settle down until I see that part of the world.' I never lost that desire. And then the war came, and my teen years were during the war, and there was not much opportunity to emigrate then. So when conditions changed I wanted to emigrate, that's when I started to think about going.[74]

Annie's perception was that living standards were much better on the other side of the Atlantic:

> Well I thought everything was much better over there than here, and the clothing – well, the clothing that came from over there too, during the war, packages would come, and we were so limited – everything was utility, dresses were really short and coats were half lined, and everything over there was so beautifully made, and fancy jewellery, and fancy shoes, and all that kind of stuff, which we didn't have access to over here. And I just thought it must be a wonderful place to be.[75]

The decision of her fiancé, Norman MacRitchie, to work on the Great Lakes also played a part in her decision:

> I had been dating the man whom I later married and we had been dating for six years, and when it came to approaching me about marriage, I told him, 'Well, I'm not going to settle down until I see the US.' And I think he was quite shocked. So we stopped seeing each other. And then we met up again maybe a couple of months later, and he had decided to sell his business and emigrate, and his brother... had already been over in the States, and he was studying in Philadelphia, in Westminster [Theological Seminary] there, and he had come to Detroit.[76]

Meanwhile, over on the west side of Lewis, Murdo MacIver was absorbing knowledge of North America and other places in a similar way to Annie. In 2007, in the first of three interviews, he remembered fondly his home village of Arnol and the window on the world that was opened through story-telling in the family home, which was a ceilidh house from his infancy:

> It was a great place to grow up. Everybody knew one another and our house was the centre of the village and there was ceilidhs there every night from Monday to Saturday. Never on a Sunday. And I heard all the stories from Canada, Australia, South America, Falklands, South Africa. And a lot of the people that was there had gone back from Canada in the early 1930s because of the Depression. And some of them had gone back in the First World War and was gassed in France, so they didn't bother coming back to Canada. So the stories were fantastic. And I think that's maybe why I'm here today in Canada.[77]

During a third conversation, in 2013, Murdo reiterated the significance of those fireside geography lessons, which had given him 'a knowledge of just about the whole world'. He also remarked on the high percentage of natives of Arnol who had gone to British Columbia, where he had encountered 11 in Vancouver when he first arrived and a further 16 when he visited a first cousin at Trail in the interior of the province a year later.[78]

Some interviewees reflected on the relevance of inherited or imparted wanderlust, or referred to other family members, past and present, who were scattered across the world. Ian Skinner, with whose sentiments this chapter began, had his first experience of overseas life when, as a wartime seavacuee, he spent four years in Dallas, Texas, before – as an adult – pursuing a career in shipping that took him to Hong Kong, Singapore and Japan.

Born in Egypt as the son of an RAF officer, emigration was firmly woven into his family culture:

> I was brought up in a family that had spent time overseas... I was brought up in Montrose but a lot of my parents' friends had similar experiences overseas, so a lot of the conversations were about what happened, their experiences abroad, and it seemed very natural for me to think in terms, when I grew up, that abroad was where it all happened, and it just seemed to be a natural thing.[79]

Imparted wanderlust could take the form of general encouragement from previous emigrants about the prospect of better living standards overseas. It was a recurring – if rather formulaic – refrain in the testimony of Carolina-bound passengers on the *Bachelor* in 1774, but in no case does the encouragement seem to have extended to practical assistance with the cost of relocation.[80] Nineteenth-century testimony, by contrast, is full of evidence of how chain migration was fuelled by specific support, in the shape of remittances, prepaid tickets, accommodation, investment in a farm, or a testimonial for a job. 'Large sums of money continue to be received from settlers in Upper Canada, who had previously gone out', the *Illustrated London News* observed when reporting the departure of about 1,500 emigrants from north-east Scotland in spring 1857,[81] while enquiries into Highland emigration identified the significance of ethnic networks in publicising opportunities and offering practical support. 'Many have sent home letters strongly recommending their friends to follow them', testified John Bowie to a parliamentary select committee in 1841.[82] There are several examples of such encouragement in the collection of correspondence, possibly commissioned, from Hebridean settlers in the Eastern Townships of Quebec, to their countrymen in Lewis in the 1850s. 'My dear brother', wrote Malcolm McLeod,

> I hope, before you are done reading this letter, your mind will be made up, and that you will not hesitate for a moment to say you are going to come, and we shall help you, and linger no longer on the barren soil of the poor decaying Lews'.[83]

Requests or recommendations from family and friends were particularly powerful and persuasive catalysts. It is not surprising that they feature in the testimony of interviewees, for personal exhortation carried the stamp of both authenticity and accountability. Some individuals, like Christina MacLeod, emigrated in response to a family crisis. As her daughter recalled in 2011, Christina, along with two companions, went to Canada in 1921 to look after her sick sister, after her brother-in-law had paid the passages of all three women from Portnaguaran in Lewis to Crandall, Manitoba.[84] In a later generation, family influence is particularly evident in the experience of Charlie and Molly Law, whose emigration, return and re-emigration were triggered when different family members alerted them to employment opportunities in the pulp and paper industry on both sides of the Atlantic: in 1950 Charlie, followed by Molly, went to Ocean Falls in British Columbia at the behest of his parents; in 1962 the Laws returned to Scotland after Molly's mother had sent them information about Wiggins Teape's new mill at Corpach; and their remigration to British Columbia in 1981 was sponsored by their son, who had returned from Scotland to the country of his birth five years earlier.

Meanwhile, family encouragement was blended with concern about Scotland's economic future in triggering the decision of journalist Alan Lawrie and his wife Marjory to emigrate from Edinburgh to Australia in 1966. As newlyweds in 1952, they had toyed with the idea of going to New Zealand, when Marjory's twin brother, who was working for a newspaper in Wanganui, asked the editor of the paper to write to Alan, encouraging him to emigrate. The Lawries did not follow on, partly because the less than wholehearted encouragement in the Australian-born editor's letter described New Zealand as a 'much more sleepy place' than Australia. By 1966 Alan was a successful deputy news editor at the *Scottish Daily Mail*, but the Lawries' interest in the Antipodes was rekindled by his sister and brother-in-law, who had emigrated to Australia the previous year after the latter had been head-hunted by the South Australian Fishermen's Co-operative Limited (SAFCOL). Like many others, concern for their children's future was also part of the equation:

> They [the sister and brother-in-law] seemed to be settling down well, and we started to think, 'what's left for us here?' because at that time, 1965–66, things weren't that good in the UK, especially in Scotland. The hydroelectric scheme which had been introduced after the war was going to be a great saver, but had sort of plateaued, coal mines were closing down all over the place, and industry seemed to be moving away. So we thought, 'what is there left for the kids?' And we just started thinking about it, and we spoke to – discussed it with Liz and Fred by mail, and we decided, 'okay, we'll have a go'.[85]

Destinations

It is abundantly evident that family networks, the testimony of friends, and the wider context of chain migration often determined destinations. In the first half of the 20th century, Canada remained the top choice, resuming the position it had held from the late 18th century until it had been overtaken by the United States in 1848. Of the 494,053 Scottish emigrants who went to

North America, the Antipodes and South Africa in the inter-war period, 39.4 per cent went to Canada, 36 per cent to the United States and almost 20 per cent to Australia and New Zealand.[86] Post-war emigrants continued to favour the Old Commonwealth, particularly Australia, although it is more difficult to differentiate Scottish statistics from UK emigrants as a whole.[87]

As noted in Chapter 1, most interviewees emigrated to these traditional destinations, and their observations can be amplified from testimony in other repositories. When eight-year-old Amy Dalgleish accompanied her parents to Canada in 1915, the destination was dictated by her grandmother. During an interview for an oral history project in British Columbia in 1973, she recalled:

> We were going to go to New Zealand, and in fact there was a huge drawer in a dresser filled with literature on New Zealand, and by this time, my mother's mother and... brothers were out in Canada, and my grandmother was horrified at the idea of us going to New Zealand. [She said] come to Canada if you're going to leave. So we came out to Canada.[88]

For Anne Morrison's family in the 1920s, Canada was the obvious destination for a variety of reasons:

> I think because the three emigrant ships were leaving from Lewis going to Canada, and it was direct from Stornoway, and it also was nearest, so I suppose the possibility of coming home was higher. Because my mother had an uncle that lived in Australia, and I think he possibly only came back once. So I think my uncle thought of Canada because he knew that he would be able to come back at some point and visit his family.[89]

Several interviewees mentioned that the presence of family, friends or acquaintances, or a previous experience of the country, played a part in directing their decision. In the 1920s Agnes Lawrie's workmate had relatives in Connecticut, while surgeons Roddy Campbell and William Gillespie had each been in Canada and New Zealand respectively before. Annie Matheson did not consider any alternatives to the United States, the country which had captivated her imagination as she was growing up. 'I never wanted to leave Lewis unless I would go to America. I didn't want to go to Glasgow or London to work. I would far rather stay here [Lewis], but America was first.'[90] On the other side of the world, Cathy Donald's mother had two sisters in New Zealand, and a brother-in-law who sponsored them in 1953; and while Katrine and Ian McLean emigrated from Aberdeen to New Zealand in 1961 primarily because Katrine was pregnant and the McLeans 'couldn't afford to stay' in Scotland, their decision was determined partly because they could stay initially with Ian's sister in Auckland.[91] Two years later Helen Campbell and her husband decided to emigrate primarily for the benefit of their two sons (aged seven and four) after their rented farm in Argyll was sold to the Forestry Commission and they lost the tenancy. Their choice of New Zealand as a destination was shaped by encouragement from a friend who had settled in Owaka. Helen recalled that 'my husband had a very good friend who was already out here, and his brother was also out here. They kept writing, it was really through them... they just worked on one another, I suppose.'[92]

For others, the destination was determined by a specific job offer or a particularly favourable economic climate. Two of the handful of interviewees who went to Africa, Gladys Morrice and Carrol Stewart, joined their husbands, who had secured employment in Northern and Southern Rhodesia respectively. In 1946 Gladys travelled to Luanshya, where a relative had encouraged her husband to take up work in copper mining, and in 1953 Carrol followed a similar path when her husband, head forester at Dallas in Morayshire, who had tired of waiting to fill 'dead men's shoes' in terms of promotion, applied successfully for a job near Umtali.[93] Three years later Easton Vance 'was tempted to look at Rhodesia', after hearing about the country from comrades who had been sent to RAF training camps out there, but in retrospect he commented, 'I'm sure glad I didn't' [go there].'[94] Easton's decision to leave his job as an engineer with Colville's steel works was made at a time when 'practically every country in the Commonwealth and elsewhere were calling for emigrants'. After consulting 'all the newspapers of the countries in which I was interested', he rejected New Zealand, which was 'economically in a pretty poor way'. Although Australia 'made the best deal in terms of outlay of money'[95] and he went to several Australian recruitment lectures in Glasgow, he opted instead for Canada, mainly on the grounds that it offered a good balance between earning power and cost of living. His specific choice of British Columbia was dictated by his aversion to 'extreme weather climates' and the fact that he had contacts in the city. Brian Coutts' father ultimately decided on New Zealand instead of Canada because he wanted to emigrate with his wife and family, rather than alone:

> I know that in 1951, when I was four, they considered migrating to Canada, and we were within weeks of going, I think within a couple of weeks, but it required my father to go first and set up a job and a house and then the rest of us to go, and I think at that point he wasn't prepared to do that, when it came to the crunch, because he'd spent so much time away from the family, and he wasn't going to volunteer to do it again, so at the last moment we didn't go to Canada.[96]

Echoing Easton Vance's evaluation of locations within Canada, climatic conditions also steered John and Joan Noble to Vancouver Island in 1966. They wanted to replace Aberdeen's 'abysmal' weather with a more benign environment, but they were not sure where to look. They thought first of the south of England, 'but that didn't appeal a lot'. John was keen on Australia, having received encouragement from relatives to go there, but Joan, who was very attached to her parents in Lewis, baulked at the distance, and suggested the idea of Canada, which she felt was already familiar through long-standing correspondence with a cousin in Winnipeg. When the Canadian government sent lecturers to Aberdeen to promote different provinces in three nightly lectures, Joan was 'not very taken' with the lecture she heard on tobacco growing and manufacturing in Ontario. 'It was not my idea of Canada', she recalled. John, however, had a very different experience the following evening:

> They had a marvellous film of Vancouver Island. The beaches, and the arbutus trees leaning out over the beaches, and the provincial park sites, and Sproat Lake, and places on the Lower Mainland, and everything in BC, and he came home. It was a horrible night, and he came home, and he walked in the door, and he said 'We're going' [laughs]. And I really – I got a bit of a fright. I wasn't all that serious – I didn't think we were entirely serious, and I did get a bit of a fright. So we went through a process of great excitement on my part during the day, and apprehension at night. But he was absolutely committed to it, so in the April of '66 we sailed.[97]

Vancouver Island also met John's criterion of a location with close proximity to both ocean and mountains. A decade later, Murdo MacPherson from Inverness was, like the Nobles, influenced by a mixture of environment, previous knowledge, and distance when he chose to go to Canada. 'I never considered any other places', he reflected in 2005, 'partly because I'd been to Canada, I suppose, and I *did* know people there. I liked the environment, I didn't want to go to a hot place like Australia. New Zealand was just a bit far off the beaten track.'[98] In a follow-up interview in 2017 Murdo reiterated his fascination with the environment, including 'a lot of romantic notions of conquering the wilderness', and although he ended up living in Toronto, he spent much of his time in outdoor pursuits. He was also influenced by a visit to an Invernessian friend, a bricklayer, who had emigrated to Ontario four or five years before Murdo took the plunge: 'I could visibly see his life was so much better than it would have been when he was in Inverness originally, in all sorts of ways, not just material ways, but his outlook was more open, more positive.'[99] Occasionally the choice of destination was a lottery that might be decided by chance encounters or casual conversations. As we have seen, Cathie Murray's destination changed when her letter to Canada House went unanswered and an acquaintance encouraged her to apply to New Zealand instead. Isobel Gillon's original plan to emigrate to Australia was switched to New Zealand on the recommendation of a workmate:

> Out of the blue Margaret says 'Do you fancy emigrating?' And I said, 'What?' And she says, 'Emigrating.' I says, 'Where to?' She says, 'Australia.' I says, 'Why?' She says, 'I'm ready to go. I'm fed up.' But when I went back into the mill on the next day, on the Tuesday, the wool sorter heard about this news and he said, 'Isobel, come here,' and he had a world map up on the wall, and says, 'You don't want to go to Australia, you want to go to that wee country down there, New Zealand.' So I takes the message back to Margaret, and she says, 'I'm no fussy, as long as it's somewhere.'[100]

* * *

The multi-layered complexities of the decision to emigrate have been demonstrated in testimony that covers a wide spectrum of social and geographical backgrounds, employments, and destinations. Successive generations of Scots from all parts of the country were propelled overseas by the same interaction of adversity and ambition, discontent and opportunity that had characterised their 18th and 19th century predecessors. Their wanderlust was focused and directed by job offers, word of mouth encouragement, precedent and advertising. Young adults, who had always made up the majority of emigrants, continued to dominate the outflow, but there was a greater gender balance, as independent young women took advantage of expanding opportunities for adventure as well as employment. In a century of increasing individualism, the Hebridean exodus of April 1923 was also the last fling of significant community emigration. Other changes were the eclipse of farming as the dominant occupation in both donor and host countries, and the – not unrelated – shift of attitude towards emigration, away from a permanent commitment to an experimental venture or an element in a career plan that might involve multiple relocations.

Personal recommendations and assistance from family or friends were always persuasive factors for those considering emigration. Crucial substitutes – or supplements – were the activities of governments, employers and charities that sponsored emigrants, and whose canvassing influenced both the initial decision and the choice of destination. Drawing on testimony from service providers and users alike, the role of recruitment agents is examined in the next chapter.

CHAPTER 3

Persuasion and Propaganda: Official Interventions and Reactions

MORE THAN FOUR decades after Cathie Tulloch and her husband emigrated from Morayshire to New Zealand in 1965, she remained in no doubt that it was the recruitment agent who had 'really clinched the deal for us'.[1] He rekindled their enthusiasm, which had been dampened by a year's delay between application and interview, and was, Cathie recalled, 'a lovely person' who was 'obviously well trained to sell New Zealand'.[2]

Agents, in various guises, had always played a part in mobilising and steering emigrants, especially those whose decisions were not framed by the experiences and encouragement of family, friends or community. In such circumstances, they could well have a formative influence on both the general decision and the specific destination, while emigrants who operated primarily through personal networks might seek supplementary practical information or financial assistance from recruiters representing governments, employers or charities.

The personal testimony of recruits and recruiters is woven into the key questions that frame this chapter. How did the objectives and tactics of agents in the 20th century compare with those of their predecessors? Can we identify significant variations in the approaches taken by advocates of different destinations? Were their policies influenced by any sense of Scottish exceptionalism? In what ways did globalisation and an increasingly casual attitude to emigration affect recruitment strategies and outcomes? Why were their activities often dogged by controversy? Just how important was their intervention in shaping the narrative of emigration and settlement?

Only a handful of interviewees had distinct memories of interacting with an agent, and only the Tullochs attributed their decision to emigrate unequivocally to his influence. But unanticipated encounters with two former recruiters, from Australia and Canada, led to interviews which allow us to explore the relationship from the other side of the table.[3] The testimony of Gordon Ashley and Bob Smart is supplemented by oral and written reflections from a handful of other agents, as well as the correspondence of a regiment of emigrants who acknowledged – to varying degrees – the role of professional advice and sponsorship in the conception and implementation of their decisions.

Changing patterns of recruitment

By the 20th century the recruitment of settlers was a well-established and integral part of government policy throughout the British Dominions, as well as the United States. Its foundations had been laid in the mid-1700s, when canvassing was often in the hands of former military officers who had acquired colonial land grants, or ship-owners and their agents who sought passengers for vessels that were returning to North America after delivering cargoes of tobacco to British ports. That pattern persisted during the first half of the 19th century, although the import cargo had shifted from American tobacco to Canadian timber. Localised embarkations, from ports right around Britain and Ireland, kept shipping agents on their toes, for in a climate of intense competition, emigrants could easily boycott vessels and captains that had acquired a bad reputation.

The transition from sail to steam put a greater distance between agents and their clients. As the shipping business became dominated by large companies, and embarkations became centred on Liverpool, Greenock, London and Southampton, emigrants booked their tickets through part-time passage brokers in their localities. These men were often shopkeepers, publicans or merchants, who rarely had any expertise in advising emigrants, and whose incentive for recruiting passengers was simply the commission they could earn from the shipping company or destination on each ticket they sold. In 1912 the Dominions Royal Commission identified over 3,000 of these amateur booking agents, whose activities were characterised by varying degrees of enthusiasm or inertia.[4] Meanwhile, from the mid-19th century, host countries engaged in increasingly sophisticated and competitive advertising campaigns, as salaried advocates lectured and lobbied throughout the UK, with the aid of lantern slides, agricultural exhibits and alluring posters.

Canada led the way in the intensification and professionalisation of agency activity. Two decades after London-born emigrant Thomas Rolph had returned to Britain to entice emigrants, particularly from Scotland, to the Canadas, another English emigrant, Anthony Hawke, was sent over from Toronto in 1859 to open an emigration office in Liverpool. Hawke paved the way for the appointment of William Dixon, a native of Ireland, as Canada's first emigration agent in Britain in 1866, based initially in Liverpool, then in Wolverhampton, and finally in London, where he established the new dominion's first permanent emigration office overseas.[5] It oversaw the recruitment activities of a number of regional, resident federal government appointees, who were given a fair amount of autonomy to arrange their lecturing itineraries and interviewing schedules and to liaise with provincial and railway company representatives, and local booking agents. Australia and New Zealand, which entered the field in the mid-19th century, adopted a more centralised approach, probably as a consequence of their significant and long-term financial commitment to immigration and settlement. Recruitment campaigns were generally orchestrated from the London headquarters of the various Agents-General, who took their orders from the colonial governments and kept a fairly tight rein on itinerant recruiters. Queensland dominated Australia's recruitment activity in the four decades before Confederation in 1901, notably in the 1860s and 1880s. New Zealand's biggest influx came in the 1870s, when, as part of Prime Minister Julius Vogel's national development strategy, money was poured into promoting assisted immigration, not least through the appointment of provincial agents across the UK.

As the New Zealand economy plunged into depression in the 1880s, and recruitment activity was severely pruned, the spotlight switched back to Canada, where the federal government and railway companies were stepping up their campaign to populate the prairies. During the decade after 1896 the Immigration Department, under Interior Minister Clifford Sifton, invested four million dollars in a determined effort to attract homesteaders, discourage urban settlement, and challenge American competition. Though Sifton sought experienced farmers from continental Europe as well as Britain, agents in the UK were able to capitalise on a conjunction of agricultural depression and imperial enthusiasm, and from 1905 Sifton's successor, Frank Oliver, reinstated the preference for British settlers.

The intensity of Canada's prairie-focused recruitment drive at the turn of the century helps to explain why many of the pioneers who, 50 years later, provided the Saskatchewan Archives Board with written testimony about their settlement, attributed their decisions to persuasive immigration campaigns. But, while acknowledging their significance, we should also be alert to the potentially distorting influence of the leading question posed by the archivist investigators. After asking why the immigrants had come to Canada, the questionnaire went on to suggest several possible responses: 'Through other people?' 'Reading about it?' 'Railroad or government information?' It was not surprising that the elderly respondents readily latched on to one or more of these options, sometimes simply repeating them almost verbatim.

Andrew Veitch was only two when his parents emigrated from Peterhead in 1903, after his father had learned of free homesteads from 'Canadian Government information'. Six respondents who arrived in 1906 highlighted Canadian government publications, or positive coverage in the British press.

'All over Britain papers were full of it', recalled Margaret McManus from Lanark, while Margaret Smith and her husband left Linlithgow after they 'got papers from Government telling us of the wonderful opportunity' for farming. John Allan from Kirkwall also remembered that the government information had 'painted Canada as a veritable Garden of Eden – it told us we didn't need any agricultural experience. We had only to scratch the rich virgin soil to ensure good results.' And George Craig from Beith highlighted the role of Bruce Walker, the Canadian Government Emigration Officer at Glasgow's St Enoch Square premises, who had given his father a letter of introduction. Hugh Sutherland from Inverness was unequivocal that 'Government information' had been instrumental, while other respondents whose decisions were based on the encouragement of family or friends testified to the practical guidance subsequently provided by government pamphlets. Robert Mills, originally from Dumfries, came to the prairies with the aid of government literature, but by a circuitous route. Along with a friend, he 'decided to try Canada' in order to escape the uncongenial conditions of his employment on the Central South African Railroad at Bloemfontein. He explained that 'We wrote Canada House England so I got pamphlets and maps sent us. As we sat in our tent at nights we studied the maps and settled on a place where there seemed to be a few creeks'.[6]

Oral testimony collected in British Columbia suggests that eye-catching promotional material circulated by Canada House continued to bear fruit after the First World War. Bill Christie was still a schoolboy when he had first entertained the idea of emigrating, thanks to an 'auld dominie' in Drumlithie, Kincardineshire, who 'was always talking about the colonies'. Bill decided to opt for Winnipeg rather than Australia when, during a visit to London, 'I used to go down round Canada House round Trafalgar Square and you'd see all these, *A Hundred and Sixty Acres Free*. And that's really what took me *there*.'[7] It was vivid imagery that first attracted Jane Downie from Paisley, who 'really started being interested in Canada because there was this one store I used to pass quite frequently where they had this great big coloured picture of the CPR – of Ottawa River and the bridge across, and it was advertising, it was the CPR advertising Canada'. This reinforced childhood images that she had conjured up from letters read aloud in the family home, sent by a missionary friend who described his life amongst the Blackfoot Indians. The actual opportunity to emigrate followed Jane's marriage to a disabled war veteran, who had lived in British Columbia before enlisting, and whom the Soldier Settlement Scheme sponsored to return to Canada, accompanied by his bride.[8]

The Soldier Settlement Scheme was, of course, the harbinger of the much more ambitious programme of civilian empire settlement which survived on the statute book for half a century. It generated a variety of shared funding enterprises that blurred the roles of government and charities in providing sponsorship for emigrants, and its impact on Scotland was mentioned in oral testimony from different generations. The Hebrides had been a fruitful field for recruitment before the war, and in the 1920s the islands were heavily canvassed by Australia and Canada, especially by agents William Stillman, William Noxon, and Andrew MacDonell. In February 1922, Stillman, a distinguished war veteran who had served with the Australian Imperial Force in Egypt, was sent to London to take up the post of Chief Clerk in the Australian Government's Migration and Settlement Office at a salary of £670 a year. During his three-and-a-half-year appointment, he made at least four recruitment visits to the Hebrides, where one of those who was attracted by his message was Angus Macdonald from North Uist. In 1987, when Angus (then aged 82) was interviewed for the New South Wales Bicentennial Oral History Project, he attributed his decision to the agent's offer of an advance of the £33 passage money, combined with his father's enthusiasm for Australia. Meanwhile, the neighbouring islands to the south and north were being canvassed for Canada, through the offer of assisted passages, farm work and homesteads under the auspices of the Empire Settlement Act. To the south, Andrew MacDonell, a former Benedictine priest who had founded the Scottish Immigrant Aid Society, recruited for Alberta with the aid of a handful of fellow priests who acted as sub-agents. To the north, William Noxon, Agent General for Ontario, one Major Goodliff, and Murdo MacLean, the Stornoway shipping agent, promoted Ontario in schools and village halls throughout Lewis. Mary MacFarlane from Garrabost, whose brother emigrated on the *Metagama* and paid Mary's fare four years later, remembered the illustrated lectures 'of the farmers and the wheat and all that they were growing, and this looked so wonderful'.[9] Donald MacLeod, a *Metagama* emigrant, was less impressed when Goodliff held a meeting at Lionel school. '[He] told us of the opportunities in Canada... which didn't impress us that much. It was only $30 a month, and your board you were getting' on the farm. Anyhow we felt it was a job, and better than nothing, and the mainland was closed in our face because, if there were any opportunities at all, the ex-servicemen got it.'[10] Donald's objective was to get to the United States. After two months he left farm work for fishing on the Great Lakes, and subsequently worked for General Motors in Detroit.

The clearest similarity in targeted recruitment between the pre-war period and the 1920s was the persistent, but increasingly difficult, attempt to attract farming settlers to the dominions. Peter Dawson was born three months after his parents arrived in Australia in 1928, his father – a farm worker – having probably been attracted by Australian government advertising 'at one of those horse shows, or perhaps even the feeing market'.[11] In the same era children and juveniles continued to be assisted by established and new charities like Dr Barnardo's, Quarrier's Orphan Homes, the YMCA, the Flock House Scheme and the Big Brother Movement, all of which were able to draw on the unprecedented injection of State funding. The continuation of the antipodean ten-pound passage into the 1970s was responsible, to a greater or lesser extent, for the emigration of 12 21st century interviewees in my collection, including Cathie Murray from Lewis, whose initial plan to return to the country where she had spent six childhood years was thwarted by the failure of Canada House to answer her letter of enquiry. A chance encounter with a New Zealander who was working alongside her for the NAAFI in Germany alerted her to opportunities on the other side of the world, and the New Zealand High Commission's immediate response to her letter helped to seal the deal that took her to Wellington in 1947. With an emphasis that can only be appreciated by listening to her testimony, she recalled that she simply had to fill in a form, commit herself to stay for two years, and pay 'TEN POUNDS... the best ten pounds I ever spent'.[12]

Five years later, it was again a roll of the dice that took Paddy McFarlane on an assisted passage from Edinburgh to New Zealand rather than Southern Rhodesia. As he explained:

> Back then, after the Second World War, there was a lot of emigration to Australia, New Zealand, Canada, Southern Rhodesia. A lad that I worked with had a brother in Southern Rhodesia, and [he] gave me glowing reports of living in Southern Rhodesia, which is now Zimbabwe. And it finished up, my papers arrived from New Zealand House before the Southern Rhodesian ones, and I had my medical and my interview and was accepted before the Rhodesian ones came to light, so I was probably very lucky in a way.[13]

There was a similarly haphazard element in Shona Morrison's decision to go to Australia rather than Canada in 1972:

> I just thought, 'Oh, it would be nice to go to Canada', and I actually applied to go – I was going to go on my own and I applied to go to Canada and Australia, and Australia was just as a second choice – I really wanted to go to Canada, and I got in to go, and while my application was being processed, my cousin, who was 19 at the time, said that she'd like to come with me. So she applied to go to both, and Canada turned her down because she wasn't – she wouldn't have been 21, but Australia took her, so that's how I ended up going to Australia.[14]

For Shona, the ten-pound subsidy was crucial. Without it, she emphasised, 'I probably wouldn't have gone – I probably wouldn't have even thought about it'.[15] Others, meanwhile, like Jim Wilson, Brian Coutts, Sandra Munro and Helen Bowie, found themselves in New Zealand or Australia because of parental uptake of a ten-pound passage in the 1950s and 1960s. For Helen's mother, a widow with three children, the subsidy, the advertising, and the desire for a fresh start all played a part in bringing her from Ayrshire to Queensland in 1969, as did encouragement and sponsorship from former neighbours, who had moved to Toowoomba two years earlier: 'She couldn't have afforded to do it on her own, I don't think – I don't think she would have thought about it really... She did want to come for a better future, and the advertising certainly helped: there was posters all over the place at the time.'[16]

Bob Crapnell's somewhat speculative application to emigrate to Queensland – six months earlier than the Bowies – was triggered by a newspaper advertisement, though he admitted that 'I wouldnae have had a clue about Queensland when I read it in the paper'. A shipyard joiner, Bob had worked on the QUII, but following her launch two years earlier work had become scarce:

> I just couldnae see anything in the Vale [of Leven], in Renton, to keep me in the trade that I had, and the knowledge of that trade that I had. I'd have had to have looked for another type of job, like a factory or something like that. I don't know yet what made me fill it in. I just thought, 'Hmm, this looks good, so fill it in.' I never even expected an answer.[17]

In fact, the answer came remarkably quickly, in the shape of a large package, delivered while the Crapnells were on holiday. As well as general information, it contained an invitation to an interview at Queensland House in Glasgow, and within six months the family had moved to Inala, a suburb of Brisbane. Remarkably, Bob's wife, Margaret, had been totally unaware that he had applied to emigrate until she saw the letter from Queensland House:

> All of the mail had piled up behind the letter box and I pushed in – and the two kids went running in ahead of me – and I saw a large brown envelope, and I thought 'What's *that*?' That was the largest envelope. Picked it up and read what it said on the front of it – 'Queensland Government'. Bob was coming in behind me, and I said, 'Where's Queensland?', and he said, 'Oh, I've got something to tell you.' And that was how I found out that one evening, when I was at the pictures with my mother, and he was looking after the children... he was reading the paper, he knew that work was going down in the shipyard,

> and he saw this advertisement by the Queensland government, in the local paper, and listing trades, and his trade was among this, so he filled it in, cut it out and sent it away, but he didn't tell me. And the reason why, he said 'I didn't want to disappoint you in case nothing happened.' On the contrary, they wanted us to come in two months' time. They wanted us to come really quickly, and we couldn't, because we had a house to sell.[18]

In Canada, bitter memories of interwar unemployment generated a more cautious attitude to recruitment after 1945, with a particular fear that displaced Europeans and Oriental immigrants would swamp the labour market. Government caution is reflected in Prime Minister Mackenzie King's qualified statement to Parliament in 1947. While he declared that 'the policy of the government is to foster the growth of the population of Canada by the encouragement of immigration', this was to be done 'by legislation, regulation and vigorous administration, to ensure the careful selection and permanent settlement of such numbers of immigrants as can be advantageously absorbed in our national economy'. More explicitly, he asserted that 'the people of Canada do not wish as a result of mass immigration to make a fundamental alteration in the character of our population'.[19] Eight years later JW Pickersgill, Minister of Citizenship and Immigration, confirmed the official preference for 'immigrants who will have to change their ways least in order to adapt themselves to Canadian life and to contribute to the development of the Canadian nation'.[20]

British settlers continued to be privileged until the full introduction of the points-based system in 1967. The network of federal recruitment offices which had been established almost a century earlier was maintained in the two post-war decades, along with provincial initiatives, particularly by the government of Ontario through its airlift of over 7,000 Britons in the late 1940s.[21] Although there was no subsidised transatlantic fare equivalent to the ten-pound passage, the Canadian government tried to counter antipodean competition in the 1950s and '60s by offering a scheme under which selected immigrants were offered interest-free loans on their ocean fare.[22]

Four couples whom we met in Chapter 2 were among those who encountered Canadian federal and provincial government advertising campaigns or vetting procedures. Sponsorship was often provided directly by employers, though when Ronald and Margaret Gillies Brown went to Alberta they did so under an arrangement with the Canadian National Railway, which found Ronald work with a farmer, whose land was presumably owned by or mortgaged to the company. Margaret thought that the emigration agents 'must have been in cahoots with the CNR, because it was the CNR that were going to pay for us going, if we had taken the payment'. They decided to pay their own way so that 'if we wanted to come back, we could – we weren't stuck'. Her recollection of the interview confirmed the complaints of some recruitment agents that they were not able to woo emigrants with the most up-to-date literature:

> The man, of course, was very nice, and he had a nice office, and he had all these shiny books of places to show us. We got the choice of what province we wanted to go to. We were probably advised a little on which would be the best ones, and he was a bit dubious when we did choose Alberta, because he says, 'Well, it's very new, Alberta, hasn't just quite – but no, no, it's very good, it's an up-and-coming place, there's plenty oil, and all the rest of it', so he was quite enthusiastic. And then he showed us brochures of houses we might have in the country, which were mostly the farmers' houses. But the thing was, he said, 'Well, I'm afraid I don't have any of Alberta, but I'll show you a book of ones in Saskatchewan', which all looked quite nice, actually, very romantic looking. So we were quite happy with that. And they would be furnished, because we had a family. So we wouldn't have to worry about having nowhere to go – we'd have a job, and somewhere to go to. And so, with a family, we wouldn't have to worry.[23]

Seventy miles further north, and a decade later, John and Joan Noble were, as we have seen, already thinking about moving to Canada when John attended an inspiring illustrated lecture about Vancouver Island.[24] Hamish and Isla Robertson went to Ontario in the same year that the Nobles settled in British Columbia. Having returned to Scotland in 1970 before re-emigrating four years later, the Robertsons were able to compare the immigration procedures, which 'didn't take long' in 1966, but were much more cumbersome by 1974.[25] Together, they speculated about the reasons for the delay:

> Hamish: I think they must have tightened up on the qualifications to come or something, I don't know – it just seemed to take – oh, they had moved the office to London... It used to be in Glasgow, but then they centralised everything in London...
>
> Isla: Now, we already had one Canadian-born child, so I don't know why it took so long, but we'd to go through the medicals and everything, all over again. And it seemed to be from the Canadian end that it was taking the time.
>
> Hamish: Well, maybe it was because our daughter was born in Scotland while we were there, so that made it more difficult for us to go back, because if we hadn't we could have probably just hopped on a plane and come back, but because we had Helen, that was an extra person who wasn't registered in Canada.[26]

Although their papers were stamped for Ontario, where Hamish had secured a shipbuilding job in Collingwood, by the time immigration procedures had been completed, they had decided to go to Vancouver instead, thanks to sponsorship from a friend with whom Hamish had previously worked in Montreal.

Charlie and Molly Law's second entry to Canada in 1981, when they were sponsored by their son, was also entangled in more red tape than their initial emigration in 1953. They attributed this partly to their having neglected to take out Canadian citizenship earlier:

> Molly: For us to get back to Canada, we had to be interviewed at Canada House, and there was absolutely no problem with the family, but we had to come back in a couple of weeks. So we went back in two weeks, and there was a big stamp on it [the application form], 'No adverse reports from previous residence'. But John [their son] had to sponsor us. We just never got around to taking out Canadian citizenship.[27]

When they went back to British Columbia the second time, the Laws' first step was therefore to take out citizenship for themselves and their youngest son, who had been born in Inverness. By that time the points-based entry system had been in force in Canada for 14 years. It was introduced in 1967, following a White Paper which had recommended a reduction of family-sponsored immigration and a greater emphasis on independent or economic migrants. The new regulations, which aimed to align immigration policy more closely with economic conditions, finally eradicated explicit racial discrimination in selection, confined sponsorship to a more limited range of relatives, and removed much (but not all) of the discretion that immigration officers had formerly exercised.[28]

Controversies, conflicts and impact

Recruitment strategies may have changed over time, but agents were always controversial figures, and opposition to their activities was woven into almost three centuries of Scottish emigration discourse. In 1802, Alexander Irvine, missionary minister at Kinlochrannoch, used the terminology of the press gang in an anti-emigration treatise which contained a damning indictment of the 'crimps' who he claimed were luring gullible Highlanders across the Atlantic. His diatribe was probably triggered in general by mercantilist philosophy and specifically by the colonising ventures of men like the Earl of Selkirk and Hugh Dunoon:[29] 'Highlanders,' Irvine argued, 'are strongly tempted by the flattering reports transmitted from time to time by former adventurers', who 'exaggerate their own good fortune... and depreciate the advantages of those whom they artfully address... Distance, credulity, and affection, give their misrepresentations currency and value.'[30]

More than three decades later, the temperature was still high. When ship's surgeon David Boyter toured the Highlands in the mid-1830s in search of emigrants who could be assisted to New South Wales under the colonial bounty scheme, he was criticised by destitution relief agencies for (not surprisingly) selecting the cream of the crop. In the early 1840s Thomas Rolph incurred the displeasure of the colonial authorities for the opposite policy of encouraging paupers to emigrate to British North America on the promise of receiving government aid.[31] And in the 1870s political differences fuelled a barrage of press criticism of unprincipled New Zealand agents who were allegedly squandering public money on spurious missions. In 1872 James Seaton was denounced for 'eating off his head in the west of Scotland', while a rival Canadian agent had 'met with great success' in Shetland, the field which Seaton had been excused from visiting after claiming – falsely – that smallpox was prevalent in the islands.[32] Although another New Zealand agent, Thomas Birch, visited Shetland a year later, press critics claimed that he was a 'government pet' who had been sent back to his homeland to enjoy a 'little spree in the capacity of an immigration agent'.[33] Fourteen years later Colin Allan was similarly excoriated for enjoying a free holiday at government expense when he visited his native island of Skye in pursuit of an 'absurd scheme' to recruit crofters for Otago.[34]

The main source of tension within the recruitment world was rivalry between representatives of different destinations and interests, but internal jealousies were also evident. While the New Zealand Agent-General, Isaac Featherston, described Thomas Birch, James Seaton and another agent as 'costly and useless', Birch counter-claimed that his premature return to New Zealand in 1873 was due partly to insufficient remuneration.[35] Almost half a century later, William Stillman's initial appointment in 1920 as an emigration officer for Victoria, without any others being allowed to apply, led to an 'emphatic protest' from more senior returned servicemen, who felt he was being unfairly favoured.[36] In 1923 George Fuller, Premier of New South Wales, petitioned the Australian Prime Minister, SM Bruce, to use his upcoming visit to London to press for better representation of New South Wales at Australia House, 'where the advantages of selection in the shape of migrants with capital are reaped by Western Australia and Victoria'.[37] Also in 1923, the appointment of a female agent to the Canadian government's newly-opened office in Inverness caused consternation among the traditionally male ranks of recruitment officers, while the agent herself, Anne Macdonald, was perturbed both at the cost-cutting policy of the Immigration Department in

Ottawa and the activities of Andrew MacDonell and his associates, whose questionable tactics, she claimed, were undermining the federal government's recruitment efforts.[38] In an interview recorded many years later, Lachlan MacNeill confirmed that her suspicions may have been well founded. He recalled that, as the *Marloch* ploughed its way across the Atlantic, 'One day the agent called the head of each family into his office to find out how much money each one had. He told them that if you tell me that you have more than you actually have it will be to your credit when we get to Alberta.' The MacNeill family was soon to discover this was 'a lie that backfired', and that they had been lured to Canada by naïve or even duplicitous promises.[39]

In the febrile atmosphere of 1920s Scotland, when the country lost a tenth of its population, commentators across the political spectrum vehemently condemned emigration and its advocates. Their rhetoric was reminiscent of the declamations of 18th century mercantilists, although, with the advent of political nationalism, the most vocal lament was for the loss of specifically Scottish, rather than British, brain and brawn. Three decades later, SNP activists turned their fire particularly on recruiters from the Antipodes, where ten-pound passages were attracting significant numbers. In December 1956 Douglas Henderson, who 15 years later became Deputy Leader of the SNP, pulled no punches in petitioning the Prime Minister of New Zealand to withdraw his country's emigration agents from Scotland. Alerting Sidney Holland to the 'serious effects' of his agents' campaigns, Henderson claimed that the benefits bestowed on New Zealand by Scottish settlers had been gained 'at the cost of a disastrous drain of many of the finest and best of Scotland's youth'. He went on to accuse the Westminster government of 'actively and deliberately fostering a large-scale clearance' of an 'under-populated' nation, which, in conjunction with a 'dangerous influx' from England, constituted a 'threat to the survival of our country'.[40]

Henderson's letter was written at the end of a year which had begun with nationalist opposition to an Australian publicity campaign in Edinburgh, and the sensational, but spurious, case of the poisoned pie. Hec McMillan, a native of Manly, New South Wales, who had joined the Immigration Department in 1955 as a selecting officer, was based in London at the time of the incident, but still remembered it vividly 30 years later. He had little time for the SNP, which he and his colleagues regarded 'as a lunatic fringe'. Their alleged attempt to sabotage the Australian recruitment drive in 1956 backfired, according to MacMillan:

> We were doing a publicity campaign in Edinburgh. The Scottish nationals hopped on the bandwagon and we were the recipients of a parcel containing a pie which was alleged to be poisoned.

> They felt that emigration was bleeding Scotland to death and they didn't want to see it go, as they said, the same way that Ireland went through the mass emigration of its people. They went to various lengths including violence. Several travel agencies carrying immigration posters in Glasgow and Edinburgh had bricks chucked through their windows.
>
> The Scots showed very little originality. Some few months before the Speaker of the Northern Irish Parliament had received a pie at Stormont which contained cyanide and the Scottish nationalists apparently got the idea from this but the pie they sent us was quite innocuous. It was a Wall's family sized steak and vegetable pie. Looked quite nice too but the police took it for forensic examination. That was the last we saw of it but it got us some very good publicity.[41]

McMillan subsequently encountered nationalist opposition at first hand when he was sent to run the newly opened Edinburgh office in February 1959: 'I had no sooner got the office in Edinburgh opened', he recalled, 'when a large gentleman presented himself at the counter and said, "My name is Gillespie. I am the divisional superintendent of police down at Leithwalken [sic] and this area is in my jurisdiction. In case your building is singled out by the Nationalists, we'll keep an eye on it and let you know if anything occurs." Two weeks later,' McMillan continued, 'There was an "occurrence" outside the office, when Gillespie phoned him to report that "they have painted some highly abusive slogans on your front steps and they've got a bundle of your migration literature which they have heaped into a wee pile and set fire to at St Andrew [sic] Square. They are playing the "Muckin' O' Geordie's Byre" and they're dancing an eightsome reel around it."'[42]

Recruitment agents were demonised in public and political discourse because their activities were perceived as dangerously effective. Emigrants attended their lectures, read their literature and solicited their help in booking tickets or securing employment, but rarely expressed strong views about their intervention, unless things went wrong. Among all my interviewees, Rob and Cathie Tulloch stand out as the only emigrants who ascribed their decision emphatically to the persuasive canvassing of a recruitment agent. After qualifying as a nursery nurse in Aberdeen in 1965 Cathie returned to her native Morayshire to marry Rob, who was working on a farm, and living in a tied cottage. Finding it difficult to settle after three years away, and feeling that Rob was undervalued by his employer, it was perhaps not surprising that Cathie was attracted by a newspaper advertisement for farm workers to go to New Zealand. As Cathie explained:

> CT: Shortly after that [returning from Aberdeen to Morayshire], I started to

feel there must be more to life than just what we'd seen, and there was an advert in the *Sunday Post*, a very, very small advert, which said, 'Farm workers wanted for New Zealand.' So I sent away for the information, and Rob didn't know anything about it till the information started to come in. We applied, and it took some 18 months before we actually got out there, but after about 12 months we got an interview. By that stage Rob had got a little bit tired of waiting, and had gone off the idea, but I convinced him to just go along and see the guy, and have a chat, and he convinced us that New Zealand – he sold New Zealand – and convinced us to keep going.

MH: How did he sell New Zealand? What sort of things did he say?

CT: He told us about the free and easy life out there, and how it was a country where one could really better themselves if they were prepared to work, and of course we always had worked, so that didn't daunt us any at all... The big thing too, was that he explained that class distinction wasn't a big thing in New Zealand, and workers and owners worked side by side and played side by side, more or less, which was something which we really did find out for ourselves when we got there.[43]

The Tullochs' conversation with the unnamed New Zealand government agent in an Aberdeen hotel reinforced the initial impression they had gleaned from the 'huge wad of brochures' that had been sent to them a year earlier. Cathie's comment demonstrates that, in their case, the provision of external encouragement was crucial: 'It really clinched the deal for us... We had nobody up here. We didn't know anybody in New Zealand, and so we had no information.'[44] Both came from big families – Rob was one of ten and Cathie had five siblings – 'so the thought to come away wasn't taken lightly'.[45] Rob's older brother had already emigrated to Vancouver, propelled by a desire to escape the perceived 'rut' of working in his father's carpentry business and the encouragement of former RAF comrades, but Rob did not want to follow directly in brother Bill's footsteps.

The Tullochs were particularly attracted by the prospect of an egalitarian society that was so different from their experience in Morayshire:

RT: The boss was the boss over there, and if he wanted to sack you, he could sack you, but you couldn't really leave the job without an awful lot of turmoil, and literally, you were scared to mention the fact that you – that I was planning leaving him, because I knew he would just throw a wobbly, and that would be it, so we kept it fairly quiet until we had to go into Aberdeen to be interviewed, and that's when it all came out.

MH: What did your boss say when you said you were leaving?

CT: He sacked him!

RT: [Laughs] He told me I was finished. 'You're going to New Zealand – you might as well go today.'

Evicted from their tied cottage and dismissed from his employment, Rob found a job making concrete on a building site for the six-week period between acceptance and embarkation, a short interlude which 'didn't give us any time to brood over it or think, well, are we doing the right thing?'[46]

The recruiters' perspective

So far the objectives and effects of recruitment have been discussed mainly from the perspective of clients and commentators. The view from the other side of the desk generally has to be gleaned from the official reports and letters of agents to their employers, but can be supplemented by a handful of interviews with selecting officers. This chapter is rounded off by drawing on four such interviews: one from a published collection, one from an oral history archive, and two from the bank of interviews in which this study is rooted. Three agents represented Australia, and one worked briefly for a Canadian province. Of the host countries, only Australia has so far explored the careers of former recruitment officers specifically, through a book of reminiscences, published in 1989, and an ongoing oral history project hosted by the National Library of Australia.[47]

The promotion of immigration lay at the heart of Australian government policy after the war. In the 1940s and '50s, with wartime memories of attempted Japanese invasion still fresh, the sustained recruitment of immigrants, especially from the UK, was prioritised as Australia attempted to tackle the vulnerability generated by under-population, under-development and isolation. For a quarter of a century, the ten-pound passage was immensely popular, and indeed, British migrants 'became the abiding base of Australia's immigration program until the 1980s', being offered better assisted passage conditions and hostel arrangements than other immigrants.[48] In 1989, a former migration officer, George Kiddle, described how in the 1940s people had commonly queued in the streets of London for more than an hour to visit Australia House, while such a backlog of paperwork built up that two years sometimes elapsed between application and interview.[49] Between 1947 and 1965 the number of selection officers employed increased from six to 25, not including locally engaged British staff, and Kiddle testified to 'a tremendous spirit amongst us all' as they collaborated with State government and employers, banks and housing developers to encourage suitably skilled migrants. 'It was all done with a sense of decorum', he stressed. 'We vetted their activities very carefully and didn't allow any exaggerated claims to be ventilated.'[50] Kiddle's term as Chief Migration Officer from 1965–9 saw assisted passage numbers peak, with a record 170,000 Britons emigrating under the scheme in 1968.[51]

The recruitment net was cast widely. While Australia House in The Strand was always the hub of activity, regional offices had a vital input, and the supposedly 'innovative' deployment of a 'mobile showroom' in the 1960s was a reinvention of the Canadian Immigration Department's travelling exhibition wagon half a century earlier.[52] The notable popularity of the ten-pound passage challenged Canada's traditional dominance, which was further eroded by increasingly restrictive Canadian entry requirements, and in 1963 62 per cent of UK emigrants to Australia, Canada and New Zealand chose Australia.[53] The Scottish component, particularly within the post-war exodus, is difficult to identify, but an indication of immigration from different parts of the British Isles can be gleaned by looking at countries of birth recorded in the Australian census returns between 1911 and 1971.[54] The main surge of Scottish interest in Australia had in fact been in the 1920s, when the numbers of Scots-born increased by 23,733 between the censuses of 1921 and 1933. In the same period the English-born – from a much larger population base – increased by only 40,707. After 1947 the census figures indicate that the net migration of Scots was always less than 20 per cent of the British-born in Australia, and was generally proportionate to the place of Scots in the population of Britain. In 1971, the last occasion on which the census included a detailed breakdown of birthplace statistics, there were 159,292 people of Scottish birth in Australia.[55]

We have already met Hec McMillan, one of 18 migration officers interviewed for Harry Martin's study of Australian recruitment practices in the four decades after 1945. All but one of the officers were Australian-born (the exception being Irish), while the 12 immigrant interviewees included two Scots. When the Immigration Department decided to adopt a more decentralised policy in 1959, McMillan was about to return to Australia at the end of his three-year British posting to London. He had booked a return passage for himself and his family on the *Arcadia* and was 'looking forward to a few wet nights on the boat on the way home' in the company of the English Test Cricket squad, several of whom he knew. Having agreed to extend his tour of duty by between one and two years, and after insisting on a posting to Edinburgh (rather than Manchester or Belfast), McMillan was wrong-footed when Minister of Immigration, Alexander Downer, 'jumped the gun and announced in Parliament in Canberra that the Scottish office was off and running and we didn't even have premises. So I was told to pack a bag, get on the *Flying Scotsman* and get myself up to Scotland as quick as I could'.[56] After working out of a hotel bedroom for about three months, McMillan returned to Surrey to spend Christmas with his family, who then accompanied him back to Edinburgh in January, a month before the official premises opened for business.

'When I kicked off the regional office, I was a sort of one man band as far as Australian-based staff was concerned', he recalled. He was assisted by a clerk, Jim Hill, a Dundonian who (like many Scots) had served as a police inspector in Hong Kong, and a typist, Moira Sutherland, who was 'one of the most efficient lasses that I've ever had the pleasure to work with'. When the small team was immediately overwhelmed by over a thousand enquiries during the first three days of opening, McMillan managed to secure two extra typists and two more clerks 'to handle the sheer weight of paperwork', but the office – 'a small Georgian building owned by one of the banks' – was 'literally bursting at the seams'.

After weeding out 'a fair percentage of frivolous enquiries', McMillan estimated that about 300 of the 1,000 individual and family applications proceeded to approval stage. Misunderstandings sometimes arose, and he described how one qualified plumber, on being asked for his indentures, had posted in a set of false teeth, along with a note 'saying that he couldn't quite understand why we wanted to see his dentures but he'd send in his second best pair'.[57] McMillan felt that Glasgow and its hinterland would have been a more fruitful recruitment field, which they needed to canvass assiduously in order to counteract competition from rival destinations:

> I always felt that strategically we were in the wrong place having the office situated in Edinburgh, which is as different from Glasgow as chalk is from cheese. Glasgow is a fairly dirty, somewhat seedy rambling place but there's a vibrancy, a warmth there that I totally fail to detect in the sort of more austere character of Edinburgh.
>
> The Glaswegians tended to be very earthy, tied to the Clyde and the Clydebank which is a heavy maritime shipbuilding area, and it was from there that we got the bulk of the skills which were in very, very short supply in Australia back in those times. We used to absolutely welcome these skilled workers with open arms.
>
> They had this splendidly hard headed approach. No pie in the sky as far as your average Scot was concerned. He wanted to dot all the Is [and] cross all the Ts, and you got quizzed pretty rigorously about how the unions work out in Australia and did they follow the British way to any extent? Was it a case

of last on first off? And I said, 'Well, you know, by and large that's the way it goes.'

They liked the idea of a 40-hour week. They liked the idea of the wage scales. In Glasgow they worked when they worked, about a 48 hour week. In those days the average wage of a fully-skilled fitter and turner or rigger would have been anything from £7 10s to about £9 a week.

The whole of Clydeside was pretty stagnant, and if we hadn't got them, then they would have gone to either New Zealand or Canada. So we were in what we reckoned was an open market and I don't know about my colleagues, but I went hell for leather for the best I could get.[58]

Final decisions were made in London, but it was the regional interviewers who had to face the anger and disappointment of unsuccessful applicants, as well as make challenging initial judgements. On one occasion, Hec McMillan recalled that the Australian author, dramatist and playwright, Gwen Meredith, wanted to sit in on an interview so that she could write a 'typical Scottish family' into the storyline of *Blue Hills*, a long-running radio serial in Eastern Australia. She turned up for his final consultation on a Friday morning, after two days of 'run of the mill stuff', followed by 'the cream of the crop' on Thursday, and two or three 'hopeless' cases on McMillan's final slot before he headed back to London on the midday train. He described a scene of destitution and desperation:

Anyway, the family came in and the husband was a beat up little fellow, probably weighed about seven stone wringing wet with an army great coat and boots on. The wife was a tired looking woman. The kids were scrupulously clean but the clothes had been patched and darned. The poverty stuck out a mile.

Name was Macaulay. No skills, no nothing.

Anyway, I said, 'Have you tried to get a job?'

'Aye Mr,' he said, 'I have. I get up first thing. It's then down to the newspaper office.'

They used to stick the situations vacant pages in the shop windows for the unemployed people.

He said, 'I'd see a job and I'd think, "Aye I can do that". But by the time I got (sic) there, it's always full.' He said, 'I got to walk, I haven't even got enough money for a car fare.' 'Cars' being trams in Glasgow.

I said, 'So what are you living in?'

He said, 'One room and a wee kitchen.'

I said, 'One room, the seven of you?'

He said, 'Aye, we sleep in the one bed. The rats run... and I'm worried, Mr.

> My daughter. She's coming up to be a woman and what happens when her time comes? Where are we going to give her some privacy? What's the effect going to be on the other children? What's the effect going to be on her?
>
> At the end of it I said, 'Well, if we pass you through for a medical, that is going to cost you four guineas.' And I said, 'The passage will cost you £20 and that covers you from door to door and the kids go free. But you're going to be looking at a wee bit of spending money on the ship. You're going to be looking at about £30. Can you scrape it up?'
>
> The wife spoke for about the one and only time during the interview and said, 'I have my jewellery, my engagement ring and a few things. I think it will be worth maybe £30 or £40.'[59]

The upshot was that McMillan ignored the Department's guidelines and recommended the family for acceptance. Surprisingly, they must have also been passed by Australia House, because two years later McMillan learned, in conversation with a colleague who had faced the challenge of placing them on arrival in Australia, that they had been sent to a four-bedroom house at the Williamstown Migrant Hostel in Melbourne to replace the caretaker and his wife who had left suddenly.

Sandy Fox, whom we met in Chapter 2, emigrated from Edinburgh to Australia as a teenager in 1952. He joined the Immigration Department five years after Hec McMillan's Scottish posting, having acquired a taste for agency work when he was returning to Australia in 1963 after a three-year spell back in Britain. In a long interview with the National Library's oral history unit in 2009, he explained that the Australian government offered him a free trip on a vessel full of British emigrants in return for escorting about 14 children who were travelling under the auspices of the Big Brother scheme, but that he also assisted the ship's education and welfare officers by providing a young settler's perspective in answering questions about life in Australia.[60] 'In those days there wasn't quite as much promotion being done by Australia House as was done later', he recalled. 'There was lots of information material, published material, but a lot of people weren't interested in reading. They wanted to… see pictures, but we didn't have that much money in those days to make films, so whatever we could give them was good.'[61] Ina Watson, who emigrated from Glasgow in 1951 with her husband and two children, confirmed that the recruitment procedure, including the content of the films, was fairly basic. The Watsons were living in a one-room apartment, where the outside toilet was shared among three flats and the only bathing facilities were the city's public baths. When her husband saw an advertisement for boilermakers with the State Electricity Commission in Moe, Victoria, she agreed to go because the job came along with a house. At a 'very formal' interview in Bath Street, she recalled, 'the only thing they asked me was if I was quite willing to go for two years... They showed films on Australia and actually when I think back on it, it didn't show a great lot.'[62]

Back in Adelaide, Sandy Fox initially found a job with the Fitness Council of South Australia, before joining the immigration service in 1964. His reminiscences reflect the close camaraderie and long-term friendships among recruitment officers, his discomfort with the White Australia policy which he was required to implement, and his delight when its abolition meant 'we didn't have the dulux paint chart to look at any more'.[63] During an initial spell in Adelaide, he was responsible for processing full fare-paying immigrants from Europe, accompanying them to hostels and taking them on city tours. His appetite whetted by his early encounters with immigrants, Sandy then went on a six-week training course for overseas service. He explained that: 'In those days they used to send people for orientation trips all the way round, to each State in Australia so as the migration officers were prepared for each State – they knew a bit about every State, they'd been to every capital city.'[64] He learned a lot from the course, as well as being wined and dined by employers such as BHP steel, who 'were big customers of immigration, and they wanted us to bring out as many people for the steelworks as we possibly could'.[65]

Sandy's first tour of duty was to Athens, where, encountering many traumatised applicants who had suffered during the country's wartime occupation, 'I learned that you have to learn what they've been through'.[66] Four years in Greece were followed by tours in India, Beirut, South Africa and Chile, and a short spell back in Australia. In 1979 he was offered a posting to London, where – seven years after the cessation of the ten-pound passage scheme – part of his job involved trying to reignite British interest in emigration. During Gough Whitlam's reformist premiership, the White Australia policy had been explicitly repudiated and replaced by a completely non-discriminatory approach which removed the remaining vestiges of British privilege. As a result, according to Sandy, 'the British had thought that they were no longer wanted in Australia, so we had to try and put them right'.[67] He went on to explain that economic conditions augured well for a recruitment drive:

> This is the Thatcher era, and Brits were losing jobs right, left and centre. Steel places were closing and so on. So the Department, wisely, I thought, suggested that we have 'field days', as they were called, at various centres throughout Australia [sic], particularly centres that were suffering because of the sort of, kind of depression that was on – North East England, for example, round Newcastle; Glasgow; Liverpool; Manchester, particularly Manchester; Cardiff. And we went to these places, took over hotels, and ran an open day.

And apart from ourselves – we ran it – but the participants were every known bank in Australia, used to come along, they had a stall; the housing people, Reid Murray, that famous South Australian one, South Australian Housing; BHP would come out, they were always looking for staff, and recruit staff there and then, and we'd have, oh maybe, stalls with about maybe 100 Australian people at them, you know. And the people were genuinely interested. Big adverts in the paper to come to our open day. I remember I, among others of course, had to get up and we'd be speaking to as many as two or three thousand people at a time, which was good fun.[68]

Following the formal presentations and informal conversations, applicants were referred to technical advisers and the Committee on Overseas Professionals for vetting. Australia House also liaised with the various State governments and employers who all had London offices and ran their own recruitment drives, maintaining practices which had originated in the 1940s and '50s. The federal government continued to make the final decision and undertook the administrative processing and medical examination of applicants.

Ten years before Sandy Fox's tour of duty in London, Gordon Ashley had entered the service of the Australian Immigration Department, which at that stage had a London-based staff of around 30 migration officers. By that time, Australia House had recognised the importance of the west of Scotland as a recruitment field, and had supplemented its Hanover Street office in Edinburgh with premises in Jamaica Street, Glasgow. At the beginning of my conversation with Gordon Ashley, in July 2008, he offered 'the potted version' of a career that embraced theological study, business enterprise and politics, as well as the recruitment of emigrants:

[I] grew up on a farm in South Gippsland in Victoria, studied theology in my early to mid-20s. With the need of something to do by sheer circumstance I ended up taking a position with the Department of Immigration in the late '60s and was promptly selected to go overseas to be involved in recruiting people to settle in Australia under the Ten Pound scheme. And so I arrived in London in early '69 and found myself being sent up to Glasgow for three years, and then spent two years after that back in London doing the same kind of work. The position was very restricted in terms of movement around in Scotland because most of the people who were going to Australia were going from the west of Scotland, so it was only – most of the interviews were done in Glasgow. There would be an occasional trip across to Edinburgh, if the officers there were away or on holidays. I did four trips to Northern Ireland, two before the Troubles started, two afterwards. And I'd do an occasional

> trip down to Carlisle in the three years that I was here. After that I went – I went back to Australia, worked with the Productivity Council of Australia for three years before the Secretary was, was seconded from the public service and then came back – and I was five years – and came back to the UK in '78 as Professions Adviser at Australia House. Worked for three years doing that, more at the trade, at the sub- sub-professional [sic] and professional end, engineers and sorting out those who were able to settle in Australia given that their qualifications were accepted, from those whose qualifications weren't. And then went and established a small business in personnel consulting, concentrating on finding good positions with good Australian firms for people from all over the world, but principally the UK. And I did that for ten years before I entered the Victorian Parliament, of which I was then a member for another ten years, taking me up to the beginning of 2003.[69]

Duties were shared between Gordon and a colleague, who 'basically dealt with the west of Scotland case load'.[70] The technical advisers to whom Sandy Fox had also alluded were sent up from London periodically to evaluate the qualifications, aptitude and acceptability of tradesmen, and Gordon made occasional forays to Inverness and Carlisle, where interviews were conducted either in a hotel or in the local office of the Department of Employment and Productivity. In a shift of practice from earlier generations, these labour exchanges no longer actively promoted recruitment. 'I think those days had well and truly passed', Gordon observed, because of 'a concern that that would be seen politically to be aiding and abetting the flight of skilled people, and... the government wasn't prepared to go that far anymore'.[71] He also commented on the Australian government's reluctance to accept families with a disabled child, as well as non-white British applicants. For his own part, 'I would recommend them if I felt, all other things being equal, that they'd be accepted. But that would be a case that would be referred to London, right? So that's where the sensitivity came in and [the White Australia policy] hadn't yet broken down to that point where it didn't matter.'[72]

Local officers had considerable autonomy, and only 'more contentious or problematic cases', such as applicants with criminal histories, were decided in London by the Chief or Deputy Chief Migration Officer.[73] Once an applicant had been interviewed and recommended, 'all the paraphernalia around actual going was done in Australia House'. Local doctors, engaged by the Australian High Commission, held 'pretty stringent' medicals; in some cases criminal records clearance was solicited; and train tickets were bought for the trip to Southampton, where the emigrants embarked. A few went by plane, with BOAC or Qantas.[74]

Most applicants had been alerted to Australian opportunities by 'family stories' from earlier emigrants, along with advertisements and 'travelling film shows' emanating from Australia House and the various State offices.[75] All were seeking assisted passages. About a third comprised young couples, often with families, followed by young single men, and young single women made up a tenth. By the time they appeared in Gordon's office, they had completed a form with their basic personal and occupational details, and his task was to determine their objectives, adaptability, and the veracity of their employment history. Motives were emphatically economic rather than idealistic, and concerns and questions were equally practical:

> The weather, the heat, there were issues of heat, issues of what the housing was really like, and issues of schooling, if there was a family. Health, I mean there were the things that were predictable. And the other one which one might think is predictable from an Anglo-Saxon, from an Anglo-Celtic point of view but not from an Australian point of view is – 'what about the creepy crawlies?'[76]

Most enquirers did not have a particular destination in mind, but were generally amenable to going to wherever employment prospects were best. Occasionally, 'you would get silly things', such as 'one person, I recall, wanting to go to Ayr in Queensland because they came from Ayr in Ayrshire'.[77] Gordon estimated that between 80 and 85 per cent of interviewees were accepted, although by no means all made it as far as the boat, and between 25 and 35 per cent subsequently returned from Australia. Long delays between acceptance and embarkation could be discouraging:

> It might be two to three, it might be six to ten weeks prior to interview, and it could be anything from two to two, three to 12 months afterwards. Depending upon all sorts of circumstances, how long it took them to sell their house and all those sorts of things, all those things entered into it. So all you can say is that it was simply impossible to tell in an individual case how long it would take, and an average is meaningless. But the longer it took, often the less likely it would be that it would work out positively. Because people had waited too long, they had held their lives up for too long. And the kids need school shoes, and we're hoping to get Australian school shoes, but it looks as though we're not going. And the car's broken down. Will we buy a car or will we wait to get to Australia? And that's what churned people up, and in the end, you know, put them off. And there were times, and it became worse later, where it just took far too long for people's cases to be dealt with. Just too long, and the longer it went on, the more Australia lost esteem in the minds of the people who were migrating. Why *can't* they deal with my case, or, you know, why can't they finalise it?[78]

While some of those who gave up in frustration may have switched immediately to other destinations, Gordon's perception was that they often waited a couple of years before reactivating their interest in emigrating, though not necessarily to Australia. He also mentioned the introduction, around 1970, of a 'second-time assisted passage', which cost about half the standard fare:

> [T]hat was for people who had been in Australia, come back, realised they had made a dreadful mistake and wanted to go again. And in the end that wasn't frowned upon because it – initially it was, well, you know, if you've failed, you've failed. But as time went by, people in government began to realise, 'Oh, all sorts of things happen in people's lives, gee they happen in our lives, don't they?... Well, you know, you can't hold it against people if for good reasons or even for homesick[ness] occasionally they came back. So maybe we're being silly by depriving them of an opportunity.' And that had to do with competition. And that – the introduction of that scheme – had to do with competition, the fear that, 'well, you've got a decent family, who know and understand now what Australia's about, who've learnt their lesson, or have sorted out the problems that they had to come back for, why let them drift off to another country?'[79]

It was only through such re-applications that Gordon was able to glean any feedback on outcomes. The absence of evaluation 'was one of the things I disliked intensely about the process', he commented, since it prevented the migration officers learning from their own mistakes. His description of a 'typical day' reflected the pressure that he was under to make quick decisions on the basis of a half-hour or 45-minute interview in which he was trying to elicit as well as impart information, dealing with applicants whose background reading and knowledge of Australia varied enormously. Since much of the work was repetitive as well as pressurised, it was easy to 'become slapdash', especially when reports on the day's many interviews had to be written up well into the evening.[80]

Gordon's later tour of duty, as Professions Adviser at Australia House, offered a less stressful, more varied and more open-ended portfolio than his earlier sojourn in Glasgow. Reflecting the Australian government's shift of recruitment requirements from skilled tradesmen to the professional and semi-professional sector, his interviewees came from 'professions right across the board... and small business people'. His role was to advise them on the acceptability of their qualifications and to address the naivety of a selection system that did not understand the nuances of (for example) the different systems of computer programming:

> The more I understood about UK qualifications, the more I could be helpful to people. In Glasgow there was a restriction on the fact that it was assisted passage migration, earlier stage and all the rest. Basically it was a form of interviewing that I didn't like because it was, you know, it was really the same all over again. It was very much a factory style process, where you had to ask the same questions of everyone.[81]

Competition with other destinations appears to have been more light-hearted than in earlier generations. Inter-State rivalry was 'pretty sort of brotherly sisterly',[82] and relations with Canadian recruiters were 'all very friendly.' He felt Canada – their main competitor – had missed a trick by locating its office in Edinburgh rather than Glasgow, because 'the kinds of people they must have been wanting would have been more plentiful on the ground in the west than in the east. So I never quite understood that.'[83]

Finally, what of Canada, which had blazed the trail for professional recruitment a century earlier? Insights into the policy and practice of the province which attracted most British emigrants are found in the testimony of Bob Smart, who in the 1950s spent 13 months as an interviewer and immigration counsellor for Ontario House. Ontario was, in Bob's words, 'the engine of Canada', the centre of manufacturing and finance, with resources and requirements for immigration that were not matched by any other Canadian province.[84] Although Bob's job never took him outside London, his observations are of general application and reflect – in a way that emigrant testimony does not – the evolution of recruitment strategy and the political machinations that shaped it.

In 1955 Bob was 21 years old, newly married and keen to see Britain and Europe. Arriving in London in July with a letter of introduction from his church minister to HG Donaldson, Director of Immigration at Ontario House, he was appointed at a salary of £12 10sh a week, which allowed him to rent a flat opposite Clapham Common, buy a Morris Minor, and travel around England during his time off. He worked not in Ontario House itself, but in an office at 12 New Burlington Street, Mayfair, where his up-to-date knowledge of life in the province complemented the long interviewing experience of his two colleagues, George Patten and Andy Willcox. They provided advice, rather than advocacy, but worked alongside representatives of three Ontario employers who were engaged in specific recruitment drives: the Ministry of Education, which was looking for 'trained and experienced' teachers at both elementary and secondary levels; the Avro Aircraft Company, which was looking for technicians to work on building the Avro Arrow interceptor aircraft; and Ontario Hydro, which required thermal engineers and others to help construct two coal-fired electricity stations. An interview might last for up to 45 minutes, followed by a 15 or 20 minute slot to write up an assessment, but since Bob saw only two or three applicants in a morning, the pace was much more relaxed than in Gordon Ashley's experience:

> Our principal role was to review the applications that would-be immigrants to Ontario would fill out, quite a long page, and then invite them to a conversation in a private office where they could ask any questions about what it was like, and from our point of view, we could see whether or not they had specific skills or education that might be of use to Ontario employers. We also could determine whether or not they were financially likely to be a burden or an asset to the economy of Ontario. We could tell, for example, that if they were over the age of 40, we would be inclined to discourage them, because there was already some unemployment in Ontario and adding a man who wasn't familiar with the circumstances, he's going to have a difficult job finding employment. One of our main secondary purposes was to act as a kind of funnel or sponge for specific talents and skills that were sought by Ontario employers.[85]

Once those employers had reached an agreement with a recruit, Bob and his colleagues dealt with 'anything else they needed to know', and facilitated the travel arrangements. The weakness of the Canadian dollar prevented Ontario Hydro in particular sourcing employees from across the American border, so 'the obvious answer was to come over where there were English-speaking fellows and raid, in effect, the generating CEGB, the Central Electricity Generating Board'.[86] While he did not recall that such 'raids' provoked any animosity from British employers, there were some internal conflicts of interest. On one occasion there was an incompatibility between the Ministry of Education officer's remit to fill a post in a remote settlement to which no Canadian teacher would go, and Bob's responsibility to provide realistic information and correct misconceptions. The job was in a small railway town in central Ontario between Sudbury and Thunder Bay, about three hours' train journey from the nearest town.

> Well, this enthusiastic young teacher, with his lady – who were going to marry – came in. And of course, he's down the hall talking to the education guy... And he came back up to see me... and I said, 'Why do you want to take a job in Biscotasing...?' He said, 'Well, it's right in the middle of Ontario.' And if you take a map, yes it is. But if you take a map and then look at where the roads are, they're in the lower part of the bottom third. And the top two thirds are wilderness, with lots of lakes and rivers... 'Oh well, but it'll be interesting...' However, my responsibility was also to the guy down the hall, who's trying to get a teacher in there and who *has* offered him a job. So I'm

> not going to say, 'don't go'. I can only point out that it isn't paradise, and in fact the teacher that was there last left.[87]

Misconceptions were 'extremely common', Bob recalled, not least about distance: even those who consulted an atlas often failed to realise that while the Canadian map was printed on the same size of page as that of Great Britain, the scale was entirely different. Another misconception was 'that it was like Britain but over there', demonstrating a complete unawareness of Canada's multiculturalism and climate.[88] Bob's advisory approach might mean deterring those over 40 who did not have a sponsor or a job; those with limited educational qualifications; and the naïve who had 'never been out of their county' and did not realise that emigration would entail 'a major upset in their lives'.[89] Those he encountered were mainly young couples, followed by single men, but hardly any single women, apart from a handful of nurses and teachers. Most had been educated up to secondary level, and he speculated that university graduates made their enquiries by some other route:

> We could in effect attract any person who was saying 'I don't think I have opportunities in Britain, I think I *do* have opportunities in Canada', and if they were, say, 20 to 35, then we had very few concerns about them finding something. We did suggest strongly that the father went ahead and found a job and accommodation rather than arriving in Canada with a family in tow and his first concern is shelter, and his resources are probably limited, whereas if he's there, finds a job, then gets accommodation, and it may be two or three months, but that's the safe way to do it. So that's part of the shaping, if you will, of helping them get settled with as few problems [as possible].[90]

The cautionary approach of the Ontario government differed from Australia's determined push for immigrants in the 1950s. Bob reflected on the reasons for the disparity, reiterating the significance of the wartime invasion scare:

> Australia was very nearly overrun by the Japanese in the Second World War, and was on a policy of 'let's just build the population from anywhere and anywhere [sic] and any kind'. So they were looking for heads, rather than for skilled or trained or folks with money, and Canada, and specifically Ontario... didn't require that. We were looking for people that already had the education and the skills, and in fact we were raiding the country for people that we needed, and we were prepared to pay for them.[91]

Careful selection was accompanied by investigation into the reasons for dissatisfaction among those who returned to Britain. While Australia had a return rate of between a quarter and 35 per cent, Bob noted that fewer than five per cent of those who went to Ontario through the province's involvement returned, adding that about half of them subsequently went back to Canada, after they found the UK was not as idyllic they had remembered.[92]

The non-promotional approach of the 1950s was also significantly different from Canadian agency activity in earlier generations. Bob attributed this partly to improved communications which meant that the office was furnished with current Canadian newspapers and magazines, but he felt there was also 'a greater degree of integrity' by the 1950s:

> I have seen those ads for Canadian Pacific. 'Come to the west and we'll have a farm for you... It was really just a land deal. They were just trying to fill up the land on each side of the railway tracks because that's the only way they were going to get any business... The Second World War had a lot to do with people's insight and appreciation. A lot of Canadians came over here and generally speaking you know were well received... Also I think there was a maturing that went through in Canada after the war. We had been a colony style of country and we got some political leaders who were aware that we were big enough to be part of – and we became part of a group of seven later – but we were moving from a mid-wars 'aren't we lucky to be here?' to 'we can make a contribution'.[93]

Most of the people whom Bob encountered were seeking higher incomes, better opportunities, and an enhanced style of living that was advertised – bizarrely – by Ronald Reagan, who was then still forging an acting career:

> It wasn't necessarily that they were unhappy in Britain, but it was a stagnant economy, and their potential wasn't as great as it was somewhere [else]. And they couldn't get in to the United States as easily as they could get into Canada. They had various limits, and still have [sic] quotas in the United States... We were in the middle of the 'live better electrically' campaign. That was Ronald Reagan, who went on to become the President. But he was the spokesman for General Electric. And he promised a fridge in every kitchen, and a stove and all that kind of thing, so for the woman of the couple, she was going to have a nicer home, a better equipped home, and her lifestyle was going to go up just because that was the standard there.[94]

Bob's testimony also offered a perspective on the political backdrop to recruitment programmes. When he arrived in London, the Ontario government's regional offices in Glasgow and the English Midlands (probably Birmingham)[95] had recently closed:

> There was a struggle between the federal government, which was Liberal under various prime ministers from Quebec... and their interest was in bringing over Europeans, many of whom were expected to vote Liberal, because that was their background, and Ontario, with a Conservative government, said 'We've got to keep a balance here,' and so the Ontario government placed these other offices in further cities, meaning Scot[land] and central England, and still had the opportunity for shipping arrangements – this same thing worked no matter where you lived. As the pressure from the federal government – they said, for example, you've got to have a TB exam, we don't want to have anybody that has TB, so Ontario brought over TB measuring devices, x-ray machines, and qualified doctors, and we hired in London, and the Feds said you've got to have a *federal* x-ray – a provincial x-ray isn't good enough. So this kind of political jostling was taking place. And since the Feds were bigger and they had a bigger budget, Ontario was gradually succumbing to the limits.[96]

By 1955, all emigrants were going by sea. Ontario retained 20 or 30 berths on vessels operated by the main shipping lines – Cunard, White Star, Canadian Pacific – thanks to the personal contacts of the Immigration Director, HG Donaldson. Bob also blamed the federal government for the demise of the short-lived Ontario airlift scheme under George Drew:

> There was some aeroplane traffic. Now, one of the schemes, which didn't last too long, of the earlier period in the '50s, before, let's say, the Feds got Ontario under some kind of control, was that there was a plane leaving London, and it would drop in to Glasgow, and it would drop in sometimes to Belfast, and they would be picking up people and flying across, but it was all on a ready to go, there's a job waiting, but that was expensive... They tried it and it was costly. It moved people over quickly, but as a longer term strategy it had its limitations.[97]

He added that, while immigration remained 'fairly high profile' for three or four years after he left the service, 'once the demand for skilled workers fell off and once the economy stabilised, we weren't looking for more population'. He attributed the policy shift to the advent of John Diefenbaker's Conservative government, under which 'immigration was discouraged in some ways.'[98] Bob Smart himself returned to Ontario with his wife and baby, having been offered a job with Ontario Hydro, the company with which he was to remain for the next 36 years.

* * *

Bob Smart and Gordon Ashley were part of a recruitment industry that had a long pedigree, not least in Scotland. By the mid-20th century policy was being planned and implemented in a global environment that embraced ever-increasing migrant mobility and more restrictive gate-keeping by destinations that had traditionally favoured British settlers. While Scottish selection strategies were no different from the experiences of recruits and recruiters in other parts of the UK, SNP opposition to agents' campaigns in the 1950s suggested that the controversy always associated with recruitment was particularly acute in post-war Scotland.

Some emigrants never encountered a recruitment agent. For others, migration officers were simply facilitators, whose job was complete when the interview had been held, the acceptance form had been signed or the tickets had been handed over. In a handful of cases, however, professional recruiters or sponsors played a more fundamental role: triggering decisions, shaping destinations, and overseeing after-care in a way that would have been familiar to their 18th- and 19th-century predecessors. Some of them will reappear in Chapter 5, as they helped emigrants to become immigrants, brokering the settlement process and at times addressing disparities between clients' expectations and experiences.

CHAPTER 4

Making the Transition: Leaving, Travelling, and Arriving

ANNIE MACRITCHIE WAS not alone in comparing shipboard life to a holiday in a 'floating luxury hotel'.[1] Several post-war emigrants, particularly those who had endured years of rationing, were amazed at the quantity and variety of food on offer, and their fond recollections of ocean travel, despite the persistent problem of seasickness, stood in sharp contrast to the deprivations commonly described by earlier generations of inter-continental travellers. The hardships of the actual journey from the old land to the new had been frequently and graphically described in emigrant testimony in the era when crossing oceans and continents was a lengthy and risky undertaking. As the speed and comfort of transportation increased, however, so the tendency to document the move or offer warnings and advice to others diminished. Very few interviewees pondered in detail the processes of leaving, travelling and arriving in the second half of the 20th century, especially those who travelled by air. The exceptions were those for whom the journey had been particularly memorable, or emigrants who reflected on the symbolic significance of the physical transition. Longer journeys, notably to Australia and New Zealand, evoked more recollections than transatlantic travel, while some interviewees commented on the reception arrangements at ports of landing, or onward travel experiences. In this chapter, their testimony is woven into the bigger chronological tapestry of emigrant travel accounts, and their experiences are considered within the context of the policies and procedures that governed transportation. It is notable, however, that the process of transition provided far fewer reflections from interviewees than other aspects of their emigration experience. Their relative silence is indicative of the diminishing significance of the actual journey, which had loomed so large in the memories and writings of their predecessors.

Preparing to leave

Victorian letters and travelogues were preoccupied with the careful preparations that had to be made for the voyage, irrespective of whether travel was subsidised and supervised by the British and overseas governments (as with the antipodes) or involved the less regulated transatlantic traffic. Instruction was commonly offered on packing judiciously, avoiding seasickness, behaving appropriately, and – for those going to North America – avoiding fraudsters at both ends of the journey. In the 20th century, the tone of the advice became less moralistic and more pragmatic, and instructions were delivered mainly through the handbooks of shipping companies or government agencies.

A series of Passenger Acts during the first half of the 19th century tried to tackle fraud, abuse and health hazards. Their success was limited, and improved conditions owed more to the faster passages resulting from steam technology than to government intervention. Both donor and host countries then focused on health issues, although the testimony of emigrants and officials suggests that pre-embarkation medical examinations were often perfunctory at best. W Peel Nesbitt, a ship's surgeon on the New Zealand run, complained in 1875 that the examination of passengers at the embarkation depot 'is quite insufficient to prevent death and disease on board',[2] and one emigrant described the Plymouth depot as 'a den of disease'.[3] Maintaining a healthy ship was a major challenge, particularly among steerage passengers, and those who had come from isolated locations – like the disproportionate number of St Kildans who fell victim to measles while sailing from Liverpool to Melbourne in 1852 – had no immunity to common infectious diseases.[4] Smallpox vaccination was not popular in the Highlands, so it was perhaps not surprising that a few months later 'numerous' Hebrideans aboard the *Hercules* were carried off by that disease (or by typhus) on their way to South Australia.[5] The sufferings of unwilling Highland emigrants were repeatedly woven into the contemporary writings of polemicists such as Donald McLeod and into the retrospective testimony of witnesses to the Napier Commission, though they focused primarily on the 'unfeeling and deceitful conduct' and 'shocking inhumanity' of landlords and factors in clearing tenants onto ships during the 'transporting season.'[6]

The correspondence and diaries of Victorian emigrants rarely mention initial health screening. The responses of some interviewees to questions about the pre-embarkation medical suggest that, even in the mid-1900s, it was little more than a formality, although smallpox vaccination had been a prerequisite since the mid-19th century and in the 1950s three months' passive immunity against measles (just long enough for the voyage) was given to emigrants to the Antipodes, several years before the MMR vaccine was developed.[7] Some emigrants did not remember any medical interventions. Alec Miller, who emigrated from Port Glasgow to New Zealand with his wife and three children in 1953, recalled going through to Edinburgh on a

Saturday morning for an interview and medical, but suggested that neither was taken very seriously. After producing papers relating to three engineering jobs he had held,

> [we were] shown into this room. So I'm not sure if it was a doctor or not. But they took us in to X-Ray first. And then... 'have you had any illnesses and things like that? You're not blind, or anything? Blood still warm, sort of thing?' [Laughs] So that was that, really. That was all that was done regarding coming out here.[8]

The Millers had originally intended to emigrate in 1952, but delayed their departure for a year when Alec's wife became pregnant. Margaret Gillies Brown confirmed that the preliminary medical for would-be emigrants to Canada was equally cursory. She did not divulge her pregnancy to the authorities when she was preparing to cross the Atlantic with her husband and three children in 1959, and it only became evident in mid-passage when she was so sick that she had to consult the doctor on board. She recalled going for the pre-embarkation medical:

> It was in Glasgow, and we went up a *lot* of steps, and afterwards, a long time afterwards, we were told that was because – whether this was true or not, I don't know – because if you had any heart defect or lung defect, you would know by the time you got to the top of the stairs. But I don't remember getting much more of a medical than that, except we were asked if we had things wrong with us.... They weren't too fussy with their medical or anything then, because they *were* wanting people to go... You weren't supposed to sail if you were over five months pregnant, which I was, but I hadn't told them that... But I thought, well, they're not going to put me out in the middle of the... Atlantic – they're not going to do that, so what *can* they do, and if I get over there they're not going to bring me back. So, actually when the doctor did find out, he was a bit cross to begin with, but then he was quite nice about it, and I got every help on the boat.[9]

Margaret's recollection of a perfunctory medical echoes the perception of interviewer Bob Smart, whom we met in Chapter 3, that in the 1950s the only medical requirement for entry to Canada was a chest x-ray to demonstrate the absence of tuberculosis.[10] Three years earlier, Baptist minister Arthur Russell, along with his wife and two children, had emigrated from Stirlingshire to New Brunswick. When interviewed for the Pier 21 Oral History Project in 2006, he suggested that the medical and other preliminaries were more rigorous than Margaret or Bob remembered, but stressed that the experience was very positive:

> In those days they were very strict. You had to be well. You had to be healthy... We had to go to our own doctor, and we had to go to [the] immigration doctor, and you had to get x-rays, then there was police reports and so on... Glasgow was where the office was. And they were very helpful, very supportive. In fact, it was so easy in many ways, in spite of the chore of having to go through all of this.[11]

Yet Sally Blake, who emigrated to Nova Scotia in 1957, insisted that she did not have to undergo a medical until she arrived in Digby, where it was required by her employer.[12]

Ena Macdonald from North Uist had cause to remember her medical in Glasgow in 1961, because she had an adverse reaction to the smallpox vaccination: 'I was nearly dead after it, I was so ill... I was delirious, oh, I was never so ill in my life.'[13] Ten years later Shona Morrison did not have either an interview or a specific medical before going to Australia. Everything was done 'by paperwork', and she simply had to submit proof of a smallpox vaccination (to which she also had a bad reaction) and a chest x-ray. As W. Peel Nesbitt had recommended a century earlier, the standard medical checks were therefore undertaken by local practitioners, rather than at the final stage when the emigrants were about to embark.

Neither were the administrative procedures particularly burdensome, particularly for those who were not sponsored by governments or employers. Katrine and Ian McLean, emigrating independently under their own steam to New Zealand in 1961, recalled 'no bureaucracy. We just bought our tickets and came. No applications to make'.[14] Rob and Cathie Tulloch, who went from Morayshire to New Zealand in 1965 with government sponsorship, had to wait a year between application and interview, but thereafter did not encounter significant administrative hurdles, and left six weeks later. Alison Gibson from Dumfries, who emigrated to Canada with a friend in 1967 when they were offered jobs as computer programmers with the provincial government of Nova Scotia, remembers

> ...almost nothing of the details after our interviews and the job offer. I don't remember having a medical check prior to being accepted as an immigrant, and also don't remember if we just mailed in the necessary papers, or went to the Canadian embassy, nor how we arranged our travel, which was on the *Empress of Canada*. Of course, at that time we had never come across a photocopying machine, and so kept no record of the papers we submitted, except for the handwritten copy in fountain pen of my work experience when applying for the job I obtained.[15]

Partings: poignancy and practicality

However exciting was the prospect of the new life, and however smooth the preparations, the moment of parting was often traumatic. Wistful leave-takings were a particularly common feature of Victorian testimony, but also feature in the less sentimental writings of 20th-century emigrants, as well as the recollections of a few interviewees. In other cases, it was only after the passage of time that individuals who had emigrated as young adults began to appreciate how their parents had felt as they waved them goodbye. Sheena McBean's parents were 'very supportive' of her decision to go to Australia as a young teacher in 1969. Forty-five years on, she recalled the departure with some emotion:

> We were a very close-knit family, and that's why I think it must have been really difficult. I can remember Mum – Dad couldn't come down, he saw me off at Inverness station, but Mum came down to Edinburgh with me. And I remember looking back and seeing him [audibly emotional pause] it's something – it's only me that realises it now. At the time it was such a big adventure and you didn't think about – isn't it awful? I didn't really think about the effect it was having on them.[16]

In similar vein Shona Morrison's parents did not stand in the way of her decision to go to Australia in 1972 at the age of 21, but, looking back in 2014, she thought that 'while they never, ever said anything... they were heartbroken, probably, thinking about it now'.[17]

Margaret Gillies Brown mused on her mixed emotions at leaving Scotland: the sadness at pulling up old roots but the anticipation of putting down new ones:

> I don't think it was as sad as it should have been. Ronnie was always determined that no relative would come and see us off, because he always said he thought that was the saddest thing, having somebody waving to you [with] the ship going away. And he was in the Navy during the war so he'd seen a lot of that. So he wouldn't have anybody. So the worst bit, actually, was going away in the train from Dundee, down to Liverpool. Once you were away you were away. And then I had my family with me, that was my family, and they were all with me. And there was a sense of excitement about it too.[18]

Ena Macdonald's departure, however, was devoid of any sense of excitement, perhaps because she herself had played no part in the decision to emigrate to Australia. Her anguish at leaving was never assuaged, but deepened (as we shall see later) into an inconsolable homesickness, which her husband could not comprehend. Notably, he did not feature in her account of the pre-embarkation train journey from London to Southampton, but she described being accompanied by her sister Jessie and an acquaintance from Skye who lived in Southampton, and recalled that 'I was absolutely breaking my heart crying – absolutely – I was just torn apart. It was a horrible feeling'.[19]

Very few interviewees spoke about their feelings at the point of departure. Some were only children, whose horizons were limited, but even those who emigrated as adults did not seem to remember thinking that they were entering on a life-changing enterprise. Most were probably too busy dealing with practical pressures, but it is conceivable that some, perhaps subconsciously, suppressed or erased painful or ambiguous emotions. Some simply packed their bags and left without any fanfare, family or community commemoration, either celebratory or melancholy. That pattern was probably more common among individuals who did not have close family or community ties, or were already rolling stones without roots. It was not the experience of Annie Matheson, probably because she came from a close-knit Lewis township which had seen steady emigration to Canada and the United States. Perhaps because of those long-standing transatlantic links, Annie's parents were 'quite reconciled' to her decision to emigrate, rather than being angry, as she had feared. When she left Coll for Detroit in December 1952 the whole village bade her farewell and maintained an interest in her progress thereafter. That close-knit rural community's ownership of the emigration experience had been commonplace in earlier generations but was becoming increasingly rare in the more individualistic culture of the mid-20th century:

> When I left for the States... I think I called at every house in the neighbourhood where I lived to say goodbye because I knew them all so well... We had a lot of relatives and neighbours and friends, they would all be interested. For it was a big thing, one from the community going, doing what I did. They would all ask my parents – 'well, have you heard yet, how she got on?'[20]

Life at sea

Emigrant journeys in the 19th century are well documented in personal testimony, for as an antidote to the enforced idleness and tedium of a long voyage many passengers kept diaries or wrote letters. Their 20th-century successors, benefiting from faster transport and more entertainment, were less inclined to spend time with pen and paper, but we have enough written accounts to make comparisons, and most interviewees who took an ocean passage had some recollections of the journey.

From time to time in both centuries international conflict disrupted travel. Emigrants who crossed the Atlantic during the Napoleonic Wars were advised to travel in well-armoured ships, and shipping advertisements highlighted the security provision.[21] Piracy was sometimes an issue on vessels bound for the antipodes. A clergyman sailing from Leith to Australia in 1837 noted that the main cabin of the *North Briton* was furnished with guns and cannon to deter pirates, particularly in the tropics, since 'they generally hover about this latitude and take the opportunity of attacking ships when they are becalmed and unable to flee from want of wind'. He went on to describe how these 'desperate men', including several Scots, would murder all on board, steal the cargo, and sink the vessel, often with the passengers entombed in the hold.[22]

By the 20th century pirates and the press gang were confined to folklore, but new dangers and difficulties emerged. In September 1940 the *City of Benares* was torpedoed in the Atlantic as it was shipping children to the supposed safety of Canada – a notorious incident, which resulted in the death of 77 of the 90 'seavacuees' on board, and brought the scheme to a premature end. Interviewees Ian Skinner, Peter Dawson and Agnes Lawrie all experienced travelling in wartime convoys, Ian as a seavacuee, Peter when his parents brought the family back to Scotland from Australia, and Agnes as a young bride returning from New York to Glasgow.[23] For most emigrants, however, the only effect of the world wars was to delay their departure because civilian transport ground to a halt. Shipping shortages persisted for a few years after each war, but particularly after 1945, as several vessels that had been requisitioned were destroyed during hostilities, others needed to be converted back to civilian use, and priority was given to transporting troops and displaced persons. The problem was particularly acute in Australia and New Zealand, where subsidised passages were reintroduced prematurely. But none of the interviewees mentioned any difficulty in securing a berth, probably because by the 1950s, when most of them left, the disparity between supply and demand had been resolved. The only interviewee to mention, tangentially, the impact of international relations on the voyage was Rob Tulloch, who recalled that the *Oriana* was in a group of ships escorted through the Suez Canal by the British Navy, two years before the canal was closed by Egypt at the beginning of the Six-Day War.[24]

If the dislocation caused by war features only tangentially in emigrant testimony, the misery of sea-sickness is a recurring theme. The lamentations of Victorian diarists pulled no punches about the squalor, and sometimes the tragedy, of life below decks: 'The pishpots are tumbling everywhere', wrote Charles Robertson from Monymusk in Aberdeenshire, during a mid-Atlantic storm when the sea was 'raging terribly'. It was April 1846, and Charles, his parents and six siblings had embarked on a timber ship at Aberdeen two weeks earlier, bound for Montreal. A day after that diary entry, a baby was born and died, being lowered overboard with 'two stones attached to it to make it sink'. Shortly afterwards Charles' mother succumbed to incessant seasickness, compounded by dysentery and childbirth, and was similarly committed to a watery grave.[25]

In the alien environment of a floating village, the unfamiliar rituals that accompanied ocean deaths and burials unsettled some Victorian diarists and fascinated others. More than seven decades later, Shetlander Margaret Whyte, travelling from Liverpool to Dunedin, wrote of her distress at the fate of a crew member on the SS *Dorset* who had died from blood poisoning. She could not get out of her head 'the thought of his body being tossed about in this awful sea'.[26] Her comment introduced a sombre thread into an account that was otherwise largely positive. By that time, the testimony of most emigrants tended to highlight the pleasures of the voyage, a theme that was generally echoed by interviewees, both then and in a later generation. But Cathy Timperley's account of her journey to New Zealand in 1953 (then as 10-year-old Cathy Donald) reminds us that the tragedies which were commonplace in earlier generations had not been eradicated by technological and medical advances. For Cathy's mother, the voyage was dominated by the loss of her newly born baby:

> CT: She was actually pregnant. Everything [the preparations] went through, and she got pregnant. Now, she had several miscarriages after me, so what they did was they accelerated our departure. They said, you can't go – the boat that you were booked on – you can't go on this one, you can go on this one. But unfortunately, a baby boy was born on the voyage. And they didn't tell me until it was over, but they had a little ceremony and buried him at sea.
>
> MH: Was he stillborn?
>
> CT: Well, no, he lived, apparently he lived. And they said, had he been on land, of course, they probably would have [saved him] but they couldn't, they didn't have all the equipment that they needed. I think they did put him in a – they might have had an incubator, I'm not sure. So that was really sad. And I was not really quite aware of the impact of that, I think. I guess my mother landed and that was it. They had to just get on with life. Didn't have a lot of money. And I quite admire my mother, 'cos she just – she didn't sit around and mope, and so on. But she said to me years after that every time she heard – hears the cry of a baby that used to bring back the memory of it, you know, just that little new-born cry.[27]

For most interviewees, the main hardship of the voyage was the almost ubiquitous seasickness that had similarly afflicted earlier generations of emigrants. Although the four- or six-berth cabin of a modern liner offered more privacy than the fetid hold of a sailing vessel, or even the cramped steerage of a steamship, it did not provide immunity against misery. Passengers usually succumbed early in the journey, in the North Atlantic or the Bay of Biscay, though the Great Australian Bight could catch them out towards the end of the antipodean voyage. During the third and fourth days of Annie Matheson's six-day crossing from Southampton to New York in December 1952, she remembered being 'so seasick, I didn't care if they threw me over',[28] while pregnancy probably exacerbated Margaret Gillies Brown's persistent sickness during the passage from Liverpool to Halifax aboard the two-year-old Cunarder, RMS *Sylvania,* in February 1959. When Ena Macdonald set out for Australia in January 1961 on the P&O liner *Orion* it was 'blowing a hoolie' in the Bay of Biscay, a situation which did nothing to alleviate her crushing homesickness. 'It was terrible, and I was sick for three days. Oh, was I wishing I was back home.'[29] Shona Morrison was not long out of Southampton on her six-week journey to Australia in January 1972 when she also fell victim to a raging storm in that same notorious stretch of water:

> I was very, very seasick – *very* seasick. But we shared a cabin with two ladies. One would have been well into her 70s, and the other one was well into her 80s. And they were going out to join family in New Zealand – they were going to start their lives over again at that age! And one of them – I don't remember which one it was – told me to drink brandy and port, and that cured me of my seasickness [laughs].[30]

Once they had gained their sea legs, the over-riding sentiment of almost all interviewees who spoke about the voyage, was that it was a time when – unlike many of their Victorian predecessors – they clearly enjoyed themselves. While they were undoubtedly reaping the benefits of better shipping technology and cultural changes, it is possible that the passage of time between travel and interview also filtered out recollections of more negative experiences, and perceptions were, moreover, dependent on the emigrant's age and the era in which they travelled. For ten-year-old Morag MacLeod from Balivanich in Benbecula, it was definitely an adventure to cross the Atlantic in 1923 with her parents and six older siblings, although in later life she appreciated why her parents had not shared her enthusiasm. She was one of 280 Hebridean passengers on the Canadian Pacific liner, the *Marloch*, which had embarked its first complement of passengers at Greenock before heading for the Western Isles. Until then she had never left her isolated island and was, she admitted, 'very naive, I didn't know of anything very much'. More than eight decades later, she recalled the sensory impressions associated with dense fog and (perhaps influenced by tales of the *Titanic*) huge icebergs. She was also excited by the vessel's bright illumination ('we had never seen electric lights') and its modern conveniences:

> Oh, I remember quite a bit about the voyage, the icebergs, and it was foggy, and we had to anchor. It took us about, oh my goodness, close to two weeks to cross. We were stuck in the fog. The icebergs were *huge*... Oh, I remember the blasting of the fog horn for sure, I can still hear it. And of course we didn't – we were put in the state rooms, you know, to sleep, and that – and we never had running water in Benbecula, as you know, if was just a well, and we didn't know what the bowl and the taps and all this sort of things were, you know...[31]

Four years after Morag emigrated, Donald Murray's wife and children crossed the Atlantic to join him in Prince Rupert, British Columbia. They also enjoyed the adventure of travelling on a Canadian Pacific liner, a journey which began with a ferry from Stornoway to Kyle of Lochalsh, and a train to Glasgow. At Greenock, where they embarked on the *Melita*, they were joined by their aunt, uncle and cousins, who travelled with them as far as Winnipeg, the older children keeping an eye on the young Murrays while their mother was prostrate with seasickness. Calum recalled that their 'eyes would be wide open, trying to take in as much as you could of what was going on'. Both he and Cathie spoke of large numbers of Russians 'crowded together' in the steerage, 'I suppose getting away from the Revolution or whatever'.[32] After a week or so, they disembarked at Quebec City, where they boarded the train for the long journey west.

On the other side of the border, Minnie Anne Fraser from Halladale in Sutherland and Agnes Lawrie from Whithorn in Dumfries-shire both arrived at the port of New York between the wars. As a consequence of the recent American quota legislation, they had waited two years and 18 months respectively for a berth. Minnie Anne travelled second class, which she described as being 'like the happy atmosphere of steerage, without the heat and the noise'.[33] Her daughter confirmed that Minnie Anne enjoyed 'tremendously' the voyage from Glasgow on the SS *Cameronia* in 1926. Although she and her companions from East Sutherland had a cabin, they found that 'the best fun was to be had with the steerage passengers, who were mainly Irish, they danced the same dances, sang more or less the same types of songs, and they had a fellow feeling for them'.[34] Unlike many Victorian emigrants, whose shipboard diaries ridiculed or demonised their Irish shipmates, particularly Catholics, Minnie Anne and her friends actively sought out their company.[35] Such bonds, forged between Free Church Presbyterian Highlanders and Irish Catholics, were all the more remarkable in the 1920s, a decade when a notoriously xenophobic report by the Church of Scotland had warned of the 'menace to Scottish nationality and civilisation' caused by Irish immigrants in Scotland, and had called for the wholesale repatriation of Irish Catholics.[36] Perhaps conventions and prejudices were more easily set aside at sea than on land. Agnes sailed from Liverpool on the Cunard liner *Athenia* on 29 May 1930. The ten-day journey, for which she had paid £22 10 shillings, was 'really quite a good voyage', during which she played shuffleboard and card games, 'and oh there was talks, there was always talks going on about your new life'.[37] During the next nine years she made two trips back to Scotland, in 1935 and 1938. The transatlantic crossing also played a part in her long-term destiny, for on her second return voyage to New York she met her husband-to-be, Norrie McGilvray, chief electrician on the Anchor liner *Transylvania*. Three weeks before their marriage in New York the following year, the war had broken out, and they returned to Scotland, sooner than they had intended, settling in Glasgow.

Several interviewees who crossed the Atlantic in the 1950s singled out shipboard catering for commendation. Since post-war austerity had played a big part in many decisions to emigrate in the 1950s, it is not surprising that the first tangible evidence of its absence – the quantity and quality of food at sea – elicited positive comment. For Annie Matheson, facilities on the transatlantic liner contrasted markedly with the discomfort of the long ferry and train journey from the Hebrides, via smog-filled London, to Southampton, and, in a second interview recorded two years after our first conversation, she repeated her comparison of the boat with a luxury hotel:

> It was great, it was so interesting. I went on the *Queen Elizabeth*, and we had a lovely big cabin. I was sharing it with – I think there were two war brides, and there was a girl from Italy, and a girl from India, and a girl from Glasgow... We had a nice time on the boat – it was just like a luxury hotel. Your own waiter, and all in uniform, white linen tablecloths, big white napkins that were about a yard square, and your own table, and *anything* you wanted, it didn't matter. If it wasn't on the menu they would get it for you.[38]

Les Ford left Aberdeen in July 1955 to take up employment with the Hudson's Bay Company. Although rationing had ended 12 months earlier, the passengers were still impressed by the abundance of food on the maiden voyage of the Cunard ship *Ivernia*.

> I think we all thought we'd died and gone to heaven. It was food to no end.

> Maybe special because of the maiden voyage, and so on but we'd never seen so much meat, and chicken, and all that sort of stuff. Things were still pretty tight in Aberdeen in the '50s.[39]

Passengers to South America, Australia and New Zealand in the 1950s also recalled the abundance and variety of food. Alec Miller, travelling to Dunedin in 1953, remembered that 'you could get second helpings of puddings and things you wanted.'[40] But by 1961, when Katrine McLean and her husband emigrated to New Zealand on a Dutch ship, rationing was a distant memory. In answer to a question about the food, she responded that 'It was all right – nothing – nothing spectacular' and recalled missing fresh milk.[41] Some, however, would have preferred more familiar plain fare. For Ena Macdonald, sailing to Australia the same year, the food on the *Orion* was just another poignant reminder of the life she had left behind:

> We were put at the table, and it was the first officer, I think. It wasn't the captain, it was the next one below the captain. He was at our table, I think. I used to chat away to him. We had good food, but I wasn't particularly – it wasn't things I was used to – can't even remember what it was, but I remember saying to him one day, 'Oh, you know, I'd love a plate of mince and tatties' [laughs]. I think he was agreeing with me too.[42]

Rob and Cathie Tulloch, bound for New Zealand aboard the *Oriana* in 1965, found 'the ship food was just absolutely wonderful – far too much, but absolutely wonderful, and when we got off we just wanted something really nice and plain, like baked beans on toast'.[43] Six years earlier, aboard the Pacific Steam Navigation Company's four-year-old ship, *Reina del Mar,* John MacPherson and his pregnant wife Catherine found 'the food was excellent when were able to eat it'.[44] Sailing from Liverpool to Callao (Lima) to serve as missionaries with the Free Church of Scotland, the MacPhersons encountered a number of other missionaries to South America. Most were, like them, travelling in second class, with the exception of the Salvation Army contingent, which was confined to the steerage 'and we weren't allowed to go down to visit them'. The missionaries circumvented that 'disgraceful' restriction by securing permission to organise a Sunday service on the third-class deck, complete with the Salvation Army musicians, and John also recalled entering – and winning – the ship's fancy-dress competition, along with one of the other missionaries.[45]

Entertainment featured prominently in passengers' recollections of life at sea. Even in the 19th century some diarists, at least those writing from the perspective of a cabin, described deck and parlour games, card schools and reading parties, while improved technology such as refrigeration helped to make the voyage a more pleasurable experience. By the 1920s shipping companies emphasised recreation through visual as well as written advertising. Stocks of slides were supplemented by silent films such as 'Cunard to Canada', which, with the aid of captions, showed different constituencies of passengers eating, playing deck games, and enjoying themselves in nurseries or on the dance floor. The gradual shift of emphasis from order and discipline to enjoyment and relaxation reflected wider cultural changes, such as increasingly secular attitudes and the commodification of leisure. In the inter-war era the YMCA appointed officers to organise social and educational programmes for assisted emigrants on their way to Australia and New Zealand.

By the 1950s expectations of quasi-military shipboard discipline were fading, and the general consensus was that the voyage was an extended holiday. Passengers on the *Ormonde* in 1949, for instance – 'a very large proportion' of whom were Scots – seemed to appreciate the light touch with which their life at sea was orchestrated. According to the surgeon, they frequently commented 'that they expected much more dragooning, and were pleasantly surprised to be treated as passengers rather than emigrants.'[46] Although shortened journey times meant that ships had long ceased to be the floating villages of Victorian times, there was still a sense of community, particularly on voyages to the southern hemisphere. Even on the short Atlantic crossing, however, Margaret Gillies Brown felt the different nationalities on board got together like 'a big family all going away on this adventure'.[47]

The interpersonal friction and disorderly behaviour that preoccupied some Victorian diarists and letter-writers, and featured in the reports of ships' officials through to the late 1960s, were not highlighted by any interviewees. No doubt shorter passages, roomier accommodation and better sanitation, as well as the provision of diversionary activities, played a part in shaping more positive perceptions, although there may have been an element of amnesia about minor tensions or altercations. The enforced proximity of passengers with different standards of hygiene and states of health had upset some 19th century travellers, mainly because of the spectre of epidemic. More than a century before most interviewees embarked, Jessie Campbell from Fort William had written of the 'fearful prospect' of fever breaking out on the *Blenheim,* bound for New Zealand. The link between anxiety and antipathy was particularly evident in her denunciation of the unhygienic practices of Highlanders in the steerage, and her generally disputatious attitude to the ship's two doctors, the steward, her maid, and her 'disagreeable' fellow passengers in the cabin.[48]

Shipboard disputes might also be sparked off by differences of ethnicity or religion, inflamed by the confined spaces in which most passengers were corralled. By the 20th century these boundaries were becoming less problematic, although they were sometimes replaced by different challenges. Wartime shipping losses meant that civilian emigrants and service personnel were often transported together in troop ships, not always harmoniously. As previously mentioned, since most of the post-war interviewees did not leave until the 1950s they were unaffected by shipping shortages, but even two Scottish war brides who went to Canada during or after hostilities – and who were interviewed for the Pier 21 project – did not recall particular problems. Patricia Edwards and Helen Whetstone both crossed the Atlantic in 1944, and remembered, respectively, a 'huge' ship that seemed to have far too many people for the number of lifeboats, and how they had sweltered in their woollen siren suits during an unplanned detour to the Azores to escape enemy submarines.[49] The challenge of maintaining order on the antipodean run in the late 1940s is evident from reports in the files of the Orient Steam Navigation Company, and perhaps it is a testament to their success in tackling problems that by the mid-1950s and 1960s not a single interviewee found fault with the shipboard arrangements.

The sources of friction on the long antipodean voyage reflected the less deferential society from which the post-war emigrants had come, the different standards and expectations of various generations, and the mixing of constituencies. Former ship's cook Jock Baird enjoyed being at the receiving end of steward service on the SS *Fairsky* in 1971, but commented that 'you had to watch when you hung out the baby's nappies on the line... you'd to sit and wait [for them] to dry, otherwise they'd get pinched'. He added that, having lost a dozen of their own baby's nappies at the start of the voyage, 'I stole a dozen back.'[50] Noisy, disruptive children were a recurring problem on several ships, a problem which was encapsulated in the rueful comment of the captain of the *Orion* in 1947 that 'it seems impossible to find a solution to please both parents and disgruntled old ladies'.[51] There were also complaints about overcrowding, the lack of quiet spaces for reading and writing, tourist-class passengers straying into first-class spaces, and the bad behaviour of assisted emigrants. These issues were tackled by the employment of tourist liaison officers, new settlers' welfare officers, and nursery hostesses, as well as the introduction of structured entertainment and sporting programmes, and the provision of schooling. None of the interviewees who emigrated as children recalled being schooled during the voyage, but shipping company records indicate that vessels carrying large numbers of emigrant children sometimes engaged the services of qualified teachers from among the passengers, even if those who taught the 130 children aboard the *Ormonde* in autumn 1951 gave their services 'a little grudgingly'.[52]

Adult education took the form of lectures on Australia delivered by information officers, who also had an unofficial disciplinary role in keeping under control 'the more unruly types who do not conform to any rules of the ship or of common decency, and who are a continual source of trouble and annoyance to all other persons on board'. The absence of such an individual was felt to have contributed to the *Orion*'s difficult voyage to Australia in 1962, during which there had been significant teenage vandalism, and the 546 children had been an 'unruly mob' over which their parents had exercised little or no control.[53]

Since the journey was a means to an end, most emigrants were prepared to tolerate temporary inconveniences, particularly if it meant securing a quick passage. 'The voyage was only incidental to being in Australia', commented one emigrant who was berthed along with five ex-servicemen on the *Orion* in 1947.[54] Cathy Timperley and Brian Coutts both recalled that their parents were allocated to separate male and female cabins on the *Rangitata,* which brought them to New Zealand in 1953 and 1955 respectively, but neither remembered that this separation was a problem.[55] Ten years later, Cathie and Rob Tulloch were also berthed separately, but got on well with the three other couples in the same position who shared their respective quarters. Separation was, however, identified as a cause of discontent by the Orient Steam Navigation Company, at least among some emigrants going to Australia in 1951, when both the staff commander and the purser on the *Ormonde* reported quarrels, particularly in female cabins, among women who had been separated from their husbands. Towards journey's end the strain had escalated into 'open hostility and abuse', as a result of which the purser recommended that families should be berthed together, even if it meant reducing the number of passengers carried.[56] Five years earlier, Gladys Morrice, travelling from Aberdeen to Northern Rhodesia with her two children and her mother, who had just undergone major surgery, attributed an unpleasant journey to Cape Town partly to post-war austerity, and partly to her own naivety.

> It wasn't very nice because it was 1946. We weren't treated all that well, really. I know that I was put into a cabin with my mother and my little girl and another lady and her little girl, and they weren't very nice companions... I could have had a cabin in the hospital area, but I didn't know enough about it. I was quite naïve – first time, I mean, 25, and I was travelling abroad with a sick mother and a baby.

Within just two years, however, enjoyment rather than endurance was the hallmark of the voyage. Gladys was able to reflect on significant transformations in the experience, for she made two return trips from Cape Town to Scotland in 1948 and 1953, before returning permanently to her homeland in 1957:

> Now those journeys were *very* very different. We were so well treated, there was entertainment every night, and it really was lovely. And we had fancy dress for the kids, and fancy dress for the adults, and it was really a very pleasant journey, it was part of your holiday. But I'm afraid, going out in 1946, it was anything but that.[57]

Interviewees who travelled in the 1950s and 1960s unwittingly reaped the benefits of a more relaxed culture, and the increasing provision of shipboard leisure facilities. Although the segregated spaces that had dominated Victorian voyages persisted, children were often oblivious to protocol. 'Children being children, we made friends with first class passengers', recalled Cathy Timperley. On the *Rangitata* in 1953 she played with a boy on a higher deck, whose parents 'had a really posh cabin... There were only two children in first class. They did not have anyone else to play with'.[58] In the tropics Cathy and her parents escaped the oppressive heat of their cabins by sleeping on deck, though this meant rising early to remove their mattresses before the decks were swabbed.[59]

Cathy's recollection of the heat below decks was echoed by Alec Miller. He also travelled in 1953, when the New Zealand government's free immigration scheme had been extended with the aim of bringing in a minimum of 10,000 settlers a year, including married men with families, like Alec. Interviewed in 2010, at the age of 89, he asserted that the decision was 'the best move I made', despite some discomfort during the five-week voyage on the *Captain Cook* from Glasgow to Wellington:

> It can get very warm out there, you know, you're all in this little cabin. So I often thought, well, perhaps I should have waited, and come out the proper way, rather than go out in an immigrant ship, you know. Still, we managed it... [We had] even a library, books to read and everything, a swimming pool they rigged up there, and oh, they'd deck golf and things like that they play, and also these rings of rope you threw over a net and that.[60]

For young Brian Coutts, who emigrated from Edinburgh in 1955, on the *Rangitata,* the family's adventure began in high summer with a train trip from Edinburgh to London, followed by an unanticipated two-week stay with relatives in Kent when their departure was delayed by a dockers' strike. Once aboard the vessel, the family was split into two cabins, his mother being berthed with three [probably five] other women, while Brian, his father and brother shared a cabin with another father and his two sons. Films, notably

The Dambusters and *Colditz*, were part of the entertainment, but Brian also needed to release pent-up energy:

> As an eight-year-old it was great fun. I don't remember any bad weather – when I say *bad* weather I mean stormy weather – I seem to remember grey days, but racing round the back end of the boat because we were not first-class – whatever the other bit of it was – emigrants. There was other kids to play with, there was a play area that had toys and a wind-up gramophone, and there were other boys, so we used to chase each other all round.[61]

A highlight of the antipodean trip was the opportunity to disembark and explore ports of call. Occasionally this had unforeseen consequences. In 1946 the *Rangitiki*, on which one-year-old Gail Anderson and her mother sailed to New Zealand, broke down in Panama for nine days:

> For a lot of the women who were on the ship, it was their way out of Britain, and so they had a really happy time. You know, some of them did not get back on the ship. And when they got to Wellington, there were men waiting for these fiancées, for their wives or girlfriends... and they just weren't there – they had decided to stay in Panama.[62]

Even Ena Macdonald, whose experience of emigration was almost wholly bleak, recalled a 'lovely journey' with interesting stopovers.

> We had plenty entertainment, went swimming and played deck games, and things, and got off, and I remember seeing Gibraltar, it was my first glimpse of a foreign land, and I was very excited seeing that... I came off at the Suez Canal and then we joined the ship at the other end, we went by a bus... We were riding on a camel, and saw the pyramids, I think it was on the way out. It was quite an experience. I remember being in Aden, and everything was tax free there and you could buy things for pennies in the shops. Everything was so bright... quite exciting for a 20-year-old, you know.[63]

Helen Campbell from Inveraray, along with her husband and two young sons, sailed to New Zealand on the maiden voyage of the Shaw Savill vessel *Northern Star* in 1962. It was, she remembered, a 'one class' ship, on which passengers paying economy fares had full run of the vessel. An extended stopover in South Africa was caused, in Helen's recollection, by a breakdown in the distilling plant.[64] While the shipping company flew engineers out from the Clyde to make repairs, the passengers spent a week in Cape Town and Durban respectively, and during bus tours from each location Helen became aware of the impact of apartheid: 'Whites only on buses, and seats along the beaches were whites only. It was really awful.'[65] When Shona Morrison travelled to Australia on the *Northern Star* in 1972 she did not comment on stopovers, but did commend the vessel's facilities: 'It had everything on it – cinema, two swimming pools, library, everything on it. You could literally do what you wanted to do.'[66]

Transitions in transport

At some point during an ocean voyage, the emigrants stopped looking back and began to look forward. For some, that moment coincided with their embarkation; for those going to the southern hemisphere, it might be when they crossed the Equator; for others it might be as they approached their destination. In all cases, attitudes and temperament were part of the equation. The shift of focus heightened the travellers' anticipation, but sometimes also brought apprehension. For Cathie and Rob Tulloch, the anxiety began when the ship taking them to New Zealand in 1965 disembarked its first consignment of passengers in Australia. The doubts that they had felt on the boat train from London to Southampton – but had forgotten about during a 'wonderful trip' – resurfaced. Cathie recalled:

> It was a fantastic experience, a month and a day on a beautiful ship, on the *Oriana*... It wasn't until we left Australia that we all started to think 'Wow, the next stop is ours. What [do we do] from here?' So that was a bit daunting.[67]

Emigrants who travelled by air had much less opportunity to reflect on the complexities of transition. They were also more likely to adopt a slightly different definition of migration than their predecessors. Murdo MacPherson spent almost two decades in Canada before returning to his native Highlands in 1996, but continues to make frequent visits across the Atlantic. As he explained:

> It's like I've never left... I don't really feel separated from Canada – I mean, when I go back, it's quite normal... The ease of transatlantic travel makes it less imperative to live in one place or the other. This wouldn't have been the case between the wars, you know. The 1920s or '30s, it would have been different, or even the 1950s.[68]

The key change from sea to air travel happened in the 1960s, initially in North America. As early as 1947, Ontario had pioneered emigrant air transportation when the Premier, George Drew, organised an airlift of over 7,000 Britons to boost the provincial workforce. By 1950 the federal government was offering subsidised fares to eastern Canada with Trans-Canada Airlines at £55 per head, which was slightly cheaper than the tourist-class ocean passage, but the decisive shift came only when jet engines replaced propeller-driven aircraft.[69] Scots were particularly enthusiastic about air transport. In 1962 the International Passenger Survey reported that 62 per cent of Scottish emigrants to Canada that year had travelled by air, compared with 45.5 per cent from the United Kingdom as a whole. The following year 63 per cent of Scottish emigrants to Canada went by plane, compared with 49 per cent from the UK as a whole.[70]

Even so, some emigrants still preferred the slower alternative. Alison Gibson had been working in London when she and a friend decided to emigrate in 1967, Canada's centennial year, and the year of the International and Universal Exposition (Expo 67) in Montreal. They chose to take a six-day voyage from Greenock to Montreal:

> We had the option of flying or going by boat... It was such a huge change in our life, flying seemed too simple, just to leave one whole life behind and start afresh overnight. It just seemed, if you had the opportunity, not the right way to do it, and so we went by the *Empress of Canada*, six days out of Greenock, to Montreal, hoping to get off the boat in Montreal, and see Expo on its last day. Again, no concept of how much you can fit in. We loved the sailing across, and there were so many young people, all going to all over Canada, just emigrating at that time. We had a really fun time. It was like staying in a great hotel, which we had never done before.[71]

Alison's evaluation of sea and air travel was echoed by Joan Noble. For her, the distance from Aberdeen to Vancouver Island in 1966 was measured in culture as well as miles. She felt that the Atlantic crossing, followed by the long transcontinental train journey, emphasised the family's total separation from their old life and provided a better psychological and physical preparation for settlement than the experiences of immigrants who arrived jet-lagged and disorientated after a day in the air.[72]

The benefits of sea travel on the much longer journey to Asia were also commended by Moira Campbell from Aberdeen, who spent 29 years in Taiwan as a missionary. She was among the last contingent to travel east by sea, sailing from Trieste in Italy to Singapore in 1967, just before the closure of the Suez Canal following the Six-Day War. Thereafter her organisation, OMF, switched to air travel because of the greater expense of the route round the Cape of Good Hope. Moira enjoyed the three-week voyage, during which she shared a cabin with three other missionaries: 'I was glad to sail because you got used to the heat gradually and just got used to the whole idea gradually... And for years afterwards Barbara and I just felt privileged when we just saw that the ones who flew in, well, they were exhausted when they arrived, and it was all so new to them.'[73] Cameron Tallach vouched for 'never feeling as tired as I was that night' he landed with his family in Hong Kong in 1974, after 20 hours on a cramped Dan Air charter flight from London, en route to Taiwan. Cameron had entertained 'the old-fashioned missionary expectation of sailing out by boat', but the cost had become prohibitive, whereas his recollection was that the Dan Air fare was only £90 for a family of four.[74]

The experience of air travel before it had become routine and mundane elicited comment from some interviewees. When 20-year-old Angus Pelham Burn joined the Hudson's Bay Company in May 1951, he managed to fit some sight-seeing into 'an amazing flight', the first time he had travelled by air. Nearly 60 years later, he still had vivid and detailed memories of the journey:

> I got on to a train at Keith in Banffshire, and ended up at Glasgow and then Prestwick, where I got on a Trans-Canada Airlines North Star, four droning engines, and we took off, and we flew to Keflavik in Iceland. We touched down very briefly and took straight off again, because there was such a blizzard, and I remember looking out of the window, seeing all this snow. And we then turned round and went down on the most lovely morning, early morning, down the west coast of Ireland, I can see it now, at quite a low height, and landed at Shannon. And so I'd spent the whole night flying, and I'd only got as far as Shannon, where they refuelled – we had to get out – and they refuelled. And then we had our second breakfast on the aeroplane, one going to Shannon and one heading across the Atlantic. We then went to Gander in Newfoundland, and we had about two hours' stop. And I said to a number of my fellow passengers – 'why don't we club together?' – 'cos I'd never been abroad before – 'club together and see a bit of Newfoundland in a taxi for an hour?' And none of them were in the least interested. And the taxi driver said 'Come on', and he took me for an hour round melting snow and dark forests, and we didn't see very much, but he wouldn't take anything from me for doing it. I told them I had a fiver, five pounds in my pocket, and that was it, and I had to arrive in Winnipeg with something, and he wouldn't take anything. And so I've always been very grateful to him for that. Although we didn't see very much I'd been there, and done that. Got into the aeroplane again, flew to Dorval, which was the airport for Montreal, refuelled, flew to Malton, which was the airport for Toronto, and then flew to Stevenson's Field, which was the airport for Winnipeg. And I then got into the Marlborough – I think it was called – Hotel, where the Hudson's Bay Company recruits were all put up. And

> I slept for I don't know how long – 24 hours. And then I was given a job in the basement of Hudson's Bay House, marking heaps and heaps of white stockings for the various stores, pricing them. And I was found sound asleep on them and left there and I slept all day. But eventually I recovered, but it took me about three days to recover, because I think it was 37-and-a-half hours flight.[75]

When John Wallace from Aberdeen joined the Hudson's Bay Company 15 years later, at the age of 17, he was able to fly straight from Prestwick to Winnipeg on a Boeing 707. Some of his memories were similar to those of Angus Pelham Burn, including his first sight of Iceland, and his initial accommodation at the Marlborough Hotel, although he had been more apprehensive than Angus when it came to leaving home. His parents accompanied him to Prestwick on 7 August 1966:

> The date's burnt into me. I remember my Mum and Dad taking me up to the airport. I remember my Mum giving me £10 – in those days it was probably about $35... I remember getting on the plane and flying over [Iceland]... To me, I mean, it was amazing to see Iceland. I think this was the first time I'd ever been on a plane, and looking down at Iceland. Then it kind of dawned on me. I seem to remember sitting back in my seat and thinking 'What have I done?' Seriously. 'What have I done?' I left my Mum and Dad. Left my brothers, sisters, friends. It kind of started to sink home – What *have* I done? You know. And then I thought – I started to think – well, two years, I'll stick it out, two years, and then I'll come back. Then we flew over Greenland, and that was quite amazing, just seeing all the snow-covered land, the mountains. Then in over Hudson Bay itself, into Winnipeg. It was about an eight, nine – nine-hour flight, I think.[76]

By the 1960s emigrants to the Antipodes had the choice of sea or air travel. When Bob and Margaret Crapnell emigrated from Glasgow to Queensland with their two children in January 1969, they opted for a Qantas flight that took them from London to Brisbane, via New Delhi, and Manilla, but when Margaret's 70-year-old mother joined them a year later, she came by ship, and '*loved* it'. As Margaret explained:

> That [the mode of transport] really was Bob's decision. He wanted to get here quick. He didn't want to prolong the agony. Oh, he wanted to get *right* into it. That was fine, as far as I was concerned. Possibly had I heard about what a good time some people had on board ship, as being, taking it as a last holiday... before they arrived in Australia, and really got down to it, I may have put up a question for all – what about considering ship? But I didn't know that. I didn't

> know anyone who had travelled that way, with that mindset, you know, 'we'll make this a holiday, we'll all have a holiday, on board ship'.[77]

Helen Bowie also travelled by air, on a Boeing 707, when she emigrated to Queensland with her widowed mother, two siblings, grandmother and aunt six months after the Crapnells. The family's travelling attire invested the journey with a sense of occasion, mixed with practical discomfort during refuelling stops in hot airports:

> It was very exciting because I had never been overseas. I'd been to England, but never crossed the Channel even, so to go on a plane at the age of 12 was very exciting. The funniest thing to me now is that we were dressed in our best Sunday clothes. Yes. And we had them specially bought for us before we left. They were woollen, and I had a sleeveless woollen dress, it was mustard. This is the late '60s, so it wasn't quite Mod and Rocker, but it was above my knee, it was a slight mini, and I had a cape that went with it, a woollen cape, and it was white, and it was mustard and navy check... And I had stockings on, and I had sort of navy shoes that had heels... very trendy... And I just think now, 'How crazy.' We didn't have hats on, but otherwise it was like we were going to Sunday school. And that's what we wore on the plane journey.[78]

From emigrants to immigrants: arrival and onward travel

Entry into the new land was not always straightforward. The first hurdle was passing quarantine, after which many immigrants faced a long onward journey to their final destination. Partridge Island in New Brunswick's Bay of Fundy and Grosse Île below Quebec City on the St Lawrence were Canada's main gate-keeping stations in the 19th century, but also the sites of major outbreaks of typhus and cholera. On the other side of the world, each of Australia's States also established quarantine stations, and New Zealand's four major ports built similar facilities on adjacent islands. At any of these facilities vessels harbouring contagious disease, and their human cargoes, might be detained for a month or more, until better infection control made them redundant and they closed, most in the 1920s. No interviewee mentioned a medical inspection on arrival, but Alec Miller's daughter, Rose, who was present during the interview with her father, produced her late mother's diary, from which she quoted. 'We queued for medical inspections this morning', she had written on 28 October. 'The doctor inspected our eyes and forearms.'[79] The inspection at Dunedin therefore appeared to have been just as cursory as the one in Edinburgh.

The best known gate-keeping institution was the United States' federal inspection station at Ellis Island in New York harbour, but the facility closed in 1954, so it was irrelevant to most post-war emigrants, and since both Minnie Anne Fraser and Agnes Lawrie were met by sponsors when they disembarked in 1926 and 1930 respectively, they avoided the experience. The terrors of Ellis Island, which have become part of American immigrant tradition, focus on arbitrary detention and deportation, although in fact only two per cent of arrivals were sent back. Most were admitted after a few hours, during which they were subjected to brief medical and legal checks. Marge Glasgow, one of the Scots interviewed for the Ellis Island Oral History Project, was only 15 when she emigrated in 1922. She remembered 'crying hysterically' while being inspected for trachoma, despite the reassurance of one of the doctors who 'put his arms around me and said, "Please, please don't cry so hard. We're trying to help you. We only want to help you.".'[80] Thomas and William Allan, who came out from Tillycoultry in 1927 to join their widowed father, were only seven and five respectively when they had a traumatic experience at Ellis Island. As Tom explained in an interview 57 years later:

> My brother come [sic] down with the chicken pox, and we were quarantined on the ship. And I, to no avail, was trying to tell them that I already had chicken pox and there was no need for me to be quarantined, but being of young age, my argument didn't stand water. Because of that, we were sent to Ellis Island and quarantined... And naturally I was a very angry young Scots lad. This is not the America that I was led to believe it was going to be, and here I was literally a prisoner... and I escaped from that ward, and I remember it created quite a hue and cry and it seemed like everybody in America was trying to chase me down, and how far I got I don't remember, but it was in one of the other buildings, and they got me cornered in a corner, and a big guard grabbed me, and he was carrying me over his shoulder, and I was screaming bloody murder... And I remember I was so angry at America I kept singing, 'Hail [sic] Britannia, Britannia rules the waves.' And I wanted to go back to bonnie Scotland.[81]

By the time Annie Matheson arrived in New York in December 1952, Ellis Island was coming to the end of its working life, and she made no mention of it in her interviews. Her first impressions of America were of searingly cold temperatures and kaleidoscopic colour that reinforced the contrast with austerity Britain:

> We left Southampton Monday morning and we arrived in New York Saturday evening, early evening. There were four tugs came to pull the boat. It couldn't get into the harbour on its own, so there was four tugs pulling it in. What I can never forget is the bridge – I don't know, would it be the Brooklyn Bridge

– with all those cars, every colour under the sun. And I was used to seeing just black or grey cars.[82]

The striking difference from her homeland continued as she travelled on to Detroit with her fiancé, who had come to New York to meet her. 'The train was so different to what we had going from Mallaig to Kyle. It was perfectly clean, a waiter came and took your order like you were in a restaurant... everything was just first class, although I wasn't travelling first class.'[83]

On the other side of the border, almost one million new arrivals in Canada were processed at Pier 21 in Halifax, Nova Scotia, between 1928 and 1971, overlapping with Grosse Île, which closed in 1937. Recollections of disembarkation in Halifax do not feature very prominently in the testimony of Scots who have been interviewed for an ongoing oral history project at Pier 21's immigration museum, but Margaret Gillies Brown remembers a less than welcoming reception, at least for her husband, when the RMS *Sylvania* docked in February 1959. While she and the children were treated very well, thanks to gifts of food and toys from volunteer workers, Ronnie Brown was being humiliated by 'a very nasty immigrant woman' as he saw their luggage through customs in a separate area of the reception shed.[84] While others were admitted after a cursory check, or even no inspection, he was ordered to open each of their securely fastened cases and trunks. Margaret's description of the incident in her book, *Far from the Rowan Tree*, echoes and expands the recollections voiced in her interview, and merits quoting *in extensor:*

> 'Open up,' she said with no preliminaries. Our cases and trunks had been securely fastened and it took some time to undo all the straps and locks.
>
> 'Hurry up – haven't got all day!' said the woman.
>
> 'Do you want me to open them all?'
>
> 'Yes all!' she snapped. 'Don't know what you effete English might have in there.' Ronald had said nothing up to this point, knew better than to argue with her but now really incensed he said,
>
> 'I'm not English.' Not that Ronald had anything against the English. He had many English friends. It was the way she said it that annoyed.
>
> 'Oh well, Scots, Irish – it's sure all the same, you're in Canada now.' Ronald kept silent while she removed everything from our carefully packed cases and trunks. She made sarcastic remarks, here and there, while doing so...
>
> At last she had come to the bottom of the last trunk where our evening clothes lay carefully wrapped in tissue paper. She took them out of their wrappings, my lacy sky blue dance dress, Ronald's evening suit. Holding our clothes at arm's length she gave a sarcastic laugh.
>
> 'Look at these, you guys!' she said to the other officials who were standing

idly by, all the other immigrants having gone. 'And he says he's going dirt farming in Alberta.'[85]

Most interviewees who went to the antipodes did not have long onward journeys after landing, although those going to New Zealand's South Island recalled taking the inter-island ferry from Wellington to Lyttleton, and then a train if their destination was Dunedin. For many who landed at Halifax, Quebec or New York, however, disembarkation was often the prelude to a long westward trek, which featured prominently in the written testimony of earlier generations of emigrants, though with decreasing degrees of hardship. It is worth comparing their (often extensive) observations with the generally more fleeting comments of interviewees.

Victorian travellers were frequently, and eloquently, preoccupied with the discomforts of transportation, even after the advent of the train. In August 1879 Robert Louis Stevenson disembarked at New York, after a ten-day passage from Greenock on the *Devonia* in the company of emigrants whom he famously described as a 'shipful of failures'. The railway had crossed the American continent about a decade earlier, and in a 'wretched little booking-office' thronged with rain-soaked emigrants,[86] Stevenson bought a ticket which took him on a 12-day trip to San Francisco over the Union Pacific Railroad, through a land which was in the throes of rapid change, and whose frontier line was still moving. But while he welcomed the new technology for the refuge it provided from the natural and man-made perils which he claimed had beset those who crossed the country by wagon, he pulled no punches about the discomfort of the train, or his uncongenial travelling companions. The comparisons he drew between the alluring images of the west and the harsh physical and economic realities of the 'God-forsaken land' through which he travelled also punctured prevalent notions of the frontier as a land of boundless opportunity.[87]

Meanwhile, in Canada, William Craig was one of many Victorian Scots who were lured west to the Canadian prairies, as they were opened up by railways and recruitment propaganda. Craig, a merchant from Lochwinnoch, his wife and five children embarked at Greenock on the SS *Canadian* on 18 May 1883 and arrived at their final destination on 7 July. They did not travel light, for their 'unusually large amount of luggage' included the complete works of Scott, Dickens and Shakespeare.[88] Throughout the journey 46-year-old William kept a diary, the purpose of which, he wrote retrospectively, was 'to afford a little information and amusement to friends at home who have never traversed the ocean highway and to whom the great rivers and forests and prairies of the west are yet but as far off dreams'.[89] After disembarking at Port Lévis, opposite Quebec City, the family travelled by train, steamboat and wagon, via Minnesota, to their destination near Prince Albert in the North West Territories. William's diary recorded meeting fellow Scots, an encounter with a skunk which 'smells like an exaggeration of a gaswork',[90] the layout and life of Winnipeg, and the challenges of an unforgiving landscape. A week into the wagon journey from Qu'Appelle, which also involved camping each night on the trail, he wrote:

> Slowly plodding over this vast plain. The sun is exceedingly hot there is not an inch of shelter and the mosquitoes are at times dreadful. We have a combination of drawbacks at present. Want of wood, scarcity of good water, excessive heat, the plague of flies and sloughs. 'It's a long lane that has no turning.' This I fear is a very long lane. As far as the eye can reach, on either side and for mile after mile on the trail there is not a tree [and] scarcely a bush to be seen.[91]

On 7 July he reflected on the epic journey, which, he wrote, had been 'no joke. It is quite an earnest affair and requires in the "voyageur" physical strength enough to undergo the exertion, a heart stout enough not to be discouraged at small dissapointments [sic] and little difficulties and a temper good enough not to be too easily crossed by trifles'.[92]

More than seven decades later, Craig's sentiments were echoed by several of the elderly pioneers who responded to the Saskatchewan Archives Board's questionnaire about settling on the prairies in the late 19th and early 20th centuries. Some, like Craig, had completed the journey on foot or by ox-drawn wagon, including Margaret McManus from Lanark, whose family party took nearly two weeks to travel 160 miles west from Saskatoon. The trip, she recalled 'was not very pleasant. It was a cold late spring of 1907, freezing every night, the two little boys & myself slept in the covered wagon, for nearly two weeks, except for three nights, when we managed to get to a stopping place'.[93] Others were disabused of the prevalent stereotypes of pugnacious natives and wild animals. The First Nations people often offered practical help to the travellers, and George Craig from Ayrshire, who had travelled the same route as Margaret McManus a few months earlier, recalled that 'the wildest beasts we encountered were mosquitoes and lice'.[94] For other pioneers, the main memories were of uncomfortable train travel: four-or five-day journeys in colonist carriages with hard slatted seats, no beds, and poor food.[95]

Train travel also featured in the testimony of some interviewees who had crossed Canada, although they were reflecting on a much shorter experience than the pioneers, and were generally much less preoccupied with the journey. Moreover, the focus had changed from endurance to enjoyment, at least for the children. Morag MacLeod had never seen a train before she travelled with the rest of the *Marloch*'s passengers, 3,000 miles west from Saint John to Red Deer, in a conveyance which she described as looking 'like little houses'.[96] When in 1927 the Murray children from Lewis disembarked the *Melita* at Quebec they immediately boarded the train on the quayside for the long journey to Prince Rupert, an experience which Chrissie remembered as 'wonderful'.[97] Almost three decades later, in Halifax, Margaret Gillies Brown recalled her children's excitement on boarding a train which was '*so* big, *so* big, really like some great monster'.[98]

As she 'looked up, up, up at the train' its size also introduced her to a different sense of scale. 'In this huge country perhaps everything was bigger', she wrote in her memoir.[99] Despite the two cramped bunks – which they shared with their children all the way to Edmonton; her advanced pregnancy; a debilitating cold; and a feeling that their formal British attire was out of place as they mingled with casually-dressed Canadians, Margaret enjoyed most of the journey to Alberta, as she absorbed the sights and sounds of the strange new country. Those who went all the way to the west coast became particularly aware of Canada's huge scale, and the distance they had traversed. Easton Vance recalled that when he and his wife emigrated from Lanarkshire to Vancouver in 1956, their ten-day ocean crossing was followed by three days and four nights on the train, as a result of which 'we seemed and felt like we were a hell of a long way away'.[100]

* * *

It is not surprising that intercontinental journeys featured less prominently in the recollections of interviewees than in the testimony of Victorian emigrants. Technological advances, a less deferential culture, and more careful attention to the care and comfort of passengers transformed the voyage from an ordeal to an adventure, although seasickness was a significant continuity, and contentment – or its absence – were determined by the wider context of the decision to emigrate. A light bureaucratic touch meant that many emigrants were unaware of the infrastructure that supported their relocation. Some did not recall pre-embarkation interviews or medicals, and immigration procedures at the other end were mentioned by only a few. Most passed painlessly into their new country, free from the anxiety-inducing enforcement of explicit gatekeeping, while onward train travel allowed them to view, in relative comfort, terrain which their predecessors had traversed by stagecoach, wagon or on foot. The advent of air transport, of course, transformed experiences and perceptions entirely, diluting, not always advantageously, the emigrants' awareness of the physical and cultural gulf that was an integral part of the whole process of emigration. Their initial impressions after arrival, and their adjustment to new worlds of school, work and leisure are explored in the next chapter.

The Emigrant statue,
Halifax, Nova Scotia

Gordon Ashley

Morag Bennett

Peter Bevan-Baker

Sally Blake Hooff

Isobel and Billy Bouman
celebrating their Golden Wedding

Helen Bowie 1969

Charlie Boyle

Allan Bruce

Helen Campbell

Moira Campbell

Roddy Campbell
in Victoria, BC, 1969

Jessie Coupland and
daughter Ann at Filaret
Farmhouse, Patagonia,
1947

Brian Coutts

Sheena Coyne (McBean)

Peter Dawson (right) and his
brother, c.1935

Les Ford, 1950s

Les Ford, 2012

Minnie Anne Fraser

Bill and Lesley Gillespie

Margaret Gillies Brown

Gail Gilmour

Elvira Gonnella Welch

Billy and Elizabeth Graham

Shona Howarth (Morrison)

David Knight

Charlie and Molly Law

Matthew Lynas

Anne McCarthy

Charlie Macdonald

Ena Macdonald

Maggie McEwan

Mary and Paddy McFarlane

Agnes Lawrie (later McGilvray) New York, 1932

Agnes McGilvray, 2009

Graham McGregor

Murdo MacIver

James Mackenzie

Ian McLean

Katrine McLean

Katherine Anne MacLeod

Sandy 'Boots' Macleod

Alison McNair (Gibson)

Catherine and John MacPherson

Murdo MacPherson

Norman MacRae

Annie (r) and Marilyn MacRitchie

Christine Matheson

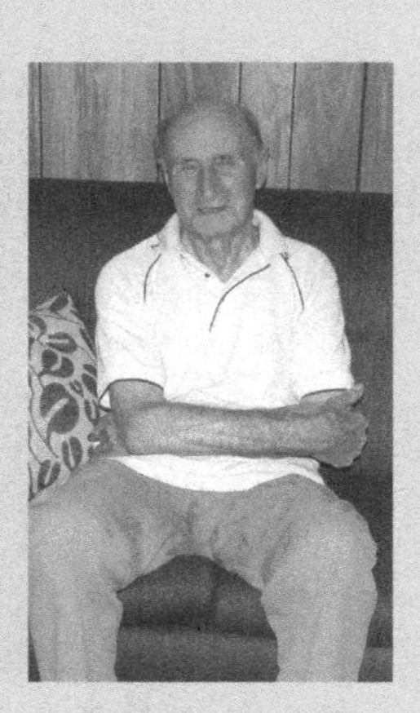

Alec Miller

Edwin Millar

Rachel Minton

Adam and Alice Moffat

Gladys Morrice

Isabel and Ken Morrison

Sandra Munro

Calum Murray

Cathie Murray

Chrissie Murray

Donald Murray's gravestone, Braigh Cemetery, Point, Isle of Lewis

John and Marion Nelson and Trish Botten

Angus Pelham Burn

Hamish and Isla Robertson

Jim Russell

Anne Lynas Shah

Ian Skinner

Bob Smart

Margaret Steventon

Brian and Carrol Stewart

Colin Tait

Cameron and Ishbel Tallach

Muriel Thorburn

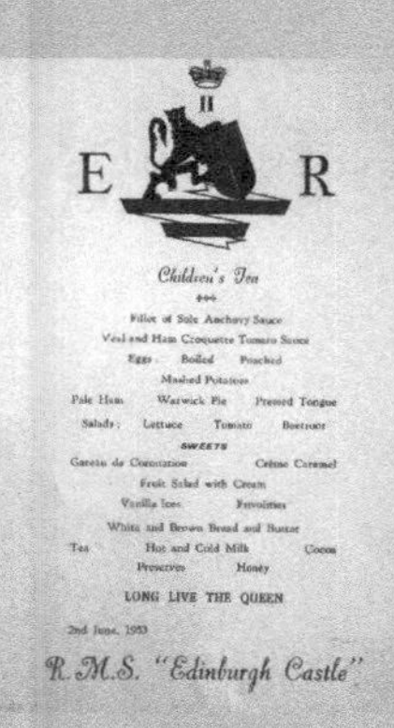

E II R

Children's Tea

Fillet of Sole Anchovy Sauce
Veal and Ham Croquette Tomato Sauce
Eggs : Boiled Poached
Mashed Potatoes
Pale Ham Warwick Pie Pressed Tongue
Salads : Lettuce Tomato Beetroot

SWEETS

Gateau de Coronation Crême Caramel
Fruit Salad with Cream
Vanilla Ices Frivolities
White and Brown Bread and Butter
Tea Hot and Cold Milk Cocoa
Preserves Honey

LONG LIVE THE QUEEN

2nd June, 1953

R.M.S. "Edinburgh Castle"

Children's Tea Menu:
RMS *Edinburgh Castle* 1953

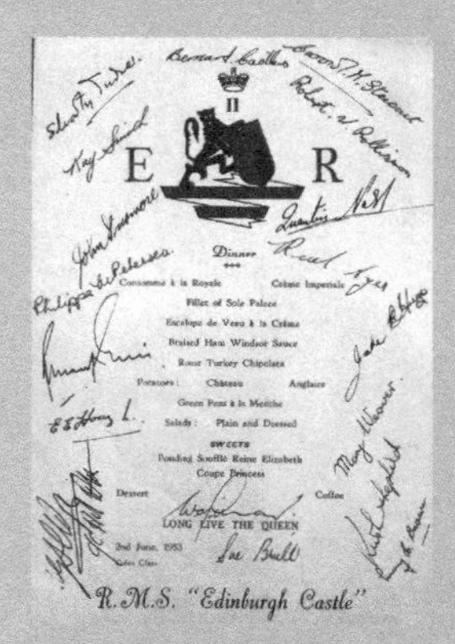

E II R

Dinner

Consommé à la Royale Crême Imperiale
Fillet of Sole Palace
Escalope de Veau à la Crême
Braised Ham Windsor Sauce
Roast Turkey Chipolata
Potatoes : Château Anglaise
Green Peas à la Menthe
Salads : Plain and Dressed

SWEETS

Pouding Soufflé Reine Elizabeth
Coupe Princess
Dessert Coffee

LONG LIVE THE QUEEN

2nd June, 1953

R.M.S. "Edinburgh Castle"

Coronation Menu:
RMS *Edinburgh Castle* 1953

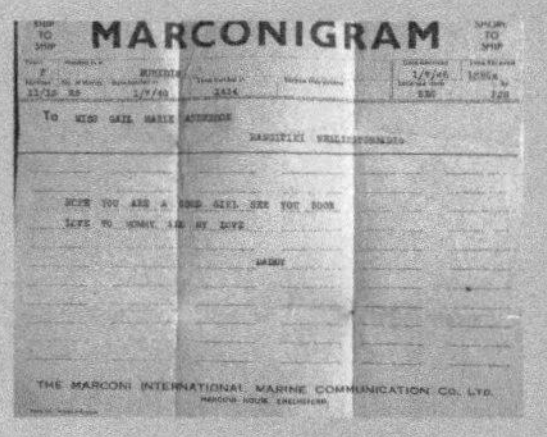

MARCONIGRAM

THE MARCONI INTERNATIONAL MARINE COMMUNICATION CO. LTD.

Telegram sent by Gail Anderson's father to Gail and her mother

Gail Anderson (later Gilmour) with her parents

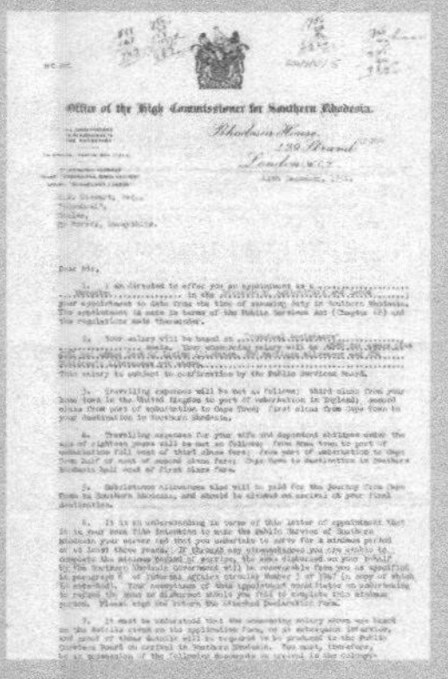

Office of the High Commissioner for Southern Rhodesia

Edward Stewart's letter of appointment to Southern Rhodesia 1952, page one

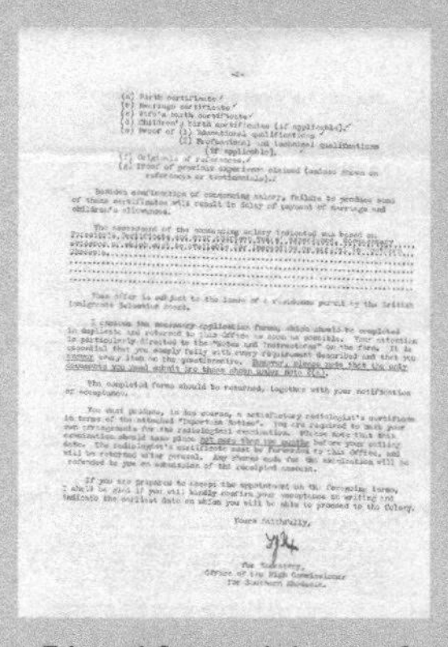

Edward Stewart's letter of appointment to Southern Rhodesia 1952, page two

NEW ZEALAND

DOCUMENT OF IDENTITY

This document is valid for a single journey only.

Document of Identity, Rob and Cathie Tulloch

Memorabilia from Sheena McBean's voyage to Australia, 1969 (courtesy Sheena Coyne) part one

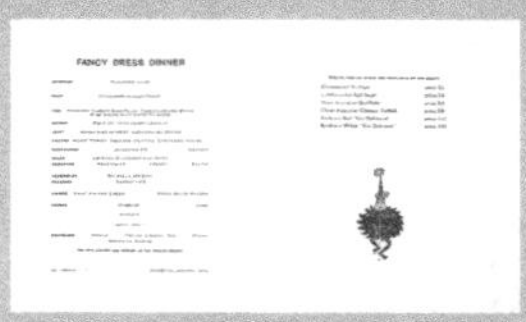

FANCY DRESS DINNER

Memorabilia from Sheena McBean's voyage to Australia, 1969 (courtesy Sheena Coyne) part two

Alison Thornton

Cathy Timperley

Sandra Train

Rob and Cathie Tulloch

Easton Vance (1955)

John and Nellie Wallace

Morag Wheeler

Jim and Jane Wilson

CHAPTER 5

Building New Lives: Impressions and Experiences

'TWICE AND TEN times bigger than I expected' was Annie Matheson's first impression of the United States, as the *Queen Elizabeth* docked against the backdrop of New York's skyscrapers in December 1952.[1] More than four decades later Colin Tait from Elgin described being 'blown away' when he arrived in Hong Kong. As a science fiction fan, he likened it to 'living in the future... you really feel you're living in a film like *Blade Runner*.'[2] Sensory perceptions triggered by climate, landscape, buildings, and food were commonly invoked in emigrants' recollections of their initial encounters with a new land. While some were enthralled at the sights, sounds, smells, tastes and overall atmosphere of their surroundings, others were daunted by the challenges of navigating an unfamiliar and bewildering environment, particularly if they had arrived as solitary strangers in a strange land. Narratives of subsequent experiences focused on the practicalities of settlement, notably housing, home-making, schooling and employment, while also offering reflective observations on the immigrants' engagement with the attitudes and values of host countries and communities.

This chapter considers a range of impressions and experiences recalled by interviewees, within the wider chronological context of two centuries of written testimony. Of course, the evidence must be handled with caution. Just as emigrants' interpretations of their motives were subject to change over time, so personal accounts of their reception and settlement were equally vulnerable to conflation or reconfiguration as the result of long residence, subsequent achievements or disappointments, wishful thinking, and the expectations of readers or listeners. Narratives – particularly in letters – might be crafted to justify controversial decisions, to encourage or warn family and friends, or to endorse or condemn the propaganda of sponsors. While oral testimony can appear to have a less explicit agenda, the articulation of settlement experiences is no less a chronicle of snapshots, whose selection is shaped by the filtered recall of particular pleasures or hardships, comparisons between old and new lands, significant encounters, and later life events. This chapter itself adds another filter, highlighting the environmental, occupational and social issues that featured most frequently in emigrants' recollections. It concentrates on the mechanics of adaptation, integration and assimilation, while issues relating to identity transfer, reconfiguration – and occasionally loss – are tackled in Chapter 6.

The natural environment

The fickle Scottish climate, while never the sole or dominant trigger in the decision to emigrate, was regularly invoked by interviewees as a contributory factor. It is therefore not surprising that the impact of a new environment on daily life and well-being was a common feature of emigrant testimony, which sometimes made direct comparisons or analogies with conditions in Scotland, or expressed shock at unanticipated climatic extremes. Generations of letter-writers told of Canadian cold, Australian heat, or a New Zealand landscape that (despite the frequent earthquakes) was comfortingly familiar.[3]

Environmental hazards were often vividly described by pioneer settlers on the Canadian prairies. William Wallace from Glasgow, newly arrived in Manitoba with his father and brother in the summer of 1881, was aware the honeymoon would not last, writing home to his sister that 'the climate, so far as we have experienced it, is simply unparalleled, but the winter will be, I am afraid, very unpleasant'.[4] The hardships of every season were very fresh in the mind of a Ross-shire emigrant when he wrote home bitterly in February 1887 of 'the dryness, the frost and hailstones' that had destroyed his crop in two successive years.[5]

More than six decades later, Robert Wood was not the only elderly respondent to the Saskatchewan Archives Board's questionnaire who mentioned the misleading propaganda of Clifford Sifton's homesteading campaign, which failed to mention the 'drought, rust, frost and hail' that beset farmers at different seasons. Having emigrated from Dundee at the age of 16, Robert had been distinctly unimpressed with the featureless landscape of Moose Jaw – where there was 'not a tree, nor even a shrub to be seen anywhere. Nothing but prairie and not even nothing' – and he also recalled how in 1899 he and his brother had been given up for dead after becoming lost in temperatures of -64F while searching for missing cattle.[6] Searing heat could be as hazardous as intense cold, and several respondents were daunted by the ferocity of prairie fires. Norman Macdonald from Benbecula and Andrew Veitch from Aberdeen lost their homes, possessions and (in Veitch's case) an entire season's crop to such infernos, although Veitch's fear of being burned in his bed was tempered by 'the beauty of watching fields of jumping flame in the various formations on hill tops, valleys and bluffs against a pitch black night.' It was, he wrote in 1954, 'the most outstanding' memory of pioneer days.[7]

How do these written recollections map onto the experiences of later 20th century interviewees? The environment certainly remained a preoccupation. Although few faced the dangers encountered by the pioneers, some felt they were ill-prepared for the severity of the Canadian winter, while others revelled in it. John Macdonald described to his son how, when he worked on hydro schemes in Ontario between the wars, 'the breath would freeze on your whiskers' in a climate that was very different from his Hebridean homeland.[8] More positively, 'really blue skies and snow everywhere' dominated Anne Lynas's impressions of Canada when she arrived at Toronto on 8 January 1970. Anne had grown up in Leith, graduated from the University of Edinburgh, and was working as an editor at W and R Chambers when she emigrated. Her initial perception of sun sparkling on pristine snow persisted throughout her 29 years in Ontario and after her return to Scotland, although she was well aware that 'it's only part of the Canadian winter'.[9] A similar image was invoked by AM, a merchant seaman from Glasgow, who emigrated to Montreal with his wife and children in 1967, and later moved to Halifax, Nova Scotia. He declared that the Canadian climate was infinitely preferable to the damp cold of the west of Scotland, with 'all these grey skies every day, and the wind and the rain'. Indeed, the weather was one of the features he missed least about his homeland, and he and his wife 'made the best of the winter' by taking up cross-country skiing:

> When we got to Montreal there was an amazing difference of climate because it's a continental climate there – it's very warm in the summer, more warm than, say, Halifax, but very cold in the winter. But when it's cold and the snow's there, that's okay, because it's blue sky a lot of the time, you see, so it cheers you up. You've got sunny days – cold, yes, but you can wrap up against the cold, and it's all geared to – it's not like Britain – we've got all the equipment for clearing snow, and everybody gets used to clearing snow, and use [sic] the snow.[10]

Further west, Edwin Millar from Dundee also liked the 'dry, crisp cold' of Edson, Alberta, where he arrived in January 1980 to take up a job in a coal mine, though he was disappointed that the snow was too dry to make snowballs.[11]

For Rachel Minton – who, at 27, was the youngest interviewee in the sample – Dunedin's winter had similar invigorating qualities:

> Nothing's really that depressing over here, even in the depths of winter... People aren't that miserable in the winter. Especially in Dunedin, we have a

lot of – it's like very hard frosts and blue sky, and I think that probably keeps people's spirits up.[12]

Of course, perceptions were significantly shaped by the interviewee's age, circumstances and responsibilities at time of arrival, and Rachel's exuberance may have owed something to her youth and circle of fun-loving friends as much as Otago's bracing climate. Looking back more than six decades on the winter playground that she had enjoyed as a ten-year-old in Alberta in the 1920s, Morag MacLeod acknowledged the very different sentiments of her relatively elderly parents, as they confronted the extremes of a continental climate and a land-locked prairie landscape that bore no resemblance to ocean-girt Benbecula. Even Morag admitted that 'we didn't like it because we loved the sea', and she realised that her parents had endured a 'terrible time' as they struggled to establish a viable farm and make a home for their seven children out of an uninsulated prefabricated wooden house where only the boards and one thin sheet of tar paper separated the residents from temperatures that in midwinter might plummet to minus 40. It was a memory confirmed by extensive and disputatious documentation about the so-called 'Stavelock houses'.[13]

More than three decades later, Margaret Gillies Brown and her family arrived in eastern Alberta in the depths of winter. While her husband was preoccupied with 'the coldness, the harshness, the loneliness of the land',[14] exacerbated by the unreasonable demands of his new employer, Margaret's sensory impressions were more positive, and her expectations less undermined by her experiences. As they embarked on the long journey west, she was struck by the contrast between the sub-zero outdoor temperatures and the well-heated buildings, especially the train stations, which were very different from their draughty Scottish counterparts.[15]

She was initially enthralled by the 'incredibly blue sky' and dazzling sun of Quebec, subsequently wearied by the grey monotony of the Canadian Shield, and ultimately inspired by her first sight of the prairies, where 'the sky was clear unhazed blue and the sun blazed on an endless white baking-board flatness'.[16]

Despite the exhausting travel, surly attitude of the employer who met them, a bewildering introduction to Canadian shopping, and primitive accommodation in a clapboard shack, Margaret was consoled by the prairie landscape. 'Never in my strangest dreams had I imagined or expected such spectacular beauty', was her memory of the *aurora borealis* as she stepped outside to pump water at 4am the day after the family arrived at their destination near Red Deer.[17]

Emigrants to Australia were more likely to remember extreme heat. Ocean travellers, who passed through a variety of climatic zones in the course of a long voyage, were perhaps more prepared for the change of hemisphere than those who stepped off a plane two or three days after leaving Scotland. In 1969 Bob and Margaret Crapnell, along with their two young children, were dressed for a Scottish winter when they left Glasgow in January 1969. They were still wearing the same clothes when their Qantas flight landed in Brisbane, so it is not surprising that their first impression of Australia was of an overpowering heat for which they were inappropriately clad. Margaret recalled that:

> when the plane landed, that awful heat hit us. And our daughter, she had a kilt on. We landed in Brisbane in January, in the January heat. She had a kilt, and a pair of tights, and a long-sleeved blouse.[18]

Bob was even more laden with apparel, which included 'a tweed suit, waistcoat, collar and tie, scarf, overcoat, hat, and gloves', and he recalled the incredulous gaze of the government official who met them as he stepped off the plane into a cauldron where 'the sun was melting the tarmac'.[19]

The contrasting climates remained the Crapnells' 'biggest impression' of the difference between Scotland and Australia.[20] Margaret was particularly grateful for the practical advice to adjust her daily routine that she received from the 'dinner ladies' at the migrant hostel:

> They would say, 'Now, you're not in Scotland any longer, dear. You get up early in the morning. When you get out to where you've got your house, you get up early in the morning, you get your work done, and you put the midday movie on at 12pm, and if you've got any sewing to do, or anything like that, do something quiet, while it's hot. And then, at 3pm, you go and collect the kids from school. Don't try and do anything between 12pm and 2.30pm.' And that was really, really good advice, because the climate was one of the biggest cultural changes that we had to get used to.[21]

Helen Bowie, who arrived in Queensland six months after the Crapnells, was less impressed with the mid-winter weather in Brisbane. 'I just remember thinking, "Oh!" I was a bit disappointed, 'cos I thought it was supposed to be sunny Australia, with blue skies and things, and it was grey, and overcast, and drizzling, and sort of feeling a bit cheated.'[22] Later, however, she summed up her childhood memory of the climatic difference between Scotland and Queensland in terms of school milk, which froze in Scotland but curdled in Australia.[23]

Matthew Lynas, Alice Moffat and Shona Morrison, who went to Australia in 1952, 1967 and 1972 respectively, each recalled, unprompted, the searing heat. When Matthew – who was born in 1932 into a 'very strong Scottish community' in County Antrim – was contemplating emigration, he opted for Australia rather than Canada (where he had relatives) on the grounds that it 'seemed warmer to me than Canada... hopefully not a flippant reason, but in the absence of guidance, that was how one tended to think. And it also illustrates that I had no idea what I was taking on'. That sense of naivety was reinforced later in the interview, when Matthew, describing his work on a stock station in the flat, treeless and arid outback of south-west Queensland, remembered having 'no notion that you get 120, 130 degrees in the shade sometimes in the Channel Country'.[24]

Alice Moffat's first impression of Auburn, New South Wales was of heat and humidity that were 'really different and strange'. Interviewed more than 40 years later, she commented, 'We still talk about it yet... So that was one thing that we found *very* difficult to handle.'[25] Shona Morrison's memories were of a 'really long, hot train journey' from Sydney to Brisbane when she and her cousin arrived in Australia, and a bad case of sunstroke on her second Christmas, when she was living in Coogee, New South Wales. She was off work for three weeks, and attributed her return to Scotland six years later partly to that unpleasant experience: 'Oh, it was horrible, so I've never been out in the sun since. And that could be a lot to do with me coming home, because I just didn't particularly like the sun.'[26]

For Matthew Lynas, Sheena McBean and James Mackenzie, the Australian environment triggered other sensory perceptions. When Matthew travelled from Brisbane to an outback sheep station at Keerongolo, his first impressions encompassed not only the intense heat and huge distances, but also the distinctive smell and frontier atmosphere of Quilpie, where the railway ended.

> I finished breakfast, went outside, and had a look around, and it was really like a cow town. There was a man walking down the road, and he had his saddle under his arm like this [demonstrates] – the Australian saddle and high heel boots. So that was my first experience in beginning to see [how] distinctive things were. One thing I should also mention – when we arrived the preceding evening, the first thing I could smell was the smell of the bore water, the Artesian bore. You could smell, probably, the gases which were coming up from these deep [wells]. It was a very, very distinctive gassy smell.[27]

Seventeen years later, when Sheena McBean disembarked at Fremantle, she immediately noticed the vibrant clothing and sense of well-being: 'Everybody seemed to be bright and perky, and I'm pretty sure, looking back now, the weather was the main reason for that. I'd come out from winter, you land in this beautiful, beautiful climate, and... everybody just seemed healthy.'[28]

James Mackenzie from Edinburgh was working as a chemical engineer for ICI in Slough when he was seconded to Melbourne in 1989 on an 18-month skills transfer visa to build a new paint factory and train local staff. He had asked for a secondment because he 'never really felt comfortable in the south east of England. There were too many people, very congested... I really missed the open spaces of Scotland and, I guess, the more sort of casual, relaxed atmosphere, whereas down in the south east of England it was very competitive, very dog eat dog.'[29] Having initially expected to be sent to Europe, it was a shock to be despatched as far as Australia, but he immediately felt a rapport with the country, and has been there ever since. He reflected that he was attracted by 'a lot of similarities to Scotland', especially in the Victorian high country, where he was able to indulge his passion for cross-country skiing, snow camping and hill walking in 'wild open spaces' that reminded him of the Cairngorms.[30]

For Moira Campbell in Taiwan, heat and humidity were the norm, though she recalled cold, wet winters when she tried to keep warm in unheated living quarters with the aid of a hot water bottle and an electric reading lamp.[31] Perhaps surprisingly, none of the five interviewees who went to Africa had particular memories of climatic novelties.

Two, however, did recall other – hazardous – aspects of the natural environment. For Gladys Morrice, living in a copper mining community in Northern Rhodesia in the 1940s and '50s, wildlife tours involved the family in two dangerously close encounters with elephants.[32] In the same era, in Southern Rhodesia, Carrol Stewart, like the prairie pioneers half a century earlier, lived with the fear of wild fires. Her husband was employed on the Stapleford Forest Reserve near the Chimanimani mountains, a coniferous region whose topography she likened to Craigellachie in Morayshire – the area to which the family returned in 1964, after an 11-year African sojourn. Carrol remembered taking Paludrine as an anti-malarial and ironing all clothing scrupulously to kill the eggs of the Putzi Fly.[33]

The memories of Carrol's son, Brian, who was only three when he went to Rhodesia, focused on the carefree outdoor life of growing up in the bush, game hunting, going to boarding school, and learning practical skills from his father at a very early age – 'the sort of things that health and safety would never permit'.[34] Two decades after leaving Africa, Brian, accompanied by his wife, returned to Zimbabwe for a brief visit. While his reflections confirmed the enduring impact of the natural environment, they went much further, indicating both the instability of memory and the disquieting sentiments triggered by revisiting locations that had been frozen in a time-warp. The interaction of childhood memories and adult experiences generated three particular sensory perceptions:

> One, a kind of reminder of the magic of Africa in some senses, you know, the blue skies and the views, the atmosphere and so on. Secondly, a curious adjustment of scale. When you're a child, things seem large. When you go back, somehow the proportions tend to differ, and places that I thought were far away seemed not to be. I'm talking about the places we used to live. I think part of it was because places that I remembered as being open space, where trees had just been planted, were now forests, and places that I remembered where you had a view – and I remembered very clearly in my mind's eye the views – but the views weren't there anymore, because there were now grown trees. And the third thing was, this curious bitter-sweet sense of familiarity with the places, the houses... We went back to three of the houses we had lived in, and in one sense it was surpris[ing] – this curious sense of déjà vu and familiarity, but, I have to say, a rather depressing sense that it was all falling to ruin. The houses were empty. What I had remembered as gardens and grounds and roads were all weed-strewn and overgrown and derelict.[35]

Housing and home life

Brian Stewart's observations remind us that the physical infrastructure of the new land also made a lasting impression on some emigrants. Depending on age, temperament, personal circumstances, and location, they might be daunted or excited by their surroundings. 'I could give experiences of our pioneer days that would fill a volume', wrote John Allan of Battleford, Saskatchewan, in response to the Saskatchewan Archives Board's questionnaire about memorable events. He described how he had lived initially under canvas when he arrived in 1909, then built sod shacks which 'were warm enough in winter but leaked badly in rainy weather' to such an extent that he erected an indoor tent over his bed to deflect the water.[36]

Letters from newly arrived emigrants described the pleasures and hardships of adjusting to unfamiliar living conditions. Domestic servant, Elspet Knowles, newly arrived in Saint John, New Brunswick in 1873, declared herself delighted with her 'nicely-furnished room', which included a full-length mirror, in a centrally-heated house, where 'you could have your clothes warm every morning if you chose'.[37] Elspet's urban experience was very different from John Allan's introduction to the prairies a generation later, and several interviewees recalled their general surroundings and specific accommodation in similarly varied terms.

In 1956 veterinary surgeon John Nelson took his family to Edmonton,

Alberta, where John had been offered a job as a meat inspector in an abattoir, prior to undertaking further studies at Ontario Veterinary College in Guelph. In conversation with one another during a joint interview in 2012, John, his wife Marion and their daughter Trish recalled that their first impression of Alberta's capital was one of relative backwardness:

> TB: I remember quite a lot about Edmonton. I thought I was in a cowboy town.
>
> JN: So did I.
>
> MN [addressing John]: You were.
>
> TB: Because I used to walk by mum, pushing the push chair, and I always thought mum was the best-dressed mother around... I used to trail behind her, just looking at the back of her, looking down at what were board walks with grass coming up.
>
> MN: Yes, nettles coming too.
>
> JN: [sidewalks were] 'a foot off the road.'[38]

Almost four decades after emigrating to Ontario at the age of 11 in 1968, Alan Blair (who later joined the Royal Canadian Air Force) still remembered the Boeing 707 on which the family travelled, and the excitement of strange surroundings. He was particularly struck by the difference in scale which had captivated Annie Matheson in New York 16 years earlier:

> It was quite late when we arrived in Toronto, and Sarnia is about a two and a half hour drive. I remember being fascinated by the size of everything, and the fact that here we were, in a country in the middle of the night, and the televisions were still on... The sheer size, the vehicles, the roads, everything appeared huge... At first light the next morning I got up. We stayed the first few nights in a hotel until the house was ready for us. I remember looking out, getting up at first light in the morning and opening up the curtains, and peering out into this foreign land, in absolute wonder. I mean, everything was new, *everything* was new, the buses going by, the people dressed differently, it just seemed – and the smells, and the birds. It was all quite remarkable.[39]

Later in the interview, Alan recalled that, despite studying the atlas before leaving Scotland, he had 'no concept of distance', and had expected it would be possible to cycle from Sarnia to Toronto, Montreal or even New York. He reiterated that he was 'flabbergasted' by Canada's sheer size, which 'continued to amaze me for a long, long time... Despite the fact that it was an English-speaking community, it felt very, very foreign – extremely foreign'.[40]

Alan Blair's childhood perceptions of scale were reinforced through an adult lens by Peter Bevan-Baker, who in 1985, as a young graduate, left a position at the Glasgow Dental Hospital to take up what he envisaged as a two-year opportunity to practise dentistry in Newfoundland. He has been in Canada ever since: in Newfoundland, Ontario and – since 2002 – in Prince Edward Island. He described his initial impressions as the plane landed:

> I remember flying into Gander, getting lower and lower, and lower and lower, and not seeing *anything* other than trees and ponds. And thinking 'either we're crash landing, or I am arriving in the middle of nowhere.' And eventually, the airport of course did come into sight, and we weren't crash landing, and it wasn't a barren landscape at all. But just the vastness of it was *immediately* apparent to me. And then we landed, it was August the 4th. It was *deadly* hot in a way that, as a Scot, I hadn't really been [expecting] [laughs] – I hadn't experienced terribly often. And everything was terribly large. The airport was grand and opulent, and the cars were huge. So my first impressions were that I am in a pretty different place here. Not an unfriendly, not an unwelcoming, not a daunting place, but just that things were very different... So that sense of vast emptiness, of humanity's fingerprints on the countryside being much less so than it is in Scotland was very clear, right from the beginning.[41]

Elsewhere in the Maritimes, Greig Macleod left Aberdeen for Halifax in 1973 to take up doctoral studies in law at Dalhousie University. He was initially struck by the city's lack of a long-established built heritage:

> One of the things that required a bit of an adjustment was that although in North American terms, Halifax was certainly an older city, if you were coming here directly from somewhere like Aberdeen, I mean there was *nothing* standing in Halifax, for obvious reasons, that was earlier than late 18th century. And if you grew up in Aberdeen, went to university in Aberdeen, round Old Aberdeen and so on, I mean, that city's just dripping with structures that are considerably older than that, and huge swathes of the city are still 19th century and late 18th century construction through parts of Aberdeen. And of course, there's none of that over here. I mean, there are one or two prominent buildings from very late 18th century, but other than that, remarkably little has survived from the 19th century.[42]

More significant than transportation, public buildings, infrastructure and the general environment, however, was the living accommodation in which the new arrivals found themselves. Those working in domestic service – like Agnes Lawrie and Minnie Anne Fraser in the 1930s, and Annie Matheson in the 1950s – were generally given board and lodging by their employers, and echoed Elspet Knowles' commendation of living conditions. In 1930 Agnes crossed the Atlantic to New York, where she immediately registered with Hutchison's recruitment agency and spent almost nine years working for a succession of wealthy households. Looking back over almost eight decades, she recalled, with audible pleasure, a lifestyle that was much freer, easier, better paid and more comfortable than her experience in either Liverpool or London, where she had worked in service after leaving her home in Whithorn. Although she had to stay on duty until 10pm, she took full advantage of the novelty of having her own key, which meant 'you could do as you like[d]' after working hours, which for Agnes meant 'going to more musicals and more theatre and more everything'.[43]

For Minnie Anne Fraser, however, 10pm was the hour of curfew in the Detroit home of the Studebaker family. In 1926 Minnie arrived in Detroit, where she worked initially in a household headed by a woollen manufacturer from Galashiels. Her second job was with an employee of the Studebakers, before she moved to work for the car manufacturers themselves, a position which gave her the opportunity to travel fairly widely in the eastern and southern States.[44] Minnie Anne returned to Scotland after six years, but a generation later, Annie Matheson followed in her footsteps, when she too worked as a nanny for an 'automobile magnate', Roy Chapin. Board and lodging went hand-in-hand with a handsome wage, and she found herself among compatriots, in a household where the cook and butler (husband and wife) were both Scots, as indeed were 'most of the workers' whom she encountered.[45]

Domestic service, which had dominated the female employment market among previous generations of immigrants, accounted for just a small proportion by the 1950s. Annie Matheson was the only post-war interviewee to experience life in service, and she soon saved enough money to marry her Lewis-born fiancé and relinquish her post. Other interviewees who had emigrated as single women usually arranged their own accommodation, though a few – like Isobel Gillon in Dunedin – stayed initially in hostels that were operated by their employers.[46] For married women like Molly Law, Margaret Gillies Brown, Elvira Gonnella Welch, Cathie Tulloch and Helen Campbell, housing was provided as part of their husbands' employment package. It was not noteworthy for any except Margaret, who recalled her horror when the family's supposedly furnished house turned out to be an unfurnished 'dilapidated shed made of clapboard', where there was a sink but no indoor plumbing.[47]

After only six weeks, and following an inspection visit from a representative of the Canadian National Railway (which had sponsored their emigration), they were unexpectedly moved to another farm with slightly better accommodation, although they were relocated again after a few months because the property was not winterised.[48] A decade later, basic accommodation was also provided for Dr Roddy Campbell when he took his family to Nakusp in British Columbia's Kootenay mountains in winter 1969. A cold house that did not have a washing machine and was heated only by one oil-fired stove played a part in their decision to move to the provincial capital, Victoria, after only a few months. According to Roddy:

> It was a pretty primitive place... The doctor rented me a house. He'd bought the house, and when my wife came over, she was not impressed. Oh, gosh, she didn't like the house that we'd been given. And it was very cold that winter. The clothes on the line were stiff and my little son, who was in his first year of life, would have blue hands in the cot, I remember that well... I thought Canada was a rich country, and that people would have excellent houses, but that's not what I found, really... It was fairly basic territory. The world had not caught up with Nakusp.[49]

In December 1967 John Black, a newly qualified chartered accountant from Aberdeen, arrived in Saskatchewan to take up a post which he had secured after responding to an advertisement in an accountancy magazine. Conditions were not what he had expected, and nearly three decades later, he could recall the incongruity of the situation in some detail:

> I laugh about it every time I think about it now, but it was a sort of a nightmare experience when it happened. We left on the 1st of December, arrived in Saskatchewan total strangers – my wife, myself and three babies, one of them about four months old – very young baby, the youngest. The position had a house – a fully modern house, I think it was described in the letter, in town, as part of the remuneration. When we arrived we found that the deal on the house had fallen through and we were driven 100 miles out of Regina, and only half way out over the frozen prairie we found out we were going out to a house about seven miles out of town in a tiny hamlet of a few other houses, but no running water, no bathroom. It did have electricity in it, and a party line telephone. When we got to this house we found a party watching the Grey Cup football game in the house. And it was so incongruous. Here was a house which had no bathroom and no running water, but it had a huge colour television in it. A group of people watching the Canadian equivalent

of the Superbowl – the Grey Cup game, in the house. We had three babies by this time who were dehydrating, had diarrhoea, just having a tough time adjusting to different water and everything else. The sanitation in the house was a honey bucket... Basically it was a bucket under the stairs which is used for the obvious purpose, and once a day the bucket is carried outside the back door, emptied smartly into a Safeway paper grocery bag, and freezes almost instantly as you do this. These bags are then wrapped up and stacked, and they had a wall built just across the yard of the house, of these unmentionable parcels which just piled up all winter. And I gather the process was about March or so when spring break-up was expected, somebody with a tractor and a cart would come along, load all these parcels into the cart, drive it about five miles out on to the frozen lake and dump them, and when the ice went through, the whole winter's accumulation disappeared into the lake.[50]

As we saw in Chapter 2, housing shortages or inadequate accommodation were significant triggers for emigrants like Jock Baird, Easton Vance and Cathy Donald's father. But expectations were not always fulfilled. Brian Coutts recalled his father's dislike of wooden houses, which he thought 'looked rather temporary', and was disgusted when he discovered he had exchanged 'the old stone atmosphere of Edinburgh', initially for 'a ramshackle wooden house with a rusty tin roof' in Ocean View, a suburb of Dunedin.[51] Early disillusionment among post-war emigrants to Australia tended to be associated with the transit accommodation in 32 hostels that was provided for assisted settlers for up to 12 months after they arrived. The shortcomings of the corrugated iron Nissan huts – supplied at first by the Department of Labour and National Service and from 1952 to 1978 by Commonwealth Hostels Ltd – have been well documented, not least in oral testimony and through websites.[52] The length of stay depended on the availability of alternative housing and the residents' adjustment to hostel life.

This project's five interviewees who encountered Australian hostel life in three different States all mentioned their experiences, which ranged from a few days to two years. The most detailed account was that of the longest resident, Sandra Munro, who was seven when she emigrated from Paisley to New South Wales in 1965 with her parents and two brothers. For two years the family lived at the Berkeley hostel in Wollongong, a facility for 800 residents which was run by the Commonwealth Department of Labour in four units of 200 people each.[53] While Sandra's memory of hostel life was largely positive, emphasising a sociability which lingered long after the hostellers had moved on, her mother had some reservations:

My mum wasn't too happy with the accommodation, which was what she described as a tin shack cut in half and you got half each – in Berkeley, in New South Wales. It was the Berkeley hostel. So my mum wasn't happy about it. I remember settling in okay, and I remember my mum settling in okay, except we didn't like the food, so a big thing that my mum went out to buy first was an electric frying pan. Everything was cooked in the electric frying pan because she just didn't like the food that we had to have in a canteen... I remember there was a stew [in the canteen], and it had crisps on the top of it. People [in Scotland] put potatoes on top of the stew, but this was just crisps. That's the only thing I remember. I always remember that. But then, saying that, my mum did get a job in the canteen, and my dad in the steel works and we settled in the hostel for two years. [That was] the waiting list for a council house. Obviously people with more money could buy a house, and moved from the hostel.

Like I say, I enjoyed the hostel, I enjoyed the experience, but there was people that just wouldn't stay there, you know, didn't like it. We were the very last hut and we were 56B, so obviously that's how many there was in the hostel. And we had a netball team and there was a lot of things organised for kids. It was just like a campsite, 'cos the showers were outside. You had to have your showers outside, obviously. The only thing I first couldn't get used to was the really hot weather. It was really hot. You just didn't feel like doing anything. You had to go to school. A lot of your school was outside, because [on a] nice day you could sit outside and do a lot of your school work. So, yeah, I enjoyed it. And then the good thing about it was you made all your friends, and then you went to school, obviously years later, and said 'Oh, we're getting a house'. 'Oh, where's your house?' And because obviously it was built in the same area, we all moved to the same area, so you still kept in touch with all your friends, 'cos all these houses were getting built at the same time.[54]

Sandra's parents applied to the New South Wales Housing Commission for a council house as soon as they arrived in Wollongong. The Commission, established in 1942, had begun its construction programme in 1944 in Sydney, Newcastle and Port Kembla, but demand vastly outstripped supply, and properties were allocated by ballot, with a Tenancy Application Committee assessing applicants' needs.[55] After two years the Munros were assigned a council house at Shellharbour, a property which they later purchased. Sandra's recollections echoed the testimony of others about the lack of indoor plumbing, which 'was the only thing my mum really didn't like about Australia'. She had a particular horror of the outside lavatory, and Sandra quoted her mother's statement that 'if I'd known we had to use the dunny can there's no way I would have went over to Australia'.[56]

Two years after the Munros went to Wollongong, the Crapnell family spent six weeks at the Yungaba State Migration Office and Reception Centre at Kangaroo Point, Brisbane, while they waited for an ex-army house in the suburb of Inala to be vacated. The Queensland government had first opened an immigrant depot at Kangaroo Point in 1887, although the building's fortunes subsequently fluctuated in tandem with the ebb and flow of arrivals, and at various times it had been as an employment agency, a shelter for destitutes, a reception centre for troops, a military hospital, and a construction workers' billet, before it finally closed in 1993. Bob and Margaret Crapnell agreed that their hostel experience was positive, although there seems to have been less interaction among residents than at Wollongong. According to Margaret:

> When we arrived, there was quite a few people in the hostel. It wasn't full, but they were mainly English people who were there. And then, when we arrived, we were the only family who arrived off this Qantas plane. We were told that there was a ship coming in, and the hostel would fill up. Over in the main building, the single men and women were housed – housed separately, and they were in a completely different area to the families. The families were in the wooden huts. They were perfectly clean – they were spotless – everything was absolutely spotless, but the families were in a different area to the single men and women, so we really didn't see them, except at lunch time. And then, when the ship came in, the hostel really filled up, mainly with English families.[57]

Bob was less complimentary about the huts, which he described as 'very, very primitive', but he confirmed the ethnic composition of the residents:

> The majority were English, much, much the majority. In fact, I can only think of us as the only Scots people there. I cannae think of anybody else that was Scottish – at that time. Course, they were coming and going regularly. There were intakes and outtakes and things like that, but the majority were English.

Shona Morrison's brief experience of Yungaba three years later was less positive. She recalled it being cramped and dark, 'not the best of places... it was like a cubicle you were in with two beds, and it didn't go all the way up to the ceiling'.[58] Shona and her cousin, 'desperate' to get out of the hostel, rented a dilapidated flat, but they fared little better, not least when Shona was comprehensively bitten by the mosquitoes that came into the bedroom during the night through the gap between the walls and the floor.[59] Meanwhile, over 1,200 miles to the south west, Jock Baird's priority at the Pennington Hostel in Adelaide was to protect his possessions from theft. Having signed on as a cook with the Royal Australian Air Force, Jock arrived from Glasgow in 1971 and spent three months at Pennington.[60] It was South Australia's longest-running hostel, which at its height housed almost 2,300 residents and Jock paid 21 dollars a week for his bed and full board:

> You'd your own cup and cutlery... and when you went to the toilet you brought your own paper. And when you went to do your washing, you took your own powder, and you had to watch what you were doing because if you didn't it got knocked off while you were standing there. That's how bad thieving [was].[61]

New Zealand's transit accommodation seems to have been more palatable. Cathie Murray worked for two years in the cafeteria of the migrant hostel in Wellington where she also lived after arriving from Lewis in 1947. This was the hostel that shortly after Cathie left featured in the New Zealand Labour Department's promotional film, *Journey for Three*. Down on the South Island, Paddy McFarlane arrived in Dunedin in 1954, and spent three happy years in a seaside hostel which had previously been a transit camp for soldiers going overseas. It offered full board in huts, with excellent catering, and 'a couple of clean sheets once a week'. Paddy made good friends at the hostel and left only because he was getting married. 'You were advised to get out as soon as you could and get flats or whatever, but there was a lot of people stayed', he recalled, citing one English immigrant who had already been there for about 12 years when Paddy arrived and was still there when he left.[62]

Securing four walls and a roof was only the initial part of home-making in a new land. Diet and housekeeping were most commonly mentioned by female interviewees. For those who had grown up in war-time or post-war Scotland, the contrast between austerity and abundance was particularly remarkable. In Detroit in the early 1950s, Annie Matheson found 'the grocery stores were just amazing. I couldn't believe the amount of stuff in the stores, things that I thought I'd never see again – cottage cheese and sour cream, stuff that you would only get on the croft at home. But there, it was if you had money to buy it was available in all the stores. Plenty of meat, everything, no scarcity of food or clothing or anything'.[63] In Alberta in the same era, newly-arrived Margaret Gillies Brown was 'overawed' by the supermarket in Red Deer where she had to buy supplies in a hurry before the brusque employer who had met them drove them out to their isolated wooden shack 20 miles from town:

> I didn't know where to begin. I did find it very difficult, because, you see, I wasn't too well, because I'd been sick all the way on the boat, and then I had that bad cold, and I was tired. I was trying to think, 'What do I need to get?'... I didn't know their money, how much things would cost. And we'd asked, and

> our boss just didn't give us any help at all. So Ronnie just handed me some dollars, and I had to find things like an alarm clock, because none of our – only our most necessary things came with us.[64]

For some interviewees, unfamiliarity with shopping produce and protocol led to miscalculations and misunderstandings. Katrine McLean recalled her first purchase from a New Zealand butcher after she had arrived in Auckland in 1961:

> I had been told that I had to put an order in, say, on the Thursday of a week, because all the shops here closed at the weekend. So I duly put in my order, which was for a small shoulder of lamb and about half a pound of mince, which was approximately what we might have ordered in Scotland. And when I went to pick up my order on the Friday, he presented me with a *huge* parcel, and when I got it home I discovered that it contained a four quarter [sic] of lamb and a pound of mince. And there were only the two of us, and I couldn't stop laughing – I had to sit down and write home and tell them all about it, because the price was exactly what we would have paid for the small shoulder of lamb and the half pound of mince at home in Scotland... That was a big surprise.[65]

Two years later, at Balclutha in New Zealand's South Island, Helen Campbell's attempt to follow her normal practice of buying stork margarine for baking met with a pugnacious response in a district whose economy relied on dairy farming and where 'everything was made with butter'. Helen recalled that 'they nearly ran me out of the shop' and 'even two or three years after that you couldn't buy margarine unless you had a doctor's line for it'.[66]

When asked to identify the most memorable difference from Scotland when they arrived in Sarnia, Ontario, in 1968, Joe and Janet Blair responded in unison: 'Food.' Joe highlighted that 'the cuts of meat were very different from what we were used to', while Janet added that 'flour was different. Baking was an absolute *disaster*'.[67] When asked what she missed most about Scotland in Taiwan, Moira Campbell replied that, 'It's hard to give up your western breakfast. Yes. Cereal and oatmeal porridge, things like that, toast.'[68] It was a sentiment echoed by David Knight, who generally enjoyed Chinese food but found breakfast 'the most difficult to adjust to'.[69] In the very different location of the Falkland Islands, Alison Inglis also highlighted a number of culinary disappointments, including the lack of fresh meat and fish, a poor range of bread products, fruit and vegetables, the high price of groceries, and the limited variety of restaurants and take-aways, though she admitted that things had improved since she arrived in 1997.[70]

The classroom

The schoolroom and the workplace were sites which often generated vivid recollections. Only four interviewees who went to North America (all to Canada) emigrated as children, and all spoke, in varying degrees of detail, about their schooling. Morag MacLeod, who arrived in Ohaton, Alberta, in 1923, 'loved' her small country school, but regretted that she had to leave after Grade 8 to help her mother on the farm.[71] Further west, and four years later, Cathie Murray enrolled in a similar one-teacher, three-grade, 20-pupil 'side school' in Prince Rupert, which in 1927 was under the charge of Miss Vickers, a second-generation English immigrant. Cathie's description invoked cinematic images:

> It was like these you see in the old films, a wooden yellow-painted [building] – one room, a cloakroom, outside toilets and one teacher... And oh, the subjects were so interesting, we loved it. And she'd one of these cars you know, [a] Ford, one of these two-seater things that you see in the old pictures, and she used to come up past our house... to the school.[72]

The higher school attended by her brother, Calum – and later by Cathie herself – was a multi-national establishment which educated the children of Scandinavian, Chinese, Japanese, American, Serbian and Greek fishermen and businessmen who had settled in Prince Rupert. It was a world away from the Murrays' Hebridean classroom experience. Like Morag MacLeod, Gaelic-speaking Calum picked up English almost immediately, and 'found everything quite easy', since the curriculum was less advanced than in Scotland. It was only when the family returned to Lewis in 1933 that they experienced problems of adjustment, not least because their Canadian accents were ridiculed by teachers and pupils alike.[73]

In the 19th century the Scottish merchant and politician, James MacAndrew, whose many offices included that of Superintendent of the Province of Otago, had been instrumental in founding a university and medical school in Dunedin, as well as spearheading the campaign for a girls' high school.[74] How did his compatriots who emigrated a century later fare in the educational system? After Ian and Helen Campbell arrived at Balclutha with their two sons in 1965, the older boy, Donald, 'had quite a hard time at school to begin with', because he and his teacher were unable to understand each other's accents. When the latter resorted to physical chastisement, Helen complained to both the headmaster and the Department of Education about the weals on her son's legs, but recalled that she 'didn't get anywhere'.[75] On the other hand, three other interviewees who went to school in New Zealand recalled an approach that was both less authoritarian and less rigorous than they had experienced in Scotland. Cathy Donald, who became a teacher herself, contrasted the passive learning and corporal punishment of her school in Burntisland with the sporting emphasis and interactivity of MacAndrew Intermediate School in Dunedin, where she was enrolled in 1953. Although she was initially 'a bit horrified' at the relaxed classroom atmosphere, which she found 'quite strange', she later came to believe that it provided a better learning environment. At the same time, however, she was bullied because her aptitude for study did not conform to an anti-academic ethos which she felt was prevalent in New Zealand in the 1950s and '60s. 'It was unfortunate for me that I was reasonably bright. I think I would have fitted in better if I had been a bit dumb', she reflected.[76] Two years later, also in Dunedin, newly-arrived Brian Coutts resented being assigned to the 'baby class' at the age of eight. After a week he simply refused to go to school until he was promoted to Standard Two in a school that had no uniform code and was less disciplined and organised than his Scottish experience, but where he benefited from an excellent teacher. Brian's 14-year-old brother, however, who arrived in New Zealand at a more difficult transitional age, 'absolutely hated' his brief schooling experience in Dunedin, and truanted frequently.[77]

Meanwhile, Alison Thornton, like Donald Campbell, was picked on by teachers who 'put a boot in' because she came from 'so far away.' Since Alison's parents, both academics, returned to Scotland for sabbaticals in 1954 and 1962, she was able to compare schooling in the two countries. Her verdict was that the Scottish system allowed her to blossom more effectively:

> The school scene [in Scotland] had a different tenor, a different energy in it. I just daundered [wandered aimlessly] along here [in New Zealand] and there, there was a sharpness in the interest. I started at something like 22nd in the class, and I got up to about 3rd or something. There was just a way of catching you. In '62 I was at George Watson's Ladies' College, and was virtually repeating what I had done in the year before here. But it was *all* so much wider. In Latin, instead of ten-line snippets of something, we read Livy – *Hannibal over the Alps* [sic] and you could get immersed in a thing. There was a kind of growing and an opening-out... It had a different depth and energy to it.[78]

From a teacher's perspective, Katrine McLean, who emigrated to New Zealand with her husband in 1961, also testified to the more informal classroom atmosphere in her school at Kaikoura, 120 miles north of Christchurch:

> The thing that I noticed most was that the relationship between the teacher and the pupils was far different – it wasn't nearly as formal as in the UK... I

> was quite astonished that the children would run up and actually touch you – grab your hand, they would crowd around you and chat away without any formality or anything like that, and it was quite different.[79]

The two interviewees who had personal or vicarious recollections of schooling in Queensland described a traditional – and relatively strict – education system. In particular, Helen Bowie's experience of Toowoomba State High School in 1969 belied the stereotype of Australia as a laid-back society with a relaxed work ethic and few rules and regulations. Helen, who was happy to immerse herself in her studies (including the novelty of learning Japanese) enjoyed school, and described her classmates as 'wonderful'. She did, however, have to get used to a more formal dress code than she had known at Irvine Royal Academy, and a regime that was reminiscent of an earlier generation in Scotland:

> The uniform was very strict. We had to wear black stockings. Grade 8s were allowed to wear socks in summer, but you had to wear black stockings in winter... And it was box pleat tunics, and white blouses, and a tie, and a blazer, and a hat, and gloves. And, of course, I wasn't used to this at all. In Scotland, you maybe wore gloves 'cos your hands were cold, but it was not an official part of your school uniform, and there was no hat, either... So it was all very new, and the prefects were so *strict*. They were in Scotland too – prefects in Scotland were strict, but it was more a behavioural thing... in Australia, especially the girl prefects, they were checking at the gate that you had your hat and your gloves on. So, anyway, that was very different. And the parades. In Scotland we didn't have parades – I don't know, 'cos it was too cold, maybe, I don't know, but in Australia there was a parade every morning, and they sang the national anthem.[80]

Seventy-nine miles to the east, in Brisbane, the Crapnell's seven-year-old daughter also had to wear a school uniform and hat, to her delight, since – her mother Margaret recalled – 'she was quite taken with this idea of having a uniform, like in picture books'. That she settled in 'surprisingly well' was attributed by Margaret to a combination of her age, the school's friendliness, and its familiarity with immigrants, who were 'coming in all the time, and she was just another immigrant child'.[81]

Work, leisure and living standards

While school life featured in the testimony of interviewees who emigrated as children, the workplace was a key forum in which adults interacted with their new environment. Occupations represented included medicine, veterinary science, teaching, the law, farming, missionary service, and a variety of skilled trades. Unexpected challenges of multi-tasking faced Roddy Campbell as soon as he took up employment as the local doctor in the remote interior of British Columbia in 1969, but his enthusiasm for frontier life was not shared by his wife:

> I found that not only was I to be the doctor, I was to be the dentist and the vet as well... and I also had to do post mortems in the surgery as well, in the little hospital in Nakusp... The High Arrow Dam was being built at the time, and this had caused a lot of people to move towards Nakusp, and the population had expanded greatly, most of them living in caravans there. There were a few native people there too, but most of them were from other parts of Canada. It was a most challenging and interesting place to be in, but my wife wasn't that keen on it, because she felt a bit trapped. I was out all day, busy, busy, doing all sorts of things which a real doctor should do, as you might say, but she didn't feel the same way about it at all. So I had to sit my exams once again because they wouldn't let me practise in the rest of British Columbia until I had passed these exams, my final exams, again, which I did in Vancouver, and having passed them, then my wife and I headed for Victoria... a very different place from Nakusp.[82]

During his few months in the mountains, Roddy had to deal with the consequences of an 'absolutely appalling' attitude to health and safety, forcing him to undertake 'things that I never thought, and I wasn't really qualified to do.' There were also six suicides, tragedies which he attributed to loneliness, particularly of women, in that semi-wilderness location.[83]

Like Roddy Campbell, William Gillespie obtained his medical qualifications at the University of Edinburgh, but whereas Roddy worked for a brief spell in Canada before returning permanently to Scotland, William's peripatetic career saw him move between different locations in Scotland, New Zealand, Australia and England before he retired to Dunedin in 2007. An orthopaedic surgeon, professor of orthopaedic surgery, and Dean of the medical schools of Dunedin and Hull York, William straddled the academic and health sectors, and pioneered the development of community-based medical education. The only part of his career he did not enjoy was a four-year stint as Professor of Orthopaedic Surgery in a newly established medical school at Newcastle, New South Wales, a place where he felt the medical profession was characterised by 'aggressive private practice' and 'a fair amount of cronyism of a very obvious kind'. But he found New Zealand 'an attractive society' where there was 'a more even relationship [with the indigenous people] than Australia' and where he was 'hugely impressed' that 'almost everyone had jobs and the gap between the haves and the have nots seemed incredibly small compared with what I'd seen in Britain'.[84]

None of the teachers interviewed said a great deal about their working lives, although Sheena McBean recalled being very impressed with the West Australian government's care for her when she arrived to take up a post as a primary teacher, initially in Perth. On the other side of Australia, when Charlie Boyle was recruited as a lecturer in Visual Arts at the University of Southern Queensland in the 1980s, his first impression was of a financial liberality that contrasted markedly with his experience in Glasgow:

> It was really quite a pleasant transition. They paid every penny involved in it. It was quite odd, because I wasn't used to that, being handed fistfuls of money like that. In Art School in Glasgow, you accounted for every penny... [but here] the money was very easily obtainable. They gave us, I think it was $1,600 sitting in an allowance, and we were in a motel for about six days or something, and then we moved into a unit. And I had spent $600 or $700 dollars. So I went to the office to give them this money back, and they thought it was the funniest thing that had ever happened. They'd never come across somebody trying to give money back.[85]

Charlie went on to explain how at that time the whole working culture was also very different, both within and beyond the university:

> It was accepted here that you knew how to do most things, like television work, like radio work, like all those things. It wasn't a case of 'Is it possible that you could possibly?' I think it was a case of 'Oh, you're on the radio at 10 in the morning.' And this is all in your first two or three months. You were introduced to the area as much as the college. You went on local television to be interviewed – 'This is the new arrival in USQ.' There was instantly a different sort of status. I remember the lecturer – the head of programme I came to work for, who was a Glaswegian, and he took me round to introduce me to the doctor, the dentist, the candlestick maker etc. He took me to the bank to change travellers' cheques and to open a bank account. And I always remember the bank manager came out, and he had little short shorts on and white socks up to his knees, and he came out and introduced himself, and you were instantly on first-name terms, right away. There was none of this 'Mr this and Mr that'. It was the same when you met the Vice-Chancellor. It was first-name terms, right through the whole thing. It was all very casual and very relaxed, and, dare I say it, very Australian.

Thanks to some bending of the rules by the local building society manager,

Charlie was soon able to secure a mortgage and buy the house where he still lives:

> Everything was so easy. It was so simple and so easy. So four months later we bought a house. Can you imagine doing that in Glasgow, even at that time? You couldnae have done it to save yourself.[86]

While Charlie Boyle's emigration experience comprised a single move from Glasgow to Toowoomba, his colleague in the Visual Arts Department, Dundonian Allan Bruce, had spent time in Sudan and Papua New Guinea before finally settling in southern Queensland. But as we shall see in Chapter 7, it was not only academics and doctors who were characterised by itineracy. So were skilled tradesmen. Charlie Law followed opportunities in the pulp and paper industry in three locations in British Columbia and Alberta between the 1950s and the 1980s, returning to similar employment in Fort William for 15 years between jobs in Ocean Falls and Kitimat. AM and Edwin Millar were both former merchant seamen who subsequently worked at a variety of jobs in different parts of Canada. When AM left the merchant navy and emigrated to Montreal in April 1967 to take up work with a stevedoring company, he had a rather rough induction into Canadian life. As he explained:

> I didn't really like my job. It was very difficult, the cultural difficulty. I'd been captain of a big ship for quite some years. Here I was now, down on the docks, with a very bolshie sort of crew. It doesn't matter where you are with stevedoring, unionised labourers are not the best sort of company to keep. I was supervising them – long, long hours, and pretty rough characters. I thought I would stay with them till the end of the year, and then I would quit. In those days Montreal shut down at the end of the year because of the ice in the St Lawrence.[87]

In fact, the decision to leave was taken out of his hands, when after only three months, and with the imminent arrival of his wife and family, he was laid off by a new manager. In the meantime he had put down a deposit on a house, and had bought a new Chevrolet. His initial response was to resort to subterfuge and pretend he was still going to work for the first week or two after his wife arrived.[88]

By August, however, both AM and his wife, a school teacher, had secured employment, though his work-related absences, and some Francophone hostility encountered by his children, meant that remained a 'stressful time' until in 1968 he changed job again. Ultimately his expectations were fulfilled, especially after the family moved to Nova Scotia, where he felt that people were more 'laid back… and accepting of people from away… This is a good country. I would recommend it to anyone – anyone from *Britain*.'[89] Edwin, too, was eventually laid off from his job in the Luscar Sterco coal mine at Edson. After a brief spell back at sea, he moved to New Brunswick to teach marine mechanics, but when he was confronted with the same culture of cronyism that Bill Gillespie encountered in Australia, he moved west again, to work for the Ford car company in Windsor, Ontario. His return to the Maritimes – and to a succession of skilled engineering jobs – was triggered when the pollution of the Windsor-Detroit area undermined the health of his young son.

Interviewees tended to focus more heavily on comparative lifestyles than on details of their actual employment. Several contrasted living standards with those they had left behind. In Detroit in 1953 Annie Matheson found 'there was plenty of work available. The economy was probably at a peak when I went out there... and wages were good compared with wages over here'.[90] On the other side of the border six years later, Jim Russell testified to better conditions in Winnipeg, where he arrived to take up a university teaching post. 'I was paid a much better salary when I started than I was earning in Scotland', he recalled, a disparity which he attributed to the 'terrible austerities' of the war. Despite his father being a senior civil servant, the family did not have a car, whereas in Manitoba it was 'the normal thing'. There was an optimism that did not exist in Scotland, he continued, 'The sky was the limit, that was really the feeling you had, and I do recall that distinctly.'[91] On Canada's east coast, Alison Gibson also perceived a better standard of living as soon as she arrived in Halifax in 1967, noting that 'a fridge was a given in North America' and most people had cars. 'They just took it for granted that everything was possible and available', and Alison herself was able to have 'very much more than I would have anticipated in the way of material things', including several transatlantic trips in the early years.[92]

Further west, in Ontario, Joe and Janet Blair stressed there was 'no question' that living standards were higher than in Scotland in 1968, noting that appliances such as refrigerators, stoves and dishwashers were 'bigger, they were better' and 'everyone had them'.[93]

When Greig Macleod arrived at Halifax, Nova Scotia, in 'wet and unpleasant weather' in early October 1973, his initial disappointment was soon overcome:

> When I first got to Halifax, I was a little bit dismayed at how provincial it seemed. It did seem to me to be a bit of a backwater at first, though this city has steadily, steadily improved over the years I've lived here. But initially my impressions were that this was rather a provincial backwater... It just seemed somewhat less vibrant, believe it or not, than Aberdeen. It really did.

At the same time, Greig found that living standards were 'noticeably higher' than in north-east Scotland, even though by 1973 the oil industry was beginning to revitalise the economy and culture of Aberdeen:

> It wasn't particularly diverse or interesting here, but standards of living were clearly very, very high. That is, I remember being just astonished when I came over here that you could walk into the equivalent of pubs – they're called taverns over here – and working men would just as a matter of course be sitting down to eat steak over here, which was available at prices that were simply unheard of in Britain, and probably still are. I mean, that was one of the things, because I remember growing up as a kid in Aberdeen, I mean, steaks were things that we very, very rarely dined on, let me tell you. And to see people just tucking into large steaks as a matter of course, I was just breath-taken by that back in the 70s. Also the proportion of people here who could at that time buy their own houses, who owned motor cars and so on, was significantly higher than it had been back home. Also, I remember when I first came over here, I mean, the bursary I was offered here to come and study for a PhD was the equivalent back in '72 of the starting salary for an assistant lecturer at this university.[94]

Like their predecessors who had grown up during rationing, some emigrants from later generations articulated comparisons in terms of food. Anne Lynas also mentioned the 'huge steak' with which she was confronted in Toronto in the early 1970s to illustrate the difference from Britain,[95] and the value of a steak similarly featured in Edwin Millar's testimony of life in Alberta a decade later. For Edwin, however, the 'most obvious' measure by which to evaluate living standards in the UK and Canada was 'the comparison of the relative value of working time'. He had previously served in the army and merchant navy, and worked as a maintenance engineer in power stations at Loch Awe and in Gloucestershire. He quantified the gulf in living standards with illustrations from gastronomy and gasoline:

> I found the only valid comparison of the respective standards of living was in the ratio of time worked against goods bought. For example, while a fitter in Oldbury-on-Severn nuclear power generating plant immediately before departure for Canada in 1980, I, as a tradesman, was on one of the top hourly rates in the country, at just over two pounds per hour. A pound of steak was about one pound a pound and petrol was in the region of 35p per litre. Doesn't take a genius in math to calculate that steak was one hour's work per pound, and petrol cost ten minutes a litre.
>
> When I arrived here, the exchange rate was around $3 to the pound and my

> hourly rate at the mine, with the two journeyman trade certificates I showed you, was $17.50 an hour. Steak was about $2 a pound and petrol was 33 cents a litre. Translating that to time, a pound of steak cost less than six minutes and a litre of petrol less than a minute.
>
> When I was a wee lad, my dad worked every Saturday morning and mum always got him a 'quarter o' steak' from the butcher for when he came home. Mum and dad visited us in Alberta in '81 after Fiona, my daughter, was born, and I made a point of barbecuing a full slice round steak, one inch thick, just for him. It was so big, it overflowed his dinner plate all around. He couldn't finish, it of course, got through less than half. I gave his leftovers to my Alsatian (who came with us from Dundee) to make the point 'we're OK here dad, we have a good life, a rich life, a life where we eat well and live well and have some to spare'.[96]

Scots who went to the other side of the world generally testified to similarly improved living standards, whatever decade they arrived. Steak in particular and cuisine in general featured in the first impressions of Matthew Lynas in 1952. Describing his first meal after disembarking at Sydney, he recalled that 'coming from what was still very much a tight post-war situation, the size of the steak astounded me... The variety was totally beyond my comprehension.'[97]

Sandra Munro, speaking vicariously about her parents' experiences in the 1960s, declared emphatically that, having exchanged a two-bedroom flat in a rough area of Paisley for a four-bedroom house near the beach in Shellharbour: 'there would have been no way they would have come back to Scotland. They had a better life in Australia'.[98] While Shona Morrison, like Matthew Lynas, referred to the variety and quality of food in Australia in the 1970s, her main measure of a better lifestyle was the increased freedom she enjoyed:

> We went out and ate a lot, an awful lot. We went to parties, we went to barbecues... [There was] much more freedom than there had been growing up in Scotland. Nobody knew you. You could do what *you* chose to do. It wouldn't reflect on your mother or father. Not that you *did* anything, but the thought was always in the back of your mind, 'well, you're free, nobody knows you here'.[99]

In the 1980s, James Mackenzie relished the multi-ethnic cuisine and culture of Victoria, which challenged his childhood image of Australia as an agricultural society:

> I also found Melbourne was very cosmopolitan, very European. A lot of Italian and Greek migrants came out after the war. Some fantastic dining, a lot

> of theatre, and really good restaurants. So, I kind of thought, 'this is the life for me'... I remember when we were at school, in George Watson's, and we had to do projects, as I guess most people did, and I remember doing projects about sheep farming and fruit farming in the Goulburn Valley ... When I arrived I was actually surprised how sophisticated it was, it was probably more sophisticated than I thought it was going to be. I was absolutely amazed at the diversity of eating and different cultures that there were, in Melbourne in particular. At the time I came across initially the buzz word then was a multicultural society, and I thought Australia, and particularly Victoria, had really achieved that.[100]

What about New Zealand? Alec Miller was emphatic that both living costs and conditions were better in Dunedin than on Clydeside in 1953, although he felt that practices in the engineering firm where he initially worked were '20 years behind the time'.[101] Paddy McFarlane, who arrived in Dunedin a year after Alec, echoed his assertion about better living standards, citing higher wages and the easier purchase of a house, while acknowledging that luxury household goods were more expensive.[102] In 1958 Isobel Gillon was sufficiently well paid to be able to send her parents a pound a week from her wages after she arrived in Dunedin. Her skills as an invisible mender had taken her from Gorebridge when she was sponsored by Dunedin's biggest manufacturer, the textile firm of Ross and Glendining. Established in 1862 by John Ross from Caithness and Robert Glendining from Dumfries, it had benefited from the opportunities provided by Otago's gold rush, expanding from a retail drapery and outfitting business to the import and distribution of clothes, and then into the manufacture of clothing, footwear and textiles in the firm's own mills, using wool from its own sheep farms. By the early 20th century the Roslyn mill, where Isobel worked, was one of several Ross and Glendining factories in New Zealand, providing employment for many Scots, not least those who already had expertise in the Borders woollen industry. Isobel was flown out at the firm's expense and spent her first six weeks in its hostel – a 'lovely old building' with a harbour view that she described as 'like magic to me'.[103]

We have already heard Katrine McLean's recollection of her first experience of shopping in Auckland. AS, who moved to New Zealand in 1972 after three years in Canada, recalled – like Charlie Boyle – the 'shorts and long socks' of the bank manager in Auckland who immediately offered her a loan to buy a car and reinforced her impression of a 'beautiful, friendly, warm and sunny country'.[104] Thirty-four years later, Rachel Minton found Dunedin appealing not so much because of the cost of living (which was generally comparable to Scotland) but because she discovered there the sort of relaxed lifestyle which had touched AS and which Shona Morrison had also enjoyed in Australia in the 1970s. It was very different from the work-dominated pressure-cooker of London, where Rachel had worked before travelling in America, Australia and New Zealand, and which cemented her decision never again to live in the UK:

'Such a laid back lifestyle and the quality of life here is far superior to anything I think I've ever had in the UK... We don't appreciate what's in our own back yards... I think people are time poor in the UK... I would never, ever, ever, contemplate moving back to the UK.'[105]

Rachel's sentiments were largely echoed by Alison Inglis, who moved from Fife to the Falkland Islands in 1997 on what she initially envisaged as a short-term sojourn in her employment as a lawyer. She had deliberately avoided reading books about the Islands in advance, as she 'didn't want to arrive with too many preconceptions'. Conversations with acquaintances – mostly ex-military – had been unhelpful, since most had disliked the climate and accommodation, but Alison had been 'very well prepared' by the Falkland Islands Government Office in London. Her initial disquiet at a brown and barren landscape that was very different from lush Argyll was assuaged by her first sight of Stanley. As she recalled, 'It was as typical summer's day, very strong winds, very blue skies, the harbour was full of shipping, and the town looked so gay with brightly coloured roofs and gorse in full bloom.' On the negative side, she subsequently encountered an element of hostility towards contract workers like herself who earned higher wages and were given easy access to housing. But, like Rachel, she liked the 'more laid back' lifestyle, and also listed qualities such as a lack of concern with fashion or status, an environmental awareness, strong community support and vibrant cultural traditions. Among the other benefits of moving from Scotland she cited the dry climate, and the absence of midges, pollution, litter, junk advertising and commercialisation of festivals like Christmas.[106]

Difficulties and disappointments

Not every interviewee testified so positively as Rachel Minton. A much earlier emigrant from Ross-shire, whose battle against the Canadian prairie climate was mentioned at the beginning of the chapter, blamed his unhappy experiences unequivocally on the 'Gaelic books' which had been distributed across the Highlands to promote Manitoba and the North-West Territories. 'I say that if those books had been published in Hell they could not have been more full of lies than they were; because they were designed to deceive the population,' he raged.[107]

Every generation of emigrants has included those who have testified to misleading promises and unfulfilled expectations. Some, like the prairie farmer, wrote from the bitterness of recent or ongoing despair or difficulty, and sought scapegoats for their misfortune. A few stored up their disappointments, resentments and woes for disclosure in retrospective testimony, but negative narratives are in the minority. The natural bias of personal testimony favours positive experiences, as correspondents and interviewees strive – usually subconsciously – to construct accounts that vindicate the decision to emigrate and highlight progress and achievement rather than hurdles and heartaches. Individuals with painful experiences are much less likely to write letters, respond to questionnaires, or put themselves forward for interview, and it is not surprising that for the vast majority of interviewees in this project the benefits of their new life outweighed, or nullified, its challenges and irritations.

Satisfactory employment was a key factor, and more was at stake for those whose housing was tied to their job. When Rob and Cathie Tulloch went to Whangarei, their employer, his family and indeed the whole community 'just absolutely adopted us when we arrived, and that was just amazing, it made settling down a lot easier'.[108] By contrast, Margaret Gillies Brown and her husband were virtually imprisoned in their isolated, barely furnished prairie shack, at the mercy of a harsh employer, whose suitability had clearly not been investigated adequately by the sponsor, the Canadian National Railway. But as Margaret reflected, there was probably disappointment on both sides. The farmer and his wife had 'been through very hard times themselves', including living in a hen house after their home had burned down, and they were anticipating the arrival of impoverished continental European immigrants who would work with grateful diligence rather than a family that 'looked as though they had a better life' and might be dissatisfied and lazy:

> Ronnie was always quite smartly dressed, and he had a camel coat on. 'They're not what I'm wanting. They're not the hard working people that I'm looking for.' That's what he would think. Whereas he would think the poor Ukrainians are glad to have a home at all, and they'll work like anything. I think he thought they wouldn't mind poor conditions, and they wouldn't mind working all hours of the day and night. I'm sure he thought that. Just the sight of us, I think. And then me expecting and that. He just wasn't happy, he wasn't a happy man.[109]

Charlie Boyle and James Mackenzie both encountered obstruction from the Australian consulate in Edinburgh in the 1980s, Charlie's challenge coming while he was still trying to arrange his move in 1980. After being interviewed at Queensland House in London, and being offered the post for which he had applied, the actual arrangements were in the hands of the Edinburgh consulate, which he found 'obstructive, pedantic and dilatory, and characterised by a latent sense of aggression'.[110] James Mackenzie's administrative 'nightmare' arose when he was trying to secure permanent residency after having been in Australia for some time. A formerly straightforward procedure had been complicated by a government clampdown on immigration – and constantly changing regulations – at the very time he applied. As a result his initial application was refused and he spent several months in 'limbo', mainly in Edinburgh, where the consul was initially 'adamant' in refusing to grant him a visa to return to Melbourne, even to collect his possessions and relinquish his flat:

> The system was ridiculous, 'cos I'd already worked in Australia for four years, I'd already proved my skills were necessary, I'd proved that I was employable, and yet I was forced to return to my country of origin, get a health check, have my degree certified, have someone do an assessment of my work ability – would I be employable – and start the process as if I was a brand new migrant.[111]

The attitudes of host families and communities were crucial to successful settlement. Like some of the war brides whose experiences have been so well publicised, Gail Anderson's mother could not integrate into her husband's extended Shetland-born family when she arrived in New Zealand in 1946 with her three-year-old daughter. Already homesick and apprehensive about her reunion with a man whom she had married in Scotland, but who 'in this land was a stranger to her' (as well as his parents' favourite son), she spent three unhappy years lodging with her in-laws until the situation became 'quite intolerable'. As Gail explained, 'the last straw was my grandmother saying to her, "I know you're very homesick. I'll give you the money to go home," and Mum's eyes lit up, she said, "but you leave Gail here." How could grandmother say that? So from that day on – that day – she decided to look for a house, and [they] moved out.'[112]

Disillusionment or vexation – whether fleeting or persistent – could be attributable to temperament as well as external circumstances and family dynamics. The allegedly inferior accommodation which irritated Brian Coutts' father in Otago was just one manifestation of a deep-seated disgruntlement and a conviction that life had dealt him a bad hand. Perhaps that negative attitude played a part in his decision to leave Scotland, as well as in his subsequent complaint that he had emigrated under false pretences to a country that was more backward than the one he had left.

> My father was angry and he stayed angry till the day he died... [He was angry with] everybody and anybody. He was an angry person anyway. He was angry at Hitler. He was angry at the people because of the Depression. I guess he was angry maybe at his parents too because he had to go out and work when he was 14 because he was the eldest in the family. He was angry at the people who started the war from [sic] taking him away from a marriage that was only [recently begun] – I think war was declared a week after my mum and dad got married, and away from his newly-born son and all that.[113]

But although Brian's father denigrated New Zealand 'at any and every opportunity', his son painted a picture of progress rather than regression:

> The reality was that within three or four years we owned a quarter-acre section with a brick house that had pretty large rooms compared with what we'd come from and each of us boys had a room of our own. [With a] quarter-acre section, we ate well – there was no shortage of food. So if you stop to think about those sorts of things – we had a car, certainly within six months of being in Invercargill. Things that we would never have had. Whatever their view was, the reality was that the standard of living had improved.[114]

Very few interviewees found themselves in places of political unrest. The exceptions were two missionary couples, both working with the Free Church of Scotland. We have already mentioned (in Chapter 4) John and Catherine MacPherson's journey to Lima in 1959.[115] For 18 years John taught at the *Colegio San Andres* before returning to Scotland to take up ministry in Dornoch. When he went back to Lima as the school's headmaster in 1988, the political and economic situation was critical. Not only was the Shining Path Maoist insurgency perpetrating acts of terrorism across the country; Lima faced a cholera epidemic, exacerbated by erratic water supplies (a consequence of the destruction of electricity generating stations); and an inflation rate of 7,500 per cent put huge pressures on a private school which depended on fees paid by parents who were losing their jobs. John admitted that the four years they spent there 'were difficult in many ways' in the midst of terrorism and military coups'.[116]

Meanwhile in South Africa, Billy and Elizabeth Graham were living in the midst of the increasing tensions and protests that preceded the end of apartheid. As Elizabeth explained:

> When we went there first, because Bill was a minister we had to go down to the police and be re-examined and registered every six months. We weren't allowed to be citizens or anything like that for a long time. So they kept an

> eye on us, and we knew that if we put a foot wrong, like complaining about their treatment of the Blacks or anything, we were home. So we had to weigh [it] up. And the African people themselves said, 'Just don't get political, don't preach politics, we're all different...' So we just kept our heads down as far as politics were concerned, and never allied ourselves on one side or the other. We just kept going so that we could stay there, and so we didn't do anything on the political side ourselves, and we had to keep being registered all the time.[117]

After a lull in the early 1980s, things got 'really bad' in 1986. Meetings at the Dimbaza Bible School had to be suspended because people were afraid to come from the villages, it was sometimes too dangerous for Billy to go to work, and near to election times huge crowds of up to 60,000 people would surge along the main road past the Grahams' house, clashing with the police. In the midst of the difficulties, however, they were heartened that the work – especially the Bible School's distance learning courses – went on. Billy recalled:

> It was quite an emotional thing for me, during the very troubled times in South Africa, to realise that in the midst of say, Soweto, which was 1,000 miles away from where we were, that there would be people studying the correspondence courses there. When you would read in the newspaper of things going up in smoke or the riots and so on, there was somebody in the middle of it all sitting down and writing responses to the Bible studies and... theological studies.[118]

* * *

We shall see in sharper focus in Chapter 6 that anxiety and disappointment were more likely to be associated with emotions than with specific experiences, although negative incidents might well trigger or exacerbate feelings of alienation, displacement and identity loss. As Charlie Boyle observed, 'It's not all gain, particularly initially'. He went on to suggest that the reason 'some people don't totally settle' was closely linked to their motives for emigrating, with those who were pursuing adventure, new challenges and fresh experiences being more likely to enjoy the change than those whose driving force was purely economic.[119]

It is difficult to identify patterns and trends from the testimony of such a wide variety of emigrants, whose experiences encompassed many decades and destinations. Interviewees' perspectives and recommendations echoed those of previous generations of letter-writers, sometimes linking environmental, occupational and cultural factors in a 'lifestyle' approach that became much more common at the end of the 20th century. Several spoke of new sensory perceptions, before recalling their specific living, schooling, working and social surroundings. Most, not surprisingly, told stories of success rather than mere survival, emphasising that their quality of life had improved, though Morag MacLeod's assertion that her parents simply worked and slept and 'didn't have any' social life suggests that they had simply exchanged the hardships of crofting for the equally challenging life of prairie farming.[120]

One striking omission from virtually all accounts is any reference to health issues, perhaps because most of the interviewees were young and healthy when they emigrated. Only Margaret Gillies Brown mentioned an encounter with the Canadian hospital system, when she gave birth to her fourth child shortly after arriving in Alberta. Some interviewees were able to reflect on economic, social and cultural changes that had taken place over years and decades, such as the recalibration of comparative living costs, or shifts between authoritarian and liberal attitudes. Their testimony therefore differed from that of letter-writers, who generally wrote 'in the moment', focusing on immediate impressions and recent events. In all types of testimony, however, the recollection of practical issues was seamlessly interwoven with reflections about emotions, identities, and attitudes, and it is to these issues of adjustment that we turn in the next chapter.

CHAPTER 6

Migrant Identities: Retention, Reconfiguration and Abandonment

'YOU'RE NEITHER FLESH nor fowl... I don't think you ever fully become integrated.'[1] Elvira Gonnella Welch's observation, articulated more than half a century after leaving Scotland for Canada, reflects the cultural ambiguity that sometimes accompanied emigration – in Elvira's case, initially to Moose Jaw, Saskatchewan, in 1960. Bob Crapnell, resident in Brisbane since 1969, expressed his personal ambivalence in terms of a reconfigured ethnic identity: 'I don't want *not* to be Scottish, but I don't like to be *completely* Scottish', he explained, when interviewed 46 years after arriving in Australia.[2] Each end of the identity spectrum was embodied by other interviewees who insisted that they were either lifelong Scots or wholehearted citizens of their adopted lands, while a range of intermediate positions was represented by those who regarded themselves as hyphenated Scots, occasional Scots, or multicultural, unclassified citizens of the world.

Chapter 5 considered some of the first impressions of newly-arrived immigrants, as well as the practical adjustments associated with living and working in a new land. But sensory-based emotions and the mechanics of settlement were often inseparable from issues of culture and identity, which could manifest themselves in terms of speech, diet, material culture, the cultivation of local and international networks, political involvements, and – negatively – the crippling pain of homesickness. Through the prism of personal testimony, this chapter highlights and compares some of the ways in which ethnic identities were perceived and proclaimed by different constituencies of settlers and sojourners in public and private places across the Scottish diaspora. What strategies were adopted to address rootlessness, assuage homesickness and reconfigure identities? Have time and technology effected significant changes in objectives and emotions, or can we trace recurring patterns of adjustment across the generations? Did attitudes and experiences depend on age, sex, family composition, financial circumstances, occupation, or location? Did single, stage, serial and return migration engender different cultural outlooks and outcomes?

Debates about identity and culture transfer are permeated with contradictions and complexities that are by no means confined to modern migration narratives. More than two centuries ago, Samuel Johnson bewailed the departure of thousands of Highlanders to North America, but was inconsistent in his evaluation of the impact of that 'epidemick desire of wandering'. On the one hand, he asserted that the emigrants 'carry with them their language, their opinions, their popular songs, and hereditary merriment: they change nothing but the place of their abode'. Yet a few pages later in the published account of his tour in the Highlands and Hebrides in 1773, he declared that those who were 'scattered in the boundless regions of America' were like 'rays diverging from a focus', whose heat and power had been destroyed as a consequence of their dispersal.[3] His observations are no less relevant when applied to the mainly 20th-century characters whose diverse views shape this chapter.

Objective evaluation of issues relating to identity and adjustment remains particularly difficult, since the concepts are associated with a greater degree of introspection and retrospective interpretation than questions about the practical dimensions of departure, arrival or settlement. While interviewees were very willing to discuss intangible concepts such as adaptation, integration, assimilation and alienation, few spoke unprompted about such theories in terms of their own experiences. At the time of transition, many immigrants were too busy with the day-to-day demands of their new life to contemplate its wider cultural and psychological context, and so their reflections about identity tended to be articulated much later, as part of a narrative that might be constructed predominantly in the light of their subsequent experiences or environments. Those who had underestimated the stress generated by packing up their old life and putting down roots in unfamiliar surroundings might be able to describe and interpret their difficulties only after a considerable time had elapsed, although specific problems of adjustment were often catalogued in their correspondence at the time.

Maintaining lines of communication

When asked what they missed most about Scotland, many interviewees echoed the sentiments of emigrants in previous generations in citing the pain of separation, on which we touched in Chapter 4. Some did so more emphatically than others. 'Severing those ties was definitely the most painful part of moving,' was Peter Bevan-Baker's response. 'Without any doubt or hesitation, I can say that.'[4] Anne McCallum, who, like Peter, settled in Prince Edward Island, set her own experience – especially of homesickness triggered by childbirth – in a wider context:

> People don't, I think when they emigrate to other countries, they don't anticipate what they're giving up. It's only [when] – they think about the new thing they're going to – in my case it was a new life with my husband. I still regret that I had to give up the family life that I had known in Scotland. Even though I was moving away from it anyway, I still missed it my whole life.[5]

Keeping in touch was therefore vital for all but a few, and until relatively recently, letter-writing, supplemented by the occasional phone call, was the predominant medium of communication. It was an emotional as well as a practical lifeline for every generation of emigrants, and any delay or cessation in the receipt of letters – in both directions – could cause immense anxiety or exacerbate homesickness. In Katanning, Western Australia, in 1970, Sheena McBean 'felt really alone' when she received no Christmas post, until the problem was traced to a rogue postman who had been throwing mail over the hedge instead of delivering it.[6] A century earlier, James Thomson from Aberdeenshire, prospecting in the Cariboo in the 1860s, testified that 'amidst all the toil and anxiety and privations experienced in this country', the lack of news from his wife back in Upper Canada was 'hardest of all to bear',[7] while David Laing, an itinerant day labourer in the United States, made no secret of his homesickness when he wrote to his sister in 1873 that 'I have read your letter at least 20 times since I received it'.[8] Nowhere is the anguish over unanswered letters more clearly demonstrated than in the petitions that were submitted to the Scottish courts under the so-called 'Presumption of Life Limitation Acts' of 1881 and 1891. Although some petitioners had mercenary motives in seeking to secure a death certificate and secure an inheritance, many were distraught about the disappearance, and presumed demise, of family members, most commonly overseas.[9]

Sometimes it was those in Scotland who failed to keep in touch. Moira Campbell's fortnightly letters to her parents during her 29 years in Taiwan were not always answered, most notably during a three-month period when (unknown to her) they were wintering in the Mediterranean. Her parents were always opposed to her 'crazy' career choice, her mother being particularly vociferous in her opposition. 'To go and be a missionary, what a disgrace!... We'll just have to close down our business. Nobody will come to our shop if they know that our daughter is a missionary.'[10] Their lack of interest made letter-writing difficult, as Moira explained:

> I couldn't tell them about my work 'cos they weren't interested, so I told them about the Chinese food I was eating. And then my mother complained that all I was doing was eating delicious Chinese food, and why should I spend all this money going all this way overseas in order to eat Chinese food?[11]

Moira's experience was unusual among interviewees, however, and, as we noted in Chapter 1, letters were generally a vital two-way conduit of information.[12] Their significance was demonstrated most remarkably in Annie MacRitchie's fond memory that her daily treat after she went to Detroit in 1953 was the receipt of mail from family and friends. Her treasure trove of correspondence, sent as well as received, was still giving her pleasure six decades later:

> That was my favourite hobby, waiting for the mail man to come, where I worked. I used to go to that front door, to see if he was at the end of the street. Couldn't wait for the mail. My mother wrote, my sisters and all my friends, and relatives. And for the last number of years I started saving letters, because they're few and far between any more. So I have boxes of letters. And I love to read them – I love to go through them once in a while... They're in a suitcase there. They [her parents] saved all my stuff, and it's in boxes.[13]

Annie's sister-in-law Marilyn, Detroit-born but resident in Stornoway since 1966, echoed the pleasure bestowed by the receipt of a letter from her family at 'home' in the USA:

> MM: My Mum wrote wonderful letters, telling me everything that was doing. I wasn't as good a correspondent as Annie, but – yeah – it was wonderful having word – news from home.
>
> MH: Did you keep the letters?
>
> MM: Yes, I did, yes, and my Dad – my Dad had a flair for writing poetry, and all his letters were in verse, very witty and very, very good, so I've got all those.[14]

For most emigrants, the prohibitive cost of phone calls meant that all but the most urgent communication was made by letter. In New Zealand, Rob and Cathie Tulloch wrote to their parents every Sunday, but since – at £1 per minute – a phone call could soon consume a week's wages, they telephoned only once a year, or to announce the birth of their children.[15] John and Catherine MacPherson spent a total of 18 years in Lima with the Free Church of Scotland, between 1959 and 1977, and again from 1988 to 1992. While they were overseas, John recalled, 'we never once spoke by phone with our family, and we missed that'.[16] Their experience was similar to that of their fellow missionaries, Billy and Elizabeth Graham, who in 1976 went out to the Eastern Cape, returning permanently to Scotland 20 years later. For them too, as Elizabeth explained, 'there were frequent letters, 'cos we couldn't phone – it was too expensive and by the minute – you just spoke for your two or three minutes if you had to say something.' As well as missing their friends, wider family circle, and home congregation, the Grahams had occasional qualms about having removed their two daughters from 'a friends and family environment and putting them here, where they had other friends, but they weren't family, and we felt they had missed out on the family side of it'.[17]

Elvira Gonnella Welch, whose observation on migrant displacement introduced this chapter, also testified to the role of correspondence in maintaining links with her homeland. She contrasted the letter writing which was virtually her only means of keeping in touch with Scotland during her first spell in Canada with the development of multiple, instantaneous communication devices in recent years:

> There was no feeling of homesickness at that point. The connection with home was much less than it would be today, because of course there was no skype or cell phones or anything of that sort. We just didn't phone that much. A lot of letter writing, of course.[18]

Was the unstated – perhaps subconscious – implication a sense of surprise that limited communication did not trigger homesickness, or, alternatively, that letter-writing was an adequate mechanism for keeping in touch? Although Elvira did not make any comparisons, it is arguable that modern technologies and ever-changing communications platforms can exacerbate rather than alleviate some emigrants' homesickness and impede adjustment to their new surroundings by shackling them to a computer or phone screen which, at the press of a button, exudes visual and verbal reminders of the lives they have not been able to leave behind.[19]

In Asia, David Knight reflected on the way in which instantaneous communication with the homeland had, perhaps paradoxically, encouraged a sense of disengagement with host communities in a way that had not been possible in a pre-internet age:

> In '91 when I went to Beijing, you could make international phone calls, but they were expensive. There were no mobile phones, there was no internet – I don't mean in China, there was no *internet*, not for any practical purposes. So, when you were in China, when you were in Hong Kong, all your communication was either just by writing or with the local society. Now you could live – particularly in Hong Kong more than in China – you could live a very expatriate lifestyle, but even then, you weren't spending the evening doing your bank accounts in English, you weren't listening to the BBC. You

> could listen to the BBC on the radio, but you weren't downloading things from iPlayer and watching movies all the time on your computer. I think one of the huge advantages I had in '91 was I was just working in a Chinese hospital, so most of my day-to-day interaction was with Chinese people.[20]

The former sense of separation, he continued, had been eroded by a combination of faster communications and more mobile lifestyles.

> You don't leave your home in the way that you did before. In '91 you just had to get on with it. And 20 years, 30 years before that, it was even worse. Because I mean, in '91, if I got really fed up or there was some crisis back home, I could have just got on a plane, but in '51, which is not that long ago, it was six weeks to get back – well, six weeks, or extremely expensive. So basically you just had to get on with it... It's not just homesickness – it's just we are less involved timewise as much as anything. You don't need to commit yourself so much to the local culture. You can maintain links with the UK or whichever home country it is, much more easily.[21]

Adjusting and articulating identities: adaptation, integration and assimilation

Levels of commitment to the host land, or disengagement from its culture clearly shaped emigrants' perceptions of their identity overseas. All the interviewees mentioned above referred to their native land as 'home'. Some used the term subconsciously but others were aware of both its semantic significance and its ambiguity. Previous generations of emigrant letter-writers – settlers and sojourners alike – had habitually referred to Scotland as 'home', but the prairie pioneers who responded to the Saskatchewan Archives Board's questionnaire in the 1950s were more likely to use the term in relation to Canada, both because they were writing long after the event and because most of them had emigrated with the intention of turning a homestead into a home.[22]

The attitudes of missionary interviewees were clearly shaped by their sense of calling and commitment to the communities in which they worked, as well as by their theological worldview. During his first nine months in Taiwan, Cameron Tallach suffered from 'very significant cultural shock', to a greater extent than his wife, a native Gaelic speaker, who could accept more easily the need to learn Mandarin.[23] It was only when – still with very limited language skills – Cameron attended a Mandarin service and recognised the hymn tunes, that 'it just suddenly came over me, that here we were in Taiwan with all these people that we didn't know, Chinese people, worshipping the same

God that we had worshipped back in Scotland. And the sense of strangeness, which was a significant part of this cultural shock, just lifted, and I felt at home, and I did from then on'.[24]

In Lima, John and Catherine MacPherson felt that they 'proceeded from adaptation to integration – seamlessly', though they never assimilated. Their own, and their children's, temperaments were such that they never found it difficult to adapt, whether they were living in Lima, London or the rural Highlands of Scotland. Their three children, all of whom were born in Lima, have dual Peruvian and British citizenship, and a clear international outlook. As Catherine explained:

> Well, the truth is, we have always felt at home wherever we are. That's the only way to answer it. Our daughter, when she was still in school, just finishing, John was editor of the missionary magazine at the time, and he asked her to write an article about what it was like to be a 'mish' kid. And it was entitled 'Peru was home'. We had managed to communicate to our children, wherever we were, that was home. We never talked when we came home, saying 'we're going home.' We always said, 'We're going to Scotland.' We never, deliberately – well, we didn't deliberately *not* say it, but we never said, 'We're going home,' 'cos home was where our home was, and that's what we believed, and that's what we inculcated into our children.[25]

The MacPhersons' fellow Free Church missionaries in South Africa, Billy and Elizabeth Graham, spoke fluent Xhosa and identified fully with the people among whom they worked, while simultaneously accepting that they would ultimately step back from a role that was focused on training up indigenous leaders of the church. At the same time they had to contend with the complexities and tensions of the political situation in South Africa. 'I think we adapted, but I don't think we ever integrated,' Elizabeth reflected. 'We did in many ways, but we knew that we weren't there for life... We were there to get them going so they could do their own things.'[26] Similarities to their Highland childhoods also helped to make them feel at ease, as Elizabeth explained:

> We felt as if we had gone back to our youth, because there were general stores with paraffin lamps, 'cos it was all paraffin, and the smell of paraffin, and you could get different things for lamps, things like that. Meal – big things of meal and so on. And then when we went out to get to know the people, we found, oh, hey were *so* like the Sutherland people... so that we found that we had a real rapport with the country people, because we came from country places, especially Billy's people, on crofts and farms, and the people were just the

same, so we felt completely at home with them. And the shops were still selling stuff that they had when we were little.[27]

Billy reflected further on issues of adjustment, differentiating between easy adaptation, partial integration, and non-assimilation:

> Adapting was not difficult, I think because, after all, we were going to a settled, English-speaking town that had many of the same facilities as here, and we were given a very warm introduction to the Black churches that we were working in, so that it was easy to adapt. But integrate – South Africa was such a complicated society, and to get inside the Afrikaans mind and English-speaking people too – they were lovely people and yet they were the same people who kept the Africans in their place, and what I've seen the police doing sometimes, white police to black people, would make you ashamed to be a white person. So to integrate into that situation, you know, you could go so far, but just so far, because your mind could not really settle itself in thinking, 'I'm one of these people', and yet probably in the eyes of many of the Black people you *were* one of these people. So that you integrated as far as you could, and that was good, and we were helped to integrate, simply because many of the people really put their arms round us, and accepted us in that way. Assimilate? Aha, that's different, because we were, in one sense we were people of two worlds. We wanted to be as much part of the African church as we could be, and yet, as it were, at night we came home to a different culture, so that there was always that barrier, I think, that stopped you from assimilating everything, and I don't think I could ever say that I assimilated everything South African.[28]

For the Grahams and the MacPhersons, language was a key ingredient in the process of adjustment, as it was for those, like the Tallachs, who settled or sojourned in Asia. Its significance depended both on workplace requirements and on the social milieu in which the emigrants moved. When Alexander Morrison joined the Hong Kong Police Force as an inspector in 1946, it was essential that he learn Chinese in order to achieve promotion. He had left school at 14, and after working initially as a fish delivery boy in Bainsford, Stirlingshire, he joined the Glasgow Police, specialising in forensic investigation. When he went to Hong Kong he was newly married to Jessie Porteous from Bonnybridge, and had never been out of Scotland. A few years later he was put in charge of traffic for Hong Kong, and subsequently became Assistant Commissioner of Police, in charge of the New Territories at a time of particularly delicate relations with mainland China in the 1950s. His fluency in Chinese hugely facilitated his integration into the local community, where he was well known and respected, and the letters 'AM' are still reserved for the registration plates on government vehicles in Hong Kong.

Alexander's enthusiasm for integration was passed on to his son, Ken, who was born in Hong Kong in 1951 and initially schooled there. He completed his education in Scotland, at Dollar Academy and then Edinburgh University, where he studied law. In 1976, having taken a further, more portable, qualification as a chartered accountant, he returned to Hong Kong, eight years after his parents had reluctantly retired back to Scotland. In 1979 Ken married a former schoolmate, Isobel Lobo, whose Macau-born father, Sir Roger Lobo, was of mixed Portuguese and Scottish descent.[29] Ken worked for a number of international accountancy firms until in 1985 he set up his own company, which, now as part of an international group, Mazars, had 300 staff in Hong Kong and 2,500 in mainland China at the time he was interviewed in January 2017.[30] Ken felt his own integration was helped by having been born and brought up in Hong Kong, as well as his marriage to Isabel, but the couple maintain strong links with Scotland, where they have a house, and where their four sons (one of whom played rugby for Scotland) were educated. Ken pondered whether Hong Kong's more recent Scottish arrivals have been less willing to commit themselves to the local community – linguistically and otherwise:

> For those that *do* hang together it might be a limiting factor to them integrating more into the community. They don't speak any Chinese. Nor do they want to. Nor do they have any interest to. And if it became difficult here, they'd be off, they'd be back in Scotland, maybe not in Scotland, but they certainly wouldn't stay, because there isn't the same tie to here that there might be otherwise.[31]

Colin Tait from Elgin, whom we met briefly in Chapter 5, was a member of that later generation of Scottish emigrants to Hong Kong, but has never cultivated the sort of ethnic networks identified by Ken Morrison. Colin, who began travelling in Asia in the early 1990s, has been in Hong Kong since 1997, and when interviewed was teaching in the Centre for Applied English Studies at the University of Hong Kong. Despite trying to learn Cantonese for 20 years, he felt he had never attained a high level of proficiency. He attributed the poor linguistic skills of Scots not to their own laziness or arrogance but to the enthusiasm of host communities to improve their English, an objective which was in turn shaped by globalisation and politics.

> My experience has been that language may not be as significant a barrier to integration as it might be in other parts of China or East Asia. Most HK Chinese can speak English at least at a basic level and most seem quite happy

to talk and socialise in English. Many HK Chinese I know personally have also studied or spent time abroad and in the current political climate many HKers, particularly the younger and highly educated, look more to the West than to China (i.e. they see themselves as quite westernised).[32]

As Colin hinted, and Billy Graham indicated, and as we also saw in Chapter 5, the ease of adjustment to a different culture and environment also depended on the response of the host community. Most interviewees who reflected on their reception had been embraced rather than excluded, even if there were difficulties, such as Ronald Brown's uncongenial employers.[33] In some places the Scottish connection – institutional as well as personal – was highly prized, not least in Lima, where John MacPherson spoke in positive terms about consistent Peruvian support for the *Colegio San Andres*. Although John had wanted to bring about indigenisation of the school in the 1980s, he had been 'unanimously' advised by Peruvian church leaders that the time was not right, and that parents and former pupils 'would be distressed if they felt it was being abandoned'.[34] He also referred to the surprise of those who visited Scotland that the church which had founded the school was such a small denomination in its home country.

Some of our former pupils came over to Scotland… They always heard about the Free Church of Scotland, *La Iglesia Libre de Escocia,* and they came here, and they couldn't believe it was such a tiny, almost on the fringes denomination in Scotland, because it had founded a school that had such standing and had sent a constant stream of Scottish teachers. The four houses, the old English system, all have Scottish names… Mackay, Macgregor, Douglas and Stewart… So the Scottish influence is woven through the school, and I think it will always be there.[35]

It is perhaps unsurprising that temporary migrants displayed dual or multiple identities, but those who remained permanently in the diaspora yet had close family bonds in two or more locations were also unlikely to assimilate fully. Les Ford, who joined the Hudson's Bay Company in 1955, settled in Manitoba after marrying a Canadian, but returned frequently to north-east Scotland to visit his family. Interviewed in January 2012, during a visit to his sister in Aberdeen, and only a week before he passed away suddenly back in Winnipeg, he reflected on his malleable identity and the emotional challenge of being away both from his three sons and grandchildren in Canada, and his siblings in Aberdeen:

LF: I think of myself as Scots Canadian, I *guess*. It's different here, you know, being here [I am] 100 per cent Scottish. I think back in Canada probably 50-50. I was 17 when I left, but it's still a strong, strong pull… I still say home is here.

MH: And when you're here, and you're about to go back, would you say 'I'm going back to Canada' or 'I'm going home'?

LF: I guess I would say going home too, so, I guess – what's the word? Dichotomy. That's difficult. It's difficult.[36]

In similar vein, Alison McNair acknowledged that 'whichever country I'm in, I will talk about home as the other'. For Alison, distance and time have imparted an enchantment to Scotland that was definitely not present 'when I was growing up, and felt confined'. After initially visiting her native land approximately every four years, she has since 1985 returned annually to Dumfries, where she had inherited a property. Her identification with Scotland has strengthened and 'I have just enjoyed coming back more and more each time'.[37]

Alison's increasing empathy with Scotland as the years passed was echoed by Marilyn MacRitchie, who was emphatic that, despite having lived in Stornoway for more than four decades, the United States remained her home:

I think, as we get older, our roots are – go – deeper and stronger… You learn so much in the early years of your life and when you get older you remember better the things you did when you were young.[38]

That there may be a generational dimension to emigrants' perceptions of their identity was reiterated by Marilyn's Detroit-based sister-in-law, whose enduring connection to Lewis had been cemented not only by memories of her youth, but by frequent, extended, trips back to the island, where in earlier years the American-born family integrated easily into the local community.

Well, I refer to this [Lewis] as home. And I always say to the children, 'Well, I think I'll go home in December, I think I'll go home in June, or I think I'll go home.' And they accept it from me. Once in a while, they'll say 'This is your home.' But in a way I still think this is home. What you experience in your childhood – and I was 23, 24 years old when I went over there – and this is the place where I was raised… And of course we always made an effort to come over with the children when they were young, and the former emigrants weren't able to do that. Fortunately, we were. We came home a few times as a family, and the children attended school over here for three months in the

> winter, and they got to know their relatives, and they love to come... But I don't think they consider it home. They consider Detroit or Livonia, where they were raised, their home... They like to come over and vacation, but I don't think, they would give up their – It wouldn't faze me to give up my luxuries in America to come here today, but my family, I wouldn't dream of purposely staying over here and leaving my family there.[39]

As a child, Cathy Donald had berated her mother for using the term 'home' with reference to Scotland after the family had emigrated to Dunedin. But after over five decades in New Zealand, punctuated by five years in England in the 1970s, Cathy admitted in 2010 that 'I still struggle with my identity', and suggested that such ambiguity was associated with getting older. There was also an environmental ingredient, for Cathy only felt comfortable once she and her English-born husband had moved from the humidity and congestion of Auckland to the fresher climate and open spaces of Dunedin. She described the feeling as 'like slipping on an old comfortable jersey'.[40] Later in the interview, she reflected further on her desire to maintain her Scottish identity, despite having left the country when she was ten and having no ties with her birthplace of Burntisland.

> Identity is something that's exercised me quite a lot lately... I always identify as Scots. I would never, ever identify as being English. And that attitude to English, I mean, England was a foreign country – 'She's living in *England* now', with, again, that [disapproving] sort of tone of voice. I probably would call myself a Scottish New Zealander, and I care really passionately about New Zealand, and I care passionately about Dunedin, it's a *wonderful* city. And I know so little about modern Scotland, in what it's like, and what its culture is now, that I don't even know whether I would fit into some place like Edinburgh. But, as you say, you play the pipes, and these are sort of superficial things, but they tap into – songs always tap into memories of childhood. And I think if I didn't have arthritis I probably would have joined Scottish country dancing, because I always enjoyed that. But I can't get away from my Scottishness, and that was why I did Angela's paper on Scottish history when I first retired [course run by Professor Angela McCarthy, University of Otago], because I really wanted to fill in the gaps, 'cos I know there's myth and there's reality. And so, if someone asks me who I am, I don't know that I could just say I'm a New Zealander. Because I was born in Scotland I feel that I have to put Scotland first. It's probably a nostalgic thing – it's more of a nostalgia than something that's logical. Sometimes I feel that there's something missing, a longing. I'd love Scotland to be as close as Australia, and then I would be able to afford to travel to it.[41]

At the younger end of the age spectrum, Rachel Minton, who emigrated to New Zealand in 2006, interpreted a subtle shift in her perception of 'home' as confirmation that she wanted to settle in Dunedin, where, at the time of the interview, she was also planning to hold her wedding:

> I'm really proud of the fact that I'm from Scotland, and I love my background and I love the fact that I came from a farm, and I'm from the Highlands – I love that part of it, especially... But I do believe in, like, embracing the culture that you're living in, and, like, I love New Zealand, like, equally as much. And the funniest thing I find is that when we visited Scotland I was referring to 'home' but I was meaning New Zealand, and it was kind of then when it hit me, it was like 'I'm there to stay, and that is where I will be for my foreseeable future...' When I'm speaking to people from Scotland, I always say – I don't say 'I'm going to come home', I always say 'I'm coming over for a visit.' Like, it's no longer like I'm coming back to somewhere where I lived, 'cos I no longer live there.[42]

Still in Dunedin, but in an earlier generation, Brian Coutts' parents remained 'absolutely Scottish, without question', their son recalled, not from nostalgia but for the unequivocally negative reason that Brian's father felt he had made the wrong decision. 'He was angry about New Zealand and he professed to hate the place from the day we arrived until he died, so there was no way he was ever going to admit to being a New Zealander.'[43] Brian's mother's ashes were scattered in Scotland in 1989.

Sporting loyalties sometimes reflected changing or ambiguous identities. 'The first time I realised that I was a New Zealander', AS recalled, 'was when New Zealand were playing football – rugby – against Scotland, and I wanted New Zealand to win. I thought, well, that shows I'm a New Zealander.'[44] Journalist Alan Lawrie, interviewed for the Australian Oral History Project in 2013, 57 years after leaving Scotland, identified himself first and foremost as an Australian but still rooted for Scotland in sporting contests and earlier that year had boasted of Andy Murray's first Wimbledon title 'as if I'd had something to do with it'.[45] Peter Bevan-Baker, however, on asking himself 'Who is my allegiance to?', when Murray played (and beat) the Canadian, Milos Raonich, in the 2016 Wimbledon final, found that he 'didn't feel strongly either way'. It was, he reflected, 'quite revealing that I don't find myself overtly on one side of that fence or another'. Peter admitted that 'I'm not one for attaching labels to people, therefore I haven't really thought of attaching one to myself, but I think of the two that you offered [Scottish Canadian or Canadian Scot], Canadian Scot would seem to fit better.'[46]

Citizenship

A more profound and practical indicator of emigrants' attitudes towards identity was whether they took out citizenship in their adopted country, although the issue is far from straightforward. From opposite ends of the spectrum, it is not surprising that Brian Coutts' parents never considered naturalisation or that Helen Bowie, who 'wanted to assimilate as soon as possible' after arriving in Queensland at the age of 11, saw it as the obvious step to take:

'I denied that I was Scottish for years and years and years. I was Australian. And I became a naturalised Australian the minute I could.' Her brother and sister, on the other hand, who worked for the Commonwealth Public Service, 'became Australian because they had to'. While they also retained their British citizenship, Helen relinquished her British passport. 'I never even thought about having one,' she explained, reiterating that her objective from the outset was 'just to assimilate, I didn't want to stand out... I just wanted to blend in, not being conspicuous.'[47]

Murdo MacPherson took out Canadian citizenship after about eight years for the very practical reason that it was a prerequisite for a federal government job, although he felt it was 'ridiculous' to have to swear allegiance to the Queen and avoided saying the words of the oath at the ceremony.[48] Anne McCallum's decision to take out Canadian citizenship came only after she had been long resident in the country and, like Helen Bowie's siblings and Murdo MacPherson, it was triggered by her employment. She remains tentative about her identity.

> A Canadian Scot, I think. I'm very proud of coming from Scotland, and I've never wanted to give that up. I mean, I have dual nationality but I only did that after living here, for 25 years or something, and it was for a specific reason – I wanted to apply for a federal government job and I had to be a Canadian citizen in order to do it. But I never wanted Canadian citizenship – I always wanted to keep my Scottish identity, so – yeah, but I love Canada, I love my life here, and I'm particularly fond of this part of Canada, so, I think – what did I say in the first place, Scottish Canadian, Canadian Scot, what would be the difference?[49]

There were other practical reasons for becoming naturalised. Alison Thornton's father lived in Dunedin for many years, but always regarded himself as a career migrant, who retained a nostalgic sense of his Scottish identity, and never took out New Zealand citizenship. Perhaps that attitude influenced Alison, who, despite coming to Dunedin at the age of 17 months, had some qualms about becoming naturalised in the 1970s, when she was studying for a PhD in Germany and needed to have citizenship in order to return. As she explained:

> Inwardly, it felt difficult, but gradually after that, I thought, 'Ah well, I've grown up here, and Glenorchy matters and Dunedin matters.' I had the idea that you could be a Scoto-Kiwi. I couldn't deny my background, where I had started, and that we didn't *have* any relatives here – they were all in Scotland and in Germany, and yet we had people... who mattered very much to us. So, I mean, that's the kind of duality – dichotomy – you live with.[50]

For two interviewees – in Canada and Australia respectively – naturalisation presented no problems. 'Well, of *course*', was AM's initial rejoinder to being asked whether he had taken out Canadian citizenship, though he immediately modified his statement by adding, 'I don't know why I said "of course"', adding that he knew of some Scots who never naturalised because 'they want to remain Scottish'.[51] Neither did Charlie Boyle have any hesitation in taking out Australian citizenship:

> I couldn't get it quick enough, and particularly as you could have dual citizenship. We have the privilege of dual citizenship. Why would you not take it out? It just seems logical. It's like a commitment thing. To me, it was just part of the commitment of being here.[52]

Others took longer to act. For Bob and Margaret Crapnell, the decision to seek Australian citizenship after several years in the country marked an equalisation in the balance of their hybrid identities, particularly for Margaret. As she explained, taking out citizenship was both the cause and effect of her change of attitude: 'Originally very much Scottish. Very, *very* much Scottish. And it took a *long*, long time. Naturalisation was one thing that made a shift.'[53] The reorientation was less clear-cut for Bob, who has 'never attempted to be an Australian. I'm a Scotsman in Australia... I want to do Australian things, but I still want to be a Scotsman'.[54] Meanwhile Margaret's mother, who at the age of 70 joined the family in Brisbane a year after they emigrated, and lived there until her death at the age of 98, threw herself into Australian life and never wanted to revisit Scotland, nevertheless refused to take out citizenship. 'I'm a Scot and going to die a Scot!' she responded when her daughter asked if she wanted to join them in becoming naturalised.[55] Her attitude echoed that of Sandra Munro's parents, who had taken their family from Paisley to New South Wales in 1965. Although there was 'no way' they would ever have come back to Scotland, they did not take out Australian citizenship, because 'they would never give up being Scottish – they didn't want to say, "Oh, I'm Australian.".'[56]

Similar sentiments were expressed by Greig Macleod and Alan Blair in Canada and Isobel Bouman in New Zealand. Despite feeling 'less dramatically Scottish over the years' that he had lived in Nova Scotia, Greig attributed his decision not to become a Canadian citizen to a lingering 'family loyalty to Britain'. Alan, a retired Colonel in the Royal Canadian Air Force with dual nationality, commented: 'I don't think, as an immigrant, you can ever say that you're 100 per cent a citizen or you're 100 per cent Canadian. There's always a part – you have this strange attraction, almost poetic draw, to Scotland'.[57] While Isobel Bouman's Dutch-born husband had taken out New Zealand citizenship, she declared emphatically, 'I'm still Scottish. I've never naturalised. I'm not giving up my Scottish nationality.'[58] Although she had no desire to live back in Scotland, she still missed her extended family, and acknowledged an increasing nostalgia for her birthplace as she got older. Like two other Dunedin interviewees, Graham McGregor and Paddy McFarlane, she wanted her ashes to be scattered back in Scotland. Her desire was expressed with a mixture of emotion and humour, as she had envisaged her late nephew 'going up to the parapet at Edinburgh Castle on a nice day, not telling anyone, and just saying, "There you are, Auntie Isobel – there's Princes Street on a nice day.".'[59] Though neither Graham, Paddy nor Isobel mentioned Robert Louis Stevenson, their sentiments echoed part of his paradoxical observations on his homeland, penned from California in 1883, that, 'though I think I would rather die elsewhere, yet in my heart of hearts I long to be buried among good Scots clods'.[60]

The shape of Scotland: politics and the constitution

The changing political landscape of Scotland, particularly the 2014 independence referendum and its ongoing repercussions, has given Scots in the diaspora a heightened awareness of their identity. While some interviewees reflected on these issues well before the first referendum was on the horizon, the constitutional debate has allowed new areas to be explored in more recent discussions, and where possible, follow-up interviews or email conversations have been conducted with earlier participants.

Back in December 2007, Jim Russell likened the 'great deal more colour and more variety in Scottish politics' that had characterised the post-devolution decade to his perception of the 'different identities' that were represented in the Canadian political scene after he arrived in 1959. Cathy Timperley (formerly Donald), interviewed four years before the 2014 referendum, speculated that a corrosive blame culture – whose validity was at variance with the findings of her own recent studies in Scottish history – contributed to the country's persistent socio-economic problems, but was uncertain about the influence of greater political autonomy:

> I know that my life was much better for coming here. I think it's quite sad. I mean, I don't know what Scotland's like at the moment, where devolution will lead it. But it was all very well, people would blame the English for things. I mean, the English were blamed for the Highland Clearances… it was the wicked English who were supposed to have done it, and it's just nonsense… It seems that Scotland always struggles for prosperity.[61]

In the aftermath of the 2014 referendum, Jock Baird in Toowoomba was 'angry' about the possibility of independence, which he felt posed a threat to Scotland's economic security and defence capability,[62] while, in the same town, James Mackenzie had canvassed online for Scotland to remain in the UK. He felt, however, that he was in a minority among his Scottish acquaintances in Australia, most of whom had come out much earlier than he had, as children, and who nurtured 'the romantic notion that it would be great for Scotland to be separate and stand on their own'.[63] Charlie Boyle, who had also emigrated to Toowoomba as an adult, acknowledged the variety of views about independence, and expressed his own opinion in robust terms:

> A lot of us think there's something gone wrong with the water or something. There seems to be some sort of element of madness in the air. Most of us don't understand how Scotland's going to survive financially, for a start. Now, maybe we're being pragmatic because we're seeing it from a distance, or maybe less romantic than the locals, but it just seems in general, the opinion is, how can you survive financially?[64]

Like James, he testified to the influence of romantic nostalgia, which he compared to a strong thread of myth-making in his own family history. His maternal grandfather, who had emigrated from Lithuania to Blantyre to work as a coal miner, subscribed to a deep-rooted west of Scotland myth that the Lithuanians were introduced as strike-breakers. At the same time, his paternal great-uncle fabricated a narrative of expulsion from his Irish homeland, whereas the family had actually been in Scotland for two or three generations. Charlie and his wife have 'never found it necessary' to go back to Scotland, and he regarded the independence debate as 'not my argument'.[65]

If Charlie Boyle did not endorse an 'ingrained attitude' of anti-English rhetoric which he had seen demonstrated in his own family, Allan Bruce was more comfortable with a narrative of economic exploitation to which he had subscribed while growing up in Dundee in the 1960s. He supported the decentralisation of power, and thought the Scottish Parliament was a 'marvellous building'.[66] In Prince Edward Island, Anne McCallum echoed Allan's perception that the pessimism and fatalism that seemed to have characterised Scotland in her youth had been transformed into a confident optimism in the decades since she had left. She had been 'fascinated' by the referendum, and 'very excited to see how engaged people were in the process', an engagement which seemed to her to be very different from the political apathy of the country in which she had grown up. Yet she was unsure about the best way forward: 'You know when I lived there I would have voted yes, but now that all this time has passed by, I wasn't very sure... I was afraid for Scotland, that they would make the wrong decision somehow, but you know I was really excited as well.'[67] She felt that Scottish self-confidence was vested in something other – and more significant – than its constitutional position, and feared that the realities and responsibilities of independence might, paradoxically, undermine the nation's sense of identity by removing the key obstacle against which it was often defined.

> I don't actually believe the feeling of Scottishness is anything to do with whether you're part of the UK or not. Well, for me Scotland's about the language, and music, the sensibility of the people, the geography, the beauty of the place, the humour, and it seems to me if it's survived this long, well, being connected to the rest of the UK, how can it be lost? Why does it – how can I phrase that? I don't know that separating makes it any stronger. It seems strong already to me. And also sometimes it's pretty useful to have that thing that you define yourself against. Maybe if Scotland got independence they wouldn't be as happy with it as they would be with the dream of independence. You know, there's a big difference between thinking it's a great idea and living with the reality of it.[68]

Peter Bevan-Baker, who when interviewed in 2016 was leader of the Green Party in PEI, shared Anne's belief that Scotland had developed a much greater and more explicit cultural self-confidence in recent years.

> It strikes me that Scotland has a very strong sense of itself, and a deep self-confidence and cultural identity which I think has always been there. I think there's more of a pride in that now than when I was there... My pride as a Scot when I lived there was expressed by walking with waves of people to Hampden Park... but that was how Scottish pride, to me, was expressed. And now I see a pride in the sort of the musical, artistic culture of Scotland, and the

> uniqueness and how special that is. And I think again, that was probably there when I was 20 but I wasn't as interested in it as I am now.[69]

Another PEI interviewee, Sally Blake Hooff, was – as an artist – 'tickled pink' by the architecture of the Parliament building, but although she had voted SNP before emigrating to Canada in 1957, in conversation 60 years later she was sceptical about the feasibility of independence.[70] Sally's late father was the journalist and novelist, George Blake, whose best-known book, *The Shipbuilders,* portrayed the industrial conflict and hopelessness of those who worked in a declining industry, factors which were a significant trigger for emigration during the interwar years. Sally, who described herself as 'born a Red Clydesider', recalled that after they returned from a spell in London in the 1920s, Scottish nationalism had played a 'big part' in the lives of her parents, who were both steeped in the history, traditions and traumas of shipbuilding in their native Greenock.[71]

In the final interview conducted before this book went to press, Alan Blair suggested that the outcome of the EU referendum in June 2016 had triggered a shift in attitudes towards Scottish constitutional issues among expatriates, at least those of his acquaintance. Having been a firm opponent of independence on economic grounds in 2014, he had shifted his position as a result of Brexit. As he explained,

> 2014 – I felt, again, that it was more of an emotional issue for Scots, and that they weren't looking at things logically, and it wasn't a logical move. However, since then, with the Brexit referendum south of the border I've changed my mind. I think that was the single most foolish action by a population that I've seen in probably my lifetime, and I'm now, actually, I'm more disposed towards Scottish independence or some form of disassociation from the United Kingdom as a result of the Brexit outcome. And again, talking that up amongst the expats here, that's a fairly common opinion amongst them as well, so it's been really interesting how this has all played out in the last few years.[72]

Attitudes to Scottish independence in the Falklands have been coloured by the Islands' relationship with the UK as a whole, particularly since the conflict with Argentina in 1982. Alison Inglis observed that while the Brexit vote in 2016 'upset the vast majority of Falkland Islanders' because of its implications for exports to the EU, there had been no support for Scottish independence two years earlier because of the conviction that the Falklands 'needs a strong, united Britain'. Yet interest in the Scottish referendum had been more 'detached' in a place that did not explicitly commemorate its links with Scotland through associational culture. While Alison herself had assimilated to the Falklands' society and shared the prevailing view, she admitted that on Referendum night 'I was surprised by how strongly my emotions were engaged and how much I supported a Yes vote'.[73]

In Hong Kong the constitutional debate had an extra edge because of 'budding pro-independence sentiment' among those who claimed Hong Kong's status under 'one country, two systems' was being eroded by China's alleged manipulation of the election of the chief executive in 2017.[74] Colin Tait referred to a number of negative editorials in the *South China Morning Post*, and added that some of his pro-independence students were 'curious' about Scottish parallels. Ken Morrison reflected the concern of the business community about the independence movement, highlighting a damaging isolationism which he felt also characterised Scottish nationalism and Brexit:

> With the devolution taking place in Scotland, in many ways Scotland has quite a high degree of autonomy, which is the words that are used in Hong Kong. One country, two systems – Hong Kong would have a high degree of autonomy, that's what it says in the Basic Law. And in Scotland, within Britain, Scotland has a high degree of autonomy. And isn't that the best of both worlds? And can't you contribute to make things better in that context, where you have a seat at the table, whereas if you don't have a seat at the table you don't have an influence in the debate and discussion? Same with Europe.[75]

The spoken word

Ken Morrison is audibly Scottish, perhaps because he spent much of his childhood in Scotland but perhaps also because he is comfortable with multiple identifications in the strikingly international environment of Hong Kong. A particularly intriguing marker of identity which can be evaluated only by actually listening to oral testimony is the loss or retention of a language, accent or dialect. A determination to blend in linguistically was a recurring thread in the testimony of those who emigrated as children, sometimes because of the embarrassment of being audibly different. When Morag MacLeod went to Alberta in 1923, she continued to speak Gaelic at home, but at school she and her siblings 'wanted to be like the other children, and we didn't think much of the Gaelic language at that particular stage'.[76] More than 40 years later, Alan Blair explained that altering his speech was also key to his strategy for settling into school in Sarnia, Ontario:

> Everyone does it somewhat differently. My mechanism was to adapt and blend in as quickly as I could. As you can tell from my accent at the moment, there's very little, if any, Scots there on a day-to-day basis. I do still have the accent,

> though – I file it away and I bring it out on special occasions. I blended in – it wasn't that I was maltreated or mistreated, but I didn't like being the centre of attention, and I was certainly the centre of attention for the first part of that first school year. So probably by Christmas of that first year I was a proper little Canadian and indistinguishable from the Canadians on either side of me in the schoolroom.[77]

While his father Joe attributed the decision to Alan's age ('12 seems to be the magic age over here whether you keep or lose an accent'), and commented that the three younger children automatically adopted Canadian accents,[78] Alan himself thought it was associated more with temperament.

> I think it depends a lot on your personality, whether you enjoy being – relish being the centre of attention, don't mind being the centre of attention, or whether you, like me, just wanted to be one of the group, didn't want to stand out from the rest of them. I think it's very personality-dependent, how you end up coping and adapting.[79]

Alan's description of his self-conscious determination to become Canadianised was confirmed by his mother, Janet, who recalled how 'he practised his accent in front of the mirror. You know, he *really* wanted to be Canadian'.[80] In much the same way, but at a younger age, Isla and Hamish Robertson's two children wanted to lose 'that funny accent straight away' after the family emigrated to Vancouver in 1969. To this day, 'they don't really want to hear all about Scotland', Isla added, 'and aren't what I'd call "born again Scots"'.[81]

Also in 1969, and with a similar embarrassment about standing out from the crowd, Helen Bowie made a persistent effort to become Australian as soon as she arrived in Toowoomba.

> Everybody says, 'Oh, your accent, it's so interesting', or 'it's so funny...' And so they'd get you to say things – 'Say this again', and 'say that'. And they'd laugh if you pronounced something wrong. So both of us [she and her sister], and my brother I suppose too, learnt to speak with an accent, an Australian accent, as soon as possible. We used to practise speaking Aussie.[82]

Brian Coutts, who also emigrated as a child, maintained a dual linguistic identity for many years, not least because of his father's lifelong anger at having taken the family to Dunedin. As Brian explained:

> I got quite a hard time about having a Scottish accent, and so I lost that in

> public very quickly. I retained it for being at home, 'cos it was either being teased at home or being teased at school, so I decided I didn't like either, so I picked up a New Zealand accent as quickly as possible for school and I spoke to my parents with a Scottish accent. In fact the last of that disappeared when my father died.[83]

As we saw in Chapter 5, mutual incomprehension between Donald Campbell and his teacher in Dunedin resulted in Donald suffering corporal punishment.[84] That extreme reaction was confirmed in a taxi driver's anecdote. Following my interview with Helen Campbell, in which she had told me about her son's experience, the cab driver who collected me from Helen's home described how, when his wife had emigrated from Scotland to Dunedin in 1950, her teacher had hit her with a ruler because of her Scottish accent.

Graham McGregor, an interviewee who is also a linguistics professor in Dunedin, blended professional theory with personal experience in explaining the reasons for retention or loss of accent. His comments echoed and amplified Ken Morrison's observation that the deployment of an accent might reflect an attempt by those who did not feel comfortable about themselves 'to gain the approval of others by adapting to them.'[85] Graham has retained his Scottish accent, and, with his finely tuned ear, he admitted that when he came to New Zealand, 'I missed the voices. It took me a long time to adjust to a very, very different linguistic system.'[86] Turning to theory, Graham explained that convergence and divergence are the terms used by linguists to describe the deliberate decision to associate – or not – with the host culture or the expectations of others.

> It's choice... My kids first addressed me when we first came here, I was 'Dad'. 'Hello Dad, how are you Dad?' Within a very short period of time I was no longer 'Dad'. I became 'Ded'. And I kept teasing them, saying 'I'm not dead, I'm alive.' The peer pressure at school – you've either got to want to be different, or you change. And you say, we are maximally like you.[87]

Graham illustrated the opposite choice – to remain distinctive – from his own experience during an interview for a lecturing post while he was still in the UK. Having been told that, if he got the job, he would be expected to adopt received pronunciation, he reacted by emphasising his distinctiveness in a similar way to some emigrants who felt their identity was being criticised or threatened:

> So what I did in that situation was not convergence as it's called in linguistics, but divergence. And I found myself getting further and further away from that

particular way of speaking to a much more Scottish voice, to say maximally, 'Hey mate, I'm not actually like you, I'm different, I have a different history, I have a different culture, I have a different ethnicity, I have a different musicology, I have a different sense of education, I have a different religious upbringing, I have a different past, I have a different history, and I remember it and we're not the same.'[88]

On arriving in New Zealand, Graham – an ardent Scottish nationalist and republican who refused to take out citizenship because it involved swearing an oath of allegiance to the Queen – had made a conscious choice that his identity was going to be 'marked and known' through the way he spoke.[89] Turning back to theory, he also explained that language can also function in a more complex way than as simply a mechanism for assimilation or distinctiveness. It can be a vehicle for establishing networks, and a verbal means of conveying an identity that might equally be expressed through clothing or food. Scots, he asserted, differed from New Zealanders in establishing mutual credibility through language rather than through family or community connections:

That notion, that you will name the place and that you have identified yourself by the way that you speak, is incredibly powerful and strong. And it may be there's not a huge conversation happens thereafter... There is a kind of linguistic acknowledgment of others, without necessarily establishing a relationship or having a huge brouhaha about the Scottish society. It's more likely to happen quietly, in people's homes, rather than 'let's form a group of ourselves and do this Scottish thing'. For many, many Scots that's the way you are, this is who I am, this is the way I speak, and that's, I suppose, the linguistic equivalent of wearing a tartan scarf or listening to the bagpipes or whatever the other stereotypes are, or having haggis for breakfast, you know, whatever it is we're supposed to do... it's a statement, definitely. And it's one way too that I think we retain the connect [ion] with Scotland and with other Scots, even although we're not in their company, because you're never quite sure where one's going to turn up.[90]

As some of Graham's examples implied, linguistic convergence or divergence was relevant not only to those who emigrated as children. He referred to another Dunedin Scot, and interviewee, Isobel Bouman, as having 'not a hint or trace of Kiwi at all', while Isobel herself explained that she had not deliberately tried to keep her accent, but had consciously modified her dialect 'because it was silly to try and use it because you knew people couldn't understand it.'[91] Her explanation was echoed by Cathie and Rob Tulloch, whose speech patterns varied according to context. Cathie, who had done 'a fair bit of public speaking' in New Zealand, demonstrated a much more obvious convergence in her intonation than Rob, who had clearly retained his Morayshire accent, though she suggested that her hybrid accent was also due to having an English mother and to the relatively formal setting of an interview with someone she had never met.[92]

Meanwhile, back in Canada, Anne McCallum and Peter Bevan-Baker both cited a desire to fit in as a consideration in their loss of a Scottish accent. Anne was 'puzzled' by the disappearance of her accent, which, 'as far as I can tell, hardly happens to Scots people', but she attributed it partly to having an English husband, and partly to shyness: 'I'm a fairly shy, quiet person, and I hate having to repeat things.'[93] Peter echoed her sentiments:

> I'm one that likes to fit in. I like to feel – I don't like to stand out. I like to be liked, so I'm very aware if I am not fitting in with the group where I am. And part of that of course would be an overt Scottish accent [which he then demonstrated]... I think it was part of my desire to belong and to feel like part of the place in which I lived.[94]

Perhaps the retention or adoption of language or accent was also influenced by place of origin, as well as by the circles in which the emigrants moved. After living in Canada for more than 80 years, and marrying a Canadian, Morag MacLeod could still speak Gaelic. Annie Matheson and Murdo MacIver, whose first language was also Gaelic, married fellow Gaelic speakers, mixed with other Hebrideans in the Free Church of Scotland in Detroit and the Highland Society of Vancouver respectively, and made frequent visits to their native island of Lewis. After more than half a century in North America, both retained their Gaelic language and continued to speak English with a strong Hebridean accent and idiom. Despite being born and living all her life in Winnipeg, Katherine Anne MacLeod identified strongly with her parents' birthplace of Lewis. Angus and Christina MacLeod were emigrants from Portnaguran and Bayble who met in Manitoba and married there in 1925. Brought up in a large Gaelic-speaking community, Katherine learnt the language as a child, and in her 80s she was still attending a language class in Winnipeg.[95]

As the daughter of immigrants from the western isles who had spent most of their lives in a Hebridean community in Canada, Katherine Anne MacLeod exemplified the 'intergenerational commitment to their ancestral homelands' that is a key marker of diasporic consciousness.[96] The persistence of a cultural commitment to Scotland among both first-generation and ancestral Scots was also evident in the popularity of Scottish societies and institutions, as well as through what the immigrants ate, read and listened to. Interviewees who spoke about ethnic associations and identifications displayed a range of responses. For most, these symbols of their Scottish origins were simply optional threads in the multi-hued tapestry of their social lives rather than cornerstones of their reconfigured identities. Others deliberately repudiated any connection with what they regarded as self-indulgent, contrived and spurious Scottish sentimentality, which they felt could block their integration into the host society. For a few, however, reminders of Scotland triggered not cosmetic nostalgia, but crushing homesickness, which in extreme cases could thwart adjustment and even bring about a return to their homeland.

Cultural and institutional networking and nostalgia: association and divergence

In 1998 the folklorist and ethnologist Margaret Bennett published *Oatmeal and the Catechism,* a cultural history of Scottish Gaelic settlers in the Eastern Townships of Quebec.[97] Drawing mainly on oral testimony, she documented the lives of the Hebridean pioneers who in the mid-19th century had dominated the Eastern Townships but who by the 1990s were barely remembered in an area that was rapidly becoming homogeneously French-speaking. Her book demonstrates the fragility of the Gaelic culture, for even in the 1930s the region may have boasted up to 50,000 Gaelic speakers, and it was not unusual for children to be 'quite unaware that there was any other language in the world but Gaelic'.[98] Although the log cabin replaced the black house, tangible memories of the Hebrides were preserved in the furniture, books and portraits that adorned the settlers' Canadian homes, and a blend of old and new worlds was evident in the combination of stone walls and cedar rail fences that marked the farm boundaries. Recipes and medical remedies too were imported, and although both subsequently absorbed French Canadian, First Nations and American influences, food traditions in particular retained a vital role in reflecting the Scottish heritage of the Eastern Townships, to a much greater extent than language.[99]

We saw in Chapter 5 that some emigrants – especially those who came from a background of rationing – were amazed at the variety, quality and quantity of food on offer.[100] Others, however, missed the comforting familiarity of traditional Scottish fare, or looked forward to imported treats. Despite being 2,000 miles from the sea, the Eastern Township settlers and their descendants studied by Margaret Bennett regarded salt herring as an essential part of their diet. For some of the Lewis settlers in Detroit a century later, salted guga (gannet chick) was an annual delicacy, as Marilyn and Annie MacRitchie explained:

MM: They kept their customs and traditions. I'll just tell this wee bit. The *Niseachs* – there were a lot of people from Ness there – were sent the famous gugas, these are seabirds, like, that they relished. They were sent them from Lewis, and so they had a big feast every year, and the minister was guest of honour. And although he [Murdo MacRitchie, Marilyn's husband] was never accustomed to eating guga, he soon got a taste for them...

AM: Some of them used to get these birds at the same time every year, and they used to have a get together in one house or another and enjoy it that way. Those that didn't like those birds would have salt herring...

MM: One time there was a seamen's strike and so the gugas laid on some pier for a long period of time. When they finally arrived, well, they were finished, I mean, months I think, before they arrived. And the story went that one of the men thought he'd play a trick on one of his friends, and had it delivered to his home, and it smelt so bad, and he was so angry when he got it, he threw it into the furnace, which put a smell through the whole house and the dog went away and never came back.[101]

On board the boat taking her back to Australia in 1965 after a spell back in North Uist and the birth of her son, homesick Ena Macdonald longed for a simple 'plate of mince and tatties', rather than the sophisticated, unfamiliar menus of the P&O liner *Orion*.[102] In Dunedin, Graham McGregor missed 'stupid things like Arbroath smokies, Finnan haddie and real haggis'.[103] Generally, the consumption of haggis was more a ritual than a culinary treat, as Burns' clubs across the world went to elaborate lengths to import the authentic article from Scotland. On the Northern Rhodesian Copper Belt in the 1940s and '50s, for instance, Gladys Morrice recalled that the haggis was brought out from Scotland by Luanshya's 'huge Caledonian Society', as it was when Gavin and Aileen McEwen from Aberdeen were involved in the Caledonian Society of Nairobi (and other Scottish networks) during a two-year spell in Kenya in the 1980s.[104] In Hong Kong, the popularity of haggis among both Scots and Chinese means that it – and Stornoway black pudding – are readily available locally, although the large ceremonial haggis for Burns' Night is still flown in, along with Scottish newspapers.[105]

Traditionally, of course, churches and schools had been perceived as central pillars of Scottish identity in the diaspora. The strict Presbyterianism of the Eastern Township Hebrideans described by Margaret Bennett was a common feature of Scottish settlements. When George Elmslie left Aberdeen in 1834 to prepare the way for a subsequent exodus of Aberdonians to a new township in southern Ontario (then Upper Canada), those who waited behind instructed him to check not only the quality of the land, but to ensure that church and school were both within 'reasonable distance' of the proposed settlement.[106] Novelists like Ralph Connor and Sir Andrew Macphail put the influence of those institutions at the heart of their fictional portrayals of Scottish immigrant life in Ontario and Prince Edward Island respectively,[107] while in 1920, a report on the Scots Church in Colombo, Ceylon, described it as 'a rallying-point for Scottish sentiment and tradition'.[108]

In an increasingly secular age, religious rallying-points have become largely obsolete, ignored by recent generations of emigrants. From the mid-20th century institutional religion no longer took centre stage as an indispensable marker of identity, though a few interviewees still joined churches for spiritual succour, social support or ethnic or denominational networking. In Toowoomba, St Stephen's Presbyterian Church was a lifeline to Helen Bowie's mother, grandmother and great-aunt, while in Brisbane, Bob Crapnell quickly became involved with the St Vincent de Paul Society, an international Catholic poverty-relief organisation, ultimately becoming supervisor for the Society's Brisbane stores.[109] The Free Church of Scotland in Livonia, Detroit, was a gathering place for the large community of *Leodhasachs* and has been at the heart of Annie MacRitchie's life since she emigrated in 1953.[110]

Burns' clubs, Caledonian societies and their more regionally-based equivalents were the traditional vehicles for the formal commemoration of secular Scottish associationalism. They had generally been founded with charitable objectives: assisting distressed Scots in the diaspora and donating to deserving causes back in Scotland were combined with celebrating Scottish culture. By the mid-20th century philanthropy had generally been eclipsed by entertainment, a trait which Samuel Johnson had noticed two centuries earlier, when he commented that Highland emigrants carried with them 'their popular songs, and hereditary merriment'.[111] Gladys Morrice's description of the scene at Luanshya in the 1940s and 50s suggests that a mixture of distortion, exaggeration and dilution had accompanied the export of Scottish popular culture:

> Every year we had a big fête. We'd Scottish country dancing, and we had all sorts of things – dog shows, I mean – we tried to emulate to a large degree what went on at home, and what we enjoyed at home. And it was lovely to see the country dancers on the stage, you know, in the kilt, and all this sort of thing... I was secretary of the Caledonian Society, and I had a lot of photographs of all the men there in their kilts. When we went to dances we all wore our white frocks with the tartan sashes. I think we were more Scottish in Africa than we are in Scotland, but that was just the way of us.[112]

In 2001 Gavin and Aileen McEwen left Aberdeen for Nairobi, where Gavin had been seconded for two years by Pricewaterhouse Coopers. In the event they stayed for seven years, and from the start were heavily involved in the Caledonian Society. As Aileen explained, this allowed them to meet people and integrate quickly, thanks to an organisation that married social activities with an ongoing philanthropic agenda:

> The Caledonian Society was started in Kenya in 1903. Again, it was just to give Scots in Kenya a real focus and probably a memory of history and culture, or – for us – a place to go to, to meet other Scots. It helped Scots. Its ethos was to look after Scottish people, particularly people who were hitting hard times. To do that, they had to have some money, so the money was made by doing different sorts of Scottish activities – for instance the Highland Games, Burns' suppers and the Caledonian Ball – St Andrew's Night Ball. So these are three examples of the sorts of things that raised the money to allow [benefactions] – we were benefactor to people who were in straitened times. That is probably the ethos – is to continue Scottish culture in a foreign land and to help one another.[113]

Before long, both Gavin and Aileen were serving on the committee, Aileen as secretary and Gavin ultimately as Chieftain. Like many Caledonian societies faced with dwindling memberships, it had steadily slackened its entry requirements and – eventually – admitted women to its ranks. Aileen explained the change of rules:

> Initially, Scots-born, and it developed into having Scots parents, or grandparents. Associate membership would have started in, I think, the '50s... of just having an interest in things Scottish. Because there are fewer Scots there now than there were before, just by people not going – people don't emigrate to Kenya very readily – so that being in a Scottish family is sufficient to be a member of the Caledonian Society. Until fairly recently women were not members. I think that happened in the '90s, when membership was extended to women... but the membership was much more a domestic membership, making tea at the various events, or joining in to make up the numbers.[114]

Formal Scottish associationalism in Hong Kong has remained vibrant, partly because, as Ken Morrison explained, the roots of Scottish involvement in business, government and administration were deep and wide. Long-established firms like Lowe, Bingham and Matthews (now part of PricewaterhouseCoopers) adopted the practice of sending partners to Scotland each year to recruit a new batch of trainees. For Ken's father's generation, however, adjustment from the very different world of Bonnybridge and Falkirk was facilitated more by an international network whose members were 'all launching forth together' to grasp the new opportunities of the post-war world. But Ken went on to qualify that statement slightly, before speculating that the emphasis has changed in recent years, when he has seen Scots congregate at the Hong Kong Club, or in the British Chamber of Commerce's Scottish Business Group:

> I don't think that there was a seeking out of just Scottish community, but, having said that, there were enclaves of Scottishness... A lot of the Masonic halls were packed full of Scots; Union Church, where we attend, was founded by a Scotsman from Aberdeen, James Legge, but there was very much a Scottish mafia in the church, and they used to have Burns' suppers and Highland dancing every week, and so forth. Very strong community. Many of the people at Taikoo dockyard here were Scottish. The utility companies, and the engineering companies and so forth, many of them were Scottish, so there was a very strong community. And so the St Andrew's Society was very active, and that's really where the Scots did get together for different occasions, particularly the St Andrew's Ball in November every year, and the Burns' Supper in January. And that's when [a] huge gathering of Scots would come together, far more than any of the other – St David's, or St George's, or St Patrick's societies.
>
> So, was it overtly Scottish? I don't think so. I didn't have that feeling. I think that there are aspects of that present now because there's fewer Scots, so in some respects they seem to seek each other out more now.[115]

Back in Canada, Murdo MacIver's involvement with the Gaelic Society of Vancouver persisted from the time of his emigration to the city in 1953 until his death in 2016. It was at the Society that he met his wife, Mary, a Gaelic-speaking emigrant from Acharacle, and while they were both proud of their adopted land, they were equally committed to maintaining their Highland culture and heritage. Both served as Chief of the Gaelic Society – Mary once and Murdo three times. The Gaelic choir which they started in 1969 still meets weekly, and Murdo was also involved with the Vancouver St Andrew's and Caledonian societies. Over the years the couple made several visits back to Scotland, and Murdo, who was widowed in 1994, continued to return to his native village of Arnol in Lewis to visit his sister until her passing in 2011. From the start, he cultivated a network of Arnol connections across British Columbia, and remembered vividly how, on his first trip to the interior of the province in 1954, he had encountered 14 fellow villagers in the Kootenay region. A natural *seanchaidh* (story-teller) and bard, Murdo's spellbinding oratory made him a star, bilingual contributor to 'Scottish Voices from the West', the oral history project of Simon Fraser University's Centre for Scottish Studies.[116] I also interviewed him on three occasions between 2007 and 2013, our conversations covering a total of six hours.[117] During the final interview, he described – as he had done on previous occasions – his early encounters with fellow islanders:

> There was a lot of people from Arnol in Vancouver when I came. It was amazing. And some of them – well I think I told you the story about one of them before. But there was [sic] 11 people from Arnol and myself here when I came here in 1953. Then I went up to Trail. Between Trail and Nelson and Procter there was another 16 people from Arnol. And Arnol's not a big village. I think there was 46 numbers and about four other houses in my day, growing up. So the whole population of Arnol would have been about – well, guessing, averaging five for each house – five 50s, 250.[118]

Jim Russell, like Murdo, was interviewed at length, in 2004, for SFU's 'Scottish Voices from the West', and, more briefly for this project in 2007.[119] During that latter conversation, he reflected on the 'fossilised' mindset of emigrants (including himself), the spurious nature of some celebratory 'Scottishness', and his own tongue-in-cheek participation in the activities of the Burns' Club.[120] His attitude to his Scottish roots has been more calculating, and – to an extent – self-deprecatory, than Murdo's. Across the border in the United States, he observed, 'I am always treated as slightly exotic, as a Scot, and I do capitalise on that. I wear my kilt from time to time and make a bit of a show of it because it's always appreciated and so on. So it's been good fun being a Scot, I think, in North America.'[121]

Also in Vancouver, Banffshire-born Hamish and Isla Robertson made some initial contacts through the Gaelic Association, but were then introduced to the Moray, Nairn and Banff Association, where 'it was a big help to meet people from your own area' and 'hear your own tongue', as well as to get practical assistance with navigating an unfamiliar schooling system for their two children.[122] That Society, founded in 1931, is still going strong but Jim Russell testified to the steady decline of other examples of formal Scottish associationalism in Vancouver. His testimony was echoed by other interviewees elsewhere in the diaspora, sometimes at a much earlier date. When Annie Matheson arrived in Detroit in 1952, the once thriving Lewis Society of Detroit was in terminal decline. It was finally wound up in 1972, and its records were repatriated to Lewis in 2007. By the time John and Catherine MacPherson went to Lima in 1959, the Caledonian Society numbered 'very few' native Scots among its membership. Yet to this day it remains 'very keen' to maintain its connection with *Colegio San Andres,* where it still awards an annual prize, the Caledonian Shield, for cooperation.[123] It was not just in Lima or Nairobi that Scottish societies relaxed their rules in an attempt to attract those with a cultural interest, rather than necessarily a birthplace in Scotland, and some have continued to flourish under a more inclusive umbrella.[124]

Some interviewees, like Easton Vance, deliberately avoided involvement with Scottish organisations, on the basis that their members – mostly older Scots – were 'in a time warp', and those who belonged to the Burns' Club in particular were 'maudlin'.[125] For similar reasons Cathy Donald's father would not join the Dunedin Burns' Club. She recalled his observation that 'All they do is sit around, weeping and being nostalgic about their old home, and they've forgotten why they left it in the first place.'[126] In Sarnia, Ontario, Joe and Janet Blair initially attended the Overseas Club, but soon decided to move beyond that default ethnic comfort zone and develop a wider circle of friends.[127] In Toronto, Murdo MacPherson patronised the TRANZAC Club and 'deliberately tried to avoid' fellow Scots. As well as not joining Scottish organisations, Murdo mentioned 'a couple of Scottish pubs which I avoided like the plague, 'cos I didn't want to end up with the usual tartanism that people end up with, more Scottish than they ever were before.' His encounter with a White Supremacist countryman in Northern Ontario, who 'thought, because I was a Scot, I would somehow identify with his views', reinforced his caution, and also challenged Robert Louis Stevenson's famous claim that when Scots met in 'some far country', their domestic differences were eclipsed by a 'ready-made affection' based on their common ethnicity.[128]

Jim Russell has demonstrated his lingering attachment to Scotland through regular visits and subscriptions to Scottish publications, while being fully aware of the temptation to preserve his image of the country – and his own identity – in aspic.

> You never feel that you're anything other than a Scot at one level, and yet, when you go back, you become very conscious that you have a whole different dimension to life, having lived in Canada, and that you're a Canadian – you're different. You're not the same as what the locals are any more... What is the relationship with the Old Country? It's still – and I'm still – we get the *Banner*, we get the *Celtic Connection*, we get the *Scots Magazine*. We read the stuff voraciously. We get *History Scotland*... So we keep completely in touch. But somehow you lose this – the country has changed. What you go back to in your mind is still the Scotland of the year that you emigrated. It never ceases to be that. All the changes, you somehow don't incorporate them into your being the way that would happen if you lived there.[129]

A handful of New Zealand interviewees preserved elements of their Scottish culture in informal ways, rather than by joining ethnic associations. In Brian Coutts' opinion, 'Dunedin's Scottish heritage is more in the talking than the doing', but while his parents were not interested in Scottish societies, they did 'amass a group of Scottish friends' in Invercargill, and Brian remembered a Scottish aunt's occasional gifts of tartan towels and the annual arrival of *The Scotsman* calendar.[130] Most of Cathy Donald's childhood books had to be left behind when the family emigrated, but, as was customary among Scottish emigrants in earlier generations, her parents did pack a volume of Robert Burns' poetry. Cathy was also surrounded by Scottish music at school and home alike:

> When we came here and had records, we often had Andy Stewart and, of course, Kenneth McKellar... When people got together, they sang, so I know all those Scots songs – they were very much part of my growing up. But coming to a city like Dunedin, you always had people who would sing Scots songs. I mean, we learnt them too, at school.[131]

Elsewhere in Dunedin, Isobel Gillon received copies of the *Sunday Post* from home, and listened to Scottish music on the radio. For Isobel, however, the tunes were a trigger for homesickness, as were Gaelic waltzes – and other Scottish music – for Ena Macdonald in Australia, who described her reaction:

> Oh aye, another thing I remember too when I was over there, that song was really on the top, 'There was a soldier, a Scottish soldier', Andy Stewart. Oh, every time I turned on the radio that was on, and I used to sit and I would cry. Oh, it was just magic... I can remember going to a Scottish ball, and this couple we went around with a few times, he was also, he was homesick, more homesick than his wife. I think they both came from Glasgow. And I remember us all holding hands, 'Will ye no come back again?' – 'I'll be back, I'll be back', he was saying.[132]

Andy Stewart's sentimental 'Scottish Soldier' topped the charts in Canada and New Zealand, as well as Australia, in 1961. For Margaret Gillies Brown in Alberta, the release of that record coincided with the birth of her fourth son. Childbirth, away from the supportive environment of the wider family, is a well-attested trigger for homesickness, and Margaret, who was always so busy that she generally 'hadn't thought too much about home,' found listening to Stewart's record 'just so overwhelming'.[133] A visit by the Queen to their nearest town provoked another unexpected bout of homesickness, which Margaret described in her book:

> I was taken by surprise by the strength of my own emotion. This wouldn't have happened at home but here, in this alien place, she seemed part of all that I was part of, all that I remembered from the beginning. She epitomised home. For one fleeing second I wished that Ronald and I and our family could get on that train with her and travel east over the long lonely terrain to the sea and beyond, back to our native shores.[134]

Revisiting that incident in conversation, Margaret added that 'at home I probably wouldn't have gone to see her'.[135]

Traditional festivals did not always translate easily into new environments. Anne McCallum has 'always disliked New Year's Eve in Canada because it's not Hogmanay in Scotland'.[136] Nostalgia and dislocation were more acute where the seasons were upside down, and several interviewees testified to the challenges of celebrating Christmas in the southern hemisphere. Even Rachel Minton's upbeat endorsement of Dunedin was modified slightly by her admission that she missed 'Christmas in winter'. Describing how she had cooked a roast dinner on a day when the mercury hit 32 degrees, she declared that 'I don't think I'll ever get my head around a summer Christmas'.[137] The incongruity of Christmas in summer could also trigger homesickness, even among those who were happily settled, like James Mackenzie in Australia, who likened it to being 'caught between two worlds':

> The whole time I've been here [26 years at time of interview] I've never felt that Christmas in the middle of summer is Christmas. And I say to Judy [his wife], it's just not Christmas, you can call it what you like, it's the 25th of December, but it's not Christmas because it's hot, and it's not Christmas unless it's cold and drizzly outside... When I first came out I was desperately homesick at Christmas time.[138]

Alice Moffat and her footballer husband Adam arrived in Auburn, New South Wales, in 1967, more than two decades before James Mackenzie went to Melbourne. Despite her successful integration, aided by a strong network of compatriots from Fife, and in recent years the birth of grandchildren, Alice still becomes nostalgic – even homesick – at Christmas and New Year.

> First Christmas – 'cos we got there in November, I mean, the first Christmas, och, it was terrible. We got some friends to come over to the flat, 'cos we were in a flat. So of course, I'm doing everything that you do in Scotland and England, you know – roast potatoes, mince pies, you know, all the trimmings, Christmas dinner. Nobody could eat it – it was too hot. That was pretty upsetting. But I'll tell you something, even after all this – all these years in

> Australia, I still don't like Christmas. It's not the same, you know, it's too hot... Even to this day I still get homesick at New Year, especially when you watch the Tattoo and things like that. Yes, still play the Scottish music, but the thing is now, all the grand kids are there now, you know what I mean? But some – I've got Scottish friends that said, 'Oh, I don't think about Scotland, you know, no, no.' But I do. My husband and I both do.[139]

Alice's sentiments echo Cathy Timperley's recollections of emigration to New Zealand in the 1950s, not least her mother's seasonally-induced homesickness:

> Christmas and New Year was a *huge* change. Because of the summer holidays here, everybody disappeared, and even – it was more in the '50s, where New Zealand closed down for three weeks. All the factories closed down and so on, and people went away. So where was the family and friends to have Christmas? And New Year was another huge change. I mean, my mother *really* missed the First Footing. And what she found here was that you had to organise a party. So there wasn't that same excitement of midnight, and you take the calendars down, and the house has been polished and shined from top to toe, that smells of shortbread having been baked, those smells of New Year. Well, of course, everyone's outside having a barbecue, in their camping grounds, doing the traditional Kiwi holidays in those days. And my mother really missed that season, and never ever, I don't think, got used to Christmas being like it was.[140]

* * *

The visceral and cerebral response of immigrants to their new surroundings, and the lens through which they viewed Scotland, depended on many overlapping influences: the physical environment; age and family circumstances; the social, cultural and political milieu in which they found themselves; the nature of their employment; the permanence or otherwise of their settlement; and their own personalities. Such factors determined the blend – or singularity – of adaptation, integration, assimilation, or dislocation in their experiences. As we have seen, multiple identifications and networks were juggled with varying degrees of conviction and convenience, and some interviewees testified to the ambiguities and contradictions inherent in attempting to pin down unstable concepts of home and identity.

Neither the interviewees' recollections, nor the wider historiography of migrant adjustment, provides us with a clear theoretical framework within which to explain attitudes and responses. Some recurring sentiments were voiced, notably a recognition of hybrid identities, the sensory triggers for nostalgia or homesickness, and – among recent interviewees – an awareness of Scotland's changing political and constitutional landscape. At the same time, the institutional vehicles through which diasporic ethnicity had been articulated until the mid-20th century – the church, the school and the Scottish association – waned steadily in significance. In terms of emotional adjustments, no male interviewee admitted to having experienced homesickness, though some, like Murdo MacIver, cherished and cultivated their Scottish networks for decades after leaving Scotland. While younger interviewees generally adjusted with the greatest ease, and older ones – especially women – were more likely to ponder the essence of their identity, temperament and context were more significant than age. Margaret Crapnell's mother had 'the time of her life' when, at the age of 70, she emigrated to Brisbane. She never suffered a pang of homesickness or expressed any desire to return to Scotland, whereas Ena Macdonald, who was only 21 when she emigrated, was consumed by homesickness, a malady that she had first experienced during a year at boarding school in Inverness. To make matters worse, she had played no part in the decision to go to Australia, which had been orchestrated by her mother-in-law. On the other hand, the absence of close family bonds worked to the advantage of AS. She had been a solitary, self-reliant child, who always felt distant from her four older siblings, and did not therefore feel any emotional attachment to Scotland after she had emigrated. Those of her acquaintance who had returned, she observed, generally did so because of 'family attachments'.[141]

There were, of course, many other reasons for return migration, and the causes and repercussions of 'homecoming' are examined in the next chapter. As we shall see, those who came back to Scotland, whether temporarily or permanently, could face – sometimes unexpectedly – challenges of adjustment and acculturation that echoed the experiences of those who had gone in the opposite direction.

CHAPTER 7

Reverse Migration: Resettling and Reconnecting

IN 2000 THE geographer Russell King drew attention to 'the great unwritten chapter in the history of migration'.[1] The black hole to which he was referring was return migration, which had been neglected by scholars, despite being printed indelibly on the whole history – and ongoing experience – of demographic upheaval across the world. As 'homecomers' have begun to be rescued from obscurity in recent years, their stories have demonstrated not only the significance of return, but also its complexity and diversity. Just as outward migration involves individuals, families and communities engaging in one-time, one-stage settlement or constant wandering; and short-distance or global mobility, so 'return' has always encompassed a range of objectives and experiences. Moving on or moving back might take place as an unforeseen response to disappointed expectations or insatiable wanderlust; to fulfil family responsibilities, claim an inheritance, or retire; as part of a planned strategy of career advancement or self-improvement; or in the pursuit of leisure and recreation, including ancestral tourism. These goals are variously demonstrated in seasonal, serial, sequential or boomerang migration; occasional trips to visit family or enjoy a holiday; and permanent return to the place of origin.

This chapter explores the causes and consequences of return migration through the testimony of Scots who experienced its various manifestations, either personally or vicariously through immediate family members or ancestors. Interviewees' experiences are contextualised within the wider documented history of 'homecoming', for very few emigrants locked and bolted the door irreversibly when they left Scotland. About a third of those who emigrated in the 19th and 20th centuries returned permanently,[2] while many others visited their place of origin or ancestry, sometimes repeatedly. The diverse narratives of interviewees and the bigger supporting cast are scrutinised with reference to continuities and changes among returners in different generations, and comparisons of the motives and experiences of outward-bound and returning migrants.

We begin by looking at those whose return was not part of the original plan: the homesick, dislocated and disappointed, and those for whom changed family circumstances necessitated retracing their steps. Economic objectives were always an integral part of temporary sojourning, and we look next at the career emigrants whose occupations in an increasingly internationalised labour market took them backwards and forwards between one location and Scotland, or through a series of job-related staging posts before their eventual return. In a handful of cases, departure and return were caused or facilitated by external circumstances and government policies, such as war and subsidies, and in all cases mobility was eased by improvements in technology. Long-distance holiday-making was a notable beneficiary of easier and cheaper travel, and ancestral tourism has become a highly marketable commodity, particularly since the Scottish government's first 'Year of Homecoming' in 2009.

Just as those who constituted the diaspora might wrestle with alien environments and attitudes, some returning migrants also felt that they were strangers in a strange land. Reverse culture shock was particularly challenging if it was unexpected, and not all 'homecomers' adjusted seamlessly to a new Caledonia that was different from the land they had left. The consequences of return are explored through the eyes of individuals who testified to a sense of displacement, as well as those who reintegrated easily, or whose reflections focused on practical comparisons, usually of living standards. The equally important, but more elusive question of the returners' impact on their families, communities and – collectively – on Scotland itself is rarely addressed in personal testimony, but can sometimes be glimpsed in the observations of onlookers.

Unplanned return: homesickness, disenchantment and family responsibilities

We saw in Chapter 6 that there was a fine line between tolerable or even pleasurable nostalgia and agonising homesickness. It was not just a modern malady: emigrant correspondence across the centuries testifies to the intensity of what the Welsh call *hiraeth* – a poignant word which conveys a deep, insatiable longing for home. In advising settlers in New Zealand in the 1870s how to adjust to life on the other side of the world, Scottish pioneer and recruitment agent James Adam warned readers of his guidebook to expect bouts of homesickness. It was, he wrote,

> a disease common to emigrants, and one that is sometimes very difficult to

cure. The new land, new scenes, new pursuits, may for a time preserve the strangers from home-sickness, but come it must, sooner or later. The new faces that look upon the emigrant are not familiar ones... No amount of kindness or sympathy can heal the wrench of home-separation. Like sorrow for the death of a child, its cure is a thing of time.[3]

After estimating that the cure took an average of 18 months to effect, Adam suggested various remedies, including keeping busy, and writing regularly to friends and relatives, not least with news of success. He took patriarchal credit for the self-help strategy that had cured his own wife's homesickness a quarter of a century earlier. 'We must give the country a fair trial,' he had instructed her. 'If you don't like it at the end of a year I will send you home again, on condition that you make as much as will pay your own passage':

This was considered a great concession, and satisfied my guidwife, who had been a dressmaker on her own account. She at once set to work, and in six months enough had been made to pay her passage to Britain. This result of the needle produced an effect quite opposite to what had been intended, for no sooner did my wife and her sister discover that they possessed the power of returning home at pleasure than the desire to do so left them. They were astonished at the rewards of their own industry, and wisely concluded that a country which could reward the hands of the diligent with such liberality, was not a country to be left for the silly qualms of home-sickness. That was the author's experience of home-sickness. It was never heard of again, and was soon effectively disposed of.[4]

James Adam's parsimonious last-resort remedy of sending his wife back to Scotland reappeared in the mid-20th century in the guise of what became known as the thousand-dollar cure. The term was initially coined in respect of disgruntled war brides, whose expectations of their new life were not matched by their experience of their husbands' home countries and communities. But it was also used to describe a wider constituency of post-war emigrants – mainly women – who retraced their steps, only to discover that the overseas environment and lifestyle were preferable to the low wages, rationing and dismal weather of Britain in the decade after 1945. It was a strategy adopted – and recommended – by one interviewee, and observed by another.

Just after the war ended, Gladys Morrice's husband took up a position with the Roan Antelope Copper Mine in Luanshya, Northern Rhodesia, where Gladys' aunt – who had emigrated in 1914 – ran a boarding house. Gladys and their baby daughter followed in 1946, but within three years they were back in Aberdeen. As she explained,

> That was really because I was so homesick. I couldn't settle, and we decided we'd come home. Took a lot of my stuff with me. Arrived at the Aberdeen Joint Station, came out, had a look round, and I said to Arthur, 'Look, I could retrace my steps and board the train and go right back to Africa.' As soon as I saw the dull, dark, grey day, and people all muffled up with big coats and scarves and everything, I wanted the sunshine again. And that cured me. I was here for a while, a few months, and then back we went. And I never looked back. I would say to anyone who went abroad and was homesick, make one journey home, and that *will* cure you.[5]

During their 14-year sojourn in Northern Rhodesia, the Morrices made two further visits to Aberdeen, but on each occasion Gladys eagerly anticipated her return to Luanshya, where she had been joined by her parents, as well as her sister and brother-in-law, with their two children. 'Oh the happy day, the day that we set off to go back to Africa. I *loved* Africa. I really did. I did love Africa,'[6] she emphasised. When they all decided to return permanently to Scotland in 1960, Gladys was 'broken hearted – I wept for days' and initially found it very difficult to settle back in Aberdeen.[7]

Janet Blair, speaking from Sarnia, Ontario, in 2006, described the rationale for the thousand-dollar cure in the country where the term was first coined, but added that it sometimes backfired:

> Oh yes, quite a number [returned], particularly women, who would go home on their own or with their kids every year, and then decide that they did not want to stay here [Canada]. Their husbands used to call it the 1000-dollar cure at one time, in the '60s. You know, send them back and they would come back and decide to stay here, but a lot of them didn't, a lot of them went back home.[8]

Whereas Janet's husband, Joe, had made about 15 visits back to Scotland since emigrating in 1968, Janet had returned only once to a country with which she had almost no family connection. Her testimony, and the very different experience of Ena Macdonald, reinforce Anne Simpson's speculation that return was closely connected to the strength of family attachments.

Ena Macdonald's attempt to deploy the thousand-dollar cure resonated more with Janet Blair's description than with Gladys Morrice's experience. After three miserable years in Australia, Ena made an extended visit back to her parents in North Uist. She returned briefly to Australia with her newborn son, Angus, and a cutting from her mother's bizzie lizzie which she had smuggled in to remind her of home. Her poignant memory of how 'I loved that plant, I felt it was something alive'[9] reflected her persistent anguish, the only remedy for which was to leave her husband and return permanently to the family croft in 1966. As the white cliffs of Dover came into sight, the eponymous song generated very different emotions from the Scottish melodies which had tugged at her heartstrings during her five years in Sydney and Ipswich (Queensland):

> It must have been when I was coming back with Angus for good, and I can remember going down to the toilet on the liner, getting ready to come off, and seeing the cliffs of Dover. Every time I hear that song, I cry, even yet. I'm seeing, looking out through – there was a porthole there. And I'm crying my eyes out. And this woman – 'Are you not happy to be back, seeing England?' I says, 'I'm happy, I'm happy, I'm so happy I can't stop crying. Of course I'm happy', I said. I don't think she understood why I was so happy.[10]

In some respects Ena was following in the footsteps of her parents, both of whom had sojourned, separately, in Canada in the mid-1920s. Archie Macdonald and Morag (Sarah) Miller met and married in Toronto in 1930, before returning to North Uist with a two-year-old daughter, Flora, in 1933. Her mother's homesickness in particular may have subconsciously coloured Ena's own attitude to emigration, or alternatively, she may have projected her own negative experiences back on to the previous generation. Morag, like her younger daughter 36 years later, had emigrated under pressure, rather than of her own volition, and Ena's description of her parents' experiences in Canada emphasised adversity rather than adventure:

> My mother was born in Mull, and she told me that when she was in her early 20s she was working in Dundee in a big house, cooking. Then her sister – her eldest sister, Mary, she emigrated to Canada. And her father – my grandfather – he was very worried about Mary going over there. I think she must have gone on her own, and [he] kept nagging my mother to go and sort of look after her, be company. Anyway my mother didn't really want to go, but she did go. And shortly after she arrived in Toronto, sister Mary decided she would go to America... Well, my father must have emigrated about the same time, I think. And my mother was cooking in a big house again over there, and my father worked on the railway, so they told me. And they met at a party or something in a house belonging to someone who had left North Uist... And then in the '30s, that was the big Depression over there. And my father was sure he was going to be made redundant, and lots of their friends were out of work, and my mother used to be trying to feed them, and things were difficult. And then out of the blue a letter came from my grandfather, who was next door here,

that the people who lived in the croft where I am now... were moving to Bernera, and he asked my father, did he want to put his name down for the croft? So he did. And my mother was determined she wouldn't say anything, because my father asked her 'What do you think?' and she said, 'Well, it's your decision.' She was worried in case if things didn't go well, she would be partly to blame, so she left the decision to him. And she was delighted when he said they would come here.[11]

Ena's father 'never talked that much' about Canada, perhaps a reflection that he had no regrets about the life he had left behind. Her own sentiments are injected into her observation about her father and the 'crowd' of islanders with whom he had emigrated.

I think he was quite happy to be back here anyway. Most of the people that did emigrate were always homesick anyway. Some made a good life but deep down in their hearts I'm sure most of them would prefer to be back in the islands, or back in Scotland.[12]

In the same year that Ena Macdonald returned from Australia to Scotland Anne McCarthy (also aged 26) flew out in the opposite direction. Originally from Kirkcudbrightshire, she had met and married a dentist from Brisbane in 1964 while they were both working in London, and by the time they emigrated – a decision triggered by the sudden death of Anne's father-in-law – they had an infant daughter. Although, like Ena, Anne was accompanying her husband rather than implementing a personal decision, she adjusted well, was welcomed into her husband's 'large extended Irish Catholic family',[13] and insisted that she did not feel homesick. 'I had no huge desire to go to Australia *per se* but I was quite happy to go,' she explained, adding that 'I never thought of myself as an emigrant, because I went as a family member... I think to be an emigrant, you initiate the choice to some extent.'[14] Anne's nostalgia for her homeland manifested itself five years later, after the family, now with three children, had spent Christmas with Anne's parents, and in 1972 – on her husband's suggestion – they returned permanently to Scotland:

I'd had very little negative feeling about going to Australia the first time. When we came back and then returned, it was awful. I felt very bereft about leaving the second time. I don't quite know – I think, very much more, I thought I was leaving things behind, rather than going to something new... It wasn't a feeling that I was going back to something I was rejecting, but it was more that I was leaving behind things that were more important to me, I think than I had maybe realised initially.[15]

A decade earlier, nine-year-old Christine Matheson and her siblings had been brought back to Scotland from New Zealand only three years after leaving Invergordon. The family had emigrated – ostensibly permanently – in 1959, when Christine's father secured employment as a mathematics teacher in Gisborne. Although the children were shielded from discussions and decision-making, she believed it was her mother's homesickness that was the crucial factor in their return. It was also the reason why the family never went on holiday in their adopted land, as her mother was saving up to go back to Scotland:

> My father really, really loved it. He enjoyed teaching at the High School... but I don't think my mother ever really settled. I think when we went to New Zealand I think you thought that was it, and you'd possibly never see your family again, and I think she probably felt very homesick, although she wouldn't have expressed that to us.[16]

That homesickness was demonstrated not in emotional outbursts, but in a persistent criticism of Gisborne's climate and lifestyle. Her husband looked forward, but she looked back, a difference in temperament perhaps suggested by Christine's recollection that while her father probably 'wrote a total of three letters in his time in New Zealand', her mother, who was the second youngest of seven siblings, wrote home 'religiously' each week both to her elderly parents and to her mother-in-law.[17] James Adam's assurance more than 80 years earlier, that regular letter-writing cured homesickness, was therefore not fool proof.

All the individuals interviewed or cited who had returned to Scotland because of homesickness were female. Another who fell into that category was Roddy Campbell's wife, whom we met (through Roddy) in Chapter 5, struggling to adjust to primitive conditions and loneliness in the mountainous interior of British Columbia while her husband enjoyed the challenges of practising medicine in a frontier environment.[18] Even after they moved to Victoria, where Roddy worked in partnership with another Scots-born doctor, Scott Wallace from Leven, she remained unsettled, and persuaded him to come back to Scotland after ten years in Canada. Roddy took out Canadian citizenship just a few weeks before leaving for good in 1977, 'because I was not sure how things would work out for me back here [Scotland] and I might want to return'.[19] His younger son, born in British Columbia, was a Canadian citizen, but not his wife nor his older son:

> We were there to stay in Canada. [But] it just – the feeling was that we didn't want to grow old there. That was it. I thoroughly enjoyed it – Victoria's a

> beautiful place, and I was a very successful doctor there, and plenty of money, if I wanted to go to Scotland I could hop on the plane three times a year if I wanted, but in practice I didn't do that… I did very much enjoy it, and I think if my wife had different ideas I think I might have stayed, but in the end I agreed with her it wasn't home, and back we came.[20]

Homesickness was a very specific form of discontent, which several interviewees were ready to acknowledge. Perhaps not surprisingly, none admitted to having returned because of a more general disappointment with the emigrant life. It was not only that such individuals were unwilling to recall their overseas sojourn and therefore unlikely to put themselves forward for interview: to acknowledge disillusionment might be to imply there had been poor initial judgement in decision-making, or a subsequent failure to adjust that was the fault of the settler rather than the host society. But the absence of such testimony distorts the overall picture of a movement in which disenchantment had always played a significant part. On 20 May 2016 the BBC reported that more than 7,000 British people a year were turning their backs on the beaches and barbecues of Australia to return to the UK for good, and nearly half on permanent migration visas returned home within five years.[21] Among their complaints were traffic congestion in a country with a poor public transport infrastructure, high living costs, difficulties in finding employment, long working hours, and other unexpected cultural differences that made it difficult to make friends and develop a social life.

It is even less surprising that we lack any testimony from emigrants who had no choice but to return. A small minority was sent back by the immigration authorities of the country where they wished to settle, after being denied entry on arrival, or subsequently deported, on the grounds of mental or physical illness or disability, criminality, or unemployment. Narratives of enforced return are rarely articulated by those who were sent back, but have to be sought in press reports and official documentation.[22] Others chose to come home because of illness. The Lewis Society of Detroit was one of the Scottish associations which periodically subsidised the repatriation of sick or destitute members, not least during the Depression. On five occasions between 1924 and 1933 the Society subsidised the fares of those who wished to recuperate – or die – back in their homeland. They included Joseph McDonald, who in 1924 was 'sick in New Mexico with malaria and tuberculosis', and another consumptive, Kenneth MacLeod, who, the Minutes recorded in 1933, 'hasn't got long to live and wants to die in his native home'.[23]

Not all unplanned return was the result of homesickness, disillusionment, denial of entry or illness. Changes in family circumstances such as bereavement, marriage and inheritance had always triggered homecoming, and these factors were well represented among interviewees. In 1933 Margaret Murray brought her children back to Lewis after almost six years in Canada. Her husband, Donald, had been killed in an accident in Prince Rupert at the beginning of that year, and although Margaret initially moved to Calgary, where her two sisters and three brothers lived, she could not tolerate the hot summer, and longed for the temperate climate of the Hebrides.

A year earlier, Minnie Anne Fraser returned to Halladale on four months' leave from her position with the Studebaker family. She had been in Detroit since 1926, and although she fully intended to return to the United States, her mother had other ideas. Having lost her husband and three sons in the previous five years, she told her daughter, 'you've had your time away, home is where you are to be'.[25] At the age of 93, Minnie Anne recalled alighting from the train at Forsinard, where she greeted – with an American accent and idiom – the man who three years later was to become her husband. She also spoke of the reluctance with which she relinquished her return ticket to the US, and the resentment of some young women in Halladale when she captured the heart of Donald Macdonald:

> And there was a few came and shook hands with me and welcomed me back. And one of them was a young gentleman who said to me, 'And how are you, Minnie?' And I'm supposed to have said, 'I'm just mighty fine.' And I was going to go back to America in November but my dad had died while I was away, and my mother was a widow and she wished me to stay because my sister at home wasn't well. So I said I'd stay for a wee while, but my sister wasn't getting over her sickness, so I had to stay on and eventually I just had to give up the idea of going back to America, and look after my mother and be with her. And years passed, and three years after that I was married to this young gentleman whom I had told I was mighty fine. [We] settled in Halladale on the croft, which was very strange to me after all these years being away. Sometimes I think I wasn't just exactly welcomed by all the young ladies that was on the strath, but they had just to accept that they'd done nothing in 12 years, so that was that.[26]

Carrol and Edward Stewart and their two children left Morayshire for Southern Rhodesia in 1953 when Edward secured a promoted post as a forester near Umtali. They put down roots and took out Rhodesian citizenship, with every intention of staying permanently. In 1964, however, after Edward became ill, they came back to Craigellachie, where Edward had inherited the family home. Carrol recalled their dilemma:

> We had to think carefully about coming back. You see, being with a government

> department, we had a house. It went with the job – it was a tied house. And my husband, I knew, would have to be on medication, which would mean we'd have to move, either into a town, I would have to get a job of some kind... Being a government department, you got what was called medical aid, which did help a bit, you were allowed so much, not like the NHS, but you were allowed so much, but whether the fact that he would have been not working for the government – but he never actually worked again – I would have had to get a job, the children – well, would they have stayed on at school, at boarding school, or would we have had to move so they went as day scholars? But there was this home here, which actually belonged to him anyway... we had something to come home to. And of course, there was the National Health.[27]

Murdo MacPherson and his wife had been considering moving from Toronto to 'somewhere smaller and a bit more remote' when his father died back in Scotland and Murdo came home on a year's leave of absence in 1996, partly to settle his father's affairs. A new high school had recently opened at Kinlochbervie in north-west Sutherland, and Murdo made a snap decision to apply (successfully) for a teaching post. The location met the MacPhersons' criterion of accessible remoteness, 'wild' land which was not 'wilderness'. As he explained, 'That's why we came and stayed here. Otherwise we'd probably be somewhere in Northern Ontario.'[28] He added that if he were to live in a city, he would live in Toronto rather than in any Scottish – or British – city, 'so if I can't live in an area like this in Scotland I'll go back to Canada, which I may do, eventually. I'll maybe retire back to Canada.'[28]

When re-interviewed in 2017, Murdo had retired but he and his wife were still living happily in Kinlochbervie. The decision to stay in Scotland, he explained, was attributable to a combination of the 'phenomenal' cost of housing in cities like Toronto or Vancouver, their ability to blend rural living in north-west Sutherland with access to increasingly good facilities in Inverness, and the ease of travel which, as we noted in Chapter 4, helped them feel at home on both sides of the Atlantic.[29]

During the 12 years that had elapsed between the two interviews, Murdo had become heavily involved in developing a formal link between Kinlochbervie and Vancouver through the memorialisation of a World War I recipient of the Victoria Cross, Robert McBeath. Having emigrated to Vancouver after the war, McBeath joined the Police Department, was fatally shot in the line of duty in 1922, and his funeral was a major public affair. As part of the commemoration, Murdo led two school trips to Vancouver, and in 2009 a commemorative plaque was dedicated in Kinlochbervie.[30]

Economic imperatives and incentives: career emigrants and the international labour market

Murdo MacPherson's priorities were environmental, but it was the offer of employment that actually took him to Kinlochbervie. Patterns of migration and return were most commonly shaped by career opportunities, which for centuries had seen Scottish soldiers, scholars, tradesmen and others from all levels of society play the international labour market in varying patterns of circular and step migration. Until the mid-20th century the British empire was often perceived as a treasure house to be exploited or a career ladder whose rungs could be ascended with relative ease. The intention to retire home as soon as possible with an improved status and bank balance was sharpened if the location was characterised by dangerous pathogens or unstable politics. But while some sojourned overseas in order to feather their own nests, others remitted their earnings, from casual labour to contract work, to support their dependents back home. Sojourning was also a quest for adventure, not least among those for whom payments flowed in the opposite direction – the so-called 'remittance men' whose exploits have been widely satirised in song and story, as well as subjected to scholarly scrutiny.[31]

Some interviewees testified – personally or vicariously – to traditions of sojourning and networking that straddled the generations and were also firmly embedded in their home communities and families. Donald Murray had worked on grain elevators among fellow Hebrideans at Thunder Bay in Ontario before returning to Lewis during the First World War to join the naval reserve, resume fishing, and get married. As we have seen, his second sojourn in Canada was cut short by his untimely death at the age of 51. His son, Calum, felt that, however long they had been away, men like his father 'always at the back of their minds' expected to return to Lewis, and he recalled a conversation in which Donald had expressed that intention: 'Some people [were] in visiting, and he was talking about that, when he'd been pensioned off, he'd be coming back here. And at that time he had spent a good part of his life in Canada.'[32] Calum himself initially joined the merchant navy, but 22 years after his father's death, he followed in his footsteps by returning to Canada. In 1954, through the good offices of an uncle out there, he embarked on a 30-year career as a transatlantic commuter, freighting grain on the Great Lakes during the summer and returning to his wife and family in Lewis in the winter, until he finally retired to Lewis in the 1980s. 'I don't know. I just fancied it. I always had the idea that I'd like to go back there', he explained in response to the question of why he chose that career path.[33] His sister Cathie, meanwhile, emigrated in 1948 to New Zealand, where she spent two happy years working in an immigrant hostel in Wellington, followed by ten years employed in a nurses' home in Auckland. Her decision to return to Lewis was made – somewhat reluctantly – because of her mother's increasing frailty, but she worked her way back to the island over four years, with sojourns in the United States and Canada. As she explained, the years then passed, and her goal of returning to New Zealand was never fulfilled:

> Well, I came home. I'd been away for about 16 years, so I worked my way back home, and by this time my mother was crippled with rheumatism, and she couldn't be left on her own all day, and I fully intended going back, but, you know, as I'd no steady job that tied me down or nothing that I kept year after year after year. I was here till she died, which was about nine to ten years. And then, of course, starting all over again. By this time my friends in New Zealand were all married and scattered and I thought I'd better stay in this country then.[34]

During his three decades of retirement in Lewis Calum Murray regularly reminisced with fellow islanders who had also worked on the Great Lakes, on each side of the American–Canadian border. It was just as common an occupation for Highlanders as was service in the merchant navy, but with a more focused location, in either Detroit or Windsor. Norman MacRae's father had emigrated on the *Metagama* in 1923, and worked initially as a security officer for the Ford Motor Company in Detroit before transferring to a job on cargo boats on the Lakes. In 1933 he married a fellow emigrant from his home island, whom he had met at the Lewis Society of Detroit, and Norman, born in 1941, was the youngest of their three children. In 1947, when Norman's paternal grandparents were in failing health, his mother returned to Lewis with the children to look after her in-laws while his father continued to work on the Lakes, coming home only during the winter freeze-up, until he eventually retired to his home village of Back in 1960.[35] Norman, like his father before him, has never relinquished his American citizenship, but we should not read complex questions about identity into that status, which he attributed to inertia rather than a deliberate choice to remain an American. After almost 70 years in Scotland, he has never found his American citizenship an impediment, although he was a little concerned that he might be drafted during the Vietnam War. Although he has visited the US regularly, he was in no doubt about his Scottish identity: 'This is my home, this is what I consider my home, and to all intents and purposes, I don't consider myself anything other than a Scotsman, a Lewisman.'[36]

Multi-directional and serial intercontinental mobility was also second nature to some Scots well before the days of fast transport. Kenneth Mackenzie was one of seven siblings from Melvaig, Gairloch, all but two of whom are buried overseas. Kenneth initially went to Patagonia with his brother John, probably in the 1890s, to join an uncle who had a ranch. At that time Patagonia was a favourite sojourning place for Scots, especially for Hebrideans and West Highlanders though Jessie Coupland and her husband Bill were among a sizeable contingent from Dumfries-shire, going out in 1913 (Bill) and 1934 (Jessie). While some estancias employed recruitment agents in Scotland, word-of-mouth recommendations and family networks were probably more significant.[377]

On his second visit home Kenneth married Mary Mackenzie, and two daughters were born. If he had remained a bachelor, his daughter speculated, he would probably have returned to the South Atlantic, which he loved, and where his brother remained for the rest of his life. But, believing that Patagonia 'wasn't a place for a young family',[38] in 1930 or 1931 Kenneth took his family to Providence, Rhode Island, where he already had two sisters. Kenneth and Mary's third daughter, Alexandrina (Alice) was born in Providence in 1932 and testified to growing up in a 'very, very happy home', despite her father, a joiner, not being to find work at his trade during the Depression. It was her mother who – as a cleaner in the local bank – was the initial breadwinner. In January 1946 the family returned to Ross-shire, where they named their house in Poolewe after the last Patagonian ranch on which Kenneth had worked. His daughter believed the decision to return was made for the sake of her mother, who 'always called Scotland home' although she was not explicitly homesick. Alice attributed her parents' contrasting attitudes to 'home' to their different experiences: whereas Kenneth, who was 15 years older than his wife, had been back and forth from Patagonia twice as an independent economic sojourner before going to the United States, Mary's only experience of life in the diaspora was as a young wife and mother, who missed her sister in Scotland, and looked forward avidly to her letters.[39]

Ian Skinner, like Kenneth Mackenzie, was born into a family which regarded overseas sojourning as part of the normal warp and weft of life. Ian's father was an RAF officer who had spent time in India and also in Egypt, where Ian was born in 1933. 'Picnics at the pyramids' and a very active social life meant that his parents 'found things were a bit dull' when they were posted back to Montrose in 1935, but Ian himself absorbed from infancy their images of the colourful life of the mobile Scot:

> A lot of my parents' friends had similar experiences overseas, so a lot of the conversations were about what happened, their experiences abroad, and it seemed very natural for me to think in terms when I grew up, that 'abroad was where it all happened' and that seemed to be a natural thing.[40]

With National Service on the horizon, but no obvious path to follow thereafter,

Ian 'began to wonder what I should do with myself':

> When I tried to decide what to do leaving school, there was nothing in this country – no sort of career place in this country that excited me, I suppose because I couldn't see myself going to university. That was for the high flyers in those days. And – what else? We didn't have a family business. My father being RAF, we didn't have a family business that I could find my way in. We didn't have a farm or anything like that. I needed to look further afield.

Ian's own assumptions, and those of his family and school, that 'abroad was where it all happened' suggest that the expectations of public schoolboys and the strategies of recruitment agencies in the closing days of empire were not dissimilar to the assumptions and strategies that had steered young adventurers overseas in that empire's heyday. His leisure-time reading diet of Rider Haggard and John Buchan was reinforced by a school curriculum that celebrated the lifestyle, opportunities and responsibilities of empire.

> I think the public school ethos was always based on that, that you're training people to go and run the world. There was something in that, in the sort of books you were reading, the John Buchans and so forth, that was where you had to go to get some action... Your history was the history of the empire.[41]

By the 1950s, opportunities in the increasingly truncated Colonial Service were giving way to a new emphasis on business and industry, the route ultimately followed by Ian. When he was in his final year at Loretto School, he attended three interviews set up by the Public Schools Appointments Bureau: one with a trading firm operating in Burma, another with the Anglo Iranian Oil Company (later BP), and the third with the Ben Line Shipping Company, all of which suggested that he get in touch when he had completed his National Service. Two years later Ian opted to join the Leith-based Ben Line as a management trainee, and in 1955 he was sent out to Singapore, 'the key-point of Far Eastern trade'.[42] In 1959 he was transferred to Hong Kong, the scene of his National Service and a location which had given him a taste for Asia, then in 1962, by which time he was married, he was transferred to Japan. His five-year sojourn there came to a premature end because his infant daughter needed surgery that could not be performed locally, so the family returned to Edinburgh, where Ian spent the rest of his career in the Ben Line's head office.

Muriel Thorburn also had experience of the Ben Line, but from the perspective of an employee's wife. In 1961 she and her husband arrived in Singapore, after he had been appointed as co-ordinator of the Company's Far East fleet. For 23 years she lived there as an ex-patriate, involving herself in charity work, raising their son, and using their home leaves to make regular trips back to Scotland to visit relatives. 'I suppose it was quite a lonely life', she mused, 'but I didn't find it lonely, because I can manage on my own, but I think if you were the sort of person who needed a lot of people, it could have been devastating.'[43] Muriel's self-reliance was to stand her in good stead, for after she and her husband made an unsuccessful attempt to retire to Majorca, she returned alone to Edinburgh to start a new life, working initially in a bookshop and then taking up the reins of her nursing career, retiring eventually at the age of 74. Having not associated particularly with Scots while she was in Singapore, her main friends are now former Ben Line employees and their wives whom she had first known in the Far East in the 1960s.

'Perhaps it's what set me on the path of global travel!' was Brian Stewart's analysis of the impact of a sea voyage to Cape Town at the age of three, followed by a childhood in Southern Rhodesia.[44] After finishing his secondary schooling in Morayshire, Brian studied geography and politics at Keele University and then became a career diplomat. Like Ian Skinner, Brian was enticed rather than exiled overseas, spending 35 years working for the Foreign and Commonwealth Office in a variety of Middle Eastern and North African locations, as well as Singapore. Overseas postings were interspersed with home assignments in Whitehall, and Brian ultimately spent a year (2004–5) as British Ambassador to Algeria before he retired.[45]

Charlie and Molly Law's 'ping pong' movement between Scotland and Canada was attributable to a blend of job opportunities in the international paper industry, family influences and an external event. We saw in Chapter 2 that in 1953 Charlie was encouraged by his parents to join them in Ocean Falls, British Columbia, where he secured a job in the paper mill that dominated the town.[46] Molly, a nurse, went out a year later, and they married and had four children. In 1965, however, alerted to opportunities in the pulp mill that was under construction at Corpach, they decided to 'give it a try'. Their decision was also influenced by a fatal landslip in Ocean Falls on 13 January 1965, which cut the town in two, rendered the Laws temporarily homeless, and killed seven neighbours. Even after they were back in their house and life had assumed a semblance of normality, they still felt unsettled.

> CL: It still preyed on our minds. Molly, I said, 'Not another winter, please'. Charlie: We'll have to get out of here before winter again.
>
> ML: And of course, my mother was pushing it as well, as sending columns from the *Evening Express*, written by Pearl Murray.[47]

Back in Scotland, the Laws were given the pick of a road of newly built council houses. They ended up staying in Corpach for 15 years, until a downturn in the industry took them back to Canada, initially to Kitimat in BC, where their eldest son and his Morar-born wife had emigrated in 1976, and for his final eight years of employment to a new pulp mill in Peace River, Northern Alberta. They have retired alongside their daughter and son-in-law on British Columbia's Sunshine Coast, where their friends are mainly Scots and Welsh, but they return to Fort William every year, where they are still well known. Molly acknowledged that their comings and goings have given them a hybrid identity.

> Are we Scots or are we Canadians? I really don't know. We're a mixture… It's a very true saying, that 'home is where the heart is', so if we're here it's home, if we're there, it's home, so where would we like to be? Midway between them both? I don't know.[48]

External circumstances: war, subsidies and communications

Occasionally, the return to Scotland was a consequence of external events that impinged, unexpectedly, on the lives of the individuals concerned. When the First World War broke out, David Cooper, a joiner from Dundee, had been in New York for about 16 years, punctuated with two short visits home. Having become an American citizen, he was conscripted and in 1918 found himself in France. His impulsive decision to absent himself without leave meant that his third visit back to Dundee became an enforced – and reluctant – permanent return. As his daughter reflected, 'If he hadn't gone AWOL, I think he would have been there to the end of his days', for 'he regretted very much the fact that he had burned his boats'.[49]

For three interviewees, it was the Second World War that played a part in their comings and goings. Agnes McGilvray (who celebrated her 101st birthday three weeks after being interviewed in 2009) had been working in New York for nine years and was newly married when she made a premature return to Scotland in October 1939. She had met her husband, Norrie, a Glaswegian and chief electrician with the Anchor Line, while returning to the United States after a visit home. Their wedding, at New York City Hall, had taken place just after the outbreak of war, and their original intention was that Agnes should carry on working in New York for a year to save money, seeing Norrie whenever his ship was in port. That plan was rapidly revised when transatlantic shipping was disrupted and Norrie found a shore-based job in ship repair back in Scotland. Agnes packed up rapidly and sailed to

Southampton, presumably in a convoy, before taking a train to Glasgow for a reunion with her husband.[50]

Eleven-year-old Peter Dawson also landed in Southampton in the early days of the war when unsettled international conditions, and a failed business venture, led his parents to bring their family back to Scotland after 11 years in Australia and New Zealand. The ship, the Orient liner *Orcades*, took a zig-zag route from Sydney, crossing the Equator three times and picking up a large contingent of Senegalese troops at Dakar before docking in Southampton on 18 June, shortly after the Dunkirk evacuation. Peter's main memories were of being issued with gas masks, the darkness of the blackout at Waterloo Station, and the long journey north to his grandparents' home near Coupar Angus.

Ian Skinner was the same age as Peter when he returned from the United States to Scotland four years later, in June 1944, just after the Normandy landings. It was because of the war that he had been in America in the first place. Ian was one of 3,500 British children who were evacuated overseas during the early days of the conflict, an experience which he felt 'didn't do me any long-term harm'.[51] The plan was devised in the aftermath of Dunkirk, when the fear of invasion was at its height, and implemented from July to September 1940. It was abandoned after the *City of Benares*, carrying 90 children to Canada, was torpedoed in the Atlantic on 17 September with the loss of 262 lives, 87 of them children. Most 'seavacuees' were sent to Canada, Australia, South Africa and New Zealand by a government agency, the Children's Overseas Reception Board, but 838, including Ian, went to the United States under private arrangements.[52] Paternal cousins in Dallas had suggested he be sent there, and seven-year-old Ian duly sailed on the *Cameronia* in a convoy from Glasgow to New York. He remembered little about the trip, although, like many emigrants before him, the sight of the Statue of Liberty against the backdrop of New York harbour made a lasting impression. The Scottish children were ordered to wear their kilts to disembark, and Ian's recollection of their arrival is corroborated by the *New York Times*, which on 11 September 1940 reported the arrival of the *Cameronia*, 'crowded with kilted children of Scotland and several hundred German refugees'.[53] Ian thought there were about 60 children on board, but the newspaper claimed there were 300, including 200 Scots, 'most of them ruddy-cheeked youngsters from the highland country, sturdy and bright-faced, and wearing a variety of tartan skirts and kilts that made a little brighter the drab liner's voyage up-river'.[54]

Ian was met at New York by his guardian (a friend of his father's cousin) and they flew to Texas, where he spent the next four years. Initially he was paraded publicly by his guardians, who had their own, rather disingenuous, agenda:

I didn't actually stay with my father's cousins. They had a family of their own who were teenagers, early 20s at that stage. They didn't really think that they wanted to take on me in their own family. But they had some 'good friends' – and I put that in inverted commas, because it then became a bit nasty. They were some friends of theirs who were childless and very anxious to adopt or to take me on. So I was put with this family... They were quite wealthy, quite well off, with political ambitions. And it transpired – I learnt about this many, many years later, that their main reason for taking me on was to further their political ambitions, to be seen to be generous and open hearted, and taking on an evacuee child.[55]

The guardian was a former Attorney General of Texas who had ambitions to be State Governor:

The first year they were all over me, and they sent me to the posh school, a very posh school, I remember this. But then when his political thing didn't work out, they said, 'Oh well, we can't be bothered with this', so they took me away from this school and sent me to the sort of little local thing down the road. And I was very conscious that this was moving down market, even at eight years old. I thought this is funny, why have they done this? And I thought, perhaps they're a bit short of money but they didn't seem to be. They still had three cars in the garage, that sort of thing, and servants in the house.

The family's connections meant that Ian, whose only image of America was of 'cowboys and Indians', was able to meet his hero, Gene Autry, at Dallas airport, but he also remembered eating all his meals with the servants in the kitchen (never with the family), and travelling into the city centre on segregated buses, along with the maid, who had to sit at the back while Ian sat at the front, thinking, even at age eight, 'This is strange, this isn't right'.[56] When the guardians lost interest in Ian, his father's cousin stepped in. The consequence was that he spent his final two years, much more happily, at a boarding school in Dallas and at American summer camp in the south of Texas, where he remembered encountering one other seavacuee. His guardian's wife reappeared to accompany him on the train trip to New York, where they spent two or three weeks in a hotel awaiting a phone call to tell them that a ship was available:

Obviously we were low priority, and eventually they found that there was an escort carrier, one of these escort carriers, which was being used to transport aeroplanes across the Atlantic from the US to Britain. And this aircraft carrier – I remember the decks were just covered in aeroplanes and the hangars were covered in aeroplanes, so it was obviously not operational as an aircraft

> carrier, so the air crew accommodation was empty, so we took over the air crew accommodation.[57]

Ian embarked with about 25 or 30 returning seavacuees, all boys, who had been gathered from different parts of North America, mainly Canada, and they crossed the Atlantic in a large convoy. Coming into bomb-blitzed Liverpool was 'a bit of a shock' for Ian, whose life in the United States – not least his final fortnight in the brightness and bustle of New York City – had cushioned him from the devastation of the war. The whole transatlantic operation had been kept secret, and it was only once the ship had docked that his parents were telephoned to come from Montrose to collect him. Ian had suffered no pangs of homesickness at any time during his American sojourn, perhaps because he had already dealt with that experience during an unhappy year at boarding school in Aberdeen at the tender age of six. As he explained, when he became a candidate for seavacuation, he was 'not perturbed' in the least about going to the United States, 'since anything was better than going back to Aberdeen Grammar School.'[58] When he came back to Scotland, his recollection of reconnecting with his parents echoed the experiences of many seavacuees, though in his case the sense of dislocation was fleeting and did not lead to the strained relationships and resentments which some returning children experienced:

> It was strange, I suppose – yes, it *was* strange. I didn't really know them at all. We'd exchanged letters, obviously throughout the time, but we had to sort of get to know each other again, I think.[59]

For almost three decades after the war, the easy availability of the ten-pound passage to the Antipodes gave many people the unprecedented opportunity of a subsidised two-year holiday, on which they embarked either as a deliberate strategy, or as an experiment that could be reversed without too much financial pain as long as they could last out the 24 months. It was an attitude that did not always go down well in Australia, where one survey estimated that 29 per cent of those admitted in 1959 had returned to Britain by 1966.[60] While the bean counters were concerned at such a poor return for a heavy investment in assisted migration, the press attacked the attitudes of 'whingeing Poms' whose tales of disappointed expectations were undermining the recruiters' alluring images. Of the five interviewees settled back in Scotland after being in receipt of ten-pound passages, only the desperately homesick Ena Macdonald regretted the venture. The others – Cathie Murray in New Zealand, and Matthew Lynas and Shona Morrison in Australia – were youthful adventurers whose thoroughly enjoyable experiences enriched their subsequent lives.

Sandra Munro, whose parents had taken the family to New South Wales on a ten-pound passage when Sandra was only seven, returned to Scotland in her 20s, and although she has lived in Ullapool since 1984, she still thinks of Australia as 'home' and would like to go back.[61]

Even without the subsided antipodean fares, developments in technology – notably the dawn of mass global air travel – were making return migration, and regular inter-continental visiting affordable options for a wide spectrum of emigrants and their families. The initiative was more commonly taken by those who had left than by those who had remained behind, a pattern confirmed in the testimony of older interviewees.

During the 63 years that Murdo MacIver lived in Vancouver, he made numerous (ultimately biennial) trips back to Arnol in Lewis to visit his extended family, sometimes with his wife and children, and on at least four occasions to attend the Mòd. Unlike previous generations of returning emigrants, he was able to take advantage of faster communications. In his first interview in 2007 he recalled the inception of Wardair charter flights to Scotland in 1957.

> In the olden days we used to go by Wardair. That was a charter flight. And they spoiled us, because they gave you the best service you could ever think possible on any aircraft. They even had Doulton china and stuff, serving you.[62]

Max Ward, founder of Wardair, was a Canadian from Alberta, but it was a Hebridean in Vancouver, Norman Finlayson, whose business acumen helped to inaugurate charter flights to Scotland. In 1923 21-year-old Norman had left his home at Brue in the Isle of Lewis, bound for Canada on the iconic emigrant ship, the *Metagama*. From Ontario he worked his way west, labouring on farms and sending home money to his parents on the croft, until in 1928 he arrived in Vancouver, where he married another Lewis emigrant, Anne MacIver. Interviewed for a television programme in 2014, his daughter Anna Daniels recalled Norman's role in securing cheap air travel for homeward-bound Scots living in the Pacific North-West:

> He started the first charter flights to Scotland. There were enough Scottish people here that wanted to go back home and visit, so he set up a charter with a company called Wardair, in those years. And they flew from Vancouver to Prestwick. And they always referred to Lewis as home, yeah. And he passed away in Vancouver on 21st April 1983, exactly 60 years to the day he left home.[63]

Strangers in a strange land? Reverse culture shock

Re-engaging with people and surroundings in Scotland was not always straightforward, particularly for those who had been away for a long time. It was probably more acute in previous generations, when frequent returns and reunions were much less common than they became in the late 20th century. The mixed feelings of returners in an earlier era were encapsulated in the reflections of Thomas Henderson, a former mayor of Rockhampton, Queensland, who visited Edinburgh and the surrounding area with his wife in 1905, 20 years after leaving. His letter was published in the *Dalkeith Advertiser* in January 1906, just after the Hendersons had embarked on the return trip to Australia:

> 'Coming home' is not an unmixed joy by any means. Two thirds or three fourths of the 'old identities' are either dead or removed to other parts, and I felt like a stranger in a strange land. Bonnyrigg itself has not altered quite so much. The suburbs of miners' cottages, largely inhabited, I believe, by Poles, have not improved it. But the streets are better paved and cleaner than I remember them, and it is as tidy and prosperous-looking a little town as I have seen in my travels. Dalkeith has hardly altered at all, and certainly not for the better. Musselburgh has, however, gone ahead considerably. Edinburgh has not changed much, and except about the North Bridge has not progressed as it ought to have done. I took a run out to Clovenfords, near Galashiels, a country I used to know well. The moorland solitudes around looked as peaceful as ever in their spring verdure, and the Tweed and its tributary streams still sang their lullaby as of yore – a sound particularly sweet to a dweller in a riverless land.[64]

Some interviewees took up the theme of change and continuity. When Morag Bennett and her brother visited Benbecula in the 1990s she felt little had changed in terms of living standards or culture since she had emigrated in 1923. Although she had severed most of her links with her birthplace, and the relatives whom she visited were 'total strangers', she was still able to follow all the conversations in the Gaelic language which she had not used in seven decades.[65]

Morag's memories of Benbecula in the 1920s were of a croft with no indoor sanitation, a not dissimilar scenario to that encountered by Norman MacRae when he arrived at his grandparents' croft in Lewis in 1947. Six-year-old Norman, who had experienced nothing other than the urban environment of Detroit, was confronted with a significant drop in living standards. He recalled that:

> When we left the States, as many of the others who left these shores and went to the States, we had done reasonably well. We had a car, we had all modern

> conveniences, but when we came back to Lewis here, outside Stornoway there was no electricity, there was no running water, and of course the house we went to, it didn't have electricity, it didn't have an inside toilet even. The nearest place of convenience was the byre, which was I suppose a bit of an adventure for youngsters, not so much for my mother. But she knew what she was coming back to. Having left the island she knew exactly what she was coming back to, and she must have been willing enough to come back.[66]

Alan Blair, who as an 11-year-old had been captivated by the sheer scale of Canada, found his native Lanarkshire much bleaker than he had remembered. When the RCAF sent him on a three-year exchange tour to Britain from 2001 to 2004, Alan was based in the south of England, but brought his two daughters on one trip north to show them around. He corrected himself: 'I *tried* to show them around some of the places where I grew up, but so much has changed', he explained, citing the disappearance of Wishaw Public School and the closure of Law Hospital.[67]

> To be honest, I found Motherwell very depressing, and I think that's part of the reason that I didn't go up there very often. That whole area to the east of Glasgow – Motherwell, Hamilton, Bellshill, Wishaw, it's just very drab, very depressing. I really didn't enjoy it very much at all. I enjoyed seeing family members and what not, but [I was] very very pleased that I didn't live there any more... Very grey and drab and dull and industrial, graffiti and lots of garbage. You know, like a place that had lost its self-respect... It was an interesting experience, but it confirmed in my mind that my parents certainly made the right decision.[68]

Eleven years later, Alan's overriding impression of Motherwell and its environs was still of a monotone, depressing drabness, where 'even if it doesn't look grey, it feels grey'.[69]

While there seemed to be greater parity in living standards, Alan thought that the high cost of living made it difficult to maintain a good lifestyle in Scotland, and he was still struck by small-scale infrastructure and attitudes in the UK as a whole:

> The size issue again, I keep coming back to that, but that was again the biggest thing that struck me, going back and actually living there, was how small everything is in comparison. I mean, the houses are small, the rooms in the houses are small. Vehicles are smaller, roads are smaller. Standards of living – I think it's improved, one would hope. There's not a lot of difference, I don't believe – not *as* much difference between standards of living now, Canada

> versus the UK as there was back in the '60s. But one thing did strike me. People in North America tend to have a lot of things. We have big houses and we fill them. We have a lot of clothes, we have a lot of televisions, we have a lot of everything. And it struck me that although the standards of living are quite similar, that people in Britain tended not to have as many possessions.[70]

While Alan Blair was slightly surprised at the shabbiness of Lanarkshire, other interviewees who remembered leaving a land of leaden skies and limited horizons found that return visits simply confirmed those recollections. Despite Isobel Bouman's persistent nostalgia for a Scottish homeland which she had revisited four times, she singled out the drab uniformity of its housing schemes as a negative factor, which contrasted starkly with the colourful rooftops of her adopted country. 'You know what?' she had remarked to her daughter as they rode a bus through an Edinburgh housing estate one winter. 'I'm so pleased we've got a return fare to New Zealand paid for.'[71]

Murdo MacPherson's Canadian-born wife was more comfortable with Inverness than he was with a place which he felt had lost its distinctiveness during the 19 years he had spent in Canada. Murdo's political leanings were perhaps evident in some of his comments. He pulled no punches in claiming that Inverness was 'a badly run, badly managed town' which was 'pro-development of any sort', and had 'lost a sense of itself, lost a sense of its character. It's torn down its best architecture. It's shoved roads through inappropriately. It's tried to modernise in a way which has not worked.'[72] In the wider context, he felt that Canadian cities (at least while he was there) had far better municipal facilities and a much better sense of civic responsibility than in Britain, where the ethos was one of 'build, build, modernise, privatise'. In Toronto, Montreal or Vancouver, he argued, transit systems, parks and municipal garbage systems were all better organised – and sometimes free: 'You don't expect to pay to go into a swimming pool there, for example; you wouldn't expect to pay to go into an ice rink. These are all public facilities.'[73]

Murdo went on to make some cultural comparisons, in which Scotland again came off second best. While admitting there was racism in Canada, he felt its longer history of multiculturalism contributed to 'a greater acceptance of variety and difference'. On returning to Scotland, he had also been struck by the deferential acquiescence in a class hierarchy which he had not noticed as he was growing up: 'It was there obviously but I wasn't aware of its existence. Having been in Canada and come back I noticed its existence more... There may be anger and dislike within it but there's still this deference goes on which you tend not to get there.'[74]

Anne Lynas Shah spent almost three decades in Toronto, working in publishing. During that period she came back to Edinburgh every year –

sometimes more frequently – before returning permanently in 1979. She found her homecoming 'far more difficult' than she had expected, not least because people in Toronto had been 'much more open and easy to talk to' than her compatriots.[75] While she greatly appreciated the 'the cultural thing, the scenery, the history, the ease of travel to Europe',[76] as well as the temperate climate and better welfare provision for senior citizens, she also felt there was 'an ugliness about life' in Scotland that manifested itself in a lack of civic pride and a generally 'negative feeling' about life.

> When we first came back we lived in Stockbridge, and we lived in a narrow street, Raeburn Street, off Raeburn Place. And there would be a garden full of roses and outside of it dog dirt and rubbish. You don't get so many lovely gardens in Toronto, but you didn't get the dirt either. I would say about life in Britain, we feel this, it's much more extreme. The goods are really good and the bads are really bad.[77]

Anne also echoed Murdo MacPherson's opinion that Toronto was well run and resident friendly:

> Our lifestyle wasn't fabulous. But what it is, it's just more comfortable, whatever level you're at, it's probably more comfortable. For instance, the apartments are all warm. We've got a nice flat here, and we've got central heating, and we're comfortable but everything's more of a struggle here.[78]

She explained that her return had triggered a conflict of emotions:

> When people say, 'Do you regret going to Canada?' I say, 'Absolutely not!' And when people say, 'Do you regret coming back to Britain?' I have to say, 'To some extent'... Really [the best thing about return was], the sense of being where I grew up. But that's mixed, 'cos I wasn't all that happy when I left here about my life here, so unfortunately it also opens up memories of things you didn't like, that you'd forgotten. I thought I was much more secure in myself till I got back here, and discovered I wasn't quite.[79]

In 1970, the year that Anne Lynas Shah left Edinburgh for Toronto, Cathy Timperley and AS both returned to Scotland for a brief visit, from Canada and New Zealand respectively. For Cathy, who had emigrated in 1953, 'it was still a very old-fashioned society',[80] while AS, who had only been away for a year, recalled the same attitude of defeatism and passivity identified by Murdo MacPherson and Anne Lynas Shah. Her sense that 'everything was grey' was perhaps partly attributable to it being December, but her criticism extended to the demeanour of the people, who 'wore grey, and their faces were grey. And they whinged. They whine [sic] about everything, and they didn't seem to have any will to do anything. They didn't think that they would be able to change anything.'[81]

AS did add, however, that 'since they got the Parliament people have had more of a feeling that they can do something about things'.[82] Similar sentiments emerged in other testimony, particularly in interviews conducted after 2007, the year in which the SNP became the largest party at Holyrood and formed a minority government. Graham McGregor, who had emigrated to New Zealand in 1989, became very aware of the impact of devolution when he visited Scotland in 2009. Graham is an advocate of Scottish independence, and a member of *Alba Otago*, which he describes as a 'group of 15 or so of the Dunedin diaspora', formed in 2015 'to share ideas and opinions about the independence vote.'[83] In conversation five years earlier, he reflected on changes he had observed during his visit in 2009, when he had travelled in the country and attended a debate in the ten-year-old Scottish Parliament, at a time when he was aware of 'all kinds of reviews going on about Scotland and what was happening to it.'[84]

> When I got to the border I'd never before seen bilingual signs, in Gaelic and in English. When we got to Jedburgh I was astounded by the number of Saltires that were flying. I was really, really surprised. I had never seen St Andrew's flags being displayed publicly in quite that way before. I was also struck by the conversations I had with some English people, south of the border, who felt that life and things that were happening in Scotland were much better than they had because of access to EU funding and initiatives, and [there was] a little bit of a green eye. Now, that had always been the reverse for me – we always looked to the south to say, 'It's better down there, they've got a better standard of living, they've got a better quality of life.'[85]

Anne McCallum, who has been in Canada since 1973, but returns to Scotland once or twice every year, feels that people are better off and more optimistic than when she left. 'When I lived there what I remember is that people didn't seem to have any way to reach their potential', she said.[86] Her comments were echoed by Peter Bevan-Baker and Alan Blair. Peter – like Anne – lives in Prince Edward Island, and, as a politician himself, welcomed the 'strong sense of self identity and a willingness to be self-sufficient' that characterised the modern Scottish political scene.[87] Alan, now retired from the RCAF, identified in an interview in 2017 'more of a sense of self amongst the Scots' than he recalled from visiting in the early 2000s, a trend towards cosmopolitanism which he attributed partly to Scotland's association with Europe.[88]

Murdo MacPherson was similarly upbeat, despite his sense of a lingering deference in Scottish attitudes. Indeed, he declared that changes in perspectives and politics had been instrumental in persuading him to remain in Scotland in 1996. 'If Scotland *was* the same as when I left, I would be less inclined to stay here. There's an excitement, a dynamism which is here now which was not here then.'[89] During his time in Canada Murdo had supported the aspirations of the Parti Québécois, which had helped to hone his views on Scottish separatism. As he explained:

> Certainly when I came back to Scotland, my attitude towards the lack of power exercised by a Scottish devolved Parliament, even though devolution I did see as a good thing for Scotland, I didn't see it as sufficient. So, by being in Canada, I wasn't a nationalist prior to leaving, and I'm not a nationalist as such now, but I certainly see that Scotland needs to take more control over its own affairs. And that is what I've been very pleased about coming back, that I see that Scotland has grown up politically, *is* growing up politically. There's a more open discussion over politics, a much greater understanding of the issues that affect the lives of the people of Scotland and the need for more control over that. A debate is here which was not here when I left.[90]

Murdo's sense that Scotland had developed a more international perspective and a 'bigger view of the world' was not shared by other interviewees. When Anne McCarthy had been in Australia, she remembered 'having a very specific feeling' that if Scotland ever attained devolution, 'I would want to be here and be part of it', but she changed her view in the light of subsequent political developments.[91] Although Ken Morrison and David Knight live in Asia, they return regularly to a country which they felt had become more isolationist rather than outward-looking.

David attributed the introspection partly to Britain's vastly diminished – and diminishing – role on the world stage, and a connected abdication of a recognition of the concept of a shared planet. 'Sadly, I think people are becoming less aware of a world out there and that they have a responsibility for that world. I think that's what working abroad and living abroad gives you – a concept that there is another world out there.'[92] While Ken's concern that Scottish political life was becoming 'too narrow and myopic' did not affect his sense of Scottish identity, he anticipated that in the event of independence, the family might sell their property in Edinburgh and so 'our roots with Scotland would be loosened'.[93]

Returners were not just observers of lifestyles, attitudes and politics. Reverse homesickness could be a problem for those who replanted their roots in Scottish soil. Gladys Morrice, we saw, had been 'broken hearted' when she finally left Northern Rhodesia, but it was worse for her teenaged son Gavin, who 'missed the wide open spaces' of the African bush and found it 'very, very difficult to settle'.[94] Several interviewees who returned as children testified to difficulties – albeit usually minor – in adjusting. Sometimes school could be a difficult place. Just as linguistic distinctiveness was an issue for some Scottish children in the diaspora, so those who returned with American or Antipodean accents might find themselves singled out by teachers or fellow pupils. Calum Murray 'didn't find it very easy for a start' when in 1933 his widowed mother brought Calum and his younger siblings back to Lewis, where the way of life 'was all different'. Calum, who at 15 was coming to the end of his school career, recalled a teacher disputing his pronunciation of the capital of Saskatchewan. 'It's not Regina, it's RegEEna. Don't come here with your Canadian accents,' she berated him. His younger sister Cathie also encountered classroom curiosity:

> Oh I had a teacher who was a pest. All he used to do was make me stand and read, you know, so that they could hear me talk [laughs]. Maclean, Mr Maclean. Down in Aird school, down there. And every chance anything had to be read, he used to make me do the reading. And at first I never noticed, you know, how the kids would be, and then they'd have a little giggle, you know, how we pronounced different words. However, I got over it.[95]

Alison Thornton spent two years (1954 and 1962) at school in Edinburgh when her father was on sabbatical from his post at the University of Otago. She remembered that 'the girls were basically very friendly', and that cutting remarks came more from teachers, who 'put a boot in'.[96] Alison's observation was echoed in the experience of Christine Matheson. When Christine and her siblings returned from New Zealand to the Highlands in 1962, they stayed for the first nine months with their paternal grandmother in Cromarty, while her father, who had returned without a job, found a teaching post initially in Ullapool and then in Grantown, where the whole family moved in 1963. Christine's schooling in Gisborne had been largely positive, where the experience was 'far more relaxed' than in Scotland; 'It wasn't learning through fear. I can't remember anybody getting punished for not being able to do something.' Re-entry into the Scottish system was, she recalled, a 'terrible, terrible' experience, which included the teacher ridiculing their alleged backwardness in front of a colleague:

> We went to Cromarty School, and it was the biggest culture shock we ever had. You know, the children were chanting the tables backwards and forwards. They were very good at mental arithmetic. Every day they had to learn bits of

> the Bible, a paraphrase or a psalm. The minister would come in to catechise them. This was just totally new. The teacher was ferocious and she used the strap very liberally. She punished children if they couldn't do something. We were terrified of her. We thought, 'There must be a mistake here, she's not young and glamorous, like teachers should be... I barely opened my mouth. I remember she ranted and raved about how backward we were, and she gave us special homework.'[97]

When Brian Stewart was growing up in Rhodesia, he had 'a curious sort of pride' in his Scottish roots, but without any sense that Scotland was home: 'On the contrary,' he recalled, 'although I knew I had been born in Scotland, my identity, and my framework, my terms of reference were completely African.'[98] Moving to Morayshire, where he went to school in Aberlour and then Keith, involved considerable adjustment:

> The shock to the system, and it's the mirror image of my parents going out to Rhodesia from post-war Scotland, my experience and my culture shock at the age of 15 was returning – well not returning – it was being transplanted from this lifestyle in the relatively remote bush of Africa, 'cos we lived in very, very remote rural circumstances, surrounded by forests and farms and so on, but in big open spaces, and to return as a 15-year-old from that environment, that climate, that lifestyle, those conditions, which were, in a sense, all I had known, to return to Britain, to the UK, was an *astonishing* shock.[99]

Elements of that shock included the constricted landscape, so different from the African bush; his 'Crocodile Dundee moment' when he was confronted for the first time by an escalator (in London); the purchase of an anorak ('The idea that I was going to have to wear this strange piece of kit in order to put up with the Scottish climate was a bit daunting');[100] and the strange school attire of his fellow pupils at Aberlour (long trousers and jackets rather than khaki shorts and shirts). His preference for running barefoot at sports events (pre Zola Budd) attracted attention, and he quickly became aware that, having been at boarding school from the age of seven, he was more self-reliant than his contemporaries who had never left Speyside.

Reverse dislocation also affected adults. When Cameron and Ishbel Tallach settled back in Scotland for family reasons in 2003, he experienced again, but with greater intensity, the sense of strangeness which he had felt when he first went to Taiwan in 1974. 'It was very dislocating', he recalled, 'and I only really discovered that when we came back to this country.'[101] Growing a beard was a visual reflection of his displacement. As he explained, it was difficult to sever professional and social bonds with people whose language they had learned and with whom they had interacted for many years, and it was equally challenging to return to collaborative general practice after running Peace Clinic almost single-handedly for many years. They also came back to an island where most of the people they had previously known were no longer around:

> When we came back in 2004 I just felt so disturbed and not caring what people thought, [so] I said, 'Och well, I'll let it grow.' And that's how it came, and I haven't taken it off since... It did feel as though I'd been torn away from the place I most wanted to be, and it took several years for that to kind of settle down... I didn't have these bonds back here. In fact, the thought of going into general practice in Scotland terrified me. That's not too strong a word – it terrified me... I was very, very nervous about going into that situation. So, I suppose that aggravated the whole sense of strangeness that should have been otherwise, coming back to my own country. But I just felt I had left something that I was familiar with, and where I felt comfortable in, and that I enjoyed, and where I felt accepted. All of that was left behind. I was going into this new experience.[102]

Margaret Steventon, who – with her family – spent a year in New Zealand in 2004–5, also found it very difficult to return to Scotland. Margaret and her husband had been running a mussel farm at Kinlochbervie for 14 years when they decided to emigrate, with a view to settling permanently. Margaret's profession of optometry allowed them to fast-track their entry on a talent visa, which required her to stay with the same employer for two years. She secured a position in Nelson, and enjoyed her work, but her earnings were only about a third of what she had been paid in Scotland, the cost of living was higher than they had expected, and they struggled financially. Margaret's husband had difficulty finding work, was pessimistic about the prospects of the New Zealand economy over the next decade, and did not settle easily into kiwi culture. He was also very concerned about the carcinogenic effect of high UV levels on their children, having been struck by the prevalence of skin cancer in New Zealand. Within a year they had made the 'very hard decision' to return to Scotland, this time to Ullapool. As Margaret explained, by that time she and the two children had 'made a complete transformation, and the kids were kiwis, basically.'[103] Her teenaged son in particular, who had been frustrated with the isolation of Kinlochbervie, adapted immediately to the more sociable environment of New Zealand and made good friends, and was initially very angry about returning to Scotland. His 11-year-old sister, on the other hand, who had been happy in remote north-west Sutherland, also settled well in Nelson, but surprised her mother by saying after they got back: 'I'm really glad we went to New Zealand and I really enjoyed it, but

I never really felt it was my home.'[104] Margaret herself was, like several other interviewees, dispirited by the prevalent greyness of the Scottish winter:

> It took me a long time to settle back down. The first kind of gloomy spell in the winter... everything just seemed to be grey, you know, that way, and you just think, ugh – and I got my laptop out, and I'd all my photographs of New Zealand, and I just printed them off, I printed off screeds and screeds of photographs, which were all blue sky, green trees, beautiful beaches and smiley faces, and I just put them all over the house. I thought, 'Aah! There's somewhere else out there that's not grey.' When I went to New Zealand it was almost instant when I got on the plane where I just looked forward to what was ahead. Coming back, I would say it took me about a year where [sic] I felt the urge to go back to New Zealand die down a bit. But that first year, if a plane had landed at the door going to New Zealand, I'd have been straight on it.[105]

Impacts and interactions: family, community and nation

It is more difficult to ascertain, at least from personal testimony, the impact of an overseas sojourn on the individual sojourner and the community to which they returned. The repatriation of money could be significant for individuals, families and – usually through bequests – for wider communities. A handful who came home with fortunes sometimes invested their money in bolstering family coffers, making charitable donations or reshaping the built heritage of their native parish. The *Statistical Account of Scotland* is peppered with references to individuals whose overseas sojourns in the 18th century had 'been of service to their relations', or whose fortunes had endowed handsome civic buildings. Their 19th century successors also repatriated funds to support family farms or businesses, endow hospitals or schools in their places of birth or upbringing, or occasionally – in the case of exceptional individuals like Andrew Carnegie – make an impact on the nation at large through the disbursement of immense wealth. While none of the interviewees made reference to personal repatriation of funds, two commented on its significance to their fathers, both of whom had returned from the United States. According to David Cooper's daughter, Margaret Penley, the savings he had accumulated while working as a joiner in New York before the First World War enabled him to pay cash for a flat in Dundee when he married in the 1920s, and then to keep his family above the breadline when his brothers pushed him out of the family antique business during the Depression.[106] On the other side of the country, Sandy Macleod's father was one of many Highland sheep herders who returned from Montana in the inter-war years, in his case having 'made a bit of money' which he used to purchase most of Tanera Mor, the largest of the Summer Isles, for fishing, cattle and sheep grazing.[107] It is also alleged that so many Highlanders returned to the Coigach area that silver dollars were for many years used as currency in local pubs.[108] It was not unknown for so-called 'returned Yanks' to generate caustic comments, especially in Ireland, where returners were sometimes ridiculed for opinionated vanity and ostentatious flaunting of their wealth. No interviewees encountered such hostility, but Kenneth Mackenzie from Melvaig was concerned to demonstrate that his overseas experiences had made no difference to his interaction with people in the local community. According to his daughter, he felt 'terribly bad' on his first visit home from Patagonia, when he discovered he had lost his fluency in Gaelic and feared that his neighbours would 'think I'm just putting on airs and graces' and was only pretending to have forgotten his mother tongue because it was more prestigious to speak in English.[109]

Homecomers might be received with open arms or complete indifference. While Murdo MacIver developed his global geographical knowledge and personal wanderlust by soaking up tales of the Americas, the Antipodes and Africa from global travellers who had returned to Lewis in the 1930s, Cathie and Rob Tulloch discovered that acquaintances in Morayshire had narrower horizons, being more interested in telling them about their own experiences than in asking about New Zealand. When they were about to make their first visit to Morayshire six years after emigrating in 1965, Cathie was given a piece of advice by a longer-term Scottish settler:

> She said, 'When you go back to Scotland be prepared to listen, but also be prepared that they may not want to know what you've been doing.' And that was really true, wasn't it? [Rob: Yes.] Cathie: Like one lady, she said, 'Oh, hello, I've been away since you left.' And I said, 'Oh, that's nice, where have you been?' She said, 'I went to Canada.' I said, 'How long did you go for?' 'One week.' And she talked non-stop for about 15, 20 minutes about her week in Canada. And she said, 'Oh well, I'll see you later. If I don't see you before you go, I'll see you next time.'[110]

Elvira Gonnella Welch's sense of not fully belonging in either Canada or Scotland – the ambiguity of identity that we addressed in Chapter 6 – was partly a consequence of a similar indifference that she encountered when visiting her homeland. As she explained:

> You go home with the idea that you're going to impress everyone with the wonderful experience you've had in this new country, and they're not

> impressed. They're polite, but they're not really impressed, and you realise that you can't go back, that you're neither flesh nor fowl.[111]

A handful of interviewees reflected on the impact of their overseas experiences on their own lives. Margaret Gillies Brown was convinced that her time in Canada, not least its hardships, had tutored her in self-sufficiency. When her father-in-law decided to retire from farming in 1962, Margaret and Ronald had to decide whether to sell up in Scotland and invest in a property in Canada, or return to take over the reins of the family farm in the Carse of Gowrie. They were still undecided when the Edmonton real estate company for which Ronald worked suddenly closed down, creating an acrimonious situation which made it easier for him to make up his mind. Margaret, unlike many returners, came back to a better standard of living, and with a new confidence that 'nothing was impossible', an attitude that she attributed to the 'get-up-and-go-ness' that she had learned from her Canadian neighbours. Her three-year sojourn had been long enough for her to learn these lessons, but not so long that her sense of identity was undermined. As she explained in conversation in 2012, 'I still have the same affection for Canada but because I came back soon enough, I haven't [the] "I should be there" feeling, which I think would have happened if I'd stayed in Canada – I wouldn't have quite known where I should be.'[112] Margaret also offered an eloquent summary of the positive legacy of her Canadian experience in the closing paragraphs of her book, *Far from the Rowan Tree:*

> I was going back home a different person. Canada had taught me a great deal about myself and what were really the most important things in life. It had taught me that most things can be done without, provided there is enough food, water and heat. Many things I might have thought of as essential at home weren't really, even tables and chairs... I was going back to Scotland a much more confident person – one who would find it less difficult to hold her head up and speak in public – one who would be able to cope with most situations. Going back also with much more appreciation of the British way of life and the Scottish in particular. It was perhaps we who had been in the doldrums not the country. But not anymore – after Canada anything seemed possible. I would, however, appreciate the feeling of safety I had always felt at home which we never quite felt in Canada with its nine months of winter when so much had to close down because of the severity of the climate.[113]

Margaret Gillies Brown's endorsement of the character-building qualities of Canadian frontier life was echoed by Angus Pelham Burn, who attributed his achievements in many decades of business and public service in Scotland to the seven years he had spent in the employment of the Hudson's Bay Company in the 1950s. After learning the ropes, Angus, still in his early 20s, was initially put in charge of a trading post at South Indian Lake in Manitoba. After two years he was promoted to the much larger trading post of Big Trout Lake in Northern Ontario, where he produced an annual profit through trading pelts and fur with up to 1,600 Cree in a relationship of mutual trust and respect.[114] He returned to Scotland in 1959 because he was starting to think about marriage, a change of status which he felt was incompatible with living in the Canadian North:

> When I left for home it was with a heavy heart but I felt I was doing the right thing making that decision; it was right because the experience I had in Canada with people taught me, in a natural way, to live with everyone at all levels in a company scenario such as The Bank of Scotland and Aberdeen Asset [Management] for example... I like to think, because I think it is true, that my paths in later life worked out because of my ability, and joy, of talking to everyone regardless of who they were or what they did. It might seem strange, but that situation was entirely due to working with Cree Indians, who were nice, honest and genuine people, and if one applied that outlook to everything it – somehow – worked.[115]

***

Within Scotland's long-standing tradition of mobility, narratives of return migration, like those of outward movement, do not conform to a single pattern. On the contrary, they are made up of a patchwork of one-time, occasional, seasonal, step and boomerang relocations. Some experiences have common roots irrespective of direction, for homecoming is often triggered by the same economic objectives and career ambitions that prompt the initial departure from Scotland. Other influences, such as a quest for adventure in *terra incognita*, are generally associated primarily with initial departure, while loneliness, bereavement, and family responsibilities are more likely to play a part in the decision to return.

In a globalised environment of ceaseless mobility and instability, the simple linear implications of terms such as migration and return have lost much of their meaning. While there have always been rolling stones whose lifelong saga is one of movement and who are uncertain of the meaning of 'home', that category of 'transilient' citizens of the world has mushroomed in recent years, bringing with it not only multiple international opportunities but also an unprecedented potential for multiple and malleable identities.

Scotland is by no means exceptional in its diversity of 'homecomings'. The causes and consequences of return described by interviewees would generally be familiar to those who have revisited or resettled in their homelands, wherever they might be. The injection of an element of distinctiveness into the wider story may, however, be found in the attitudes of roots tourists who 'return' to a country which they had never left, but with which they feel a deep affinity. While no interviewees fell into that category, the anthropologist Paul Basu has demonstrated that these 'genealogical pilgrims' sometimes visit Scotland with a particular agenda and set of expectations,[116] and their commercial potential has inspired much of the government-driven 'Homecoming' phenomenon. Just as nine-year-old Ian Skinner had expected the streets of New York to be patrolled by cowboys from the western plains, so some visitors to Scotland expect to encounter the romantic landscape of Sir Walter Scott-land, or the ghosts of cleared Highlanders. Those who come in search of victims and villains in their ancestry are also, perhaps, most likely to be disenchanted when their experiences do not conform to their anticipated stereotypes, and their hosts are dismissive of or indifferent to their quest. 'Homecoming' is not always a comfortable or affirming experience.

CHAPTER 8

Postscript: Commemorations, Mirror Images and Reflections

THE TESTIMONIES OF transition that populate this book are but a drop in the ocean of Scottish emigrants' experiences. They provide a tiny chronological and geographical snapshot of a diaspora whose roots lie in the middle ages, and whose territorial reach came to embrace every part of the globe. The focus is on the well-worn path to North America and the Antipodes in the decades since 1945, with an injection of insights from Africa, Asia and South America, and a smattering of narratives from the inter-war era.

Commemorations

Oral testimony can be corroborated, embellished or challenged by a wealth of documentary evidence generated by politicians, the press, sponsors and opponents of emigration, as well as the writings of the participants themselves. The Scottish diaspora has also been extensively commemorated in song and story. From the *Canadian Boat Song*'s anonymous lament for Highland exile and *The Proclaimers*' depiction of a post-industrial urban wilderness, to the short stories of Alistair MacLeod and Alice Munro, the causes and consequences of emigration have been condemned and celebrated, particularly in a North American context.[1] But while fictional portrayals and poetic interpretations offer a dramatised lens through which to view the lives of emigrants, settlers and sojourners, the story can equally be told in stone, for the diasporic legacy of many centuries is woven indelibly into the landscape and architecture of Scotland. Estates such as Poltalloch in Argyll and Fyrish in Easter Ross were modernised with profits from West and East Indian enterprises respectively; Glasgow's Merchant City was built on the wealth generated from Caribbean sugar and Virginian tobacco; public buildings throughout the country were financed by riches repatriated from the Empire and beyond; and private mansions (or more modest houses) built with overseas earnings were often named after the locations where those assets had been acquired.

Only a handful of emigrants made or bequeathed fortunes, but thousands of anonymous individuals who never returned physically to Scotland are commonly remembered in the cemeteries of their native land. Just inside the gate of St Andrew's churchyard in Golspie, Sutherland, bordering the main road to the north coast, the global reach of the Scottish diaspora is graphically encapsulated in a single weathered inscription. The Grant family headstone does not tell us where Hugh and Annie Grant's two daughters passed away, but of their six sons, only two died in Scotland, one in Golspie and the other in Glasgow. John passed away in Colombo, Ceylon, in 1871, aged 36; Donald in Queensland, Australia in 1887, aged 50; James in New Zealand in 1923, aged 81; and William in New York in 1929, aged 74. For the Grants, as for countless other families across the length and breadth of Scotland, ties with the homeland were not completely severed by the physical departure of the emigrants, even if they were never seen again after they went overseas. Cemetery inscriptions – some of which also record the circumstances of the deceased's demise – are a poignant reminder of the desire of those who stayed in Scotland to memorialise and restore to the family circle the sons, daughters and siblings who found their lasting resting place thousands of miles from their homeland.

Memorialisation was, of course, a two-way process, as has been demonstrated to particularly good effect in Patricia Lim's exhaustive study of the 'ordinary people' buried in Hong Kong's Happy Valley cemetery between the 1840s and the 1970s. Among the 8,000 graves identified by Lim are several Scots: indeed, Scots comprised the largest minority group (16 per cent) of the 150 individuals who died between 1887 and 1912 and are buried in Section 23 of the cemetery.[2] Occupations were not always recorded, but service in the Hong Kong Police Force seems to have been the most common employment, with recruits drawn from all over Scotland, including particular clusters from Aberdeenshire and Dundee. When Robert Mark, an engineer from Port Glasgow, died at Hong Kong in 1901, aged 22, his headstone was, according to the inscription, 'erected by his town's people in the east.' And although Dumbarton-born James Liddell, Superintendent of Kowloon Dock, died back in West Kilbride, North Ayrshire, in 1929, his death is commemorated in Happy Valley by a stone which also records the passing of his wife, Mary, at Kowloon in 1882, and their 18-month-old daughter in Greenock in 1883.[3]

The diaspora in stone has traditionally memorialised notable individuals. The first overseas statue to Robert Burns was unveiled in New York's Central Park in 1880, where it joined an earlier sculpture of Sir Walter Scott on the Literary Walk. It was followed by the dedication of over 60 statues and busts of Burns across the world, including seven in both Canada and Australia, and four in New Zealand, part of the movement that has turned the Bard into an enduring poster boy for Scottish identity.[4] Lesser-known or even anonymous individuals and groups from the emigrant constituency have sometimes been similarly commemorated by statues, plaques or cairns, not least on the north-eastern fringe of Scotland. Twenty-two miles north of Golspie, on the same A9 road that skirts St Andrew's church with its Grant family memorial, and just into Caithness, lies the abandoned village of Badbea. One large monument stands above the ruins of former croft houses from whose stones it was constructed in 1911. Commemorating the long-gone 'people of Badbea', it was commissioned by David Sutherland of Wellington, ten years after he had visited the birthplace of his father, who had emigrated to New Zealand with his family in 1839.[5] Six miles to the south, also on the A9, and overlooking the village of Helmsdale, is the much more politically explicit Emigrants' Statue. It was commissioned by Dennis MacLeod, a native of Helmsdale, who emigrated to Zambia in 1965 and subsequently made his fortune in mineral mining in South Africa and Canada. A year after the Helmsdale statue was unveiled by the then First Minister of Scotland, Alex Salmond, a matching statue, the Selkirk Settlers' Monument – also commissioned by MacLeod – was unveiled in Winnipeg. Together, the two statues depict the notorious Sutherland clearances, and in particular, the emigration of over 100 people who, having been evicted from the strath of Kildonan in 1813, settled, under the auspices of the fifth earl of Selkirk, on land that now forms part of the city of Winnipeg. Among those forced into that arduous journey were the Bannermans, great-grandparents of John Diefenbaker, Canada's 13th prime minister. During a visit to Sutherland in 1968, Diefenbaker unveiled a plaque and a cairn in two separate locations: the plaque is embedded in the wall of the old Kildonan church, and commemorates the clearance that had brought his ancestors to Canada, while the cairn, 30 miles to the south in the parish of Rogart, is constructed from stone taken from the house of the grandparents of Sir John A. Macdonald, Canada's first prime minister.[6]

Mirror images

Visual memorialisation still continues, most recently in the Scottish Diaspora Tapestry. Comprising more than 300 embroidered panels, it attracted participants from 34 countries, and has, since its launch in 2014, toured widely in Europe, the Antipodes and North America, as well as being displayed at various venues in Scotland and England. But the tapestry does not only depict the outward flow of Scots. Through its portrayal of the Irish, Italian, Lithuanian and Asian communities that have settled in Scotland, it reminds us that Scotland's story of migration is also that of an inward movement, which in recent years has been swelled by refugees and asylum seekers, as well as free migrants. The causes and consequences of the in-migration of Asians, Lithuanians, Poles, and English in the 20th century have been explored to varying degrees in a handful of books, while recent studies have provided an overview of migration to Scotland in general, and to the Highlands and Islands specifically.[7]

There is undoubtedly scope for further research in this area, not least in order to inform contemporary policy-making. As part of its analysis of migrants' experiences in Scotland, the SSAMIS initiative has recorded 207 interviews with migrants in Aberdeenshire and Angus, conversations which have revealed striking similarities with some of the sentiments expressed by Scots overseas.[8] The ambivalence of identity that was expressed by interviewees like Elvira Gonnella Welch in Canada and Bob Crapnell in Australia was echoed by several Eastern European migrants whose testimony features in geographer Sergei Shubin's study of mobility and religion in rural Scotland. Velna, from Latvia, felt that 'In Scotland, I am at home among strangers and a stranger at home. I left Latvia but I have not quite arrived to Scotland yet' while Donatas, from Lithuania, commented that 'You just have to manage to live "in-between": one leg is here, another there.'[9] Annie MacRitchie's endorsement of the centrality of the Free Church of Scotland to her life in Detroit was echoed – from a very different denominational tradition – by several of Shubin's interviewees. 'The Catholic church here reconnects me with Poland altogether, the Polish way of living,' was the testimony of Margita, a young migrant, who went on to explain that the incorporation of specific Polish celebrations into religious festivals encouraged her to become involved in the church, 'to mentally move back home... You feel stability in the church. In our church in Scotland we break Christmas wafer like we do in Poland. When I go to church it just feels very normal because the mass is exactly the same as it is in Poland. You just fit in.'[10] Her sentiments were echoed by another Polish migrant, Magdalena, for whom churchgoing offered a sense of community and safety. 'I can move back home mentally even though I cannot be there physically,' she explained.[11]

In collecting 'testimonies of transition', there was no intention to extend the survey to the experiences of immigrants to Scotland. On one occasion, however, the opportunity to do so presented itself serendipitously, when Annie MacRitchie, who emigrated from Lewis to Detroit in 1953, agreed to be interviewed while visiting the home of her sister-in-law, Marilyn MacRitchie, in Stornoway in 2011. Marilyn's experience, as mentioned earlier, was the exact reverse of Annie's, for she had left Detroit for Lewis in 1966, when her late husband became the minister of Stornoway Free Church. She has lived in the town ever since. Until she settled in Scotland her only experience had been of the cosmopolitan environments of Detroit, her birthplace, and

Princeton, New Jersey, where she went to college. Coming to Lewis set her on a steep learning curve, both practically and culturally. While her sister-in-law Annie (and other interviewees) noted the much bigger scale and volume of buildings and commodities on the other side of the Atlantic, Marilyn was struck by how 'how everything seemed to be so much smaller here than in America'.[12] She was also initially taken aback by the bleak, treeless moorland, though 'after living here for a time I realised it had a beauty all its own... I suppose I expected more like Brigadoon, softer, but I think Scotland is very majestic, much more so than England.'[13] The whole town of Stornoway, she remembered, smelt strongly of fish, and she wondered how she was ever going to handle the 'slippery, slimy' herring that were frequently donated to the family.[14] She also had to get used to the damp climate, which made her 'cold all the time', exacerbated by living in a huge manse with no central heating, where she had to learn to make fires with peat and coal. 'I felt like a charwoman from morning till night,' she recalled. 'I had smudges all over my face from the coal and peats.'[15] The local people were very kind, however, 'and very understanding [laughs]. They had to overlook a lot, 'cos my ways were so different to theirs.'[16] When visiting country areas, she 'would feel a little bit out of it' because of her inability to speak Gaelic, though she added that people were 'very appreciative' of her efforts to learn a few words 'that would get me by.'[17]

Writing from the Falklands in 2017, Alison Inglis commented that the downside of the Islands 'is you live in a goldfish bowl: everybody gossips about everybody else'.[18] It was an analogy also used by Marilyn MacRitchie in identifying the main cultural challenge of moving from a large, anonymous and cosmopolitan city to a small town many years earlier. 'I felt I was in a fish bowl, everybody watching me swim around.'[19] As the minister's wife, she would have been under particular scrutiny, and she regretted the negative attitude of the Free Church community towards secular music which inhibited her from sending her children to classes in instrumental music. A trained musician herself, Marilyn 'felt that very much'.[20] Like Alison, however, Marilyn emphasised that the benefits of community spirit and mutual support in Lewis far outweighed the challenges created by a lack of anonymity or a narrow cultural outlook: 'It was a good place to bring up your children. I felt it was safe, and people looked out for one another very, very much.'[21]

A year after Marilyn and Murdo MacRitchie moved from Detroit to Stornoway, Australian Gloria MacKillop arrived at a more southerly Hebridean location, when in May 1967 she took up a three-month post as relief district nurse in Berneray, North Uist. Aged 33, she was coming to the end of a two-year working trip to Scotland before returning to her home in the 'hot, dry, dusty centre of New South Wales'. A year after arriving on the 'island of bachelors', however, she married Donald Alick ('Splash') MacKillop, a crofter, lobster fisherman and relief ferryman, and assimilated quickly and totally to island life, 'because of the way a community reached out and was always there to help. It's been the most wonderful thing', she reflected in an interview with Loriana Pauli in 2013, adding that 'I was an absolute disgrace as far as the Gaelic language was concerned, but I can sing the songs, and do the dances'.[22]

In a telephone conversation in March 2017, when I asked Gloria to reflect further on her adjustment to the Hebridean environment, she identified 'culture, language and tradition' as the three key ways in which life was 'just all so different'. She described how, in the absence of an undertaker, islanders taught her 'how to place remains in coffins' and prepare bodies for burial, an experience that she had never encountered in Australia, where all her work had been in hospitals. Living on a small island, surrounded on all sides by the sound and sense of the sea, she missed to some extent the 'wide open spaces' of her homeland, where Berneray could have fitted into a paddock, 'with acres still to spare'. In an era when phone calls cost £5 or £6 a minute, Gloria – like Marilyn MacRitchie – treasured the air mail letters which kept her in regular touch with her family, and described reading her mother's missives as 'like going home for cups of tea'.[23]

Reflections

There is clearly a rich harvest to be reaped in terms of collecting and analysing the testimony of immigrants to Scotland. Equally, there are innumerable Scots scattered throughout the diaspora whose stories remain untold, and many areas of the world that have barely been touched by this study. Although we have dipped a toe into the South Atlantic with some reflections from the Falkland Islands, and incorporated a Patagonian and a Peruvian example, the experiences of Scots in vast swathes of South and Central America await systematic and detailed study. So does the Scottish diaspora in Africa and Asia, particularly the Indian sub-continent, where Scots had a deep-rooted tradition of service in the East India Company, as well as significant involvement in the plantation economy. More attention needs to be paid to the 'vitally important'[24] issue of language learning in non-English-speaking locations, in contrast to countries like New Zealand, which Rachel Minton favoured partly because of the easier transition to a place where 'everyone speaks the language'.[25]

Yet, with 106 interviewees drawn from five continents, supplemented by published collections and documentary evidence, enough testimony has been amassed to identify significant recurring themes in the unbroken story of

Scottish emigration. These include the quest for adventure, the significance of inherited and imparted wanderlust, the complexity surrounding identity transfer, and an emphasis (not surprising, in a largely self-selecting group) on successful adjustment. The most obvious practical change in the narrative is the impact of transport facilities and communications technology on the ability of emigrants to interact with family and friends. For instance, since Alison Inglis emigrated to the Falkland Islands in 1997, her parents have visited her seven times, and she has been back to Scotland on 16 occasions, a constant to-ing and fro-ing that would have been beyond the reach of previous generations of Scots in the South Atlantic. Telephone calls that in the post-war decades were only made when there was urgent news to transmit had become cheap and commonplace by the end of the century, and have been supplemented and superseded by audio-visual internet communication. As Cathie Murray observed in 2005, 'It's not a big wide world anymore.'[26]

In recent years, issues of identity, normally confined to the cultural sphere, have taken on a political dimension, although interviewees rarely raised the Scottish independence question unprompted. In some cases, emigrants had never reflected on culture and identity until the mooring rope that attached them to Scotland was cut. Anne McCarthy defined culture as 'background, it's all the things that you take for granted that are part of your background really. All that you base your thinking on'.[27] Several interviewees defined 'home' in multiple and multifaceted ways, depending on where they were and what they were doing, and the degree to which they adapted, integrated or assimilated was shaped by a combination of their objectives in going overseas, their encounters with host cultures and communities, and their own circumstances and personalities.

Only in Hong Kong was the concept of Scottish exceptionalism touched upon, when Ken Morrison attributed the emigrants' notable role in business and administration in Asia to an entrepreneurial attitude generated by the Scottish educational system. Quoting Tennyson, he observed that 'There is something in the Scottish spirit which is to strive and not to yield... if employment in Scotland was a problem they wouldn't just bury themselves under a rock, they would actually go out and try and make something of their lives, and generally with that spirit of "can do".'[28] David Knight speculated that the same visionary trait was shared by the people among whom the Scots settled in Asia.

> I think there is perhaps something in the Scottish character and the Chinese character – there is an overlap, in that the Scots who go abroad, particularly in the past, but probably still, are the ones who are ambitious and who really want to do things. I think that in China as well, and Hong Kong, there's that

desire to succeed, desire to progress.[29]

Was emigration a public or a private phenomenon? To those involved it was very much a personal or family story. It was only many years after she had returned from Australia to Scotland in 1972 that Anne McCarthy read a book about Scottish emigration and came to realise she had been part of a much bigger movement that had a significant public face.

AM: I never thought of myself as an emigrant.

MH: Why?

AM: I presume because I went as a family member... I had never quite thought of myself in those terms. I thought of myself as coming from somewhere different, but that's not the same thing to me. And I think to be an emigrant, you initiate the choice, to some extent, anyway... I would never have gone had it not been for the family circumstances.[30]

Immersed in personal decision-making and in the practicalities of making the transition, most emigrants were unaware of the parallel public and political narrative that surrounded emigration, or the controversy in which it was steeped. As we saw in Chapter 3, recruitment had always been a contentious practice, not least in the post-war decades, when there was huge concern about the depopulation of Scotland, and at times overt opposition to the canvassing activities of agents. Occasionally that concern also emerged in indirect comments in obscure sources, such as a press report of a Shetland wedding in 1964. When Ina Priest and Robert Nevin tied the knot, the *Shetland Times* reported that, while the festivities concluded with the singing of Auld Lang Syne, 'for most of us the most happy note of all was the knowledge that this capable young couple have chosen to make their home in Uyeasound'. Their decision, the newspaper continued, 'does more to boost the morale and give the lie to the pessimists than all the commissions and committees from here to St Andrew's House. May they find happiness and prosperity in the future and be justified in their decision to "stay put" in this district, where they can at least be certain of the friendship and respect of all'.[31]

Within host lands, internal political tensions of which the emigrants were usually totally unaware also shaped recruitment strategy. Among the interviewees, Bob Smart's testimony offered a rare glimpse into that world of 'political jostling', as he explained how, in 1950s Canada, the objective of a Liberal federal government to recruit Europeans who would share their political perspective was countered by the strategy of the Conservative-dominated provincial government of Ontario.[32] And another interviewee, Matthew Lynas, looking back after more than six decades on his three-year Australian sojourn in the 1950s, drew on his personal experience to question the extent to which oral history has successfully democratised perceptions of the past. The dominant narrative, in his opinion, remains that of the 'Ten Pound Poms', a constituency which he defined as largely 'elite', at least in terms of official supervision and support. At the other end of the spectrum are the much publicised accounts of institutional abuse suffered by former child migrants, articulated most recently in witness evidence to government committees. Matthew, however, did not fit either profile. As a 19-year-old left to fend for himself in a 'brutal, barbarous place' – 12,000 miles from home and 2,000 miles into the outback – he neither enjoyed the protection of a government scheme nor suffered the trauma of enforced juvenile emigration and the criminal mistreatment that often accompanied it.[33] His story was, he felt, the largely untold experience of those who had to contend with a culture of ingrained pugnacity and private brutality for which he, at least, had been ill-prepared.

Most participants, however, did not view emigration through a theoretical or political lens and were unaware of the wider context within which their decision was perceived as either a problem or an opportunity. For them, benefits and challenges (usually in that order) were defined in terms of practical considerations and cultural or emotional adjustments that were played out at an individual or family level. From the mosaic produced by the testimony in this book we may be able to identify a number of common themes, but for the narrators the story was always primarily a personal journey. While its ups and downs can be articulated and analysed on the printed page, the excitement – and occasionally the anguish – of the experience can be appreciated in much greater depth by listening to the voices of interviewees as they recall their part in the ongoing tradition of migration and diaspora that is such a central feature of Scottish identity.

APPENDIX I

Table of Interviewees

NAME	DATE	LOCATION
AM (anon.)	2011	Canada
Ashley, Gordon	2008	Australia
Baird, Jock (pseudonym)	2016	Australia
Beaton, Alice (née Mackenzie) and Mhairi	2014	USA
Bennett, Morag (née MacLeod) (d.)	2005	Canada
Bevan-Baker, Peter	2016	Canada
Black, John (video interview)	1995	Canada
Blair, Alan	2006, 2017	Canada
Blair, Janet and Joe (d.)	2006	Canada
Blake Hooff, Sally	2017	Canada
Bouman, Isobel (née Gillon) and Billy	2010	New Zealand
Bourne, Helen (née Bowie)	2015	Australia
Boyle, Charlie	2015	Australia
Bruce, Allan	2015	Australia
Campbell, Helen	2010	New Zealand
Campbell, Moira	2017	Taiwan
Campbell, Roddy	2010	Canada
Coupland, Jessie (née Morrison) (d.)	1994, 1996	Patagonia
Coutts, Brian	2010	New Zealand
Coyne, Sheena (née McBean)	2014	Australia
Crapnell, Bob and Margaret (née Harvey)	2016	Australia
Dawson, Peter	2009	Australia
Ford, Les (d.)	2012	Canada
Gillespie, William	2010	New Zealand and Australia
Gillies Brown, Margaret	2012	Canada
Gilmour, Gail (née Anderson)	2010	New Zealand

NAME	DATE	LOCATION
Gonnella Welch, Elvira	2011	Canada
Graham, Billy and Elizabeth (née Mackay)	2016	South Africa
Howarth, Shona (née Morrison)	2014	Australia
Knight, David	2013	China
Law, Charlie and Molly (née Lennie)	2012	Canada
Lynas, Matthew	2014	Australia
McCallum, Anne	2016	Canada
McCarthy, Anne	2017	Australia
MacDonald, Charlie	2011	Canada
Macdonald, Ena	2011	Australia
McEwan, Maggie	2014	Canada
McEwen, Aileen and Gavin	2013	Kenya
McFarlane, Mary and Paddy	2010	New Zealand
McGilvray, Agnes (née Lawrie) (d.)	2009	USA
McGregor, Graham	2010	New Zealand
MacIver, Murdo (d.)	2007, 2012, 2013	Canada
Mackenzie, James	2015	Australia
McLean, Katrine and Ian	2010	New Zealand
Macleod, Greig (d.)	2006	Canada
MacLeod, Katherine Anne	2011	Canada
Macleod, Sandy ('Boots')	2009	USA
McNair, Alison (née Gibson)	2005	Canada
MacPherson, Catherine (née Leitch) and John	2016	Peru
MacPherson, Murdo	2005, 2017	Canada
MacRae, Norman	2009	USA
MacRitchie, Annie (née Matheson)	2009, 2011	USA
MacRitchie, Marilyn (née Thomson)	2011	Scotland (from USA)
Matheson, Christine	2014	New Zealand
Millar, Edwin	2011	Canada
Miller, Alec	2010	New Zealand
Minton, Rachel	2010	New Zealand

NAME	DATE	LOCATION
Moffat, Alice	2014	Australia
Morrice, Gladys (née Keir) (d.)	2014	Northern Rhodesia (Zambia)
Morrison, Anne	2009	Canada
Morrison, Isabel and Ken	2017	Hong Kong
Munro, Sandra	2009	Australia
Murray, Calum (d.), Cathie and Chrissie	2005	Canada and New Zealand
Nelson, John, Marion and Trish (Botten)	2012	Canada
Pelham Burn, Angus	2010	Canada
Penley, Margaret	2001	USA
Robertson, Hamish and Isla	2007	Canada
Russell, Jim	2007	Canada
Shah, Anne Lynas	2006	Canada
AS	2010	New Zealand and Canada
Skinner, Ian	2016	Hong Kong, Singa-pore and Japan
Smart, Bob	2014	Canada
Steventon, Margaret	2009	New Zealand
Stewart, Carrol (d.) and Brian	2012	Southern Rhodesia (Zimbabwe)
Tait, Colin	2017	Hong Kong
Tallach, Cameron	2017	Hong Kong
Thorburn, Muriel	2016	Singapore
Thornton, Alison	2010	New Zealand
Timperley, Cathy (née Donald)	2010	New Zealand
Train, Sandra (née Macdonald)	2010	USA
Tulloch, Cathie and Rob	2010, 2012	New Zealand
Vance, Easton	2008	Canada
Wallace, Nellie (d.) and John	2010	Canada
Wheeler, Morag (née Callander)	2010	New Zealand
Wilson, Jim and Jane	2010	New Zealand

Informal conversations and email communications

NAME	DATE	LOCATION	MEDIUM
Inglis, Alison	2017	Falkland Islands	Email
Macdonald, Allan Forbes	2017	Hong Kong	Skype
Mackillop, Gloria	2017	Berneray, North Uist	Phone
Macleod, Donna	2009	Stornoway, Lewis	Face to face
Vance, Easton	2017	Thetis Island, British Columbia	Phone

APPENDIX 2

Interviews from other collections

PRIVATE COLLECTION (SANDRA TRAIN)
Macdonald Minnie Anne (née Fraser)

ELLIS ISLAND ORAL HISTORY PROJECT

Allan, Tom; Hansen, Helen; Kirk, Margaret Jack; Quinn, Anne; Schilling, Agnes; Will, John

PROVINCIAL ARCHIVES OF BRITISH COLUMBIA, REYNOLDSTON RESEARCH AND STUDIES COLLECTION
Anderson, George Bowman; Donaldson, John; Downie, Jane

SIMON FRASER UNIVERSITY: SCOTTISH VOICES FROM THE WEST
Noble, Joan; Russell, Jim

NATIONAL LIBRARY OF AUSTRALIA, SCOTS IN AUSTRALIA PILOT ORAL HISTORY PROJECT
Lawrie, Alan and Marjory

NATIONAL LIBRARY OF AUSTRALIA, ORAL HISTORY COLLECTION
Fox, Alexander (Sandy)

CANADIAN MUSEUM OF IMMIGRATION AT PIER 21, ORAL HISTORY COLLECTION
Edwards, N Patricia; Russell, Arthur Morris; Whetstone, Helen

Select Bibliography

Armitage, David, 'The Scottish Diaspora', in Jenny Wormald (ed.), *Scotland: A History* (Oxford: Oxford University Press, 2005).

Barber, Marilyn, and Watson, Murray, *Invisible Immigrants: The English in Canada Since 1945* (Winnipeg: University of Manitoba Press, 2015).

Basu, Paul, *Highland Homecomings: Genealogy and Heritage Tourism in the Scottish Diaspora* (London and New York: Routledge, 2007).

Bueltmann, Tanja, Hinson, Andrew and Morton, Graeme (eds), *Ties of Bluid, Kin and Countrie: Scottish Associational Culture in the Diaspora* (Guelph, Ontario: Centre for Scottish Studies, 2009).
The Scottish Diaspora (Edinburgh: Edinburgh University Press, 2013).

Devine, TM, *To the Ends of the Earth: Scotland's Global Diaspora 1750–2010* (London, 2011).

Gillies Brown, Margaret, *Far from the Rowan Tree* (Glendaruel, Argyll: Argyll Publishing, 1997).

Glass, Bryan, and MacKenzie, John M., *Scotland, Empire and Decolonisation in the Twentieth Century* (Manchester: Manchester University Press, 2015).

Hammerton, A. James and Thomson, Alistair, *Ten Pound Poms: Australia's Invisible Migrants: A Life History of British Postwar Emigration to Australia* (Manchester: Manchester University Press, 2005).

Harper, Marjory (ed.), *Emigrant Homecomings: The Return Movement of Emigrants 1600–2000* (Manchester: Manchester University Press, 2005).
Scotland No More? The Scots Who Left Scotland in the Twentieth Century (Edinburgh: Luath, 2012).

Harper, Marjory and Evans, Nicholas, 'Socio-economic dislocation and inter-war emigration to Canada and the United States: a Scottish snapshot', *Journal of Imperial and Commonwealth History*, 34: 4 (2006), 529-52.

Harper, Marjory, and Constantine, Stephen, *Migration and Empire* (Oxford: Oxford University Press, 2010).

Hutching, Megan, *Long Journey for Sevenpence: An Oral History of Assisted Immigration to New Zealand from the United Kingdom, 1947–1975* (Wellington: Victoria University Press in association with Historical Branch, Department of Internal Affairs, 1999).

Jupp, James, *Immigration* (Oxford: Oxford University Press, 1995).

McCarthy, Angela, *Personal Narratives of Irish and Scottish Migration, 1921–65: 'For Spirit and Adventure'* (Manchester: Manchester University Press, 2007).

McCarthy, Angela (ed.), *A Global Clan: Scottish Migrant Networks and Identities since the Eighteenth Century* (London and New York, 2006).

McCarthy, Angela, and MacKenzie, John M (eds), *Global Migrations. The Scottish Diaspora since 1600* (Edinburgh: Edinburgh University Press, 2016).

MacKenzie, Greta, *Why Patagonia?* (Stornoway: Stornoway Gazette, 1995).

MacKenzie, John M., and Devine, TM (eds), *Scotland and Empire* (Oxford: Oxford University Press, 2011).

Perks, Robert and Thomson, Alistair, *The Oral History Reader* (New York: Routledge, 2006).

Ritchie, Donald A, *The Oxford Handbook of Oral History* (Oxford: Oxford University Press, 2011).

Sim, Duncan, *American Scots: The Scottish Diaspora and the USA* (Edinburgh: Dunedin Academic Press, 2011).

Sim, Duncan, and Leith, Murray Stewart (eds), *The Modern Scottish Diaspora: Contemporary Debates and Perspectives* (Edinburgh: Edinburgh University Press, 2014).

Thompson, Paul, *Voices of the Past: Oral History* (Oxford: Oxford University Press, 2000).

Wilkie, Benjamin, *The Scots in Australia 1788–1938* (Martlesham: The Boydell Press, 2017).

Wilkie, Jim, *Metagama: A Journey from Lewis to the New World* (Edinburgh: Birlinn, 2001).

Endnotes

Chapter 1. Listening to Emigrants: Evaluating Personal Testimony

1 Throughout the book the terms 'emigrant' and 'emigration' are used when the focus is on the donor country; 'immigrant' and 'immigration' are used when the scene shifts to the host land(s). The more generic term 'migrant' is used, often with qualifying adjectives such as 'serial', 'boomerang' or 'return', to denote the general movement of people within and beyond their native country.

2 Author's telephone interview with Murdo MacIver, Vancouver, 7 December 2007; author's interview with Ena Macdonald, Bayhead, North Uist, 7 September 2011.

3 Scotland Week Gateway, 2015 http://www.scotland.org/whats-on/scotland-week/about-scotland-week/ [date accessed 19 January 2016].

4 Jim Gilchrist, 'Stories of Homecoming: we're on the march with Argentina's Scots', *The Scotsman*, 15 December 2008, p. 18; Tom Shields, 'We hold the reason for this holiday to be self-evident', *Sunday Herald*, 20 March 2008, p. 36. See also Mark Horne, 'No flies on Alex as Tartan Week goes walkabout', *Scotland on Sunday*, 30 March 2008, 3.

5 Marjory Harper, 'Homecoming emigrants as tourists: reconnecting the Scottish diaspora', in Sabine Marschall (ed.), *Tourism and Memories of Home* (Bristol: Channel View, 2016), 45, 48.

6 Chris J Wrigley, *AJP Taylor, Radical Historian of Europe* (London and New York: Tauris, 2006), 265; also quoted in Brian Harrison, 'Oral history and recent political history', *Oral History* 3 (1972), 46.

7 Paul Thompson, *Voice of the Past: Oral History* (Oxford: Oxford University Press, 2000); Rob Perks and Alistair Thomson (eds), *The Oral History Reader* (New York: Routledge, 2006); Alessandro Portelli, *The Death of Luigi Trastulli and Other Stories: Form and Meaning in Oral History* (Albany, NY: State University of New York Press, 1991). The interest has fuelled a huge publications industry. A bibliographical search on 'oral history' on the online catalogue WorldCAT on 20 January 2016 produced 194,084 hits.

8 Alessandro Portelli, 'A Dialogical Relationship. An approach to oral history', *http://www.swaraj.org/shikshantar/expressions_portelli.pdf* [date accessed 15 March 2017], 1.

9 Alistair Thomson, 'Moving stories: oral history and migration studies', *Oral History*, 7: 1 (Spring 1999), 24-37. The quote is on page 24.

10 Ibid., 29, 34-5.

11 The most recent publication is Marilyn Barber and Murray Watson, *Invisible Immigrants. The English in Canada since 1945* (Winnipeg: University of Manitoba Press, 2015). See also A. James Hammerton and Alistair Thomson, *Ten Pound Poms: Australia's Invisible Immigrants* (Manchester: Manchester University Press, 2005); Angela McCarthy, *Personal Narratives of Irish and Scottish Migration, 1921–65: 'For Spirit and Adventure'* (Manchester: Manchester University Press, 2007).

12 The interviews were conducted between 2000 and 2011. Thanks to Sinisa Obradovic, Oral History Researcher, Pier 21, for this information.

13 For Ellis Island, see https://www.nps.gov/elis/learn/historyculture/oral-history-collection.htm; for Pier 21, see https://www.pier21.ca/research/oral-history/oral-history and http://www.pier21.ca/search-our-online-collections; for 'Scottish Voices from the West', see http://cufts2.lib.sfu.ca/CRDB4/BVAS/resource/12092; for 'Scots in Australia', see Alan and Marjory Lawrie, interviewed by Rob Linn http://catalogue.nla.gov.au/Record/6382498 [all accessed 2 March 2017].

14 State Library of New South Wales, *http://www.sl.nsw.gov.au/about/collections/oral_history.html* [date accessed 2 March 2017].

15 Judith Winternitz, 'Telling the migrant experience: the oral history project of the Ethnic Affairs Commission of NSW', *Oral History Association of Australia Journal*, 6 (1984), 45.

16 Gould P Colman, 'Oral history – an appeal for more systematic procedures', *American Archivist*, 28: 1 (January 1965), 79-83.

17 Donald A. Ritchie (ed.), *The Oxford Handbook of Oral History* (Oxford: Oxford University Press, 2011), 9.

18 Gordon Donaldson, *The Scots Overseas* (London: Hale, 1966).

19 TC Smout, 'The state of oral history', *Oral History. The Journal of the Oral History Society*, 2:1 (1973), 14.

20 Alexander Freund, *Oral History and Ethnic History* (Ottawa: The Canadian Historical Association, Immigration and Ethnicity in Canada Series, Booklet no. 32), 2014, 3.

21 WT Couch (ed.), *These Are Our Lives* (Chapel Hill, NC: University of North Carolina Press, 1939); Ann Banks (ed.), *First Person America* (New York and London: WW Norton & Co., 1980). The Federal Writers' Project 'life histories' were used to good effect by Mario Varricchio in his doctoral dissertation, 'From the Mother Country. Oral Narratives of British Emigration to the United States, 1860–1940' (University of Edinburgh: unpublished PhD, 2011).

22 See in particular House of Commons Parliamentary Papers [hereafter HCPP] 1826–7 (237), V, *First, Second and Third Reports from the Select Committee on Emigration from the United Kingdom;* HCPP 1841 (182) (333), VI, *First and Second Reports from the Select Committee on Emigration, Scotland*; HCPP 1884 [C 3980] XXXII, *Report of the Commission of Inquiry into the Condition of Crofters and Cottars in the Highlands and Islands of Scotland.*

23 The structure and findings of the questionnaires are discussed in Marjory Harper, 'Pioneering on the prairies: a survey of settlement in Saskatchewan, 1887-1914', *Saskatchewan History*, 52: 2 (Fall 2000), 28-46. See also *http://www.saskarchives.com/using-archives/family-history-research/pioneer-questionnaires* [date accessed 10 February 2016].

24 Megan Hutching, *Long Journey for Sevenpence: An Oral History of Assisted Immigration to New Zealand from the United Kingdom, 1947–1975* (Wellington: Victoria University Press in association with Historical

Branch, Department of Internal Affairs, 1999). The questionnaires can be consulted in the National Library of New Zealand, Alexander Turnbull Library (MS-Papers-8653/1-3).

25 Valerie Raleigh Yow, *Recording Oral History: A Guide for the Humanities and Social Sciences*, 4.

26 For discussion of the anxiety caused by the cessation of correspondence, see Marjory Harper, 'Missing emigrants: gleanings from petitions presented under the Presumption of Life Limitation (Scotland) Acts', *Scottish Archives*, 22 (2016), 17-38.

27 James Adam, *Twenty-five Years of Emigrant Life in the South of New Zealand* (Edinburgh: Bell and Bradfute, 1876), 34.

28 Barber and Watson, *Invisible Immigrants*, 194.

29 Author's telephone interview with Annie MacRitchie (née Matheson), Stornoway, Isle of Lewis, 19 October 2009; author's face-to-face interview with Annie MacRitchie, Stornoway, 6 September 2011. Also quoted in Marjory Harper, *Scotland No More? The Scots who left Scotland in the Twentieth Century* (Edinburgh: Luath, 2012), 187.

30 Bruce S. Elliott, David A Gerber, and Suzanne M Sinke (eds), *Letters across Borders. The Epistolary Practices of International Migrants* (New York: Palgrave Macmillan, 2006), 3.

31 Jock Phillips and Terry Hearn, *Settlers. New Zealand Immigrants from England, Ireland & Scotland, 1800–1945* (Auckland: Auckland University Press, 2008), 5, quoting *Appendices to the Journals of the House of Representatives*, 1886, vol. 2, F-1, 13, *Report of the Post Office and Telegraph Department, 1885*, table 15.

32 David A Gerber, *Authors of their Lives. The Personal Correspondence of British Immigrants to North America in the Nineteenth Century* (New York: New York University Press, 2006), 5.

33 *Aberdeen Journal*, 12 May 1852, p6, c4-5.

34 Gerber, *Authors of their Lives*, 2.

35 'The uses of immigrant letters', *The German Historical Institute Bulletin*, no. 31 (Fall 2007) http://www.ghi-dc.org/files/publications/bulletin/bu041/137.pdf [date accessed 21 January 2016].

36 Mary Chamberlain, 'Narratives of exile and return', in *Communicating Experience: Proceedings of the IX International Oral History Conference* (Goteborg: International Oral History Committee, 1996) (Section 1: Migration and Ethnic Identity), 1-13.

37 See, for instance, the letters that were published regularly in *The Imperial Colonist: The Official Organ of the British Women's Emigration Association and the South African Expansion Committee* (London, 1902–27); *A Narrative of Facts relative to work done for Christ in connection with the Orphan and Destitute Children's Emigration Homes, Glasgow* (Glasgow, 1872–1939); *Letters from Successful Scottish Ploughmen* (Ottawa: Department of the Interior, 1909).

38 Charlotte Erickson, *Invisible Immigrants: The Adaptation of English and Scottish Immigrants in Nineteenth-century America* (London: Weidenfeld and Nicolson, 1972), 3-4.

39 See Richard Jensen, 'Oral history, quantification and the new social history', *Oral History Review*, 9 (1981), 13-25; Barber and Watson, *Invisible Immigrants*, 7-8.

40 Enoch Powell, 'Old men forget', *The Times*, 5 November 1981, 11, reviewing Anthony Seldon, *Churchill's Indian Summer: The Conservative Government, 1951–55* (London, 1981); Patrick O'Farrell, 'Oral history: facts and fiction', *Quadrant*, 23: 11 (November 1979), 4-8.

41 Since its inception in 2008, the journal *Memory Studies* has discussed some of these theoretical issues. See, for instance, Paul Connerton, 'Seven types of forgetting', *Memory Studies*, 1: 1, January 2008, 59-71; Jefferson A. Singer and Martin A. Conway, 'Should we forget forgetting?', *Memory Studies*, 1:3, September 2008, 279-85. For a Scottish perspective, see Andrew Blaikie, 'Imagining the face of a nation: Scotland, modernity and the places of memory', *Memory Studies*, 4: 4, October 2011, 416-31.

42 Alessandro Portelli, 'What makes oral history different', in Perks and Thompson, *The Oral History Reader*, 33. See also Portelli, 'A Dialogical Relationship', 5.

43 Colman, 'Oral history', 83.

44 Portelli, 'What makes oral history different', 39; Paul Thompson, *The Voice of the Past*, 129-37, 157-9, 173-89.

45 Portelli, 'What makes oral history different', 37.

46 Alistair Thomson, 'Anzac memories: putting popular memory theory into practice in Australia', in Perks and Thomson (eds), *The Oral History Reader*, 244-54.

47 Harper, *Scotland No More?*, 194-230.

48 Four interviewees (Calum and Cathie Murray, Ian Skinner, and Brian Stewart) had emigrated initially as children, and later as adults.

49 Carrol and Brian Stewart; Nellie and John Wallace.

50 Calum, Cathie and Chrissie Murray.

51 A full list of names, dates of interviews and locations covered is given in Appendix 1, while Appendix 2 provides details of informal conversations.

52 According to a parliamentary report in 1963, 'Scottish oversea emigration continues to be mainly to Australia, Canada, New Zealand and the USA, and at a higher rate proportionately to her population than for Britain as a whole.' HCPP 1964-65, Cmnd. 2555, *Commonwealth Relations Office. Oversea Migration Board. Statistics for 1963*, tables based on International Passenger Survey. 1963, Table 4, 109, 'Scottish Emigration'.

53 See, for instance, Barber and Watson, *Invisible Immigrants*; McCarthy, *Personal Narratives*; Varricchio, 'From the Mother Country'.

54 See, *inter alia*, Tanja Bueltmann, Andrew Hinson and Graeme Morton (eds), *Ties of Bluid, Kin and Countrie: Scottish Associational Culture in the Diaspora* (Guelph: Centre for Scottish Studies, 2009); Tanja Bueltmann, *Scottish Ethnicity and the Making of New Zealand Society, 1850 to 1930* (Edinburgh: Edinburgh University Press, 2011). A recent general study of the Scottish diaspora is Angela McCarthy and John M. MacKenzie (eds), *Global Migrations. The Scottish Diaspora since 1600* (Edinburgh: Edinburgh University Press, 2016).

55 Barber and Watson, *Invisible Immigrants*; Hammerton and Thomson, *Ten Pound Poms*.

56 Thomson, 'Moving stories', 29.

57 Author's interview with Calum, Cathie and Chrissie Murray, Shader, Isle of Lewis, 25 February 2005.

58 Janis Wilton, 'Oral history and ethnic community studies in Australia', unpublished paper delivered at the International Conference on Oral History, New York, 1994, quoted in Thomson, 'Moving stories', 29.

59 All but four interviews in the collection were conducted by the author, the exceptions being the interviews with Helen Bourne, Bob and Margaret Crapnell and Jock Baird, which were conducted in Queensland, Australia by Kirstie Moar in 2015 and 2016. I am immensely grateful to Dr Lauren Brancaz, Kirk Reid and Kirstie

Moar, who respectively prepared 14, seven and four summaries of interviews that appear in this book. The process of summarising interviews is still underway, but a short précis of content is available for interviews for which a full summary has not yet been prepared.

Chapter 2. Pulling Up the Roots: The Smorgasbord of Decision-Making

1 *House of Commons Parliamentary Papers* [hereafter HCPP], 1964–65, Cmnd. 2555, *Commonwealth Relations Office. Oversea Migration Board. Statistics for 1963*, tables based on International Passenger Survey. 1963, Table 4, 109, 'Scottish Emigration'. Scotland comprised 10 per cent of the population of Britain, but between 1956 and 1962 it accounted for an average of just over 12 per cent of emigrants from Britain.

2 The National Archives [hereafter TNA], T47/12, *Register of Emigrants, 1774–1775*, quoted in Viola R. Cameron, *Emigrants from Scotland to America, 1774–1775* (Baltimore: Genealogical Publishing Company, 1965), 6-7, 'Report of the examination of the emigrants from the counties of Caithness and Sutherland on board the ship *Bachelor* of Leith bound for Wilmington, North Carolina. In the event, the ship was repeatedly damaged by storms, and did not cross the Atlantic.

3 Saskatchewan Archives Questionnaires [hereafter SAQ], no. 2, Pioneer Experiences: A General Questionnaire, Box 10, 1906: Padgham, Mrs AH.

4 Author's telephone interview with Morag Bennett (née MacLeod), Sechelt, British Columbia, 21 February 2005, 01:17–01:28; 06:31.

5 Ellis Island Oral History Project, New York Statue of Liberty/Ellis Island National Monument [hereafter Ellis Island Interviews], Helen Hansen (née Baxter) interviewed by Andrew Phillips, 26 May 21989, DP Series 46; John Will interviewed by Elysa Matsen, 16 September 1994, EI Series 547; Anne Quinn (née Reilly) interviewed by Dennis Cloutier and Peter Kaplan, 8 December 1983, NPS Series 146. See also Marjory Harper, *Emigration from Scotland between the Wars* (Manchester: Manchester University Press, 1998), 42-6; Angela McCarthy, *Personal Narratives of Irish and Scottish Migration, 1921–65: 'For Spirit and Adventure'* (Manchester: Manchester University Press, 2007) for further extracts from the Ellis Island interviews.

6 Author's interview with Cathy Timperley (née Donald), Dunedin, 30 November 2010, 06:00–06:39.

7 Author's interview with Morag Wheeler (née Callander), Dunedin, 30 November 2010, track 1, 01:01–01:18.

8 Author's interview with Brian Coutts, Dunedin, 20 November 2010, 03:03–03:51.

9 Author's interview with Jim Wilson, Dunedin, 26 November 2010, track 1, 01:07–01:53.

10 TNA, T47/12, quoted in Cameron, *Emigrants from Scotland to America*, 5-23, 67-9.

11 HCPP, C-3980, 1884, XXXII–XXXVI, *Royal Commission of Inquiry into the Condition of Crofters and Cottars in the Highlands and Islands of Scotland* [hereafter Napier Commission], Minutes of Evidence, Bettyhill, Sutherland, 25 July 1883, question 26030, written statement by Angus MacKay, crofter's son, Cattlefield, Farr. See also AD Cameron, *Go Listen to the Crofters. The Napier Commission and Crofting a Century Ago* (Stornoway: Acair Ltd, 1986).

12 Provincial Archives of British Columbia, Reynoldston Research and Studies Collection. Item AAAB0275, accession number T0238-0001, George Bowman Anderson interviewed by Marlene Karnouk, 26 November 1973; item AAAB0193, accession number T0167, John Donaldson interviewed by William James Langlois, April 1973.

13 George Malcolm Thomson, *Caledonia, or The Future of the Scots* (London: Kegan Paul, Trench, Trubner and Co Ltd, 1927), 6, 21. See also George McKechnie, *George Malcolm Thomson: The Best-Hated Man: Intellectuals and the Condition of Scotland between the Wars* (Glendaruel: Argyll Publishing, 2013).

14 McCarthy, *Personal Narratives*, 35-63.

15 John MacLeod, *When I Heard the Bell: the loss of the* Iolaire (Edinburgh: Birlinn, 2010); Marjory Harper, *Scotland No More? The Scots Who Left Scotland in the Twentieth Century* (Edinburgh: Luath, 2012), 55.

16 Author's (unrecorded) conversation with Donna Macleod, Stornoway, Isle of Lewis, 18 November 2009. Murdo's daughters thought that their mother had also been unaware of the *Iolaire* disaster.

17 Author's interview with Alison Thornton, Dunedin, 30 November 2010, 09:34–10:27.

18 Author's interview with Alec Miller, Dunedin, 29 November 2010, 14:38–15:37. See also below, Chapter 5, 96, 139, for Alec's comment on extra puddings and Katrine McLean's experience in Auckland.

19 Author's telephone interview with Annie MacRitchie (née Matheson), Stornoway, Isle of Lewis, 19 October 2009, 12:05–13:08. See also Harper, *Scotland No More?*, 207-8.

20 Author's interview with Margaret Gillies Brown, East Inchmichael, Errol, 21 December 2012, track 2, 00:37–01:14.

21 Author's interview with John and Marion Nelson and Patricia Botten (daughter), Aignish, Isle of Lewis, 7 September 2012, track 1, 15:59–16:06; 20:52–21:03; 21:25–21:31.

22 Scottish Catholic Archives, PL3/6/10, Rev. Angus MacEachran, St Andrews, Prince Edward Island, to Alexander Cameron, Coadjutor Bishop of the Lowland Vicariate, Edinburgh, 14 December 1807. See also Charles Dunn, *Highland Settler. A Portrait of the Scottish Gael in Cape Breton and Eastern Nova Scotia* (Wreck Cove, Nova Scotia: Breton Books, 2003), first published 1953; Andrew Mackillop, *More Fruitful than the Soil: Army, Empire and the Scottish Highlands, 1715–1815* (East Linton: Tuckwell Press, 2000); Allan I Macinnes, Marjory-Ann D Harper and Linda G Fryer (eds), *Scotland and the Americas, c. 1650–c. 1939: A Documentary Source Book* (Edinburgh: Scottish History Society, 2002), Chapter 4, 'The Military Emigrant'.

23 Bernard Kelly, '"Masters in Their Own House": Britain, the Dominions and the 1946 Ex-Service Free Passage Scheme', *Journal of Imperial and Commonwealth History*, 2015, 1-19.

24 Author's interview with Charlie and Molly Law (née Lennie), Banavie, Fort William, 13 October 2012, 02:21–03:39.

25 National Library of Australia, Oral History Collection, Chief Migration Officers' oral history project, Alexander (Sandy) Fox interviewed by Ann-Mari Jordens, 26 February 2009, 01:35–02:21.

26 Author's interview with Christine Matheson, Inverness, 14 June 2014, 03:48–04:00.

27 Author's interview with Paddy McFarlane, Dunedin, 28 November 2010, 02:02.
28 Author's telephone interview with Easton Vance, Thetis Island, British Columbia, 9 July 2008, track 1, 10:00–10:20. Easton's National Service took him to Sardinia and Malta.
29 Author's telephone interview with Easton Vance, Thetis Island, British Columbia, 27 March 2017, 00:49-01:04; 03:15-03:29.
30 Jock Baird (pseudonym), Toowoomba, Queensland, interviewed by Kirstie Moar, 20 January 2016, 08:01.
31 Joan Noble, Victoria, Vancouver Island, interviewed by Ron Sutherland, for the Simon Fraser University 'Scottish Lives in the West' Oral History Project, 12 May 2012, 44:22–45:21.
32 Author's interview with Allan Bruce, Toowoomba, Queensland, 2 June 2015, track 1, 03:04–03:06; 09:30–09:56.
33 Author's interview with AS, Dunedin, 29 November 2010, 02:53–03:43.
34 Alison Campsie, 'Six Scots living abroad tell us what they miss (and don't miss) about home', *The Scotsman*, 12 April 2016. *http://www.scotsman.com/lifestyle/travel/six-scots-living-abroad-tell-us-what-they-miss-and-don-t-miss-about-home-1-4097895#comments-area* [date accessed 25 August 2016].
35 Although 51.6 per cent of those who voted did vote 'yes', the figure represented less than a third of the whole electorate. See, *inter alia*, TM Devine, *The Scottish Nation 1700–2000* (London: Penguin, 1999), 588; Richard J Finlay, *Modern Scotland, 1914–2000* (London: Profile, 2004), 335-41.
36 Author's interview with Edwin Millar, Ottawa, 9 November 2011, 19:34-21:50.
37 Harper, *Scotland No More?*, 70, 71-2.
38 Ellis Island Interviews, Agnes Schilling, interviewed by Janet Levine, 16 June 1992, EI Series 172.
39 Ibid., Margaret Jack Kirk, interviewed by Paul E Sigrist, 25 February 1994, EI Series 440. Also quoted in McCarthy, *Personal Narratives*, 53. See, in addition, Peter Morton Coan, *Ellis Island Interviews. In Their Own Words* (New York: Checkmark Books, 1997), 135.
40 Minnie Anne Macdonald (née Fraser) interviewed by Sandra Train (her daughter), Bayview House, Thurso, 17 July 1996, track 1, 02:06.
41 Ibid., 02:14–04:26.
42 Ibid., 07:07.
43 Author's telephone interview with Sally Blake Hooff, Kensington, Prince Edward Island, 30 March 2017, 11:16–11:23.
44 Ibid., 12:54–13:56.
45 Author's interview with Alison McNair (née Gibson), Kintore, Aberdeenshire, 12 September 2005, track 1, 04:56–05:16.
46 Ibid., 09:20–12:04.
47 Author's interview with Isobel Bouman (née Gillon), Dunedin, 29 November 2010, 02:50–04:08.
48 Author's interview with Rachel Minton, Dunedin, 29 November 2010, 01:23–01:48.
49 Emails from Alison Inglis to author, 20 February, 5 March 2017.
50 Author's interview with Angus Pelham Burn, Dess, Aberdeenshire, 6 April 2010, 01:16–01:42.
51 Author's interview with Les Ford, Aberdeen, 25 January 2012, 03:09. At 1955 exchange rates, the HBC wage was the equivalent of £34 per week, compared with the British Rail weekly wage of £1.8sh (£1.40).
52 Author's interview with John and Nellie Wallace, Aberdeen, 24 April 2010, 06:47–06:58.
53 Interview with Charlie and Molly Law, 04:16–06:50.
54 Author's interview with Isla and Hamish Robertson, Vancouver, 7 December 2007, 04:26–04:58; 10:14–11:00; 13:19. See also below, Chapter 3.
55 Author's interview with Roddy Campbell, Inverness, 8 October 2010, 01:16–02:03.
56 James Kyle, 'The Hong Kong College of Medicine, 1887–1915', *British Medical Journal*, 21979, 1, 1474-1476. https://www.ncbi.nlm.nih.gov/pmc/articles/PMC1599052/pdf/brmedj00075-0038.pdf [date accessed 16 February 2017].
57 Interview with Alison Thornton, 11:05–11:09.
58 Scottish Catholic Archives, DA9/44/5, Alexander, Archbishop of St Boniface, Manitoba, to Bishop Angus MacDonald, Oban, 18 May 1844; Harper, *Scotland No More?*, 170.
59 Reverend Arthur Morris Russell, interviewed by Steve Schwinghamer, 16 May 2006, *Our Canadian Stories*, catalogue no. 06.05.16, Canadian Museum of Immigration at Pier 21, Halifax, Nova Scotia.
60 John M MacPherson, *At the Roots of a Nation: the story of San Andres School in Lima, Peru* (Edinburgh: The Knox Press, 1993); John Mackay Metzger, *The Hand and the Road: the Life and Times of John A. Mackay* (Louisville, KY: Westminster John Knox Press, 2010).
61 Author's interview with Moira Campbell, Aberdeen, 9 February 2017.
62 Author's interview with Cameron Tallach, Breakish, Isle of Skye, 10 April 2017. See also below, 218-19.
63 *Johnson's Journey to the Western Islands of Scotland, and Boswell's Journal of a Tour to the Hebrides with Samuel Johnson*, edited by RW Chapman (Oxford: Oxford University Press, 1984), originally published 1924, 87, 345-6.
64 Marjory Harper, 'Crofter colonists in Canada: an experiment in empire settlement in the 1920s', *Northern Scotland*, 14 (1994), 69-108.
65 Author's interview with Anne Morrison, Cumbernauld, 2 July 2009, track 1, 01:23–01:25. Anne's uncle emigrated from Portvoller, Lewis, allegedly on the *Metagama*, but his name does not appear on the passenger list.
66 Author's interview with Charlie Macdonald, Carinish, North Uist, 8 September 2011, track 1, 01:17–01:21.
67 Marjory Harper and Nicholas J Evans, 'Socio-economic dislocation and inter-war emigration to Canada and the United States: a Scottish snapshot', *Journal of Imperial and Commonwealth History*, 34: 4 (December 2006), 529-52.
68 Author's interview with Sandra Train, Halladale, Sutherland, 5 November 2010, 00:59–01:06.
69 Harper, *Scotland No More?*, 198.
70 Author's interview with Maggie McEwan, Aberdeen, 29 April 2014, 03:38–04:24.
71 Author's interview with Shona Howarth (née Morrison), Culbokie, Ross-shire, 13 June 2014, 03:01–03:47.
72 Author's interview with Calum, Cathie and Chrissie Murray, Shader, Isle of Lewis, 25 February 2005, 36:48–36:52. Calum speaking.
73 Interview with Calum, Cathie and Chrissie Murray, 43:02–44:20. Cathie speaking; Harper, *Scotland No More?*, 219.
74 Author's face-to-face interview with Annie MacRitchie (née Matheson), Stornoway, Isle of Lewis,

6 September 2011, track 1, 04:07–05:36; 04:34–05:35.
75 Ibid., track 2, 00:24–01:07.
76 Ibid., 04:34–05:35.
77 Author's face-to-face interview with Murdo MacIver, Vancouver, 22 May 2012, track 1, 01:24–02:21. See also author's telephone interview with Murdo MacIver, Vancouver, 7 December 2007, track 2, 10:34–13:10; and Harper, *Scotland No More?*, 225.
78 Author's face-to-face interview with Murdo MacIver, Vancouver, 24 June 2013, 09:05–09:42. See also below, 185.
79 Author's interview with Ian Skinner, Edinburgh, 2 March 2016, 01:49–02:53.
80 Cameron, *Emigrants from Scotland to America*, 6-24.
81 *Illustrated London News*, 25 April 1857, 384.
82 HCPP 1841, *Select Committee on Emigration*, question 222, John Bowie, WS.
83 Malcolm McLeod, County Sherbrooke, to John McLeod, Swainbost, Lewis, 27 September 1851, quoted in Napier Commission, Appendix A, 'Extracts from Letters from Lews Emigrants in Canada to Friends in Lews, 1851 and 1854', letter III.
84 Author's telephone interview with Katherine Anne MacLeod (Christina's daughter), Winnipeg, 8 February 2011, 01:48–02:38.
85 National Library of Australia, Scots in Australia Pilot Oral History Project, Alan and Marjory Lawrie interviewed by Rob Linn, Brighton, South Australia, 18 September 2013, session 2, 01:22–02:46.
86 Norman H Carrier and James R Jeffery, *External Migration: A Survey of the Available Statistics, 1815–1950* (London: HMSO, 1953), 96, 100.
87 James Jupp (ed.), *The Australian People: An Encyclopaedia of the Nation, its People and Their Origins* (Cambridge: Cambridge University Press, 2001), 62-5. See also Malcolm Prentis, '"It's a long way to the bottom": the insignificance of "the Scots" in Australia', *Immigrants and Minorities*, 29: 2 (2011), 195-219. See also below, Chapter 3.
88 British Columbia Provincial Archives, Reynoldston Research and Studies Collection, item AAAB0238, accession number T0204, Amy Dalgleish interviewed by Marlene Karnouk, 4 May 1973.
89 Interview with Anne Morrison, 04:06–04:35.
90 Interview with Annie MacRitchie, 6 September 2011, track 2, 14:26–14:37.
91 Author's telephone interview with Katrine McLean, Auckland, New Zealand, 3 November 2010, track 1, 02:57; 05:30–05:37.
92 Author's interview with Helen Campbell, Dunedin, 1 December 2010, track 1, 03:58; 05:05–05:07.
93 Author's interview with Gladys Morrice (née Keir), Aberdeen, 4 December 2014, track 1, 08:27; author's interview with Carrol and Brian Stewart, Craigellachie, 9 April 2012, 06:58–07:14.
94 Interview with Easton Vance, 9 July 2008, track 1, 02:46–02:53.
95 Interview with Easton Vance, 27 March 2017, 11:41-11:47.
96 Interview with Brian Coutts, 03:52–04:28.
97 Joan Noble, interviewed by Ron Sutherland, 46:57–47:58.
98 Author's interview with Murdo MacPherson, Kinlochbervie, Sutherland, 24 February 2005, track 1, 02:37–02:53. See also Harper, *Scotland No More?*, 203.
99 Author's interview with Murdo MacPherson, Dornoch, Sutherland, 18 January 2017, track 1, 19:10–19:16; 19:49–20:05.
100 Interview with Isobel Bouman, 01:18–02:06.

Chapter 3. Persuasion and Propaganda: Official Interventions and Reactions

1 Author's telephone interview with Cathie and Rob Tulloch, Whangarei, New Zealand, 2 November 2010, 16:19.
2 Author's face-to-face interview with Cathie and Rob Tulloch, Kintore, Aberdeenshire, 14 August 2012, 03:17–03:21.
3 I was one of two historians approached by Gordon Ashley for background advice when he was preparing to write a novel on the Highland Clearances. While discussing that project he mentioned, in passing, that he had once worked as an emigration agent for Australia. Bob Smart, who was employed briefly by the Ontario government in London, initially made himself known to me after a public lecture in Guelph, Ontario.
4 HCPP 1912-13, XVII [Cd. 6516], *First Interim Report of the Royal Commission on the Natural Resources, Trade and Legislation of Certain Portions of His Majesty's Dominions [Dominions Royal Commission]. Minutes of evidence taken in London during October and November 1912, Part I, Migration*, p. 154, q. 2954, R. Courtney, passenger agent.
5 *Dictionary of Canadian Biography* [hereafter DCB], http://www.biographi.ca/en/bio/rolph_thomas_8E.html and http://www.biographi.ca/en/bio/hawke_anthony_bewden_9E.html and http://www.biographi.ca/en/bio/dixon_william_10E.html [date accessed 3 May 2016].
6 Saskatchewan Archives Questionnaires [hereafter SAQ], no. 2, Pioneer Experiences: A General Questionnaire, Box 6, 1903: Veitch, Andrew; Box 10, 1906: McManus, Margaret; Box 9, 1906: Smith, Margaret; Box 9, 1906: Allan, John; Box 9, 1906: Craig, George; Box 10, 1906: Mills, Robert. For the combination of family encouragement and government advice, see Box 3, 1891: Fraser, Peter; Box 10, 1906: Padgham, Mrs AH; Box 11, 1907: Maxwell, Alexander.
7 Provincial Archives of British Columbia [hereafter PABC], 'Now You Are My Brother: Missionaries in British Columbia' collection, item AAAB3927, call number T3534:0001, William (Bill) Christie, interviewed by Margaret Mary Whitehead, June 1979.
8 PABC, The Reynoldston Research and Studies Oral History Collection, item AAAB0085, accession number T0083:0001, Jane Downie, interviewed by Cheryl Pierson, July 1972.
9 Jim Wilkie, *Metagama: A Journey from Lewis to the New World* (Edinburgh: Birlinn, 2001, originally published 1987), 123.
10 Ibid., 100.
11 Author's interview with Peter Dawson, Fochabers, 27 March 2009, 00:57–01:10.
12 Author's interview with Calum, Cathie and Chrissie Murray, Shader, Isle of Lewis, February 2005, 44:12–44:21. See also Marjory Harper, *Scotland No More? The Scots Who Left Scotland in the Twentieth Century* (Edinburgh: Luath, 2012), 219.
13 Author's interview with Paddy McFarlane, Dunedin, 28 November 2010, 02:14–03:07.
14 Author's interview with Shona Howarth (née Morrison), Culbokie, Ross-shire, 13 June 2014, 03:12–03:46.
15 Ibid., 12:10–12:22.
16 Helen Bourne (née Bowie), Springfield Lakes, Queensland, interviewed by Kirstie Moar,

17 December 2015, track 1, 50:21–54:13. After Helen's father, a GP in Irvine, died suddenly at the age of 33, his replacement was the neighbour who emigrated to Toowoomba in 1967, and who, with his wife, offered to sponsor the Bowie family.

17 Bob Crapnell, Brisbane, Queensland, interviewed by Kirstie Moar, 18 January 2016, 19:32–20:30.

18 Margaret Crapnell (née Harvey), Brisbane, Queensland, interviewed by Kirstie Moar, 18 January 2016, 16:43–19:51.

19 Canada, *House of Commons Debates*, Ottawa, 1 May 1947, 2644-7, quoted in Ninette Kelley and Michael Trebilcock, *The Making of the Mosaic: A History of Canadian Immigration Policy* (Toronto: University of Toronto Press, 1998), 312.

20 Canada, *House of Commons Debates*, Ottawa, 1955, 1254.

21 See below, Chapter 4, 83.

22 Marilyn Barber and Murray Watson, *Invisible Immigrants. The English in Canada since 1945* (Winnipeg: University of Manitoba Press, 2015), 26.

23 Author's interview with Margaret Gillies Brown, East Inchmichael, Errol, 21 December 2012, track 2, 02:02–05:10.

24 See above, Chapter 2, 53.

25 Author's interview with Hamish and Isla Robertson, Vancouver, 7 December 2007, 10:34.

26 Ibid., 14:51–16:06.

27 Author's interview with Charlie and Molly Law, Banavie, Fort William, 12 October 2012, 19:21–19:57.

28 Kelley and Trebilcock, *The Making of the Mosaic*, 348-9, 351-2, 360, 380.

29 John M Bumsted, *The People's Clearance: Highland Emigration to British North America 1770–1815* (Edinburgh: Edinburgh University Press, 1982), 119-22, 88-95. For Selkirk, see Lucille H Campey, *The Silver Chief: Lord Selkirk and the Scottish Pioneers of Belfast, Baldoon and Red River* (Toronto: Natural Heritage, 2003).

30 Alexander Irvine, *An Inquiry into the Causes and Effects of Emigration from the Highlands and Western Islands of Scotland, with Observations on the Means to be Employed for Preventing It* (Edinburgh: Mundell and Son, 1802), 65-6.

31 Marjory Harper, *Adventurers and Exiles: The Great Scottish Exodus* (London: Profile, 2003), 133; *DCB*, http://www.biographi.ca/en/bio/rolph_thomas_8E.html.

32 *Otago Daily Times*, 19 August 1872, 2f-g.

33 *Bruce Herald*, 10 April 1872, 6d; *Wellington Independent*, 8 October 1873, 2e.

34 *Timaru Herald*, 13 July 1886, 3f; *Tuapeka Times*, 22 September 1886, 2d-e.

35 *Appendices to the Journals of the House of Representatives*, 1874, D1, p2, correspondence of Agent General, no. 2, G. Maurice O'Rorke to Agent General, 29 September 1873; *Wellington Independent*, 8 October 1873.

36 National Library of Australia, 20/3647/3, General Secretary, Commonwealth Public Service Clerical Association, to WM Hughes, Prime Minister of the Commonwealth of Australia, 17 December 1920. My thanks to Graham Hannaford, Canberra, for supplying me with these and other papers relating to Stillman.

37 National Archives of Australia, CP103/12, Bundle 10/20, Merchandise Marks Act, George Fuller, Premier of New South Wales, to SM Bruce, Prime Minister of the Commonwealth of Australia, 27 August 1923.

38 Harper, *Scotland No More?*, 63.

39 'Scotland: The Promised Land', Programme 3, 'Homes Fit For Heroes', BBC Scotland, 2016, audio recording of an interview with Lachlan MacNeill. The 'agent' to whom he referred would have been one of Andrew MacDonell's clerical collaborators: Donald MacIntyre, James Gillies or John MacMillan, all of whom accompanied the emigrants on the *Marloch*.

40 Archives New Zealand, L1, 22/1/28, Suggestions and Criticisms, Pt 2, Douglas Henderson, National Secretary, The Nationalist Party of Scotland [sic], to Sidney Holland, 18 December 1956. See also Harper, *Scotland No More?*, 166, for a fuller version of Henderson's letter.

41 Hec McMillan, quoted in Harry Martin, *Angels and Arrogant Gods: Migration Officers and Migrants Reminisce* (Canberra: Australian Government Publication Service, 1989), 52-3.

42 Quoted in Martin, *Angels and Arrogant Gods*, 54. The incident does not seem to have been recorded in either *The Scotsman* or *The Times*, both of which have been consulted for February and March 1959.

43 Interview with Cathie and Rob Tulloch, 14 August 2012, 01:54–03:45.

44 Telephone interview with Cathie and Rob Tulloch, 2 November 2010, 16:27–16:36.

45 Ibid., 03:11–03:15.

46 Ibid., Rob Tulloch, 14:15–14.20.

47 Martin, *Angels and Arrogant Gods*; National Library of Australia, Chief Migration Officers' Oral History Project. See, inter alia, https://www.youtube.com.watch?v=R1JY32qYqRN8 [date accessed 3 March 2017].

48 James Jupp (ed.), *The Australian People: An Encyclopedia of the Nation, Its People and Their Origins* (Cambridge: Cambridge University Press, 2001), 63.

49 Martin, *Angels and Arrogant Gods*, 2. See also George Kiddle interviewed by Ann-Mari Jordens in the Chief Migration Officers' oral history project, National Library of Australia, http://trove.nla.gov.au/work/33815090 [date accessed 3 March 2017]. See also Ann-Mari Jordens, *Alien to Citizen: Settling Migrants in Australia, 1945–1975* (St Leonards: Allen & Unwin, 1997).

50 Martin, *Angels and Arrogant Gods*, 12-13.

51 Ibid., 64.

52 Ibid., 63.

53 *House of Commons Parliamentary Papers* [hereafter HCPP], 1964–65, Cmnd. 2555, *Commonwealth Relations Office. Oversea Migration Board. Statistics for 1963*, tables based on International Passenger Survey. 1963, Table 1, p. 283.

54 Of course, the census figures do not take account of return migration, mortality, and individuals who did not emigrate directly from Scotland to Australia, but despite their limitations, they give a longer-term picture of migration trends than the various statistics generated in Britain. Carrier and Jeffery's survey ends in 1950, and the International Passenger Survey, which began in 1961, does not disaggregate passengers' origins. For these census statistics, see Australian Bureau of Statistics, *Census of the Commonwealth of Australia, 1911–61*; *Census of Population and Housing, 1966–71*. http://www.abs.gov.au/AUSSTATS/abs@.nsf/ViewContent?readform&viewProductsbyCatalogue&Action=Expand&Num=2.2 [date accessed 7 April 2017].

55 Australian Bureau of Statistics, Census of

Population and Housing, 1971, Bulletin 1, Summary of Population, Part 9, Birthplace, p. 2. http://www.ausstats.abs.gov.au/ausstats/free.nfs/0/b5a50c9901b6140fca25788100004ac56/$File/1971%20Census%20Bulletin%20n0%201%20-%20Summary%20of%20Population%20-%20Part%209%20AUSTRALIA.pdf [date accessed 7 April 2017].
56 Martin, *Angels and Arrogant Gods*, 53.
57 Ibid., 55.
58 Ibid., 55-6.
59 Ibid., 57-8.
60 National Library of Australia, Oral History Collection, Chief Migration Officers' oral history project, Alexander (Sandy) Fox, interviewed by Ann-Mari Jordens, 26 February 2009, track 1, 09:21-09:50.
61 Ibid., track 1, 10:43–11:11.
62 Quoted in Martin, *Angels and Arrogant Gods*, 24.
63 Interview with Sandy Fox, track 2, 00:33–00:36.
64 Ibid., track 1, 18:30–18:41.
65 Ibid., 23:11–23:25.
66 Ibid., 52:22.
67 Ibid., track 2, c. 01:05:47–01:05:52. Two of the former migration officers interviewed by Harry Martin testified to a significant loss of morale and collegiality under Whitlam's regime, as officers with practical expertise lost out to empire builders, 'high fliers... who knew nothing about immigration but had read about it in a book.' (Martin, *Angels and Arrogant Gods*, 96-7).
68 Interview with Sandy Fox, track 2, 01:05:59–01:07:28.
69 Author's interview with Gordon Ashley, 10 July 2008, Carnoustie, Angus, 00:41–03:31.
70 Ibid., 05:02–05:10.
71 Ibid., 16:04–16:24.
72 Ibid., 39:50–40:11.
73 Ibid., 16:40–16:50.
74 Ibid., 32:12; 33:43.
75 Ibid., 10:34–10:44.
76 Ibid., 24:44–25:15.
77 Ibid., 25:50–25:56.
78 Ibid., 28:23–30:00.
79 Ibid., 30:34; 30:46–31:43.
80 For Gordon's full description of a 'typical day', see Harper, *Scotland No More?*, 205 and interview, 06:35–08:29.
81 Interview with Gordon Ashley, 51:21–51:55.
82 Ibid., 23:55.
83 Ibid., 19:20–19:29.
84 Author's interview with Bob Smart, Aberdeen, 29 April 2014, 57:48–57:53.
85 Ibid., 03:56–05:09.
86 Ibid., 06:44–06:54.
87 Ibid., 18:11–19:56. For Sally Blake Hooff's reflections on the recruitment of teachers for Nova Scotia in 1957, see above, Chapter 2, 38.
88 Interview with Bob Smart, 23:40.
89 Ibid., 15:10–15:26.
90 Ibid., 13:19–14:12.
91 Ibid., 27:03–27:43.
92 Ibid., 31:27–32:00.
93 Ibid., 38:22–40:35.
94 Ibid., 33:45–34:06; 35:06–35:36.
95 Bob could not remember in which English city the office had been located, other than that it was in the Midlands.
96 Interview with Bob Smart, 10:40–12:01.
97 Ibid., 58:06–59:01.
98 01:06:24–01:06:40.

Chapter 4. Making the Transition: Leaving, Travelling and Arriving

1 Author's telephone interview with Annie MacRitchie (née Matheson), Stornoway, Isle of Lewis, 19 October 2009, 09:18. See also *Marjory Harper, Scotland No More? The Scots Who Left Scotland in the Twentieth Century* (Edinburgh: Luath, 2012), 207-8.
2 *Appendices to the Journals of the House of Representatives*, 1875, Session 1, D-01, no. 46, enclosure 3, W. Peel Nesbitt to Immigration Officer, Auckland, 31 January 1875.
3 John H Hillary, *Westland: Journal of John Hillary, emigrant to New Zealand*, 1879 (Fakenham: Acorn Editions, 1979), 4. Diary entry for 12 March 1880.
4 Eric Richards, *From Hirta to Port Phillip: the St Kilda Emigration to Australia in 1852* (Kershader, Isle of Lewis: The Islands Book Trust, 2010); Richards, 'St Kilda and Australia: emigrants at peril, 1852-3', *Scottish Historical Review*, LXXI (1992), 129-55.
5 Eric Richards, 'Highland emigrants to South Australia in the 1850s', Northern Scotland, 5 (1982–3), 1-29.
6 Donald McLeod, *Gloomy Memories in the Highlands of Scotland: versus Mrs Harriet Beecher Stowe's Sunny Memories in (England) a Foreign Land: or a faithful picture of the Extirpation of the Celtic Race from the Highlands of Scotland* (Toronto: Thompson, 1857), 164; HCPP C-3980, 1884, XXXII-XXXVI, Royal Commission of Inquiry into the Condition of the Crofters and Cottars in the Highlands and Islands of Scotland [hereafter Napier Commission], XXXI, Appendix A, p. 123.
7 Thanks to Hilary Hinton, librarian at Aberdeen Medico-Chirurgical Society, for this information.
8 Author's interview with Alec Miller, Dunedin, 29 November 2010, 12:10–12:33.
9 Author's interview with Margaret Gillies Brown, Each Inchmichael, Errol, 21 December 2012, track 2, 03:38–04:01; track 1, 25:05–25:09; 25:50–26:33.
10 Author's interview with Bob Smart, Aberdeen, 29 April 2014, 46:26–47:08.
11 Reverend Arthur Morris Russell, interviewed by Steve Schwinghamer, 16 May 2006, Our Canadian Stories, catalogue no. 06.05.16, Canadian Museum of Immigration at Pier 21, Halifax, Nova Scotia.
12 Author's telephone interview with Sally Blake Hooff, Kensington, Prince Edward Island, 30 March 2017, 17:33–1743.
13 Author's interview with Ena Macdonald, Bayhead, North Uist, 7 September 2011, track 2, 26:14–26:24.
14 Author's telephone interview with Katrine McLean, Auckland, New Zealand, 3 November, 2010, track 1, 11:57–12:06.
15 Email from Alison McNair to author, 10 February 2016.
16 Author's interview with Sheena Coyne (née McBean), Inverness, 12 November 2014, 10:35–11:10.
17 Author's interview with Shona Howarth (née Morrison), Culbokie, Ross-shire, 13 June 2014, 10:25–10:34.
18 Interview with Margaret Gillies Brown, track 2, 09:40–10:24.
19 Interview with Ena Macdonald, track 2, 29:42–29:50.
20 Telephone interview with Annie MacRitchie, 43:54.
21 See, for instance, the *Inverness Journal* of 22 March 1811, which advertised a 'well-armed' vessel about to sail from Stornoway to Prince Edward Island.

22 National Library of Australia, MS 1412, diary of the Reverend Mr Tait, 1837.
23 See below, 206.
24 Author's telephone interview with Cathie and Rob Tulloch, Whangarei, New Zealand, 2 November 2010, track 1, 25:51–26:30.
25 Library and Archives Canada, MG24 I 193, Diary of Charles Robertson, 27, 28, 30 April, 3 May 1846.
26 National Library of Scotland, Acc. 12493, Diary of Margaret Whyte, 4 February 1922.
27 Author's interview with Cathy Timperley (née Donald), Dunedin, 30 November 2010, 08:45–10:13. See also Harper, *Scotland No More?*, 208-9.
28 Author's face-to-face interview with Annie MacRitchie (née Matheson), Stornoway, Isle of Lewis, 6 September 2011, 12:42.
29 Interview with Ena Macdonald, track 2, 30:59–31:07.
30 Interview with Shona Howarth, 06:44–07:16.
31 Author's telephone interview with Morag Bennett (née MacLeod), Sechelt, British Columbia, 21 February 2005, 04:19–04:34; 05:29–05:51.
32 Author's interview with Calum, Cathie, and Chrissie Murray, Shader, Isle of Lewis, 25 February 2005; 06:28–06:35; 06:56–07:15; 11:38–11:41.
33 Minnie Anne Macdonald (née Fraser), interviewed by Sandra Train, Bayview House, Thurso, 17 July 1996, track 1, 12:49–12:55.
34 Author's interview with Sandra Train, Halladale, Sutherland, 5 November 2010, 06:19–06:57; email communication with Sandra Train, 12 February 2016.
35 See, for instance, National Library of New Zealand, Alexander Turnbull Library, MS Papers 1678, diary of Jane Findlayson, 1876.
36 Church of Scotland, CH1/2/359, Report of the Church and Nation Committee, 1926: Appendix on Irish Immigration and Scottish Emigration.
37 Author's interview with Agnes McGilvray (née Lawrie), West Kilbride, 18 July 2009, track 7, 03:06–03:32.
38 Telephone interview with Annie MacRitchie, 11:39–12:34.
39 Author's interview with Les Ford, Aberdeen, 25 January 2012, 05:00–05:16.
40 Interview with Alec Miller, 15:33–15:40.
41 Interview with Katrine McLean, track 1, 12:19–12:32.
42 Interview with Ena Macdonald, track two, 30:15–30:48.
43 Telephone interview with Cathie and Rob Tulloch, track 1, 21:38–21:54.
44 Author's interview with John and Catherine MacPherson, Edinburgh, 30 May 2016, 21:49. Catherine speaking.
45 Interview with John and Catherine MacPherson, 18:53–20:26. John speaking.
46 CL, NMM, OSN/12/6, voyage reports and logs of the *Ormonde*, voyage 64, April to July 1949, surgeon's report.
47 Interview with Margaret Gillies Brown, track 2, 11:17–11:22.
48 Marjory Harper, *Adventurers and Exiles: The Great Scottish Exodus* (London: Profile, 2003), 226.
49 N Patricia Edwards, interviewed by Cassidy Bankson, 13 December 2010, Canadian Museum of Immigration at Pier 21, Oral History Collection, 10.12.13PE; Helen Whetstone, interviewed by Amy Coleman, 21 June 2001, Canadian Museum of Immigration at Pier 21, Oral History Collection, 01.06.21HW.
50 Jock Baird (pseudonym), Toowoomba, Queensland, interviewed by Kirstie Moar, 20 January 2016, 35:48–36:16.
51 Caird Library, National Maritime Museum, OSN/12/1, no. 12, captain's report on the voyage of the *Orion*, Gravesend to Sydney and back, September to December 1947. The comment was actually made in respect of the return voyage.
52 CL, NMM, OSN/12/6, voyage reports and logs of the *Ormonde*, voyage 72, September to December 1951, Staff Commander's Report.
53 CL, NMM, OSN/12/9, voyage reports and logs of the *Orion*, voyage 62, 1962, Reports by Staff Commander and Captain.
54 CL, NMM, OSN/12/1, voyage reports and logs of the *Orion*, voyage 11, 1947, newspaper clippings, *Herald*, 4 July 1947.
55 Interview with Cathy Timperley, 11:40–12:05; author's interview with Brian Coutts, Dunedin, 30 November 2010, 10:20–10:58.
56 CL, NMM, OSN/12/6, voyage reports and logs of the *Ormonde*, voyage 70, February to May 1951, staff commander's and purser's reports.
57 Author's interview with Gladys Morrice (née Keir), Aberdeen, 4 December 2014, track 2, 00:00–01:38.
58 Interview with Cathy Timperley, 12:18–13:08.
59 Ibid., 14:17–14:30.
60 Interview with Alec Miller, 13:24–14:00.
61 Interview with Brian Coutts 08:25–09:02.
62 Author's interview with Gail Gilmour (née Anderson), Dunedin, 26 November 2010, track 1, 03:59–04:26.
63 Interview with Ena Macdonald, track 2, 31:10–32:23.
64 According to a New Zealand maritime website, the delay was caused by a fault in the high pressure turbine in both the port and starboard engines http://www.nzmaritime.co.nz/nstar.htm [date accessed 17 January 2018].
65 Author's interview with Helen Campbell, Dunedin, 1 December 2010, track 1, 13:00–13:12.
66 Interview with Shona Howarth, 07:48–08:00.
67 Author's face-to-face interview with Cathie and Rob Tulloch, Kintore, Aberdeenshire, 14 August 2012, 08:13–08:35.
68 Author's interview with Murdo MacPherson, Dornoch, Sutherland, 18 January 2017, track 1, 02:45, 03:40; 04:10–04:29.
69 Marilyn Barber and Murray Watson, *Invisible Immigrants. The English in Canada since 1945* (Winnipeg: University of Manitoba Press, 2015), 94.
70 House of Commons Parliamentary Papers [hereafter HCPP], 1963-64, Cmnd. 2217, Commonwealth Relations Office. Oversea Migration Board. Statistics for 1962, tables based on International Passenger Survey. 1962, Table 4, 155, 'Scottish Emigration; HCPP, 1964-65, Cmnd. 2555, Commonwealth Relations Office. Oversea Migration Board. Statistics for 1963, tables based on International Passenger Survey. 1963, Table 4, 109.
71 Author's interview with Alison McNair (née Gibson), Kintore, Aberdeenshire, 12 September 2005, track 1, 19:33–20:45.
72 Email from Joan Noble to author, 22 July 2013.
73 Author's interview with Moira Campbell, Aberdeen, 9 February 2017, 13:19–13:58.
74 Author's interview with Cameron Tallach, Breakish, Isle of Skye, 10 April 2017, track 1, 13:47-14:39.
75 Author's interview with Angus Pelham Burn, Dess, Aberdeenshire, 6 April 2010, 02:43–05:36.
76 Author's interview with John and Nellie Wallace, Aberdeen, 24 April 2010, 14:21–16:20.
77 Margaret Crapnell (née Harvey), Brisbane, Queensland,

interviewed by Kirstie Moar, 18 January 2016, track 1, 23:22–24:24.

78 Helen Bourne (née Bowie), Springfield Lakes, Queensland, interviewed by Kirstie Moar, 17 December 2015, 00:43–02:25.

79 Interview with Alec Miller, 57:26; 59:25.

80 Peter Morton Coan, Ellis Island Interviews. *In Their Own Words* (New York, 1997), 136-7.

81 Ellis Island Oral History Project, interview NPS-149, Tom Allan, interviewed by Jean Kolva, 16 July 1984.

82 Telephone interview with Annie MacRitchie, 13:09–13:38.

83 Ibid., 14:02–14:15.

84 Interview with Margaret Gillies Brown, track 2, 17:39–17:47.

85 Margaret Gillies Brown, *Far from the Rowan Tree* (Glendaruel, Argyll: Argyll Publishing, 1997), 21.

86 Robert Louis Stevenson, *From Scotland to Silverado* (Cambridge, Mass: John Harvard Library, 1966), 12, 100.

87 Ibid., 127, 133-7.

88 *Their Dreams, Our Memories. A History of Duck Lake and District*, volume 1 (Duck Lake, Sask: Duck Lake History Committee, 1988), 284.

89 Saskatchewan Archives Board, A802, William Craig Papers, 'Rough Notes by the way. Narrative of a journey from Scotland to the North West Territory, Dominion of Canada', 14 July 1883. See also *Their Dreams, Our Memories*, 283-4.

90 'Rough Notes', 27 June 1883.

91 Ibid.

92 Ibid., 7 July 1883.

93 Saskatchewan Archives Board Questionnaires, no. 2, Pioneer Experiences: A General Questionnaire [hereafter SAQ], Box 10, 1906: McManus, Margaret.

94 SAQ, Box 9, 1906: Craig, George.

95 For examples, see Marjory Harper, 'Probing the pioneer questionnaires: British settlement in Saskatchewan, 1887–1914', *Saskatchewan History*, 52: 2 (Fall 2000), 28-46.

96 Interview with Morag Bennett, 11:06.

97 Interview with Calum, Cathie and Chrissie Murray, 13:17.

98 Interview with Margaret Gillies Brown, track 2, 20:19–20:27.

99 Gillies Brown, *Far from the Rowan Tree*, 24.

100 Author's telephone interview with Easton Vance, Thetis Island, British Columbia, 9 July 2008, track 1, 10:54–11:00.

Chapter 5. Building New Lives: Impressions and Experiences

1 Author's face-to-face interview with Annie MacRitchie (née Matheson), Stornoway, Isle of Lewis, 6 September 2011, 24:57.

2 Author's interview with Colin Tait, Hong Kong, 1 February 2017, track 1, 09:93.

3 See, inter alia, letter from 'Tom' in Dunedin in *John O'Groat Journal*, 22 April 1849. 'I like the climate very much. It is like home, but rather warmer.'

4 William Wallace, My Dear Maggie: *Letters from a Western Manitoba Pioneer*, edited by Kenneth S Coates and William R. Morrison (Regina, Sask., 1991), pp. 20-22, letter dated 29 June 1881.

5 *Scottish Highlander*, 17 February 1887, 2b.

6 Saskatchewan Archives Questionnaires [hereafter SAQ], no. 2, Pioneer Experiences: A General Questionnaire, Box 4, 1892: Wood, Robert Golder.

7 Ibid., Box 6, 1903: Veitch, Andrew M.; Box 1, 1883: Macdonald, Norman.

8 Author's interview with Charles Macdonald, Carinish, North Uist, 8 September 2011, 02:23.

9 Author's interview with Anne Lynas Shah, Edinburgh, 10 January 2006, 14:02–14:04; 15:01.

10 Author's telephone interview with AM, Halifax, Nova Scotia, 17 November 2011, 39:17–40:02.

11 Author's interview with Edwin Millar, Ottawa, 9 November 2011, 32:33–32.50.

12 Author's interview with Rachel Minton, Dunedin, 29 November 2010, 08:07–08:40.

13 Author's telephone interview with Morag Bennett (née MacLeod), Sechelt, British Columbia, 21 February 2005, 10:56. See also Scottish Catholic Archives, DA9/26 Father RA MacDonell, OSB, 'British Immigration Schemes in Alberta', Stavelock Lumber Company.

14 Margaret Gillies Brown, *Far from the Rowan Tree* (Glendaruel, Argyll: Argyll Publishing, 1998), 40.

15 Author's interview with Margaret Gillies Brown, East Inchmichael, Errol, 21 December 2012, track 2, 19:37–20:00.

16 Gillies Brown, *Far from the Rowan Tree*, 25, 31, 32, 11.

17 Ibid., 40, 43.

18 Margaret Crapnell (née Harvey), Brisbane, Queensland, interviewed by Kirstie Moar, 18 January 2016, 30:47–31:07.

19 Bob Crapnell, Brisbane, Queensland, interviewed by Kirstie Moar, 18 January 2016, 48:21–48:56.

20 Bob Crapnell, 54:57.

21 Margaret Crapnell, 35:29–36:24.

22 Helen Bourne (née Bowie), Springfield Lakes, Queensland, interviewed by Kirstie Moar, 17 December 2015, track 2, 12:38–12:50.

23 Helen Bourne, track 1, 29:23–30:24.

24 Author's interview with Matthew Lynas, Aberdeen, 5 December 2014, track 1, 00:53, 10:54–11:16; track 2, 43:00–43:15. Matthew's recollection of a temperature of 130 Fahrenheit is not confirmed by the statistics, which indicate a record high of just under 120 Fahrenheit in Birdsville, Channel Country.

25 Author's Skype interview with Alice Moffatt, Auburn, NSW, but in Kiltarlity, Inverness-shire, 5 August 2014, 03:19–03:54.

26 Author's interview with Shona Howarth (née Morrison), Culbokie, Ross-shire, 13 June 2014, 13:18–13:21; 01:04:34–01:04:46.

27 Interview with Matthew Lynas, track 21:19–22:35.

28 Author's interview with Sheena Coyne (née McBean), Inverness, 12 November 2014, 29:19–30:57.

29 Author's interview with James Mackenzie, Toowoomba, Queensland, 2 June 2015, 04:04–04:30.

30 Ibid., 06:47–07:03.

31 Author's interview with Moira Campbell, Aberdeen, 9 February 2017, 21:41.

32 Author's interview with Gladys Morrice (née Keir), Aberdeen, 4 December 2014, 27:12–29:50.

33 Author's interview with Carrol and Brian Stewart, Craigellachie, 9 April 2012, 27:29–32:20. The fly's eggs, laid in clothing hanging out to dry, hatch on contact with human skin. The larvae burrow into the flesh and develop into maggots, creating abscesses in the human host, a condition known as myiasis.

34 Author's interview with Brian Stewart, Craigellachie, 9 April 2012, 01:25:17–01:25:21.

35 Ibid., 02:53:46–02:55:42.

36 SAQ, no. 2, Box 6, 1906: Allan, John Macdonald.
37 *Stonehaven Journal*, 13 March 1873, 3e. Elspet's recommendations should be taken with a pinch of salt, as she was promoting New Brunswick's so-called 'Scotch Colony', which was launched in Spring 1873 by William Brown, a native of Stonehaven. For details of the settlement, and the controversy that surrounded it, see Marjory Harper, 'A family affair: the colonisation of New Kincardineshire', *History Today*, 37, October 1987, 42-8.
38 Author's interview with John and Marion Nelson and Trish Botten (daughter), Aignish, Isle of Lewis, 7 September 2012, track 1, 29:40–30:25.
39 Author's telephone interview with Alan Blair, Halifax, Nova Scotia, 12 January 2006, 08:53–10:26.
40 Ibid., 20:33–21:56.
41 Author's Skype interview with Peter Bevan-Baker, Hampton, Prince Edward Island, 29:19–31:37.
42 Author's telephone interview with Greig Macleod, Halifax, Nova Scotia, 13 January 2006, 11:35–12:35
43 Author's interview with Agnes McGilvray (née Lawrie), West Kilbride, 18 July 2009, track 3, 31:22–31:29.
44 Minnie Anne Macdonald (née Fraser), interviewed by Sandra Train (her daughter), Bayview House, Thurso, 17 July 1996, 18:20, 25:50.
45 Interview with Annie MacRitchie, 6 September 2011, track 2, 0:00–08:55.
46 See below, 149.
47 Interview with Margaret Gillies Brown, track 3, 04:12–04:16.
48 Gillies Brown, *Far from the Rowan Tree*, 83-4; interview with Margaret Gillies Brown, track 3, 14:12–16:19.
49 Author's interview with Roddy Campbell, Inverness, 8 October 2010, 32:21–33:45.
50 Author's video interview with John Black, 'The Emigrant Experience', University of Aberdeen, Department of Medical Illustration, 95c/012, 1995. The Grey Cup is the championship game of the Canadian Football League. It was also mentioned by Edwin Millar, who remembered it being on television when he arrived in Edmonton in 1980.
51 Author's interview with Brian Coutts, Dunedin, 30 November 2010, 12:41–14:56; 33:25–35:05. After two weeks in the Ocean View 'bach', the family moved to rented accommodation in Dunedin, where they stayed for six months before moving south to Invercargill.
52 A James Hammerton and Alistair Thomson, *Ten Pound Poms: Australia's Invisible Migrants* (Manchester: Manchester University Press, 2005), Chapter 5, '"Butlins without the laughs": life on the hostel'.
53 Meredith Walker, 'First accommodation for migrants arriving in Wollongong post World War 2', Wollongong's Migration Heritage Thematic Study, 'Places Project', 7. http://www.mhpillawarra.com/docs/places_accommodation_essay.pdf [date accessed 17 January 2018]. The Berkeley hostel, one of three migrant workers' hostels in Wollangong, closed in 1969 and was demolished a year later.
54 Author's interview with Sandra Munro, Ullapool, 26 March 2009, 02:11–04:32.
55 Walker, 'First accommodation', 31.
56 Interview with Sandra Munro, 04:44–04:48. See also Beryl Fletcher (nee Child), http://www.migrationheritage.nsw.gov.au/exhibition/belongings/fletcher/index.html [date accessed 17 January 2018].
57 Margaret Crapnell, track 1, 37:31–38:56.
58 Interview with Shona Howarth, 13:31-13:32; 17:13-17:23.
59 Ibid., 13:48; 14:42–14:55.
60 https://southaustralianhistory.com.au/hostel.htm [date accessed 17 January 2018].
61 Jock Baird (pseudonym), Toowoomba, Queensland, interviewed by Kirstie Moar, 20 January 2016, 40:22.
62 Author's interview with Paddy McFarlane, Dunedin, 28 November 2010, 09:00–10:00.
63 Interview with Annie MacRitchie, 6 September 2011, 03:34–04:02.
64 Interview with Margaret Gillies Brown, track 2, 245:05–25:01.
65 Author's telephone interview with Katrine McLean, Auckland, 3 November 2010, track 1, 06:17–07:28. See also, above, Chapter 2, 31, for Alec Miller's similar experience in Dunedin eight years earlier.
66 Author's interview with Helen Campbell, Dunedin, 1 December 2010, track 1, 18:40–19:36. See also Harper, *Scotland No More? The Scots Who Left Scotland in the Twentieth Century* (Edinburgh: Luath, 2012), 212-13.
67 Author's telephone interview with Joe and Janet Blair, Sarnia, Ontario, 10 February 2006, 12:39–12:57.
68 Interview with Moira Campbell, 30:10–30:23.
69 Email from David Knight to author, 13 February 2017.
70 Email from Alison Inglis to author, 20 February 2017. Response to questionnaire.
71 Author's telephone interview with Morag Bennett (née MacLeod), Sechelt, British Columbia, 21 February 2005, 37:46.
72 Author's interview with Calum, Cathie and Chrissie Murray, Shader, Isle of Lewis, 25 February 2005, Cathie speaking, 22:08–22:54.
73 Ibid., Calum speaking, 24:06.
74 http://www.teara.govt.nz/en/biographies/1m1/macandrew-james [date accessed 1 September 2016].
75 Interview with Helen Campbell, track 1, 23:06–23:14.
76 Author's interview with Cathy Timperley (née Donald), Dunedin, 30 November 2010, 25:41–25:46; 27:12–27:16; 28:20–28:34.
77 Interview with Brian Coutts, 17:34–21:20.
78 Author's interview with Alison Thornton, Dunedin, 30 November 2010, 33:49–35:25.
79 Interview with Katrine McLean, track 1, 18:13–19:09.
80 Helen Bourne, track 2, 27:48–29:16.
81 Margaret Crapnell, 39:15–40:16.
82 Interview with Roddy Campbell, 02:12–03:57. The High Arrow Dam was in fact completed in 1968 and renamed the Hugh Keenleyside Dam in 1969.
83 Interview with Roddy Campbell, 35:25–35:29; 16:01; 16:40–17:11.
84 Author's interview with William Gillespie, Dunedin, 26 November 2010, 10:21–10:47; 05:49–06:47.
85 Author's interview with Charlie Boyle, Toowoomba, Queensland, 2 June 2015, track 1, 05:46–06:49.
86 Ibid., 24:28–24:41.
87 Interview with AM, 07:53–08:38.
88 Ibid., 11:46–12:15.
89 Ibid., 41:20–42:19.
90 Author's telephone interview with Annie MacRitchie (née Matheson), 19 October 2009, 04:37–04:41; face-to-face interview with Annie MacRitchie, 6 September 2011, 00:23–01:05.
91 Author's telephone interview with Jim Russell, Vancouver, 8 December 2007, track 1, 12:05–13:58.
92 Author's interview with Alison McNair (née Gibson), Kintore, Aberdeenshire, 12 September 2005, track 2, 22:09–22:14; 22:28–22:32; 22:50–22:54.

93 Interview with Joe and Janet Blair, 13:25–13:52.
94 Interview with Greig Macleod, 13:15–14:30.
95 Interview with Anne Lynas Shah, 17:30.
96 Email from Edwin Millar to author, 11 November 2011.
97 Interview with Matthew Lynas, track 2, 05:10–05:47.
98 Interview with Sandra Munro, 13:27–13:32.
99 Interview with Shona Howarth, 57:15–58:35.
100 Author's interview with James Mackenzie, Toowoomba, Queensland, 2 June 2015, 07:26–07:41; 08:22–08:51.
101 Author's interview with Alec Miller, Dunedin, 29 November 2010, 35:26, 42:05.
102 Author's interview with Paddy McFarlane, Dunedin, 28 November 2010, 27:10–28:10; 28:21–28:30.
103 SRH Jones, *Doing Well and Doing Good. Ross and Glendining. Scottish Enterprise in New Zealand* (Dunedin: Otago University Press, 2010).
104 Author's interview with AS, Dunedin, 29 November 2010, 06:38–06:45; 09:37–09:40.
105 Author's interview with Rachel Minton, Dunedin, 29 November 2010, 02:16–02:25; 06:00–06:16; 17:40–17:45.
106 Email from Alison Inglis to author, 20 February 2017.
107 *Scottish Highlander*, 17 February 1887, 2b.
108 Author's telephone interview with Cathie and Rob Tulloch, Whangerei, New Zealand, 2 November 2010, track 1, 20:30–20:40.
109 Interview with Margaret Gillies Brown, track 2, 28:55–29:41.
110 Interview with Charlie Boyle, track 1, 29:00–35:30.
111 Interview with James Mackenzie, 17:55–18:17.
112 Author's interview with Gail Gilmour (née Anderson), Dunedin, 26 November 2010, track 1, 07:47–09:16.
113 Interview with Brian Coutts, 14:48–15:25.
114 Ibid., 35:20–36:14.
115 See above, Chapter 4, 96.
116 Author's interview with John and Catherine MacPherson, Edinburgh, 30 May 2016, 53:21-56:30.
117 Author's interview with Billy and Elizabeth Graham, Edinburgh, 30 May 2016, track 2, 47:10–48:15. Elizabeth speaking.
118 Ibid., 45:42–46:27. Billy speaking.
119 Interview with Charlie Boyle, track 1, 37:15–37:19; 38:57.
120 Interview with Morag Bennett, 22:56.

Chapter 6. Migrant Identities: Retention, Reconfiguration and Abandonment

1 Author's interview with Elvira Gonnella Welch, Halifax, NS, 1 November 2011, 41:26–41:28; 42:45–42:50
2 Bob Crapnell, interviewed by Kirstie Moar, Brisbane, 18 January 2016, 42:00–42:06.
3 Johnson's *Journey to the Western Islands of Scotland*, and Boswell's *Journal of a Tour to the Hebrides with Samuel Johnson*, edited by RW Chapman (Oxford: Oxford University Press, 1984), 87, 119.
4 Author's Skype interview with Peter Bevan-Baker, Prince Edward Island, 20 September 2016, 16:55–17:26.
5 Author's telephone interview with Anne McCallum, Prince Edward Island, 28 September 2016, track 1, 44:16–44:43.
6 Author's interview with Sheena Coyne (née McBean), 12 November 2014, 44:50–45:12.
7 James Thomson, *For Friends at Home: An Emigrant's Letters from Canada, California and the Cariboo, 1844–1864*, edited by Richard Preston (Montreal: McGill-Queen's University Press, 1974), 297.
8 David Laing to his sister, 19 February 1873, quoted in Charlotte Erickson, *Invisible Immigrants: The Adaptation of English and Scottish Immigrants in Nineteenth-century* America (Ithaca, NY: Cornell University Press, 1990), 362.
9 Marjory Harper, 'Missing Emigrants: Gleanings from Petitions Presented under the Presumption of Life Limitation (Scotland) Acts', *Scottish Archives*, 22 (2016), 17-38.
10 Author's interview with Moira Campbell, Aberdeen, 9 February 2017, 07:33–07:37; 07:50–07:59.
11 Ibid., 37:00–37:19.
12 See above, Chapter 1, 13-14.
13 Author's interview with Annie MacRitchie, Stornoway, 6 September 2011, track 2, 33:39–34:43. See also above, Chapter 1, 14.
14 Author's interview with Marilyn MacRitchie (née Thomson), Stornoway, 6 September 2011, track 2, 34:46–35:30.
15 Author's interview with Cathie and Rob Tulloch, Kintore, 14 August 2012, 19:20–20:00.
16 Author's interview with John and Catherine MacPherson, Edinburgh, 30 May 2016, 34:05. When their three children were born, the news was sent to Scotland by telegram.
17 Author's interview with Billy and Elizabeth Graham, Edinburgh, 30 May 2016, track 2, 01:11:01-01:11:41.
18 Interview with Elvira Gonnella Welch, 13:45–14:18.
19 Marjory Harper, *Scotland No More? The Scots Who Left Scotland in the 20th Century* (Edinburgh: Luath, 2012), 154.
20 Author's interview with David Knight, Hong Kong, 31 January 2017, track 2, 13:38–14:49.
21 Ibid., 16:26–16:58; 17:12–17:38.
22 See, inter alia, Saskatchewan Archives Questionnaires [hereafter SAQ], no. 2, Pioneer Experiences: A General Questionnaire, Box 12, 1909: Keslick, Mrs Frank. In answer to the question, 'What were your reasons for coming west?', she responded, 'To establish a home in a new country'. In answer to a later question about the response of those left behind, she recalled that 'our relatives were sorry to see us leave the old home Scotland'.
23 Author's interview with Cameron Tallach, Breakish, Isle of Skye, 10 April 2017, track 1, 16:54–16:56; track 2, 55:20–55:45. Cameron commented, 'It was as if my brain hadn't accepted that there were different ways of expressing things.'
24 Ibid., track 1, 17:34–17:59.
25 Interview with John and Catherine MacPherson, 01:54:31–01:55:15. 'Mish kids' are part of the wider category known as 'TCKs' (Three Culture Kids).
26 Interview with Billy and Elizabeth Graham, track 2, 01:14:54–01:15:47.
27 Ibid., 22:19–23:07.
28 Ibid., 01:16:14–01:19:37.
29 Sir Roger Lobo (1923–2015) moved from Macau to Hong Kong in 1945 and had a distinguished career in public service. His Scottish great-grandfather had worked for the East India Company. Author's interview with Ken and Isabel Morrison, Hong Kong, 30 January 2017, 27:06. http://macaudailytimes.com.mo/macau-born-roger-lobo-dies-at-91.html [date accessed 13 February 2017].
30 For details of Ken's career, see http://www.mazars.com/Users/Our-team/Kenneth-Morrison

[date accessed 13 February 2017].
31 Interview with Ken and Isabel Morrison, 53:58–54:27.
32 Email from Colin Tait to author, 7 February 2017.
33 Author's interview with Calum, Cathie and Chrissie Murray, Shader, Isle of Lewis, 25 February 2005, 01:01:27-01:01:46.
34 Interview with John and Catherine MacPherson, 01:07:30–01:08:01.The school was handed over to a local Board of Governors in 2012.
35 Interview with John and Catherine MacPherson, 01:10:12–01:11:37.
36 Author's interview with Les Ford, Aberdeen, 25 January 2012, 53:46–56:36.
37 Author's interview with Alison McNair (née Gibson), Kintore, Aberdeenshire, 12 September 2006, track 2, 11:28–11:33; 11:46–11:50; 12:39–12:41.
38 Interview with Marilyn MacRitchie, track 2, 31:19–31.27; 32:46.
39 Interview with Annie MacRitchie, track 2, 30:41–31:20; 31:29–32:32.
40 Author's interview with Cathy Timperley (née Donald), Dunedin, 30 November 2010, 37:40–38:08; 54:20.
41 Ibid., 47:49–50:30.
42 Author's interview with Rachel Minton, Dunedin, 29 November 2010, 21:27–22:35.
43 Author's interview with Brian Coutts, Dunedin, 30 November 2010, 21:33–21:56.
44 Author's interview with AS, Dunedin, 29 November 2010, 16:12–16:30.
45 Alan Lawrie, interviewed by Rob Linn for the Scots in Australia pilot oral history project, Brighton, South Australia, 9 October 2013, file 3, 01:02:25.
46 Interview with Peter Bevan-Baker, 11:40–12:41.
47 Helen Bourne (née Bowie), interviewed by Kirstie Moar, 17 December 2015, track 2, 31:46–33:25.
48 Author's interview with Murdo MacPherson, Dornoch, 18 January 2017, track 2, 10:50–12:16.
49 Interview with Anne McCallum, track 1, 16:10–17:05.
50 Author's interview with Alison Thornton, Dunedin, 30 November 2010, 31:37–32:25. Glenorchy is the small settlement in Central Otago where the Thorntons spent their holidays.
51 Author's telephone interview with AM, Halifax, Nova Scotia, 17 November 2011, 43:50–44:10.
52 Author's interview with Charlie Boyle, Toowoomba, Queensland, 2 June 2015, track 2, 35:04–35:21.
53 Margaret Crapnell (née Harvey), Brisbane, interviewed by Kirstie Moar, 18 January 2016, track 1, 59:21–59:39.
54 Bob Crapnell, 39:35–40:02.
55 Margaret Crapnell, 59:11.
56 Author's interview with Sandra Munro, Ullapool, 26 March 2009, 13:27; 23:24–23:30.
57 Author's telephone interview with Alan Blair, Halifax, Nova Scotia, 12 January 2006, 38:58–39:31.
58 Author's interview with Isobel Bouman (née Gillon), Dunedin, 29 November 2010, 15:05–15:11.
59 Ibid., 15:04–16:30.
60 Robert Louis Stevenson, *The Silverado Squatters* (New York: Scribner, 1899), 41. https://babel.hathitrust.org/cgi/pt?id=hvd.32044086812294;view=1up;seq=9 [date accessed 9 March 2017].
61 Interview with Cathy Timperley, 55:15–56:08.
62 Jock Baird (pseudonym), Toowoomba, Queensland, interviewed by Kirstie Moar, 20 January 2016, 56:11.
63 Author's interview with James Mackenzie, Toowoomba, Queensland, 2 June 2015, 25:35–25:45.
64 Interview with Charlie Boyle, 28:50–29:20.
65 Ibid., 32:44, 33:44.
66 Author's interview with Allan Bruce, Toowoomba, Queensland, 2 June 2015, track 3, 13:31.
67 Interview with Anne McCallum, track 1, 25:38–25:57; 32:08–32:17.
68 Ibid., 33:00–34:13.
69 Interview with Peter Bevan-Baker, 21:28–22:46.
70 Author's telephone interview with Sally Blake Hooff, Kensington, Prince Edward Island, 30 March 2017, 32:25–32:29; 32:51–32:54.
71 Ibid., 29:04; 30:24.
72 Author's telephone interview with Alan Blair, Halifax, Nova Scotia, 12 April 2017, track 2, 0015–01:28.
73 Email from Alison Inglis to author, 20 February 2017.
74 http://www.scmp.com/news/hong-kong/politics/article/1937727/beijing-frets-pro-independence-movement-could-worsen-or [date accessed 13 February 2017].
75 Interview with Ken Morrison, 35:05–35:45.
76 Author's telephone interview with Morag Bennett (née MacLeod), 21 February 2006, 13:44–13:48.
77 Interview with Alan Blair, 12 January 2006, 10:39–11:40.
78 Author's telephone interview with Joe and Janet Blair, 12 February 2006, 11:48–12:11.
79 Interview with Alan Blair, 12 January 2006, 12:50–13:22.
80 Interview with Joe and Janet Blair, 11:34–11:42.
81 Author's interview with Isla and Hamish Robertson, Vancouver, 7 December 2007, 36:24–37:05.
82 Helen Bourne, track 2, 30:17–30:47.
83 Interview with Brian Coutts, 19:12–19:46.
84 See above, Chapter 5, 173, 174.
85 Interview with Ken Morrison, 59:35–01:00.
86 Author's interview with Graham McGregor, Dunedin, 26 November 2010, 28:33–28:38.
87 Ibid., 13:54–14:35.
88 Ibid., 16:00–16:58.
89 Ibid., 17:53–18:02.
90 Ibid., 12:33–12:48; 13:07–13:36; 19:27–20:07.
91 Interview with Graham McGregor; 18:41–18:54; interview with Isobel Bouman, 22:47–22:51.
92 Interview with Cathie and Rob Tulloch, 33:20–33:53.
93 Interview with Anne McCallum, 14:08–14:50.
94 Interview with Peter Bevan-Baker, 42:14–42:53.
95 Author's telephone interview with Katherine Anne MacLeod, Winnipeg, 8 February 2011, 16:21–17:35.
96 The quote is from Elena Fiddian-Qasmiyeh's review of *Diaspora and Transnationalism: Concepts, Theories and Methods*, edited by Rainer Bauböck and Thomas Faist (Amsterdam: IMISCOE Research/Amsterdam University Press, 2010), in *International Affairs*, 87: 2, 2011, 176-7.
97 Margaret Bennett, *Oatmeal and the Catechism. Scottish Gaelic Settlers in Quebec* (Edinburgh and Montreal: McGill-Queen's University Press, 1998).
98 Bennett, *Oatmeal and the Catechism*, 277.
99 For further discussion of food culture, see Anje Merkies, 'Cookbooks as Sources of Scottish-Canadian Identity, 1845–1934', *The Great Lakes Journal of Undergraduate History*, 2: 1 (2014), 21-38.
100 See above, Chapter 5, 138.
101 Interview with Marilyn and Annie MacRitchie, Stornoway, Lewis, 6 September 2011, 04:38–09:32.
102 Author's interview with Ena Macdonald, Kyles, Bayhead, North Uist, 7 September 2011, track 2: 28:07.
103 Interview with Graham McGregor, 28:05–28:10.
104 Author's interview with Gladys Morrice (née Keir), Aberdeen, 4 December 2014, track 1, 25:58; author's interview with Gavin McEwen and Aileen McEwen,

Aberdeen, 21 February 2013, track 1 (Aileen), 11:15–22:56; track 2 (Gavin), 00:10–05:50.

105 Author's unrecorded Skype conversation with Alan Macdonald, former Chieftain of the St Andrew's Society of Hong Kong, 14 February 2017.

106 Marjory Harper, *Adventurers and Exiles: The Great Scottish Exodus* (London: Profile, 2003), 353.

107 Ralph Connor, *The Man from Glengarry: A Tale of the Ottawa* (Toronto: McClelland & Stewart, 2009); *Sir Andrew Macphail, The Master's Wife* (Charlottetown: Institute of Island Studies, 1994).

108 *Reports on the Schemes of the Church of Scotland, with the Legislative Acts passed by the General Assembly, Colonial Committee Report, 1920.*

109 Bob Crapnell, 15:15–15:32; Helen Bourne, track 2, 34:55–35:05; 47:59–48:28.

110 Author's telephone interview with Annie MacRitchie, Stornoway, 19 October 2009, 49:37–50:00; Harper, *Scotland No More?*, 226.

111 Johnson, *A Journey to the Western Islands of Scotland*, 87.

112 Interview with Gladys Morrice, 20:53–21:43.

113 Interview with Aileen McEwen, 21 February 2013, 11:14–12:32.

114 Ibid., 15:57–17:00.

115 Interview with Ken Morrison, 19:36–22:03. For a detailed account of James Legge's career, see Marilyn Bowman, *James Legge and the Chinese Classics: a brilliant Scot in the turmoil of Hong Kong* (Victoria, BC, FriesenPress, 2016).

116 http://digital.lib.sfu.ca/soh-21/interview-murdo-macivor-1-2 [date accessed 17 January 2018]. Murdo was interviewed for a total of almost six hours.

117 Author's telephone interview with Murdo MacIver, Vancouver, 7 December 2007; author's face-to-face interviews with Murdo MacIver, 22 May 2012, 24 June 2013.

118 Interview with Murdo MacIver, 24 June 2013, 08:52–09:42.

119 Jim Russell, interviewed by Harry McGrath and Ron Sutherland, Vancouver, 11 May 2004. http://digital.lib.sfu.ca/soh-6/interview-james-russell-interview [date accessed 27 February 2017]. The total interview time was six hours and 38 minutes.

120 Harper, *Scotland No More?* 221, 227.

121 Author's telephone interview with Jim Russell, Vancouver, 8 December 2007, 18:23–18:41.

122 Interview with Isla and Hamish Robertson, 22:41–23:33.

123 Interview with John and Catherine MacPherson. 43:08–43:20; John M MacPherson, *At the Roots of a Nation: The Story of San Andres School in Lima, Peru* (Edinburgh: The Knox Press, 1993), 9-10.

124 For an academic study of Scottish associationalism, see Tanja Bueltmann, Andrew Hinson and Graeme Morton (eds), *Ties of Bluid, Kin and Countrie: Scottish Associational Culture in the Diaspora* (Guelph, Ontario: Centre for Scottish Studies, University of Guelph, 2009).

125 Author's telephone interview with Easton Vance, Thetis Island, BC, 9 July 2008, track 2, 20:36–20:40; Harper, *Scotland No More?*, 223.

126 Interview with Cathy Timperley, 18:25–18:34.

127 Interview with Joe and Janet Blair, 06:54–07:17; Harper, *Scotland No More?*, 222.

128 Interview with Murdo MacPherson, 24 February 2005, 20:21; 22:18–22:28; 23:04–20:17; Stevenson, *The Silverado Squatters*, 40.

129 Jim Russell, Vancouver, interviewed by Harry McGrath and Ron Sutherland, for the Simon Fraser University, 'Scottish Lives in the West' Oral History Project, 11 May 2004, 05:58:36–05:58:57; 05:59:54–06:00:40. http://digital.lib.sfu.ca/soh-52/interview-james-russell-interview [date accessed 17 January 2018].

130 Interview with Brian Coutts, 23:34–23:40; 23:54; 25:06–25:12.

131 Interview with Cathy Timperley, 51:14–52:05.

132 Interview with Ena Macdonald, track 2, 01:27:51–01:28:42.

133 Author's interview with Margaret Gillies Brown, East Inchmichael, Errol, 21 December 2012, track 3, 20:25–20:30; 22:21.

134 Margaret Gillies Brown, *Far from the Rowan Tree*, 151.

135 Interview with Margaret Gillies Brown, track 3, 20:55–20:58.

136 Interview with Anne McCallum, track 1, 46:09–46:16.

137 Interview with Rachel Minton, 20:34.

138 Interview with James Mackenzie, 36:46–37:40.

139 Author's Skype interview with Alice Moffatt, Auburn, NSW, but in Kiltarlity, Inverness-shire, 5 August 2014, 17:21–18:04; 18:25–18:58.

140 Interview with Cathy Timperley, 56:44–57:57.

141 Interview with AS, 29:59–30:18.

Chapter 7. Reverse Migration: Resettling and Reconnecting

1 Russell King, 'Generalisations from the history of return migration', in Bimal Ghosh (ed.), *Return Migration: Journey of Hope or Despair?* (Geneva: International Organization for Migration, 2000), 7.

2 TM Devine, *To the Ends of the Earth. Scotland's Global Diaspora 1750–2010* (London: Allen Lane, 2011), 93.

3 James Adam, *Twenty-five Years of Emigrant Life in the South of New Zealand* (Edinburgh and London: Bell and Bradfute, 1874), 34.

4 Ibid., 35.

5 Author's interview with Gladys Morrice (née Keir), Aberdeen, 4 December 2014, track 3, 01:10–02:04. She was unsure whether they came back in 1948 or 1949.

6 Ibid., 02:28–03:03.

7 Ibid., track 4, 30:15.

8 Author's telephone interview with Joe and Janet Blair, Sarnia, Ontario, 2 February 2006, 07:46–08:19.

9 Author's interview with Ena Macdonald, Bayhead, North Uist, 7 September 2011, track 2, 01:32:19.

10 Ibid., track 2, 01:27:11–01:27:50.

11 Ibid, track 1, 00:44–01:08; track 2, 00:01–03:18.

12 Ibid., track 2, 05:02–05:25.

13 Author's interview with Anne McCarthy, Edinburgh, 7 February 2017, 11:29.

14 Ibid., 07:04–07:15; 31:32.

15 Ibid., 20:28–20:58; 30:35–30:54.

16 Author's interview with Christine Matheson, Inverness, 13 June 2014, track 1, 18:57–19:26.

17 Ibid., track 2, 08:00.

18 See above, Chapter 5, 134, 143.

19 Email from Roddy Campbell to author, 19 December 2016.

20 Author's interview with Roddy Campbell, Inverness, 8 October 2010, 18:17–18:40; 39:42–39:57.

21 '"Boomerang Poms" flee Australia's traffic and TV', http://www.bbc.co.uk/news/world-australia-36299682 [date accessed 1 December 2016].

22 See, for instance, J, a miner from Glasgow, and M,

a domestic servant from Aberdeenshire, who were deported in 1906 and 1909 respectively, after being committed to the British Columbia Provincial Asylum. These, and other, cases are discussed in Marjory Harper, 'Minds on the Edge: immigration and insanity among Scots and Irish in Canada, 1867-1914' (*Journal of Irish and Scottish Studies*, 8: 1 (Autumn 2014), 56-79 https://www.abdn.ac.uk/riiss/documents/JISS_EdgeOpenAccess.pdf). For a much later example, see the case of Archibald 'Mad Dog' McCafferty, a multiple murderer, who was deported from Australia to Scotland in 1997, and, after re-emigrating to New Zealand, was deported from there in 2002 after failing to declare his criminal convictions. Details are given in Marjory Harper and Stephen Constantine, *Migration and Empire* (Oxford: Oxford University Press, 2012), 322; and in the *New Zealand Herald*, 23 July 2002.

23 Lewis Society of Detroit, GD2/2/1. Minute Book, 1923–1936; 28 June 1924; January 1933. http://www.tasglann.org.uk/training/sample_catalogue_-_lewis_society_detroit.pdf

24 Author's interview with Sandra Train (née Macdonald), Halladale, Sutherland, 5 November 2010, 05:08.

25 Minnie Anne Macdonald (née Fraser) interviewed by Sandra Train (her daughter), Halladale, Sutherland, 5 December 1997, 02:20–04:20.

26 Author's interview with Carrol and Brian Stewart, Craigellachie, 9 April 2012, 01:02:40–01:04:14.

27 Author's interview with Murdo MacPherson, Kinlochbervie, Sutherland, 24 February 2005, 07:10–07:20.

28 Ibid., 09:11–09:20.

29 Author's interview with Murdo MacPherson, Dornoch, Sutherland, 18 January 2017, track 1, 01:26. See also above, Chapter 4, 102.

30 For details of McBeath's career, see http://www.kinlochbervie.info/scripts/gallery.asp?Root=mcbeath [date accessed 23 January 2017].

31 For satire and romanticisation, see Robert Service, 'The Ballad of the Ice Worm Cocktail', 'The Rhyme of the Remittance Man' and 'The Younger Son'. For remittance men, see Patrick Dunae, *Gentlemen Emigrants: From the British Public Schools to the Canadian Frontier* (Manchester: Manchester University Press, 1981).

32 Author's interview with Calum, Cathy and Chrissie Murray, Shader, Isle of Lewis, 25 February 2005, 01:01:30–01:02:00.

33 Ibid., 36:10–36:24.

34 Ibid., 44:40–45:27.

35 Marjory Harper, *Scotland No More? The Scots Who Left Scotland in the Twentieth Century* (Edinburgh: Luath, 2012), 219-20.

36 Author's interview with Norman MacRae, Back, Isle of Lewis, 17 November 2009, track 4, 04:47–05:03.

37 For another example of family networking in Scottish emigration to Patagonia, see Marjory Harper, *Emigration from Scotland Between the Wars: Opportunity or Exile?* (Manchester: Manchester University Press, 1998), 93-4, and interviews with Mrs JA Coupland, Aberdeen, 26 July 1994, 16 October 1996. See also Greta MacKenzie, *Why Patagonia?* (Stornoway: *Stornoway Gazette*, 1995) for Scottish involvement. For more general background on Patagonia, see Robert Barrett, *A Yankee in Patagonia: Edward Chace: His Thirty Years There 1898–1928* (Cambridge, Heffer, 1931) and Hesketh Vernon H. Pritchard, *Through the Heart of Patagonia* (London: Thomas Nelson, 1912).

38 Author's interview with Alice Beaton (née Mackenzie) and Mhairi Beaton, Aberdeen, 20 January 2014, 02:14-02:17.

39 Ibid., 49:39, 53:13–53:19.

40 Author's interview with Ian Skinner, Edinburgh, 2 March 2016, 02:26–02:54.

41 Interview with Ian Skinner, 01:17:56–01:18:33; Roy Lowe, *Education in the Post-War Years: A Social History* (Abingdon: Routledge, 1988), 123.

42 George Blake, *The Ben Line: The History of Wm Thomson & Co. of Leith and Edinburgh, and of the ships owned and managed by them, 1825–1955* (London: Thomas Nelson and Sons, 1956), 179.

43 Author's interview with Muriel Thorburn, Edinburgh, 16 March 2016, 40:19–40:35.

44 Interview with Brian Stewart, 01:18:14–01:18:17.

45 See https://www.keele.ac.uk/alumni/keeliteofthemonth/brianstewart/ [date accessed 12 December 2016].

46 See above, Chapter 2, 5, 129-30.

47 Author's interview with Charlie and Molly Law, Banavie, Fort William, 13 October 2012, 01:33:19–01:33:35. Strangely, there was another, more minor, landslip in the now largely deserted town of Ocean Falls almost 50 years to the day after the one experienced by the Laws. See *Coast Mountain News*, 13 February 2015. http://www.coastmountainnews.com/news/291885771.html [Date accessed 13 December 2016].

48 Interview with Charlie and Molly Law, 02:00:26–02:01:50.

49 Author's interview with Margaret Penley, Inchmarlo, Banchory, 24 July 2001, 19:33–19:38; 25:23–25:30.

50 Author's interview with Agnes McGilvray (née Lawrie), West Kilbride, 18 July 2009, track 7, 11:23–1200; 13:43–14:49.

51 Interview with Ian Skinner, 01:30:00.

52 The short-lived 'seavacuation' experiment is described in Michael Fethney, *The Absurd and the Brave. CORB – The True Account of the British Government's World War II Evacuation of Children Overseas* (Lewes, Sussex: The Book Guild Ltd, 2000). For the Scottish dimension, see Harper, *Scotland No More?*, 108-15.

53 *New York Times*, 11 September 1940, p27, c1.

54 Interview with Ian Skinner, 03:52–05:14.

55 Ibid., 01:27:47.

56 Ibid., 07:45–08:24.

57 Ibid., 01:30:00.

58 Ibid., 11:14–11:34.

59 Ian's story features in Michael Henderson, *See You After the Duration: The Story of British Evacuees to North America in World War II* (Baltimore: Publish America, 2004), 106, 153.

60 Reg Appleyard, Alison Ray and Allan Segal, *The Ten Pound Immigrants* (London: Boxtree, 1988), 103.

61 Author's interview with Sandra Munro, Ullapool, 26 March 2009, 21:50. The impediment to Sandra's return is that she does not have Australian citizenship.

62 Author's telephone interview with Murdo MacIver, Vancouver, 7 December 2007, track 2, 23:47–24:14. See also author's face-to-face interview with Murdo MacIver, Vancouver, 24 June 2013, track 1, 31:27.

63 'Scotland: The Promised Land: Homes for Highland Heroes', 0:46:26–0:46:55 http://subsaga.com/bbc/documentaries/history/scotland-the-promised-land/2-homes-for-highland-heroes.html [date accessed 29 November 2016]. See also Norman's entry in The Scottish Emigration Database, www.abdn.ac.uk/emigration.

64 'Notes by a Queensland Visitor', *Dalkeith Advertiser*, 4 January 1906, 2d.

65 Author's telephone interview with Morag Bennett (née MacLeod), Sechelt, British Columbia, 21 February 2005, 18:24.
66 Interview with Norman MacRae, track 1, 06:14–07:19.
67 Author's telephone interview with Alan Blair, Halifax, Nova Scotia, 12 January 2006, 28:06–28:26.
68 Ibid., 29:09–31:10.
69 Author's telephone interview with Alan Blair, Halifax, Nova Scotia, 12 April 2017, track 1, 31:36–31:38.
70 Interview with Alan Blair, 12 January 2006, 36:01–37:28.
71 Author's interview with Isobel Bouman (née Gillon), Dunedin, 29 November 2010, 20:44.
72 Interview with Murdo MacPherson, 24 February 2005, 14:53–15:15.
73 Ibid., 15:50–17:05.
74 Ibid., 17:21–17:39 and 18:20–19:12.
75 Author's interview with Anne Lynas Shah, Edinburgh, 10 January 2006, track 2, 20:15.
76 Ibid., 09:00.
77 Ibid., 12:50–13:14.
78 Ibid., 06:39–07:04. Anne accepted, however, that recent feedback from friends in Toronto suggested that her memories of a comfortable lifestyle might be out of date, and she herself had noticed a decline in the infrastructure during a recent trip back there (03:56).
79 Ibid., 09:43–09:53; 11:29–11:40.
80 Author's interview with Cathy Timperley (née Donald), Dunedin, 44:35.
81 Author's interview with AS, Dunedin, 29 November 2010, 03:08–03:34.
82 Ibid., 03:54–04:02.
83 Email from Graham McGregor to author, 15 April 2015.
84 Author's interview with Graham McGregor, Dunedin, 26 November 2010, 24:11–24:13.
85 Ibid., 22:18–23:27.
86 Author's telephone interview with Anne McCallum, Hunter River, Prince Edward Island, 28 September 2016, 22:49, 23:35.
87 Author's telephone interview with Peter Bevan-Baker, Hampton, Prince Edward Island, 20 September 2016, 23:10–23:16.
88 Interview with Alan Blair, 12 April 2017, track 2, 02:46–03:13.
89 Interview with Murdo MacPherson, 18 January 2017, track 2, 08:22–08:34.
90 Ibid., 05:12–06:13.
91 Interview with Anne McCarthy, 7 February 2017, 41:28–42:12.
92 Author's interview with David Knight, Hong Kong, 31 January 2017, track 2, 24:58–25:13.
93 Author's interview with Ken and Isabel Morrison, Hong Kong, 30 January 2017, 36:25–36:41. Ken speaking.
94 Author's interview with Gladys Morrice (née Keir), Aberdeen, 4 December 2014, track 4, 04:34–04:43.
95 Interview with Calum, Chrissie and Cathie Murray, 34:18–34:47.
96 Author's interview with Alison Thornton, Dunedin, 30 November 2010, 37:39, 39:29.
97 Interview with Christine Matheson, track 2, 05:08; 17:51.
98 Interview with Brian Stewart, 01:44:19–01:44:29.
99 Ibid., 01:44:54–01:46:04.
100 Ibid., 01:47:47, 01:50:15.
101 Author's interview with Cameron Tallach, Breakish, Isle of Skye, 10 April 2017, track 2, 34:50–34:58.
102 Ibid., 35:11–35:25; 35:41–35:51; 37:44–37:55; 39:04–39:37.
103 Author's interview with Margaret Steventon, Ullapool, 9 September 2009, track 6, 02:19, 02:31–02:36.
104 Ibid., 09:52–09:59.
105 Ibid. 12:49–14:09.
106 Interview with Margaret Penley, 22:50–23:05.
107 Author's interview with Sandy 'Boots' Macleod, Ullapool, 27 March 2009, 06:05–07:11.
108 Tom Bryan, 'Tracking the Rocky Mountain Men of Coigach', *West Highland Free Press*, 28 January 1994.
109 Interview with Alice Beaton, 56:28–56:30.
110 Author's interview with Cathie and Rob Tulloch, Kintore, Aberdeenshire, 14 August 2012, 24:34–25:17.
111 Author's interview with Elvira Gonnella Welch, Halifax, Nova Scotia, 1 November 2011, 41:01–41:36. See also above, Chapter 6, 156.
112 Author's interview with Margaret Gillies Brown, East Inchmichael, Errol, 21 December 2012, track 3, 22:37.
113 Margaret Gillies Brown, *Far From the Rowan Tree* (Glendaruel, Argyll: Argyll Publishing, 1998), 239.
114 Harper, *Scotland No More?*, 116-17, 119-20.
115 Email from Angus Pelham Burn to author, 9 December 2016.
116 Paul Basu, Highland *Homecomings: Genealogy and Heritage Tourism in the Scottish Diaspora* (London & New York: Routledge, 2007).

Chapter 8. Postscript: Commemorations, Mirror Images and Reflections

1 Anon., 'Canadian Boat Song – from the Gaelic', *Blackwood's Edinburgh Magazine*, XLVI, September 1829, 400; The Proclaimers, 'A Letter from America', Album, *This is the Story*, 1987; Alistair MacLeod, *The Lost Salt Gift of Blood* (London: Flamingo, 1993); Alice Munro, *The View from Castle Rock: Stories* (London: Vintage, 2007). See also Ivan Doig, *Dancing at the Rascal Fair* (New York: Atheneum, 1987).
2 Patricia Lim, *Forgotten Souls: A Social History of the Hong Kong Cemetery* (Hong Kong: Hong Kong University Press, 2011), 453.
3 Gwulo: Old Hong Kong, 'Inscription for cemetery sections 01-09', https://gwulo.com/node/8739 [date accessed 9 March 2017]; Lim, *Forgotten Souls*, 455.
4 http://www.scotsman.com/heritage/more-heritage/the-history-of-robert-burns-statues-around-the-world-1-4007818; http://www.bbc.co.uk/guides/zswpsbk [date accessed 22 February 2017].
5 Marjory Harper and Stephen Constantine, *Migration and Empire* (Oxford: Oxford University Press, 2010), 334.
6 John A Macdonald was born in Glasgow, where his father was a merchant, but the family emigrated to Canada when he was five years old.
7 See, inter alia, Bashir Maan, *The New Scots: The Story of Asians in Scotland* (Edinburgh: John Donald, 1992); John Millar, *The Lithuanians in Scotland: A Personal View* (Isle of Colonsay: House of Lochar, 1998); Tomasz Ziarski-Kernberg, *The Polish Community in Scotland* (Hove: Caldra House, 2000); Murray Watson, *Being English in Scotland* (Edinburgh: Edinburgh University Press, 2003); Carlos Vargas-Silva, *Migrants in Scotland: An Overview* (Oxford: Migration Observatory, 2013); RB Macleod, *Where I Eat My Bread: Stories of In-Migration to the Highlands and Islands* (np, 2016).

8 Social Support and Migration in Scotland, University of Glasgow http://www.gla.ac.uk/research/az/gramnet/research/ssamis/background/ [date accessed 23 January 2017].

9 Quoted in Sergei Shubin, 'Living on the Move: mobility, religion and exclusion of Eastern European migrants in rural Scotland', *Population, Space and Place*, 18: 5 (September/October 2012), 615-27. The extracts are on page 619. All names are pseudonyms. Velna and Donatas were interviewed in 2009.

10 Ibid., 620, 621. Margita was interviewed on 23 April 2010. I am grateful to Dr Sergei Shubin for enlightening conversations on the relationship between faith and migration.

11 Ibid., 621. Magdalena was interviewed on 6 June 2009.

12 Author's interview with Marilyn MacRitchie (née Thomson), Stornoway, Isle of Lewis, 6 September 2011, track 1, 21:24.

13 Ibid., track 2, 00:57–01:40.

14 Ibid., track 1, 22:37–23:30.

15 Ibid., 12:32–12:45; 16:04–16:06.

16 Ibid., 10:56–11:08.

17 Ibid., 12:45–13:13.

18 Email from Alison Inglis to author, 20 February 2017.

19 Interview with Marilyn MacRitchie, track 1, 11:49–12:05.

20 Ibid., track 2, 02:30–03:13.

21 Ibid., track 1, 13:27–13:38.

22 Gloria MacKillop, interviewed by Loriana Pauli, 2013, 00:25–00:31; 03:43; 24:21–24:40. https://lorianapauli.wordpress.com/2013/04/04/interview-with-gloria-mackillop-in-berneray/ [date accessed 3 March 2017]. Gloria and Splash were responsible for keeping secret the island's most famous visitor, when in 1987 and 1991 Prince Charles was a guest at their home while taking on, for a week, the life of a crofter. It was in that same home that I was most hospitably entertained in 2012, three years after Splash passed away, and in 2017 I renewed my friendship with Gloria as I was completing this book.

23 Author's telephone conversation with Gloria MacKillop, Berneray, 10 March 2017. For Marilyn MacRitchie's comment on her mother's letters, see above, Chapter 6, 159.

24 Author's interview with David Knight, Hong Kong, 30 January 2017, track 2, 10:20–10:29.

25 Author's interview with Rachel Minton, Dunedin, 29 November 2010, 01:37–01:39.

26 Author's interview with Calum, Cathie and Chrissie Murray, Shader, Isle of Lewis, 25 February 2005, Cathie speaking, 51:34–51:37.

27 Author's interview with Anne McCarthy, Edinburgh, 7 February 2017, 35:38–36:53.

28 Author's interview with Ken and Isabel Morrison, Hong Kong, 30 January 2017, 46:08–46:48. The quote from Tennyson is from the final line of 'Ulysses': 'To strive, to seek, to find, and not to yield'.

29 Interview with David Knight, track 2, 09:02–09:34.

30 Interview with Anne McCarthy, 31:32–32:40.

31 *Shetland Times*, 1 May 1964. Thanks to Angus Johnston, Shetland Archives, for passing on this item.

32 See above, Chapter 3, 79-83.

33 Author's interview with Matthew Lynas, Aberdeen, 5 December 2914, 58:49–58:53, and subsequent conversation, 20 March 2017.

Index

Also published by **Luath Press**

Scotland No More?
The Scots who Left Scotland in the Twentieth Century
Marjory Harper
ISBN 978-1-908373-35-9 PBK £14.99

In this groundbreaking history, awarded the Frank Watson Book Prize by the University of Guelph in Ontario, Marjory Harper uses untapped archival sources and oral testimony to brings to life the individual experiences of men, women and children who settled or sojourned overseas in the last century.

Scotland No More? explores the causes and consequences of the persistent restlessness which has left few Scots families untouched. Emigration was not always and easy option – controversy, catharsis and contradiction are all part of this multi-stranded history.

Luath Press Limited

committed to publishing well written books worth reading

LUATH PRESS takes its name from Robert Burns, whose little collie Luath (*Gael.*, swift or nimble) tripped up Jean Armour at a wedding and gave him the chance to speak to the woman who was to be his wife and the abiding love of his life. Burns called one of the 'Twa Dogs' Luath after Cuchullin's hunting dog in Ossian's *Fingal*.
Luath Press was established in 1981 in the heart of Burns country, and is now based a few steps up the road from Burns' first lodgings on Edinburgh's Royal Mile. Luath offers you distinctive writing with a hint of unexpected pleasures.
Most bookshops in the UK, the US, Canada, Australia, New Zealand and parts of Europe, either carry our books in stock or can order them for you. To order direct from us, please send a £sterling cheque, postal order, international money order or your credit card details (number, address of cardholder and expiry date) to us at the address below. Please add post and packing as follows: UK – £1.00 per delivery address; overseas surface mail – £2.50 per delivery address; overseas airmail – £3.50 for the first book to each delivery address, plus £1.00 for each additional book by airmail to the same address. If your order is a gift, we will happily enclose your card or message at no extra charge.

ILLUSTRATION: IAN KELLAS

Luath Press Limited
543/2 Castlehill
The Royal Mile
Edinburgh EH1 2ND
Scotland
Telephone: +44 (0)131 225 4326 (24 hours)
Email: sales@luath. co.uk
Website: www. luath.co.uk